SIDNEY X

THE PIRATE

B.R. EMRICK

ROGUE PUBLISHING GROUP

SIDNEY X THE PIRATE

By B.R. Emrick

Emrick-Caribbean, Rogue Publishing Group, PO Box 503195, St. Thomas, Virgin Islands 00805-3195

Email: Lagoonie@lagoonieville.com

www.lagoonieville.com

ISBN: 978-0-9891982-0-2

Printed in the United States of America

Dedicated to my Son

BERT RICHARD EMRICK IV

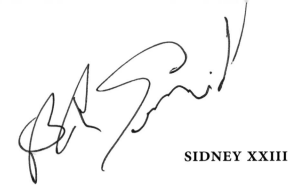

SIDNEY XXIII

IF ANYONE COULD EVER FIND ANYTHING GOOD TO SAY ABOUT SIDNEY, IT would be that he had a great body and was in fantastic shape—for his age and lifestyle. To find anything else good to say about him would take an extremely good imagination. Even that would be difficult, as no one knew him. He was the paradigm of a lone-wolf.

Unfortunately, it was not a dark and stormy night, Sidney's preferred scenario for his type of work. With minimal light from the stars over the Caribbean, Sidney moved in the shadows of a cargo ship's main deck. He moved so slowly that even when in view of a guard, the observer's eyes wouldn't detect him.

The only lights on the *Abraham*, a 550-foot tanker, were the running lights and red night-lights in the wheelhouse, as she pushed her bulk through the dark night at twenty knots off the north coast of Puerto Rico. She was bound for the Arabian oil fields in the Red Sea.

The *Abraham* had pumped its load of crude oil in Santo Domingo the day before and was headed back for more. Keeping a monthly supply of Zurrah crude to Jamaica and the Dominican Republic had been her only job for years. The captain had made the trip so many times the passage was boring. The crew kept busy doing their day-to-day duties on board, maintaining the ship's plumbing and wiring and the 150 gate valves above the water line and another 50 sea cocks below. It was just a job, a rather monotonous job, not a cruise and certainly not an adventure.

The crew's monotony was exactly what Sidney counted on to make his job easier. He slowly made his way from the deck and up the ladder to the wheelhouse. The door had been left open to get fresh air inside. Sidney slipped into the house when the man on watch turned to take a look at the radar screen. He really didn't expect to see anything on the screen; it was just habit and part of the job.

Very quietly, Sidney moved behind the man and with a short motion of his right hand, knocked the man unconscious. There was no sound of contact on the man's skull from the black leather blackjack, filled with lead pellets. That was Sid's preferred choice of weapons that he had named *Billy*—when he was only six years old.

He fished a small roll of duct tape out of his pack and put a strip over the unconscious man's eyes, then another to cover his mouth. He then taped his hands and feet together and to a well-worn safety rail to keep him from moving.

Sidney left the bridge and quietly moved down the red lighted corridor until he found the door with words "Ship's Master" on it. The door was unlocked and he slowly cracked it open while listening for breathing sounds from the captain. The man's breathing was shallow, slow with an occasional snore. The breathing pattern was a sign that the captain was enjoying a deep sleep.

Sidney looked around in the cabin, moving and searching everything without the slightest sound. After searching, he found only one of the two things he needed. The ship's safe was concealed behind a fake steel wall panel. That didn't take a lot of genius though, as most ships designed by Matthews Ship and Iron Works used the same arrangement. The safe had a combination lock; he looked around the usual hiding places for a secret combination but he found nothing.

He pulled Billy out for the second time that night and gave a rap to the sleeping captain's skull. It wasn't a hard hit but it was exactly the force needed to keep the man unconscious until Sidney was ready for the captain to be alert. The roll of tape came out again and the captain was bound like the man on the bridge. The only differences were his left forearm was taped to the man's right knee, and the right arm to his left knee, leaving his hand free to write the safe's combination. An extra strip of tape was stuck on the tip of the captain's nose.

With everything ready, Sidney woke the captain up with several soft slaps on his cheeks. When the captain appeared to realize what was happening, Sidney put the tape over his nostrils, cutting off his air supply. The man fought against the tape, struggling to get free to get air. His screams were muffled.

Just before the man passed out, Sidney pulled the tape off his nose. Frantically, the man's empty lungs sucked in as much air as physically possible through nostrils much too small. It took a few panicky moments before the captain was able to pull in and expel enough air to regain a sufficient oxygen level.

After the captain settled down, Sid whispered in his ear, "I am going to put a pencil in your hand and I'm going to hold a pad for you to write the safe's combination on. If you refuse, the tape will be put back over your nose."

The captain was trying to yell for help or talk to him, Sidney couldn't tell which, but very little came out through his taped mouth. The sounds of the ship moving through the water, engines and all of the other equipment running, made it impossible to hear his pleas, no more than a few feet away.

The captain refused to hold the pencil or write anything. Sidney closed off his air supply again. As before, when the man's struggling slowed just before passing out, the tape was removed. Sidney gave him the same message but in Italian, Spanish, Norwegian and Portuguese languages. Again, the captain refused, and again, the tape went back over the nostrils.

When the captain stabilized again, Sid whispered once more, "If you refuse me this time I'll leave the tape on. I do not have the time to baby you." He repeated the warning in the languages until the man acknowledged. He scribbled the combination—and he wrote *Barracuda?*

Sidney tried the combination; the safe opened. The captain was given the right touch from Billy that would give him several hours of deep sleep. The tape was removed. The safe's cash was stuffed into his pack and he quietly closed the door behind him.

He checked the man on the bridge; he was still out. Checking the wall clock, it was 0145, leaving another two hours and fifteen minutes before the next watch came on duty—just as Sidney had planned.

He slowly worked his way back to the vessel's stern, and slipped over the safety rail. He had tied a double nylon braid line to the bottom of a stanchion. Using the line he lowered himself to the little Avon rubber boat attached to the other end of the line. He quickly untied one end of the line and pulled it free of the ship, leaving him in the ship's wake. He watched the giant black shape of the ship's stern get smaller as the massive propellers churned away, pushing the huge vessel across the Atlantic Ocean.

Sidney finally turned his attention away from the diminishing ship and to the little boat's outboard engine. The twenty-five horse power Mercury was started and the dinghy was pointed straight to the distant lights of Puerto Rico. The weather was good and the seas were only three feet so he could be on shore in thirty minutes—if in a hurry.

Looking at his folded chart he knew he was due north of the Carolina area—just as planned. He was in no hurry, so he kept the boat off plane and enjoyed the night's sky.

Halfway to shore, he took a small break from Mother Nature's beauty to check the contents of his pack. The ship yielded forty thousand dollars in cash and another forty-five thousand in travelers checks made out to Captain Bent. It was customary for ships to have a lot of cash on board. Duties to local Customs had to be paid in United States dollars, and if repairs were needed, then cash was the only acceptable means of payment. Traveler's checks were in case more money was needed for emergencies.

The traveler's checks were rolled up into a fist-size roll and stuffed into his pants pocket. His black sweat pants and shirt were removed, leaving him completely naked. His clothes were then wrapped up and duct-taped to a grapefruit size rock that he had picked up on the beach before taking the dingy to sea only a few hours ago. The clothes with traveler's checks included were dropped into water well over a thousand feet deep never to be seen again.

He cut through the stainless cable that attached the boat to the engine with his recently stolen and soon to be discarded cable cutter. The cable was supposed to prevent engine theft and was long enough to attach to a dock to prevent dinghy theft, too. That end had been cut hours ago when he had stolen the dinghy.

He pulled a pair of shorts and a tee shirt out of his pack and then dressed. A pair of cheap flip-flops completed his ensemble. With everything all set, he had time to light up a Cuban Cohiba, his preferred cigar, for a relaxing smoke before he reached the beach.

As Sidney approached the Puerto Rican shore he turned eastward, then ran parallel to the rocky shoreline for a mile before he heard the sound he wanted. The seas were not rough, but they were high enough to break on the rocky shore. When the waves run up on a sandy beach, the breakers sound more like a whoosh as they glide up the slope. A wave hitting rocks was abrupt and made a crashing sound. He followed the whooshing sound until he could see the refection of the starlit night on white sand. As the shore came into sight, he was able to pick the spot he wanted to land.

He disconnected the fuel line to the engine and loosened the engine's transom clamps. With the engine free, he picked it up and dropped it overboard. He finished his trip to the beach with the dinghy's oars.

He stepped ashore, hardly getting a flip-flop wet, and let the boat fend for itself in the mild surf. It might or might not be found in a day or two. The police would think that someone had stolen the dinghy to get the engine, a common practice in the Caribbean.

Sidney walked straight into the jungle knowing there was a paved road that ran the length of the beach that would lead him to the town of Carolina. It'd be a nice walk, the weather was good and there was enough of a breeze to keep the mosquitoes away.

As he walked into the outskirts of town the sun began rising over the horizon. People were up and moving about in their homes, getting ready for work or getting the kids ready for school. A small restaurant was just opening and he went in for breakfast; he was starved.

The man working in the little restaurant tried to get a conversation going with Sidney but he shook his head and said, "No speaky Spanish," and pointed to the menu that listed *gallo pinto ~y huevo con tocino*. He felt like sitting there after breakfast to enjoy several more cups of coffee and enjoy another cigar but decided to keep moving.

He continued walking until he found a telephone booth and then called for a taxi. The taxi driver was paid to take him to the Holiday Inn, east of San Juan. From there he walked down into the community of Isla Verde. It was too early for any of the businesses to be open, but he needed to buy a change of clothes and then find a post office. After he located both, he went into a restaurant and sat in a quiet corner booth. He ordered a cold *Medalla* and read the morning newspaper bought at the cashier's station.

While he was leisurely reading the paper, enjoying a cigar, and sipping on the beer, the waitress took notice. She was annoyed at the cigar smoke and openly showed her resentment. When he ordered another beer she coughed in his face, making no effort to cover her mouth while looking directly at him. He seemed not to notice or care.

The waitress, determined to have her way, stood there browbeating as best she could, and said, "Cigar smoking is not permitted in this restaurant."

He looked up at her with a nondescript expression and said, "No speaky Spanish."

She repeated it in English.

With the same nondescript look, Sidney said, "No speaky English," and went back to his newspaper.

When it was late enough to go shopping, he left and the only tip was the soggy end of a dead, smelly cigar on the table. That didn't please the already agitated waitress. She muttered, "The start of another shitty day in paradise."

She followed him to the door, banged on the plate glass window and yelled, "This is a nice place. We don't want people like you hanging around. Be sure to take your smelly ass to some other place next time."

Sidney ignored her. She hated his indifference and wanted him to feel that he was unwanted and rejected as a human being. She had no idea that Sidney wasn't trying to piss her off, he was just being himself. He didn't care about other people or what they said, and certainly not what they might be thinking.

He bought a pair of tennis shoes, lightweight slacks and a cotton pullover shirt. As usual, when he went shopping, the clothes he had been wearing when he walked in remained there when he left.

At the post office he bought a heavyweight photograph-mailing envelope. It was addressed to Mr. S. Xavier, Hamilton Marina, St. Croix, VI. Then he placed thirty-five thousand dollars into the envelope, sealed it and dropped it into the mail slot.

He called another taxi to take him to Fajardo, a boating community on the East Coast of Puerto Rico, and found a small hotel that he checked into for the night. There he made several telephone calls until he found a yacht charter company that could furnish a captain to take him sailing the next morning.

That afternoon, after a four-hour nap, he got up, showered and put his only set of clothes back on. He headed for the waterfront, where there was an abundance of bars, restaurants and, hopefully, a hooker or two. When he entered a bar he felt right at home; it was dark and the woodwork, chairs, floor and even the glasses smelled of years of smoke. Everything was covered with a yellow stain. Salsa music was blaring from a giant boom box on one corner of the bar. On the other side of the bar was a fan blowing the stale air down the bar's length.

The bartender was a heavy woman who looked like she had lived a very rough life. But, she flashed a big warm smile when Sidney entered the bar and sat down on a rickety barstool. As she waddled over, her huge tits swayed back and forth, seemingly trying to pull her off balance with each step.

Sidney noticed a bottle of tequila on the bar where she had been standing. In perfect Spanish, he said "I'll have some of that," pointing to the tequila, "if you'll join me."

She was delighted. Two guys in the back yelled for her to bring them some more beers and she, in her best bar talk, said, "Go fuck yourselves! Can't you assholes see I'm serving a gentleman?"

One of the two men walked up behind the bar and got two beers himself. Good naturedly, he said, "If this is a self-service bar, then I ought to be getting a discount."

She said, "Shit, Juan, you're lucky that I allow a scumbag like you and your pals in the place. And how the hell am I supposed to give you a discount when you never tip me anyway?"

With her attention back on the stranger, Sidney said, "Pour us a couple of big ones; no ice for me."

"That's just the way I like it. I haven't seen you around here. You with the military?" She asked.

"Nope," he answered, and then downed his drink. He slid the empty glass towards her saying "Another."

She poured more tequila until the glass was full, and said, "You're a thirsty hombre ain't you?"

"Yep."

"Well, what's your name, thirsty stranger?" she asked pleasantly.

"Sidney."

"Do you live around here or just passing through? This is off the beaten path the tourists usually take."

"Nope."

She waited for some kind of a follow up in conversation from her new customer but got none. She asked again if he was just passing through.

"Yep," and he lit his cigar, taking his time, impervious to her watching him. After it was properly lit he inhaled a deep pull of smoke into his lungs, holding it for a few seconds before exhaling.

She thought she could see how much he enjoyed that smoke by an expression on his face. It wasn't a happy expression, but it was a look that wasn't as rigid as any he had shown since his arrival. She couldn't have possibly known, but a good cigar was one of the few pleasures in Sidney's life. After exhaling the cigar smoke, he gulped down his drink and pushed the glass towards the tequila bottle for another. He indicated that she should do the same.

With a new drink in hand he finally spoke, "Any girls around here?"

She took advantage of the opportunity to get even and said "Yep," then she poured more tequila on top of her drink with no expression or effort to carry the conversation further.

He didn't either. They sat silent and drank more tequila, neither saying a word to each other. They finished the first bottle and were on the second before the next customer came in. He sat down next to Sidney and said, "Hello."

Sidney got up without acknowledging the man and without asking how much, put a fifty-dollar bill on the bar and gestured goodbye to the bartender with a single index finger.

He walked down a dirty street looking for another place to get a drink and a woman, and maybe some food, too. All he saw in the streets were a bunch of loose dogs, peeing on everything vertical, inviting even more flies. In a few minutes he was sitting at Rosa's Bar, a twin bar to the one he had just left. The big difference was the bartender was a man, and he had been hitting the booze hard that afternoon. He didn't appear to be a very social kind of guy and he didn't bother looking at Sidney but in an irritated voice asked, "What do you want?"

The man's attitude made no difference to Sidney. He said, "Tequila."

Sidney had a couple of drinks, saying nothing to the bartender. The bartender said nothing to him or to another man sitting quietly at the other end of the bar. There was a television mounted high up on the wall behind the bar, showing the endless rotation of the news on Fox News. Sidney and the other man stared dumbly at the TV screen, not caring what was being said. They were just looking at it out of boredom. Sidney paid the bartender and asked, "Where can I get a woman?"

"Duffy's, down the street," as he pointed to the door.

Duffy's was a noisy place, but cleaner than the previous two places, and had several people sitting at the bar. Three of them, thank God, were hookers. As Sidney walked in, the three batted their cheaply painted eyelids and kept eye contact with him all the way to his barstool, which was next to the best looking hooker.

"Get me a tequila and anything the girls want," he said. That was all that was needed for the three working girls to go into action. In their business, they've learned that when an interested guy comes in, zero in and close the deal before the next girl comes in. The girls competed with each other trying to make conversation with him. He didn't say much, just kept ordering drinks for the four of them. More people started coming into the bar, including a couple of other girls. They were no better looking than the three he had, but his companions felt threatened and started getting more direct.

The heavy girl on the end said, "I can show you a really good time. You interested?"

The middle girl was doing her best to look sexy, leaned over and looked into Sidney's face. She slowly licked her lips with an unusually long tongue while putting her hand on his lap and murmured sexually, "You can have me if you like." *Have* wasn't exactly what she meant.

He didn't need to be sold; he had been ready since he woke up from his afternoon nap. He said, "All of you drink up, I'm ready." He bought a bottle of tequila and a bottle of Cruzan Rum to take back to his hotel room.

The four of them walked to his room with the girls happily joking with each other. Each laughing, feeling the effects of the booze and relieved that they all were to be winners that night. They also felt safer in numbers, which only added to their frolicking antics. Sidney didn't give a shit, he just wanted a blow job from the fat one and some hard fucking on the other two.

They drank booze and fucked most of the night. The fat girl gave outstanding head, the middle girl was a little uncertain about how she should act, and the looker was a great piece of ass and knew how to present the package as well as what to do with it.

When Sidney had enough he gave them each a one hundred-dollar bill and said, "Party's over. Time for you to leave," and those were the first words he had spoken since they entered his room.

The looker took the money but said, "Hey, that's not enough. I always get three hundred dollars."

Sidney didn't bother to say anything, he just looked at her. His look told her that he somehow knew she hadn't done a hundred dollar trick since she was fourteen. He gently guided them out of his room. After a long hot shower he was in bed alone, thinking of tomorrow's plans.

ST. CROIX, VIRGIN ISLANDS

"He'll be back tomorrow," Sally, a forty-year-old, but matronly looking mother, said to her two teenage daughters. "You kids are going to have to be quiet. You know he doesn't like children and the noise from your stereos and television, and keep the loud arguments down, too. You know how easy it'd be to make us move."

Christy, the thirteen-year-old, said, "Kids?... Mom, he doesn't like anybody."

"He's entitled to like whomever he wants. He lets me run this place as I please, and keep the profits after the bills are paid. All I have to do for him is take care of his mail. This is his place and for a forty-year-old woman without a husband this is a perfect place for us. So behave!"

Christy asked, "Those mail packets are kind of creepy. He's gone for maybe six months and sends a few of them. What are they, Mom?"

"They are news stories that he's working on."

"But if he's gone for six months they can't be news any longer."

"How do you know, young lady. You don't have any idea how news reporters work, do you?"

Honey, the twelve-year-old, said, "He doesn't look like a reporter to me. I saw him in the back of the marina one morning without his shirt on. You said he's forty, but he's built like a twenty-year-old athlete."

Christy couldn't keep quiet and blathered out, "Yeah and his chest is covered with thick black hair and you should see all of the scars on his chest and back. He must have been in a war or something. He scares me, Mom."

"Just stay away from him; he won't hurt you. I'm sure he'll only be here a few days and have another news story to cover, and then we can relax again."

Honey said, "Mom, you're crazy. Believing he's a news reporter is about as nutty as believing he's a successful New York advertising executive. He's the most anti-social person I've ever seen. Even after all of the years we've been here he has never said more than one or two words. I think he inherited his money or is a crook."

"He's a gangster?" Christy asked with big, questioning eyes.

"You kids stop it. Mr. Xavier is a news reporter, and I know that for a fact, now you kids get out of here and go do your homework."

She knew there was something wrong with his story of being a reporter. She had never seen him express emotions like laughter, sorrow or even anger. He seemed to hold all of his thoughts and feelings to himself. And from her experience, reporters were usually liberals and everybody knows you almost have to shoot a liberal to shut him or her up. Liberals' emotions lived not in their brains but on their tongues. She'd never admit it to the kids, but she was afraid of him, too. She had seen his body and besides arousing the woman in her, it frightened her that a man could be so fit and looks so mean and still be walking the streets as a free man.

In time, she had realized that she had nothing to fear as long as she did her job. She received packages for him from all parts of the Caribbean and put them in a hidden concrete vault. He'd suddenly come home for a few days and if she needed money to build an extension to the bar or replace pilings or anything else, she had only to ask. He gave her the cash without question. In the beginning he told her it would be that way and all he expected in return was her loyalty. He had always received it.

Occasionally, she thought about what was going to happen when he stopped coming back or sold the place. She'd be back on the streets again, and couldn't live under the impoverished conditions she had before Mr. Xavier found her. It bothered her so much she had asked him on one of his visits if he had plans to sell the marina. In one of Sidney's longest exchanges of words, he said, "I won't sell it Sally... for any price. I like the way you do things and I'll never need the money. Do you feel at ease now?"

Sidney had made a good life possible for her and her children and she truly appreciated the mysterious, but scary man for it.

FAJARDO, PUERTO RICO

THE NEXT MORNING, SIDNEY WAS UP BEFORE DAWN, AS USUAL. HE WAS out on the deserted streets doing his three-mile run. He traveled light and he ran light. Most people jog, but Sid ran hard giving it his full effort. While most joggers seen on the streets wear their color-coordinated outfits, with sweatbands on their heads and hands and expensive running shoes, Sidney wears the shorts he has on and runs with bare feet. His normal foot attire is none, or flip-flops, so his feet have been toughened over the years.

The reason he doesn't wear clothes or shoes is not because he travels light, but he prefers the feeling of personal freedom that being nearly naked gives him. When sailing he is always naked, and sometimes he runs naked if he's sure no one will see him. He had to be sure the cops didn't stop him, as Sidney had never owned anything that could identify him including a driver's license, birth certificate, or passport—and he never would. If the police ever stopped him, for any reason, it would create problems and injury to a hapless policeman or woman.

After his run and a long cold shower, he quickly dressed. Walking to the charter company, he found a dingy little place for breakfast. It was a crummy place, but Sid didn't notice. He gulped down a huge breakfast and washed it down with a cold beer. Of course, he had to have another beer with his morning cigar and in that dumpy little place there was no surly waitress to piss and bitch about his stinking cigar—he didn't notice that, either.

ST. CROIX

Sidney arrived at the charter broker's office promptly at eight thirty as planned on the telephone the day before. The sailboat was ready to sail, but the captain didn't show up until nine. He paid cash for a two day charter with the captain. A blond woman in her thirties, wearing a red Kmart backpack to carry her necessities for an overnight trip, was introduced as his captain. Sid shook hands without discussion and motioned for her to lead the way.

On board, Captain Samantha Smith said, "On my charters I always like to have my crew learn about sailing as well as enjoying the experience. And the only way to learn is by doing," and she smiled. "Now we need to untie the boat from the dock after I get the engine running. You can do that for me, okay?" She gave him a motherly smile.

With a complete lack of interest in anything his perky little captain had to say, he fought off telling her to fuck off at the dock. He untied the boat while she started the engine. When the boat was well away from the dock, he moved behind the steering wheel, pushing her aside with his hip.

He shut the engine off and said, "Go below, Captain, and let me sail in peace."

"I can't do that. I'm responsible for this boat. Besides, what do you know about the water and sailing?"

"Lady, I've been sailing single-handed since age six. Now go below."

She started to protest, but thought what the hell; if he gets into trouble it's his own fault. She went to the galley and muttered, "Mr. Grumpy Smartass can pay for damages. Piss on him, he can't do anything I can't swim away from." She made coffee and could hear the sails being hoisted and then could feel the power of the boat as the sails caught the wind and heel the boat over on her starboard side.

She poked her head out of the hatch and looked around. "Keep the compass steering on a course of 80 degrees in order to keep clear of a reef offshore."

Sidney said, "Yes, Captain," but headed the boat to 110 degrees. He wanted to take advantage of the slightly sheltered wind from the northeast for as long as possible while behind in the lee of the Passage Islands, then turn to St. Croix on a fast beam reach.

With coffee cup in hand she started up the companionway steps only to be shocked at the sight of Sidney standing at the helm—completely nude.

He said, "They didn't tell you?"

She turned around and responded indignantly, "No, they certainly did not," and went back into the cabin from where she yelled, "You better not get any funny ideas! I'm a black belt!"

She spent the rest of the day in the cabin fighting off, unsuccessfully, being seasick. When she became aware of the shore sounds, she made her way back outside. Her troublesome customer had put his clothes back on and the red marker outside of Christiansted Harbor was off the starboard beam.

Sidney pulled the boat into Gallows Bay and backed her into an open transit slip using only the sail for power. After the boat was tied up, he gave his captain a two hundred-dollar tip and said, "I won't be going back with you." He stepped off the boat and onto the dock.

She objected, saying that was not what her instructions were. She wasn't really anxious to sail back alone and said, "We have to clear Customs before you can stay here."

Sidney continued on his way. She had no way of knowing Sidney had traveled all over the world and had never gone through Customs for any country. She soon resigned herself that she was going to have to make the return trip by herself.

He called a taxi from a pay telephone near a patio bar, and then he went in for a cold beer to wait for the hack. He always felt good coming back to St. Croix. This was home, where his possessions were, including the marina where his employee, Sally, secured his prized mail. He had found her tending bar in a St. Croix waterfront dive sixteen years ago. She was a little on the hard side of friendly, a feature he rated as a quality.

His marina was in a lagoon where mostly live-aboard sailboat types frequented. It certainly wasn't the kind of place any self-respecting sport-fisherman or fancy yacht would be seen. That suited Sidney; he had no use for uppity assholes.

It was almost dark when he arrived at the Hamilton Marina. On the way to his apartment, he saw Sally scurrying from the Deck Bar to greet him. She helped out as bartender and cook when things were busy, and the bar looked busy that evening.

She greeted him warmly with a handshake and cheerful smile. She was full of the usual pleasantries, telling him how well he was looking and how nice it was to have him back home. Also, as always, she said it would be nice if he could stay longer this trip. They had a new cook at the bar that specialized in New Orleans cuisine; she was sure he'd enjoy the lobster jambalaya, the cook's specialty.

Sidney responded by asking, "Did you get a package today?"

Sally would never get used to talking to someone who never said more than the minimum words, but she had come to expect it from Mr. Xavier. She told him nothing had come for him since a Federal Express package about a month ago. She added that it was handled as usual. Sidney had continued walking to his apartment without further comment.

In his apartment, he took off the clothes he had been wearing for two days and dropped them on the floor, knowing Sally would find them after he left and wash them and add them to the collection in the closet. After a long hot-water shower, something the islanders didn't usually get to appreciate because of a constant water shortage, he laid down to relax. After twenty minutes and feeling refreshed, he dressed in shorts and a tee shirt, no shoes, and went to the bar.

There were a lot of people in the bar drinking and laughing. The core of the laughter was coming from a guy that Sidney recognized as one of the boat owners who rented a slip in the marina. He was telling everyone about his problems on a recent trip to St. Thomas. Apparently the story had been told before as his buddies reminded him occasionally to tell 'em this or that. Nobody minded; the story was better than the boredom of quietness. He had just about finished telling the story when he saw Sidney at the bar.

The storyteller took another big gulp of beer from his bottle and said, while he pointed a finger at Sidney, "Hey, that's the guy I need to talk to; he owns this place."

Sidney didn't hate many things, but attention of any kind was number one on his fuck-you list.

The storyteller said, "Hey Sidney, when are you going to dredge out the inlet out there? I ran aground there and spent two days lying on my side." He was laughing, but continued, "I pay big bucks every month to keep my boat floating in your marina, not lying up on my sides, trying to get over that shallow spot you got out there."

The crowd laughed and Sidney looked at the bartender and ordered a rum, straight, ignoring the storyteller. The storyteller could tell the man didn't appreciate being put on the spot and he wasn't drunk enough to let it bother him, so he went on to another part of the humorous story.

Sidney had several more drinks, then ordered the lobster specialty for dinner. He drank a bottle of cheap white wine with the lobster concoction. The wine might have been cheap but in Sidney's mind, it was a hell of a lot better than that fancy fucking lobster jambalaya.

He listened to the good times everyone was having until around ten that evening, then he returned to his apartment. He thought about going into Christiansted for some late night action, but the trio of hookers last night had done their job well enough for him to justify staying in and catch up on his sleep.

By five-thirty the next morning, he had finished his run and had showered. He drove the marina's Jeep into town for his morning breakfast. His favorite place in St. Croix was the Pig's Puss. A small place where there were never any tourists.

The local newspaper was still full of everything but the news. It covered all of the local gossip and events that concerned only the radically racial folks who, for some reason, thought they were still the stolen and enslaved victims forcefully captured and stolen from Africa, the land of lazy, by the white devils. The majority, however, like the few whites on the island, thought the radicals were full of unfortunate shit who sucked the tits of the evil Uncle Sam.

Sidney didn't dwell on social concerns but knew that ninety-nine percent of those people had never been there, and two or three hundred years had passed since their ancestors had been there. For some reason he couldn't fathom, because they had black skin, they wanted to act and talk like they were displaced people. Most of them, given a choice to live in the Caribbean or return to the ancestral homeland would fight to the death to stay where they were. For some reason or another they didn't want to take credit for being the people that had been born and raised in the islands that their forefathers had developed. It was not fashionable and to Sidney that was stupid. Hell, everyone was a descendant of a slave of one kind of another, even the elite. And there is not a single person in all of the Caribbean and Americas whose family had not originated from another land—even the early Indians came from some other place.

The only part of the newspaper Sidney was interested in that morning was the classified advertisement section. He wanted to buy a sailboat, and only one boat was of interest to him. After a greasy breakfast, a cup of bitter coffee and two beers, he called about the boat. It sounded like it was rigged the way he wanted and had the right equipment. Arrangements were made to see the boat later in the afternoon.

Usually when Sidney wanted a boat or to get from one island to another, he would just steal a boat, but he would not do that in St. Croix. He never left a trail to the safe harbor his family had used for two hundred years.

On the way back to his apartment, he stopped by the rum factory to restock his dwindling supply. Only at the factory could he buy a ten-gallon cask of the local squeeze, which by his definition was the best made anywhere. Fifteen minutes later, he found an old paper cup under one of the Jeep's seats, blew some of the dirt out and poured it half full of the golden rum to be sure it wasn't a bad batch. It was another excellent year, or fifteen minutes, whichever it took to make the rum.

Before he pulled into the marina's driveway he had poured a second sample of rum into the cup. As he got out of the Jeep, Sally walked over to say hello and informed him that his package had arrived. She had opened a secret panel in a wall and dropped his mail down a stainless steel mail slot. She had no idea where it went or why. She did care, but she would never ask.

Sidney only nodded that he received the information and continued to his apartment. Inside, he refilled the dirty paper cup with rum, and after closing the window louvers to insure his privacy, he went into a walk-in closet.

He removed hanging clothes off the nine-foot closet rod. The closet floor, like the rest of his apartment, was concrete covered with large sections of red Spanish title. The tile had no regular pattern as it had been broken in to smaller pieces before being grouted into place. There were many cracks in the tile, but the cracks were small and almost unnoticeable. The nine-foot clothes rod required an extra vertical rod that was mounted to the floor to support the weight of the clothes. With his knife blade, he loosened three screws holding the vertical support to the floor. He swung the rod up and out of his way to reveal an elongated key hole in the floor.

Sidney removed his only piece of so-called jewelry, an old tarnished key on a leather strap that he wore around his neck. The key was inserted and unlocked a dead-bolt lock on a trapdoor that concealed a compartment two feet wide and six feet long. He had built the building himself years ago and designed it to be a secure mail drop and a place he could crawl into if he ever felt the need to hide. A stainless steel mail drop was on the other side of the wall hidden by a false wall inside a cabinet.

With a little careful jiggling he opened the floor door. He held a small flashlight in his mouth, and reached inside the opening. One at a time, he passed up four thick envelops. After retrieving the packages, he checked the original seals to see if any had been tampered with. He also checked the very slight slice marks, made with fingernails on every seam for signs of tampering. All was okay, nobody had gotten nosy.

He opened the packages one at a time to examine the contents. The first opened was dated five months ago. It contained 120,000 United States dollars.

He counted it out, sorting it by denomination. He refilled the same dirty cup with his demon rum and played with the cash much like a kid or a collector would his newly acquired stamps or coins to be added to a collection.

That was one of the few pleasures afforded to Sidney since he was seven years old. It was his moment to realize the fruits of his work, his purpose in life, as it had been for his father, his dad's father and every Sidney X fathers back to the year of 1523 when the first Sidney decided to go into the pirating business. The open packet represented a quick profit with almost none of the exhaustive planning required for many of his raids.

He opened the second and larger pack. It had been mailed ten days after the first. That one hadn't been so easy to acquire. To take that prize required some luck, a lot of listening to dock workers and plenty of guts and physical abilities. Before the opportunity to take the money away from the smugglers had presented itself, Sidney had gone to Ocho Rios in Jamaica to study the landing frequencies of three cruise ships. Each of the ships was in the Caribbean on lengthy cruises from New York through several stops in the Caribbean and then ending in Spain. Two weeks later the ships would be back in the Caribbean again but going the other direction, returning to New York.

Sidney wanted the return run, but had to let the current conditions determine which cruise he would get. He had been in no hurry; the rum was good, the sun was warm; the water was clear, and the women were as cheap as anywhere else he wanted to be. And the Jamaicans rolled a decent cigar, too. Finally, the ship, *Tropical Sun,* came in directly from Madrid with just a quick stop in San Juan to re-provision. And Sidney was delighted to empty two of their safes.

SICILY

A FAX SLID ACROSS THE BIG HIGHLY POLISHED DESK OF ANTHONY "*Tony-the-Pop*" Castero by his secretary. Her solemn expression told the other man sitting across from Tony the Pop that it contained adverse news. After a few seconds, Tony confirmed that was the case with some well-chosen words, by Italian standards. "Those cocksuckers are fucking dead. They think this shit is going to pass without heads rolling?"

He looked at the man sitting across from him as he asked the question. The other man had no idea what Tony was talking about so he sat there with a blank expression, waiting to be told what had gone wrong.

"Those cocksuckers are fucking dead, Vincenzo… and I want you to do it!"

"Sure Tony, but who exactly, am I supposed to pop?"

"How the fuck do I know? If I knew, I'd pop the cocksuckers myself." He threw the fax across the desk towards him; it didn't make the trip, and instead, fell off the desk. Vincenzo "The Sicilian" Jones was quick to pick it up. He read it and said, "They hit another one of our ships! This has been happening more frequently, hasn't it?"

"Fuck yes! This is the fourteenth in the last five years. It has to be by the same motherfuckers. They fuck up the captain to get combinations to the safes and thump or kill everyone who might identify them. There has never been a fucking eyewitness. I want you to find those motherfuckers and painfully show them that nobody fucks with us and lives to talk about it."

"I know you want them found and dealt with, but who am I looking for, Tony?"

"I don't know… you're our problem solver, so use those skills you have developed to find your target and end the problem. They might be drug runners who occasionally need money to buy a load. That would make them small timers, probably users themselves, and that would be why they don't keep enough cash to floor plan their own deals. It could be those bastards out of Columbia. They could be fucking with us to drive us out of the Caribbean."

Vincenzo said, "I thought the Ortegas and your family were long-time friends."

"We are, but that has nothing to do with power and money. Maybe they want to start washing their cash through their own casinos."

Tony thought for a moment and said, "It could be one of the radical political groups that want to save the fucking world, but are a few bucks short. All I do know, is I want those cocksuckers found and fucking dead. Drop anything else that you got going and get me some information. If it is Ortega, let me know before you kill him."

Vincenzo said, "You know, boss, that's a tall order with no leads to work on."

"Find the fucking leads you asshole, you know how to do it. Quit trying to break my balls and find those… motherfucking… bastards!"

"Might take some time Tony, cruising around the beautiful Caribbean, rum and tonic in hand, sweet young things under my arms so I don't stick out like a man looking for something," he said with a pleasant smile.

"Drink yourself stupid and fuck 'til your dick falls off, I don't give a shit, but you better find those cocksuckers before the Circle of Fifteen removes me. I got a lot of confidence in you, Vincenzo; you never let me down before so don't start now. If word gets out that someone is targeting the Mafia and getting away with it we'll lose respect, and next thing you know everyone will start fucking with us. You know as well as I do, we need that fear to keep the chumps away."

ST. CROIX

WHILE TONY-THE-POP WAS BELLOWING INSTRUCTIONS TO VINCENZO over the huge office table in Sicily, Sidney sat at his cheap dining table in St. Croix. His dirty paper cup was refilled again as he was sorting the contents of the second package. There was 230,000 United States dollars stuffed in it. The third package, also from the same cruise ship, contained another 173,000 dollars. About a third of that currency was Euros. The jewelry was looked at, but there was nothing spectacular in the collection, nevertheless it was treasure so he kept it.

The fourth package was opened and spread out as the others had been. Sidney, sitting there with a little buzz-on from the rum and looking at his treasure, had the feeling of what a great life it was. The memories of the pain and fear he caused other people to experience had never existed in his mind—not even for a second. He went to the closet and replaced the trapdoor and the closet rod.

He shoved a couple handfuls of one hundred-dollar bills, which he guessed was about twenty thousand dollars, into his backpack. The rest he put into a garbage bag and used a twist tie to keep it shut. He tossed the black bag over his shoulder as he walked out of the apartment's back door, taking his old dirty cup with him.

The mountain slope was nearly forty degrees of trees and Virgin Islands catch-and-keep thorn bushes. He made his way three-quarters of the way up the mountain. It was a journey he was very familiar with as he made the trip several times a year. In fact he had been making the same trip since he was a child following his father. The only difference was that his father had carried a canvas sack over his shoulder since plastic garbage bags didn't exist, at least in the islands. Nothing much else had changed with the passage of time. The difficult walk up the mountain, the same no-see-ums and hungry mosquitoes still swarmed over him.

He finally came to a small outcropping of rocks that was his destination. Sidney sat down on one of the rocks. Not to rest but to look around. He was stone-still for a while and listened for movement in the woods around him. After he was satisfied that he was the only human around, he stood up, turned around and began digging underneath the rock he had been sitting on. Sticking his hands beneath it, the one hundred twenty pound rock wasn't difficult for him to pick up and move, exposing a twenty-inch hole that it had covered. The exposed bottom of the rock had a rope attached to an iron eyebolt buried in the rock.

It wasn't just a hole; it was the entrance to the *Cave of Snakes.* Only male members of the Sidney X family have known of the cave for hundreds of years. The entrance shaft went straight down for fifty feet without getting any larger and the rope had to be used to enter or leave the cavern. Before going down he dropped the plastic bag full of cash and jewelry down the black hole.

For someone to go down a narrow hole like that, for the first time, would be extremely unlikely, it was too claustrophobic for anyone with any sense in his head. And nobody would want to be lowered headfirst so they could see what is below waiting for them. Going feet first they would be unable to see what kind of snake pit could be waiting. That would bring out the worst kind of claustrophobia. Sidney knew exactly what was below and was not the least apprehensive.

The vertical shaft led to a cavern that had a ceiling about five feet high. In the years past, there had been a stick wrapped with weeds or cloth and soaked with oil to be lit for light in the cavern. This had been replaced with oil lanterns and they, in turn, were replaced with battery-powered lanterns. Batteries were easier to replace than lugging fuel up the mountain. He turned on the first lantern. The light, blinding at first, bathed the rock walls with its yellow glow. The light quickly faded to blackness in the hollow of the tunnel.

He had to walk hunched over to keep from banging his head on the rock ceiling. The cavern angled down, going deep into the belly of the mountain for a quarter of a mile, and then another branch turned back up again, almost vertically. Going up wasn't difficult, as his forefathers had carved steps in the rock. The vertical climb leveled off at a larger cavern. The room was about fifty feet round and was ten to fifteen feet high. It was not an ordinary cavern; it was cluttered with all kinds of glittering things.

The clutter consisted of several old wooden chests with brass shackles and tangs that had tarnished to dark, ages ago. Five of them were the large sea-chests issued to the Royal British Naval Ships during the seventeenth and eighteenth centuries. Those were full of all kinds of trinkets, as Sidney called them. The trinkets were coins of gold and silver and every kind of jewelry imaginable. Dozens of smaller chests were scattered everywhere and all contained pretty much the same contents. Also scattered around were enough weapons to mount an assault on a sizeable group of men. Very few of those weapons, however, were produced much after the Spanish American War. Also cluttering up the room were dozens of bulging plastic garbage bags just like the one Sidney had brought with him.

He walked into the room and casually tossed the bag full of money into a corner heaped up with several other bags. He found and lit two other lanterns in the room, changing the dark shapes of chests and treasures to sparkling and brightly shining objects. Everything in the room was sacred to him, as it had been for his ancestors. The room was the history and testimony of the accomplishments of Sidney Xavier, the first through the twenty-third... It was proof of the Sidneys' legacy of piracy; they were, without a doubt, the Kings of the Sea, known to seamen throughout the ages as the phantom, Barracuda.

Somewhere else in the old cavern was another legacy... the old pirate tradition of *tresure guarden*. The Cave of Snakes had the bones of a very ferocious pirate, known as the Snake in Sidney XIV's day, that were placed inside the original entrance and had to be buried when civilization began cluttering up the island.

CAVE OF SNAKES

IN THE STILL SILENCE OF THE CAVERN AND LANTERN'S YELLOW GLOW, Sidney opened one of the large chests and pulled out an old and thick book with a tattered leather cover. It was centuries old with worn and faded letters on the cover that read *HMS Good Hope*. It had been the ship's log for that vessel, a 173-foot square rigger. It was one of the many ships' logs converted to the Sidneys' Logbook. All raids, successful or unsuccessful, had been entered in a log since the family went into business. It was an important family tradition to enter all actions and thoughts that occurred during the taking of the prize for the future generations of the Sidneys. Every Sidney had used it to come to terms with his failures, guilt on the occasional too-bloody raids, and to measure their conquests with the Sidneys who had gone to join the others in Davy Jones's locker.

The first three pages were handwritten by the captain of the *Good Hope* describing her maiden voyage. It listed the problems experienced, the performance obtained, names of the ship's crew, weather and navigational records. The first entry in the log by the Sidney was on page four. It described briefly the brutal way the captain and crew had been dispatched, the fiery death of the *HMS Good Hope,* and the handsome treasure taken by Sidney XI.

Sidney XXIII, as all of his ancestors, faithfully maintained the log. He found the first blank page and wrote in his best, but unpracticed, hand:

January 16 ~ Sidney XXIII is presented with a quick prize with none of the exhaustive planning required for most raids. I was sitting in a bar in the town of Ocho Rios, Jamaica, when I overheard part of a conversation. Two men were giving instruction to another in hushed tones. The only reason to be so quiet with a tense conversation had to indicate something was happening that could be dangerous or costly to the party doing the talking. Once in a while the other man nodded his head indicating that he understood. Also the two men doing the talking had several drinks while the lone man had only coffee. The two men left the attaché they had carried in when they left the bar. It was placed on the other man's side of the booth, and that was enough to confirm my suspicions.

I hastily went outside and watched the two men leaving the parking lot, and then I pushed my body through a thick growth of banana trees and the wild overgrowth and patiently waited. From my vantage point I could see if anyone entered or left the bar. In less than two minutes the lone man emerged with the attaché in hand. He walked away from me, presenting his back, and his attention was focused on finding his car. Using the skills passed on to me through my father, I moved without a sound at three times the speed of the other man. I stayed in the shadows and was invisible except to the most attentive observer. As the man reached out to unlock his car door, I laid Billy on the right rear of his head, causing his body to twist to the left and almost hand the attaché to me.

Without breaking stride, I caught the case handle in midair and kept walking to another clump of dark shadows. I worked my way well back into the jungle before opening the case. It was locked, but my trusty knife popped the catches open. I wasn't surprised to find that it was full of U.S. dollars, which I transferred to my backpack, leaving the case behind. Before discarding the case, however, I wiped it to remove my fingerprints.

It is with pleasure to add the prize of 120,000 U.S. dollars to the Sidneys' Cave of Snakes.

Sid put a match to a cigar and took a swig from the rum cask that was nearly empty before he made his next entry.

January 22 ~ Sidney XXIII, after much research and lying in wait for the passenger ship *Sea Flower*, of the Italian Sicilya Lines, to arrive in the port of Ocho Rios, she dropped her anchor at 0400 a quarter-mile offshore. The deck crew was busy readying the ferryboats that would take the passengers to the shops on the beach after the sun was well up. A waning half-moon with clouds helped cut out the night light.

In my hotel room, I dressed in a black wetsuit with my pack snugly strapped to my back. I gained the ocean by walking unobserved across the beach by staying in the shadows of sea grape trees. Then I swam at a slow silent pace being careful not to splash lest the deckhands see someone swimming as I approached the ship.

At the ship's anchor chain I used a short piece of nylon string to tie my left hand to the chain. I must relax my muscles after the long swim so when I pulled my body weight up the chain the muscles would not cramp. I floated on my back for five minutes concentrating on the sky with the constellation Orion almost overhead. It fully relaxed me. I used the string to tie my swim fins to the chain, dry my hands the best I could on the chain and then pulled myself out of the water and up fifty feet of chain, hand over hand and with ease.

When I reached the deck level no one was near the bow. White lights were on in the wheelhouse. I'm exposed for only five seconds to pull myself through the hawsehole to get on deck and in the shadow of the anchor windlass. I make my way to the bridge by climbing on railings up three more decks. Three men were working in the bridge. The decks below were getting busy, however, mainly it was the ship's cooks and crew getting things set up for the six o'clock feeding of the fat hungry tourists.

I crouched in shadows, watching the men in the house. They were Norwegian and talking while tending to their duties. One man was sitting at a small desk facing the rear bulkhead doing paperwork. Another had a mop and was cleaning the bridge's floor. The last had his head and shoulders buried in an electrical cabinet, doing maintenance.

I waited until the floor cleaner had turned his back and then I quickly opened the door, took six steps and laid Billy on his right rear skull. I grabbed him and the mop to keep the sound of them hitting the floor from alerting the other men. I quickly lowered him to the floor and then laid Billy on the desk man. Another eight steps and I was at the maintenance man. He heard the thump of the paper worker's head hitting the desk, but before he could turn to see he was out cold and lying on the floor.

I taped the men up securely and stuffed them into the bridge's equipment room to keep them out of view in case someone came by. That wasn't likely though, as most ship crews take advantage of every minute when on anchor to sleep. I found the crew's room assignments on the bulkhead where the man doing the paperwork was sitting. The captain was in room 456, the purser in room 448. All officers were on the same deck just behind the bridge. I had no trouble finding the purser; unfortunately, his cabin door was locked. I didn't have time to find a master key so I went back to the bridge and called the purser's cabin on the ship's phone. The man answered with a tired, gruff voice.

Using Norwegian, I said, "This is the bridge. The captain wants you here now, and on the double." Then I went back down the hall and stood beside the purser's door until it opened. As he started to come out, I stick the point of my trusty blade at the man's throat, and with my other hand I put a finger to the purser's lips signaling him stay quiet. I walked into the room pushing the purser back with the blade's point. I pulled off the six-inch piece of tape I had already torn and had stuck to my stomach, and put it over his mouth. Then I used my roll of duct tape to secure his hands and feet, then another piece over his eyes. I lowered him to the floor and sat on his chest. Only then did I speak, he was frightened.

"If you make any moves to get away, or cause me any trouble, you're going to lose body parts with every attempt, starting with one of your ears. Nod your head if you understand."

The gagged and blinded man nodded his head. I said, "You are going to open both of the ship's safes. I want the casino safe and the ship's operating safe. After I have the money I will release you, unharmed. If you offer any resistance you'll lose body parts until you fully cooperate. If you pass out or faint, I will kill you. If I kill you then I will get the captain to open the safes for me, and I will still walk away with the ship's cash, and you will either be mutilated for life or be dead. It is entirely your decision. Do you understand?"

Another series of grunts and head nodding told me the man understood his position. I told him, "I am going to remove the tape from your mouth, and want you to whisper where the money is kept." The tape is pulled off. The man was either very frightened or mad as his whole body was trembling. In a shaky voice he said, "You must be crazy, you can't steal from these people. You had better think about what you are doing. The people that own this ship are not the kind of people that take being robbed very kindly. They are very powerful and revengeful. You cannot possibly get away with this."

If he only knew, I laughed to myself, but I only said, "Where is the money?" I grabbed an ear and put my blade on it.

The man said nothing. I put the tape back over his mouth. His attitude cost him an ear. He went berserk. Then I punched the man in his stomach knocking the wind out of him. He stopped thrashing about. The panicked man was trying desperately to get air into his lungs through only his nostrils. My weight on his chest didn't help.

I said to him, "You were warned and you ignored me. You just lost an ear." Then I reached over with my other hand to touch the other ear with my blade. The man was going wild with fear, and he still was unable to get a decent breath of air. The lack of air combined with the real and imaginary pain and fear was causing him much anxiety. An older man would have died. I let the wound bleed for effect then slapped a piece of tape over the hole to slow the blood flow—I didn't want to lose him yet.

I let the man calm down for a moment, then said, "I am going to take the tape off your mouth again. I want directions to the safes. If you resist, then you are going to lose the other ear, and after that it will be your nose. Protecting money for some greasy Italians who steal from others and have lots of money is going to make you a very freaky and ugly looking man. Maybe with plastic surgery they can stick some plastic parts back on your head. Although I don't believe I've ever heard of a plastic penis. Have you?"

When the tape was pulled off, the man spoke in a coarse voice, but was totally submissive and said, "The safes are in the administrator's office on the next deck down. There is a floor plan of that deck on my table."

I asked him, "Are they keyed safes or combinations?"

The man answered, "Combinations," and then he stiffened in anticipation of the next question from his sadistic torturer. "What are the combinations?"

The man refused to reply until I started putting the tape back over his mouth. The purser quickly changed his mind. In a resigned voice he told me the combinations. He also volunteered that the key to the office was the gold one on his key ring.

I thanked him and said, "I'm going to give you a little thump that will put you to sleep for a few minutes while I go down to the safes. If the numbers you gave me are right then you will not have to deal with me again. If they are not the right numbers then I'll be back to finish mutilating you."

The purser made no attempt to change the numbers so I felt they must be right. I laid Billy in just the right spot to put the man out for an hour.

In less than two minutes I was working the first safe. I only had another twenty minutes until daylight started creeping in. The combinations were right. Both safes were full of money, jewels and passports from the passengers for safekeeping. I stuffed my pack full of the cash and put several pieces of jewelry in another zip-lock bag. Then I went back to the purser. He was unconscious when I slipped my trusty blade into his heart. He had seen my face so he had to die. Then I hid the bag of jewelry in a box in the closet, thinking the cops would probably find it and blame it on an employee for the theft and murder.

Five minutes later, I was at the anchor chain and lowering myself over the side and down the chain, hand over hand, back to the black water. I quietly swam away in the darkness until I felt bottom about twenty feet from shore. The sky and water were the same shade of early morning gray; the only color I saw was the dull green of the normally lush green jungle behind rocks separating us. I didn't go back to the hotel, for there was no need. Instead I made landfall about a half a mile away in an isolated area. In the jungle I took off the wetsuit, and from a baggy in my pack, I took out dry clothes and dressed.

In few minutes I was downtown in Ocho Rios at the bus station waiting for the bus to Montego Bay. By ten that morning I was in Montego Bay eating a huge breakfast washed down with Red Stripe and a Cohiba.

It is with pleasure that I add 403,000 U.S. dollars and Euros plus jewelry and a notable diamond necklace to the Sydneys' Cave of Snakes.

The log was the family's history—the records were true. The tricks used and brutality described only added to the information they'd have to use when it was a new Sidney's turn to add to the treasure and continue building their tradition.

Sidney put the log down and thought about the events that started his ancient grandfather in the business of pirating. Sidney the first was born into a poor seaman's family in Belfast, Ireland. His father, Patrick, lost a leg when injured when the cargo shifted on the merchantman he sailed on as quartermaster. He lived the rest of his life in bitter resentment towards the rich ship owners who couldn't care less about him or the other seamen injured or lost at sea.

At a young age, Sidney went to sea, not as a seaman, but as a pirate seeking revenge for his father. With only vengeance in his heart, he was good at killing and pillaging, and soon was known as the Barracuda because he would strike suddenly without notice and not much would be left of the crew when he took his prize. He died at the ripe old age of forty-six owning a sizable estate in Scotland—and had more gold than he wished to spend.

Sidney's brothers had followed his father's calling; the brothers were all killed in separate incidences at sea as ordinary seamen, and, true to tradition, the owners didn't give a damn.

Sidney's two sons began learning the new family business at the age of six, when their mother died. He made sure that the boys would never be a slave to another man.

By the time they were grown they had proven time again that their father had taught them well. One brother, Patrick, was killed protecting his younger brother, Sidney Jr, during a raid.

Since then, all first-born sons were named Sidney and were taught that no man, or government of men, had any right to tell them how to live or what to like and dislike. Rules were made by the weak for the benefit of the weak who were too cowardly to risk life to live like men and seek adventure and fortune.

All Sidneys since were taught the same lessons which started intensely at age six. It wasn't about money, it was about lifestyle, total freedom, adventure, and to uphold the family name and reputation in the maritime universe.

Sidney XXII had taken his son at age six, from his mother, a Venezuelan whore. He began learning the trade that same day. He soon forgot his mother and later in life he had no idea who she was or where he had been born.

Sidney XXIII had paid several Dominican whores to give him a son. The first boys proved faulty; they didn't demonstrate raw courage or toughness, they cried continually. The last boy had those qualities, but he was only five years old, but soon to be six.

Sidney, as most all Sidneys, had no concept what that stuff called love was all about. The idea of sharing his life with a woman was as foreign and unnatural as eating meatloaf would be to the average woodpecker.

Sidney XXIII had certainly lived up to the role of the Barracuda. He enjoyed the danger, the thrill of the chase, and taking the prize. He would soon pass those skills and knowledge on to his son, Sidney XXIV.

He wanted to spend the day in the cave reading the old log but knew it would have to wait; he had to be on the other side of the island soon to buy the boat he needed for his next attack on the Italians. He put the log away in its protective bag, turned out the lamps, and headed back to the cave's entrance. It used to have two entrances, a large opening into the cave was down the mountain near his marina, but it had been sealed off a hundred years ago.

The Sidneys had owned the mountain and all land within five miles of it in all directions for almost two hundred years. It was purchased from the Dutch, when they claimed the island. Ownership meant privacy and that meant security for their treasure cave. The only structures ever built there was the marina and a two-unit apartment building that Sidney XXII had made. They only reason he made both was because he liked to party, and the apartment building was his private whorehouse. The only other thing on the property was his father's house near the mountaintop in the jungle.

Sidney secured the Cave of Snakes' entrance and he went back to his apartment. A quick wipe-down to remove the dirt and grime from the cave's entrance and a big swig from the rum keg was all he needed before going to buy the catamaran. He stuffed thirty thousand dollars into his pack and left. Twenty thousand was all he was going to pay for the boat; the rest was going to his father to live on until he returned.

His father could not get into the cave any longer as he was confined to a wheelchair. Sidney XXIII was hoping to get his father to keep the boy when he turned six-years old. His dad could start the training, and the boy could make cash runs for the old man—that is, if the kid survived the horrid jungle test.

ST. MAARTEN

VINCENZO "THE SICILIAN" JONES HAD ARRIVED ON THE LAST FLIGHT from Europe the night before. That morning he was sitting by the luxurious swimming pool of the Tropical Sea Resort Hotel and Casino. His Bloody Mary, more than half empty, had been sitting untouched for the last twenty minutes.

He was engrossed in a map he had stretched out on the poolside table. The map covered all of the West Indies and he had two other maps showing all routes cruise ships traveled, and another showed routes used by commercial shipping. He was carefully drawing both routes on the overall detailed map. His next step was to put little marks at every incidence where the mob's ships and other businesses had been hit. He hoped that after everything was marked he'd be able to see a pattern.

The Sicilian's concentration was interrupted by a shapely young thing who strutted by making a poolside flirt. All eyes followed as she made a slow trip all the way around the pool, showing everyone what they were missing, and returned to Vincenzo's table where she sat down with all of the grace and sexuality possible to put into a twenty-three year old body.

"Rita, drum up business on your own time; you are on mine now."

She answered with a pout on her soft sexy face, "Oh, Al, you know I'm only trying to get your attention. You're all the man I want, darling."

"Yeah, sure I am, unless the bell man or the fucking cleaning crew has the fifteen hundred a day to sweat up that beautiful fucking body of yours. I thought you were going to sleep in this morning."

"I tried, darling, but I got so horny thinking about you giving me a good old fashioned horsefucking that I couldn't stand it. I wanted to make you want me. Don't you want to take a little break—those maps won't change, but I will. I might not be able to handle your rejection and hurt my creamy pussy on the bedroom doorknob."

Her sexy presentation only confirmed why she was worth every dime of the fifteen hundred a day, and he gathered up his maps, thinking only about her naked body being next to his. The beautiful vista of the Caribbean Sea and swaying palms and cool breeze of the tropical tradewind before him were all lost to him. His mind was already in bed with sexy little Rita.

ST. CROIX

EARLY RETIREMENT WAS HARD ON SIDNEY'S FATHER. BAD LUCK FOUND him swimming to shore with a backpack heavily laden with three gold bars he had liberated from a cruising sailboat off the north coast of St. Maarten.

Using an established family tactic, he sailed up behind the cruising boat with a fast little Hobie Cat that he had stolen from a hotel's beach. That night, neither the sailor nor his wife had a clue that he was approaching. The faster catamaran sailed up to and slightly past the transom of the big sailboat. When in the right position, his father stepped off of the cat and onto the cruiser. He quickly moved forward to the center cockpit, and slipped his knife deep into the back of the cruiser's skull, where the spinal cord meets the head. The man died not feeling a thing or making a sound.

His wife was below and asleep in her berth. She would never wake up. He had been tracking the boat since Martinique where the couple had arrived from Sicily. They had made a fatal error by spending too much money everywhere they went. On one occasion and over too many cocktails, they bragged to all who cared to listen that they had gone to a bank to take a couple of chips off one of their gold bars to re-stock their cruising kitty. Too bad; they had made a grave mistake, and didn't know that experienced cruisers go out of their way to appear poor. Those people had asked for it as far as Sidney XXII was concerned—besides, they were Italian—and probably mafia.

His plan was to take the gold and steer the cruising boat in close to shore. When he was within swimming distance, the autopilot was set to take the boat out into the Atlantic. He jumped overboard for a quick swim to shore; all went as planned — except in the dark waters, on a dark night, a passing Tiger shark felt the vibrations of kicking feet working hard to support the weight of the gold. Surely the shark thought he was hearing a damaged fish. With one chomp, his father lost both feet that night, but the gold bars were safely resting in one of the family's chests in the Cave of Snakes.

Forced off his own boat, *Veinte Dos Barracoutas,* because he refused to crawl on his knees to get around, he built a house on his mountaintop. Life had changed drastically for him. He longed for the sea, adventure, danger and the feeling of taking the prize; it was the only life he had ever known or expected. Now his thrills were reduced to chasing one whore or another around his house in his wheelchair.

The highlight in life now was when his son returned from a raid. He didn't care about the son, only the adventurous details of the raids that he was obligated to tell him. There were no emotional bonds between the father and son, other than profound respect for upholding the family tradition. The only emotion Sidney XXII had was envy—envy of the all action his son was experiencing.

SIDNEY XXIII FILLED A GLASS WITH RUM AND HEADED OUT TO THE JEEP. It was time to start working on his next raid. He met the man who advertised the boat and concluded the deal without haggling. The man was paid in cash, on the spot. Sidney told him to hold the title because he was leaving the island and would call him with an address to send it to later. Sidney didn't want the title and sure as hell didn't want his name connected to it.

With the quick deal concluded, Sidney left the boat where it was and drove up to his father's house. His mind was on convincing his dad to help train the boy so he could spend his time raiding the family's favorite enemy, the Italian Mafia. His father had done a good job teaching him and he rationalized it would be good for him to have some responsibility in raising the boy. He hadn't talked about it to his father, but it was on his mind more and more as time drew nearer to the day he'd become a dad.

Sidney knew that if he asked his father for help outright, he'd certainly refuse and it would be a closed subject forever. He had never outsmarted the old pirate, but he had to find a way where his father would think that it was his own idea. His father had never married and lived alone except for a constant flow of hookers who moved in and out. He paid them for sex, cooking and cleaning his house; to dear old dad, he had a perfect life.

Sidney XXIII didn't bother knocking on the door; he opened the screen door and walked in. He and his father didn't have a father/son relationship; they were more like co-workers or maybe acquaintances who had worked together for years. Neither of them showed emotions because neither was capable of feeling emotions. The closest thing they experienced that could be called an emotion was the feeling that the other was the only person they wouldn't want to fight; it was fear without a name.

Although Sidney never consciously thought about it, he was always glad to see his father. He damn sure respected him as he had been a hell of a pirate before he lost his feet. Reading some of the log entries his father had written made Sidney have a strange feeling inside; unknown to him, that feeling wasn't only respect— it was admiration.

No one was in sight in the big house so he called out, "Sid, you here?" A gruff voice answered, "I'll be with you in a minute. I heard you were back."

There was another hushed voice talking to his father. Sidney heard him answer the voice, "Relax, it's only my kid, now shut up and fuck."

A few minutes later his father was pushed into the sitting room by a beautiful woman with the blackest skin Sidney had ever seen. His father introduced her. "She's Anna, the best damn fuck in the entire world. She has been living here for a couple of months."

That was very unusual as he either ran the girls off in a couple of days or they fled as soon as they had enough money. He was a little hard on the ladies with his incessant hard-on.

The Sidneys didn't shake hands; they just nodded to each other.

"Did you have a successful trip?"

Nonchalantly, his son answered, "Yeah."

Number twenty-two told Anna to bring them a couple of beers. When she returned with the beers she was then told to go outside and take a long walk. She got the message that the two men didn't want to be disturbed for a while and left after kissing the older man on the cheek and completely ignoring the younger. She played the game like the expert she was.

The next hour was the time his father had been looking forward to. It was also the only time that Sidney would ever talk to anybody and use more than just one or two words or grunts. As part of his family's heritage, Sidney must enter his raids in the log for all Sidneys to know, but since his father didn't have access, he had to be told every detail.

Sid senior listened and reacted like a child watching an enjoyable program on television. It was as if he was living the experiences being told to him by his son. Once in a while he would interrupt Sidney with a question or a suggestion on what he would have done, but for the most part he was silent and attentive to every word.

Reading about his father, grandfathers, and his own daring accomplishments had always been very special to Sid senior. He had asked his son to bring him the log so he could read it once in a while, but Sidney had always refused. They both knew the log could never be put into a position where it could be damaged or read by another person. It was the one thing sacred to their family. Besides, if the law ever found it, they both would be executed; the treasure found and confiscated by government thieves; their land confiscated, and it would be the end of one of the longest recorded family in history. Sidney X would cease to exist. While he knew his son was correct in refusing to bring the log, he would drop the subject—until the next visit.

After he was filled in with the details of his son's raids, he surprised Sidney by saying, "Our family has some history to it kid, and you damn sure have contributed. Speaking of family history, when are you going to produce a son to take over?"

Sidney shrugged his shoulder.

After a brief silence, Senior said, "You think you're going to slip him in on me, don't you?"

There was no expression on his face for Sidney to read. He said "No," reasoning there was no sense in telling him now and get into an argument; he would play it the way he had planned. Sidney went for more beers hoping to stop the conversation. When he came back he fished the money out of his pack and gave it to the older Sidney. He kept a single one hundred dollar bill that would be needed to cover his expenses until he pulled off the next raid.

Sid senior said, "You realize how stupid you are for delaying your responsibility any longer? Death comes without warning in this line of business, and if it happens to you then the long line of Sidneys will have ended, and there will be no one to guard the family fortune."

"I'm aware of my responsibility. Remember when I stayed in the Dominican Republic for over a year? Well, I was looking for the right women. Whenever I found one with the right spirit and temperament I offered her ten thousand dollars to have sex with only me to produce a male child in good health. If she produced my son and it was proven to be mine with a blood test, she'd get another ten thousand dollars. Part of the deal was that she kept the child until his sixth birthday, and then she'd have to turn him over to me. When she does, she'll be paid another ten thousand dollars."

"Damn boy, you're spoiling them. Shit, I only paid the woman who had you three thousand—total."

"I don't care about the money; I just don't want to fuck with the details. I figured if I paid too much then she's not going to get fucking emotional when I take him away."

"So did you do any good?"

"I have four sons and three daughters with seven different women."

"I'll be damnd. Why didn't you tell me? Are any of them good enough?"

"I've seen the boys each year to observe which of them exhibit the qualities needed. Two of the four boys are in the running and both are about the same age. I haven't decided which to choose. I might take them both and see who prevails."

"That might not be a good idea. If they are equal in spirit they might kill each other in the competition. These aren't children's games you know."

"I'm aware of what happens. I'll make the decision when I go there in a few months. If something happened to me now at least you can train one of them. I'll write the names and how to find them for you before I leave."

The elder Sidney wasn't concerned with how he'd get money if his son was killed. He'd hire a patsy to go into the cave, bring him the money, and then kill him on the spot.

Sidney finished his beer while listening to his father tell him about what had been going on in his life. When he started running out of things to say, Sidney got up and said, "I have to go. I'm making a run to St. Maarten. I've been hitting the sea lanes pretty hard, and thought I would do a couple of banks."

His father said, "That's smart; let it cool down for a year or so. Are you still pissing on the legs of the Italians?"

"Yep."

"Good."

That was the pattern the Sidneys had used for the last hundred years or so. Keep moving; don't raid just one type of vessel or business. Make it hard if not impossible for the law to establish a pattern. And, as far as the law was concerned, most of the raids the Sidneys did were thought to be inside jobs. No one had ever been able to give a description of him. That, too, had been family tradition since the beginning. If somebody saw a Sidney before he could lay Billy on them, they had to be killed. Quite often the body would be dumped overboard and never found, giving rise to speculation that the person or persons had committed the crime. Back in the early days, especially for the first Sidney, entire crews and their ships would disappear. That Sidney had a flare for sinking ships to cover his tracks.

For the last few years, Sidney XXIII had been hitting businesses owned by the Mafia. He had nothing against Italian people, but couldn't tolerate the swaggering and obnoxious attitudes the wise guys openly demonstrated. It all started when Sidney went into a wharf side bar in New York. He listened to loud mouth thugs, all Italians, bragging about what big time criminals they were. Big time criminals don't admit their crimes, only lowly liars and cheats who were living off the reputations of the few who were exceptional criminals.

That gave Sidney the idea to go after the wealth the mob was raking in. The world's law enforcement communities would not spend their time and budgets trying to return stolen property to thieves and murderers. Also, the mob would do everything possible to keep it quiet that someone was casually ripping them off. It would be a terrible marinara whip-slap on their spaghetti-sucking faces.

Sidney headed back to his marina with a powerful thirst for some demon rum. A little demon woman would be nice, too. Things were happening at the deck bar; half of the people were drunk and the other half were rapidly getting there. The loud mouth who tried to put Sidney on the spot was there and telling another story that everyone seemed to enjoy.

He thought it was a shame that man lived in the marina because if he were on any other island, he'd stick the loud show-off with his blade. A couple inches of cold steel would take that cockiness out of him. But, Sidney never did anything to attract attention, especially on his island.

Sitting at the bar, he saw absolutely no prospects at getting laid. There were only three women and each had a man attached. With little chance for a lusty romp in the sack being offered, he concluded it was a good excuse to get blasted. He liked to get drunk, and frequently did, but never when in pursuit of a prize. Starting tomorrow he'd be on the hunt, scouting out the area, the bank and the personnel working there. His plan made him chuckle every time he thought of it. He'd have some fun while taking a lot of cash away from a certain bank in St. Maarten.

That night he sat at the bar until closing, not speaking to anyone, just getting drunk—he did a good job. The next morning when he woke up, only his head and torso were face down on the bed, his legs were on the floor.

He struggled to clear his thoughts; his present position indicated that he had come home on remote control last night. Another indication confirming what he suspected was a large pool of rum on the floor. Apparently, he had poured himself another glass of rum from his newly purchased keg and forgot to turn the spigot off. Yet another indication was a reading table and chair that were lying on their sides. He sort of remembered knocking them over, as he tried to stagger around them.

Yep, he felt like shit as he surveyed the damage. With a blank expression on his face he mumbled, "Fuck it." Five minutes in a cold water shower later, he dressed in a fresh pair of shorts, thanks to Sally, and was on his way to the deck bar for breakfast.

After a huge breakfast, Sid felt great and had the bartender /cook that morning, who was Sally, call him a taxi. When the taxi arrived, he stood up and said, "Sally, I'll be gone for a while."

She nooded her head and sincerely said, "Mr. Xavier, have a pleasant trip, but hurry back." Her farewell message never changed.

Sidney had the taxi driver stop at a grocery store where he bought a sack of canned food and two gallons of black paint and a roller. He didn't want to be seen any more than necessary in St. Maarten so he would eat on the boat until he took his prize.

He didn't bother checking the fuel level or the water on board the boat. He disconnected the water hose off of the boat next to him and pumped water into the tank for about two minutes. After throwing the hose back on the other boat, he untied the dock lines and was gone. Ten minutes later, he was stark naked and sailing a direct tack to where St. Maarten would be. Sidney didn't need a compass or a fancy GPS; he knew where the island was even though he didn't use a chart.

He had been sailing since he was six years old and was taught the art of navigation by dead reckoning—reading and understanding the natural signs such as wind and sea swell directions, the sun and stars. He navigated just like the first Sidney did, but now he had the advantage of increased knowledge about the earth, its seas, and land masses.

Sidney's travels to and from other islands was almost always done by sailboat. It was, after all, the traditional way of transportation for a pirate. Traveling the modern way was not for Sidney for other reasons, as well. Without official identification papers, a social security number, passport or driver's license, he couldn't fly or rent cars.

Sidney could very easily have bought phony documents and changed them as frequently as he wished, but he didn't bother and wouldn't just for principle. He didn't even own a wallet. A rubber band or paper clip or two was all he needed to hold his money together and that was carried either in his pant's pocket or pack, depending on how much he had on him.

While under sail, he tackled one of the two tasks he had for that day. He selected one of the big 8-D batteries and carried it up on deck. After emptying the acid overboard he used his knife and a winch handle to knock a big hole in the bottom of the battery. The lead plates were removed and the empty battery was tied to a stout line and thrown overboard to let the saltwater wash off and neutralize the acid's residue. After a good soaking, it was pulled out and put back in place in the engine room.

His next project was a strange one; he turned on the bilge pump and let it run dry while he found a loose wire. He then put the wire on both water pump terminals, which shorted out the pump and it started smoking before it shut down forever.

Next, he disconnected the two-inch diameter head's discharge hose. He pulled it loose and water gushed into the boat. He stood there and watched the water spout for a few minutes, and then put the hose back on, using a new hose clamp. He had picked up an old broken hose clamp lying around in his marina. The broken clamp was placed near the head. He had just given himself a reason for not possessing documents if stopped by the law when entering the island.

For the rest of that day and night, he sailed and took an occasional nap. During the dark night hours, Sidney had no inclination to sleep; he loved sailing at night in the Caribbean. He never tired of watching the night's sky full of bright stars. He didn't see the stars as cold distant rocks or fireballs circling the universe, he saw them as something of beauty, as well as signposts for navigation. The night was a visual gift to be watched and appreciated.

The weather was clear, and just before daylight he could pick out the glow of lights on various islands. St. Maarten, by his reckoning, was dead ahead. By eleven o'clock, he sailed into Grand Bay and dropped anchor. He then went below to get a couple hours of sleep.

ST. MAARTEN

VINCENZO, THE SICILIAN, SOMEHOW HAD MANAGED TO GET THE SHIP-ping routes accurately plotted on his chart in between the physically de-manding fucking sessions with his pretty and high-priced nymphoma-niac. He was sitting at the same poolside table trying to concentrate on the incident locations while the sexy little kitten was massaging his inner thighs. It was a lost cause; his mind was being consumed by lust. The beautiful vista of the Caribbean Sea and swaying palms and cool breeze of the tropical tradewind before him—as well as the catamaran sailboat anchored a little ways offshore and the man rowing the dinghy to shore—were completely lost to him. His mind was already in bed with sexy lit-tle Rita.

SIDNEY'S ROWING TO SHORE WAS PLEASANT AND GAVE HIS MUSCLES A slight workout. He felt a pang of guilt at the thought of exercise, which he had not done for two days. At his age, with his occupation, being in top shape was the most important thing to keep him alive.

His purpose of going to shore was to walk around Philipsburg to get the layout of various bank locations. The last time he was there was five years ago and he was sure that with all of the drug business cash going through the island, new banks were surely added. While his target was only one bank, there could be other locations if there were branches for the same bank. Another branch might offer a better location.

He pulled the dinghy up on Tropical Sea Resort's beach. The last time he was there, he had raided the casino. The prize had contributed greatly to the family treasure. He had waited until a particularly large association had their meeting there and raided it just at closing time at six in the morning. Nobody ever knew what had happened or how much money had been lost since the cashier that had counted it was found dead.

He quickly found the main Sicilya International Bank. Satisfied that he knew the town's layout, he removed his flip-flops and started jogging on the main road taking him out of town. He ran slow and easy for a mile to warm up his aging muscles. Then he put more effort into the run, increasing his speed to a half-speed for two more miles. One more mile was run at maximum effort. The trip back to town was a relaxed walk.

As he neared the outskirts of town where the poor people lived, he was approached by three scowling young men. He had noticed them watching him as he ran by earlier. He had a strong feeling that the men would probably be waiting for him when he returned—he was correct.

The men blocked his path, the smallest one said, "Hey! Gimme dollar."

Sidney didn't have a dime on him much less a dollar. He responded, "Ain't got none, and don't want no trouble wid you."

That was about nine more words than he felt like using, but he really didn't want a fight that might attract attention to his presence. If the cops got involved he would have to kill them. He didn't come here to kill cops; he wanted the prize waiting for him in the Sicilya Bank.

Under other circumstances, he would have given the men one chance to back away from him—if they didn't he would have seriously injured them—but on this occasion he had to be nice.

He held his hands up at his sides and said, "Search me."

Two of the men pulled knives out of their pockets; the third felt Sid's pockets for money.

"Dis mudderfucker an't got shit."

The three men just looked at each other until the big one said, "Where you staying?"

Sidney answered, "Tropical Seas."

The would-be robber told him they were going to take him back to his room to get his money, and if he tried to say or do anything, his friends would use their knives on him. He told Sidney in the meanest voice and expression he could muster that they had killed men before who had re-sisted so he better not get any ideas.

Sidney said, "Okay."

The men led him to a rusted out, beat up old Ford. After several at-tempts to get it started, it kicked over and they were noisily on their way. Sidney wasn't threatened and found the tough guys amusing.

When they reached the hotel, the leader told him to go in and bring them his money and again issued the death threat if he didn't. Sidney smiled as he thought, *so that's what smoking crack will do to you.*

The leader, asserting his presence over Sidney by standing too close, looked as menacing as years of mirror practice made it possible. He asked, "What you smil'n 'bout? Don't you know how close to death you be?"

Sidney said, "What happens if I don't come back?"

The smallest man stuck his knife in Sidney's face and said, "You just better mudderfucker, 'cause you can't hide from us on dis island." Then he went on to tell everybody in the car how bad he wanted to cut the smart-ass son-of-a-white-bitch up.

The leader then realized that if someone went in with the man it might be better. He told the others, "I be going to the room wid him to be sure he don't try nutten."

Before getting out of the car, he opened his knife and held it up in front of Sidney's face just like the short little idiot had done, and heralded more threats.

It was dark by then and Sidney led the man around and behind the hotel to the beachfront rooms. As they walked past a bushy clump of trees, Sidney made his move. Before the leader saw what was happening, he was on the ground and in pain. Everything around him was swirling;

he was confused and had no idea where he was or what had happened.

Sidney had turned on the man and at the same time he pushed out his open hand to hit the man in his forehead with the hard heel of his hand. It was a straight shot, impossible to fend off. The suddenness of the blow had as much effect on the man as the force of the punch. It knocked him silly.

Sidney knelt down beside him and lightly slapped his face to get his attention. When the man seemed to be able to understand, Sidney put his face close to the man, and said, "You don't want to ever see me again, understand?"

The groggy man said, "What happened? Who you? Where dis?"

Then the would-be thief started to come around and felt a hand in his pockets, taking his money. "Gonna kill you mudderfucker if you try tak'n my money," he uttered as he was regaining his senses.

"Try it," was Sidney's response. He had no intention of killing the punk, but was having second thoughts. He had planned on breaking the fingers of one hand, but realized that he and his buddies would have to come up with a tale of being attacked at the hospital. That would bring the cops into play.

Sidney counted the money he had taken. It was a whopping seventy-three cents. He put it in his pocket. Then he reached down and gave the recovering man a swift blow to his neck—crushing his windpipe. The thug silently shook and wiggled on the ground, trying desperately to get a breath of air.

Sidney stayed in the darker shadows on his way to the car. The car was easy to find in the dark; the dudes had rap playing too loudly in the car. The two young thugs were moving all of their body parts to the music.

Suddenly the passenger's door slammed open and Sidney jumped in— his body weight keeping the surprised passenger from running— while Sidney delivered another windpipe-breaking blow to the driver. He repositioned himself and sent the same blow to the passenger.

He robbed their painfully dying bodies of everything in their pockets, plus a gold chain from the driver's neck. Including the seventy-three cents, he netted a grand total of a dollar and thirty-two cents, a cheap gold chain, a house key, and a ten-inch piece of string for the day.

The next morning he could see flashing red and blue lights from police cars and ambulances. Someone had discovered the bodies. After a long swim straight out into the Caribbean Sea and leisurely return, he fixed breakfast—a can of beans and a can of sardines.

Ready for work, Sidney took the dinghy back to shore. The first thing he did was find a shop that sold Cuban cigars. The second was to go into the targeted bank for a look around. Then he walked to the telephone company and bought a five dollar phone card and used one of the booths offered to the public. He looked up the numbers of the Tropical Seas and two of the other big casinos on the island.

He told whoever answered that he wanted to reserve a room for a seven-night stay. After giving them a fictitious name and stateside address, he declined to give them a credit card number as he would be arriving early. Then he asked for the name of the bank they deal with so he could open an account to establish a credit line for the casino. All three hotels were owned by the mafia and used the Sicilya Bank, and that confirmed his target.

While at the telephone company, he called the Sea Adventures Yacht Charter Company. He learned which of their mega-yachts would be on charter in the Windward Islands. He wanted to get photos for an article in the All at Sea publication.

His next task that day was to go back to the grocery store near the beach for a couple bottles of rum for the upcoming celebration. The rest of the day would be spent polishing his raiding plan. He already knew what he was going to do—it was going to be fun. But that day he would reflect on the details and catch a few rays.

Sidney lounged around on deck most of the day, lying naked and soaking up the warm rays from the sun and the pleasure from his bottle of rum. Three of the five Cohibas were smoked, which only added to his version of a perfect day.

He was confident that his plan would work and he could control any events that might come up during the raid. Sid was smart in all ways of security and survival; he was also imaginative in planning and performing raids. He had years of first-hand experience and generations of fore-fathers' experiences to lean on when needed.

He knew the bank was covered with surveillance cameras and silent as well as non-silent alarms. He knew there was an armed security guard in the bank or very nearby in case of trouble. He also knew that people in the bank were trained in ways to get a good identification of robbers and a trick or two in apprehending them.

Sidney had never been identified by his victims and had no intention of that happening on the current raid either. He could have broken into the bank the night before the upcoming raid and disable the video cameras and the alarms, but he didn't; it would take the challenge out of the adventure, and after all, that was what it was all about.

Early the next morning, Sidney was up and eating beans again for breakfast. He would have enjoyed washing them down with a cold beer, but none were on board and he didn't have any money left to buy one. He packed his backpack with the tools he'd need: a pair of gloves, two condoms, his sunglasses, the customary roll of tape, his trusty knife, and Billy.

He wanted to be at the bank at nine o'clock as soon as it opened. Before he went into the bank, however, he had a few things to do, so he headed to town after the beans were gone and he had taken a swim in the ocean.

In town, he went to the old gas station he had found only a block away from his target. He dug out an empty paint can from a heaping trash pile behind the station and took it over to the grease pit where used oil and grease were dumped. He filled it up and left it outside when he walked into the station. The attendant was bending over with his head under the hood of an old Chevy.

Sidney walked up and gave the attendant the proper touch with Billy to keep him out for at least an hour, although he knew for sure that the man would be found before that. Sidney emptied the cash drawer for effect and took two cans of mineral spirits with him. He looked around and found an old machete. With the machete he cut a foot long section of black hose off of a roll.

In the tropics a machete was a tool certain classes of men must own. Maybe it was a symbol of the slave days on the sugar plantations, or maybe it was just a macho thing. Didn't matter, either way he had one.

With the cans and machete wrapped up in a torn piece of canvas used as an oil drop, Sid collected his can of thick black goo and walked down the street to the house he had picked out yesterday.

It was a typical low-income type of house that had been painted with leftover paint many times during its existence. Some parts were white, some yellow and some blue. The trim was red. The paint job was commonly seen in the Caribbean; tourists thought the natives did it because it was a colorful cultural thing, but actually they did it because it was a cheap way to protect their homes, and it was widely accepted to use a neighbor's leftover paint.

The house was half a block from the bank and in a thick stand of brush with brilliantly colored flowers surrounding the property, giving it lots of privacy. He moved silently through the yard into the backyard. There was a dog there, but he just wanted to be petted.

Sidney pulled himself through one of the open windows on the side of the house. He could hear a radio playing the gospel of God and a woman humming along. The woman was ironing clothes and a young child was playing at her feet. Whenever the radio preacher said something that had meaning to her she reacted with, "Yes brother! Yes, tell it true!"

It took Sidney three *"yes brothers"* before he could get into position and lay Billy on her. The child at her feet was too young to realize something was wrong. Sidney was glad about that; he had never used Billy on a little kid before —at least one that young. He unplugged the iron and moved the woman into a closet so she would be out of sight if a friend dropped by. The child was put into the closet with her.

He spread a thick layer of old newspapers on the floor. He then found a rolled up pair of socks in the laundry pile waiting to be put away. He stuffed one of the socks into the end of the foot-long black hose, leaving about a round inch sticking out. The condom was pulled over the end of the hose to make it look like the head of a black penis.

Sidney found some thread and tied it to the base of the hose. After he removed all of his clothing, he shoved his penis into the open end of the hose—it was a good fit—the thread tied around his waist to ensure that it'd stay where it was in case his penis decided to shrink in the bank's air conditioned atmosphere.

Standing on the newspaper, he took the can of black grease and covered his body with the slime. He coated his hair with it and pulled clumps of it up into the air to make him appear as a crazed Rastafarian.

The hose and thread were covered with the goo. It was impossible to tell the hose had been tied on. He picked up the telephone, and, in perfect Afro-Carib dialect, told the operator he wanted the police department. When he was put through, he told an excited story about seeing three men go into the gas station and kill a man. He acted very excited. The cops were equally excited and would not waste time getting there.

He put on the sunglasses and gloves and started to leave the house when he saw his refection in a full-length mirror. He chuckled thinking that the raid would be a fun one for the young Sidneys to read. He picked up the machete and quickly left on a hard run to the bank.

He was still running when he hit the main doors of the bank just thirty seconds after nine o'clock. He entered the bank screaming in a loud, wild-~ pitched voice. "Yo' tief 'n be tek'n me an' mah cush!. Yo' likkrish burka crabit leav'n us cush cush! Yo' tief'n souls de shaft mules dis land! Uo tek'n de wittle from me chil gut! Yo' got de money and tief'n de life from dem wha' need it mo'! Can't tek mo' dis! Can't tek mo' dis! Go'n kill de rich! Go'n kill de rich! Can't tek mo' dis! Go'n kill de rich!"

The few white people had trouble understanding the raving lunatic, but very clearly understood the meaning behind the wild man's actions. The black people mostly understood and knew another dope-head had freaked out and was not to be messed with.

Sidney continually yelled while waving the machete in the air, and as he ran up to people he took a wild swing at them with the machete and yelled into their faces. There was not one second of silence in the bank as he ranted and screamed at everything.

People in the bank were scared shitless, thinking they were about to be killed. They also didn't know whether to look at the man's face or the giant penis that was wildly swinging around with every movement. Sidney had been successful in hiding any possible way to describe the machete maniac.

He made a straight line for the bank's vault, tearing a woman's dress off on the way. He threw the dress on the floor and shoveled armful loads of cash out of the vault's shelves onto the dress. When the dress was covered with all of the cash it'd hold, he scooped it up in a bundle and ran out the backdoor still screaming, hopping around, and waving the machete.

Everyone in the bank was stunned—even the armed guard. They had been frightened, but the main reason no one moved was they had never seen or heard of anything like it, and didn't know how to react. Besides, it happened so quickly, it seemed like only seconds had passed. Two of the women tellers were in hysterics over the wild man.

Finally, someone said, "Hey! We have been robbed! Did anybody set the alarm off?"

It had not been activated, but it wouldn't have mattered anyway; the cops were on their way to the gas station—and Sid was already off the streets and back in the borrowed house.

Sidney went into the shower and poured the mineral sprints over him to cleanse the oil and grease off. It took both cans, but it all came off. A hot soapy shower removed most of the petroleum smell. The shower was scrubbed clean, and then wiped dry with a towel. The towel was put in his backpack to be disposed of later. He used the lady's blow dryer to dry his hair, and he then got dressed.

The cash was stuffed into his pack. The dirty newspapers were wadded up and stuffed in the backpack, too. The lady was carried back out to the ironing board. The iron was plugged in and the child was left to fend for herself.

The cleaning-up process only took about or six five minutes and he was on the street before the cops arrived at the gas station. He walked casually on the street, where there were sirens everywhere in the town. People were out in the streets looking around to see what was going on. Most thought it was a big fire since there were so many sirens.

Sidney had a fifty-dollar bill in his pants from the prize and stopped at the store for a fresh supply of rum and Cuban cigars. As he was leaving the store, a passing police Jeep slowed down long enough to ask if anyone had seen a naked Rastafarian running around. Sidney, in perfect British English, responded that he had not.

A funny thing happened to Sidney on the beach; some asshole had stolen his dinghy. He chuckled at the irony as he swam, using the scissor-kick style, out to his boat with one arm out of the water holding the plastic bag containing his cigars. The backpack left a slight oil slick behind.

CARIBBEAN SEA

ON BOARD, HE HAULED ANCHOR, AND THEN RAISED THE SAILS AND SET A course of due south. Sidney separated the oily newspaper from his easily earned prize. The paper was set afire in the boat's gimbaled oven, a page at a time. The empty mineral spirit and paint cans were filled with water and dropped overboard to sink. Any dollars that felt or smelled like petroleum were soaked in a bucket containing a mixture of soap and a vinaigrette salad dressing that had been on board.

With his laundry done, he spread the wet bills out in the salon to dry. As the boat sailed away from shore, he did his favorite things: soaked up rum, sun, and the flavor of an outstanding cigar. Life was good, but would have been perfect if he had a woman.

By noon, he was five miles off the shoreline and was feeling fine. With his ocean void of other boats, he went below to examine his prize. He formed the customary stacks of dominations to count his booty. He was happy to see that in his flash through the bank he was able to liberate $488,000 from the Italians.

He put about nine thousand dollars into his backpack. The rest of the bills were stuffed into the big 8-D battery. The battery full of cash was put back in place with the cables hooked up.

As darkness took over from the fading light of sunset, Sidney XXIII was drunk and ready for a nap. He slacked the sails, and then stood on the deck to take a piss. He started thinking about how he must have looked in the bank that morning, and started laughing so hard that he lost his balance and fell overboard.

The shock of cool water sobered him enough to be thankful that he had slacked the sails. It would have a very long swim to the closest land.

After he caught the boat he swam around awhile, enjoying the cool water and the refreshing feeling of regaining his senses.

He made an instant decision to get back aboard when he saw a dark shape of a large fin on top of a wave, heading in his direction. The memory of what happened to his father flashed into his mind and he quickly got back aboard.

He laid down on a cockpit cushion to get an hour's sleep. As he faded into sleep he had a final thought: it'll be nice to hit the north coast of South America for some hot women and cheap booze… someplace to have some fun.

Later that night, Sidney was sailing over five-foot swells in a twenty-knot breeze. It was great sailing under the canopy of a billion stars. The night seemed to pass without notice, and, before he was ready for it to end, the red sky of dawn was beginning to show on the eastern horizon. Dawn was one of the prettiest times of the day, but it was also the hardest time to stay awake after being awake all night. He learned at an early age that when the sun starts up, the eyelids start down.

He decided not to fight it, so he shortened the mainsail and reduced the roller furling jib to slow the boat down. He tied the steering wheel off to maintain his southerly course, and then he sat down to watch the yellow-orange ball jump up out of the sea. Minutes later, he was fast asleep and snoring in the cockpit.

He woke up an hour later feeling rested. He scanned the horizon for other vessels and saw nothing but ocean and sky. *This is where I belong*, he thought, *out in an open sea. No person or thing to bother me. No laws, no rules, no obligations, no noise other than nature.*

It was great out there, but thinking of some of life's pleasures—pussy and cold beers were waiting for him—prompted him to set full sails again.

During the day, Sidney spent his time, when not sailing, going over all of the fittings on the boat's rigging. Checking and tuning the rigging was an art that he had perfected before he was ten years old. The boat's rig was maxed out and it would have been impossible for anyone to get more out of that boat than she was doing. He went below to be sure everything was correctly stored, as the beautiful red sky that morning had been a sign that he could expect some stormy activity later that day and he didn't want things flying around in the cabin.

Sidney wasn't concerned about stormy weather; he felt as comfortable in the blowing rain of a gale as under a lazy summer sky. Contrary to what most people said about the weather being unpredictable, it was very predictable in the Caribbean—to those who paid attention to nature. Weather killed very few people. It was the rocks on the shoreline, or the sea from drowning if caught in an ill-prepared boat, or a seaman unwilling to accept, know, and love the sea for whatever it offered. Tsunamis didn't count since they were not weather related.

The sea was made and controlled by the same force as a butterfly or a warm summer breeze over a small pond in the country. It was the force that controlled the minister of a fine church and the actions of a serial killer. Weather was a complicated living entity. Storms weren't bad or good; they happened because some action in the atmosphere was doing something to cause the reaction. To appreciate that force, Sidney knew he had to realize what can be harmful and avoid generating a contest with any of the elements that always have the advantage over man.

That afternoon, clouds began forming on the horizon and as they grew nearer they appeared bigger, with their billowing tops at twenty thousand feet and rising. The bases of the clouds were almost black and gradually turned lighter with elevation. It was early in the hurricane season, and Sidney was watching the season's first tropical wave forming. A wave today, perhaps a depression tomorrow, a tropical storm the next day, and if all the conditions were met, a hurricane a day or two later.

The developing storm hit with a sudden shift of wind and a torrent of heavy rain but passed in an hour, leaving big rolling glassy calm seas without a ripple on the surface. His wind was gone and the sails were banging back and forth as the boat rode over the ocean swells that had been on the move since they left the African coast.

He was in the doldrums of the passing tropical wave. Any wind would be light and would come from the south. It would last for a day, and then the disturbed trade wind would return. It was so calm Sid pulled the sail down to stop the noise caused by the sail and the rigging. If he was going to be drifting, he might as well do it with some peace and quiet. The thought of starting the diesel engine to continue his passage never occurred to him; he was a sailor, not a boater, and he had never motored anywhere. Besides, he didn't have a battery.

In Sidney's world, if it was too calm to sail, then it was supposed to be calm and meant he had time to do something else. Things like raising hell on the north coast of South America. The first thing he did as a becalmed sailor was to stretch out in the cockpit and take a long leisurely nap.

It was dark and the stars were bright in the clear sky when he awoke. The gentle rocking motion as the boat rode over the swells was very restful. Everything was at peace in his universe. Lying on his back and looking at the night sky, he thanked God for giving him that experience.

Sidney wasn't a religious man but he did believe very strongly in God. His God was the maker of all nature. He was not the god that man had a hand in forming and made everyone believe in what man preached. He treasured his feelings about the world and everything in it, animal, plant or mineral. Whenever he killed a person, it was because it was meant to be that way. All living creatures killed other creatures to satisfy a need. Everything lived and died.

He felt more respect toward the natural order of things than any preacher man could understand. The preacher would call Sidney the devil in the flesh. He had much different values concerning life and property. As all of his forefathers, he believed that property didn't belong to any one person. A man might possess it for a while, but only for a while. All property that wasn't disposable had passed through countless owners since there was such a thing called property.

Life was the same. It was given with only one rule: it was only temporary. It would be yanked from them, preacher or killer. And then they would go to the place they were before conception. Man didn't design life; why should he feel compelled to control those that it was given to. Who gave him the intelligence to make judgments over the laws of nature?

SICILY

Tony the Pop, in his lavish office, sat at his desk shaking his head in disbelief as he listened to the telephone. He hung the phone up and said to his secretary, "I can't believe this shit. One of our banks in St. Maarten has been robbed in broad daylight by some fucking local crack-head walking around naked. There's no respect for us at all. Well, it stops right here. I want an example made out of that fucking freak.

"Call Vincenzo and tell him to temporarily stop his search for the big boys and find that Rastafarian. He shouldn't be too hard to find—the guy has a twelve-inch dick and damn near a half million dollars. You tell Al to kill him in a manner that makes a strong statement about fucking with any business owned by Italians. Tell him to cut that dick off and shove it down his throat. And tell Vincenzo I want him dead in twenty-four hours."

WITH NOTHING TO DO AND NO RUM TO DRINK, THERE WAS PLENTY OF time for thought. Sidney smiled at the memory of the bank robbery. He could still see the faces of surprised horror in the people who were trying so hard not to look at his foot long pecker swinging freely in the breeze.

It had been a clever plan, but its origin was seeded centuries ago. Sidneys' Log wasn't only a written history of the family's exploits at sea; it also served as their only companion in their solitary world. He knew everything about his family and he would soon pass it all to the boy who would take his place.

Each boy was taught the trade and everything about every family member—and that family history had played a part in his raid on the bank. When he was thinking of a way to do it he had been struck by the memory of the seventh Sidney who had used the idea successfully several times. In fact, he had taught the tactic to another man who became famous for his adaptation.

In the sixteen hundreds, a handful of privateers had begun operating off the coast of North Carolina in the New World. They were mostly active along the coastline from Charleston to the Chesapeake. The Sidney was living in France at the time, and like most seamen, had heard about their activities and decided to take advantage of it. Keeping with the family tradition, the other pirates would unknowingly act as a cover for his raids.

To cloak his real business was simple; he paid his passage aboard an English merchant ship to start a new business in the New World. Like all areas that experienced piracy, the coast would be full of merchants selling goods the pirates were taking. The pirates sold their bounty to the merchants for very little of the real worth and the merchants would turn around and resell them at greatly reduced prices, beating their legitimate competitors.

Sidney chose something to sell that would not compete with existing businesses or attract attention to his absence when he was at sea. He assumed the role of a drummer, a salesman for a company that made heavy equipment used in making iron ingots out of raw material. There were no iron mills in the New World at that time, which was even better.

He went to the pubs and got drunk every night to presumably convince everyone to work together to get one built in Charleston. Of course, nothing ever came of this half-hearted attempt, but it provided him with a good cover for his time away and a legitimate source for his income, and justified his flamboyant lifestyle. He also learned of all upcoming shipping activities in the pubs.

As far as any man knew, he was just a drummer, nothing more. However, in time, he knew most of the pirates operating on the coast, and if not personally, then he surely knew them by name and reputation.

He started raiding the ships of his choice, and let the known privateers take the credit for his bloody raids. During the years, he operated in the area there were only three men out of the bands of privateers who learned that the drummer Sidney was really the legendary phantom, Barracuda. Many more people found out at one time or another, but under very unfortunate circumstances. That Sidney rarely left anyone alive to tell of his secret.

Like the rest of the pirates, he occasionally had a need to brag about his exploits; however, he was disciplined enough to know who he could confide in and who he shouldn't. The three who knew him placed him far above any other man of the sea; most pirate captains boasted they were the "Prince of the Sea" or "King of the Sea," but in his case they knew whom to call King.

The first man he confided in happened by accident, but it was also necessary. He had booked a passage to go from Charleston to the Chesapeake on a merchantman that he had learned was carrying a fair amount of gold. He had planned to take the prize and scuttle the ship while the crew slept. Before he could put his plan into action, however, the ship was boarded at night by a bunch of wild pirates. Sid heard the commotion on deck and realized that someone had beaten him to his prize. He waited until the fighting stopped before venturing out of his cabin and going on deck.

As he stepped out of the main companionway, he found the muzzles of two pistols held by a huge, burly but younger man. There was a look of amusement in the man's eyes, but also a look that illuminated the mean ruthless mind behind them. The eyes also told of an appreciation of humor, but warned there was none at that moment; it was strictly time for business.

The heavily armed man was over a foot taller than Sidney and had a hundred pounds on him—none of it fat. He asked with a loud deep roar, "Well, who do we have here? A dandy or a business man with a heavy chest of gold? A royal with his treasure looking for land in the New World? Or is it a government representative that begs to feel the steel of my sword?"

Everything the big man said, his crew responded with a loud and enthusiastic "Aye!" They had found a dandy, a plaything to be robbed, tortured then playfully killed for their amusement.

The big man instructed one of his men to watch the pansy until they had unloaded all of the ship's cargo and treasure, then he would attend to the coxcomb. Sid didn't like being called names like dandy or pansy, but he dressed the part to substantiate his cover.

Sid didn't do or say anything until the ship was unloaded. The pirate leader asked the captured ship's crew if any of them wanted to join up with Black Drummond; he was looking for some good able hands. About a dozen sailors crossed the line and boarded the pirate's ship. He then asked his crew if any of the defeated crew should be killed for protecting the ship's cargo by putting up undue resistance; only two men were pointed out. The pirate captain then gave the order to his quartermaster who casually walked up to them and hacked them to death with his cutlass. The bodies were thrown overboard while the pirates hooted and cheered.

The rowdy captain bellowed a curse on the ship's owner for risking all of the sailors' lives to safeguard their cargo. Cargo intended to make the fat and already rich men in Europe sitting safely on their asses, richer men. Pirates didn't particularly like rich men who made money off the sweat of others, especially seamen. And Sidney shared that sentiment.

The burly captain came over to Sidney and then yelled out to the crew what they should do with the dandy. He let them yell and carry on, offering suggestions on how to dispose of him. While all of that was going on, the captain was watching the dandy's eyes—there was no hint of fear.

The captain, bewildered by this lack of fear, got his men to be quiet and bellowed loud for all to hear, "It is like this fancy man has not the good sense to know what we do with his type… or he doesn't care!"

Everyone on deck laughed at the situation—even Sidney. He laughed because actually it was true—the captain would be dead before he felt Sidney's steel in his back.

The captain asked, "Well, dandy, in what manner do you want to taste death?"

Sid's quick answer was, "I want to taste the lips of every whore in Charleston while being fucked to death."

The crowd yelled an enthusiastically, but friendly, "Nay!"

The captain looked at him and said, "Sorry, dandy, what's your next choice?"

"If you will give me just one minute of your time in private conversation I'll be happy to let the crew decide." The crew howled their approval.

And that was enough to arouse the curiosity in the captain; it had to be information about more treasure and he was willing to bargain with it for his life. Captain Drummond took him below deck out of sight of the crew, and said, "Okay little dandy, what do want to tell me?"

Sid said, "It will be in your best interest to let me go with the captured ship's crew."

That brought a big laugh from the captain, but he wasn't amused, and asked, "Why don't you tell me why?"

Sid moved so quickly that the big man couldn't respond. He got behind him, pulled his knife out, and stuck the point about an eighth of an inch into the big man's muscular neck. The captain didn't move; it had happened too quickly to fend the smaller man away and the point of pain was only a finger away from his jugular; any move would cost him his life.

Sid told him, "I will show you the generosity you have shown me. You have a choice; you can die totally helplessly as you are now, or you can fight me, man to man. If I win the fight, I go free. If I lose, then you can throw me to the crew."

That was good news to the captain; he was as mad as he had ever been. Letting the smaller man, a dandy, catch him, Edward Drummond, who had never been beaten in a fight, was an embarrassment. He had *never* been in a fair fight; his viciousness and nasty trickiness was becoming well known up and down the American Coast.

He gave his word and Sid released the captain and stepped back a step or two. The captain didn't feel the sting of the cut on his neck—he felt only rage.

In anger he growled, "Now, little dandy, I'm going to teach you a very hard lesson," and swung his huge right hand at him. He was so quick that Sid barely saw his move to grab one of the knives out of his waistband. The swinging knife missed Sid by inches as he side-stepped the blow and jabbed his own knife into the captain's cheek.

That made Drummond even madder, and he charged Sid with his full body, not caring if he got stuck with the other man's blade or not. He just wanted to get his powerful hands on the aggravating dandy. As he charged he yelled again, "I'll teach you."

The big man was quick for his size, but he ran into a powerful fist that caught him on the nose. The blow was so forceful it instantly dropped him to his knees. It was a position the captain had never been in before; he was in serious trouble for the first time in his life. He was aware that if it was a good deck fight he'd be dead by then. But the dandy just stood there waiting for more.

Sidney said, "You are fighting someone with infinitely more experience in hand-to-hand combat. Don't let my clothes be the reason for your death. I'll be happy to give you another chance at me and with any weapon of your choosing. But be warned that I will be obliged to kill you on your next attempt."

Drummond had never given up, but that look he had seen in the man's eyes earlier on deck registered. It was the look of an unrestrained spirit. The way he had handled himself, the ice-cold, dead look in his eyes now, and the ease with which he had beaten him proclaimed who was the better man.

Drummond got up and said, "You have skill. What is your name?"

"It is not dandy, but you wouldn't know me. I wanted you out of view of your men so you wouldn't be embarrassed or be killed in front of them. Also I'm sure one of them would have put a lead ball in me if I murdered their captain."

"For someone to have so much confidence requires much experience, and there are not many with the ability to take me so easily. Who do you fight for?"

"Let me just say that we're in the same business, but I am captain and crew of my own ship. I work alone and nobody on any ocean knows me. I intend to keep it that way, and if I have your word of silence, you will be the first to gain my trust. I have already told you more than any other man in my twenty years as King of the Seas. If you refuse to give your word here and now I will kill you no matter what you do or how many men you call. And if I ever hear any tales about me later, I will do the same thing as soon as I find you."

The big man believed him, and chuckled, "You have no concern from me. I would never admit to being taken by a dandy."

Mean and rugged men like other men who are mean and rugged, just like wimpy little men like other wimpy men, and the man before him was the roughest son of a bitch that he had ever encountered.

The captain tried to get a name out of Sid, but he refused, saying, "Names are not important. You'll know me the next time you see me, and you can call me anything you want—except dandy. I'll know who you are and will call you Captain Teach since you were so sure you had something to *teach* me."

Then he quickly rolled up his right shirtsleeve and showed him the tattoo of a red flag. On the flag was a man's skull with a boarding knife used in the fifteen hundreds was sticking out of an eye socket; a shattered leg bone was sticking out of the other eye. Along the inboard edge of the, flag were seven white bones.

Sid said, "This is me, and you'll never see another tattoo like it unless the mate is my son, and to prove that, he will know of this day. If he doesn't know of this day, then kill the son of a bitch for wearing my colors."

The captain stared at the tattoo. The men in their trade had not used the red flag for over a hundred years. The black flag was used, as it was easier to see from a distance when hoisted. As a child, he had heard old stories about a man wearing the red flag with a skull on his right arm from his grandfather. This couldn't be the man grandfather knew, but the other had only five bones; the seven bones might mean there had been others. And the man his grandfather talked about had no name either, but he was called the Barracuda by his victims because of his deadly speed and ruthless, treacherous actions.

"I think I have heard of you. Would you be the phantom, Barracuda?"

Sid's only response was a smile.

The two men walked out on deck, the pirate crew waiting impatiently for the fun to begin. Few noticed the cut on Drummond's cheek or the blood on his collar or the swelling on his face. The loud roar of the crowd quieted enough for the captain to speak.

He yelled, "This man is free to do as he chooses. Any man attacks him, attacks me, today and forever. If any man wants explanations, come forward and face me. I'll teach him a thing or two about bad judgment."

As soon as he said that, Sid laughed. The crowd started laughing with him. They had heard the threat of being taught something most every day for as long as the big captain had been around.

Sid said, "Okay men; let's hear it for Captain Teach. Best you not be needing some learning from this man."

The name stuck with him for a while as Captain Teach on sea and Edward Teach on shore. The name changed later to Blackbeard, and he was *almost* the meanest son of a bitch on the seas.

Sid had met him again in a little town of Bath after he had scuttled the Danish brig *Scrotum* the night before. Most of the crew was able to swim to shore and he had mingled in with them. Some had gathered a bundle of their possessions. Sid had had time to bundle up more gold than he could swim with, the jewels from a wealthy noble lady on board, and what was supposed to be a map of the treasure locations of the pirate, Major Bonnet.

The Sidneys had developed a procedure to be able to swim heavy loads to shore if the distance was not too great. A basket would be taken from the galley and prepared for the swim. A few goatskin bags, the number depending on the prize being taken, would be attached. Each was corked to prevent air from escaping. The basket would be hung over the side, empty, and secured with a rope that would be used to lower the prize into the basket, and serve as a line for the Sidney to slide off of the ship. They had learned long ago not to jump overboard; the splash could alert a sentry that someone had gone over the side.

As each load of the prize came on deck it was put into the basket. After the basket was loaded, a piece of canvas was tied over the top to prevent parts of the prize from falling out or being washed away. The basket would be lowered the rest of the way to the water. If he had figured the bags right then the basket would sink, but be neutral in buoyancy. If there was too much flotation, a bag's cork would be opened to allow air to escape. It couldn't be seen from ship or shore, and after reaching shore, the basket would be dragged up on the beach and hidden. In cases like the *Scrotum* where there were other people about, he tied it to a rock below the surface until he could come back for it after the surviving crew was off of the beach.

The second meeting with the big captain was by chance and in a pub. All of the survivors and many of the town's men were there listening to the account of the sinking. Sid came in later after most of the stories about what had happened had been told a few dozen times. He was unnoticed by all except for one.

Captain Blackbeard watched the man walk through the room, being careful not to disturb anyone, and he fetched a large ale, then another. After the two ales, the newcomer looked around at the other men. When his eyes met Blackbeard's, they locked for only a second, while it registered whom those big mean black eyes belonged to, then he winked. Blackbeard then realized what had really happened to the *Scrotum*.

Sidney VII spent a few weeks in Bath and got to know Blackbeard and some of the other pirates who lived and worked out of the little town pretty well. But only Blackbeard knew who he was. They all got together every day and night to drink, fight, eat, and catch wenches. During one of those nights, Sid had told him about a trick his father had used to get into a heavily guarded cabin aboard the French warship *La Justice pour Tours*. He could not just charge them as the chances were good that one of the four guards would have gotten to him with a blade which would have hampered his ability to grab the prize and run. The prize was a sword made of solid gold that was to be presented to the King of England from the Queen of France.

He decided that the best defense was to cause confusion and panic in the defenders. He wrapped wet goatskins around his arms and chest then put a dry shirt on over them. He had twisted up several pieces of cloth and tied them in place on his head. He then put cooking oil on his hair and the dry shirt and lit it with fire from a lantern just before entering the cabin's corridor. He ran at the men waving his flaming arms, his hair blazing and yelling and acting crazy. The four guards couldn't get out of his way fast enough and ran out on deck. The crazy man, on a dead run, hit the locked door and knocked it down.

In the privacy of the cabin, he found the sword and took it with him as he jumped out of the rear window into the sea. As the ship sailed away he took off what was left of the shirt and goatskins. One was inflated enough to give him added flotation to swim the seven miles to a lee shore. Being covered with oil gave him protection from the fire as only the oil was burning, not his flesh as it appeared.

Those days were so much fun that Sid almost decided to join up with

Blackbeard's band of rowdy mates. Good judgment and family tradition prevailed, however, and he moved on to resume doing things the Sidneys' way. He did remain in that area for a few years with Blackbeard and a few other bands of pirates getting the blame for his actions. It provided a very nice cover until he decided it was time to move to the Caribbean.

A few months later, the infamous Blackbeard struck even more fear into the hearts of his victims. He began boarding vessels with his hair and huge black beard, complete with flaming red twisted ribbons. The sight of the huge charging bull, with the wild black eyes and flaming hair, scared many a man enough to jump overboard without a fight. The sight of the flaming bull emptied the bowels of many tough men.

Sidney XXIII had remembered that account when planning the St. Maarten bank raid, but wanted to use a different method; he wasn't too crazy about setting himself on fire.

After dwelling on his ancestors and a refreshing sunrise nap, Sidney could see the gray shapes of mountains on the horizon. He judged his distance as forty miles and thought he might as well maintain his present course. Chances were as good straight ahead as they would be to the east or west of finding a good bar.

Three miles offshore, he could see nothing but jungle where he was headed, so he turned east-southeast to sail on a close reach. If he should run into shallow water while venturing in, he could turn downwind to escape the reef. Another reason for easting close to shore was that the wind would blow from a better angle to allow a faster passage to the east.

In a couple of hours, he saw a small fishing village and continued heading for it. He arrived to find a sandy bottom and dropped his anchor about thirty yards off the beach in ten feet of sparkling, crystal clear water. He swam to shore with another line and tied the stern to one of the many swaying coconut trees.

As he waded out of the gentle surf, a couple of fishermen and a throng of noisy and naked children met him. The children were jumping around him; begging for a boat ride and jabbering happily with questions: who was he, what did he want, where did he come from, what was his name, and a hundred more queries. The kids were having fun; the stranger on their beach provided them with something new in their otherwise repetitive daily existence.

Sidney spent a lot of time in the so-called undeveloped areas of the world and had seen that scene many times, so the children's behavior wasn't unusual and he didn't mind the annoyance.

He asked the fishermen, "Where's the nearest store? I'm looking for food, rum and cigars."

One of them pointed and both said at the same time, "Go to Gaspar's. It's over there, behind that line of coconut palms."

As he approached the shack, he heard the static of an AM radio station without benefit of an adequate antenna, playing the Venezuelan National Anthem. He poked his head in the doorway and was happy to see a little bar sparsely stocked with dusty cans and boxed food supplies on dusty shelves. Also there were the very basic items you might expect to find in a remote little drugstore: locally made rum bottled in Coke bottles, ketchup bottles, and any other container that could be found on the beach. Every bottle had a handmade cork plugged into it; each was labeled depicting who had made that batch.

An old man behind the bar was talking to two other men, leaving one rickety stool open. The bar top had been made of a several well-worn and beaten-up planks that obviously had once been part of an old boat's deck. By its appearance, with a thousand worm holes in it, it had been adrift at sea for a long time before being washed up on their beach.

The front wall of the bar was made of weatherworn wooden planks of shipping pallets that were constantly found floating in all seas. Barstools were carved out of mahogany tree limbs; their seats, woven palm fronds like the hats found in the tourist areas.

The few shelves were made from more of the pallet planks. The floor was made of sand. A beautiful piece of mahogany driftwood was nailed to the fragile back wall. Carved into its surface was the word *Gaspar's*.

Sidney sat down nodding recognition to the other men in the bar as he said, "Rum."

The bartender blew sandy dust off a glass that had been on the shelf and unused for a long time. He filled it half full with the local rum. There was no ice, but water was offered. Sidney declined. It wasn't uncommon to find quality rum made in the villages around the Caribbean. After all, it had been made in the same villages ever since man planted sugar cane and imported slaves to cut it. The technique had been improved and refined over the generations. But there were terrible rums, too, as some makers were only interested in the money. The bartender watched Sidney for a sign of appreciation for their village's prized rum. Sidney, of course, made no sign of appreciation, other than drinking it down and saying, "Another."

One of the men asked, "Where you sailing to? What prompted you to stop here?"

Sidney, in no hurry to answer, downed a big gulp of rum and replied, "I wasn't going anywhere. This is the first village I saw."

The other man, leery of strangers, asked, "How long you plan on staying around here?"

Sidney said, "Don't know," and that was the end of the conversation for a while.

After two more drinks, Sidney threw a fifty-dollar bill on the bar and told the bartender, "I'm buying all the drinks today."

The number of men in the bar grew from three to ten in a very short period of time after word got out that the stranger was buying. Money was almost nonexistent in that village; everyone bartered with fish, fruits, garden grown vegetables, wild animal meats, rum and eggs from most any egg-laying animal.

Every man thanked him each time they were served another drink. Sidney liked the people; they were not trying to take advantage of a stranger, they were just happy that someone was giving them something without asking for hard labor in return.

Every man and several of the older boys in the village ended up in the bar before nightfall until the bartender ran out of rum and the few bottles of warm beer he had stashed for his own consumption. They all went back to their shacks feeling very happy and very drunk.

The village was noisy with laughter that evening and Sidney was invited by Juan, one of villagers, to come to his home for more drinks. The man's wife, Anna, was pleasant, but Sid had caught the hateful glare she kept giving her drunken husband. Her husband could care less, and so did Sidney; there was rum to be drunk. When that was gone, Sidney staggered down to the water's edge under the bright light of the moon, waded into the cool water and swam to his boat. In his condition, getting into the boat without a boarding ladder was no easy task.

Hours later he woke before dawn and swam to shore. The seas were still, the sky clear. The noise of laughter, which wafted through the village only hours before, had gone. The only sounds that morning were snoring coming from one shack or another as he walked along the beach. Roosters were doing their morning thing and a few young goats were making the only noise they could, but it sounded like a child crying *help*. He wondered if that was why young goats were called kids.

The village dogs were slowly walking around covering their usual trails while looking for anything they could eat that might have been dropped during the evening before. Everything else was still.

The first hint of light appeared on the horizon as he started his run. The beach extended for miles with an occasional section of jungle that grew out to water's edge where the beach had been eroded away. A shallow river that emptied into the sea wasn't too far from the village. It was only six feet deep and less than thirty feet wide; he had no trouble swimming it. Most of the river's mouth had been shoaled in by sand, but there was a section about eight feet wide with six feet of water that curved through the sand.

Sidney ran a range of different speeds for three hours without stopping. He only stopped when he plunged into the surf and bobbed around, taking a leisurely swim. Afterward, he lay on the sandy beach and basked in the warm sun until he drifted into a lengthy nap. He awoke to the sound of breaking waves. The wind had picked up to twenty knots and it was blowing onshore.

He had not anticipated a strong onshore wind, but knew it had to be caused by a fast moving high-pressure system. He had not put out enough scope on the anchor rode to ride out that kind of wind, as he had planned to be there only an hour yesterday while he bought his supplies. He had forgotten, and being too drunk that night to think about anything, put his boat in severe danger of grounding.

He ran into the water and quickly rinsed the sand off, then started his run back to the village. As he rounded a bend on the beach, he had a distant view of the village—something was wrong. His boat was gone. And it was not washed up on the beach. He thought that someone in the village had stolen it, or maybe the government confiscated it for violating one of their stupid rules. It was bad enough that they took his boat—but they had his prize, too. Taking a prize from the Barracuda was never tolerated. Whoever had it was fucked.

As he entered the village, the first to notice his arrival were the village dogs that came running out to greet him with wagging tails and unrelenting barking. The children, with their sandy naked bottoms and shrill chatter and laughter, were next. They all had something to say, but the biggest of the children grabbed Sid's hand and tried to lead him off the beach into the jungle behind the village. All the other kids were giggling; the adults were watching with amusement.

Sidney cooled his anger and decided to go into the jungle to see their big surprise. Breaking heads could wait a little longer, but as the gang of kids took him into the jungle his senses were on full alert in case the friendly village people had turned out to be a bunch of thieves—or cannibals.

They ran around a thick clump of tangled bushes where the path opened to a beautifully green grassy meadow surrounding a pond. There were several fishing skiffs pulled up on the grass; several old tattered seine nets were pulled up on sticks and drying—and his sailboat was floating on her anchor.

A man working on his net looked up at Sidney's arrival. He had a big friendly grin on his face that was short several front teeth, and told him they moved his boat that morning when the weather started to change. He explained the lagoon was part of the river that dumped into the beach.

Sidney was relieved, not only about the boat not being stolen by the villagers, but that they had moved it to a well-hidden and secure anchorage. *Hell*, he thought, *now if I can just get laid here. I've found a great spot to call home in this part of the world... for a while. It would have taken every man in the village to pull the boat around.*

In an uncommon display of friendliness, Sidney smiled and said, "Thanks for moving the boat. The party is on me tonight if Gaspar has been able to restock his rum."

The fisherman gave him an even bigger smile and said, "Gaspar has already made a new batch and has restocked the rum. Also a large pig had been killed in a trap last night and there is going to be a big party tonight anyway."

Sidney waded into the lagoon to swim to the boat when the children began yelling a warning, "Cocodrilo! Cocodrilo!"

The fisherman said, "There is a line tied to the back of the boat," and then pointed to a small line tied to a tree. "The river is full of crocodiles and it's too dangerous to swim in there. Every few days a goat, dog, or occasionally a child, is grabbed by them. They are used to eating people now; it is a dangerous place."

Sidney noticed that none of the kids got any closer than five feet from the water's edge and still kept an eye out for any movement. He pulled the boat to shore with the stern line, getting only his feet wet.

Later, dark clouds were building over the tops of the trees' thick canopies. He thought, *let it blow. This little cove is a perfect hurricane hole. Just don't fuck up the pig roast tonight.*

When the rain started, he went below to take a nap. His last thought before drifting off was of the village and its friendly people. Normally, Sidney didn't think about people, they were just objects in life that he had to put up with to satisfy his current needs. These village people were different. Without being asked, or without the promise of reward, they waded and swam his sailboat down the coast a half mile and then up into a crocodile-infested river—just because it was the right thing to do. They were not even aware that they had done him a favor.

After a long nap, he took a very long rainwater shower standing on the aft deck of the boat in the downpour. It hadn't stopped raining since it started four hours earlier. He thought the pig feast would certainly be called off, but since Gaspar had restocked the bar with rum he could at least get some drinks and maybe even buy some rice and beans and maybe even a chicken.

As he walked into the clearing of the village's center, he saw that a shelter had been built out of freshly cut young trees; the top was covered with palm fronds. Under the shelter was a big pig on a wooden spit over hot coals. Children were taking turns rotating the spit.

Men and women stood around in the rain watching the pig slowly roast while the children played. As he approached, the people greeted him like just another member of the village. Most of them had sipped a little rum during the day while watching the pig being cooked, so everyone had a joyful temperament.

Sidney made his way into Gaspar's little bar. The place was packed; there were more people waiting for the pig than lived in the village. Apparently, families living in the smaller jungle villages had heard about the feast and decided to join in the festivities.

There was standing room only in the little bar. The smell of damp bodies, sweating in the confines of the cramped, humid shack, compelled him to take his jelly glass of rum outside in the rain. It was much cooler, and, by covering the top of his glass with his hand, he could keep most of the rain from diluting the rum.

He stood by the fire with several other people who were transfixed on the cooking pig while feeling the welcomed warmth from the bed of hot coals. He listened to the laughter of children and relaxed buffoonery of the adults. He was happy and lost in time until someone brought him back to reality by loudly declaring that the pig was ready. His glass had been dry for a while and that surprised him, too. He felt something completely foreign to him, its name: contentment.

Everyone headed for a pile of banana leaves stacked near one of the shacks. A line formed and, with a big leaf on both hands, each man, woman and child went from one shack to another helping themselves to food that had been prepared in each home. The line ended at the pig. By the time he made the loop through the village shacks, his leaf was almost too full to carry.

Steam was rising off his portion of pork as he found his way through the rain. He found shelter under an old mahogany tree on the edge of the village. He ate his food off the leaf like eating a wedge of watermelon and his face was soon covered with grease from the pork and small pieces of food stuck to the growth of his stubbled beard. The bare but greasy leaf was discarded in the brush, and his empty glass was retrieved from his pocket as he went to the bar.

The bar was still full of people, but not as bad as before, as many of the villagers had gone to their shacks to eat. A woman sitting on one of the barstools got up and indicated that he should sit there. The man sitting on the next stool confirmed the woman's invitation to sit down, and then offered to buy him a drink. Both the man and woman were easily recognized as non-villagers by their dress and attitudes. The man appeared to be someone who carried the weight of respect and authority or admiration—or maybe fear—from the villagers.

He introduced himself. "I am Jose Ortega. I own a hacienda about ten miles from here. We don't have many strangers visit this village since it's so remote. When I heard of a man sailing directly into the village from the Caribbean, I naturally was curious why someone would come here."

After that statement, Ortega remained quiet, waiting for Sidney's response. Sidney never bowed to authority-types and damn sure wasn't afraid of that man or his power, but he liked it there and decided to be civil.

"I'm just sailing around."

"What prompted you to sail here? Do you mind if I ask your name?"

"I was off the coast of Grenada; got drunk and passed out. A storm blew me out into the Caribbean. I just happened to land here."

While the man laughed at his story, he didn't believe it. He was suspicious of anything out of the ordinary and thought that the lone sailor was a small-time drug runner looking for fresh resources. Ortega was very aware of all of the wannabe drug runners that roamed the shores of Central and South America. Every one of them was trying to score a deal on cocaine or marijuana to take to the Virgin Islands or Puerto Rico. He could also be an undercover DEA agent.

Jose Ortega knew it would be easy enough to find out who the stranger really was and what he wanted. When Sidney sat down, the woman had beckoned to another man and the two of them left the bar.

That other man was now standing guard at the lagoon while the woman went aboard Sidney's boat searching for anything that might give clues to the stranger's reasons for being there.

She was an expert at finding things. Her boss, Jose Ortega, had hired her years ago when he was told that she had some kind of sixth sense. Call it ESP or any of the other terms for psychic awareness, but she had something going for her. She had been instrumental in detecting persons within Ortega's business who felt differences in opinions or harbored ill feelings or even had planned to take advantage of many situations. She was also quite good at recovering lost objects and finding things that were hidden.

By the way the boat was provisioned, and his meager, at best, possessions, she felt the man was probably just another Caribbean boat bum. A man who had worked most of his life and probably lost his family to too many hours of everyday work; too much stress about family and work matters and too much booze while looking for relief.

She found an estimated twenty thousand dollars in cash; some was stashed in the pockets of a pair of dirty shorts, the rest was in an empty dark rum bottle. She wasn't sure how much was in the bottle, as she would have to break it to count the money, but it wasn't enough to be making substantial drug buys. No hidden compartments were found that could stash any quantity of drugs. Also, according to the villagers, the man was a loner. The usual guy trying to set up a drug score was usually a loud party animal, a good-time Charlie and always with friends, always with someone to boost his self-esteem. Drug dealers generally felt that image was important; they always needed an audience. The stranger drinking rum with her boss had not given her those vibrations. In fact, he had given her the opinion he was just the opposite. Considering all of this, she was sure the man was no threat to the Ortega Cartel.

She returned to Gaspar's bar and signaled Jose Ortega, by scratching her right ear, that the stranger appeared to be okay. Sidney and Ortega had several more rums and both were starting to feel the effects, and both were very much aware of how the other was reacting. It was turning into an unspoken challenge between the men. One was going to show the other that he could handle booze better and that he was the better man. There wasn't much conversation between them — just drinking and listening to the crowd. Mostly any attempt for Ortega to open a dialog turned into competitive responses.

It had started when Ortega said, "I went fishing last week and boarded a five hundred pound blue marlin."

Sidney responded, "I speared a six-foot Jew fish last week."

"That marlin of mine fed an entire village bigger than this one for a week."

"I ate one meal from the Jew fish and left the rest to feed the ants."

The verbal swaggering, human male chest-thumping, real or not, pertained to male physical prowess, never about business. Before the night was over, Gaspar's bar had been emptied of everything to drink again except two bottles of YooHoo and a half dozen cans of sardines.

The next morning, Sidney woke up face down in his bunk, wondering if he had won the drinking bout. He liked Ortega; the man had stood his ground, and apparently, like Sidney, looked forward to a challenge.

When he rolled over he became aware of a body next to him—a body just as naked as his and she was softly snoring, untroubled by anything. Looking at the restful expression on her beautiful face he thought, *wonder if she'll be so relaxed when she wakes and faces a naked stranger. I can't even remember talking to her much less bringing her to the boat, or fucking her*. It was Ortega's woman friend.

He watched her slow rhythmic breathing, the swelling of her chest; her nipples were dark on her pale white skin. Her jet-black hair was long and thick. She was of Spanish ancestry, and in her early thirties. He felt her skin with his fingers; she was warm and soft, creamy white, no blemishes, no scars or stretch marks from childbirth. Her body was perfect.

He reached over and gently pulled her legs apart and softly caressed her thighs while slowly moving his hand to the furry black mound. There was a hint of dampness, and he gently massaged her until she moved slightly and the dampness changed to moist, and went to wet in seconds. Then she moved to hold him as he roughly caressed her. Her body movements increased, her pelvis thrust against his hand and he positioned himself over her and replaced his fingers with his penis. She was as ready as he was, and both seemed to climax within a few seconds of each other.

What a great way to wake up, he thought as he looked, for the first time, into her dark eyes; he said nothing. She murmured as if she had had the same thought.

Then she rolled out of the bunk and said, "Excuse me; may I use your head?"

He pointed the way. She said, "I know. I used it last night, remember?" She doubted that he did as both machos had been very drunk.

While she was in the head, Sidney went on deck and hosed down any crocodiles that might have been lurking at the boat's waterline. They both returned to bed and before either got up again had made love twice more.

While getting dressed the woman said, "Good morning, Sidney, my name is Maria. My boss, Señor Ortega, wanted me to ask you to come to his hacienda today. I really didn't want to have to drive back here this morning on that horrible road so I decided to spend the night with you instead. I hope you don't mind?"

Sidney didn't reply, but looked at her with a silly grin that made an absolute statement that he thought it had been a great idea.

What Maria didn't tell him was that Ortega had instructed her to stick with him. He wanted to know everything the stranger did. Ortega, regardless of Maria's feelings about the sailor, still felt there was something not quite right about him. It was possible that he was an undercover cop or a small time drug dealer, or was sent by Ortega's competition to check out his operation; maybe even to spearhead a takeover. Being in Ortega's line of work had a tendency to make a person paranoid. And it cost nothing to play it safe. And, of course, there was another possibility: he was as he said, a boat bum just playing around in the tropics; however, he didn't look the playful type.

Maria expected him to ask about last night, but he said nothing about personal matters. She didn't bother telling Sidney that he had fared better than her boss. That was something she had never seen happen before.

Sidney said, "Thanks for the invitation, but I won't be going to Ortega's today."

Worried, she replied, "It might be in your best interest to accept the invitation. Señor Ortega is a very powerful man. He's a man that could mean the difference between being rich and poor, or even worse—if you understand what I mean."

Sidney said, "I know what you mean, but I'm not interested in being poor or rich—or even worse."

He got out of bed, but didn't bother to put clothes on. He walked over to the galley where he found a used glass in the sink. A generous splash of rum was poured into it, and then he poured it down his mouth.

Maria said, "You look a little rough this morning. If that shot helps, maybe I should take one, too. I'm feeling groggy from all the stuff I drank yesterday."

She poured about the same amount of rum into the same glass and then tossed it down equally as well as Sidney had. He wasn't impressed—but he was affected by the fullness of her breast as she stood there in her panties. He approached her and caressed her breast briefly before trying to lead her back to bed.

Maria, with the look of a woman in heat said, "I want you, too, but it will have to wait. I am very late in getting back to the hacienda."

She used all of her womanly skills during the kissing and caressing that followed as she attempted to convince him that she would be his as soon as they came back from Ortega's place. He wanted her now, but she was strong in her resolve to get him to Ortega's first.

Sidney was his own man, and had lived his life doing only what he wanted, when he wanted. He was in the business of taking things that he wanted away from people who didn't want to lose them. And many a woman's virtue had always been just another prize to him. But he didn't want to take her unwillingly.

Sidney didn't take, and for once he gave in. He had decided to come back to this village with his son. Part of the boy's training was to be able to survive in the wilds without tools or outside help. The jungles around that village ran for hundreds of miles into the interior and were inaccessible to ordinary man. Not many men, if any, had ever ventured into that area.

That would be an excellent proving ground for the next Sidney X. After he dropped the kid off he could come back to spend the next few months in the village—while the kid taught himself how to survive.

Best of all, Maria's grade "A" sex would be nearby.

SIDNEY REMEMBERED HIS SURVIVAL EXPERIENCE LIKE IT HAD HAPPENED yesterday. It had been a nightmarish experience for a seven-year-old boy, but the things he had learned had proven invaluable—countless times.

He always thought his father should have been more helpful by giving him some idea what was needed to survive or hints on what or where to look for food, shelter and most importantly, water. Fear had been a big factor as well. For weeks he had been terrified of the menacing darkness and the carnivorous animals that hunted the forest floor every night. He finally conquered his fear, but only after gaining the knowledge and confidence that he alone controlled his ability to live any damn where he wanted.

The only groundwork given him was at age six when his father started teaching him how to fight—and *never* lose. At first he fought with bare hands, then with knives and an old sword. For three hundred sixty-five days, he didn't do a thing but fight and learn about weapons.

He didn't attend school or play with other kids. There were no other kids living around his St Croix mountain hideaway. After a few months, his father started bringing assault men by once in a while and paid them to fight little Sidney.

During that year, little Sidney got beat up a lot. The men were told they would be paid only if they won. Sid didn't stand a chance the first twenty or thirty fights. Eventually, he realized that to stop the beatings he had to think about what his opponent was doing and what he was about to do. Then Sid started using tricks his father taught him. He managed to win his first fight with a grown man. His father was proud—and if he had had a mother—she would have died in horror.

The man had punched him a few times in the face before he decided what he had to do. He sidestepped a hard swing from the man's right fist and kicked him as hard as he could in his groin. It had been a direct hit, reducing the man to a crouched-over lump of moaning flesh. His father had tossed him a knife and told him to finish him. Sidney was a tough little boy, but certainly had never planned on killing anybody, so he shook his head no. That day, nothing else was said.

On his seventh birthday, his father told him to pack some clothes; he was going on a camping trip for his birthday. On his father's sloop, they sailed from St. Croix downwind for days until they reached a wilderness shoreline covered with dense jungle. He had no idea where they were. Even if he had been told that he was about to be thrust upon the shores of Nicaragua, he wouldn't have known. Like his father, he had never been to school or taught how to read. Reading and navigation would be learned later—if he survived the jungle.

When they were within swimming distance to shore, his father lowered the sails. The boat slowly drifted along the shoreline, and his father said, "Get your pack. Look carefully at the shoreline and remember exactly where you are right now. See that huge tree sticking above the forest's canopy?"

Young Sidney pointed to it.

His father said, "You are going to swim to shore now, and stay there by yourself for six months."

Little Sidney had always been afraid of his father, and he started to cry.

His father said, "Okay, little baby, if you want to cry instead of listening to what you better do, go ahead, it's your problem. I'm going to tell you a couple of things then toss your ass overboard, so you better listen."

Sidney tried to listen, but the fear in him wouldn't let him stop crying.

"Do you know what six months are?" Sidney whimpered no. Big Sid then pulled out a new shiny twelve-inch knife from a bag and gave it to him.

"This is your last birthday present. Take very good care of it like I've taught you and use it well. You put a mark on the same tree every morning as soon as you wake up. When you have one hundred eighty marks on that tree you need to be back at this place. I'll be here on that day to take you home. If I don't show up within two days, it's because I'm dead. You'll have to walk out of here and make a life for yourself."

Sidney couldn't believe his father was serious. He was a mean man, but surely not *that* mean.

The older Sidney said, "I'm doing this because you have to learn how to live off of the land. When I was your age, my father made me do this, too, as every single one of your forefathers have. I made it and so did your grandfathers so there's no reason for you not to make it. There are animals and even plants in the jungle that can kill you so you must always stay alert. And equally important—be tough and learn how to be the meanest thing in *your* jungle. You have natural, aggressive instincts to guide you, just open your mind and listen to them. If you don't, then you will not survive and learn the great secret of our family."

Little Sidney, still crying but trying to act brave, was picked up by his father and was tossed overboard without ceremony. He clamped both hands around his father's arms trying to prevent the inevitable. But his father pried the ten little fingers open and let the boy drop into the sea, without saying a damn thing.

He plunged into the cool water, and by the time he surfaced, the boat had moved enough to be out of reach. He tried swimming for the boat but his father was pulling the sail up and it was making more speed over the bottom than he could hope to swim.

That moment, the feeling of total hopelessness made him mad. Mad enough to stop crying and to start hating. He said nothing, but knew he was going to stay alive, just to get even with that mean old man. The feeling of hate slowly, ever so slowly, turned to a kind of appreciation after four months alone in the jungle. He realized that his father had done it to make a man out of him, something that could not be taught to one man by another; you had to know what the life and death experience was all about from personal seasoning.

Equally important was that he had learned respect and developed an understanding for nature. He learned not to see the big animals as monsters, but as equal creatures to himself. They both had exactly the same day-to-day requirements: finding something to eat and drink, and sleeping in a safe place were the only things that mattered in their universe. Most people think of the big meat-eaters as terrible creatures of the wild, but they should see the damage a man in the wild can do to survive. He killed many more animals than the four-legged variety of beast would ever do.

In fact, until he lost his deep-seated fear of the wild animals, he killed everything he saw with weapons he had made. He killed whether he wanted to eat it or not; he didn't want anything sharing his space. Things like bugs on the ground, a spider in a tree, anything from ants to the big jungle cats were not safe in his presence.

Later in life, that attitude raised the question in his mind about who or what was really civilized. Man thinks he is at the top of an otherwise stupid world of animals and plants. Modern man thinks these animals are here only for amusement or food, and offer nothing to the important aspects of life. Some people are aware of the very important balance they offer, but even in those humans, they appreciate nature only because it suits their humanistic need.

He particularly didn't care for the people who assumed they knew what was best for the wild animals because they had sat for a few years in college classrooms studying films and going out on field trips with all the modern conveniences. Understanding real nature could only be achieved by living as an equal to it—fully naked—for an extended time and without any of the comforts of home.

Then there's another group of people that pissed him off. They worry about the last of a breed disappearing from the world. In their smug, self-centered existence, they could never understand that those things were only natural. If a species disappears because of man, then the fucking thing was supposed to. If it cannot survive in the real world, putting up with mankind or the jaguar, it makes no difference. Both forces offer destruction and creation by their existence, and both are programmed to do and act in specified ways as the world develops. Everything improves with every change—for something or somebody.

Sidney XXIII didn't look forward to dumping his boy into the wilds; he knew the terror of the first few days, but he, like the other Sidneys, had survived. If he did not make it, then Sidney would have to knock up another batch of females.

THE JEEP RIDE THROUGH THE ROUGH JUNGLE ROAD TOOK ALMOST A half-hour to cover the ten-mile distance. The rain from the day before had flooded several areas and turned a once dusty, hard, dirt road into a slippery ten mile mud puddle. The rain had also increased the mosquito population from one to ten per cubic foot of air space. In the jungle there was no breeze, the air hung heavily with steamy moisture and it was hot. Sidney loved the jungle, but not on days like that one.

When they approached Ortega's hacienda, he wasn't surprised to see a high rock and concrete wall surrounding the large estate. Two men were standing guard duty at the gate with AK-47 automatic rifles strapped to their backs. There was only one gate—only one way in or out of the compound. Ortega was outside putting something that looked like a rifle in a Jeep.

Ortega flashed a broad smile when he saw that Sidney had accepted his invitation. He approached Sidney as they got out of the Jeep, and after hugging Maria, he cordially shook Sid's hand.

Ortega said, "I have a few activities planned for the day along with some great food and a special bottle or two. I hope the day will be as enjoyable for you as it will be for me."

He held up a couple of rifles he had placed in the Jeep and asked, "Do you enjoy hunting?"

Sidney, without saying anything, nodded his head indicating the affirmative. He did like to hunt, but not with a gun. He had his knife and that was all he needed. The knife was extremely deadly in his hands and he could use it to fashion any weapon needed to kill anything.

Ortega, seeing that Sidney was dressed in shorts, a tee shirt and flip-flops on his feet, showed Sidney to a guest room and said, "I suggest that you find some clothes more suited to hunting in the jungle. In the closet you'll find stacks of clean army fatigue pants and shirts. Also there are jungle boots and socks of various sizes. We do a lot of entertaining here, so I keep plenty of hunting clothes so my guests can enjoy their outings more."

Sid looked at Ortega and said, "Thanks, but I'll go as I am."

Ortega, obviously concerned for Sidney's limited knowledge of a jungle, if not safety, responded, "Sidney, the bugs are going to eat you alive out there. Thorns of the sticky-me bush growing everywhere in the jungle will tear your skin up. I can assure you flip-flops will be no protection against the thorns and the other thick ground clutter."

Sidney said, "I'll be okay."

Ortega smiled uneasily at Sidney. *He's either stupid or a stubborn son of a bitch. He obviously has no idea how rough it is in the wilds, but screw him. He'll learn soon enough. I'll be able to shove that cockiness up his ass a little later this afternoon.*

As they returned to Ortega's Jeep, Maria was dressed in jungle attire and had been joined by another woman. She was a strikingly beautiful woman in her late twenties who looked to be a mixture of Norwegian and Chinese. Her hair and height was Nordic; her skin was perfect, without a blemish, and was an ivory color. Her facial features gave her a mysterious appearance with almond-shaped eyes with brilliant green pupils and predominately high oriental cheekbones.

Ortega introduced her, "This is Jandy and she's my special assistant and the person responsible for the feast we'll surely enjoy later today."

As they pulled out of the compound, Maria produced a bottle of Blue Diamond Rum that had been on ice since the night before. After she twisted the cap off, she made a ceremony of throwing the cap out of the window, and then offered the bottle to Sidney. He accepted the bottle and took a big mouthful of golden rum before swallowing. The ice-cold and mellow flavor of the quality rum was a perfect way to get started. Sidney handed the bottle to Ortega and he did the same. The bottle was passed to Jandy, then Maria, and the cycle was repeated until the empty bottle was thrown out of the Jeep into the thick walls of the jungle's growth.

The women in the backseat were having a good time and laughing at everything. Ortega was happy; he lived for those outings and was singing

Some Enchanted Evening out loud and out of key. His baritone voice was totally untrained. Sidney sat there in silence. Another iced bottle of rum was brought out of the cooler and passed around again, but more slowly that time. Ortega wanted to be able to focus on his gun sights when the hunt began, so he declined every other pass of the bottle. Sidney didn't care about focus and drank at his usual thirsty pace. The girls also continued drinking and enjoying their day.

It took about an hour to reach the spot selected by Ortega to make their day camp. It was a scene only seen in science-fiction pictures. A forty-yard section of the jungle abruptly ended fifty feet from a sheer drop off of a thousand feet to the tangled green jungle valley below. The horizon was filled with a picturesque view of rugged mountains and jungle. Everything in sight was green, from light green to almost yellow, to the darkest and deepest greens imaginable. The only other color was a beautiful, clear blue sky. Not a house or any other sign of civilization could be seen anywhere. With its remoteness and the immense view, Sidney felt unreal, like he was standing on another planet—called Paradise.

Sidney appreciated beauty, whether in a woman or in nature, and he certainly appreciated that moment. He thought about looking for a cave, and, if found, buy the land. *St. Croix had probably been this way when that Sidney moved there*, he thought.

His admiration of the area's panorama was interrupted when Ortega asked, "Ready for the hunt? In order for us to eat today, something will have to be killed. Our main course is out there still on the hoof, so to speak. Anything big enough to feed the four of us is all we need. How does that sound to you, Sid?"

Both girls were smiling; they had seen Ortega do this on most every occasion he brought someone out there. Usually the guest's reaction to eating freshly killed wild animals was good for a few laughs.

Sidney nonchalantly and without expression said, "Okay."

Ortega continued, "There are plenty of big cats, wild boars, tapir, and all kinds of things here. Be careful Sid, the boars are a nasty lot; the cats aren't much of a problem in the daytime, unless you corner one or surprise it."

Then he offered other warnings, "There are thirty-seven varieties of snakes in the jungle and twenty-seven of those are very poisonous, so be careful where you walk. If you should bag something, be very alert. If a panther gets the scent of a fresh kill, he'll take it from you and probably leave you behind badly wounded or worse." He then recounted a couple of tales that had happened. In one instance, his guest had been badly mauled.

Sidney smiled inwardly, but looked indifferent. *I developed a taste for jaguar when I was a seven-year old boy, partly because they're so easy to get.* He had learned that big cats always try to take a fresh kill away from any other predator if given a chance. So he would wound a rat or another small animal then tie its leg to a tree with a vine. The animal would trash around in the brush, and the sound was more than any cat could resist. It didn't make a difference if they were hungry or not because they were so inquisitive. Sidney would lie very still, under the cover of leaves, letting the wounded rodent squeal and run around the brush. Suddenly there would be a crash of something hurling through the foliage, then a nerve-shattering snarl to tell the world to stay away from the cat's prize.

Before the cat could take it to his liar, Sidney would jerk the dead animal away from the cat with the vine. And every time, the cat would pounce on it just like a kitten and a piece of string. He would jerk it away again, bringing it closer and closer to his concealed position. His skin and clothes, if he wore any, had long since been covered with mud and rubbed with crushed leaves and the flowers growing in the area to hide his scent.

The big cat was no different than an ordinary housecat when it came to playing. Like all animals, when they play—they get stupid. The cat would end his game as he pounced into a sharply pointed spear made by Sidney; it's deadly point just hidden by the leaves around his hiding place. The cat would be impaled on the spear, usually in the neck or mouth area, long enough for him to pounce on the cat and bury his twelve-inch knife deep into the cat, and then he had to hang on to its back for a few seconds while keeping away from its razor-like claws until it dropped dead.

Ortega offered Sidney a rifle, but it was declined. Ortega was perplexed. He muttered to Jandy, "Damn, I didn't consider the possibility

SIDNEY X THE PIRATE

that this guy might not like killing. I should have guessed that he wasn't an outdoorsman. He's probably just another pansy-ass sailor. Damn, and I was really looking forward to a little sport today." It was a possibility that Ortega couldn't understand since it had always been his favorite way to use his free time. He had thought that any other adventuresome man, sailing the oceans by himself, would be of the same nature.

Sidney, seeing a look of disappointment in his host's face, said, "I hunt with my knife." He pulled the twelve-inch blade out of its sheath. It wasn't his original knife; the one his father had given to him was lost at sea when he was only fifteen years old during the boarding of a charter fishing boat off the coast of San Juan. But the knife was identical and bought at the same store in Caracas.

Ortega asked, "What do you think you'll get with only a knife?"

Sidney responded, "I'm all set. You go your way, I'll go mine."

Ortega loved competition and suggested, "Okay. The one who fails to bring back game should pay a penalty. Will you agree to that?"

Sidney responded, "Okay." He was mildly curious what kind of penalty Ortega had in mind, but he didn't ask—it didn't matter.

Ortega said, "What do you say if we wager some money on this?"

"Okay."

Ortega thought *I'll have some fun with him. I know how much money he has stashed on his boat.* And he offered, "Well, let's make this interesting. What about a twenty-thousand-dollar bet? And we will meet back here in three hours. I'll bring back an animal large enough for the four of us to eat and you try to do the same. The first one back wins."

Sidney didn't register any reaction, but quickly agreed. It bothered Ortega that a man sailing alone in a remote area with very little provisions aboard his vessel, was willing to lose all of his money on a heavily lopsided bet. It didn't make sense, and that raised the yellow flag of caution. While Ortega wanted to go hunting, his real reason was to learn who the mystery man was and what he was up to. He was getting more and more curious.

Ortega said, "We'll divide the jungle in half while facing the cliff. You get to choose the left or right side. In the interest of sportsmanship, Sid, I confess that I have hunted on both sides. Both are equal in the availability of game."

Sidney noticed that the trees at the bottom of a hill on the left side appeared a little thicker than most of the other vegetation indicating the presence of a creek. The creek would be where larger animals would come for water. He chose the left.

Ortega looked at his watch and said, "It is now one-thirty; we must be back here no later than four-thirty, okay?"

Sid nodded his agreement, stepped out of his flip-flops and walked to the edge of the jungle where he silently disappeared into the brush.

Ortega was amazed at his guest's audacity—or was it stupidity. "This is going to be the easiest twenty grand I ever made. The stupid fucker can't go in there in bare feet, and I warned him about the thorns."

ST. MAARTEN

ABOARD THE *SWEET SEA,* ONE OF THE ITALIAN'S SHIPS NOT ATTACKED BY the raiders, was Vincenzo the Sicilian. His map was completed. Also, he had acquired a list of the other sizable raids where there had been a witness during the last five years.

A young Jamaican girl, who was his traveling companion for the week, suddenly interrupted his attention for the rest of the day. Vincenzo admitted to himself that if he ever ran out of money he might speed up catching his target, but what the hell, enjoy. The eighteen-year-old, long-legged beauty was worth every fucking dime and extra time.

THE JUNGLE

AN HOUR AND A HALF HAD PASSED BEFORE SIDNEY REAPPEARED IN THE grassy clearing. He left the dense jungle as easily and as quietly as he had entered. Slung over his back was a wild boar, its legs tied together with vines to keep it from kicking him with its razor-sharp hooves. A big leaf had been tied over its head with another small vine to prevent it from seeing, and it calmed the captured animal.

Sidney respected nature by not killing anything that didn't need to be killed. It wasn't because he was opposed to killing, but it would have been a waste of an animal, as he was sure Ortega would bring in something. Probably another boar since there were so many of them in the area. He knew Ortega had something, as he had heard gunfire in the distance, and a man who enjoyed hunting in that rugged terrain would be a very good hunter.

Jandy and Maria ran gleefully like children to meet Sid as he appeared. The girls had been in the rum, and, by the remains of white dust on their nostrils, some cocaine as well. They were having a good time. When they realized the pig was still alive, they petted it and talked baby talk to it.

"Poor piggy. Did the mean old man hurt you? Poor thing, all tied up and can't run away. Poor little piggy—do you have a family the mean man took you away from?"

A bottle of the iced rum was offered and Sidney took several slugs before giving it back to the girls. Despite the boozing and snorting, they had been busy. They found lots of firewood and had started a big open fire with plenty of logs to feed it.

Sidney thought, *nice fire, but they've got enough wood to cook a fucking elephant. I'd compliment them, but they'd probably just get chatty and expect me to talk about it. Fuck 'em.*

Jandy eagerly asked, "That's a wild boar! How did you catch that thing without getting torn to pieces?"

Sidney, without elaborating as usual, said, "He was sleeping."

He found the rum again and helped himself to another big gulp. Maria motioned Sidney over to the fender of the Jeep where a large sandwich-sized baggie was filled with the white powder of power. She poured some of it on the fender; the hood blocked the slight breeze from blowing the powder around. She laid out a few lines of the dope and a golden tube was offered to him for a snort or two.

Uninterested, he said, "Fuck that shit."

Both girls looked at him in disbelief. Jandy said, "You've got to be kidding man; this is the world's capital for premium blow. This is our national product. Why, people here just do this stuff because it is good for the economy, if for no other reason."

Sidney said, "Fuck the economy."

Jandy laughed then said, "Well that's good; it leaves more for me." She took the tube and filled her nose to the brim with the stuff that impossible dreams were made of.

Maria was puzzled as she didn't understand why a man who drinks like he did wouldn't do a little harmless social blow.

Sidney had no feelings for or against dope. It offered an escape from reality, and he found nothing wrong with reality. Mother rum provided a ticket to Happyville quite nicely. *If these people wanted to feel a real high they should experience serious danger, now there's where the real highs live.*

His thoughts about dope ended when Ortega yelled from deep in the brush, "Hey Jandy! Give me a hand! I've been dragging this thing for a half mile."

Sidney and the girls responded and found Ortega sitting on a big dead tree, huffing and puffing for a breath of air. He was covered with mosquitoes even though he had applied several applications of bug spray, and the hot humid air of the rain forest was getting to him.

The man looks in shape, but apparently he enjoys the easy life more than he should, Sidney thought. Ortega's shoulders, and the front and back of his shirt were soaked, bloody, and filthy. Blood and guts, seeping from stomach wounds of the wild boar that he had shot and carried back, covered him.

Sidney was amused. *It's funny that a seven-year old boy can figure out that it is better to carry an animal alive rather than dead weight over your shoulders. It's less messy, too.*

Ortega's clothes were torn from the jungle's thorns; his arms were covered with deep scratches. He looked at Sidney, who was as fresh as when they had started.

Ortega said. "Well, I see you let good sense prevail when you found out how rugged it is in here. I don't blame you for giving up."

The girls roared with laughter and said, "No way! He came back a half hour ago and brought a boar in, too, same as yours—but his is alive."

Ortega said, "There's no way," as he sat there sucking for air. He looked up at Sidney to see an amused look on his face. Sidney had won the bet.

Back at the fire, Ortega stood over Sidney's boar that was still tied up and lying quietly on its side. He asked, "How the hell did you do that?"

Sidney said, "He was asleep."

Ortega said, "Bullshit! You don't have a scratch on you. What did you use to capture him?"

Seeing the frustration in Ortega, Sidney smiled and said, "He and I had an understanding." Ortega, still in disbelief and scowling, said, "These fucking animals are very dangerous in the brush. Nobody can sneak up on one and tie it up before it wakes up. I have hunted and killed a lot of these animals. I know from first-hand experience how vicious they are." He felt anger at the boat bum for being so superior about the boar—but had to respect any man that could navigate the jungle in his clothes, and barefooted, and bring in a male boar alive. He had obviously misjudged the man's hunting ability.

Sidney sensed that Ortega was annoyed at being beaten at his own game. And he was beaten in such a way that destroyed his image as "the great white hunter" in front of his friends.

He decided to ease up, and said, "Don't feel bad, Ortega. I've been hunting all of my life with only my knife. I use the jungle to my advantage."

Ortega, still exhausted, said, "Well, that doesn't explain how you caught it and brought it back alive. Something is not right with this picture."

Reluctantly, Sidney explained, "There were signs of boars and a jaguar. I followed the tracks until I found one or the other. The boar lost when he charged me from out of the brush."

"Bullshit, Sid! How the hell did you capture the fucking thing? There's no defense from a charging boar."

Sidney said, "There is if you're expecting the charge."

Ortega was getting pissed at the stranger's refusal to tell him. He yelled, "So damn it! Tell me!"

"I slapped him with a thorn branch." Sidney reached for the rum and swallowed a mouthful.

"Sid, quit fucking with me. That would just piss him off."

"Not if you coat the thorns with tree sap."

"Putting sap on thorns is supposed to scare the fucking pig to sleep?"

"Yeah, if you get the right tree sap."

In disbelief, Ortega looked at Jandy and muttered, "Can you believe this guy? He thinks I'm going to believe that the prick of a thorn is going to put the brute out."

Jandy said, "Well, as they say, the proof is in the pudding."

"I don't believe this shit!" muttered Ortega. "Did I make a hunting bet with another fucking Tarzan? How did you know how to do that shit?"

"Experience."

"How the hell can you go in there the way you're dressed and come out looking like you went for a stroll through the park? Shit, man, that's some rough country in there."

"I crushed some plants and smeared them on my skin to hide my smell and to keep the bugs away. I'm used to walking around really rough areas."

That was not what Ortega wanted to hear. And he said nothing more since Sidney's incomplete responses to his questions made him feel more like a novice with every answer.

Sidney took another gulp and thought, *I should tell him I enjoy the jungle as much as they enjoy that stuff they suck up their nose and shoot into veins, but fuck him.*

Ortega wanted to regain his position of alpha male, but in another tack. He said, "That's an incredible story. But what would you have done if there were no animals to track and you were going to lose the bet?"

Without hesitation, Sidney answered, "I would have ambushed you on your way back to camp."

They all laughed, but Ortega wasn't so sure that Sidney was kidding. Sidney knew he wasn't. He had never lost any part of his prize to anyone and damn sure wouldn't over a stupid bet.

Sidney said, "This pig on the ground is yours, Ortega, to do with as you like. You just paid twenty thousand dollars for him."

The girls roared with laughter, Ortega reluctantly smiled, taking his defeat as a good sport. Twenty thousand dollars meant about the same as an American quarter to the average American. He had more cash than he could ever use or even wanted. In fact it was his biggest problem, how to get rid of all the cash. It wasn't the money, however, that he resented—being beaten was—and for the second time by the same man.

Everyone was drinking rum while Ortega butchered his boar. Maria and Jandy were preparing fresh vegetables brought from the hacienda. Sidney was admiring Maria's big tits. The girls were doing a lot of cocaine and Ortega had joined in, too. No one minded that Sidney didn't; he seemed happy enough with the rum.

Ortega's dead pig was cut into strips and wrapped in separate pieces of aluminum foil along with pieces of potato, garlic, onion, cabbage, and a turnip. The dozen or so hunks of foil were then covered with more pieces of wood that would soon cover them with more coals. Leftover pig parts were thrown over the side of the cliff to be considered as a feast for millions of insects and small animals.

As sunlight began to fade, noise from the pesky night fliers started to build. The night fliers were the multitudes of insects that feed at night on animals, plants and other insects. Maria covered herself with bug spray; Jandy did as well, and handed the can to Ortega. Sidney stopped him and pulled leaves out of a pocket and said, "Rub this on your skin, instead."

Ortega did, but couldn't smell anything other than a faint hint of chlorophyll that all green plants have. Ortega said, "This isn't going to work. There's no smell to repel the little bastards."

Sidney assured him the bugs could smell it.

Maria giggled, "Let me know if it works. I don't like smelling like something in a can."

With an abundance of rum and all of the blow a really huge nose could hold, thoughts turned to sex before the food was ready to eat. Jandy started it by running across the grassy opening and tackling Ortega as he was walking towards the fire from the Jeep. She was giggling and horny. After a brief period of playfully wrestling and rolling around on the thick cushion of grass, Jandy pulled his pants off, then her shorts. She mounted him like the original Rough Rider cowboy. Ortega was into it as much as she was, but Jandy was more vocal. Sitting on top of him and her knees up in the air, she moved back and forth, up and down, and grunted like an old buckaroo sitting on a wild mustang.

Sidney missed the show as he had grabbed Maria and they, too, rolled around on the bed of grass, not making love, but his own rough and animalistic style of fucking.

Mother Nature apparently was looking out for the four. The bugs were not bad and the boar was ready to eat as soon as their passion had cooled. The meal was eaten in silence under a dark night sky filled with millions of twinkling stars. Each sat cross-legged on the thick grass-covered ground. Grease from the wild meat smeared their faces and ran down their hands and arms unnoticed.

Smoldering coals produced enough light to see the swarming mosquitoes that kept circling them, wanting to dive bomb them for a taste, but the leaves Sidney used on them all did their job. Maria had opened four chilled bottles of white burgundy, one for each to enjoy with the feast. And it was a feast fit for kings but without benefit of glasses, plates, silverware or napkins. The funny thing was—the feast *really* was for kings—and neither king could guess that the other man had his own kingdom.

Ortega's family had controlled the world's largest smuggling business for three hundred years, and in every part of the world. They owned the property, the politicians, the power and the wealth to establish their position in the underworld of untouchable criminals.

Sidney's fortune, however, was built up over five hundred years and was hidden in a dark, unknown cave.

As they sat in the firelight tearing at the boar's tough flesh, neither man knew their histories were so similar, and if they had it wouldn't have made the forming bond between them any stronger. There was an unspoken understanding between the two that demanded respect for each other. That feeling didn't occur very often with Ortega, and never for Sidney. Both were expected to have things go their way always, and neither gave in to the other. It was a refreshing feeling to be with another powerful man and it was the closest thing to a friend Sidney ever had.

Sidney knew of the word *friend*, but not the true meaning. He had already spent more time with Ortega and the women than he had with any other humans, other than his father. Ortega liked the same things he did and was fun to be with. He wasn't afraid of action or reactions. He was

SIDNEY X THE PIRATE

sure the man was from a strong Spanish family who either controlled a vast business, or were smugglers.

Ortega dominated, as he openly demonstrated his power over the village elders. And his lavish compound in the jungle wasn't built with wages of a working man. The armed guards suggested there was something on the outside of the perimeter wall beside the jungle cats that had better stay away. He had the air of belonging about him wherever he went; he was as much at home in the jungle, or in a dirt floor bar in a third world village, as he would be in New York City's grandest.

After their fill of food and wine, Ortega said, "I suggest we head back to the compound. The smell of a dead boar might encourage a hungry jaguar to come into the camp for a snack." He looked at Jandy with a teasing smile and added, "It might even decide to take a bite out of Jandy instead."

Jandy jumped to her feet and instantly said, "Let's go!"

The trip back to the compound was as much fun as the trip out. The Jeep bounced around the rough trail with everyone laughing and hanging onto anything they could reach. Ricocheting around the Jeep or being thrown out wouldn't be so funny. Leftover wine was discarded for the iced rum and was passed around until they were all thoroughly drunk—again. Ortega missed staying on the trail a couple of times and knocked down some small trees. At one point, the Jeep, four-wheel drive and all, became stuck in the mud.

Three of them got out in the mud to dig the wheels free and then rock the car back and forth to free it from the suction of the red, slippery mud. Maria got behind the wheel. It didn't take long before one of the drunks slipped and fell into the mud, face first. That produced spontaneous laughter from the other three.

As soon as Jandy, covered from face to toe with slimly mud, was able to get on her feet, she jumped on Ortega's back, causing him to fall face first in the deep mud.

Sidney smiled. There was one of the most beautiful and sophisticated women he had ever seen rolling around in thick mud and snorting like a pig between wild bursts of laughter. She was a lot of woman.

Sidney had never had so much fun and was actually laughing out loud. Ortega grabbed his leg and pulled him down into the slippery mud to join them in the messy ooze. Jandy, the head piglet, crawled on her hands and knees snorting, then jumped on him to be sure he was thoroughly covered. The only clean member of the party was Maria, who was behind the steering wheel. She tried to get them to stop without getting out of the car, lest they grab her, too.

She commanded, "Quit floundering around and get serious, you guys. We have to get unstuck from this mud hole." Her words were wasted. She soon realized they were having too much fun wallowing around like pigs to care—so she yelled, "Geronimo!" and dove into the pile of slimy bodies and immediately started snorting like the other little piggies.

After several minutes of exhaustive play, they rolled over and laid on their backs resting, letting the moment of insanity pass. Finally, Ortega got to his feet and reached into the cooler for more rum. The cap from the last bottle joined the caps of the other bottles that day and he took a big drink, mud and all.

One by one, the others stood and had a drink as well. Occasionally, someone would start laughing at the thought of them standing there completely covered in rapidly drying mud with no way to wash it off. Or they laughed at the memory of them squirming around in the mud snorting like pigs.

Finally Ortega realized that they were going to be stuck out in the jungle all night unless they got the Jeep moving again. Everyone resumed their roll in the efforts to get free. After piling some grass and broken limbs in front of the four wheels they were able to get free from the slime trap.

Being encased in dry mud wasn't comfortable. Maria stayed behind the steering wheel as Ortega and Sidney seemed determined to drink everything in sight, and she was very much ready for a long hot, soaking bath. Jandy either fell asleep or passed out in the front seat. The men in the back seats drank and laughed at Ortega's jokes that Maria had heard many times before, which was good, as it kept her interest on the slippery road.

They finally arrived at the well-lighted compound. Big yellow lights spaced every fifty feet were partly obscured with thousands of flying insects, each of them circling the light constantly. The guard looked concerned when he saw the mud-caked condition of his boss and the other three, but soon realized after hearing the laughter that everything was alright. The perplexed expression on the guard's face provoked even more laughter from the muddy four.

Unable to speak because of the uncontrolled laughing, Ortega tried to tell the guards with hand signals that they were okay, but quit in desperation as every move made only produced more spontaneous laughter from his companions and more confusion for the guards. Then the guards found themselves caught up in the mood and soon joined in the folly, but only until one of them realized who he was laughing at, Don Ortega's oldest son and heir to the Don title.

As they came to a stop in front of the hacienda, the girls leaped out and ran. Ortega stood on wobbly legs, holding the empty bottle of rum in the air and loudly declared, "Everybody to the swimming pool!"

Maria objected at first, she was tired and desperately wanted that hot steamy soak her tub offered—right after she answered the call of nature.

Sidney got out of the Jeep then lost his balance and fell down, which caused him to start laughing again. The others helped him get to his feet and steered him to the swimming pool.

Ortega was yelling for the housekeeper to bring more rum as he plunged belly first into the beautiful clear water, leaving a mushroom shape cloud of mud in the water. They all plunged into the water, feeling grateful to shed their mud casings.

Nobody drowned that night and two more bottles of rum were either consumed or spilled. The sun was just peeping over the horizon before Ortega, sitting in a pool chaise, finally dropped off. The girls had disappeared sometime during the night's festivities without being noticed. Sidney had been very drunk, but managed to drink himself sober. After Ortega dropped off, Sidney found the kitchen and cooked himself a whopping big breakfast of several eggs, bacon and big chunk of fresh French bread, piled high with butter. As he finished eating, Ortega's cook came into the kitchen. It was time for her to go to work.

Sidney told the cook, "Tell Ortega that I took his Jeep back to my boat. If he wants it back, come get it."

She thought he was crazy talking that way to Don Ortega's oldest son, but said nothing, only nodding her head that she understood.

Sidney added, "Tell him to bring my money with him."

Now she objected; that was not her place to speak to Ortega in that manner. "Señor, you should wait until the guards get here. If Señor Ortega is still asleep you can tell them. I can't say these things to him."

Sidney was ready to leave and paid no attention to her complaint. He pulled Ortega's Jeep up to what looked to be the maintenance barn in the compound. He was looking for a gas pump; the Jeep was empty. He found the pumps unlocked and filled the Jeep's tank.

When he reached the trail's crossroads, leading to either the village or back to the scene of yesterday's party, he stopped. Yesterday's activities really made an impact on Sidney. That was the only time since he was a little kid that he had played and acted foolishly and it had been fun. It was the first time he had laughed until his eyes watered—and certainly the first time he had wallowed in the mud and grunted like a giggling pig-idiot. He had been embarrassed at acting like a kid, but he was drunk enough not to care. He had fun, and fun was very strange.

As he drove into the village that early morning, everyone waved while showing their usual friendly grins. His boat was tied short to the lagoon's edge exactly as it had been left: wide open, unlocked and untouched by the locals.

Sidney felt like doing something good for the village people, but the thought quickly ended as the sleepies attacked. He plopped down on his berth and easily drifted into a deep sleep. Even the sound of uniformed men yelling to him from shore didn't wake him.

SIDNEY WAS DREAMING OF MARIA'S LOVELY BODY WHEN HE WAS ROUGH-ly awakened. Someone held him by his shoulder and was shaking him hard enough to realize that the person had lost his patience. Four armed men were standing over him; their guns pointed directly his way. Uniforms suggested they were members of the country's militia.

He awoke fully prepared to kill each of them, but remembered his thoughts of moving into the area, and decided to play along. Those men were found in the cities and countryside of all nations and their main function was to be sure that nothing illegal went on unless authorized by the political elite. They also would be on hand to help the general population in time of national disasters, as long as it didn't interfere with their responsibility to their own families or create discomfort to themselves. They were the lowest rung on the graft and corruption ladder, but were, and maybe more so, as dangerous as those standing on the highest rung.

They had little to lose by killing the wrong person and most were too stupid to know the difference anyway. You could buy your way out of any problem with those men, but the price would keep going up as the news reached higher echelons of the government. Sidney had lots of experience with that type of person. Generally, they were in the same type of work as he was, but they were allowed to rob and hurt people with the governments' protection. It was the way developing governments could afford the protection of an army. Since the start of time, people had to contend with those people, and every government in the world had condoned their activity at one time or another. To Sidney, they were his enemy and in most cases were dealt with severely.

That day, however, was different. It took him a moment or two to get things in perspective after being shaken awake. He sat on the edge of the bunk, clearing the cobwebs and the effects of empty rum bottles out of his head. Two soldiers searched the boat while another kept his AK-47 trained at his mid-section.

The oldest of the bunch was doing all of the talking. "I'm Sergeant Manual of the National Militia and have been sent to investigate the area for any wrong doings. I want to see your passport and documents giving you permission to be in Venezuela. I want also to know where you cleared into Customs and Immigration."

Sidney, confident that he could talk his way out of anything if he remained calm, told the sergeant, "I arrived a couple of days ago, but have not been able to get anywhere that has a Customs Office."

That brought on a look of suspicion followed by an attitude that suggested he was in for some trouble.

Sidney continued, "I was caught in a storm a day before I landed here. During the storm my boat started taking on water so bad I thought it was sinking. I deployed my life raft and loaded it with all my papers, passport and navigation charts."

He then quickly added and put special emphases on it, "*And my money. The raft's painter pulled loose when I went below to make a last check for possessions before abandoning ship. By the time I got topside the raft was gone. It had blown away."

The sergeant asked, "Where are you from and where were you going?"

Sidney responded, "I have been sailing from Costa Rica enroute to Grenada, where I had intended to buy some land."

"So why are you still here? And how is it you managed to be here, floating in the hidden Lagoon of Crocodiles, in a boat that was quickly sinking from under your feet?"

Sidney explained, "I managed to find the problem. A discharge hose from the head came off of its fitting. It is a two inch hose that let a lot of water into the boat."

The sergeant pointed at one of his men and said, "Go inspect the hose and take a very good look."

Sidney continued with his story, "After I pumped the water out I was able to ride out the storm. When the winds eased I decided to sail due south to find land. I needed to find out where the hell I was. I spotted this village, anchored and got too drunk to leave that night. The next day I went for a run and while I was away the wind came up and the villagers moved my boat around to the lagoon. I didn't even know it was here. It was too rough to leave that day and the next day a big man in these parts wanted me to go to his hacienda. I thought he was part of the government so I went. I just returned from his place this morning."

Then he added, "Since I have been here, however, I have decided to buy land here instead. I like this place."

The sergeant already knew of his visit to the hacienda and asked, "How long have you known Don Jose Ortega?"

Sid asked, "Who is this man Ortega? Does he have something to do with the government?"

The sergeant said, "You, be quiet. I am the one asking the questions."

The man sent to check on the head's discharge hose came back with a rusted and broken hose clamp. He said, "It looks like this clamp broke off and there's a new one on the hose now."

Sidney remained silent, waiting for the next question from the sergeant and the discovery of the twenty thousand dollars by the others. His only problem would be if the man who found the money put it into his pocket without telling the sergeant. If that happened, then he would be forced to kill them. Nobody took a prize from the Barracuda.

Soon, Sidney heard one of the searchers proclaimed he had found money in a bottle. *That's good, this means the search is over. Now it's time to buy some allies.* The men gathered around the sergeant as he broke the rum bottle. The rolled up dollars fell to the floor. He then picked them up and counted the money.

With the same distasteful expression he looked at Sidney and said, "So you lost your money with your papers Señor?"

Sid said, "That's right. I lost two hundred thousand US dollars in traveler's checks in the life raft. That money is just cash for my expenses, *chump change.*"

The sergeant put on his official air of authority and said, "It's against the law to bring this much cash into our country without declaring it. It seems you have no regard for our country's laws, Señor."

Sidney spread his arms in desperation and said, "What could I do? Where could I register? Where could I go to declare the cash?"

"That is not my concern. My concern is that you have broken our laws."

Sidney then said, "Okay, then where can I pay a reasonable fine since I find myself in a position such as this?"

The sergeant in the same arrogant attitude said, "You will be arrested and must go with us to headquarters for an investigation."

It was now the sergeant's turn to turn the screws. He said, "Señor, do not try to do anything stupid, my men are very alert and their weapons are loaded. You must now go with us. Lock this boat very carefully as the village is full of thieves who will either steal the boat and sell it in Caracas or strip everything of value before you are released from jail. It might take a long time while we check out who you really are."

Sidney knew the village people wouldn't steal, but acted indignant. He said, "They better not! I'll have them arrested!"

The sergeant said, "Perhaps I should tell you that you are a stranger here and a law breaker in our country. I doubt very seriously that anything will be done about your complaints. It's your just dessert for being in our country illegally."

Sidney played his next card and said, "Even if I have Jose Ortega's eyes looking over me?"

The question caused the sergeant to shuffle his feet and look around nervously, buying time while thinking of what he should say next. "How do you know Don Ortega?" he asked again.

Sidney answered, "We're pals. We get drunk together and chase the ladies. That is his Jeep parked out there, don't you recognize it? Or maybe you are not from around here. Or is it that you do not respect Señor Ortega?"

The sergeant responded, protecting his ass in case the stranger was a friend of Ortega's, "Of course I know of, and certainly respect him. He is a great man. Señor Ortega has done many wonderful things for our communities, as his family has for many years. The Ortega family is one of the most respected in Venezuela."

The sergeant hesitated long enough for effect then added, "He also frequently demonstrates his appreciation of the militia whenever possible."

That was all Sidney needed. He asked the sergeant, "Please, Sergeant Manual, let's you and I step outside for a minute to get some fresh air."

Outside, Sidney said, "I appreciate the job you and your men must do and know it isn't easy to keep the area free from the type of people who have no respect for you and your government. Since arriving here, I have developed a fondness for your country and especially this area. I plan to buy a large section of land here to grow a crop called kenaf. This is a new export crop and will be very good for the local economy and your government. This will be a sizable investment and I would feel more at ease spending the kind of money that will be required to set up and maintain this operation if I knew I could count on your presence occasionally to keep the undesirables away. I know you can't make guarantees because you have a boss that may not let you come to this area very often. So if you and your men would not be insulted, I would like to pay for a monthly visit when I get started. I assure you I'm a generous man."

Sidney reached over and took the wad of cash from the sergeant and said, "If you're not offended by this proposal then I would like to give you a thousand dollars for you to distribute to your men as you see fit—starting now."

He counted out the money and pushed it into the sergeant's palm. It angered Sidney to lose his money, but after all, he was getting something in return. It was like buying a boat for cash to use to take a prize then sinking it. It was all the same no matter what occupation—it was the cost of doing business.

The sergeant quickly assumed his new role, the veil of bullshit was down and the men knew the rules and agreed to them. He asked, "I can assure you, Señor, everything will be fine for you now. My men and I appreciate your understanding of our problems. We want to do everything possible to help your new project be a success and your generosity will certainly help us do just that. Is there anything we can do to help you today?"

Sidney said, "I'll be leaving in a couple of days and will be gone for a while. I want to buy some land from Ortega. If he doesn't have the land that I want then I'd appreciate it if you can find someone who can help me. I'll want about one thousand hectares to start."

The sergeant said, "Señor, I know many people with very good land. I am sure I can find you a very good deal, but please do not lose your passport again; it would be very difficult to purchase land here without proper identification."

Sidney said, "I have confidence that you'll find a way, Sergeant."

That made Sergeant Manual even happier; he was going to make a lot of money with the man from Costa Rica, or wherever the hell he was from. The sullen attitudes of the other men changed to willing cooperation as soon as they saw the expression on their sergeant's face. They were proud of their sergeant; he always made money for them. However, had they known they were only given two hundred dollars each out of the thousand they would be pleased to kill the thieving prick. As the proud men left the boat, Sidney made his best effort at waving a friendly good-bye.

ST. MAARTEN

VINCENZO WAS SITTING IN THE BANK PRESIDENT'S CHAIR. AS PART OF his investigation he was talking to every victim and witness. In this case, he was laughing at the whole scenario surrounding the robbery. A wild, crazy man, with either a huge pecker or something resembling one, suddenly appeared waving a machete around and yelling crazy talk and then took a lot of the mob's money without one person lifting a finger to stop him. Nobody even bothered to sound the silent alarm until after he left.

All of the witnesses responded with either: "He had a huge thing and was crazy." "He had a huge dick and was scary." "He had a huge thing and was filthy." One woman said, "He had a huge dick and got grease on me when he tore my dress off." That was as much of a description as he could get; no size, no weight, no age and nothing for certain for his race, but all used the description of Rastafarian at some time during their interview. There was no reason to think he was a Rasta as his hair was pointed into the air in spikes and wasn't in dreadlocks.

He interviewed the gas station attendant that might have somehow been involved. At the time of the robbery, the police had been called there to investigate a call about a murder that hadn't happened. A local black man had placed the call, but nobody knew who it was. When the police arrived they found the attendant unconscious and leaning over the fender of the car he had been working on. It took a while to revive the man, so he was cleared of any involvement.

The attendant could only remember working on Mrs. Clyde's Chevy. The next thing he knew, the police had him on the ground and paramedics were caring for him. He had a hell of a headache and a good-sized lump on his head. He had treated a lady for the same symptoms a few minutes later. The woman had been ironing her clothes when she suddenly came to and was lying on the floor. Her head hurt and she had a nice lump on her noggin, too. No other harm had been done to her; she hadn't been molested or robbed, but whoever gave her the lump had stolen her husband's only pair of black socks.

The police were sure it was an isolated crime. There had never been a robbery of a pair of socks, or an obviously well-planned wild man robbery. It was probably done by a man off one of the cruise ships. When word got out that the police were looking for a man with a *huge thing* their doors were jammed with drunken men bragging by demanding it wasn't them. Local women showed up to laugh at the men and disproved every claim. The locals had a lot of fun with the search for the mystery man for almost a week.

Had the incident not happened to a family owned bank, Vincenzo would have given the robber a thumbs-up for an excellent job. Instead he was making every effort to connect it to his current mission. And he had remembered something important. There had been headaches and lumps on heads on many of the other reports he had read. And all had been robberies by unseen assailants.

He was starting to piece together bits of information. He started a facts sheet to cross check similarities.

Robberies done in Caribbean: Victims knocked unconscious from behind, leaving headaches and lumps on their heads. Tape was used to cut off air from the victims to get information on many jobs. Only one man was involved and several cruise ship victims had only heard one man's voice, but that same voice spoke several languages.

THE HACIENDA

Jose Ortega slept undisturbed for six hours on a poolside chaise lounge. The household staff knew better than to wake him when he was sleeping off a drunk. The housekeeper was concerned that he would have an aching back when he awoke but that was too bad, she too wasn't going to disturb him.

Jandy had made her appearance around three that afternoon to find Maria fixing Bloody Marys for herself and Ortega. Jandy declined Maria's offer to fix her one, too. Their relationship was a strange one: they both worked for the same man; both had made love to him on several occasions; both regarded him with the utmost respect, and they liked him personally. They liked each other personally as well and showed the respect they each deserved. Neither had a tendency to become a lover of the other, both enjoyed their normal sexual preference: a hard dick, even if it was on another woman's husband.

Ortega appreciated each woman's skills and made sure they never felt threatened by the other. Both knew he would never form an emotional bond with any woman other than his wife. She seldom came to Venezuela unless she stayed in their huge ultra-modern condominium in Caracas. She wanted nothing to do with her husband's "jungle shanty" as she called it. She spent most of her time proving to be a good mother to their six children, living either at the Virgin Island compound or the old family hacienda in the mountains of Columbia.

Maria lived permanently in the Venezuela compound except when Ortega made her travel, which happened frequently when he needed her extraordinary skills. She thoroughly enjoyed her status in life and it would have been impossible for anyone to buy her loyalty.

Jandy's home was on St. Thomas, but she was rarely there as she traveled with Ortega everywhere he went. She was his personal secretary, travel agent, salesman, whore, spy or anything else he needed to get his job accomplished. She was a person that Ortega counted on to keep him organized and she did an outstanding job. She had been with him for years and, like Maria, could not have been bought for any amount of money.

Ortega improved their lives so much, financially and psychologically that both would die rather than betray him. Both made more money than they thought possible and had their own Swiss bank accounts. Also they were respected and well treated by all of Ortega's friends and business connections, which were considerable, both in quantity and preeminence.

With a couple of sips of the Bloody Mary cooling Ortega's pipes a bit, he asked Maria, "What are your thoughts about our new friend, Sidney?"

"I have a very definite feeling that he is not a man to take lightly. He has always been a loner and is very capable of being a bad character. I do not feel threatened by him nor do I think any of us has any reason to be concerned. He genuinely seems to like us, maybe even quite a lot, in fact. His laughter yesterday seemed to be a curious thing to him, as if he rarely ever laughed. I really felt that his laughter even surprised him. The strongest things I keep getting from him are he seems to be almost without emotions, and has absolutely no doubts about himself. Even his lovemaking is done just for him. His technique and the brutal animal within him, however, make up for his lack of affection and turns out to be one hell of a romp in the old sack." She giggled with slight embarrassment.

Maria went on, "With this unrestricted self-confidence, he also has no feeling of fear. His performance yesterday, when he bet all of his money on the hunt and the way he hunted the jungle with only a knife, proves that point. The fact that he brought the boar in alive indicates that, while he is capable of controlling and killing, he doesn't kill without a reason. This tells me he is intelligent, but you would never be able to tell that from conversations. I have never seen a man who talks so little, especially from a man with his looks, physique and self-confidence. Normally, those attributes would produce a cocky and overbearing man."

"Is he really a good fuck?" asked Jandy.

Ortega snapped, "Jandy, be quiet. I want to hear more from Maria. You can compare notes later."

Maria continued, "His drinking could indicate that he spends a lot of time by himself and has no one to share his troubles or happy times with, or he's just a drunk with a heavy habit. Either way, he does appear to enjoy his rum."

Ortega said, "Well, what the hell's wrong with that?"

Maria said, "Sure, you like to drink and sometimes you drink a lot, too, but you shut down when there are things to do. You might go for a week at a time without drinking and hardly even notice it when you're busy. I don't think Sidney has much to do. His hands are tough like a working man's hands, but the way he carries himself and with his attitude, I don't see him working for another man as a laborer— or for anyone. The fact that he has time to sail around in his own boat and has that much cash on board also tends to indicate that he doesn't work. At least he doesn't work in the conventional way."

"That could mean that he might be dealing in the drug or people smuggling business?" asked Ortega.

"I don't get that from his actions. He was offered cocaine and he refused, saying 'Fuck that shit.' If he were in the drug business he might still refuse, but would have phrased it differently, not relating to the negative 'shit' to the fruit of his income.

Jandy put her thoughts out for the others to reflect on. She asked, "Have you ever looked deep into his eyes? I did, on several occasions, and was frightened by the hardness and coldness in them. It's like his eyes are not connected to his thoughts. It is uncomfortable to look into those eyes."

Both Ortega and Maria agreed.

Maria added one more thing by saying, "He has the strangest looking tattoo on his shoulder. It is a scary looking skull with a big knife stuck through one eye socket and a broken leg bone in the other, which forms a cross-bone image of a pirate. A barracuda is curled around them as if it's saying, "Approach at grave risk." The skull is resting on a bunch of small bones. For some reason, I felt those small bones meant something and I counted them; there were twenty-three bones. A red flag with tattered edges was the tattoo's background."

Ortega remarked, "That sounds like a modified pirate flag, doesn't it? Was it a recent tattoo?"

Maria said, "No. It looked old and faded as if he has had it most of his life. I just happened to see it as I had a good vantage point while in bed when he was making love to me." She briefly paused, then said, "Scratch that part about making love. I should have said ravishing me."

Jandy had a little laugh and said as if interested, "Really?"

Maria could tell that Jandy wanted some sack time with the beast from the boat.

"Jandy, keep your legs closed and your mind open; we need to find out about this guy. Anyway Maria, could he be a cop?" asked Ortega.

"No way," was Maria's immediate response.

Jandy added, "An undercover cop down in this country would go out of his way to be nice in order to encourage contacts. This man had been civil, but certainly didn't want a thing from us. He wouldn't have accepted his invitation to join us had Maria not put the pussy whammy on him. The same would be true if he worked for your competition. If there is any still around," she added with a coy smile.

Maria continued, "I think that if anything, he's on the run from someone or some country. He's vague about his past. All I know about him is that he said he was coming from Costa Rica, but his Spanish doesn't reflect that. I am not able to say exactly what Spanish he speaks as he, for one thing, doesn't talk much, and he uses dialects and words from Spain, Puerto Rico and Cuba as well as South America."

Ortega asked if he spoke another language. No one had heard him say anything. That gave Jandy an idea. She offered, "Why don't I go over to the village to get the Jeep and I'll see if he understands any other language?"

Maria said, "Yeah, you would love to make the beast bark, wouldn't you?" and she laughed.

Jandy, smiling, said, "Who me? Why no, Maria, whatever gave you that idea?" Then she blushed with the memory that Maria was able read her very well.

Ortega got up and announced, "Relax girls, we all will go to the village in a little while. Maybe we'll just sit down and ask our friend who the hell he is and what he is up to."

Jandy asked, "What are you going to do about the twenty thousand dollar bet?"

Ortega replied, "I took his fingerprints off of the glass he used and emailed them to Miami, San Jose, and Bogota this morning. Our people there are going through the procedures to find out who he is and what he has been up to. Until I know that, I won't pay him and he won't leave here until I do. That has got to be a lot of money to him. Who knows, maybe I'll double it for him by giving him a job, depending on his check out."

Jandy said, "I'll volunteer to babysit him if needed."

"Oh, no you don't, I got him first, he is mine," snapped Maria, a little more serious that time.

Ortega said, "Hey, you two, stop being so horny. I don't want anybody to get careless around Sid yet. His prints could be identified this afternoon. Then we will be able to scheme intelligently on our plan of action. For today, we will just drink, party and have fun. Fun means no catfights between the two of you over the boat beast as Maria calls him. I want her to be with him to give us more insight on the guy."

Playfully, Jandy stuck her bottom lip out in a pout and whined, "Okay, daddy."

Ortega thought he'd finish the conversation by saying, "I don't know why, but I like the man. He appears to be a real standup guy. I hope his record substantiates that feeling. The fact that he doesn't have much to say isn't a bad trait either. In fact it leaves more time for my brilliant words to be heard by all, hey girls?"

Jandy added, "It was ballsy for him just to take the Jeep without even asking. Are you going to let him get away with that?"

Maria's last words were, "Let's go; my Sidney needs his iced rum."

THE VILLAGE

SIDNEY WAS SITTING ON THE BOW OF HIS BOAT WITH A COIL OF LINE IN hand that had a hook with a small shiner on the other end. He was trying to lure something up for dinner. Earlier, he had used the same line with a smaller hook, baited with a bean, one of the several that had been soaking in a can of tuna fish juice. The bean soaked up the fish odor but remained hard enough to stay on the hook. It had taken only a few seconds to land the fighting minnow, which upon boarding, Sidney toasted the wiggling three-inch fish with a big gulp of rum. He respected the minnow's life as much as he would when he caught the bigger fish destined to be his dinner.

Ortega's other Jeep came bouncing into the village on the rough dirt road. Sidney's mind had gone slack after twenty minutes of waiting for his dinner to bite the minnow. His eyes followed the Jeep, but his mind was lost in the beautiful greens of the jungle and its reflections on the calm, peaceful water of the lagoon. Suddenly, he had a hard jerk on his fishing line and the abruptness of the hit almost pulled the line out of his hand.

Señor Fish was in a mad rush to get away from whatever was in his mouth. It hurt and he couldn't shake it out or get away from it. He swam in a wide circle, diving to the bottom then surfacing to leap clear from the water. On the big silver fish's first jump he cleared the water's surface by three feet, which gave Sidney ample time to see he had hooked a three-foot snook, the favored fish on his list of good things to eat. They were among the top in fighting as well. If the fish had been caught on a light rod he would have had a tough fight bringing him in. Snook were good at finding something like a coral head, stump, or piling to swim around in order to wrap the line. It would then be only a matter of seconds before he would slice the line off with its razor-sharp gills to be free once again.

The hand line, however, was different. It would be easy to keep the fish away from the anchor line since there was a direct pull from the strength of man to that of a twenty pound piece of swimming muscle.

As Ortega and his troop pulled up to the lagoon, Sidney landed the fish and held it high for them to see. The trio started walking toward Sidney lugging two bottles of iced rum in a small canvas cooler bag.

Ortega better have my twenty grand. If he didn't bring it, he better have a damn good excuse... Hell, it's not prize money; I'll probably give it to the village anyway. — Damn, I am getting soft. Then he almost smiled at another thought. *But that money will become prize status if Ortega tries not to pay.*

Maria gave him a warm hug with kisses on his lips and cheek, showing a little more affection than she normally would—just to mark her territory for Jandy. Jandy hugged him and pecked a light kiss on his cheek.

Ortega was last aboard, and after the last two affectionate greetings he said, "Don't expect any kisses from me. Instead, how about this?" and held out a bottle of iced rum with its cap missing.

It was an offering Sidney had never refused. He listened a few minutes to the chit-chat from the three of them about yesterday's fun and what they could do to top it. He then excused himself and said, without fanfare "I'm cooking the fish."

He threw a handful of rice in a pot of boiling water on his galley stove and did the same with some black beans. On the aft deck he quickly killed and gutted the fish, and cut the fish into three sections to make it fit in his largest frying pan. He poured milk from two coconuts that came from the lagoon's edge into the pan. Then he added a big splash of rum. The fish sections were the last in. After two glasses of rum, dinner was ready. The fish was excellent; the taste of rum and coconut added an unusual flavor. The rice and beans were ordinary, maybe even tough, and if you looked close enough you'd see a few tiny bugs. But everything was hot, nourishing, and filling and that's all that mattered to Sidney.

For dessert the coconut milk and rum mixture was spiked with more rum and offered hot. Its hint of a seafood taste barely overpowered the coconut and rum and was probably the best part of the meal. After dessert, Ortega produced a couple of cigars and said, "I brought these along. I thought you might enjoy a good smoke after such a unique dinner." Sidney was delighted, especially since they were Cohibas.

During the lighting rituals that some men like to go through with exceptional cigars, Jandy said, "Hey, let's go to Gaspar's and dance and have some fun."

Both girls cheered, but Ortega said, "Why don't you girls go on over; Sid and I have some business to discuss."

After the girls had gone, Ortega asked, "How long are you going to be around here, Sidney?"

Sidney answered, "Leaving tomorrow."

Ortega, looking disappointed, said, "Well, I don't have your money yet, and don't expect it to be here for three of four more days. I don't want you to think that I'm trying to welsh on our bet; believe me, I'm not. I just don't keep that kind of cash around. After all, what could I possibly spend it on out here in the middle of a jungle?"

That wasn't a surprise to Sidney. He knew very well that Ortega had plenty of cash at his hacienda. He had to have cash living in the jungle. There are no banks so people don't take checks. Cash or product is all they have. Also, Sidney was almost sure Ortega was in the smuggling business, and at his level, he would always maintain large amounts of cash. Every transaction he made had to be cash so as not to leave paper trails.

"I know where you're going with this story, Ortega. That won't do."

"Well, why not, Sid; can't you stick around a little longer?"

"No."

"You are putting me in a bad situation here. Why can't you wait?"

"I have to be somewhere that requires my departure by noon tomorrow."

Ortega said, "Well, then, I guess you'll have to take a check. You can cash it in Caracas if you are going east."

Sidney said, "No checks."

Ortega gestured a hopeless situation by spreading his arms at his side and holding both palms facing upwards. "What can I do?" he asked.

"Just pay your debt. You made the bet. You lost. Now pay." Sidney wasn't acting angry, just talking in a matter-of-fact tone of voice.

Ortega asked, "Why not stay until the money arrives and just postpone your meeting with whomever it is you are to see. After all, twenty thousand bucks is surely a lot of money to you."

Sidney said, "It's impossible to postpone my meeting."

Ortega then said, "Tell you what! If you wait for the cash to arrive, I'll have my helicopter take you to Caracas. Then my private plane will take you to your meeting. The pilot will wait for you and bring you back to your boat. How does that sound?"

Sidney said, "Can't do it, Ortega. I'm leaving tomorrow, on my boat."

Ortega asked, "Why?"

That pissed Sidney off. He didn't usually have conversations with people and he never argued. Nobody ever had tried to make him do something he didn't want to do.

Ortega said, "Well Sid, it appears we have some kind of problem here."

"I don't. You have the problem."

"What do you mean I have the problem, Sid? I own this part of the world. If I didn't pay you there is nothing you could do. That, however, is not the case. I'm willing to pay you, but you are going to have to wait for a day or two for the money to arrive."

Unimpressed, Sidney had just shifted the wager money to prize status. He said, "It's your problem, Ortega, and it is going to be resolved before you leave my boat."

Ortega smiled, showing his lack of concern for implied threats, and said, "What's to keep me from jumping overboard, swimming the short distance to shore and getting the men of the village to take care of you for me? I do support this village you know."

Sidney with his deadly cold black eyes staring at Ortega said without emotion, "Dead men don't swim."

This made Ortega realize that he *was* in a situation. For the first time in many years he was not totally in control and was running out of options. He wished he had brought his pistol along; that would have put the balance of power where it should be —even if it meant shooting Sidney.

Sidney stood still, not saying or doing anything, waiting for Ortega to back down or make a move to leave the boat. If Ortega had a gun and made a move to pull it out, Sidney's knife would sever his jugular in the same instant. Sidney, however, did not want to kill him as it would make enemies for him. That place offered a good place to spend time while the boy was in the bush, and possibly find a new cave.

Sidney decided to help Ortega out of his perilous position and said, "Okay, I'll take your Jeep instead of the cash."

Ortega, somewhat relieved, said, "That's fine with me, but how do you expect to take it with you?"

Sid said, "I'll leave it here. When I return I can come over to your place for another party trip to your hunting grounds. Besides, I'm sure you'll give me another chance to take another twenty thousand from you."

Ortega was pleased that the situation had worked out okay, and that the dangerous stranger would return. By then Ortega would know who he was dealing with. His respect for Sidney had increased by his show of strength during their negations. He felt very sure that Sidney was not making an idle threat about dead men not swimming, but he didn't hold it against him —after all, it was he who had not paid the bet.

Ortega said, "Let's head for Gaspar's. I'll write you a bill of sale in front of the bartender so you have a witness."

Sidney said, "I don't need a paper. I have your word."

"By the way, Sid, that fucking Jeep cost me close to thirty thousand dollars with the fees and duties I had to pay to get it in here."

Sid smiled and said, "You can afford it. Let's get shit-faced."

Ortega's curiosity was almost out of control; *I have to know who this guy is. Who the hell is this guy who sailed in on a small boat with a measly twenty grand and a few sacks of beans and rice to his name? The only thing the guy visibly has is pair of cast iron balls… and okay, a talent for hunting. I'm too fucking rich and powerful to be denied by this guy. I'll damn sure end up getting my way over the stubborn prick—one way or another.*

Putting his consternation aside, Ortega and Sidney entered the dingy little bar to see the girls laughing, yelling, and shouting the sounds of Latin America bravo while dancing to the fast pace of salsa music blaring on the rusty old AM radio. The bartender and a customer were offering their encouragement with applause and cheers whenever one of the girls demonstrated her feminine skills of the dance.   Sidney noticed the Igloo cooler behind the bar that Ortega had brought with him that was supposedly stocked with several bottles of rum being turned icy cold. Gaspar didn't wait for the men to order and gave each an almost clean glass, filled half way up with their favorite beverage. Out of respect, the only other customer got off his stool, a fifty-gallon barrel that washed up on the beach that morning, and moved to the end of the bar, leaving four barstools available to the Don and his guests.

The remainder of the evening was spent looking at the world through the bottom of an almost clean glass in varying stages of empty. The girls danced, Ortega sang, and children of the village sat in the doorway and watched. It was fun to watch, as there were no televisions or movies for entertainment. The village men went to the little bar to have a drink and talk to friends after a hard day of fishing. Usually they were too tired to dance and sing and act silly. The children were having as much fun as the drunken adults inside.

At one point, Maria asked Ortega to dance with her, it was a slow dance. Sidney was occupied, listening to Jandy talk about anything, which she did incessantly when drunk.

Maria asked Ortega, "How did the deal work out about paying Sid?"

"You were right, Maria; the man is someone to be reckoned with. I feel sure that he was prepared to kill me if I tried to wiggle out of paying the bet. I tried every move I could think of, even an implied threat, but couldn't get him to back down or make any concessions. Maria, toward the end of our negotiations, I became concerned for my life and there was not a damn thing I could do about it."

Sensing Ortega's feeling of disappointment, Maria was sympathetic. It was a rare event when Ortega didn't have complete control over his position, but she still had her job to evaluate and advise Ortega.

She told him, "You're wrong, Ortega. You did have control; all you had to do was pay the man what you owed him."

That brought a quick look of resentment from Ortega, but it soon passed, as he knew she was right. He had a hell of a lot more cash at the hacienda than the twenty thousand.

She continued, "God knows, you might have that much money lying around as spare change on top of your dresser drawers."

Ortega said, "It wasn't the money, Maria, it was winning the negotiation that became important."

She laughed and said, "There we go again with the old male chest-thumping shit again."

Ortega responded, "Call it what you like, but it's fucking important. You can only have so many roosters in a given barnyard, you know."

Resigned to accept the silliness, Maria said, "Cock a doodle do."

They danced for a brief period saying nothing. Finally, Maria asked, "So?"

"So what?" Ortega responded.

"So how did you get out of the deal? Did you bring the money to pay him?"

He answered, "Of course not," and then took Maria over to the bar and asked the bartender for a pen and piece of paper.

All Gaspar had was a used envelope from the only letter he had ever received. It had been a notice from the Army that his son had been killed. He treasured the envelope as well as the letter inside it, but gave it freely to the generous patron.

Ortega wrote, "This blue Jeep, formally owned by Jose Ortega of Hacienda de Caribe, now belongs to Sidney." He stopped writing, looked up and asked Sidney, "What the hell is your last name anyway?"

Sidney answered, "Forget it."

Ortega looked to Maria. "I traded my Jeep for one wild boar." Only then did he realize that they had left the pig at the hunt site, lying on the ground and still tied up.

"Poor pig," he said. "Here is to the now dead little piggy we left in the bush hog-tied; even its scared little eyes covered so he could only hear the silent approach of the big jungle cat, breathing excitedly on his quest to rip the little piggy apart with its razor-like claws and pointed white teeth behind the evil smile of a mighty night killer."

Both girls were horrified that they had forgotten all about the captured boar, and their horror turned into sadness as both started crying at the thought of what must have happened to the poor pig.

Sidney said, "Here's to you, porky," and downed his glass of rum. That was as close as possible for Sidney to be humorous. He wasn't concerned about the pig; he had cut it loose as they were feasting on the other. He enjoyed seeing their sorrow and didn't tell them Porky was still doing *boaring* things in the jungle.

Sidney took the incomplete envelope, and then asked Gaspar "Can you drive?"

The bartender told him that he had moved to Caracas as a young man and had learned to drive a taxi.

Ortega said, "That's not driving. That's just a bunch of people surviving in bumper cars."

Sidney wrote on the envelope that the car belonged to Gaspar in exchange for the right to use it whenever he was there and one glass of rum. He signed it, Sidney, and slid the envelope back to the bartender with the empty glass of rum. Gaspar read the envelope; re-read it and looked around at Sidney then Ortega, thinking the machos were playing a trick on him.

Ortega took the envelope to see what had been written. He was pissed, and said, "You stupid shit! You can't do this. This is worth more money than that man could make in his lifetime. You scare the shit out of me over some stupid bet; make me sign over a thirty thousand dollar Jeep, and you just give it away?"

He was getting madder and the rum in him made it worse. He started to tear up the envelope, but Sidney instantly grabbed it from him before

Ortega was even aware he had moved.

To calm him down, Sidney said, "I intend to use the Jeep, but I want Gaspar to take care of it while I'm away. It's his to use, not sell."

"Wow, another long sentence from Sid," Jandy said to Maria. Maria didn't reply, she was concerned; she rarely saw Ortega get mad, but when he did someone always paid the price.

In any other part of the world Ortega always had his *valentóns* as he called them. In reality, they were his bodyguards and enforcers and did *anything* Ortega asked. She was glad they weren't there; they could have dragged Sidney out of the bar, killed him, and dumped his body into the lagoon for the crocs to munch on.

She thought if the bodyguards had been there Sidney would not have made it off of the boat after their chest-thumping negotiations. Ortega was a nice man, but he was not a man to argue with. His way was the right way and if it wasn't, then he'd make it the right way by any means available.

Then Sidney shocked all that knew him in the little bar by saying, "Anyway Ortega, the bet was your idea not mine. You had your reason to make such a large bet with a guy you never met before, but apparently assumed by my demeanor and appearance that I'm a drifter. Obviously, you mistook the fact that someone dressed in skimpy attire, not in the latest jungle fashions, had no idea of what it would be like in the jungle. When I refused the gun, you must have been certain you had an easy mark. I'm sure you figured I had no experience as a hunter.

"I didn't question your reasons for the bet, but I took it in good faith. The amount of the bet amused me, as well. It told me that you knew more about what I had on my boat than you should. That didn't bother me. I can imagine you have a certain need and the right to know who is moving into your territory. I have no right to judge your actions. And you have no right to criticize my actions now or what I choose to do with my winnings just because you miscalculated your advantage and lost the foolish bet."

Ortega, Jandy, Maria, and even Gaspar were impressed with the long string of words from the mouth of the quiet one. They sat almost stunned, with mouths open until Ortega said, "You know, Sid, you are absolutely right. I got carried away about this and I apologize. Fuck it, let's have some fun."

Ortega raised his almost empty glass to Gaspar and said, "Enjoy your new car, my friend," and downed the remaining rum.

Gaspar was noticeably relieved that the Don had relented and allowed him to keep the car. That car meant he was the most prominent man in the village. It was a symbol of prosperity and more importantly, it had been given to him by the Don Jose Ortega personally. The fact that it had come directly from Sidney didn't even enter the picture. However, it had given a special place for Sidney in the community, as well. Sidney didn't know it, but he would never want for anything in that village.

Both girls didn't believe Ortega admitted he was wrong on a matter over money or who had the last say in something. They both cheered and Jandy gave Ortega a huge kiss. Maria said, "Sidney, I didn't think you knew so many words. Wow, you do talk!"

Sidney grunted and turned back to the drink before him. Then they drank up everything in the little bar and returned to the boat. Everyone was tired, still feeling the effects of last night's lack of sleep. Soon all were in one bunk or another fast asleep, except Sidney, who was on top of Maria, pumping away.

ABOARD TROPICAL SUN

VINCENZO THE SICILIAN WAS DOING SOME PUMPING OF HIS OWN AT THAT same time in the very early morning hours; however, it wasn't with a sweaty belly over some expensive whore. He had reached a level in his investigation where he could feel he was on the right track, but couldn't get the right information to flow from any of the previous victims. He realized it wasn't by design, but rather a defensive measure provided by Mother Nature to cause people to gloss over or forget details of traumatic experiences.

Before him sat a ship's purser, recently known by his close friends as Lefty because of the noticeably missing right ear. He had also been stabbed in the heart; luckily, the blade only nicked the vital organ. It had been a very long night for him that night and the night he was going through right then. His face was bleeding from the punches thrown in exasperation, not anger, by Vincenzo. He needed more information and Michael wanted to give him more, but there wasn't anything left to give. The Sicilian refused to believe it and the questions, the shouting, and threats, along with the pounding fist, kept coming all night.

"Tell me again about the jewels that were found in the closet. Who on board would have been that stupid to hide them in your room?"

"I don't know! But they were not found for two days. Someone might have brought them back. I don't know!" he screamed out of frustration.

"Who had keys to that office besides the thief that you admitted giving them to?"

"Only the captain and the casino manager, who is… "

"Which is who? What were you going to say?"

"Which is Seregio Sanara; he's one of you!"

"Your ass. Seregio is one of nobody now; he's fucking dead. He didn't steal the money and jewels from the *Tropical Sun*'s safes, but he's still dead. He was supposed to guard against such things like that from happening—just like you were trusted with the keys and combinations that contained not your valuables, but ours. As the purser, you knew what that job's responsibilities entailed, and you took our money every payday to be sure that job was properly done. But what did you give us for all of our money? Nothing! But you did give the thieves the keys *and* the fucking combinations, *too!* And that means you gave our money away!"

"I gave up my ear for you. He promised me he would keep cutting body parts off of me until I gave him what he wanted. I tried to resist, but when he sat down on my chest I was helpless, and then I felt him effortlessly slicing my ear off. He held it in front of my eyes and made me look at it. He seemed to not care if I told him or not; he would be happy to keep cutting. There wasn't anything I could do! He said when he finished me off he would just move to the captain's room and get the information from him. Showing my mutilated body to the captain would make his job a lot easier anyway."

"Yeah, yeah, I've heard all of that cry-baby bullshit before. You whiney little faggot. Why didn't you tell him a phony number and get away when he went to the office?"

"He said he was going to give me a thump that would put me out while he went below to check if it was the right number. If it was not then I would regain consciousness with him whittling my body parts off. There was nothing else I could do!"

Finally, a new bit of information has surfaced, thought Vincenzo. Getting thumped to put him out for a brief time while he checked the combination was new. It means the guy knew exactly what he was doing with a sap. The other three men had been knocked out, too. All of them had the same experience as the mechanic and the ironing lady in St. Maarten. They were alert and doing something until they suddenly awoke with a lump and a headache. All three, like the other two, had been hit on the same spot of the skull.

He asked the whimpering man in a kinder tone, "Okay, you're sure it was only one man, but try harder to see his face, remember any little detail, anything."

"I didn't see his face. He had the point of his knife puncturing my neck. It really hurt. I had my eyes closed in pain."

"And you couldn't tell what color of skin even though he had pressed a finger against your lips to tell you to be quiet?"

"I told you. I was half-asleep and on my way to see the captain, and when I felt the pain in my neck my eyes closed."

"And you think he is a Norwegian."

"He's from Norway or has spent a lot of time there. He speaks the language perfectly."

Vincenzo rubbed his chin while thinking, I *guess I can understand how the little faggot got confused with an ear cut off and a promise for more. Now I know the thief knew who owned the ship because the purser had tried to scare him off with a threat of the owners. It wasn't news to him and he wasn't impressed. He had no fucking respect for us.*

As the morning light shone through portholes of the cruise ship *Tropical Sun,* Vincenzo knew he had all he would get from this man. He untied him and said, "I apologize for hurting you but it's the only way we're going to catch this son-of-a-bitch. And when we do, he'll curse the day he fucked with the family."

"I understand, Vincenzo. Please let me be there when he's punished."

Vincenzo went through the passenger list as well as the essential and unessential crew list. He got the names of every vendor that had come aboard the ship at its last port of call and the next. Tracking all of those people down for a face-to-face was not going to be fun. The one thing that furnished the drive to do it, however, was the satisfaction of nailing the bastard. And if there was one thing he was sure of, it was that he would do it.

Vincenzo the Sicilian felt like going to bed but went to the bar that early morning. He ordered a breakfast wine and worked on his list.

Jobs done in Caribbean.

Victims knocked unconscious from behind, leaving headaches and lumps. Apparently knows how to use a sap or billy club to put someone down for a controlled amount of time.

Tape used to cut off air from the victims to get information.

One man involved. Several cruise ship victims had only heard one man's voice. The man spoke Caribbean-Afro in St. Maarten and Norwegian on *Tropical Sun* and several other languages on other ships.

He knows who owns the ships and casinos.

THE VILLAGE

SID WAS THE FIRST UP THE NEXT MORNING. HE MADE COFFEE IN AN OPEN pan by pouring instant coffee into it and letting it boil for a few minutes, then simmer until consumed. He loved the smell of fresh brewing coffee in the morning. The instant didn't produce much of an aroma, but it was better than nothing. While that was brewing, he went on the back deck and looked around for a croc or two floating around. Seeing none, he dove into the cool water. After a quick swim around the boat to wake up, he headed for shore.

On land, he started his morning run slowly at first then at mid-speed followed by a mile at full power. The two-mile walk back was pleasant, with a gentle breeze and small waves lapping at the shoreline.

He was back on the boat in twenty minutes after diving overboard, and only Jandy was up. She had found the coffee and a plastic cup decorated with little pictures of nautical flags all around it. A common thing bought by first time boaters as "the ship's servings."

Sidney poured himself a cup and joined her on the aft deck. She was talking about what the flags on the cup meant and asked him if he knew.

He said, "No," he lied. It wasn't the answer she had anticipated, but Sidney didn't want to waste words talking about flags.

She playfully said, "Maria told me about your tattoo of a flag on your shoulder. Can I see it?"

Sidney pulled his shirt off. She was amazed at all of the big scars on his muscular body. *God,* she thought, *looks like he was in a machete fight armed only with a toothpick. Someone has done a job on him.* She couldn't have known that the scars had been accumulating since he was a six-year-old boy.

"Where did you get all those scars, Sidney?"

It was a question he heard every time he got laid, and said, "I used to work in a glass factory where everybody gets cut."

She didn't believe that was true but let it go, since it was a personal thing anyway. She examined, even touched, some of the scars. Her first impression was that his body felt like a rock; everywhere—he was hard muscle.

She asked, "What in the world does that represent?" as she touched his tattoo.

"Nothing."

"Why did you put it on if it means nothing, and when did you do it; looks like it has been there for a long time."

Sid answered, "No reason. I was a kid."

Jandy grimaced at the short answer. Well, the bastard is back to his normal pattern of communicating. No more long-winded conversations of two or more sentences. God, how can someone refrain from talking like that? It would drive me nuts to be that quiet.

She continued her line of questioning that Ortega had instructed her to do last night. She said, "Ortega told me you were planning to leave today. Do you really have to go?"

Before Sidney could give her another one-syllable answer she continued, "Where are you going, anyway?"

Sidney answered, "Grenada."

"Why don't you ask Maria to go with you? She loves to sail. Wouldn't you like to have some company?"

"Nope."

"When are you coming back?"

"Don't know."

Jandy got up and poured another cup of coffee for both of them. When she returned she said, "Ortega must like you to let you get away with what you did last night."

Sid took another sip of coffee and said nothing.

Getting no response, Jandy tried another tack. "He doesn't like very many people; you should feel honored. He would like to know when you are coming back so he can plan on being here. That hunting trip was really a lot of fun, even if we did end up forgetting that poor pig."

Sid just took another sip and shook his head to agree.

Jandy was angered at his indifference. *I've taken all the silence I'm going to take from this obstinate bastard. And I'm going to tell him what a jerk he is.*

"Damn you, Sidney, I'm sitting out here trying to talk to you. I was hoping for a little friendly chat. All of us like you and want to become better acquainted, but you offer nothing in the way of conversation about yourself or your interest or even show any interest in us. Don't you know what friendship is all about? It's about sharing parts of your life with others. Don't you like or think of us as your friends? You sure seem to have fun whenever we are around, but it's hard to say for sure, since you never say anything except, yep, nope, yes, no, I guess so, maybe. Until last night your longest conversation was 'I don't do that shit.' Christ, it looks like you might have experienced your first bout of laughter the other night rolling around in the mud. What's with you? Were you an abused child or something?"

Getting all of that off her chest, she felt better but was apprehensive that she might have offended him. She remained silent waiting for an explanation and wanting an apology from him for making her act so mean to him.

Sidney finished his coffee. He almost laughed at the abused child question. She would've shit in her britches had she known how the Sidney boys were brought up. He looked at her and asked, "Want some beans?" and he headed for the galley to make beans for breakfast.

Jandy sat out on the deck, fuming that she couldn't get the man to open up to her. Most men would fall all over themselves to have a personal conversation with her. She couldn't understand a man rejecting her. *By God, next time I'll get him to talk if I have to screw every word out of him. Umm, on second thought that might not be such a bad idea anyway. He does something that turns Maria on and that's rare. I've never seen a harder body— he's so damn masculine.* She finally went in to offer her help with the beans, but found them boiling away in the same unwashed pot as used the night before.

Ortega was up and wanted to know where the head was. Sid pointed the way. Maria was up, sitting like a zombie at the dinette table with her head in her hands, eyes closed.

Jandy slid in next to her and said, "What's the matter little girl, too much candy yesterday?"

She nodded her head to say yes, and then said, "I'll never drink like that again."

"Too bad you slept in this morning; you could have enjoyed the conversation of one on the deck," and she looked at Sidney with scorn.

Ortega and the girls declined the beans breakfast stating they would get something later. Ortega asked, "Sidney, can't you stick around a while longer? We can go after a marlin on the coast. I know a man there that makes the best damn rum in this country. We'll have a hell of a time."

"Nope. Have to go."

"Well, maybe when you get back. When do you think you'll return?"

"Don't know."

"Okay. Why don't you call this number when you know you are coming back? I'd like to try to get my money back on another bet."

Sidney waved from the bow deck as Ortega and crew loaded up in his remaining Jeep. Then he waved goodbye to the children playing and the few fishermen repairing nets and pulled up his anchor. The mainsail and jib were set in the gentle breeze and the boat began moving out of the picturesque little lagoon.

As the catamaran left the confines of the small jungle river, he felt the fresh smell of the sea. The open horizon was calling him to get to where he belonged—offshore and away from whining women, conniving men and from the laws of mankind and the people entrusted to enforce them.

He didn't mind the bullshit with Ortega; he had won, but he knew Ortega was not through with him yet; he wanted something. Whatever it was, he'd have to wait until he returned with his son.

Jandy made a big fucking deal about me not talking. If she only knew. It might have been worth it to answer her questions and then watch her reactions. Wonder what she'll say to me if she knew I'm going to dump a seven year old boy out in a jungle filled with all sorts of things that would love nothing better than to eat a fresh, young, and defenseless human. And if he survives the jungle, the years of training him to be the most dangerous son of a bitch found on any ocean his sails upon.

He chuckled and muttered, "Wonder if she would have lectured me if she had any idea how rich the scruffy and scared man sitting next to her was?"

As the boat got further offshore, the sails caught more wind and the cat rapidly picked up speed. He sailed due north until he was out of sight of land then turned to the east-north-east to give the appearance that he was headed east, if anybody cared. When the tall sail was out of sight of land he turned to the west. He was on a tack that would take him to his rendezvous with the mega-yacht, *Golden Boy*.

He knew of its owner and had marked him for a raid. By observing the man over a three-year period, he knew he would be aboard the yacht for an annual working vacation. The yacht made the same run every year. The owner, Vito Meridino, owned hotels and casinos in the islands of Aruba, Bonaire, and Curacao. His legitimate business was an Import Export Company in the Bronx borough of New York City. His true business, however, was being the head of the largest gambling family in organized crime. His family either owned every casino in the Caribbean and most of Europe or received sizable monthly contributions in order to operate.

Golden Boy was a one hundred seventy-foot, custom-built schooner. It was one of the most beautiful sailboats to be found anywhere in the world. Vito Meridino had worked with a naval architect in its design and hired a special crew to do much of the interior work.

Sidney had never been inside the yacht, but had been told of its richly-finished features. He had, however, managed to break into the designer's office and steal a set of the ship's construction plans. The plans had several areas that were shown as blank areas with a notation of "B.O.", which he reasoned was meant to mean, "By Owner." That indicated there would be something in those areas that Vito didn't want known to the builders. Knowing the business he was in, those areas could produce a very nice prize and this was the year it would be taken.

He sailed to the west under mainsail only. He wasn't in a hurry. The next morning he would hoist everything and begin his search for the Islas de Aves, a string of small islands. He slept off and on that night in the cockpit. The VHF radio had been turned on to listen for a possible call to or from *Golden Boy*. The radio was as quiet as the night.

When the morning sun started its leap off the sea's horizon, he dropped the main and went below. He always got sleepy at that time of day so he had learned years ago not to fight it, instead enjoy it, especially when it might be the last chance to get prone in a comfortable bed for a day or two.

He woke up after sleeping almost two hours, feeling alert and ready for some action. That night the Barracuda would run down and capture yet another ship at sea. And, as always, he would be heavily outnumbered. He estimated there would be a crew of ten. Vito and his wife, two heavies who were bodyguards, and at least four more guests made a total of eighteen people he had to avoid or control.

Golden Boy's crew in the past had been made up of college-age kids, probably from families who were Vito's friends. Three or four professionals, including the captain, were responsible for managing the yacht and crew. The chef and his crew would be the family's fulltime staff who traveled with them wherever they went. The heavies would be relaxed and not expecting trouble offshore, but they would be taken out first, anyway. If there were an alarm, the heavies would certainly know how to react. Sidney could do better than hold his own with any man, but those guys didn't mind shooting first and not bother with questions. Sidney never ignored potential risks in his raid plans. His plan was to scare Vito enough to get all of the goodies without bothering the guests or crew—other than the bodyguards.

The cat's sails were raised and wind was getting stronger after the Caribbean's nightly slack in the trades. *Barracouta* was running downwind at hull speed in short order and by early afternoon he spotted the first of many cays of the Islas de Aves. The sun was high over the water, which gave him excellent visibility of the rapidly approaching bottom as he neared the rocky island. His eyes scanned not only the bottom, but also tree and rock formations on the little islands. When he found the terrain he was looking for, he headed the boat towards the area, paying close attention to the coral heads and rocks jutting up from the ocean's floor. The next time he came over this area it would be pitch black, and he would be traveling at full speed in the fast catamaran. If everything went as it had on previous years, *Golden Boy* should pass by there around three o'clock the next morning.

Judging by water colors, there was adequate water depth up to the shoreline of the uninhabited and rocky cay that he had selected. Nevertheless, Sidney dowsed the jib and reefed the main to slow the boat down before coming into the shallows. He found the right place to wait for his intended prey and then dropped anchor. Looking around confirmed that he was the only human within miles of his secluded anchorage; his only company was the thousands of sea birds that roost on the cays. After a brief, but refreshing swim in the beautifully clear water, he let the sun dry him with the yellow heat from its penetrating rays.

He quickly dried, and then he went below and brought the cans of black paint and roller that he had purchased in St Croix. He slopped some of the un-stirred paint onto the deck of the bow section. With the roller full of paint, he reached over the side of the deck and began painting the freeboard. He finished the starboard side then covered the white deck with the paint. The swirling streaks of black and gray of the oil-based paint mixed with the white deck was either hideously ugly or tastefully artistic. Sidney saw neither; he just saw the boat as being invisible at night. Paint was smeared to cover the entire hull in an hour. The pretty sailing catamaran had transmogrified into an angry looking raiding vessel, the *Barracouta*.

Next, the mainsail was hoisted three feet at a time into the air. Both sides of the sail got a coat of the paint. The sail was allowed to stay up until the paint dried two hours later in the hot tropical sun. The jib was lowered and spread out on the trampoline between the two hulls of the catamaran. It, too, was hoisted again a few feet at a time and given the same paint job. Sidney was also covered with paint, not as part of the plan, but because it was a messy job.

He sat on the aft deck with a bucket of smelly diesel fuel and removed paint from his skin. Then he dove to the bottom with a bucket to retrieve sand. Scrubbing his skin with a mixture of sand and Joy soap finished his clean up. Then he dove into the sea again. He swam as if searching for something, then found it only a few feet off the bottom, a blowfish about ten inches long. He teased and challenged the fish with aggressive motions and the little puffer had pumped himself up to three times its body's circumference.

Waiting for his prey could have been much easier if he was part of modern generation of sailor/pirate. He would have had long-range radar to track anything moving. A SSB radio would be aboard so he could call and listen for his target. A GPS to tell him exactly where it was by coordinates. But he wasn't modern; he didn't even own a chart. But he knew where he was and where he was going and how far it was to where he wanted to go. Everything about sailing to him was how much time are you away from where you want to be. Everything in his navigational planning was keyed on when he wanted to arrive.

When the estimated time drew closer, Sidney started calling on his VHF every fifteen minutes. During the first hour, he called, "Any station, any station, any station; this is the motor yacht Rachel calling for a radio check." Every hour he would change his call sign to new one.

Between VHF calls, he spent his time making poison darts out of strands of his standing rigging. The ends were filed to a point and one of them would be stuck into a wad of kapok from a life vest. The wad was wrapped just tight enough with thread to keep it on the stainless steel splinter, but not enough to keep it from slamming forward when it came into contact with whatever stopped the dart. The aft end of the dart had about a half inch of fluffy material sticking out of the threaded area to act as the stabilizer. The pointed end protruded out almost an inch. Three darts were made.

The little puffer fish had died. Sidney cut it open and quickly found the organ he needed. Each of the darts was stuck into the tiny piece of meat allowing the toxin to saturate the fiber. The darts were then allowed to air dry, allowing the poison coat to set on the shaft. Then he rolled a piece of paper the exact size of the thread-wrapped wadding and taped it up to complete his blowgun. It was an effective gun for a distance of almost twenty feet.

Finally, at two the next morning, a response came back on channel sixteen from *Golden Boy*. They had responded to a *pan, pan* call about a huge floating tree in their vicinity. Sidney had initiated the broadcast. When *Golden Boy's* captain asked for his position, Sidney told him he was ten miles from his actual location. That made the captain feel better, the danger didn't concern them. *Golden Boy's* position was eight miles east of the cays and about three miles north of the reef line. That was the same route they had used before, and put them right on target.

Before he started the chase, he ran over his plan once more, for after the assault began his full concentration would be needed for high speed sailing in the moonless night. *The yacht will take about forty-five minutes to be directly abeam my position. I'll wait until the boat is off my beam then close in on her stern. No one will be on deck at this time of night and if there are, they'll be looking forward. Nobody's interested in looking where they've been. My only potential problem is if the person tending the autopilot looks at the radar screen and it picks up the boat.*

If I'm spotted, I'll have plenty of notice as men will surely be on the aft deck looking for the boat. In this darkness the black boat will be almost impossible to see, and I can abort the raid at any time right up to the point when a spotlight is trained on me.

He went into the engine room and removed his knapsack from the phony battery. The black wetsuit was put on and he made sure Billy was secure as was the tape and the bank's prize. Then he waited.

When he saw the red running light of *Golden Boy* was directly north of him, he walked forward and cut the anchor line. Sails had already been hoisted and were flying loose in the wind. On his way back to the cockpit, he checked to be sure everything was off the deck; it needed to be clear when he went forward to board the *Golden Boy*.

As the wind blew the bow off the eye of the wind, he pulled the main sheet in tight, then the jib's sheet. As she came around, he eased the main sheet a little until after he adjusted the foresail. Boat speed increased as he steered it to make the best direction to close the distance while reducing white spray from his bow wake. He definitely had speed on the larger boat, so his first point of concern had passed.

He slowly closed the distance between the boats while moving in behind to get between the waves of the big boat's wake. When Sid was about two hundred feet away he felt more relaxed because at that distance the ship's radar wouldn't be able to pick up his boat, as it would be lost in the ground clutter.

When only one hundred feet from *Golden Boy's* transom, a bright deck light was turned on illuminating the aft deck. Sidney reacted by crouching low in the cockpit and pulled the sheets in to flatten sails and slow the boat. Only one man came out; he walked to the stern, unzipped his pants and took a leak. The light was so bright on deck that it would have been impossible to see the *Queen Mary*. After a few shakes too many, the man went back in the rear door and the light was turned off.

Sidney was irritated. *Fucking bright light has ruined my night vision. I'll have to slow it down until they become adjusted again.* It took several minutes to make the adjustment then he let the sheets out to catch more wind and resumed his pursuit of the prize.

When his bow was only feet away from the big blue transom with golden letters spelling *Golden Boy*, Sidney yanked hard on a double braided line he had rigged to the raw water intake of the engine. The first pull didn't do anything but the second caused the seawater hose to pull off letting water spew into the boat through the two inch hose. The wheel had been tied to keep the boat running straight and Sidney quickly moved to the forepeak of the windward hull of the catamaran. Riding roller coaster-like over four and five foot seas he waited for the catamaran to get as close as possible to the transom.

Three feet was all that separated the two undulating boats; water pouring into his boat started slowing it down, producing a widening gap. Sidney had one chance. If he missed, then he would fall in front of his own boat and surely be killed. If not killed instantly, then slowly as he tried to swim against the coastal current and the big seas to find one of the uninhabited cays, now miles away.

Standing on the anchor pulpit outside of the safety rail, he crouched low and sprung forward as the bigger boat's transom started down on the backside of a wave. He landed on top of the transom and quickly pulled his body into the safety of the life rail. He lowered himself to the deck then laid still in the shadow, listening for the sounds of running feet. He watched the cat's bow to be sure it didn't bump the boat. That would have alerted someone. The catamaran was six feet back and slowing even faster as it got heavier.

When he was sure the widening distance between the two was unchangeable, he started moving in his brand of slow-motion speed to the pilothouse. His eyes searched for forms of sleeping bodies on deck or a sleeping dog. Many families took their pets along on sailing vacations, as they were effective as a security alarm. He had prepared for a dog or two with the poison darts he had made. Nothing alive was found on deck.

Inside the pilothouse a young pretty woman sat in front of the radar screen talking to the helmsman. They were intent on impressing one another, and both seemed to be doing a good job of it. The man's back was to Sid while the girl was facing him. The red night-light in the pilothouse reflected off of the glass windows except for the front window as it was tilted to prevent reflection. Sidney, wearing his black clothes and face blacked was invisible as long as he stayed out of the red light.

His target was Vito, but everyone between he and Vito had to be dealt with, and since there were so many people on board, their communications had to be first to go. Radios could be used to call for help should anything go wrong. The radios were in the pilothouse so he waited for a few minutes, hoping the girl would move from her perch on the radar cabinet and sit beside the pilot in the large, leather helmsman's chair.

She didn't budge, so he felt for the door's handle. It was unlocked. Then, in one seemingly fluid motion, the door was opened and Sidney crossed the ten-feet to the girl. Her eyes saw the approach of the dark shape of a man in black, but she kept on chatting; her mind had not expected to see such a thing, and didn't acknowledge it in time.

Billy caught her a little too hard in the center of her forehead, causing the skull bones to fracture, sending slivers of bone into her brain. She had been the only daughter of the chairman of the board of the largest insurance company in the United States. Before she could drop, Sidney's return blow, the back swing, had placed Billy on the temple of the pilot who, unfortunately, saw it coming and tried to duck, making Sidney miss the spot that would have put him asleep for a couple hours. The blow to his temple, as the one to the girl, was fatal.

No choice—a frontal hit was always dangerous. There wasn't time to maneuver and the pilot was ready to scream. Both bodies were laid out side by side between the helmsman's seat and the steering bulkhead.

He located the circuit control panel. A separate switch for every piece of important equipment on board had an engraved teakwood label. He opened the back side, exposing all of the wires; he cut the wires to each piece of radio equipment. Also the alarm switch was disabled. With the control room secured, he went down the mahogany and brass spiral stairway into the main saloon, and began working his way aft. The master stateroom was the furthest aft. The two bodyguards should be close to the master suite.

As shown on the stolen plans, the corridor ended at the master's cabin door. Cabin doors were on both sides of the corridor, which he thought would be the guards. The door on the starboard side was locked; the other was not. He didn't want to open the door slowly in case the man inside was awake enough to detect movement. Sidney was sure he would be armed, and there was no sense in giving him time to get ready. He knew where the berth was supposed to be, so he opened the door and quickly moved in without making a sound.

Billy found his target asleep, but gave him a good thump anyway. His mouth, arms, legs and body were taped to a handrail by the berth.

Before leaving the room, he sat silently for a moment, listening to every sound in the boat. All was quiet except snoring coming from the master's stateroom.

Its door wasn't locked; he opened it very slowly then slipped inside as he listened to two sets of breathing. The door was closed behind him. He approached the woman first as the snoring man was obviously in a much deeper sleep. Billy gave her a perfect thump. She'd wake up tomorrow with a lump and a headache, but no memory of the night's events—if everything went according to plan.

The man was approached and Sidney had to turn him slightly to get a good shot at the right part of his skull. His thump should keep him quiet for about an hour, or until awakened with a splash of water. His eyes and mouth were taped shut and his hands were taped to opposing feet.

Sidney skipped the other bodyguard's locked door and went down the corridor. Two guest's staterooms were empty; four were not. All occupants became acquainted with Billy and the tape. He had been on board for twenty minutes.

He moved to the forward cabins, which were reserved for the crew. He could hear the sound of a shower running in a port side cabin and the smell of someone smoking a joint was coming from another. Sidney smiled with the thought *what would Vito have to say if he knew his beautiful Golden Boy was under the hands of a dope smoking, ten-dollar-an-hour jerk.*

A light appeared in the second of the three port cabins. The plans had shown there to be two berths per cabin on the port side. The starboard side had only two cabins. One for the captain and his wife; the other was for the chef and his wife. The door at the end of the corridor led to the storage and anchor lockers.

He started with the forward-most cabin on the port side. Two sleeping men were thumped and taped. The next cabin had lights on, indicating they were getting ready to relieve the dead crew in the wheelhouse, who had occupied the third stateroom. One of them had just gotten up and was getting ready for a quick shower, he was the pot smoker, his back was to Sidney and he didn't have a clue that he was about to be thumped—and thumped and taped he was.

The shower was still running in the last cabin. Sid opened the door to the head to see a lovely young girl in the shower. The lights were on and she turned her head at the sound of the door opening. She had been nervous anyway about sharing living quarters with the opposite sex, but had been assured by her ultra-liberal mother that it was okay. After all, this was the new age; there should be no difference between the sexes. Her mother surely felt that way as she had moved another woman into her house shortly after the divorce from her father.

Unfortunately for the girl, she was already spooked and reacted to the man approaching her. She raised her hands to protect her and took a deep breath to scream. By moving her hands up, Sidney had no choice but to hit her in the mouth with Billy, breaking all her front teeth and upper jaw, silencing the intended scream. The second blow from Billy was much kinder and put the young girl and her broken teeth out for hours.

That left the potentially dangerous bodyguard behind the locked door. As he silently approached the guard's door he saw that it was ajar. That could mean that he went on deck, therefore he would have discovered the dead crewmembers. If that were the case, then he'd instantly head down to his boss's room or the other guard's room. Having nothing to lose but his life, Sidney opened Vito's door and stepped inside.

The cold steel of a gun's barrel pressed on the back quarter of his skull. The man in a calm but gruff voice loudly said, "Don't even think about moving. Who the… "

Sidney didn't *think* about moving, he *did* move. His mind had been prepared for everything that could happen when he opened the door and had already done all of his thinking. His knife had been carried close to the leg on the door's side in case someone was waiting. As the guard reached for the light switch, Sid's knife hand swung backwards and caught the man in the lower stomach for the first stroke. As the gun fired, Sid dropped straight down, pulling the knife and immediately thrust it upward again cutting the guard's throat. With a quick flip and twist of the wrist, the man fell dead, spilling his blood upon the elegant hand-woven Persian carpet that covered bulkhead to bulkhead floor.

Sidney left the lights on to see Vito squirming to get free from the tape. He had no idea what was going on, but did know he had entered the well-known world of shit. Sidney stood behind the door for a minute waiting to see if he might have missed someone. If he did, the sound of gunfire would bring them running. No one appeared and the sounds of the boat had not changed.

He went to the bed and lifted Vito out of the bed. He cut the tape holding his ankles together, but kept his hands taped. He then taped his elbows to his rib cage to keep the arms under control. With this done, he pulled the tape covering his eyes off. Vito's eyes were blinking in the room's light, trying to adjust. He was constantly mumbling under the tape over his mouth.

Sidney wasn't the least bit interested. He led the man to the first area that had been marked "BO" on the plans. In the stateroom there was a wall; a small round mahogany side table that matched the rest of the wood in the cabin, and two comfortable-looking lounge chairs. He looked the area over, but could find nothing that would suggest a hidden compartment.

He pushed Vito into one of the chairs and leaned over to look into his face. He told Vito in English, "I know there's a hidden compartment in this room, and before I leave here I will know its contents. Everyone aboard your yacht is either in the same position as your wife or your trusted guard lying on the floor."

He grabbed Vito's head and pointed it to the bed where his wife lay taped up, and then he moved the head to see the guard as he spoke. Vito had stopped murmuring and was listening to every word. Sidney had his attention. Vito understood the situation.

"I am going to ask you to tell me how to get into this secret place; if there is nothing here I want you to tell me where your valuables are. I'm going to pull the tape off for your answer. If you do not answer then I am going to your wife's bed and cut off the little finger on her left hand. Do you understand?"

Vito's eyes were wide with terror, but nodded that he did. The tape came off and Vito said, "Who the hell are you? Do you know who you are dealing with, scum bag?"

The tape was put back over his mouth. "That talk isn't going to do you any good. You have just played your mulligan in the game of your wife's pain. Now tell me what I want to know."

When the tape came off again, Vito reluctantly said, "There's nothing here, but there is a safe on the other wall, behind the framed chart."

He pulled Vito to his feet and let him lead the way. They went to the chart and Sid pushed it over his head on its hinges; there was a wall safe. Vito reluctantly told him the combination. There was close to twenty thousand in cash and a few pieces of jewelry.

Sidney stuffed it into a pillowcase taken off of Vito's bed and asked, "What else, Vito?"

"I have some money in my wallet and the passengers and crew might have some, but it wouldn't be much. I don't carry money with me; I can get all I want every place I travel."

As he had walked through the blood, Vito didn't seem too concerned with the dead guard bleeding all over his expensive carpet. Sid skirted the blood; he would never leave anything behind on his raids, including footprints.

As Vito emptied his wallet, Sidney looked disappointed and asked, "Are you sure there is nothing over there?" He pointed to the area.

Irritated, Vito said, "There's nothing there. Go fucking look if you don't believe me. Vito was led back to the chair and a piece of tape was put around his chest and the chair to keep him there. Tape was put back over Vito's mouth, but not over his eyes.

Sidney walked to the bed and then lifted the limp left hand of the unconscious woman. With a slow, but deliberate move, he pulled his big knife out and put it between the little finger and the next one. With a quick jerk, the blade easily severed the pinky off at the first knuckle. Blood shot out at first, then began oozing down her raised arm. Sidney dropped her hand onto the silk bed sheet and returned his attention to Vito.

Vito was bouncing in the chair trying desperately to get loose while screaming muffled curses from behind the tape holding his mouth shut. Sidney leaned down in front of the man to let him look into the eyes of the man that had cut the lovely finger off of his beautiful wife's hand. The eyes and expression made Vito realize that this man didn't give a shit about him, his wife, or what he had just done to her. The thief had nothing to fear, nothing to lose, and he somehow knew there was a secret place in his stateroom.

After Vito quieted down, Sidney said, "You cut that finger off with the dull edge of stupidity, Vito. She has more fingers, toes, nipples, nose, ears, and lips to lose before I leave this boat. Then I'll start on your guests and keep cutting. You'll be the last to go, Vito. I will know what is in this compartment before I leave *Golden Boy*. Remember you are far out at sea with no chance of outside help and I'm in no hurry. Now the tape comes off again. It's your choice; do you give me your property now, or watch me slowly mutilate your beautiful wife and friends or give it to me before I start removing your body parts?"

The tape came off; Vito knew the man before him had somehow learned of the safe; there was no sense trying to hide it any longer.

He told Sidney, "Remove the two screws that secure the side table to the floor. That will release a locking mechanism that's concealed in the storage vault behind the wall panel."

Vito even told Sidney where to find the screwdriver. With tool in hand, the two screws were removed, and then he heard a metallic click and the bottom section of a mahogany panel slowly opened. Sidney looked in to see a fireproof cabinet about a foot deep and three feet square. The key to open the safe was hanging on a convenient hook above the cabinet's door. After all, who would ever steal anything from Vito's secret compartment, especially since only he and two other trusted men knew it was there.

The cabinet's open door revealed stacks of one hundred-dollar bills, all United States currency. Sidney wasn't interested in counting; it was a lot and that was all that was important. Another pillowcase was stuffed full with the money.

Once again, Sidney turned his attention to Vito and asked him, "Isn't that a lot better than causing so much damage or death to your wife and friends?"

Vito didn't respond—he was busy remembering every detail about this man. He didn't bother telling Sidney that he was a walking dead man for stealing family money from one of the most powerful men in the Mafia. He didn't waste his breath, as the assailant must have already known. He not only knew where to find him at sea, but where his secret compartment was, too. He hoped that was all he knew. Vito had a strong suspicion that this man had to be the man the Sicilian family wanted so badly to find and kill. His only concern was to stay alive so he could get his revenge. It might take a while, but eventually their network would find this man and he would deal with him personally.

Vito's gratifying thoughts of retribution was interrupted by Sidney's voice saying, "Now we're going to the salon and do the same thing again."

Those words were Vito's worst fear; the man knew everything. He was picked up by the powerful pirate, thrown over his shoulder and taken down the corridor to the salon. He was dumped on the floor in the vicinity of the floor safe.

Vito couldn't force himself to give that one up without a fight. After the same question and instructions were put to him and the tape was pulled off, Vito could no longer contain his temper. He had never been treated that way—even as a kid, people had respected him or they paid a terrible price. He had become a made-man while still a teenager, and nobody, not even his enemies had ever treated him like that. His self-respect would not allow any more to go on.

"Go blow yourself, cocksucker. You are a worthless piece of shit coming on my yacht and cutting my wife's finger off, threatening me, Vito Meridino. I step on your kind every day just like the fucking cockroach you are. Your slut of a mother should have taught you better than to mess with people like me. You have gone way over your head thinking you can fuck with me and mine. So you go ahead, chicken shit. You fucking coward, keep me tied up and you can do whatever you want to do to anybody on this boat, I'm not telling you shit."

Sidney put the tape back on him to shut him up. Then he said, "I believe you, but I'll still give you two more chances to change your mind. The first will be when I bring your naked wife in here and cut off another finger. If you don't tell me, then I'll cut off her left ear. That is the last chance you're going to get. To me, it will mean that whatever is concealed here is more important that your wife's ears and fingers. If you, as you said, 'don't give a shit', then there'd be no sense in cutting her nipples and lips off, you obviously *don't give a shit*. I'll just get the fire ax and tear the entire area up to find this compartment. After I do, then I'll change the autopilot course to take your boat further offshore. Several seawater lines will be cut, the pumps turned off, the EPIRBs destroyed, and you can sit here with your wife and everybody else on board and feel *Golden Boy* slide beneath the ocean's surface. Maybe you'll still be alive and feel it settle on the ocean floor five miles under water. You all will be lost forever, even fuel slicks won't stay together at that depth. The families, yours and your friends, and the crew's, will never know what happened. Your memory will be blamed for their losses. And Vito, it won't bother me in the least. This is what I have done for a living since I was thirteen years old. Believe me, I have sent many ships to the bottom and many souls back to their hell."

With his final longwinded warning out of the way, he removed the tape long enough to hear, "You sick fuck! I'm the Mafia! You'll never live long enough to spend—"

Sidney cut him off in mid-threat by putting the tape over his mouth. Vito was a very pissed-off Italian. It looked as if blood vessels in his head were going to explode.

With no expression on Sidney's face, he said, "There's no need to scare me with tales of the Mafia. That's why I'm here. I've been pulling your greasy Italian pants down around your ankles to show everyone what sissies you are. I've also taken a lot of money away from you for years. Now you just sit there looking stupid while I get back to work."

He carried Vito's wife to the salon and roughly stripped her in front of Vito. That only added to his rage. The little finger on her right hand was quickly sliced off and thrown onto Vito's lap.

Sidney waited for Vito's eyes to resume to their normal size and his muffled screaming to subside before removing the gag once more. Vito had only unpleasant things to say about Sidney's ancestry, relating them to shit-eating dogs and such, so the tape was reapplied. Sidney then held the lovely woman's unconscious head in his one hand, and without delay, sliced off one of her ears. It, too, was tossed onto Vito's lap.

Vito was puking behind the tape and painfully choking to death. His efforts to swallow the vomit against the convulsing stomach muscles were not very effective. His eyes were bugging out of their sockets. Sidney waited for a moment before releasing the tape. When the tape was removed he jumped out of the way, knowing a gush of last night's pasta and red wine would be forthcoming.

He gave the man a moment to recover then said, "Vito you have come to your last chance. If saving the contents is worth the death of your wife and friends and destruction of this beautiful yacht, then refuse to tell me just one more time."

Vito had been giving that a lot of thought. Why die for money, there's plenty more around. Why die for ego; so I got beat once, it's no big deal. Also there's my wife and little Rosy, the daughter of my best friend. Besides, there isn't anything I can do to stop it. He'll tear up the boat until he finds it then find a way to get into the safe anyway. Who would ever suspect being pirated in this day and age? This is the son of a bitch that's been hitting us… he's not stupid enough to leave me alive to identify him so at least I won't have to face the circle as a coward. Oh, well, I lived the good life longer than I should have.

Resigned to defeat, Vito weakly said, "Can you give me any reassurance that you will not hurt my wife or friends if I tell you?"

"I give you my word that everyone, who has not seen my face, will be alive when I leave your yacht. I may be a ruthless pirate but I guard my word as much as my treasure."

Vito hesitated then said, "Remove the base of the cocktail table. There is a compartment under it."

With the table's twelve-inch base removed, a trap door eight inches in diameter was revealed. Sidney was perplexed why he would fight so hard to hold out on this little safe when he had given up so much already. Under the trapdoor was a combination safe.

Before he could ask what the combination was Vito said, "Thirteen left, thirteen right, thirteen right and thirteen left," in a soft, beaten voice. He didn't care anymore; he just wanted the man to be done with his torturous attack.

As Sidney spun through the combination he said, "Too bad you didn't do this earlier, it would have saved me time—and someone else's body parts."

Under the safe's door was a Tee-handle to pull the inner liner and its contents out. Looking into the container he saw only folded paper. The liner was pulled out; it was four feet long and six inches in diameter. He poured the contents into the pillow case. After the rolled up paper work fell out, a flooding stream of diamonds of all shapes and sizes followed it.

Sidney said, "No wonder you fought so hard." It was a treasure in itself worth millions of dollars.

He tied both pillowcases shut then walked over to the silent and vanquished Vito. He taped his mouth again. He said, "You know what I have to do to you. Your wife and everyone else on board are safe and will be rescued. You saved their lives by telling me."

Then, in a flash, he cut Vito's jugular vein, life's blood spurted out—he was dead in seconds. He checked Vito's wife, she was still out and the bleeding had almost coagulated around areas where her missing parts used to be. He stopped the blood flow by wrapping tape over her severed fingers and ear hole. He taped her mouth, hands and feet and went topsides to the pilothouse. Every step was taken with extreme caution in case someone had managed to get free and was waiting for him.

He checked his position with the GPS and plotted a course to the island of Aruba on the chart lying on the navigation station's table. He set the autopilot on that course. He then turned on the switch that activated the two thirty foot Cigarette speed boats on deck davits.

Outside, he checked the fuel levels on both speedboats; both were full. With the davits control switches he lowered the first boat so that it was in the water and being towed by the davit cable. The same was done for the second after throwing his prize into it. Both boats were bouncing around, bashing into the polished freeboard of *Golden Boy* at ten knots of speed.

When the speedboat was at its highest peak on a wave top, Sidney jumped the five feet down to it. In the boat, he started the engine and pulled forward enough to cause the rear davit wire to be slack. The rear wire was unhooked. He made his way forward on the bouncing deck and disconnected the bow wire, letting the speedboat fall off and behind the constant momentum of *Golden Boy's* sailing speed.

He then drove the boat up behind the other boat still tethered by davit wires, and then tied his boat to its stern. He transferred to the other boat and repeated the process of getting free from the big yacht.

Finally, both boats were free from the mother ship and Sidney shut down the engines to watch *Golden Boy's* stern light fade into the night. He assumed someone would get free or the yacht would stop its uncontrolled run to nowhere when she ran aground on Aruba's shore.

Thanks, Mafia, he thought. *Hope this pisses you off enough to stay out of my ocean.* He opened the bag containing the diamonds and ran his hands through the precious stones, looking individually at one or two of the largest under the glow of his flashlight. He grabbed the documents and was about to toss them overboard then stopped. *They might offer a clue to another prize since they were stored in a place of honor.* He stuffed them back into the pillowcase.

Looking around, he found the onboard tool kit. The boat's rudder was put into amidships position and the engine hatch was raised. Sid used the hammer to put a dent in the steering tube, making it difficult to turn the steering wheel or rudder. He pulled the other boat up alongside and transferred his treasure into it. After starting the boat to be sure it ran okay, he started the other, put it in forward at half throttle, and watched it roar off into the night. Its course and destination was somewhere in the middle of the Caribbean Sea, before it would run out of fuel.

Sidney had taken both speedboats to make the authorities think a gang had been responsible for the raid.

VENEZUELA

J{OSE} O{RTEGA} {LOUNGED UNDER THE SHADE OF A HUGE} B{ANYAN} T{REE}. The tree was so old that a tangled network of feeder roots extended out a radius of eighty feet. The vertical feeder root system was twenty feet high and was the only thing to prevent gravity from breaking the huge limbs off.

He was reading a very brief report on the stranger's fingerprints. Apparently, his new found friend didn't exist. There were no fingerprints, so with no known last name he could not check for social security numbers or passports or driver's license. Sidney had become a very interesting person in Jose Ortega's world.

Jandy told him about her one-sided conversation she had with Sidney. She, complete with exaggerated expressions to poke fun at his reluctance to talk, said she thought that he had stayed quiet just to make her angry. Ortega stopped her after she described the tattoo and asked her to describe it again.

"It is a red flag with a skull that has a sword sticking in one eye and a shattered leg bone in the other. A vicious looking barracuda is circling it like he's guarding it. It's faded, but terribly frightening. Oh! And there were a bunch of bones under the skull."

Ortega was quiet, something familiar was associated with that picture in his mind, but he couldn't place it. It's the same description that Maria had given him, but that, too, had struck a tone in his memory. Maybe it was the booze. He muttered, "I'll call father to see if the tattoo means anything to him. There's not much he doesn't know and if he doesn't, he can damn sure find someone who does."

His father, Don Ziguia Ortega, was the undisputed boss of the Ortega Cartel and was the man Jose or one of his brothers would replace—if they outlived him. Don Ziguia Ortega gladly left an important meeting to take his son's call. After the usual father-son pleasantries, Jose told him why he called.

"That tattoo seems oddly familiar to me, too, but don't know why. I'll ask around the brotherhood."

ABOARD THE CIGARETTE

SIDNEY CAREFULLY PILOTED HIS WAY THROUGH THE LINE OF CAYS HE had hidden in while waiting for his prize. Starlight offered enough light to make way between the coral heads and rocks that rose to the surface at near vertical angles.

He didn't stop to play with his new prize. He had to stay on schedule. When the yacht was discovered, there would be a swarm of mad Italians combing the Caribbean with vengeance in their every thought.

After clearing the little islands, he ran at three-quarters throttle to get the best mileage from the fuel on board. He had a nice easy ride; ocean swells were five feet but spaced far apart and on his beam. The night was dark with an overcast which made it hard to distinguish the difference between the sea and sky where they met on the horizon.

Three hours later, a distant glow from the lights of civilization was very apparent. An hour after sighting the lights he was off-plane and idling, looking for a place to make landfall. The wind had steadily gotten stronger in the last hour and was blowing around twenty knots. Seas had turned from lumpy to rough. Breakers formed in the rapidly shallowing water; the spray from their curling tops covered him with saltwater mist. He was truly in his element; the warm water felt good, the smell of sea was heightened by the breaker's mist, and the sound of crashing breakers reminded him of the wonder of being alive. He was having fun.

However, there was another side of reality: the shoreline was all rocks and wind-blown seas that pounded the shore and made it dangerous to make a landing. Danger only heightened his exhilaration but he kept running southward, parallel to the shoreline while looking for an area where the land turned away from the wind.

Darkness was quickly turning gray and he made a turn in the shore-line. The boat was driven in very slowly while carefully reading the breakers around him that would indicate rocks just below the surface.

The best way to make landfall was to stay in the boat, and let it take the beating, but he couldn't afford that luxury. The boat could not be found on that island— or anywhere else.

His prize and knapsack were very snugly tied to three life vests. He would bodysurf to shore on his newly acquired treasure. The boat was turned to point out to sea, and once again, he took the hammer to the steering tube. Then he sat on the gunwale while waiting to get closer to his targeted boulder. When he reached the right position he went below and kicked the head's discharge fitting causing it to break and water started pouring into the sleek ocean racer. The throttle was opened enough to maintain forward movement then he bailed out and bodysurfed with the progression of big seas to the shoreline.

His landing was as rough as he had anticipated. Forceful waves bounced him around, smashed him against barnacle encrusted rocks, tried to separate him from his prize and drown him, but even the sea was no match for the Barracuda. He finally got his feet on solid ground and was able to get out of the breaking surf with only a few minor bruises and cuts. His only concern was that something had come loose from his bundle and was lost to Davy Jones's treasure locker.

Sidney built a fire in the stiff breeze the old fashion way, by rubbing sticks together. There was no shortage of dead wood and seaweed around, but he kept the fire small and hidden between large boulders. The heat felt good and he sat on a rounded rock in the lee of the wind and counted his cash. He had $100,000 dollars.

"Not a bad night's work. Wonder what all those diamonds are worth," he muttered to himself.

The diamond's worth didn't matter, anyway; the only thing that did, was that they now belonged to the Sidneys.

Looking at the sparkling stones, he found two of the large stones that were identical. In a fleeting moment of generosity, he decided to give them to Maria and Jandy. *There's something I like about them... they're fun. It's odd knowing people I enjoy.*

He was soon dry from the hot little fire. The black wetsuit was tossed into the sea and he was reduced to wearing the only thing in his wardrobe once again, shorts, tee shirt, and flip-flops. The life preservers were tossed back into the growth of brush where they would never be seen.

He followed the shore to the south knowing that one good thing about islands was he could follow the coast line in either direction and find civilization. He knew the island and had landed on it as it was the closest little island with a low population. But he had never been on it.

Walking in flip-flops wasn't easy over the rocky terrain. He kept slipping and sliding on the rocks. The sandals were added to the backpack and he continued on barefoot. He walked along the shoreline, as the dense brush was much sparser. About an hour after the first hint of daybreak, he came to a dirt road that led to a road that had been paved with asphalt, but now was mostly pot holes. That road led him closer to civilization and soon he could hear sounds of an occasional car on another paved road, maybe a mile away. The town of Kralendijk was to the west so he went in that direction.

Fifteen minutes passed since the last car went past, and he could see a small house that served as both a home and a restaurant. He walked through the yard and was greeted by two big, tick-eaten, floppy eared dogs. Both were happy to see him.

An enormously fat man sat out on the porch talking to two other men eating breakfast at a small and well-worn table. The trio was talking about last night's cricket test, and what should be done to the batsman that caused their defeat. All were glad to see the stranger walk up. It would give them something else to judge and discuss after he left.

The huge man in his mixed language of Spanish and Dutch said. "Good morning, mon. You here to eat?"

Sidney answered in the same dialect that he was there for breakfast, and sat at the other small rickety table. The big man went into the kitchen, and standing behind a wall that separated the dining area from the family's kitchen, he asked, "You want the big breakfast or the small one?"

"Big."

The fat cook said, "It don't matter none, I'll feed you anyway, but you got money to pay for it?"

"Yep."

The man's daughter came out of the kitchen and poured him a glass of water, which he really wanted more than food at that moment. She then poured hot coffee from a very old tin pot into a well-stained mug, complete with chips around the edges. Both the water and the coffee were the best he had ever tasted.

When a sneeze came from inside, the fat man yelled, "Is stat you, Myrtle?"

A young woman's sing-song voice replied, "Yes, Pa."

"Need your help, Myrtle."

The girl went to the open serving window that had been cut into the wall. Like the chef's window, it had been cut with a saber saw used by a carpenter with very little skills.

She served two plates full of food. When the fat man said big breakfast, he meant *big*. One plate had sweet potatoes fried in bacon fat with a mound of scrambled eggs on top, and on top of that a thick heap of melted goat cheese. A handful of bacon was thrown on the side. The other plate had salt-fish, a Caribbean delicacy, with a big piece of bread from a French loaf and a huge glob of butter smeared on it. There was a pile of small onions and peppers and yucca on the side.

Sidney hadn't eaten in a day or so and ate everything on both plates but he couldn't have eaten another bite. He leaned back in the old, weathered chair to finish his coffee before becoming aware that the other two men were staring at him. They didn't believe that he had eaten the whole thing.

The fat cook came out and said, "See there you wimps, now there's a man who knows how to treat food. You don't play with it, you eat it up."

He looked at Sidney and said, "Usually folks don't finish my *big* breakfast, but I make a big one anyway."

One of the other men said, "Yeah that way he gets to eat anything left over."

The big man laughed and said, "Well, it's sinful to throw food away, and I share with the dogs."

The other man said, "By the looks of the skinny old dogs you got around here not much ever leaves the kitchen."

His companion got a big kick out of that and laughed. Apparently this was an ongoing repartee between those men. The fat man asked Sidney if he wanted anything else.

Sid answered, "Got any cigars?"

The fat man said he didn't, but one of the guys at the other table said he had an extra and offered it to Sidney.

"Thanks," he lit the cigar and inhaled the cheap smoke. He thought *life just keeps getting better.* He finished the cigar and coffee while listening to the men tease one another for some of the stupid things mankind had been programmed to do.

When Sidney asked for the bill, the fat man said, "Just pay me what you think it's worth," and he was sincere.

Sidney left a damp one hundred-dollar bill on the table under the old and tarnished salt shaker that had more rice in it than salt. The commotion he heard coming from the porch made it clear the money was appreciated. But it wasn't left to be appreciated, all he had on him were damp Benjamin Franklins and he knew there wasn't enough money there to change it.

Back on the road again, he had another half-hour walk before another road started feeding other cars on to it. A pick-up truck stopped and its passenger told him to hop in the back if he wanted a ride. Without conversation Sidney jumped in. As they came into town the driver shouted back, "Where do you want to go?"

Sidney answered, "A hotel. Doesn't matter which one."

The driver stopped in front of The Whistler's Inn. It was an old wooden two-story inn, painted white and looked like someone worked hard to keep it looking the way it did. Rooms were available and Sidney took one for a week. When asked what he did for a living by the old lady that owned the inn, he said, "I'm a writer trying to get over a block."

The old lady behind the desk felt better since he had an honorable job, and that he wasn't a smuggler waiting on refugees seeking a ride to the US Virgin Islands to get their free food stamps and U.S. government money—or a dope smuggler, both prevalent occupations in the islands off Venezuela. She didn't get many people just walking off the street to stay with them. Most foreigners stayed in town, in the big hotel with the fancy rooms and gambling casino. Every once in a while, they would get one or even a pair of young eggheads, hiking around in their fancy boots trying to fit in with the poor. There was nothing fancy about the man standing there in his beat up flip-flops.

Sidney asked, "Is there a kid around who can go buy me some things?"

She called out, "Minnie! Come here."

Minnie was five feet tall and weighed about 90 pounds and was the old lady's sister. She slipped a piece of paper and a pen over to Sidney and said, "You better write it down… she can't remember shit."

Sidney asked, "Is this a problem?"

Minnie chirped up in a sweet little voice, "Hell no! It ain't no bother, mister. I need the exercise anyway. Shit, if I couldn't run to the store, I'd just sit around here all day like some lazy folks I know," while casting a telling glance towards her sister.

Her sister was not one to be ridiculed and shot back, "Yeah! How do you know what I do all day? And what makes you think you don't sit around all day? You can't remember shit, you old biddy."

Minnie was not to be robbed of the last word and shot back, "Well, at least I remember to button up my blouse, you shameless hussy." Minnie snatched the list from Sid's hand and was gone before her sister, Alice, could retaliate.

Alice said, "We'll charge the things on your list and put it on the bill."

Sidney was shown to his room and the bathroom down the hall. Alice didn't stop talking about her sister except to point out a piece of furniture or object that had special significance to her.

Sidney, clothes and all, stepped into the shower and stood there, first washing his clothes then his body. It was a long shower, since the low water pressure produced not much more than a slight stream of sun-warmed water. After drying himself, he wrapped the towel around his waist for the trip back to his room.

Minnie had returned already and was in his room putting his things neatly in order on top of the antique dresser drawer. A bottle of rum, two cigars, a toothbrush and toothpaste didn't take up a lot of room. But she arranged and rearranged everything to her satisfaction.

Sidney realized how fortunate he was to have taken the knapsack into the bathroom with him. Minnie would have probably tried to unpack its contents too.

For the moment, his main need was to lie down and sleep—his eyes were burning from the lack of it. He had very little energy but he knew it was only surface fatigue and it could be ignored until he had finished doing what must be done.

He asked for instructions to the nearest postal service. Minnie told him she would be happy to show him. It was only a couple of miles down the main road. Sidney as usual, didn't want company and declined her offer.

With the knapsack and two bundles loaded on his shoulders, he started the two-mile walk. Along the way, he looked for an area that would discourage people, especially kids, to go into. Almost a mile from Whistlers Inn, he found an isolated area heavily overgrown with century plants and thick brush in between. He carefully worked his way up through the needle sharp points of the century plant's leaves, while being careful not to leave a trail. He worked his way in about fifty yards and was completely hidden from the road.

With his knife, he dug a deep hole under one of the giant centuries. The top layer of soil was set aside from the rest of the dirt. The documents, which he still hadn't read, were removed from the pillowcase full of diamonds and about half of the cash. The bag full of his prize was buried. He threw the excess dirt into the air to scatter it around. The surface soil was replaced and pieces of grass and dead leaves were scattered on top so that it was impossible to see there had been a disturbance. A small circle was carved under a century plant leaf that pointed to the road. Mother Nature's safe would not easily give up his treasure.

Express mail packets were picked up at the small postal service. He took the padded envelopes to the privacy of a nearby park where he sat unobserved and casually loaded four pouches with one-hundred dollar bills. The outside was marked *manuscript-rejected* and the return address was Omega Films Ltd. with an Aruba address of the building he was looking at across the park, Smiley's Ice Cream Shoppe.

If the money didn't get through, he'd know it soon enough from the local talk of Smiley's being busted for sending an illegal amount of money. If they didn't mess with Smiley, then he could be sure it would arrive at Mr. Xavier in St. Croix. He still had fifty thousand dollars that would be needed later. He could stash that much easily and almost anywhere.

Sidney pushed his reserves and jogged back to the Inn. He fell on the bed and was asleep almost instantly without hearing cheerful Minnie calling him to come down to the dining room—it was time for lunch. He also didn't hear her when she announced dinner as well, so she and Alice, using the master key, entered his room to find their masculine guest sound asleep, face down on the bed. They walked on tiptoes as to not wake him up. On the way out, Minnie had to stop Alice from peeking into their new guest's knapsack, his only luggage, the two pillow cases he had were gone. Alice was by nature a very inquisitive person—nosy, if you asked Minnie.

Sidney woke up feeling totally renewed at ten o'clock that evening. Normally he didn't need that much sleep, but every two or three weeks, especially after stretching it for a few days, he would fall into a very deep sleep, letting mind and body get a well-deserved rest. He cleaned himself and left the silent and dark inn, to look for some action.

He had passed two neighborhood bars on the way to town earlier. The first one had already closed for the evening, but the other was open and busy. He found a barstool next to an older man with big thick side burns, a huge nose, and bushy eyebrows, and wearing a faded-out seaman's cap. His head was massive compared to the skinny body that supported it. He had a Scottish accent, which wasn't too uncommon, as the Dutch Government owned the island.

The Scotsman had been in his whiskey for a few too many and was offering challenges to every man, woman or child to bet him that he could whip every man in the bar. There were no takers; everyone on the island, especially the regulars in the bar, had heard this before and knew it was just the old man's way to feel young again. Tomorrow he would be back aboard his fishing scow, headed out for the day's catch to be sold to finance tomorrow night's drinking while sitting on the same barstool, and begging for the attention he had deserved so many years ago.

As soon as Sidney sat down, he realized that he had made a mistake in choosing that particular barstool. The old Scot, realizing that a warm body had sat next to him, slowly turned to see who had the audacity to sit next to Bear Wiggins — without being invited. The Scot sat there staring at the stranger who had both forearms on the bar, and a glass of rum before him.

Sidney decided not to acknowledge the man's stare, knowing it would only further infuriate the old man to be ignored. He didn't know why he did it, maybe he just felt like seeing what the old man still had in him. A murmur floated around the bar as the stare continued. Everyone tried to conceal their delight that a stranger was about to get whacked by the Bear.

He took another drink, and as he put the glass on the bar, he was surprised by the old man's quickness with his right hand. Sidney had no time to raise an arm in defense. He was also surprised because the skinny old man had the strength of a young and powerful man. His quick right hand had caught Sidney squarely on his left cheekbone, knocking him off the barstool. Sidney was amazed: he was on his back with his feet sticking up in the air resting on the overturned barstool— and he laughed hardily.

His instinct for deadly retaliation had lasted only milliseconds as he realized that he had asked for the punch. He had hoped there was something besides bullshit left in the old man and had decided to find out. He had his answer, and after a few more chuckles at himself, he got to his feet. As he stood, the old man jumped off his stool facing Sidney, man-to-man.

The old man in his thick brogue said, "What kind of man is it who would dare to sit next to Bear Wiggins without being asked by myself?" He put his hands up; he was ready for a good, old-fashioned fight.

Sidney replied, "A better man than you." Sidney thought, *I'm doing it again. Don't want to hurt the old man. Aww, what the hell, he can't hurt me, let him have some fun.* Bear sent a flashing left jab shooting towards Sidney's chin, but he was ready for it and it hurt only a little when it landed.

Bear pronounced for all to hear, "*Not* a better man, but certainly an impertinent, stupid man by the looks of it—you foreign bastard," and he positioned himself to send the next blow.

While Sid rubbed his chin as if it hurt, he thought, *be careful. If I tank the fight the old man will lose face in front of his friends. In their own way, these people are probably proud to have such a salty old character as part of their community. If I hurt him, I'd have to fight every man in the bar to-*

night. Submitting to the old man will only enhance my statues around here and make my stay here a lot easier.

Sidney dodged the blows enough to take most of the sting out of them, but it looked good to the crowd. He swung at the old man a few times, missing or pulling back just before impact to be sure the Scot didn't get hurt. After letting the old man land a dozen blows, the enthusiastic cheers of the crowd had told him the old man was once again, not just the town's has-been, but still the fighting spirit of old.

Sidney raised his hands and said, "Okay, Mr. Wiggins—you win. I've had enough."

The old man's eyes were alight with life again, his insides were full of pride; he was once again his own man.

Sidney said, "I apologize for my bad manners. Do you mind if I sit next to you. I'd like the honor of buying you a drink."

The old man, to further show his dominance over the younger adversary said, "For you, it'll cost you three drinks."

"My pleasure, Mr. Wiggins, and if I'm incorrect in any further actions, I would appreciate you telling me before correcting me with that iron fist you swing."

The two of them sat down while the crowd stood on their feet applauding the old Scotsman, who was doing everything he could to suppress the tears that were being forced against his will to fill his eyes. Being so close to emotion, the old man didn't dare try to speak, as his voice would have betrayed the tough image he was so proud of. Without turning to face the crowd, he waved his arm in a downward motion indicating the crowd to be quiet

By the second drink, Bear was talking to Sidney, telling his life story about all of the dragons in his life that lay slain. By drink five, there was not much that Sidney didn't know about the old man. Also by drink five, the Scot had decided that he liked the stranger and whispered, "I know you took it easy on me during our fight and I'm going to buy you the next drink, just to say thanks. But if you ever say you took it easy, I'll find you and beat you till the moon turns blue and the ocean is dry."

Sidney said, "It's an honor to know a warrior like you. You can always count on me, Bear, no matter what you need." They stayed there, Bear talking and Sidney listening until the bar closed

That was the first time he had ever done something good for a fellow human. There were no available women in the bar and probably never would be; this was that type of community, so he settled in on just getting drunk. While listening to a story heard twice before, a thought surfaced in his drunken brain. *Wonder what Minnie would do to repel my advances. Shit, I'm drunk. Fuck 80 year-old Minnie? I'm worse than drunk, must be brain rum-rot. Wonder what bedding both Minnie and Alice at the same time would be like. Yep! It's rum-rot and I'm too fucking drunk to be out on the streets.*

When the bar shut down, Bear seemed to become more sober the instant his feet touched the floor. He stood erect and walked out and down the narrow dark road to his old wooden sloop that had been his home and only means of support for fifty-three years.

Sidney headed back to his room and passed out as his head touched the pillow.

Sidney's fight with Bear had made him a member of the community. Everyone accepted him, most were aware that he allowed himself to be beaten rather than humiliate the old man. After all, anyone could look at Sid and see nothing but hard muscle—and he didn't have what could be called a Sunday-school demeanor.

He spent a lot of time that week helping Bear work on his badly neglected boat. The old man had taken very good care of his boat, but was too poor to buy materials needed for repairs. Sidney enjoyed working on the old wooden boat, drinking rum, and listening and re-listening to the old man's tales.

The old man, like Sidney, had spent his life around the sea; it was his first love and a love he could not do without, but would deny that to the day he died. He openly cussed the sea for the miserable little fish, the rough seas, and the salt that destroyed everything on board. Old men have to have something to be grouchy about, and the sea made a good subject for Bear.

One day Sidney made a deal with Bear to take him on an extended sail and he would advance all of the money up front to make the repairs. That spark of decency and compassion Sidney was feeling was still foreign to him. He was doing something unnatural; he usually would steal a boat. But those feelings didn't bother him that much; he could stop fooling around very easily. He had time to kill, no more raids for a while, and he didn't have to pick up his son for another month. He was comfortable there; the old ladies were making sure he was always well fed and looked after. His time with the old man was enjoyable, so he just hung out.

Bear Wiggins made up a little poem one night when he was plastered. He remembered it the next morning and told it to Sidney every time they had a few drinks and he caught Sid looking at one of the women. The melody changed almost every time.

"*Drinking rum by day when the sky is bright;*
the sun's heat is warming Sidney's miserable plight.
Drinking rum by the gallons all during the night
in fear of Bear's iron fist, be it left or his right
brings the sting of memory of Bear's terrible might.
No women in sight for Sidney's delight today and tonight,
and that, my friends, is Sidney's woeful plight.
So get ready Miss Fist, you ain't pretty, but at least you're tight."

The old man hadn't been laid in many years, and could only remember how much he used to enjoy it. Then he would start telling stories about all of the women he had since his Lulu died twenty four and a half years ago.

Eventually, Bear's boat was back in good shape and Sidney had had enough of life in civilization. It was time to move on, he was ready for a change; however, he wasn't quite ready for the big change to his life that picking up his son would bring. He had only lived by himself and now he would have to be with the boy. He wasn't looking forward to meeting his sons and making the decision on which of the two boys would make the best Sidney XXIV. According to his deal, both boys had been named Sidney at birth, but neither would have a last name until the selection was made. The boy not chosen would belong to his mother who could name him, keep him, or put him in an orphanage—it didn't matter to Sidney.

Time was rapidly nearing when the training would have to begin. He had put it off too long and had put his family tradition and hierarchy at risk by waiting so long to produce an heir. If anything had happened to him, centuries of tradition would have died with him, or dear old dad would have to knock up a few whores.

I'll have to settle down for six years then it'll be up to the boy to contribute to our tradition, fortune, and to produce an heir. Maybe it'll be fun to teach a kid how to be the meanest son-of-a-bitch wherever he goes. It'd be interesting watching him become King of the Seas. A title he was born to, if he has the Sidney X in him.

ABOARD GOLDEN BOY

Talk about a pissed off Italian; Vincenzo, the Sicilian, had reached his point of endurance. The hatred he felt toward the people he had been looking for had reached a level that bordered on obsessive. His passion for vengeance had germinated when he first received the telephone call from Tony the Pop. Tony had instructed him to get down to Aruba in the Netherlands Antilles. Their old friend, Vito Meridino, and his wife, had become victims of the thieves.

Vito and three others were dead; his wife had been disfigured by torture. Nobody knew what happened or how many people were involved, but Vito was carrying ten million dollars in diamonds plus a hundred thousand dollars in cash. The secret safes he had on board the *Golden Boy* were left open and were empty.

A new-found passion matured ten hours later as he stood on the red stained Persian carpet in Vito's stateroom. The blood from Vito's wife's mutilation covered the creamy satin sheets. One finger lay on the floor, obviously not seen by the Aruban police force that had given the crime scene their usual half-ass investigation. That was okay with Vincenzo as he fully intended to find out exactly what had happened.

The captain of the yacht was the first to tell him what he knew. "I was asleep when apparently I was hit on the head and gagged and taped to the railing behind my bunk. When I woke up it was daylight outside, and the boat was moving at the same cruising speed. I had a terrible headache, and found it impossible to move. I did everything to get free during that day and night. I was sure we had been kidnapped, and the people responsible were taking the boat somewhere else because we should have run into Bonaire by daylight that first morning. There were no sounds or noises. Nobody came in my room, and I didn't hear any voices."

"Did you hear any voices or anything unusual during the night before you were attacked?" asked Vincenzo.

"Nothing at all. I got off watch, and went directly to bed. From the time I woke up bound that morning, I didn't hear a thing until I heard the hailer from the Coast Guard cutter alongside ordering us to stop."

"What did you think was happening then?"

"Since they were threatening to open fire if we didn't stop, I figured they were going to start shooting. Instead they boarded us with armed crews sent over in the ship's rubber boats. They searched the boat, and released us as they found us. I went into the main salon and couldn't believe what I saw. Mr. Meridino was sitting in the lounge chair, taped and gagged with blood all over his chest and floor. Shit, I never imagined a man could bleed that much. His throat was sliced wide open and looked like he had been dead for a couple of days."

"What makes you think that?"

"His skin was white, totally void of color and all of the blood had congealed into a mud. In 'nam I saw plenty of dead guys, and the ones that had been around for a while looked the same way, stone dead. Then I saw his wife. A medic was helping her. She had been taped and gagged, too. When the tape came off her head, I saw that an ear had been cut off. Both of her hands had fingers cut off. She was in shock. I don't think she knew of her condition or even that her husband was dead."

"Where is she now?"

"They took her to the hospital in Oranjestad. They took Liz Barret there, too. Someone had punched her in the mouth with something hard that had broken her face and teeth. They found her gagged, taped and naked in the shower. She's really fucked up. When they carried her off the boat she was frightened, confused and hysterical. Why anyone would want to hurt that sweet little girl is a real mystery. I hope I can get my hands on the sons-of-bitches who did this."

"Tell me what happened to the others?"

"Mary Colson was working with us as way to spend some time away from school. An eighteen-year-old, multi-millionaire, and the nicest person you can ever hope to meet. Someone hit her in the face, too, but she was dead. My backup captain was found dead beside her. They were on duty when they were attacked. I find it hard to believe that Jack would let anyone get close enough to him to let that happen. We've been working together for five years; he takes his work seriously. All I can figure is maybe Mary distracted him, and he didn't see another vessel approaching. They must have caught him completely off guard. That had to be the case—or it was an inside job."

"Why do you think it might have been an inside job?"

"We were out at sea. Who could have known we were there? Apparently there were valuables on board, and they knew about the safes. I didn't know about them and it's my job to know everything about *Golden Boy*."

"Who on board could have done this? Everyone was bound up or dead when the Coasties arrived."

"I don't know, but somebody certainly knew about us. It could have been someone associated with Mr. Meridino's business. Maybe they bought off George, Mr. Meridino's security guard."

"That doesn't make any sense. George was killed in the attack," replied Vincenzo with a touch of disdain in his voice.

"I know, but he could easily have approached Jack, killed them and let the others board the boat. Maybe it was part of the plan to kill him, too, so there would be no clues it was an inside job."

"What do you know about Mr. Meridino's business interests?"

"I know enough to not ask questions and keep well away of certain conversations. I've been with Mr. Meridino for years. He has told me on many occasions to keep my nose out of his business affairs and he knows that I did. He was involved with some very powerful people. I had nothing but respect for Mr. Meridino and he took good care of me and my family."

"Who, besides George, do you think was involved? Did he have any visitors aboard at his last stop? Do you know any names of persons he met with?"

"Who? Mr. Meridino, or George?"

"Vito."

"I don't have any idea. He used the satellite telephone many times, but I don't have any idea to whom he spoke. While at shore, I wouldn't have any idea if he met anyone."

"How about anyone else, *excluding* George?"

"They didn't use the sat-phone. I keep it locked up. That's the only way I can keep some of the crew from using it to call everybody they know. Some of the crew had no appreciation for the cost of satellite calls."

"Did anyone else come on board at any time since you started this cruise?"

"There was no one on the boat other than the crew. Two guys came aboard in Grenada to work on the air conditioner in the crew's quarters, but they were local working stiffs. I can't picture them doing something like this."

"Captain, you just answer the questions, I'll do the picturing. How did you happen to call those particular men?"

"They were recommended by the marina we were in."

The captain had gotten the message loud and clear. He was not there to share experiences with the man from Sicily. If he wanted his opinion he would ask; otherwise don't speculate.

"Tell me about everyone George talked to, or met, even casually on the streets, like a vendor or passing conversation between apparent strangers."

"He placed several calls to Sicily. I heard the name Tony once. I didn't see him meeting anyone."

Vincenzo talked to everyone on board; the captain had been the most help. The others had about the same experience; waking up with a thumping and a lump on the head. One man had seen a silent black form of a man approach him before the lights went out, but no descriptions were possible.

The next morning, Vincenzo went to the hospital to visit the two women. Both were gone and had been heavily sedated then flown to New York during the night.

When he reported this to Tony the Pop, the response was, "I know; I arranged it. I want them home with family and friends, not in some fucking third world roach-infested, bacteria breeding hole of a hospital. Go back to New York if you think you need to bother them. Whatever you do Vincenzo, don't upset Vito's wife or the girl, they've been through enough."

"Sure, boss. Did the other security guard go with them?"

"No, I'm bringing him here. I want to talk to him myself."

Vincenzo was beginning to get undercurrents of suspicious thoughts that included Tony. Why had George the guard called Tony personally? It certainly wouldn't be the first time one of the mafia chiefs had whacked another.

He decided to go back to the boat and question the crew again, but more intensely, and examine the boat thoroughly before going to the States. His hatred for the creeps that had attacked the yacht could be put on a back burner just a little longer.

VIRGIN ISLANDS

Sidney had been priming the old Scot to sail to the Virgin Islands to give his re-built sloop a proper test run. Over evening whiskey, every day the old man was ready to go—in fact, there was no sense in waiting; they should leave right then, he would say. He said the same thing night after night. During the day, however, he always found another reason to stay in port. Sidney was in no hurry; he had as much time as he needed. The boat had been provisioned for over a week and was ready to sail no matter what excuse Bear would come up with to stay another day.

Finally, one night after the usual evening of drinking at the bar, Bear returned to his boat and Sidney to his room. Sidney gathered his few items in the room and left. He left a thousand dollars in the old time cash register behind the desk with a note. The note said, "Thanks for your hospitality."

On the way back to the boat, he was able to locate his hidden treasure with the help of a brilliant full moon. He quietly put his knapsack and the soiled pillowcase on the old man's boat along with the dock lines. The trade winds blew the boat away from the dock as Sidney readied the mainsail and hanked on the jib. The sails were raised without much noise.

Sidney's plan was to go to St. Thomas and drop off a little package containing the matching diamonds for Ortega's girls. He thought it'd be fun to listen to their speculation about where they came from when he returned to the Venezuelan village. As a natural precaution, he'd be sure there was no trail and would sail to St. John, a close neighbor to St. Thomas. In St. John it would be easy to hire a young sailor—the place was infested with them—to go back to Aruba with Bear, if he wanted company for the return.

In St. Thomas he'd buy another boat to take him to St, Croix, but that boat would be kept. It would be the training vessel for the kid and provide some fun for him as well.

The old Scot woke up below that morning and unsteadily made his way up the companionway ladder. His old, tired, wrinkled, puffy, hungover face looked pissed. "You rascal, you decided to mutiny against the captain, did you?" he asked.

Sidney looked at him and said, "No, cap. You decided you wanted to leave last night since we had such a big full moon. Don't you remember?"

Bear scratched his bushy white hair and changed the look on his face to a smile with a twinkle in his eye and said, "Of course I do. You think I was drunk?"

Sidney didn't respond, he just pointed all around to the rippled surface of the gently rolling three-foot seas. Only five knots of wind were blowing, but it was in the right direction. It was a perfect day for a relaxed sail, and he had already stripped down to his skin to enjoy it.

He always enjoyed a challenging sail with wind blowing strong enough to dismast the boat and mountainous seas that spilled blue water over him and was trying to pull him into the dark depths—back to the center of nature—had a special meaning to him. That was when he felt closest to the real God, which, what or whoever it was. But, calm days like that were few and the peace, quietness, and sun's warmth revitalized his appreciation for a more tranquil way of life.

The old man didn't share the younger man's enthusiasm for sailing nude and told him so many times every day. Sidney would just flip him a bird and say nothing. The last morning at sea before arriving in Coral Bay on the island of St. John, the old man brought out a mug of coffee for Sidney.

He sat down then said, "We been sailing for a few days now and I know where we are and I think you do, too. With today's sailors it's unheard of to be able to know your position without charts and electronic do-dads. Where did you learn to sail?"

"My father taught me when I was a little kid, probably same as you."

Bear agreed, but said, "That kind of knowledge ain't taught."

Sidney agreed as a mountain slowly grew out of the sea and they sailed into a small harbor at the mountain's base. With the anchor set on a sandy bottom, Sidney said, "Let's go get a cold beer and a drink or two on shore. What'd you say?"

Bear acted like Sidney by not saying a word, but went over to lower his little rowing dinghy into the water. He then said, "Let's go, but we're going to have to row really fast to stay ahead of the rising tide."

As soon as the wooden dinghy touched water Sidney understood what Bear had meant by *rising tide*. A trickle of water formed first on the bottom near the keel then another on a seam, then another. They had a good quarter mile to row to reach shore. It was a good race with Sidney rowing strongly, the dinghy sinking, and Bear bailing. The dinghy won; however, only twenty yards from the shore of the beach bar, the Fat Feet Saloon.

People in the bar noticed the pair's race to shore and began cheering them on. When they didn't make it, ten guys came running out laughing and drunk and swam the submerged dinghy to shore.

Bear stopped the men from dragging the dinghy ashore. "Leave her in the water so her seams can swell shut, or at least get a little closer together so I might be able to keep up with the leaks on the trip back to *Lulu*."

He carried the painter to shore and tied it to a stick sticking up in the sand. It was a funny sight to see a floating painter leading out and disappearing into the water.

After a full afternoon and evening of drinking, the old Scot was feeling the effects and was on the verge of passing out. There wasn't a man in the little bar and harbor who didn't know that Captain Bear Wiggins was the toughest man alive. And he had told them of the whipping he had given his friend and a thousand other men in the Caribbean—there wasn't a man in the harbor who had not already adopted old Bear as one of their own.

As Sidney had expected, the bar was full of out-of-work captains and he had no trouble choosing one of them to hang out with Bear and sail back to Aruba with him. The captain was paid in cash and made to sign a statement as to his duties on the tavern's stationary, a paper drink napkin. He also made it clear that if he tried to cheat him, or the old man, it would be the end of his career, period. With Sidney's convincing voice and deadly black eyes, the hired captain knew this wasn't a man to fool with.

Sidney and the new guardian took Bear back to *Lulu* in the other captain's dinghy. Getting the cranky old drunk into his berth wasn't easy, but after a last glass of rum he went to sleep, sitting up. Sidney wrote a note for him.

Have fun and kick some of these pansies' asses around here before going home. A guy name Jed Tangy has been paid to work for you and is ready to go back to Aruba with you whenever you are ready. All of Jed's expenses have been paid including his flight back to St. Thomas.

He wrapped the note around a wad of hundred-dollar bills and taped it to the bottle of whiskey the old Scot had been nipping from. Sidney shouldered his pack and went back to the bar with Jed. It was getting ready to close down as he called a taxi. After an hour wait, the taxi arrived and took him to the Coral Bay ferry dock. The stern light was still in sight of the last departing ferryboat as they arrived. He would have to wait until the next morning. All the tourist bars were closed, but the deep base sound of Caribbean drums led him to an active little local's bar. He fit right in, got a lot drunker and even got lucky with possibly the ugliest women he had ever seen.

He was standing on the ferry dock at six the next morning waiting for the boat to take him the island of St. Thomas. People in that part of the Caribbean thought of St. Thomas as being the commercial island because there was a K-Mart there.

Sidney passed up the chance to marvel at the goods offered by K-Mart and told his taxi driver to stop at the address given to him by the Ortega's receptionist when he had called.

He ran from the taxi to the office entrance door and left the package marked for Maria and Jandy then returned to the waiting taxi. He had the driver take him to the Anchorage Inn, a pleasant place to lay up for a couple of days. He was ready to shave the thick beard off his face, buy something new to wear, look for his next boat and make plans to pick up the boy.

After getting a room looking over the anchorages of Long Bay and Elephant Bay, he took a long hot water shower to rinse the caked salt off his weathered body. His only thought as he stood under near-scalding water: *The way I feel today makes me think that I'm catching up to the old Scotsman a lot faster than I should.*

VENEZUELA

A PACKAGE WITH THE OTHER MAIL FROM ST. THOMAS WAS HAND-DELIV-ered by a cartel employee to the Venezuelan compound. It arrived just as Jose Ortega and Jandy were preparing to leave for a month's trip. Maria was scheduled to go to Chicago in a week to learn more about some new contacts at the company's distribution level.

Jandy was surprised to find a box addressed to her and Maria in the secure mail pouch. She opened it and found two identical diamonds lying side by side. No note was inside or anything else other than a wad of newspaper wrapping to keep the stones from rattling together. She called Maria to tell her of the gifts. She reacted with glee until she had a thought.

Maria said, "Bet they're fakes sent by one of the Ortega brothers or one of the other guys in St. Thomas to have a little fun. Let's play the part shall we, Jandy?"

They showed the stones to Ortega, acting overwhelmed, charmed that an unknown admirer had sent them such a precious gift, how romantic. When they tired of doing their little act for Ortega they stopped the charade and Jandy said to him, "Nice try, buster, but we know it's a joke. Real diamonds don't come this close to being a perfect pair and these have to be 10 carats each."

Ortega said, "If there's a secret admirer then he better let himself be known because he sure as hell is missing out on getting laid."

The diamonds had gotten Ortega's attention. *Damn things look real. Father might have sent them but he'd include a note. Maybe someone in the brotherhood did it as a joke. If Sam sent them, they're real, but he would've included a note, too. Fucking Charlie would send fakes as a joke. Ricardo has screwed every woman on the island and is looking for fresh meat, but he, too, would have sent a note.*

He placed a call to his father. He knew nothing about it and if one of the brotherhood was playing a joke, they all would have known. He strongly recommended that Jose find out who was responsible in case a rival smuggler was trying to get close to them.

The girls were disappointed that neither Jose Ortega nor the other men in the cartel had sent the stones, but they were secretly excited that someone had sent real sparklers. Nobody gave any thought to the possibility that the strangely quiet Sidney could have afforded the matching diamonds.

Maria decided to leave her stone in the safe rather than go through possible problem of taking it through customs in the two countries she would be visiting on her trip to the windy city of Chicago. Jandy was taking hers with her. She was going to St. Thomas and there was a jeweler there she trusted to tell her if it were a fake, and to build a wearable piece for her. She wanted a necklace made that would really show the stone off—fake or not, it was beautiful.

Maria was the first to suspect the stones might have a horrible past. During a meeting with the group in Chicago, the big topic of conversation was about an important Mafia boss in New York, Vito Meridino. His yacht had been attacked by pirates who mutilated him and his wife, and killed some other people who were sailing with him. The pirates had known he was carrying something of tremendous value on board, and the word was out to the underground world to look for anyone peddling diamonds—especially the much sought after and renowned Sparkling

Twins, a perfect pair of ten carat diamonds.

The word was out and everyone was looking to win the one million dollar reward paid by Vito's brother. The Italians were sincerely pissed-off.

Maria became upset when she heard of the diamonds and instinctually knew she had been given one; her psychic ability left no doubt about it. She called Jandy right after hearing the news and suggested she might not want to flash the stone around; it could cast suspicion on the Ortega cartel. While the cartel had no fear of the Mafia, there wasn't any sense in creating a degree of distrust between the two worldwide organizations.

Jandy thought they should do just the opposite and tell the mob about the stones. Maria's response to her suggestion was, "Are you nuts? I'm not going to turn mine over to the mob. They have enough money; let them steal some other diamonds. They'd probably say our diamonds were theirs just to get them, anyway. I don't trust those guys."

Jandy decided Maria was right, but decided to play it safe by telling Jose Ortega. At dinner that evening with the Ortega family, the horrible story about the Meridino family and the missing diamonds came up. Don Ortega was aware of the situation. The Italians had sent a man to see him asking for his help in finding the culprits.

The older Ortega, Don Zugia, told the family what really had happened, "Vito was on his annual vacation on his beautiful yacht, *Golden Boy*. They were moving some cash around without custom's interference, but more importantly, had ten million dollars worth of pure clear-grade diamonds on board. They have been turning excessive cash into diamonds. The pirates physically tortured Vito and his wife to find the hiding places for the cash and diamonds.

"After they found everything they wanted, Vito's throat was cut. Three other people were killed, also. One of them was the heiress to the Mc Known family fortune. She was only eighteen and had her skull crushed. Mc Known has gone wacko trying to find out who did it and was putting tons of heat on the Italians to find them.

"Everyone else on the boat had no idea what happened. All they knew is when each of them woke up they were gagged and bound to their bunks with tape. Mrs. Meridino apparently went off the deep end when she learned the extent of her injuries and of the brutal death of Vito. Another young girl was on a working vacation from the university she was attending. She had her front teeth knocked out, jaw broken and was found taped up naked in a shower stall. Her father is a friend of mine, Herald Golson."

The Don looked at Jose Ortega, and asked, "Do you remember the Golsons? They stayed in the St. Thomas compound with us three years ago."

Jose did remember the pretty girl and felt a flash of anger that someone would treat her like that. He would try to help the Italians find the murderers.

The senior Ortega continued, "I agreed to do everything possible to help find the people responsible. I've issued a worldwide call to all cartel members to look for diamonds and listen carefully for talk of anyone having knowledge about the *Golden Boy*. The million dollar reward is certainly enough to get information, if they'll pay it. Even if they don't, McKnown would double it without blinking an eye."

Jandy didn't usually speak to the Don unless spoken to, but said, "That's awful! It must have been someone on the yacht. How else would they have gotten on the boat out at sea?"

"For that kind of loot, they could have flown over them with a helicopter and repelled down. Those people couldn't have defended themselves from an attack like that. Or they could have slipped up behind them at night in a high-speed boat and boarded them that way. In fact, that sounds more probable since blows to the head, or a knife in Vito's case, killed the people. A helicopter raid would have announced their arrival and there would have been some serious shooting. Nobody was shot," offered Jose.

"Hey, wait *just* a minute!" the older Ortega said. Then he took a sip of red wine to wet his dry throat while fully absorbing a memory. "That's it, Jose! That's where I had heard of that peculiar tattoo you asked about. A man boarded my grandfather's yacht at night and killed him and everyone else on board except for the cook. He had been stabbed and should have died like everyone else, but didn't. Also the boat was sunk in an effort to cover up the crime, but the cook managed to find a plank that he hung on to. He floated around at sea for two days with his wounds until he was spotted and rescued by a fisherman. His story was unbelievable."

Everyone at the table, especially Jose Ortega, listened intently to the fascinating discovery. "The cook said one man did all of the killing. Alone, he took on twelve men with only his knife and a sword. After killing them, he took the gold they were carrying, and then torched the boat. The blow-by-blow account of the man's fighting ability was astonishing. The interesting thing was that he wore no shirt and the cook saw a red, tattered flag with a sword sticking in a skull."

He smiled and then added, "A barracuda circled a sword that had strange markings on its hilt. There wasn't any doubt at the time that it was a private signature for a Jolly Roger, the flag of the pirates of yesterday. Pirates always had their own colors."

Jandy asked, "When did this happen?"

Don Ortega answered, "May first in 1930."

Jandy laughed at the possibility that Sidney was a pirate in today's world. Jose didn't laugh. He had never seen a man Sid's age as fit as he was, and knew by first-hand experience that the man was cold blooded. The idea excited him; he had to find out.

Jandy said, "Well, Sidney is not that old—no one is."

The older Ortega said, "Well, young lady, some things get passed down through families. I doubt that flag design could not have been duplicated by chance."

Jandy suddenly realized that the older man was correct, some families do pass down traditions—she worked for one. The Ortega's had passed down their smuggling business for almost 300 years.

Jose asked his father, "Do you think it would be possible for a lone man to have made the raid on the Meridino yacht?"

"It might be possible for an extremely knowledgeable man, but it's very unlikely. They think it was several men. The two speedboats carried on deck were stolen as a way of making their escape. One of them was found in the middle of the Caribbean floating and out of gas. They haven't found the other one yet, but feel certain they were met by a pick-up ship to make the getaway."

That night Jose called Maria in Chicago and related the story and his questionable thoughts about Sidney. He instructed her to come to St. Thomas instead of returning to Venezuela. He wanted her to pursue the possibility of their strange new friend being the leftover of some pirate family. Maria had been unusually quiet. Usually she would interrupt Ortega when her feelings hit her in waves of certainty. She had the feeling that it was very likely he could be a pirate and that certainly explained a lot of things in her mind.

Maria didn't sleep much that night; she was too excited about her upcoming project: identify her mysterious Sidney, if that was his real name. It was much more gratifying than sitting in a room full of macho types trying to see who might have alternative motives to enter deals involving the cartel. Her mind was flashing through possibilities of where to start the search. Hours later she drifted off to sleep with the thought of a shirtless swashbuckler standing on the bow of a sailboat; his face was Sidney's.

She arrived in St. Thomas the next afternoon to find the company's limousine waiting. She had the driver take her to Ortega's office, Tropical Exports, Inc— before going to the dock. Getting to Don Ortega's compound required a fifteen-minute fast boat ride to his private island. After a quick stop by the office, she called a well-known sketch artist and made an appointment for him to be picked up the next day and brought to the compound.

When Maria arrived at the compound Jandy met her, eager to talk about Sidney. Maria refused to discuss him with her and Jose stating she needed a fresh mind for tomorrow. She also wanted the other two to think about anything other than Sidney. She didn't tell them why.

The sketch artist arrived and Maria's instructions were, "I want you to interview three people this morning. You are to make a separate sketch based only on the description given by each of us, without the others seeing what has been drawn. After the sketches, I want you to draw what you think the person looks like by combining descriptions with what you've done on each sketch. After that, all of us will critique the drawings to come up with the best likeness. Then I want a photo-like rendering done so it can be reproduced. This is a private matter and no one is to know about this or see the renderings. Any problems?"

The artist, a con man, forger, and escaped convict, was a close friend of the cartels—he could be trusted. Maria described Sidney as she remembered him: a man in his forties with a deep suntan and squint wrinkles around his eyes from spending a lifetime in the sun without sunglasses. His eyes were a little closer together than normal. They were hard, showed no emotion and the pupils were black. His eyebrows bushy, full, and black. His beard always looked like he needed a shave or let it grow; it covered his face up to his cheekbones. The only break in the black beard was a scar on his left lower jaw. It was about two inches long and straight, like it was made with a knife. The nose had been broken before; it looked like it had changed direction more than once. Cheekbones were high and had sharp, pronounced edges. Lips were thin over very white teeth. There was some discoloration between some of his front teeth, suggesting they were capped. There was no fat on his face, in fact, facial muscles could be noticed when he ate or showed expression, which was not frequent. His ears seemed to be normal size, started in line with his eyebrows, ended even with the bottom of his nose. The chin had a slight cleft and there were several small scars on it as well. His neck was thick, very muscular with a pronounced Adam's apple.

The artist sketched as Maria described Sidney until she had nothing else to volunteer. Then he asked her questions about specific features—little things that only a trained artist would look for. It took almost two hours before Maria left the room. It took another two hours for both of the others to give the artist everything they could remember. Jandy went into a lot of emotional stuff that seemed important to the artist. Jose Ortega was the worst. He didn't really see the features of the guy. He described him as a guy who needed a shave and had black, scary eyes; black hair and bushy eyebrows, and was mean looking.

After a lobster and wine lunch, they all sat down to finalize what the missing man looked like. Two days later Maria picked up the finished rendering and was shocked at the accurate portrait of Sidney. She had two hundred copies made before returning to the compound.

☠

Sɪᴅɴᴇʏ's ᴡᴀʏ ᴏғ ʟɪғᴇ ᴅɪᴄᴛᴀᴛᴇᴅ ᴛʜᴀᴛ ʜᴇ ɴᴇᴠᴇʀ ɢᴇᴛ ɪɴᴠᴏʟᴠᴇᴅ ᴡɪᴛʜ other people. Invisibility in man's world could only be achieved if nobody knows you're there. If another person knows you by sight, whether friend or enemy, they will be curious and eventually try to learn things about you. He, like all the Sidneys, had learned and passed that directive to every son who took the sword. A man without identity or country cannot survive if known by others.

His family had existed and built the treasure only by abiding by a simple rule: be nobody. Many people had been killed only because they could identify a Sidney. Now he had a very powerful group that knew him, and, true to human nature, were curious and wanted to know more. And to learn more, they were about to circulate an accurate rendering of him to see what turned up. Had he known about the drawing, the lives of his three new friends would be taken as well as anybody else who had seen the portrait. He wouldn't find out until it was too late.

Jᴏsᴇ Oʀᴛᴇɢᴀ ʜᴀᴅ Jᴀɴᴅʏ sᴇɴᴅ ᴄᴏᴘɪᴇs ᴏғ ᴛʜᴇ ᴅʀᴀᴡɪɴɢ ᴛᴏ ʜɪs ᴋᴇʏ ᴘᴇᴏ- ple in every country in the Caribbean. Instructions were simple: Notify me if seen, and maintain surveillance. Do not approach or apprehend. Do not harm. He is in very good physical condition and is about six feet tall. Scars are visible on his abdomen, back and face. Also included was the artist's sketch of the pirate flag tattoo on the bottom right corner of the flyer.

Sɪᴅɴᴇʏ ᴡᴀʟᴋᴇᴅ ᴜᴘ ᴀ ʜɪʟʟ ʙᴇʜɪɴᴅ ᴛʜᴇ ɪɴɴ ʜᴇ ᴡᴀs sᴛᴀʏɪɴɢ ɪɴ. He wanted to find a suitable hiding place for the prize; however, the growth was too sparse and didn't offer sufficient cover. He was not comfortable hiding the prize up there. He considered swimming over to nearby Hassle Island, it was completely overgrown but he wanted the prize to be where he could grab it and run if needed. *I'll keep it with me. If stopped by the cops*

or a burglar, too bad, they'll have been in the wrong place at the wrong time.

The local newspaper for the boating community had lots of sailboats for sale. He found one that would suit him. The next morning he hired a taxi to take him by the broker that had the boat he wanted. It was a heavy cruiser and would be good to teach the boy how to manage the seas and learn his skills. For work, he preferred speedy catamarans, but for teaching about the sea, the slower cruiser would be best.

He looked at it and bought the Morgan forty-six. It was a sloop rig and had been owned by a man and his wife and a parti poodle dog and a fat cat that had lived aboard, sailing and working the Caribbean together for years. The man was a part-time writer and a full-time drunk. His wife was a full-time saleswoman and a part-time drunk. The dog was a full-time barker and strictly a social drinker; the cat didn't drink but liked leaving gooey surprises on the floor—they made an interesting team. The part-time writer had finally sold a screenplay and the family had moved into a new eighty-nine foot yacht so the Morgan had just been put on the market.

The boat was in good shape and completely outfitted so nothing was required to get underway. The only problem was the forward head wasn't working, but that was of no consequence since Sid just hung it overboard when nature called anyway. He paid for the boat in cash, which aroused the broker's suspicions, but not enough to kill the deal.

While the previous owners finished moving their worldly belongings, Sidney spent the rest of the day at Dirty's Beer Joint on the east end. It was a small bar that was stuck in the mangroves by the marina where his new boat was docked. He had been there before; it was a place he liked; nobody fucked with anyone there—it was a cruising sailor's bar.

By ten o'clock that evening he was slightly blitzed and was relaxing in his new home, the newest *Barracouta*. The next day, Sidney sailed into the harbor of his St. Croix marina at noon. There was no room for the deep-draft vessel at the dock so he anchored in the lagoon. Sally, as usual, was surprised to see him and did her best to make him appreciate her. She reported that four packets had been received as she followed him to his apartment.

"Sally, is that loud-mouth guy with the red hair paid up to date? If not, give him notice to leave because he's a slow pay. I'll put my boat in that slip."

"Does this mean you are going to spend more of your time here?" she asked with a concerned expression.

"Yes. Stop worrying about your job; it's yours." This removed some of her doubts and brightened her day.

Sidney's day brightened as he sat at the dining table and played with the new addition to the family treasure. Later that afternoon, he made the trip up to the secret cave and deposited new garbage bags full of cash and diamonds in the treasure room. The diamonds were poured into one of the treasure chests. He was running out of room in the chests.

Since the main entrance was sealed up, it wasn't possible to bring in a new chest. There would be more bulky things brought there with a new young man capturing prizes.

"I'll drop some lumber down the shaft and build more boxes to hold the new Sidney's prizes," he muttered.

Sitting on one of the big chests, he entered the information about the bank and *Golden Boy's* raids in the family log. Then, as usual, he read pages picked at random from past Sidneys. It was strange and only by coincidence that he turned to a page logged by his great grandfather, Sidney XXI. He had seen that one before, but had no reason to pay any particular attention to it—until then.

The logged entry was about a raid on a big private yacht off the coast of Columbia. His grandfather had noticed that a wealthy man took the yacht out on a regular schedule. The yacht was reported to be one of the finest in South America surpassing even the boats of the corrupt dictators, kings, and presidents of all the countries in the Americas. He also had found out the man was big in mining and there were strong suspicions that he controlled most, if not all, smuggling groups.

Sidney XXI had timed his attack one night when the big yacht usually left Puerto, Colombia. He positioned himself and had waited in a rowing skiff right off of the big rocks that had to be taken close to starboard in order to sail through the turn as it was dead in the eye of the trades. When the yacht was directly abeam to his position, he had pulled on the oars with everything he had to catch her.

He had misjudged his timing slightly and almost missed catching the sizable yacht. It was necessary to leap at the last minute from the skiff to catch the yacht's gunwale rail by his fingertips. Shortly after the ship cleared the entrance channel, he was below deck and had already dispatched the off-duty crew.

The few men on-duty were stalked and killed one by one. By the time he entered the owner's cabin, there were only two men alive—the owner was one; Sidney was the other. After a brief bit of persuasion with the cutlass, the owner reluctantly gave up the chest containing gold coins as well the family heirlooms and the family bible with the hand painted name on its leather cover. The name was "The Ortega Family."

The bible was taken, not for the family tree or its historical value, but only because it happened to have been in the chest of gold and jewels. Also in the chest was a sealed letter to King Luther of Monrovia threatening to kill his entire family if the slaves he had purchased and sold to the Saudi Arabia's king were not of good quality.

The magnificent vessel, with its dead crew, was set afire and it sank with all sails up and ablaze while on a port tack in the Caribbean Sea. One of the yacht's lifeboats was excluded from the traditional death at seas for captured vessels and was used to sail him back to his *Barracouta*.

Ain't that some shit, thought Sid XXIII. *I'll bet Ortega would be delighted to know my family killed off some of his a few years ago.* He smiled and muttered, "And the Ortegas are still losing to Sidneys."

Then the comparison between the two men dawned on him. *Both of us came from families with traditions of above-the-law of governments. Ortega is in smuggling illegal goods yesteryear; probably drugs and weapons today. And mine— piracy yesterday and piracy today.*

He looked for the chest where the old Ortega bible was. He didn't mind rooting through the various chests, stirring around their shiny contents, sparkles reflecting from the lantern's yellow lights. He found the bible still well-preserved in the bone-dry environment of the cave. Looking through the information contained in the Bible, he decided to give it to Ortega when he returned to the little village. He wasn't sure how he was going to explain it, but would figure out something between now and then; he had plenty of time. He took a big handful of cash and the Bible to show to his father.

The elder Sidney seemed glad to see that his son was still alive, but not much was said. The woman who had lived with him on the last visit was gone, making way for yet another one in the constant stream of hookers, nymphomaniacs, perverts, and unstable women who balled his brains out until they could take no more.

Apparently, his father correctly read Sidney's facial expression when his new-meat made her appearance. She was uglier than the one he had banged in St. John.

The elder Sid said, "So, she's no beauty. Who gives a shit? Or are you pissed that pretty little Sheila ran off. What the hell difference does it make if I don't maintain a relationship with a woman? Shit, you never have had a relationship longer than one night. And who gives a flea turd anyway. I'm happy and I can afford to pay somebody to care for this old pirate without any feet."

Sidney smiled at the irony about his father. The guy sits on top of a mountain that they own and the treasure it contained would easily buy the entire island. He could have the world's most beautiful women brought there, but no, he liked the island women. He didn't see beauty and ugly when it came to pussy.

The live-in woman was sent for a walk and her hostile attitude could only mean one thing—she was on the short-timer's list. Sidney had a couple of beers and, after things quieted down, he told his father the details of the St. Maarten bank raid. His father rocked his wheel chair with laughter at the description of the crazy man in black grease bouncing into a civilized bank with a huge black cock a foot long swinging in the breeze. His father appreciated the ingenuity used to distract the police as well as the bank personnel.

Then Sidney went into the details of the raid on *Golden Boy*. As soon as he started the story, his father broke in to say, "I knew that was you! It had to be. You better lay off the Italians for a while."

"What do you mean, it had to be me?"

His father explained, "It made the national news in the States for over a week. They had all kinds of Navy and Coast Guard ships out patrolling the Caribbean looking for the gang that did the deed. Interviews with some very obviously Mafia types in the northeastern part of the States had only kind things to say about poor old Vito. They felt certain that his numerous friends would never rest until the culprits were found and punished. They really made a big deal out of it and interviewed not only the survivors, but also the families of the deceased, friends of the deceased, teachers of the deceased."

He chuckled, "One network even showed the pet dog from one of the deceased left to fend for himself.. Nothing but tears from those interviewed and the usual stupid questions by the media, 'How did you feel when you found out that morning that your daughter had her skull crushed and was left dead for days while the yacht sailed on, unattended'... '

What words would you have for her if you could talk to her now'... They interviewed Vito's widow, God, I guess he didn't want to give it up too easy, uh, kid?"

"That's right. The old man fought it every step of the way and he paid for his stubbornness."

"Yeah, I never could understand why some men get so stupid. Surely everyone these days knows that since the beginning of piracy, a man who fights hard to keep the prize dies hard. While, if the man gives it up easy, he'll be left alive if possible. If not, then death would be a lot easier... That practice had been intended to send a message to seamen to lay down your arms if boarded and you will live to sail another day. So many times in the olden days the captured ships' crew would not only drop their weapons, but often would join the pirates' crew.

Sidney said, "I guess Vito didn't know much about pirates. Besides, I don't like ego-driven men like Vito's on my oceans. I was going to kill him anyway. He let his wife lose a couple of fingers and an ear before he gave up a lot of cash and multi-million dollars' worth of diamonds."

His father asked, "Is there any way you can be tied to it? The mob is

— 174 —

going to have everybody looking for whoever did this."

"No connection or witnesses. No trails, as usual." Then he asked, "Did they find the two power boats yet?"

"One was found drifting at sea, out of gas. They think a tanker or another boat had met it. The search is being centered on Jamaica. I think they feel it might have been one of the big drug smugglers that operate out of there."

After hearing the full story, his father, once again remarked that he had done an excellent job. Sidney thought it was funny how his dad, as he aged, seemed to care more about his son. When he was younger, his father would have had tons of suggestions that would have made it a better raid. *Oh well, I'll probably end up doing the same shit to my kid*, he thought.

Then Sidney XXIII said, "There were some papers I took with the diamonds. I almost threw them away. Because I didn't, I now have a lead on a large Cuban treasure that has been maintained by the Italians for many years. I know now who can tell me its location."

"Holy shit! That'll stir them up. You might want to wait a little before taking that away from them."

"Fuck 'em." I have no intention in delaying the raid, but it'll take time to get one of the men who'll tell me what I need to know. This promises to be a very major prize… Maybe I'll wait seven or eight months and let my boy help carry the prize.

He then told his father of the secluded little spot he had found on the edge of the Venezuelan jungle. After describing it, his father said, "Yeah, I know the place, that little lagoon is plum full of crocodiles."

Small world, thought Sidney. He continued with the story of Ortega and friends then said, "You want to see something funny?" He produced the old bible from the knapsack and tossed it to his dad.

His father said, "Well, I'll be damn, it looks like the Ortegas had the misfortune to cross the Sidneys' path at some other time."

Sidney told him of the entry in the logbook by Sidney XXI, his dad's father. They sat around and drank beer until it was almost dark outside and his father asked, "When are you going to get your boy?"

"In a couple of days. I'll bring him here to get your help in his train-

SIDNEY X THE PIRATE

ing." He turned and walked towards the door, expecting a beer bottle to
bounce off his back and the short sentence of, "No way, asshole! I did
mine; now you do yours!"

Surprisingly, nothing was said and nothing was thrown. Sidney XXII
had finally mellowed out.

Back at the marina's deck bar, the same people were sitting there, telling the same stories, laughing at the same punch lines, and were just as
drunk. Sidney joined them in the latter.

The next morning after taking an early morning run, Sally met him
outside his apartment door. She looked worried and upset about something serious. In her hands, she twisted and fidgeted with a rolled up paper. She said, "Sidney, I need to talk to you in private."

Sidney, dreading another bout with her insecurity, ushered her inside.
She showed him a drawing. The rendering was of his face and the Sidney's
Jolly Roger at the bottom right corner.

Sidney was stunned and asked, "Where did this come from?"

"This guy I know left it in my apartment last night. He wanted me to
post it at the bar." Then hesitantly, she asked, "What can this be about? It
is not a wanted poster, is it?"

He answered, "No. It's a personal matter between the man whose
name is on the poster and me. Are any other posters around here?"

"This is the only one I've seen."

"Sally, forget about it," and he folded the poster in half then walked
over and put it into his knapsack. "I'll be back soon," he said as he hurriedly shoved her out the door.

He muttered while thinking aloud, "This is the first time I've been
the subject of a search. We've perfected the art of blending into our surroundings; why would he go through the trouble to produce a drawing
of me and why would he be looking for me? Wonder if it has anything
to do with the Golden Boy? There's a reasonable possibility that Ortega
is connected to Vito's mob. They're on the same side of the law. Or is it a
personal thing with Jose Ortega wanting to show me his power to regain
the respect he lost aboard the catamaran?

"No matter; it has to be stopped and that fucking picture destroyed.

Ortega may have a large network of employees to get anything he wants, but that isn't going to save his ass this time."

Sidney called the telephone number given to him by Ortega. The receptionist's response to his request to speak with Mr. Ortega was, "Which one, sir? Also, whom may I say is calling?"

"I want Jose Ortega."

"I must insist that I know your name before asking Mister Ortega to speak with you, sir."

That was okay with Sidney because she had told him everything he wanted to know. He hung up the telephone, grabbed his knapsack and made a quick departure to the *Barracouta*.

With the anchor pulled and secured, he set sail to St. Thomas. He had a sloppy ride with the wind off his starboard bow and the heavy spray washing everything down in salt water. But his mind was busy organizing the actions to be taken to get everything back to normal.

Later that afternoon, he glided into the Long Bay Anchorage and set the heavy CQR anchor in case he was gone longer than anticipated.

He was in the lion's den so he did everything possible to reduce the chances that someone would recognize him—thanks to that poster. That meant staying out of crowds and changing his appearance. He wore an old ball cap that had been left aboard by the previous owners. Soused Sluggers was embroidered on its front. Also sunglasses were added. Instead of rowing the dinghy to the harbor's dinghy dock, he went to an isolated section of the city's seawall and anchored the dinghy so it swung-to in knee-deep water from shore. He walked the back streets going towards the same office building he had dropped the gift off for the girls.

Whenever other people approached, he changed facial expressions by opening his mouth like a slack jaw idiot. He bought an oversized tee shirt in a tourist gift shop that told whoever happened to read it: *One of great lovers in the land of love, St. Thomas, Virgin Islands.* He threw his Soused Sluggers hat away and bought a corny, but effective, baseball cap that had hair protruding from the back to look like a ponytail. It wasn't much of a deception, but the people looking for a man important enough for Ortega to want wouldn't be looking for that type of guy.

Ortega's parking lot was full of cars, most notability, several big Mercedes parked in the spaces closest to the back entrance. That was a good indication that Jose was in there. If Jose wasn't then the other Ortegas would know where to find him. Being exposed meant every Ortega was expendable. No quarter to anyone who threatens his isolation from society. It was not only his life, but also the future of all Sidneys.

The first floor was concrete with no windows in the walls or glass panels in the front or back doors.

He studied the building and thought about his options: wait for Ortega to leave, and then grab him. If there were too many other men around, then follow him and wait for a better opportunity at the next place. Or wait for someone to use the back entrance and charge in when the door opened, which meant damage or death to the person opening the door. Or wait under the Mercedes for one of the big guys to leave, and then take him as hostage to gain entrance into the building.

He decided to wait, and crawled under a parked car that gave him a good view of the rear door and the line of four Mercedes. It was getting late in the afternoon and he expected people would start leaving soon.

The back door opened and two well-dressed men got into one of the Mercedes and left. The door opened again for a very distinguished man in his early sixties. Three men, who undoubtedly were guards, and Maria followed him. They left in another Mercedes, leaving two more Mercedes waiting for their owners.

Several other persons came from the front entrance, looking for their cars, but no one claimed the one concealing Sidney's location. Finally, the door opened again for Jandy. She was alone and carried a briefcase that was locked in a car's trunk. She returned to the building and he still waited. He was in no hurry. It was happening as he had hoped. It was important to get the job done not how fast he could do it. Fifteen minutes later, the door opened for Jandy again, but that time Jose was behind her. Both seemed preoccupied in thought and were silent.

Sidney was amused. That's unusual for talkative Jandy to be quiet.

The easiest way was to slip out from under the car and give Jandy a thump from Billy. But he didn't want to hurt her—and in all likeliness it'd produce a reaction from Jose that would require another thumping. The thumping of Jose would not only cause hard feelings, but would probably necessitate violence again by the Ortega family for the sake of vengeance and respect.

He rolled out from under the car and covered the distance in a fluid motion without attracting Jose or Jandy's attention. When he was directly behind Jose, he said, "Looking for me?"

Jose started to spin around at the shock of someone being so close to him, especially that man in particular.

Sidney quickly grabbed both of Ortega's elbows from behind and squeezed hard on pressure points to cause intense pain. That was enough to stop Jose from trying to move. When Ortega stopped trying to get away the pressure was released, but not the grip.

Sidney said, "Hi, Jandy. Get in the back seat, Jose. Jandy will drive us around while we talk."

Jose didn't argue, but Jandy refused to move until Ortega indicated it was okay by nodding his head. She drove out of the parking lot and her nervousness became obvious by her one-sided conversation.

"How have you been, Sidney?" There was no response from the back seat.

"What you been doing since we last saw you?"

"Have you seen Maria?"

"We were hoping you'd show up. We can go to the jungle for another party now, can't we?"

Ortega said, "Shut up, Jandy. I don't think Sidney is in a very congenial mood."

She instantly shut up. As the car approached a major intersection Ortega said, "Okay Sid, where to?"

Sidney answered, "Drive to the north side of the island." Then he looked at Ortega and said, "You and I need to get a few things clear. I thought it would be best if we have a private conversation. Jandy will not be part of it."

Ortega said, "It's okay to talk in front of her, she is my right hand and totally trustworthy."

Sidney said, "No Jandy."

That was all that was said by the three of them. Jose and Jandy were feeling a lot of tension, not knowing what the mysterious Sidney had on his mind. They were sure it was related to the bulletin they had circulated.

Sidney had her drive to the road's end on the northern side of the island. The road changed from being a rough paved to a narrow dirt road that was mostly overgrown with the island's scrubby trees and thorn bushes that scratched the perfect, deep finish of the Mercedes.

Jose didn't complain and Jandy remained quiet, as well. When they could go no further Sidney said, "Jandy, get out of the car and sit on the hood where I can see you. Leave your cell phone on the dash." She did as told.

Sidney reached into his knapsack and unfolded the poster. He asked, "What is this all about?"

Ortega said, "So that's what pissed you off. I was curious about you; that's all. You have no reason to be concerned about that poster. I just was trying to find out more about you."

"I find a life-like drawing of me with instructions to find, but make no effort to confront me just contact you — and you say I have no cause for concern? That's bullshit, Ortega. I am not some dumb punk fresh off the streets. You're going to tell me what I need to know or Jandy will—it's your fucking choice."

Ortega knew he was standing on extremely dangerous ground once again, but decided to push it a little further. He said, "You mean you're giving me the same option you gave to Vito and his wife?"

The statement produced no physical response from Sidney, just the cold black penetrating stare from his intimidating eyes as he calmly said, "Exactly."

That shook the shit out of Jose Ortega. He hadn't really believed it had been Sid, and if it had, he certainly didn't want him to admit it. He started sweating—by not denying his actions, Sidney had just told him that he and Jandy wouldn't live to tell anyone about it unless something drastic happened.

Ortega asked, "Christ! Who the hell are you anyway?" It was not a challenging question, but one of awe, respect and genuine curiosity.

Sidney said, "Answer my question."

The finality in which it was said told Ortega that it was time to realize the untenable position he was in and do the things necessary to get him out of danger.

"For starters, Sid, the three of us have been very curious about you. And for no other reason than you are truly a unique individual. We can't figure you out. Maria has an ability to read people and she can only draw a blank on you. All she's sure of is that you're mysterious.

"I had her search your catamaran in the lagoon that first night to find out who you are. She found no clues. She did find your twenty thousand, however, and that's why I made that bet. I wanted to see what you were made of. You really surprised me by taking what should have been an obviously weighted bet.

"We also never knew someone so damn confident and independent. We have never seen a man who has a total lack or need for outside support and companionship. So we were just curious and we liked being around you.

"Then the expensive diamond gifts arrived for Maria and Jandy with no note or name from the sender. Soon afterward, we had a visit from Vito's organization with the story about *Golden Boy* and the stolen diamonds. We were concerned they were part of the heist."

Sidney's expression remained unchanged.

"Then the final straw was the tattoo on your shoulder. It matches one on a pirate's shoulder who single-handedly had taken my grandfather's ship and crew to the bottom after removing its valuable cargo of gold."

Sidney asked, "How would you know that? Everyone perished."

If Ortega wasn't puzzled before, he damn sure was then. He was mystified and more than mildly interested in how Sid knew about his grandfather's death in 1930—many years before Sid was born. But he didn't want to distract from the issue at hand.

"All except for one man, the cook, who managed to survive," answered Ortega.

Again, no change of expression on Sidney's face. He said nothing.

Ortega said, "I learned that from my father, but how did you know that all hands were supposed to have been lost on *my grandfather's* boat in 1930?" He was not trying to make conversation, but was genuinely curious. Perhaps, further back in his mind he wanted to develop a dialog with the strange man who fascinated him.

Also, he was intrigued by the man known only as Sidney because he was a stand-up guy who never asked anyone for anything. Men who don't go around asking for favors in Ortega's world were very rare—everybody wanted something for nothing.

"Like you, I have my sources," responded Sidney.

"My past is not free from scrutiny either, Sid; maybe I'd feel the same threat from the posters as you do. I really don't have any intention of using the information I found out about you other than for my own curiosity. I have to tell you, however, the Italians are extremely intent— or maybe dedicated is a better word—about finding those responsible for Vito's demise. They will find him or them, sooner or later."

Again Ortega hesitated to see if there was some kind of response to his last statements. There was none, only the stare from cold black eyes.

Ortega continued, "By the way, if something happens to me then my family will not only join the search, but will feel sure that the man in the drawing is responsible. My family business is very large and can be found in every corner of the world. This is our way; my family has enjoyed this position for almost 300 years. If you have a death wish, then kill me, you will soon follow."

"Really," said Sidney. It wasn't a question just a diSt.erested response.

Ortega had used the threat in hopes of gaining some lost position. He said, "Now, why don't you relax, Sid; we can go to my villa here and talk things over. I'm willing to do whatever makes you feel better."

Sidney said, "Ortega, if I wanted to put an end to this silly search of yours without first giving you a chance to stop it, believe me, I would have. It would be a simple matter to eliminate anyone who had ever seen me and then drop out of sight for as long as I want. That goes for your entire family."

Ortega wanted to argue that point but wisely retreated instead, but only for the moment.

"As far as the Italians are concerned they are my business." Sidney added, as he seemed to finalize the subject.

Ortega thought, *Sid doesn't appreciate who he's going up against. How can he be so moxie and yet so ignorant? He has a way of pissing me off. How can a lone man sit there and think he can overcome two giant organizations at their own game. It only proves his ignorance.*

He said, "I'm afraid you don't realize the reach and power of who you are messing around with, Sid."

Sidney almost smiled when he said, "I guess you're going to convince me that you and little Jandy might harm me if I don't bow and beg for your pardon."

"I am not talking about just Jandy and me, Sid; I would think you understood that by now."

"Ortega, don't forget Jandy is all you have right now. Your family and friends may be everywhere in the world, but they don't happen to be here, do they?"

There was silence from Ortega and he was starting to get pissed at Sid's attitude. He seemed to be trying to tyrannize the situation.

Sidney continued, "I know who you are, Jose. Believe me—I'm not concerned about your family. I imagine my grandfather must have listened to the same boast from your ancestor only to answer him with a slashing blow of his cutlass across his throat to silence his blubbering baby pleas."

Ortega didn't like hearing those words. Sidney reached in his knapsack and pulled the old bible out and said, "You might like to see something. This belongs to your family, but the story of your ancestor's death belongs to my family. My family doesn't have a Bible, but we do have a detailed family log. Our log has been continually maintained for over five hundred forty years. That kind of puts your family in the newcomer class doesn't it?"

Jandy would occasionally turn around and look nervously to see what was going on inside the car. The sound of the engine idling, and the switching off and on of the air conditioner, blanketed the conversation from reaching her. Her mind was exploring all options to figure what was the best thing to do. She could sit there and hope that her boss would win whatever battle was going on between them. If Ortega were killed then she was sure she would be, too.

Running away was not a good idea. The only way out was on the skinny little road that brought them there or through the mass of thorn and scrub tress. She had witnessed Sidney's ability to handle rough terrain and she would just be dying in a jungle rather than on a road where at least her body would be found.

She decided to play the only hand she was going to get. If Ortega lost, she would offer Sidney anything he wanted, including her loyalty and all of Ortega's secrets.

Ortega was also exploring his options, but at a much faster rate than Jandy. *Fuck it, here I am again. At bat with two strikes with the third pitch already hurling at me and I've got dirt in my eye. I could back off and lose the game once again to the bastard.*

He said, "Sid, my flyer on you was only seen by my organization. The Italians know nothing about you. They asked for our help, and normally we would help out, but not in this case. I consider you a friend even though you have threatened me with death both times we have negotiated our differences. However, I realize that in both cases, I put myself at jeopardy; you have never instigated the problems. You obviously are not a person that loses and usually I am not either so I can and do respect you for your actions. I just picked on the wrong guy this time. I apologize if I have caused any problems for you. The poster will be brought back in and destroyed. Your actions and everything else we have discussed will remain between you and me. I assure you it will not go any further.

"The one possible exception to this is my father. I would like to give the Bible to him and tell him how I came by it—but will not if you prefer. My father is a man much like you; he will understand and not say anything. He would be very pleased to meet you.

"The Italians have nothing to offer us; we could wipe them off the face of the earth if there was a good enough reason. You have nothing to gain by killing me; you might be able to elude my family, but why live that kind of life when it's totally unnecessary?"

Ortega continued, "Apparently, we both are from very old families that maintained certain values and respect. I would like to offer my friendship to you and all it represents in exchange for yours. I can't begin to tell you how curious I am about your family's history."

Sidney understood how Ortega felt and was encouraged that Ortega had said everything he had. He didn't want to kill two people he had laughed and rolled around in a jungle mud puddle with—snorting like a pig. There had never been good times like that in his life. Killing was done to remove barriers between what he wanted and him. There was no need for killing now. Ortega offered his friendship and a promise not to interfere with Sidney... And, Jose was right; Sidney didn't need two worldwide criminal organizations looking for him while he was training the boy. It would be a hell of a challenge though, and he did love challenges.

Sidney stuck out his open hand, offering peace. Ortega shook it; he was very happy at the outcome. Once again, his talent and glib tongue had saved his arrogant ass. But, he knew Sidney had that extra sense and if he had been anything but totally sincere he wouldn't be alive at that very moment.

Ortega said, "Thanks, Sid. I won't betray your trust. Why don't you come over and stay at the villa, I really do want to introduce you to my father. I know you two will be friends. Also, Maria is there and she wants to see you."

Sidney replied, "Some other time. I'm going to keep a low profile until everyone forgets that fucking flyer you put out. I'll see Maria when I return to the lagoon if she's still around."

Ortega accepted the decline of his invitation and asked, "Who exactly are you and your family, if you don't mind me asking?"

Sidney answered, "We've always been solo pirates," very matter-of-factly.

Ortega believed him, but said, "If your family has been pirates and around that long surely there would be tales of the family told by the crews of many ships. Did your ancestors operate under another name?"

Sidney hesitated. He had never told another soul about his family, but he had an inner need to speak, "We are alone. Witnesses don't usually see us. Most of our raids have been blamed on other pirates that have come and gone. The others are unexplained losses of ships at sea. But we are not totally unknown; many generations of seamen of the world know of me and my ancestors by another name."

Ortega, uncontrollably fascinated by what he was told, had hundreds of questions for Sidney. He said, "Sid, this fascinates the shit out of me. I'd really like to hear more about your family. Mind if I ask what name you're known by to seamen?"

"Maybe someday, Jose. You know how much I appreciate my family's privacy, and I have already told you more than has been told to anyone."

He felt secure that the search for him was over and then he rolled the window down and told Jandy they were ready to leave. Ortega's repeated invitations to visit were declined, but, out of frustration, Sidney got Ortega to stop arguing by telling him that he couldn't—he had to pick up his son.

Both Jandy and Ortega were surprised that such a man would have or much less be concerned about a child. He explained that the mother died and he had to raise the boy. Jandy, as her normal self, was busy talking about everything she could think of on the way back to town.

Sidney didn't mind her chatter as it removed any possibility that he would be placed in a position to speak more or answer more questions about himself and his family that intrigued Ortega so much. Sidney, with an undercurrent of ego that he didn't understand, thought it would be fun to show Ortega his treasure, but knew that would never happen. Only the eyes of the Sidneys were permitted that honor. But it would have been fun to watch Ortega's expressions when he saw the immense treasure filling the cavern.

When they reached a little bar on the edge of town, Sidney said, "Jandy, stop here. This is where I get out."

Ortega said, "Well, at least let's go in that bar for a couple of drinks."

As he got out of the car he said, "I'll take you up on the drinks when I see you at the lagoon one day. I'll be spending a lot of time there."

Jandy told him she would be looking forward to meeting his son. *Wonder what she'll say about my plans to dump the boy in that wild jungle and leave him by himself for a half a year.*

After the big Mercedes was lost in the traffic of St. Thomas's only major through street, he went into the little bar. A rum was ordered, then another before he used the telephone to call for a taxi. One hour from the time he left Ortega he was back on deck of the *Barracouta* and the anchor was up and stowed away.

As he steered the boat out of West Gregory Channel, he calculated he'd get into Culebra Island's harbor just after dark. The little village of Dewey was a favorite place for him; not much was there except a few dingy bars and the world's greatest pizza. He never passed up an opportunity to stop for one of Charlie Chan's Chinese pizzas, which was totally out of character for the sleepy little fishing village.

The only tourists who went there were divers who had heard of the excellent reefs. The little village had not changed much over the years; even tourist dollars couldn't change it. Nobody bothered to lock their homes: boaters didn't chain their dinghies to the dock when in town; the town and its occupants were at peace.

Sidney did his best to contribute to the village's economy that night by buying a large pizza and lots of rum. He also bought lots of canned food and several gallon jugs of drinking water. He had not bothered to measure how much water he had on board the boat. He also purchased a couple of tee shirts and shorts thinking he should try to look decent when he picked up the boy.

The next morning, after a hard but invigorating swim around the harbor, he was ready to continue on westerly to Puerto Rico. His breakfast beans and room temperature beer were consumed while under sail, hugging the south shore of Culebra. He picked out two landmasses on the horizon and knew the narrow channel between them separated the main land of Puerto Rico from the string of barrier islands just offshore. Those islands served as notice that they were all that separated the Caribbean Sea from the Atlantic Ocean.

On the outside of the barrier islands, sea conditions changed. No longer was there protection from the wind by the islands, and the long waves that had been building from the African coast were readily apparent. The big ocean swells in the twenty knot breeze made for near perfect sailing in the heavy *Barracouta*. By early afternoon, the huge stone structure of Fort Morro was off his port beam and the channel leading to San Juan's harbor was before him. The fort was magnificent. He found a slip at the marina at the eastern-most end of the harbor. It wasn't his first visit; it offered a short walk to the casinos, a short walk to the whorehouse, the Happy Albatross, and there were bars all over the place. The place was perfect. For a week he relaxed; won and lost at the casinos, and screwed most of the beautiful young girls at the whorehouse.

At week's end, he was ready to set sail and resume his life of action and challenge—of babysitting a boy puppy. He hadn't left the girls of the Happy Albatross until five A.M. The downwind sail to Puerto Plata would take enough time to recover from his excessive merrymaking.

He had a small problem arriving in the Dominican Republic. Getting around Customs agents was always a problem and he wasn't able to pull directly into Puerto Plata as agents were always on the lookout for passing yachties.

They enjoyed searching boats, leering at the women, and munching on free goodies from the visiting boaters. A bribe was not always the thing to do as some of the men were very honest and took their jobs seriously—but all accepted snacks and cold drinks.

Fortunately, one of his forefathers had found an excellent little lagoon on the north shore that was only a mile away from the only road leading to Puerto Plata. That little lagoon was known only by some of the local fishermen. It didn't show up on the nautical charts so there were never visiting boats in the secluded cove. He wouldn't be bothered by the law there, but he might have a problem with thieves stripping his boat while he was away.

His other problem was to get the six and a half foot draft boat over and through the rocks that came up at the entrance. He had planned to arrive at high tide. He entered the tricky narrow cut in the rock walls about an hour before high tide. In case he didn't make it, he'd have an hour to get off before the water receded. He entered the cut at full speed with the wind on his port stern quarter. He drove the boat past the opening before swinging the bow around so the wind was blowing hard on a beam reach. The boat healed over so much that the jib winch was in the water and lifted the keel another foot off the bottom as he glided over the hard rocks below.

Safely inside the harbor, he slacked the sails and the boat coasted up to a vertical rock wall. He let go his anchor.

There wasn't another boat or person anywhere in the lagoon. He decided to wait for a fisherman before leaving the lagoon. He'd pay the man to keep the other thieves away. That night, he heard the sound of oars rubbing against wooden rails of a fishing boat.

A tired fisherman was rowing; the oars carelessly splashed into the sea. He had planned to sleep in the skiff until morning then continue towards Puerto Plata with his hand-line catch.

Sidney stood on the aft deck and said to the fisherman, "Tie your boat to me and come aboard. You can sleep in a bed and I've plenty of rum."

After a short conversation, Sidney knew the man could be trusted. He said, "I'll pay you two hundred American dollars to watch my boat for three days. That will offset your loss if your catch goes bad. All you have to do is keep people away from the boat."

The fisherman was delighted; that much money was more than a month's income. He eagerly said, "Yes, thank you. No one will bother your boat. I think my fish will be all right, they're covered with my tarp and two fifty pound blocks of ice. Will you tell the man who owns the feed store as you get into town that I'm okay? Ask him to tell my family not to worry."

Sidney celebrated his arrival in Puerto Plata only after telling the man at the Toro's Feed Store about the fisherman. Then he was off for a lengthy stay at Salty Sailor's Whorehouse and Saloon. It was run by a guy called Salty Tarp. No one knew what his real name was. Salty, an American, got fed up with the self-serving congress of baboons led by an egomaniac president who couldn't do a damn thing right, and the civilized public who let them get away with fucking over the taxpaying citizens, and short-changing the military that the politicians happily sent to some really shitty places to die so some fat cat could appease his master and get reelected. Salty came to Puerto Plata on a whim after leaving the Middle East where he had been doing a job that he refused to talk about… other than the rotten politics.

It was a fun place and the prices were right. The only rules in the joint: don't steal from the customers, don't hurt the girls, and everything else is okay. It was a place where mostly hard case sailors hung out, either passing through or dropouts like Salty. Fights between customers were frequent, but usually not serious since everyone was too drunk to do any real damage. Fights between the girls earned them huge tips from the customers. Live, drink, and fuck Mary merrily was the house's motto — every girl in the place was named Mary— Mary Jane, Mary Annette, etc.

Sidney went through several Marys and forty eight hours of drinking and eating charcoal-roasted peanuts that street-urchin boys sold before finally making arrangements to rent a car from Salty.

After a big steak breakfast he drove out to see the first woman who berthed his second choice of a son. He sat in the car with the boy's nervous mother watching the boy. He was skinny and happy and played with his three half-sisters and the family mutt. Sidney watched for a while then said to the mother, "You can have the boy."

The mother looked confused. Before she could respond, Sid pulled out the money they had agreed on and put it in her hand. Emotions that began when her bundle of joy arrived six years ago—and had been simmering and building behind a frail wall separating her love and conscience from a bought-and-paid-for promise waiting for that day—gave way. She cried openly with happiness; she wasn't going to lose the son she loved. The fact that the man had paid her enough money to make life pleasant for her family for years to come also contributed to her joy.

As Sidney drove by to see the next boy he thought, *hope he's going to make the grade. If not I'll have to start over. Can't steal one— it has to be Sidney's bloodline. I should've knocked up a dozen whores.*

No one was around when he pulled up to the little house. Its brightly blue and yellow painted exterior stood out from lush green bushes around it. The lawn, bare reddish-brown dirt, was surrounded with a piecemeal fence made up of assorted limbs, boards and broken planks. The family's goats and a dozen skinny chickens roamed freely in the yard looking for *anything* to eat.

Sidney stepped over the fence and walked up to an open window. The mother was busy cutting vegetables into small pieces for the stew pot. A small piece of raw, coarse red meat sat on the counter and was covered with flies while waiting its turn to be added to the pot.

The once beautiful woman, now beaten with the hardship of life, looked up at Sidney. As she recognized him, her eyes began to water with the sorrow she had been regretting for six years—dreading this day would arrive.

A pang of emotion that he had never felt and didn't know it had a name, compassion, sprang forth. *My mother probably looked and felt the same way. Wish I could remember what she looked like.*

He asked, "Where's the boy?"

Thousands of times during the years she had answered that question. She wanted to tell him the boy had died or run off or a lot of other things, but she was an honest Catholic woman and couldn't lie. She had been eager to make the deal seven years ago and the money had certainly made life for her family much better since that time. She had to honor the deal no matter the amount of pain it caused her and the other children. Everyone loved little Sidney.

Tears ran from her eyes as she spoke, "He is fishing. Patron… please— could you find your heart. Please release me from our bargain so long ago. He is such a little boy; a boy who loves and who needs his mother. He is loved so much by his brothers and sisters and by my husband. I will find a way to return your money. Please don't take my baby."

She could speak no more as her sadness turned into a powerful sorrow; tears that had been streaming now flowed in a torrent.

Sidney said, "I cannot, Señora. I will take care of him and will let him visit you often when he is older. You know he will have a better life if he comes with me and so will you and your other children."

He produced the promised amount of cash and spread it on the open windowsill before her. Amidst her sorrow, the promise of a much better life for her entire family created only more gut-wrenching confusion.

Sensibility, however, ruled—so much money meant the loss of her young-est child, but was for the betterment of his siblings and parents. Emotion fought to reject the fortune before her; she was overcome with sorrow and knew she could never stop crying—as she pulled the stacks of Ameri-can dollars toward her.

CACHORRO

"WHY THE FUCK WOULD YOU WANT TO LIVE IN THIS PLACE," SNORTED Vincenzo to Gino, who had driven to JFK airport to pick him up. "New York City, what a fucking dump!"

Vincenzo had never liked New York and especially disliked any New Yorker who defended the place. They all started their arguments with the same crap that Gino did, "Oh, it is a cultural place. Where else can you find so many refined restaurants? It's the world's center for entertainment, so many theaters, actors and dancers. Only in New York can you feel the electric atmosphere of excitement. It's certainly the world's meeting place for *cultured* people."

He responded to Gino exactly as he did to any other egotistical New Yorker. "Yeah, your culture in the Bowery, Bronx, and beautiful Harlem offers lots of entertainment. Especially if you are the elite on top of the pile of maggots, faggots, crack-heads, gutter whores, black street gangsters, and fucked up politicians kissing the union bosses' asses. If any of you conceited narrow minded, cocksuckers had enough balls, you'd go out to see what the real world is really about. And if you did, you wouldn't come back here unless you wanted to puke some of New York's *refined* food in the face of the people who made you believe all that bullshit. Half of the city is made up of fairies dancing and prancing, the rest of you fucking fairies just pay for the so-called privilege to watch the faggots prance. Trouble is, you fucking people believe the shit puked out by advertising agencies, and you are too full of self-imposed cultural hypercritical views and stupidity to know it. And there ain't a fucking one of you who is not a fucking whiner."

He had never made a friend in New York; with his attitude it was unlikely he ever would, and that delighted Vincenzo.

Gino dropped Vincenzo off at the entrance of Long Island's finest hospital. He offered to park the car and wait until Vincenzo was ready to go to his hotel.

Vincenzo looked at him in disdain and muttered, "No. You go ahead. I'd hate to think that you might be late to see the dancing fairies tonight at one of your fucking *cultured* events."

With apparent respect, Gino said good night as he drove away, but inside he was fuming about the crude man from Sicily. After he was well away from one of the few men who he was deathly afraid of, he boldly snarled, "What would someone from Italy know about culture and the theater anyway—asshole!"

Vincenzo wasn't able to learn which rooms Vito's wife or Lizy were in. As far as the receptionist was concerned they were not in that hospital. Vincenzo knew they were, but was unable to get her to cooperate enough to find out. She was just another fucking New Yorker.

Vincenzo, however, behaved and got directions to the hospital administrations office. Once there, he boldly walked up to that receptionist, and, over her objections, wrote his name down on the back of one of the papers on her desk. He handed the paper to her and said, "You get that tight ass of yours into the administrator's office and tell him that the man with that name is here for Mrs. Meridino."

Being a sophisticated New Yorker, she didn't move her tight little ass—she moved her skillful finger to the intercom and told the administrator's secretary, "A very belligerent, Mr. Vincenzo Jones is here and is demanding to see Mr. Clonestein."

The secretary on the other end of the intercom had the same attitude as the receptionist and everyone else in the fucking city as far as Vincenzo was concerned. Not more than a minute later; however, a scurrying Mr. Clonestein was out to meet Vincenzo. He apologized profusely for not putting his name on the restricted list of names permitted to visit the two women and personally took him to their private suites.

Stationed outside of the suite's door were two men in black suits.

These were not the Puerto Ricans Tony had fly with the women from Aruba. Yep, they were very obvious New York Italians.

As Gino, they were metro-sexuals. Their hair was exactly right, clothes were the latest fashion, and shoes highly polished as were their fingernails and faces. Everything was scrubbed and shined. Their accent, Hollywood Italian cliché, and the rude speedy manner in which they spoke, confirmed they were New York pansies—with big guns.

Vincenzo realized he was getting a little super critical and just wished he could return to Sicily where men acted as men should. He explained who he was and went into the suite. Inside were two clones of the two metro-pansies standing outside of the room.

He saw Mrs. Meridino first, but she absolutely was no help. Her head and hands were bandaged and her eyes, once beautifully blue, were now red and puffy. She was still in shock and had no idea what had happened to her or her husband of twenty years. She and Vito went to bed and she woke up on the salon floor all taped up and in pain. She had lain there naked until someone picked her up. She had heard nothing and wasn't even aware of the missing extremities until the tape was pulled off in the first hospital. During the interview she kept crying and asking, "Why? Why me?"

Lizy was in better shape mentally, but suffered physically; the blow to her face had altered her beautiful face. Her jaw was wired shut and a tube extended from her mouth as she attempted to drink some juice left by a nurse. Of course, she couldn't talk. After a long pleasant one-sided conversation to make her feel comfortable with his presence, Vincenzo asked, "Did you see the man who hurt you?"

Lizy picked up the bedside tablet she used for her only form of communication and wrote, "I saw him but very briefly. What I saw was just a shape, not features."

"How many people did you see?"

"Only one, a man."

"Was he black, white, Latino or Asian?"

She wrote, "It was so fast. I turned around in the shower and he was there. He was in black clothes and was either a black man or he had black stuff on his face. I was so afraid I don't remember which."

She shuddered at the memory and kept writing, "His eyes were from a dead man. They were black and showed nothing in them, they were horrible. I can never forget those eyes."

"What language did he speak?"

"He didn't say anything."

"Was he a big or small?"

She wrote, "Bigger than me."

Vincenzo was quiet for a moment while thinking, *well, at least she knew he has black uncaring eyes, that's new. He's taller than she is and that isn't much help; she's only five-foot three. Shit, everybody's taller.*

He decided that maybe he could learn more later after she healed and could talk. *I'll get her wound up and she'll start jabbering, something useful may pop out.*

DOMINICAN REPUBLIC

SIDNEY SAT IN THE CAR FOR TWO HOURS WAITING FOR THE BOY TO COME home. The sobbing from his mother in the house would fade only to start again when the thought of her loss overcame her once again.

When the little boy came into the yard he was with two other boys. All of them dirty, laughing and carrying fish wrapped in banana leaves. He recognized the kid from last year's brief visit. In fact, it wasn't much of a visit; it hadn't been much more than a few words spoken from the same car he had rented from Salty.

The kid recognized him and appeared happy to see his father again. Had he known the purpose of his visit was to separate him from his loving mother and family the boy would have run and hid.

Little Sid knew his father had come to see him, but always thought of him as a stepfather, not his natural dad. He was too young to understand the meanings of the words dad and father and had never heard the word stepfather. His dad, the man that took care of him and the family, was a farmer. He grew rice so the family had food to eat and they were content.

He wasn't aware that his stepdad, who loved him like his own child, was more than willing to let the rich foreigner raise the boy—especially since it would mean so much money for the rest of the family. Now they could have a decent home, buy a tractor and more land to plant enough crops each year to really provide very well for the remaining family. Over the years his stepfather had accepted that this day would arrive and why not, after all, it was the man's natural son. His wife had been expecting the child when he had met her.

The woman's husband wasn't at home that day as he was working in the fields and had no idea this was to be the day. Sidney had wanted him there, as he seemed to be more understanding and added stability to the situation. With the husband away, he figured he was going to have to listen to the woman making a big sobbing deal about the splitting up of her family. And she did and he did.

Sidney wasn't sympathetic; she had agreed, and was being well paid. The fact that he was not the least bit happy at the prospect of being saddled with a kid for the next decade didn't make him feel any degree of charitably. If he was to be miserable then she could be, too. If it had not been necessary to keep the Sidney family going, he wouldn't have considered taking the kid, much less making the boy into a man.

While she moaned, bitched, and groaned, Sidney was in thought. My father probably sat in the front yard of some house years ago, waiting for me to join the Sidneys like the twenty-one men before him. That's a strong obligation. It's more than obligation... it's the only way of the Sidneys, and that's something to be proud about. Go ahead woman, waste your fucking tears.

The mother tried her best to stop crying and act positive about the situation as she told her little boy, "You are going to live with your father for a while. This is for your own good. Your father is very rich and will be able to give you all of the things you want. You'll get to travel and see all the different places. You will have fun and you'll have all the food you want, and nice clothes to wear... Promise me you will never forget your mother."

She and the boy were standing in the back yard while she washed the naked boy with water from a pitcher. An old ragged towel was given to him to dry off while she went to get his best clothes.

When the boy came to the front yard he stood in front of the little shack that was his only home. He wore his only long pants and shirt, both strictly reserved for church on Sundays. He looked puzzled and scared and was very close to tears. He clinched his mother's hand tightly.

Sidney looked at the boy and thought, *come on you little chicken shit, let's get out of here.* He was forced to get out of the car when the mother stopped about ten feet away; she got on her knees and locked both arms around the boy in an intense hug. Her eyes were almost invisible from the swollen glands.

That's as far as she's going. She's decided not to let the boy leave. He had to do something to make her feel better, and he couldn't hurt her in front of the kid. *Got to get this fucking thing over with.*

He walked over to her, faking sympathy and hugged her. "Don't worry, Anna, the boy will come to see you often. And as he becomes older will spend even more time with you. I promise."

He, of course, was lying; the boy would never have any idea who that woman was in a few short years nor would he ever see his mother again. Motherhood didn't mix with being a Sidney.

Hugging the woman stirred Sidney. The close proximity to her caused him to remember the wild nights he had spent with her while he tried to get her pregnant. He wanted to fuck her again.

As if that thought had been heard by the woman, she sighed with resignation; it sounded like the death rattle heard by dying people. She released the boy. Sidney put his arm behind the boy's shoulders and directed him to the car. The little boy was crying then, but walked bravely as directed to the driver's side door. Sidney had to motion the boy to slide over to make room for him.

It was the kid's first car ride and it was exciting, an event he had always wanted to experience. But he hated that car and the silent man taking him away, making his mother and siblings so sad.

Eventually, the boy's crying stopped, but not because of encouragement from Sidney. He had said nothing, but he damn sure wanted to. The little crybaby was aggravating. His thoughts: *This is my new life. My days of freedom and fun are over. I'm a fucking babysitter. Gotta find a way to make Dad take him.*

The crying stopped when the boy noticed the speed as the country-side flew by. He really was going fast. Five minutes later the boy was sitting up and looking at the marvels of transportation. Five minutes after that, he was talking up a storm about his new adventure in the automobile; something none of the people he knew had ever done.

Sidney muttered, "Well kid, you ain't seen nothing yet."

When they arrived at Salty's, Sid told the kid, "Time to eat. Order anything you want to eat and drink. I'm having rum and a steak."

Little Sid said, "That's what I want, too."

He had never been to a restaurant before. Never had tasted meat other than what came off wild animals, fish or chickens, and that was in the form of shredded pieces mixed with rice. His father had often talked about eating steak like the rich people do, but they never did.

Rum also was foreign to him; neither his family nor any other people he knew drank alcoholic beverages. Instead of rum, he was served a Coke, not at Sidney's direction—the bartender had made that decision.

Sidney told her, "The boy ordered rum. Bring it."

The kid's first drink of the odd smelly drink produced the expected result. Little Sid coughed, his face muscles constricted in pain as the fiery liquid raced down his throat, and he gagged.

Sidney said, "Good, ain't it?"

"It's hot, it's burning me. Tastes bad."

"Good. Stay away from my rum supply. Wash it down with that Coke, sissy."

That was Sidney XXIV's first lesson; the boy could do or have anything he wanted—all he had to do was take it. If he didn't like it, leave it alone.

Little Sid was afraid to drink the Coke; the rum had been the worst thing he had ever had in his mouth and never tasting a soda before, thought the Coke would taste just like it. But he didn't like being called a sissy so he cautiously took a sip. It was a strange, zesty flavor and the best tasting drink he had ever experienced. He was accustomed to sweet drinks since there was an abundance of fruits around, but the carbonation was a new sensation.

The hot sizzling steak off the grill smelled delicious and made the boy ravishingly hungry. When it was served, he watched his new father cut his with a big knife that he took from his sheath, and a fork. Little Sid mimicked his father, but it was difficult to cut and his appetite grew impatient and demanded food.

Sidney remembered the first time he had eaten a steak and said, "Pick it up and eat it. You'll be able to cut it when you get a proper knife."

The boy didn't hesitate; the juicy flavor was tasty and ran freely down his chin. The thick, chewy meat was quickly gulped down to get another bite in his mouth. A jaguar couldn't have done a better job making food disappear.

After devouring the meat, he was sorry he hadn't saved a piece for his mother and father to taste, and then he remembered that he wouldn't be seeing them for a while. The thought saddened him—for a moment.

After Sidney XXIII had his fill, he paid one of Salty's people to take him down the road where he could walk through the jungle to his boat. Before he left, however, he felt compelled to say goodbye to Mary.

Little Sid was amused by all of the new things that had happened to him in the last few hours. They even seemed to overshadow the sorrow he had felt and demonstrated so tearfully in front of his mother. While he waited for his new father to come out of the room he had gone to with the woman, he sat at the bar and talked to the bartender until Sidney came out.

"Let's go, kid."

The boy was puzzled when his father directed the driver to stop the car in the middle of the narrow road. They got out and his father led him through the dense brush with ease that even his real father had not been able to do. The walk through the jungle was filled with one-sided jabber filled with unremitting questions from the boy. The boy had a bad case of the *whys?*

The fisherman was still guarding the boat. Two more boats had come into the lagoon and were tied to the *Barracouta*.

Sidney thought, *if they think they can rob me, the boy is about to get his first lesson in the art of killing.*

It turned out they were fishermen and friends of the boat-sitter who happened to stop by for a chat. Sidney paid the man and the fishermen departed, leaving them in the quiet solitude of the little lagoon for the night. It was the first night the boy had ever been away from his family; the first night the man had ever been with his son. Both were not at ease with their circumstance.

The boy, however, was fascinated with the huge boat. He had never imagined he would be on something as grand as that. He couldn't understand what anything was, but he was a bright boy so he was naturally curious about every little thing in his new life and proved it with his continual endless stream of questions.

Sidney tolerated it for a while then told him to go to his bed and sleep. He went up on deck with his last bottle of rum and sat on the transom with his legs hanging over the side. He looked at the jungle around him while listening to its inhabitants welcome nightfall.

Finally, the first peace I've had had since the little shit got in the car. The night was perfect; the breeze just enough to keep the bugs away and cool his skin. The sky filled with stars and a full moon as the rum bottle gave up its last drop. He was ready for sleep and lay down in the cockpit. He awoke when the sky began to fill with dim light.

As he slowly became aware of dawn and his return to reality from the dreams of the night, he saw a small face. It was an innocent's face, complete with big round dark eyes with no expression other than curiosity, only inches from his. Then the rush of reality swept over him as he recognized his son. *What the fuck is he doing?*

Then the sun's first rays started spilling out from the voids in the towering tropical trees. Black trees and massive boulders surrounding the peaceful lagoon were silhouetted by the glary light of morning.

He laid there for a moment looking at the boy's face that was so full of innocent honesty. There were no secrets in that face—not yet. He looked like a little puppy. *That's what I'll call him—Cachorro.*

Sitting up, he asked, "What are you doing out here?"

"I got scared being by myself down there." The boy had slept with his brothers every night since birth.

"Do you know how to swim?" Sidney asked.

The kid said, "Sure, we always play in the pond where we go fishing."

"Well, let's see how well you swim," and he jumped over the life lines into the clear water of the lagoon. The boy jumped feet first right after him, but didn't come up.

Sidney dove under water to find the boy wiggling and moving everything he had to get to the surface. He grabbed him by the hair and pulled him to the surface. The boy was scared and spurting. He didn't understand why he hadn't been able to touch bottom. In the clear water it looked as shallow as the pond everybody went to for swimming. Swimming to him meant walking around in waist-deep water while splashing each other. He had never been in deep water.

After a few minutes of struggling, the boy acted more secure in Sidney's arms and stopped fighting to get out of the water by any means possible. The only means he could think of had been to crawl on top of Sidney's head and shoulders. He wanted to be back on the dry safety of the big boat in the worst way.

Sidney said, "That's not swimming. It's drowning. You're going to learn how to swim like a fish today. I want you to get on my back and hold on to my shoulders."

Sidney swam for a while doing breaststrokes. The boy slowly gained confidence in the man's ability to keep them both afloat. Soon, he was enjoying the ride and the cool flow of water across his body as they slid freely about the lagoon. After several minutes, Sidney stopped and began treading water.

He said, "I want you to relax and trust me. I will not let you drown."

Before turning him loose he said, "I'm teaching you how to tread water so you can stay on top for a long time. Take a deep breath of air and keep your lungs full. You might sink below the water at first when I turn you loose, but if you hold your breath and move your hands the way I'm moving mine, then you will come back up. Don't be afraid, just do it."

He then demonstrated how to move his hands from side to side and asked, "Have you ever watched a frog swim with its legs?"

The boy had and kicked his legs the same way. Sidney held the boy's midsection so his head was out of the water and told him to practice his frog swim. The boy did the kick reasonably well and soon was supporting his own weight in the water. Sidney provided the stability.

"Okay, boy, you're supporting your own weight now. Start moving your hands like I did and I'm going to turn you loose. The boy whined for his dad not to turn him loose, but must have had the inbred instinct that it was going to happen so he prepared for the worst. He sucked in an enormous amount of air then held his breath as Sidney released him.

Sidney fought back the urge to laugh at the scared little kid. The boy had so much air in his lungs and mouth that he probably couldn't have pulled him under. His cheeks were puffed out with air, his face was turning red, but he was swimming. As soon as the boy realized it, he laughed, expelling his air and sank but recovered with a new breath.

Sidney gradually pulled away letting the boy get more comfortable about being alone in deep water. With every exhale, and a fast gulp of new air, the boy sank under the surface, but came bobbing back up. Finally, Sidney pulled the boy back to the boat and hoisted him aboard.

The two Sidneys sat down on the aft deck and the bigger one said, "Never forget what you just learned. It will save your life many times in the future. Even after you become a great swimmer you will have to tread water sometimes just to rest up and give your other muscles a chance to relax. Every morning this week you will practice treading water like that."

He had the boy's attention; he was eager to learn. Sidney hoped all the lessons ahead for the kid would be that easy, for both of them. That particular lesson was going easy because it was fun to swim and the boy could hardly wait to do it again.

Sidney asked, "Are you rested enough to swim some more?"

"Yes, let's go!"

With that, Sidney picked him up by the seat of his pants and tossed him over board. The boy yelled a loud protest all the way to the water. When he surfaced, he scared every fish within a mile away with his frantic splashing. Soon, however, the fear subsided, but the splashing continued. By the end of the day, the boy could tread water as well as anybody, better than most. That was the only thing Sidney wanted to teach him that day and he had learned it well.

Sid watched the boy and knew then that was why Sidneys were isolated so early in life. *We learn these lessons very quickly because there were no other kids to play with— no distractions to prevent us from learning the lessons. I could tell him that now, but it'd do no good. Best to do as I was taught. It works.*

That night dinner was beans, rice, and a lobster that Sidney caught with bare hands. The boy had never seen a lobster; he thought it was ugly. He showed the boy how to twist off the tail, and then break off the tail flipper, and push the meat out using his thumb.

When finished with the meal, Sidney announced, "We have just eaten the last of the food we have. What do you think we should do about it?"

Most kids would have responded by saying, "Go to the store." Cachorro however, hadn't been brought up with the luxury of a nearby store or even the money to buy things with. He answered, "Catch a fish… and I can find some fruit and some tubers along the shore."

Sidney had a funny feeling inside. The feeling was unknown and had no name to him, but most fathers would recognize it as a father's pride. His son was willing to go out and get his own food.

I made the right choice when I selected this boy over the other. The other boy would probably be crying and sucking his thumb, wishing he was at home playing dolls with his fucking sisters.

"Cachorro, this is salt water. Tubers are only in fresh water, like your pond."

"I'm not a puppy. I'm a boy," the kid said with a smile.

"I will call you Cachorro until you prove you aren't afraid of your surroundings, wherever you are."

Cachorro had a good feeling about himself, and, as usual, was full of chatter. Most of his questions could be answered and most were handled with a simple yes or no, allowing Sidney not to be over-burdened with conversation. Some others required more elaborate answers, which Sidney did without trying to shorten the response.

It was very important for the boy to know that he could count on every word from his father as being the truth, no matter how unpleasant the answer might be. Such a question Cachorro asked was, "Where are you taking me and how long before we come back?"

Sidney answered, "We're going to go sailing for weeks. We'll have no food or water so we will have to catch and find our own until we arrive on an island where your grandfather lives."

"My grandfather lives next door to my mother."

"This is your real grandfather; he is my father."

Next the boy asked, "How long will we be there?"

Sidney said, "For a long time. It will always be your home. Later, you will travel to many different places, but you will always return; there is something special for you there."

"What?"

"I can't tell you yet because you're not old enough and have not demonstrated your ability to guard the secret of your true family."

"When can I go see my mother?"

"You will be a lot older before you can go back. After you have learned all of the things I must teach you."

He broke up the question and answer period by telling the boy, "It's time for you to sleep. You can sleep in any berth you like. I'm sleeping on deck where it is cooler."

Lying in the cockpit, he heard the boy going from berth to berth, trying each to see which he liked best. Just as he was about to nod off, he heard the rustle of the kid curling up on the cushion next to him.

Cachorro asked in a tired voice," What if we don't catch any fish?"

"Then we are going to lose some weight," his dad answered in the middle of a big yawn.

The next morning, both of them woke up hungry. It was time for another lesson. Sitting on the deck with their legs hanging down towards the water, Sidney started telling him the basics of surviving in the type of area they were currently in.

"Most of your life you will be on the sea or in a jungle. Both have endless food offerings for you. You just have to know where to look to find them and what to eat without getting sick. At sea, you have deep-water conditions and shallow shore conditions. We are now in shore conditions and that's always best for finding food. The shallower the water, the more chances you have to find food."

"Good. Let's go get something to eat."

"In a minute. Before we get to our island, we'll be finding food in both places. Soon you'll know how feed yourself at sea for an unlimited amount of time. It isn't hard to do, you just need to think like you have been designed to do by nature and react likewise. There are several ways to get food. You can catch it with your hands in the shallow tidal pools of the rocks around the shore. You can rig up a fishing line, using lures to trick the fish into biting your hook."

The boy was all ready for that, as he loved fishing. In fact, he had spent most every day fishing with his friends; his catches provided many evening meals.

Sidney continued his lessons, "Okay, today we catch our fish, using only things we can find growing on shore. Here we go."

He dove overboard and made a special effort not to look back at the little boy standing on the deck in indecision. His father was swimming further away every second he waited and he wasn't so certain that he could swim today like he did yesterday. When Sidney failed to turn around or even acknowledge the boy's pleas to wait for him, Cachorro jumped in with legs and arms spread wide to start swimming before hitting the water. After a moment of adjusting to the water and assuring himself that, like yesterday, he could swim—but he wasn't going anywhere.

When Sid reached shore he yelled, "Angle your hands so you move in this direction."

After a bit, the boy started slowly moving and before he reached shore had figured out how to dog paddle. When the boy reached the shore, Sidney said, "That stroke has been provided to you by God, just like he has for every other living land animal that has ever lived on this planet. The best way to learn how to swim is to start drowning; necessity is a good teacher and if an animal doesn't listen to nature telling him how to survive, then it is too stupid to be alive. In that case the animal needs to die so the stupid in him will not be passed down to the offspring and theirs.

Cachorro asked, "You must be smart. Does that mean I'm smart, too?"

"I don't know yet. Ask me after I get to know you."

Sidney showed him some thorns on a small tree and said, "When I tell you things, do not be concerned about what the name is. Just remember what it looks like up close and from a distance and how to use it. Names are only words needed by those who know little about things, but must put names on everything so it means something to them. Next time you want a fishing hook, look for this tree. If you want to name it, choose your own name, do not be concerned what others might call it, even me. You will know why it is here and that is all that is important." Already, Sidney, unknowingly, was teaching his son not to worry about communicating with other people.

Sidney cut two thorns off of a branch, leaving a two inch piece of its pliable bark attached. The thorns were tied together in a "V" shape. Next he looked for and found a certain type of bush. It was chopped down with his knife, and then the branches were cut off. The bark was stripped off in quarter-inch strips and was six-feet long. He kneaded each strip until it was pliable. He then tied them end-to-end until he had a cord twenty feet long. One end was tied to the two thorns.

Next, he found flowers growing on several types of plants. He chose red and yellow flowers and rolled them between his hands, occasionally spitting on them for moisture and to add a scent until he had an elongated colorful roll.

He explained, "If spit doesn't get the fish to bite then take a shit and use some of that. In fact that always works better than the spit, but it won't last as long as the shit particles will float off of the hook."

The boy frowned and said, "I don't want to touch that stuff."

"Why not? It's inside and touching you right now. It'll always be touching you. You made it from what you put into your mouth to eat. Don't be a sissy."

"I'm not a sissy."

The red and yellow worms were hooked onto the thorns and were thrown into the water. Sidney showed him the best place to put the hook in the water when fishing and said, "Always make the lure appear natural, but at the same time, get the fish's attention. Some fish bite the lure because they are hungry, some because they are curious, the rest because they're pissed off. Those are the only three reasons why any animal will attack something. This is the most basic of all instincts."

"What does pissed off mean?"

The line jerked once, then again, but harder after Sidney slowly jerked it to cause the colorful worms to dance. A ten-inch fish was pulled up on the hand line. It wasn't huge, but it was enough for breakfast.

Sidney said, "Never eat a fish caught near shore in the tropics where coral is present unless you test it first. Some fish eat fire coral and the other fish eat those fish. They all end up with a disease caused by ingesting too much fire coral. If a human eats the fish then he gets the disease, too, and will be very sick, might even die."

He cut a strip of flesh off the fish and put it on a bed of ants living in a dead tree stump. "Now watch. First the ants will attack the meat with stingers because it is an intruder. If it's poison they'll leave it. If it's good they'll cut it up with their jaws and carry it into their underground nest to be eaten, which means you can eat it, too. Ants and cats won't eat bad fish usually, but they can be fooled sometimes, so be careful."

"What's coral?"

Sidney explained.

"What's the tropics?"

Sidney explained.

"What's an intruder?"

Sidney explained. He then picked another plant with stickers on it and said, "If you get sick from fish or anything else that produces stomach pain, the shits, or makes you puke a lot, then cut off a piece of this plant and suck on it. Eat the leaves and keep sucking on fresh sections of the stem until the problem starts going away. As soon as you start feeling better, stop using the plant. Too much of it will make you sick again.

All of this fascinated the boy, but he had heard enough for a while, he was starving. Unfortunately, he would have to wait a little longer while his dad taught him how to build a cooking fire. The building of a fire was not so hard to learn, but starting it with two pieces of wood and dead leaves and small dead twigs was difficult. After the fire was right for cooking, the fish had a single stick pushed through his mouth and out the end near his tail. Two other "Y"-shaped sticks were stuck into the ground to hold the fish over the fire. The boy was told to slowly turn the fish to evenly cook it. It took a while, but produced the best tasting fish the boy had ever eaten.

After breakfast, the two walked along the shoreline. Sidney stopped at every plant and animal including the snails that lived under rocks to tell him how to eat or use them to catch other things that could be eaten.

Sidney had a thought and said, "You better be paying attention to everything I tell you, because you're going to have to know these things. You'll be all by yourself one day very soon."

While the boy was playing with a lizard, Sidney thought, *Cachorro has a bigger advantage than my father gave me. I never had a clue that I'd to be thrown into the jungle to survive. This way the boy might pay more attention to his father than I did.*

Many of the creatures were slimy and crawly things that delighted the boy. Sidney explained that appearance had nothing to do with taste. To prove his point, he dove under the ledge of the rocks and came back with a good-sized horse conch. The boy had never seen one.

"How are you going to eat a rock?"

Sidney found some good-sized snails sliming their way around and an iguana about two feet long. The boy was sent after some big leaves.

Cachorro was of the opinion that everything there was too ugly to eat. Sidney showed him how to boil water, using the leaves as a pot. The snails were dropped in for a few minutes then removed. The hot water forced them out of their shells and Sidney began munching on them. Little Sid was not going to be outdone, however, so he ate one and was surprised. The conch was next and he was even more surprised at how tough it was, which his father said was good as all of the chewing convinced the stomach that it was full. He also showed the boy how to tenderize the meat by beating it with a bottle or a rock.

The iguana was kept alive for the dinner that night as both had eaten enough for lunch. Before going back to the boat for the evening, Sidney dove once again and brought in two lobsters.

The night was spent preparing lobsters and the lizard and discussing the plants and animals they had encountered during the day. The boy seemed to have a real interest in nature which pleased Sidney; it would certainly make his job a lot easier.

All young Sidneys had been educated in exactly the same manner. They were removed from society at the same age. The only contact they had with people was with fathers and grandfathers, if still alive.

Any other persons were men who were hired as sparring partners. There was no school to attend or other social functions as in a normal life. They were taught how to survive on their own, whether in nature or among men.

The main training the young boys went through was how to fight, kill and capture—and how to ignore fear. Their social graces were limited to four languages and basic math in order to navigate and count their booties. Navigation skills were honed by dead-reckoning in natural navigation. Their knowledge acquired would far surpass even the most advanced scholar in the coastline geography of the Caribbean.

Their education was more than substantial for the lives they led. Academic studies, other than the languages they were fluent in, would fall in generally around a sixth grade education. It wasn't important to know ninety percent of the stuff modern man was so concerned about.

In the Sidneys' world, only self-supportive survival was focused on. Natural physiology taught young Sidneys how to out-think and out-brutalize whoever or whatever would get in their way of capturing and keeping the prize.

In extended conversations, obvious flaws in Sidney's education, as in his father's, were easy to detect. Although fluent in four languages, Sidney's education was limited to the vocabulary that a teenager would be taught. Listening to other conversations between educated, modern people bothered Sidney sometimes. At those times, he wished he had a better education. Then he realize that he knew all of the words he needed so why bother to learn a bunch of fancy words just to make him look smart to other people. His lack of academic graces didn't bother him, however; if it had, he certainly could have hired any tutor in the world to educate him.

In modern society's ever-changing world, Sidney was uneducated. In his very real world, he was a genius, just as his ancestors were; and he owned the fortune to prove it.

There was no way to accurately figure the fortune's worth, but it consisted of chests overflowing into mounds of currency, gold and jewels in St. Croix. His European hideaway was an entire island with a cave filled with works of art that had been taken before the eighteenth century. When he was much younger, he flirted with the idea of getting everything appraised, just for his own satisfaction. But, why bother? Who, besides his family, would ever know? And, yes, the appraiser would have to be killed to keep the secret. He knew the reason he thought about it was an excuse to show the immense treasure to someone. He had always wanted to show it to somebody; he was very proud of it and his family's history.

It was traditional to tell young Sidneys about the treasure only after completing the six-month jungle trial. Survival there meant the boy had the stuff to carry the name and responsibility of the Sidney X tradition.

Then the boy's final test would be on his thirteenth birthday. He would be given a year to select and plan a raid that would occur on the day of his thirteenth birthday. If he succeeded, then the full name of Sidney Xavier was given to him as well as equal responsibility for the treasure. As the father grew older and became inactive, it would be entirely his to take care of and make decisions on what sums to allot for his father's retirement. It would also be his responsibility to make sure it continually grew and provide for the next heir.

The next few days were spent going through the same routines: swimming and studying nature on land around the seashore and how to catch and prepare food. By the time the anchor was raised, Cachorro was swimming Australian, breaststroke, dog paddle and underwater with all the ease that could be expected. Now, the boy needed endurance and practice to build his muscles and stamina. Exercise was one thing in his life that he would get more than he wanted. He already was required to keep swimming for an hour every morning, afternoon, and night.

Swimming the first few nights was a terror for the boy. Phosphorus trails left by fish, many of which were chased by bigger phosphorus trails, possibly barracudas or sharks were particularly intimidating. One night he thought he saw a fin cutting through the water near him. He began splashing around and screaming for help.

Sidney dove in and swam to his frightened son, and when he reached him, he hit him on top of his head with the palm of his hand and damn near knocked the boy unconscious. It stunned the boy but it quieted him down.

After the boy seemed to be responding, Sidney said, "If you ever do that again and the shark does not eat you—I will."

For once there was expression in Sidney's face. It was anger. "You are the meanest, the strongest, and the smartest animal in the water. You belong here because you want to be here. The shark is a stupid animal and is here because he has no choice. He was not given the brains or the body to let him do anything he wants. This makes you far more superior. The shark is here to prove you are more courageous, intelligent, and dangerous than he is. You can sit on the shore and kill the shark; sit on the boat and catch the shark; you can even enter the shark's own water, uninvited, and kill him any time you wish. The shark cannot do these things.

"If a shark bites you, remember the basic reasons why things get bitten. One, he is hungry and because he is so stupid he thinks you are a fish. Two, he is curious and wants a piece to see what a superior animal tastes like, which again proves that he is stupid. And if he does, then he has violated the last of the basic laws and has caused you, the superior animal, to be pissed off which surely means his death.

"When you splash around like you were doing you are telling the shark not to be afraid. It is you that is afraid and you are not the superior animal, but a frightened little baby. Your splashing around is offering your flesh to be eaten by him, the superior animal. That is bad because now you have embarrassed me, too. Now the shark thinks that maybe I'm not superior after all, as you are my offspring. This is the only warning you'll get from me on this matter. Do not embarrass yourself in front of nature's animals and more importantly, don't ever embarrass me."

Sidney's philosophy was good to believe in and was accurate in ways most people would not accept. Frantic splashing at night was a good way to get bitten by curious sharks. The words "stupid" and "superior" might be replaced when speaking with an older person with aggressive, domineering or hostile.

Swimming back to the boat, leaving the boy in the water, Sidney was thinking not of the shark, but of his stern warning. *Hope the boy accepts my belief as fact. It'll help him understand the basic laws of nature, and nature is the most important part of our lives. If ignored, the beast in water or on land will lie in wait for him to forget, or get careless, then it will consume him, and the Sidney will be recycled into the next phase of life, or death, whatever is waiting on the other side of now.*

Sidney's warning was effective to the young mind. His father's wisdom helped the boy believe he was safe as long as he wasn't stupid during the forced nightly swim in dark waters. And he was very careful not to splash.

AT SEA

SIDNEY USED THE SAME TACTIC TO LEAVE THE PROTECTED LAGOON AS HE had days ago when he entered. There was an unexpected thump and a bit of a jar as he clipped the top of one of the coral heads; however, it wasn't bad enough to be of any concern. He knew the boat was constructed to take abuse. It was designed for the charter boat industry where tourists and not-so-knowledgeable boaters would run aground on the many reefs.

The morning sun was up and bright with its rays warming the skin against the chill of the early morning trades. Leaving the coastline of the Dominican Republic, he steered a course due north to take them far out into the Atlantic Ocean. That course put a twenty-knot wind directly on his beam and the *Barracouta* was sailing at her best. The main was up, without a reef, as was the 110 percent jib, which kept the rails at the water most of the time. When a particular heavy swell was taken, blue water flowed over the side.

Cachorro was thrilled or scared; Sidney wasn't sure which. The boy's eyes were wide with amazement and wonder. That was so strange to a little farm boy with the knowledge of a world that consisted of a few people, an old house, a small pond and a few chickens and goats. He hadn't seen television, but had heard of them; had heard radios in passing cars when his mother would let him walk with her occasionally to the market to buy some vegetables, but never had one been in their home. At home they didn't even have lights at night other than candles and a kerosene lantern. No one had electricity where he lived.

The magical, powerful boat his father had was truly the most wonderful thing that he had ever experienced. He had been afraid at first when the huge mainsail was raised and the wind filled its belly, causing it to boom like thunder and throw the boom over. Then the boat started moving, slowly at first, then it began to heel over; he thought it was going to turn over. The heeling remained, but the boat kept getting faster.

As the boat reached its hull-speed, it was impossible to stand up without holding onto a handrail as the boat rode over and through the big ocean swells. Sitting down was easier, but with the full force of the wind and the big steep waves, two hands were needed to keep him from being thrown from one side of the cockpit to the other.

Terror gradually changed to amusement. Salt spray continually splashed him, wind cooled the water on his face then warm rays of sunlight warmed him between the splashes. With no exposure to speed, other than his first car ride, the boat's speed seemed unreal; his mind was unable to keep up with what was happening, and he wasn't thinking about what was happening, he was just reacting and holding on the best way he could. He was in a strange new world—that was scary-fun. However, it stayed that way all day and all night, and all day the next day and all night, and all day the next.

When he became seasick, his father offered nothing to ease his suffering other than advise, "Get used to it kid, this is your new life. If you think sick you get sick; you think fun you have fun. That's another rule of nature."

After a few more minutes of looking at the kid's unhappy face, Sidney offered, "Quit looking at the waves around you, and only see the steady, flat horizon out there."

The boy finally managed to get below, without help from his father who was behind the big stainless steering wheel wearing only a smile. Below, and out of the salt spray and wind, it seemed quieter; Cachorro felt safer and was much warmer. The boy crawled across the floor on his hands and knees to the bunk in the amidships companionway and pulled his body up on it.

The boat, however, was not ready to let him sleep. Every time he stopped thinking about throwing up and relaxed his hold on the bunk's cushion, the boat would swerve on a big wave and throw his nearly limp body onto the hard teak floor, always without warning. Luckily, nothing was broken, but he was rapidly becoming covered with bruises. It had stopped being fun too long ago.

Sidney was letting the boat ride sloppily through the seas for a reason. The boy had to learn about the sea and to learn was to understand. To understand meant knowing all the good, bad, comfortable, and uncomfortable things about it. Only then would the boy not become afraid when things got bad at sea, and if you spend time on the sea, things *will* get bad. But bad was only a word or description of an opinion, it didn't mean anything: the sea was the sea. Sometimes it was rough, sometimes not; just don't expect it to be anything other than what it is.

Eventually the boy's mind and body adjusted and he was feeling better, even good enough to ask for something to eat. Sidney told him there was no food, only water on board and it was too rough to catch a fish. He explained they would be in better water the next day then they would get something to eat.

The first lobster of the two caught that other afternoon was consumed the next day as the only meal. The second lobster was eaten the next day, and they got two days with the iguana.

Of course, the boy started whining later that he was hungry. Sidney said, "Whine as much as you want. It will not change the fact that there's nothing to eat. Being hungry won't kill you for seven to ten days as long as you have fresh water to drink. Make your mind strong, boy. Convince yourself that the feeling of hunger in your stomach actually feels good. That feeling is caused by your habit of eating at regular intervals. It was just your body's clock telling you it was time to eat. You think it feels uncomfortable because you're used to feeding it every day. Learn to control your stomach, don't let it control you."

The boy thought his dad was nuts. He was hungry and nothing he could tell his stomach was going to change that. Later, he would come to understand what his father had told him was true. His father didn't tell him anything that wasn't true.

Cachorro awoke from a mid-afternoon nap and could feel a change in the boat's handling of the seas. The big swells seemed not to be a factor any longer. When he went topsides he saw that the water was light green in contrast to the deep blue he had seen the last few days. The waves were steep, but smaller and closer together. On the horizon, directly in their path, was an island with white sand separating the breaking seas from mixed greens of trees.

An hour later, Sid maneuvered over the sand and coral banks to get behind the little island. There was still some swell left, but they were sheltered from the wind by the trees. The water's surface was almost mirror like, allowing the boy to see the bottom just as clear as if he was standing on bare ground. There were funny shapes to be seen everywhere. Giant sea fans growing out of the coral formations waved with the current; big red starfish that looked like his sister's drawing of a night star were everywhere. And fish, wow—big, small and huge were darting around in schools or by themselves.

Sidney asked, "Do you know what all of those animals have in common?"

"They live in the water?"

"No. Everything you can see down there is looking for something to eat."

"Me, too. I could eat them all!" He said excitedly. "Can we catch some food now?"

Sid explained, "We don't eat until we take care of our boat first. Always remember the boat always gets your first attention. We start by properly anchoring her."

He showed the boy how to set the anchor and back wind the sail to make sure the anchor was set.

When they dove overboard into the sparkling water, Sidney went directly to the bottom. The boy followed and Sidney pointed out a few things below the surface rather quickly since he knew the boy hadn't been swimming long enough to stay down very long. He led him out to the anchor to see if it was secure. Back on the surface, treading water, he explained how the anchor should look when properly set and what kind of bottom to avoid.

They returned to the boat and tied the sails down. He explained the importance of doing this every time, before leaving the boat unattended. "A freaky wind could start blowing and cause the sail to partly pull out because of wind resistance. After the sail is partly up, the boat will start sailing around her anchor and will eventually pull it out. If that happens, when you come back to the boat after hunting or fishing or chasing women and drinking rum, you will find your boat has left you."

The boy asked, "Did that ever happen to you?"

"No, because my father told me about it, just like I'm telling you. He never told me anything that wasn't true and I will never tell you untruths either. When you have a son, you, too, must never tell him anything that isn't true."

Little Cachorro giggled and said, "Not me. I'm not going to have kids. You have to have a wife and I don't like girls. They're no fun. Can we get some food now?"

Finally, they dove in search of lobsters. Sidney found a shallow ledge with dozens of antenna sticking out and waving about in the mild current. On the surface, he pointed to the bunch of antenna and then said, "There are lobsters behind those antenna. Watch how I catch one of them."

He sank to the bottom and slowly put his hand in front of a pair of antenna. The lobster wiggled his antenna and slowly ventured out of the hole to see what the strange object was in front of his home.

As it neared, Sid's hand closed around one antenna, and with a smooth motion of his other hand, captured the other antenna. Equal pressure on both antenna was used to pull the lobster out from under the ledge. It looked easy.

The boy dove under to do the same thing. After a few minutes, the only evidence of lobsters that remained was a strewn pile of broken antenna. The boy was mad and wanted to give up. He was tired and hungry and it was too hard to catch the powerful things. One lobster had spooked and shot out of his hole directly at the boy, causing mild heart failure and a sudden burst of an underwater scream.

On the surface he whined to his father, "It's too hard. I'm too tired and I don't know how to catch one."

Sidney replied, "That's too bad. Everybody has to take care of himself. I fed you for four days. You can't expect me to feed you everytime you get hungry. Do you think you're a little baby bird and everytime you squeak I'm supposed to fly out here to find something for you to eat just so you'll stop squeaking?"

It hurt the boy's feelings; he didn't understand. It was mothers' and fathers' jobs to feed the kids, everyone knew that. But not *that* father.

Cachorro whined, "You're mean," and then he starting crying, wishing he was back with his mother.

Sidney waved goodbye at the boy with his hand holding the lobster and he slowly swam on his back towards the boat. He yelled out, "I didn't know you were such a sissy. You can't even catch a defenseless lobster. Rules are, you have to take care of yourself, little puppy, and that means feeding, too. Instead of starving, why don't you collect all of the antenna you broke off the poor little animals. You might get enough meat out of all of them for a bite or two of food."

The boy's hurt feelings turned into anger. *I'm not a little sissy boy and I'll show that old mean man.* He made dive after dive down to the ledge. There was nothing left of the antenna on the only lobster still visible, except for short little nubs. Swarms of tropical fish were nibbling away at the broken antenna.

Persistence paid off when he decided he was going to pull one of the things out if he had to stick his hand back in the hole to do it. That's what he did and brought a big one to the surface. It took all of his strength to just hang onto the wild thing with its tail snapping open and closed with an unbelievable force. He swam back to the boat using his frog kick; his huge smile was hard to conceal. His father had difficulty hiding his pride and a smile.

Sidney took the lobster and said, "Since your lobster is bigger than mine and I'm bigger than you, I'll eat the big one."

Little Cachorro yanked it back from him and said, "No. If you wanted a bigger one you should have caught it. I could have caught a little one like you did, but didn't because I wanted more to eat."

That made Sidney even prouder; he agreed, and put them both into a pot of boiling seawater. Later, they sat on the aft deck eating everything the lobsters offered except the shell. It was delicious and it was enough. Then it was time for a nap to allow the kid time to recover from his physical exertion.

Afterward, Sidney took the boy around the deck of the boat. He pointed to one object then another until all deck hardware had been named and told what it was used for. Then he walked around the boat again and had the boy tell him the name and purpose. Sidney was amazed the Cachorro remembered each piece. Then it was time to swim to shore and find the evening meal.

It was dark when they returned to the boat with arms full and stomachs empty and ready for the feast. A big iguana had been taken and a young blue heron. A ruin of an old abandoned house was found and some remains of long forgotten crops were taken. Wild bananas were everywhere. Sid found chicory plants, Spanish bayonets, and a carambola tree.

Night after night for a week they stayed at anchor. They enjoyed the green salads made of a mixture of leaves and seaweed with a dressing made from the carambola and oil from a palm tree. Fresh greens and roots were consumed with fish, birds, or lobsters. Appetizers were prepared from sea urchins or jellyfish soured in carambola pulp. Coffee was made from the roasted roots of the chicory plants. And everything had a lesson that went along with it: eat a wide variety of foods, eat equal amounts of meats and plants, eat lots of the green plants and certain types of the seaweed.

The weather stayed near perfect and the boy was learning how to live off the land at an incredible rate. His fear of the water, and most of the creatures in it, had diminished to the point that he was comfortable enough with everything except the big Man-O-War jellyfish. Several times during the week, one had floated over him and its long tentacles armed with the stinging cells covered him without warning. The stings were painful, but he survived and learned how to minimize the pain by getting out of the water and rinsing the affected areas with his urine.

Also, during that week he learned the name and function of every part of the sailboat. Virtually no time was spent on the engine since none of the Sidneys used them anyway. It was important for the kid not to expect to use it as a means of propulsion—noisy iron engines were never needed. The Sidneys' way was the pirate's way—by wind, with guts and pride and glory. With the right planning, they could sail anywhere an engine could take them and capture any vessel, even one much faster and more powerful.

When Sidney was ready to leave the island, they stocked the *Barracouta* with provisions to last another week in case nothing new was caught. The boy brought the heavy anchor up by himself using one of the sheet winches as instructed by his father.

With sails set, Sidney put the boy behind the wheel and said, "You're in charge for the next four hours. Steer her on a heading of ninety degrees."

The boat was headed out into the Atlantic Ocean. After a few wrong turns and two jibes while trying to follow the compass needle, he learned the relation of the compass and the steering wheel.

During the next few days, the boy's four-hour watches were spent by telling him about the sea and the seamanship he needed to learn in order to survive. For seven days they had sailed out into the Atlantic. On the eighth day, Sid turned to the southeast trades and oncoming seas. Battling waves and head wind was rough and the boy learned about sailing close-hauled. He realized that when it was rough there was no fooling around; he could do the wrong thing and lose the rigging or the boat or himself or even worse, his father. If his father went overboard he never would know how to get back to land.

Cachorro, at six years old was able to control the huge boat charging through the seas and began to realize that he belonged at sea. It was a feeling he had about the open sea; its beauty, fury, and life had captured his interest. He felt a sense of belonging, pride and power; his self-esteem was overflowing. *If I could just show this to mother and my other father and my brothers and sisters. Boy, would they be proud of me.*

Sidney said, "Turn due south now. We'll stay on that course for two days then we'll see land. You have to keep track of time when on watch and keep a sharp eye out for land. It is not deep oceans that sink boats and kill sailors, it's the hard spots around the edges."

Two days later, as they were munching on the last of the food, young Sid saw three mountains on the distant horizon. Sidney told him they were the Virgin Islands, and gave him a compass heading that would take them around the unseen Anagada Island to keep them well offshore from the island's treacherous reef that extended out from shore and had caught thousands of sailors unaware. By evening, the island of Tortola was dead ahead.

He had the boy steer the boat close to Tortola's shore with its huge mountains looming, seemingly overhead. The boat was steered through a narrow pass between two dark shapes of land in the night. Little Cachorro was worried they might run up on the big rocks in the darkness, but knew his father wouldn't let that happen.

Soon the lights of civilization came into view when they sailed past a big jagged edge of the mountain that rose sharply out of the water.

There was a little bay full of sailboats anchored and the sound of Caribbean music was coming from a bright spot of red and blue lights in the dark. Music, laughter, and the voices of people enjoying themselves, were blaring from the lighted area. Cachorro had never heard such a ruckus, and certainly couldn't tell what was being said as he had never heard words before that were in languages other than the one he spoke.

After the sails were lowered and the boat was anchored, Sidney said to his naked son, "Get some clothes on. We're going to shore. Tonight is a night off; we'll eat good food, drink rum, smoke a Cuban cigar or two, and, with any luck, get laid."

"What's laid, dad?"

The dinghy was tossed into the water and rowed to shore then tied to the restaurant's dinghy dock. Tourists dressed in various shades but matching bright yellows, reds and greens, shorts and shirts, were everywhere. Their feet were covered with shoes, many with long black socks.

A sure indication a cruise ship was in the area. A few local types in old shorts with even older tee-shirts decorated with an almost faded away name of some forgotten saloon, and sandals or tired old boat shoes on their feet, drinking and staring off into the mass of lively, cheerful tourists. The locals' fingers were the only things showing life as they kept time to the reggae music.

Sidney ordered dinner. The boy wanted the same, but no rum. The boy's eyes were wide in wonder of the music being played and the rich, well-dressed Americanos. Everyone was drinking and eating fancy food that was served to them by other people. "Father, what are they saying? I can't talk those words."

"You will be able to talk those words pretty soon."

The carbonate of the Coke, as the one he had in Puerto Plata, fascinated him; it was truly a magical world. The sizzling steak only proved it. He had never seen a piece of meat so big; it would have fed his entire family.

During dinner, the boy tried talking to his father but Sidney responded with, "I don't speak your language here. You must speak only English now."

"What's English, Dad?"

Sidney gave the English name for everything that was brought to the table and occasionally made a statement in English that the boy knew meant he was saying something about the people or the place and only served as a challenge to him to learn the words of the fascinating strangers.

Back on the boat that night, Sidney talked to him in Spanish. "Two weeks ago you thought that you could not sail a boat, swim, dive underwater, catch your own food. Now you do. It is the same with the language. Two weeks from now, you'll be surprised at how well you can talk to these people." The boy accepted his father's words as fact—and he couldn't wait.

"We will leave here early in the morning because there is a government office here that checks every person who comes to the island for identification. These people are called the Customs and Immigration officials. All governments have them. If you do not have the papers they want you to have then you are breaking their law and you will be locked up in a jail."

"What's a jail, Dad?"

"It is a dark place where you are not allowed to do any of the things you want to do. It is the place where you must never let anyone take you. Since you do not have their papers, and I do not, either, we must leave here before they come to work and check boats in the harbor. Do you understand?"

He didn't; the boy was only six years old, but he did understand the part about being put into a dark place and not being able to swim, fish and hunt—the things that comprised his new way of life. He couldn't understand the differences between the life he had spent in his backyard and the huge world he found himself in.

Cachorro said, "Rules and laws in this place that put people in dark places seem mean-spirited. The only rules I ever heard of were don't go to the bathroom in the house: don't play with snakes, and stay away from the river in the rainy season. They were good rules. I had to do some extra chores when I was bad, but was never punished by being put into a dark place. Rules about having a piece of paper saying it's okay to be where you are is silly."

Sidney explained, "Many people are very afraid of true freedom because of fear of competition. Each person has been designed by God to be free; to be able to think for themselves without asking for permission from another person. Each person was created in and for exactly the same purpose: live, be happy, and reproduce.

"Two groups of people, the weak and the rich, are the people who are frightened the most. Weak people are afraid someone will hurt them and decided they needed something to protect them. Rich people had everything they ever wanted and they were afraid that someone would take that away from them. So they got together and formed a combined group that had strength in numbers. These groups are called governments and they decided that they knew what was best for everybody, whether anybody agreed or not.

"These governments created laws that said if you do not do what the weak or rich people want, then you are bad and will be punished in a jail for years or all of your life. Sometimes they will kill you by hanging you by your neck until you die, or hook you up to wires and shock you with electricity until you burn up, or inject a poison in your arm to make you die, or they'll shoot you full of holes with their guns."

"That's mean."

"They don't call it mean. They call themselves civilized, which means they think they have a properly developed culture of morals and are intellectually advanced with humanity, good taste, manners, and reasonable behavior. Those civilized people, teaching what love and God are all about with *thou shall not kill* morality, have tortured millions of people like you and me to death."

"Uh?" The boy didn't know what many of those words meant.

"People like you and me believe we should be free to live the life designed by nature and God. Our only laws are called the *laws of nature*—and those are the only laws you, me, and all of your grandfathers have, or ever will obey. I'll be showing you how these laws work and why. No man governs us or tells us what to do or think.

"We do not tell other people that they must do things the way we do because that would be infringing on their right to believe in anything they want, even though they are wrong. But most importantly, the reason we don't try to correct their way of thinking is because we don't care what they think. Our way is the Sidney way and we know it to be correct." That lecture was the last conversation in Spanish he had with the boy for a while.

"What's culture, Dad?"

Sid knew he used too many unfamiliar words, but thought getting the message out front was important. It could be refined later.

They sailed all over the Caribbean, making landfall at night, and when in civilized harbors, leaving early the next day. In the remote areas they stayed for days, hunting, fishing and foraging for plants with Sidney teaching the boy everything about survival.

The boy had picked up basic English faster than Sidney thought, and could converse on most any subject, but he needed to spend time with someone who talked more than he did to expose the boy to proper grammar. Sidney spoke in sentences to relay facts, not to have idle conversations. It was time to let Sidney XXII participate in the boy's education. He was a talker and the girls that he kept around the place would also be a source of conversation. Another reason to get his father involved was that it was time to start training the boy how to fight, not the art of self-defense, but the art of successful aggression.

The boy had become a remarkable sailor for his age. His strength had improved tremendously and he could completely sail the big boat single-handedly. Groundwork on his navigation skills were understood so that now only practice and confidence prevented his ability to sail alone. He still had much more to learn from the sea and life, but that would be between nature and him over a period of years.

ST. CROIX

They left the island of Grenada for St. Croix after walking the shores of many islands during the last six months. At sea, Sidney would pull his shift and then go below for a nap when it was the boy's turn, leaving him totally responsible for handling the boat for four hours at a time. That wasn't bad for a boy six and a half years old.

When they arrived at the entrance-buoy of his marina, Sidney directed him into the harbor. All along the way he pointed out landmarks for the kid to use when looking for their marina. In the harbor, the boy put the boat at the right spot and then went forward to handle the anchor. Then he came back to be sure it was set—all without instructions from Sidney. He had learned well, better than most grown men who sailed their expensive toys into the world's uppity harbors.

With the boat secure, Sidney took Cachorro out on the foredeck and said, "Look around. Look all the way around at the jungles and mountain and the marina."

Young Sidney turned slowly in a complete circle, surveying everything very carefully. He thought it was another test or lesson from his father. That time it was different.

Sidney said, "Everything you see here belongs to you, your grandfather and me. Your family has owned all of this land for a very long time and one day I will explain it to you. This boat we are standing on is just a small part of many other things our family owns. You've done a good job learning about sailing and living on and around the sea."

"It's fun."

"Your reward for doing well is this boat. It is yours to do anything you want. Her secret name is *Barracouta*. I'll explain later why her name is a secret. As her skipper you must always work on her to keep her beautiful and ready for hard sailing. I'll help you keep her in good shape until I know you know how. You must take pride in her condition, Sidney; that is our family's way."

Cachorro couldn't accept that he had just been given the boat. *Surely no one can afford to give something like this to a little boy*, he thought.

Sidney continued, "You can use the boat when you want, but I must be with you until you prove your knowledge of the sea and how to stay safe."

Ashore, Sally with her caring but concerned expression, met him. "I was worried. This is the first time you've been away that I didn't receive mail for you."

"I'm not surprised. This is my son. His name is Sidney."

She was surprised to learn that he had a son, and after the usual remarks that a diSt.erested person makes when meeting someone else's child, she asked, "Should I order another bed to be delivered to the apartment for him?"

Sidney said, "No. He lives on his boat."

Sally's mothering instincts made her ask, "Should I go shopping for the boy to get him things he'll need?"

"No. The boy takes care of himself. Has the dredging been completed so the boat can be brought to the dock?"

She looked pleased and said, "Yes. I managed to brow beat the lazies in permits. There's a boat in the slip now, but I told him he'd have to move when you came back."

He said, "Let him stay for a while. The boat will be on anchor," and turned his attention from Sally, dismissing her. She quickly departed.

While pouring a glass of rum he said, "Cachorro, you'll be living on the boat by yourself so you better learn how to cook and take care of yourself. I want you to swim to the dock every morning at sunrise and back at night. During the day we'll be in training."

Little Sid would never know the fun boys and girls experienced at that age; there would never be time for watching TV, playing Nintendo, going to movies, hanging out with other kids, or even playing sports; no classroom societies, obligations or the benefit. There would be no giggling at things silly, no tears at things sad. His childhood would be spent with hardened grown-up men where there was never a sign of emotion, other than anger. He'd never know love or feel affection. His youth would be spent training, training, training; training every minute of his day to become totally self-reliant—and by civilized standards, become the meanest son of a bitch on the ocean.

Sitting on his bed drinking rum, Sidney watched the boy chasing a big spider around the room. Looking at the skinny little shit with his big innocent eyes the thought of him as Sidney XXIV was inconceivable. *Father probably looked at me and said the same. I wasn't born any tougher than this one. He's already brown from exposure to the sun and has the beginnings of a physical hardness about him. By the time he reaches thirteen, his universe will revolve around only himself and the things important to Sidney tradition. He'll know that whatever he has to do to live in this world is the way it is supposed to be.* What Sidney didn't know was by the time he was a teenager, he would forever be guiltless, as Sidney hadn't felt the pangs of sorrow for anything he ever caused.

Cachorro caught the spider and was trying to teach it to sit on his shoulder. Sidney smiled at the irony: *pirates of olden day had parrots on their shoulders, this one has a spider.*

He stood up and said, "Let's go. I'm taking you to a store where we'll buy food. It will be in cans and should only be used when it's too rainy to forage or at times when you don't feel like eating fresh food. You'll have to find food by yourself for a while. Whatever you kill, do not take any of the dogs or cats in the marina. They belong to people. "

"I know how to take care of myself. Don't worry."

"I don't worry. If you can't take care of yourself then you better worry. You can eat the canned food as you please, but there will not be enough to last more than seven days. Eat lots of seafood or meat once a day. Eat lots of green plants once a day. Eat wild fruit, seeds and nuts every day you find them. Drink lots of fresh water every day. Everything else you want to eat or drink, go ahead."

The trip through the store didn't last long because Sidney half dragged the kid through the aisles. The boy had never seen so much food; his mind wanted more time to look at each item to see the canned feasts around him. *What would my mother say if she could see this? And here I am, getting anything I want. All I have to do is point at the picture on the can and it's mine.*

The feeling of wellbeing completely blocked any thoughts of being homesick. That wasn't always the case, however; many times, while standing alone steering the boat at night, he wished he were at home. He missed the sounds of his brothers and sisters all around him. He even missed the snorts and gagging sounds of his other father. At sea he missed the smell of the trees outdoors and the feel of dirt on the soles of his bare feet. Sometimes he would silently cry, hoping his father wouldn't hear him and come up to find him acting like a little girl.

Little Sidney stood before the cart while waiting to check out. *I have so much it's almost overflowing the grocery cart. And father is paying for it with money he has in a big roll. He must be a very rich man, maybe he's the richest man in the world. What other man can give his little boy such a grand boat. What other man could own all of that land?*

As the overloaded cart was pushed out to the Jeep, the little boy felt proud at the obvious wealth of his father and he was also proud to be his son.

On board the *Barracouta,* Sidney showed the boy how to use the can opener. "Remember to eat like I told you. Don't rely on store bought food to keep you alive. It's full of things that'll hurt you if it's all you eat. As long as you eat the way you have been shown it won't hurt you. If you don't eat right, I'll take it away from you and the only thing you will be able to eat is what you can find."

The boy understood. His father only told him the truth.

As Sidney got ready to board the dinghy for the trip back to shore, he told the kid, "Today is an exception. Eat anything you want to and don't worry about fresh food; pig out, try anything but be in my apartment at sunrise in the morning."

The boy did exactly that; there were so many things he wanted, so many enticing pictures on the cans. He opened and sampled three different cans and opened a big bag before he remembered how his mother used to rave about food, it wasn't to be wasted; it had always been too hard to come by.

He finished the contents of a can of black beans, a can of yams and a thick slice of Spam. He sat at the dinette feeling stuffed with a half-eaten marshmallow lodged in his cheeks.

A little later his stomach began to feel queasy and its surrounding muscles began to constrict, trying to force the food back out the way it had come from. He realized what the expression he father had used when he said *pig-out,* meant. That was the worst night in his life; he was so sick and his mother wasn't there to tell him everything was going to be all right, to comfort him, rub his back and wipe the drool from his chin. He knew that he was to die that night—all alone. Finally, he fell asleep after crying between spasms of wet and dry heaves.

NEW YORK

VINCENZO THE SICILIAN HAD BEEN IN NEW YORK FOR FIVE DAYS. He visited the hospital each morning and evening and had gotten to know the two women very well. Part of him felt sorry for them, but everything he did or said was slowly putting as much pressure on them as possible without causing more stress. He needed information and was willing to break fingers if he thought it would yield facts.

He was sitting in his room on the forty-fifth floor of the Four Seasons Hotel in his underwear and black socks. A half-full beer on the side table had a few empty cousins lying on the table and floor beneath it. The colorful screen of a laptop computer resting on his lap reflected off his granny reading glasses. He was reviewing his *Facts-Only* file. His *Speculation-Only* file was displayed in the window next to it. Each fact had a code number to reference the source of information.

1.1 ROBBERIES IN CARIBBEAN.

2.1 VICTIMS KNOCKED UNCONSCIOUS FROM BEHIND, LEAVING headaches and lumps. Lumps are usually in same spot, at rear of skull. Frontal and side hits are occasionally used, producing death.

3.0 TAPE WAS USED TO CUT OFF AIR FROM SOME OF THE VICTIMS to get information on location of money.

3.1 TAPE WAS USED TO BIND ARMS, LEGS AND IMMOBILIZE THEM by taping them to fixed objects.

3.2 SAME TYPE OF TAPE, GRAY DUCT TAPE, WAS USED ON ALL victims.

3.3 TORTURE USED BY CUTTING FINGERS OR EARS OFF OF targeted employees to get information.

4.1 ONLY ONE MAN FOR CERTAIN WAS INVOLVED. OTHER PERSONS have not been seen or heard. This is true in every case investigated to date.

4.2 HAS BEEN HEARD SPEAKING NORWEGIAN, ITALIAN, ENGLISH, Afro-Caribe, possibly Papiamento. No Italian accent.

4.3 SKILLFUL FIGHTER.

5. KNOWS HOW TO USE THE BLACKJACK VERY SKILLFULLY.

6. ALL KNOWN WEAPONS USED, KNIFE AND BLACKJACK. NO HAND-to-hand fights.

7. KILLED ONLY ONE MAN WHERE IT WAS OBVIOUS THAT HE intended to. Vito was securely bound and his jugular vein was slashed. He had no other damage or injuries, bruises, etc.

8. HAS APPARENT KNOWLEDGE OF OUR OPERATIONS. HAD detailed information on Vito's trip and his secure storage locations.

9. DESCRIPTION IS DIFFICULT, AS HE HAS BEEN SEEN ONCE. A quick glance only, as follows:

   A. TALLER THAN FIVE-FOOT THREE-INCHES.

   B. COLD OR SCARY BLACK EYES.

"Well, what the fuck am I supposed to do with this shit. Millions of people in the Caribbean, and this is all I have to work with," he said aloud and to himself.

Vincenzo wasn't in a pleasant mood that day. He had kicked out the fifth worthless prima-donna-New fucking-York-City-whore in five days from his room two hours go. Also he had an appointment to see the cops that morning and he hated cops—all cops, but Vincenzo had to get to the state attorney, Jack Castero. Jack was Anthony *"Tony-the-Pop"* Castero's first cousin and was going to run some profiles on what Vincenzo had for facts and speculation. There was a possibility the people or person responsible were hitting other people, too.

Vincenzo had been working on his own because the family didn't want law enforcement agencies to be aware that somebody had the audacity to repeatedly rob them. The law would be glad to hear it and certainly would not do a damn thing other than laugh, and the family would lose respect. The people he was seeing today wouldn't laugh; Jack Castero was firmly on the payroll.

Then he was to meet Fred Currens, who headed up the FBI's New York office, at midnight that night. Fred had worked his way up through the ranks for over twenty-three years. He was a good, honest and straight man in every way, except one. Fred was going to be bought that night, or face up to some terrible facts about his life in front of family, friends, and his superiors in the FBI.

Lunch with Jack Castero proved to be a waste of time. Vincenzo said to him, "We need your help in obtaining information on a matter that no one other than yourself is to be aware of. We do not want you to discuss this matter with anyone other than me or your cousin. Understand?"

"Sure, Al, how can I help?"

"I want you to run your computers to see if you can locate or match the facts I'm going to give you. We are looking for this person or persons." He gave him a printed out Facts List.

"I know this is kind of vague, but it is all I have. I need to know if I have anything that matches any of your present or past investigations."

After looking over the list Jack said, "Shit, Al, what's going on?"

"Somebody has been hitting some of our interests in the Caribbean for a few years. Maybe it is directed towards us, maybe not. I need to know if this sort of thing might be going on elsewhere. I don't have to tell you our family has had enough and intends to close these people down forever."

"Al, I don't see how I can be of much help. If I go to the computer people with this they are going to want to know why I have this information and what were the specific crimes and who's involved. Every one of our departments has its own rules and protocols that must be observed. They're too busy, Al; they're not in the business, nor the mood to do favors for anyone, even me. If I don't have a good, legitimate reason to insist they plug this in, then they'll tell me to go shit in my hat. Fucking unions can be a pain in the ass sometimes. If I raise hell about it they'll get other people involved who will want to know where, why, and who, and want to see crime reports. Shit, I can't tell them it's for my cousin, a Mafia boss."

The Sicilian was thinking, *it's too bad he's family; I'd like to park this fucking weenie next to Hoffa.* Then he said, "Listen, Jack, you got a couple of things wrong. First, I'm not asking, I'm fucking telling you what Tony wants. I don't give a shit what you do or say to your interdepartmental assholes, but you run this information through and tell me everything you can find out by six o'clock tomorrow afternoon. Bribe or blow somebody, I don't care which, but you damn sure better get it fucking done. Tony put you in that cushy job, so respect his needs. You are smart enough to do that—aren't you?"

"Of course, Al, I'd like to help, but I don't know what I can do. If you had somebody coming up on charges or going to trial then I could do some good for you. I hope you can understand this."

"Understand this! You and Tony aren't that close. I'm a sensible man, Counselor, but, like you, I have to follow orders. Your fucking job and reputation are going to be lost if you haven't done exactly what you've been told to do."

The A.G. stood up in anger and towered over Vincenzo and shouted, "You can't threaten me. I'll call Tony and have him send your greaseball ass back to fucking Sicily! Tony has the capacity to understand my position."

"Make that call. Use my phone; you'll be doing me a favor."

The attorney sat down and thought about the mess he was suddenly in. *All of those years, the big wad of cash every quarter, and I have done very little in return. Now Tony wants service for their payments. I'm fucked.*

Tony wouldn't want to lose the highest legal contact they have in New York. Oh, shit… maybe they got a new guy. Shit.

Vincenzo was getting tired of the bullshit and gruffly said, "Hey, asshole! Why are you just sitting there? I told you to call Tony, not sit on your ass like a fucking toadstool."

"I don't know the number. I'll call him from my office and then get back to you."

"No you're not. You're going to call from here. I don't have time to wait around for you to *get back to me*."

"I told you, Al, I don't have —."

"That's no problem. I'll dial it for you." He dialed the phone and in a few seconds said to the phone, "Hello, Tony. This is Vincenzo. Jack wants to talk to you." He gave the phone to Jack.

"Hi, Tony. Hey, I'm having little problem with Al right now."

Tony interrupted him and said, "I guess you are, Cousin, but if you have a problem with him, I doubt that it's a little one. You might improve your position right now by not calling him Al. That is too American and he hates anything American. Call him Vincenzo like I do."

"I wasn't aware of that; thanks. My problem is that he's asking me to do something that I cannot do, and he refuses to accept that. I was hoping you could intervene on my behalf. If his request concerned the legal system, I would certainly oblige him, with your approval of course, but this entails going into the state police's computer system to track down some obscure at best leads on someone's activities. I can give you the details if you wish?"

"Well, Jack, you do have a problem. If you're smart you will do exactly like Vincenzo asks. He's not one to be taken lightly and I'd never try to discourage him from doing whatever it is he is trying to do. He must have good reasons, so why don't you try to be more reasonable? Let me talk to Vincenzo."

His hopes for intervention faded rapidly as the two men spoke about soccer, wives, and children without mentioning the reason for the telephone call. *I'm fucked. They could have had the courtesy to talk in Italian if they were going to bullshit, but kept it in English just to prove how insig-*

nificant I am.

Vincenzo handed the telephone back to Jack after they had caught up on life's unimportant topics and asked, "You want to say goodbye?"

"Thanks for setting me straight on this. I'll do everything I can for Vincenzo. Goodbye, Tony."

Jack got up to leave and said, "Well, I guess I better get busy. I don't know who I am going to find, but it looks like somebody's going to get a blow job by a heterosexual New York State Attorney General."

Vincenzo smiled, but it wasn't genuine. *His reluctance to do what was asked suddenly disappeared. Jack just wants out of this room; there's another course of action in the man's mind.*

Vincenzo walked him to the door and said, "Listen, do us both a favor. Do as you have been asked. Don't come back here tomorrow with whiny excuses why you don't have my information. Come back with my information or solid proof that you searched the files for matches and there was nothing there or don't bother coming back. I'll find you."

He opened the door for the counselor and stared into his eyes the whole time, even after Jack had diverted his eyes.

Fucking ginzo was in Jack's mind, but he said, "Okay, Vincenzo, I'll see you tomorrow."

Dago wimp was on Vincenzo's mind as he went for another beer and picked up the telephone. He dialed a number and said, "This is Vincenzo. Put some eyes on Jack Castero, the A.G. I want to know everywhere he goes. He'll be leaving the Four Seasons in about five minutes, supposedly going to his office. Stay on him until I call you off. He is to be back at the Four Seasons by six tomorrow evening."

Then with cold beer in hand, he began looking over the next list. The Speculation File.

1.0 MUST BE WORKING WITH SOMEONE AT THE TOP OF THE FAMILY.

1.1 HOW ELSE WOULD HE HAVE KNOWN ABOUT VITO?

1.2 WHY ELSE WOULD AN INORDINATE AMOUNT OF ROBBERIES BE directed at family— owned casinos, ships and banks?

1.3 WHY WOULD TONY PULL IN THE SURVIVING GUARD BEFORE I had a chance to question him?

2.0 WHY WOULD A MEMBER OF THE CIRCLE OF FIFTEEN BE responsible for any reason?

2.1 COULD HE BE WORKING WITH ANOTHER GROUP TO SPLIT OFF from the main family?

3.0 COULD THE DRUGGIES BE DOING THIS TO WEAKEN OUR reputation, therefore gaining more respect from the streets and increasing their business and protection levels?

There's something about that possibility that seemed to have merit. I'll set traps without anyone other than me knowing. I'll catch the rat... just have to engineer a series of opportunities to hit. Only one person will know of each so it'll pinpoint the bastard— if it's an insider.

He had several more beers while playing with scenarios until he made definite decisions on what to do. After a late afternoon nap was interrupted by the requested wakeup call from the front desk, it was time to get ready for his late night dinner meeting with the FBI.

Fred Currens arrived on time. In fact, he stood outside of the door until his wristwatch moved to exactly midnight before he knocked on the door. He was totally surprised to have the door directly behind him open instead of the one he knocked on. *What the hell's going on? Not sure I made the right decision in coming. Police Chief McDonald insisted this would be a great career move. Hope the chief knows what he's doing.*

The police chief had told him a man had something for him that was sure to help his career. He wouldn't give any details saying that was against the rules of the deal, but he should accept; it could only help him when he entered the race for a Senate seat. The rules dictated that he come alone, wear no bugs, and don't tell anyone before or after the meeting. If he felt uncomfortable, come armed. He had complied; after all, if anybody knew the ropes in New York, it was Chief McDonald. And he was the man who had been scaring crime families and political leaders for decades.

The man in the open doorway said, "Hello, Fred, you're right on time. My name is Vincenzo and I'm happy you could make it." Without the usual pleasantries, he continued, "I've heard a lot of things about you, Fred. It appears you have done a very good job for the Bureau and still have some more room at the top for your career. I'm sure that, by the end of our dinner, you'll be ready for another opportunity."

As Fred entered the lavish room, he noticed the dining table was set and there were two silver ice-stands, chilling wine at tableside.

Vincenzo said, "Fred, there are two outstanding Italian wines chilled, a St. Joannes Xarel Lo and a St. Joannes Cabernet Sauvignon. May I pour you a glass of either before we order dinner? If a cocktail is more to your liking, then mix whatever you like at the bar," and pointed to the eight foot long, built-in, fully-stocked bar.

Fred went to the bar and found a Diet Pepsi and poured it into a glass, straight.

"You said your name is Vincenzo, but I didn't catch your last name."

"I don't like my last name, so I never use it. Just call me Vincenzo."

"How can I take this meeting serious if I don't know who I am talking to? I really would like to know who you are."

"My name is Vincenzo Jones. I came from a third generation American father and an Italian mother. I strictly prefer my Italian ancestry. I'm called Vincenzo the Sicilian."

That name produced instant recognition in Fred's mind and goose bumps on his arms. *This is one of the big time Mafia guys. Wonder if anyone knows he's in the States? Apparently, the chief does. Maybe the guy's going to roll over in exchange for something. Shit, Chief Mac's right, this will make my pay grade a lot better. Now I understand the reasoning behind the meeting rules.*

"Fred, we are going to discuss a few things of a very delicate nature. I hope you don't mind, but I have to check you for listening devices." He picked up an electronic probe and covered his body with it. Fred was clean.

"I imagine you are a little short on time, Fred, so let's go ahead and order dinner then start our conversation. Is that okay with you?"

"Sounds great, Al. How long have you been in the States?"

Looking at Fred's insincere expression, Vincenzo thought, *another fucking gumba. Fuck it, be nice.*

Vincenzo responded with, "Just arrived today, *Freddie.*"

That seemed to make Fred realize that maybe he was improper in using a nickname when he didn't know the man. And he hated "Freddie." He looked at the menu beside his plate a quickly made his decision.

He said, "I think I'll try the Latino Corvino with garlic, Vincenzo. I've heard the fish here is really very good."

Vincenzo picked up the telephone, dialed room service and ordered the Latino Corvino and an Ollie's Ohmah, a twenty-ounce tenderloin steak. During this time he was thinking. *Fucking New Yorkers. Got the best beef in the fucking world and they bitch and moan about how terrible it is to eat meat. They think that eating fucking fish from Costa Rica, which probably is full of mercury, is a better choice? Fucking New Yorkers!*

"Fred, when I told you my name, I gathered that you recognized who I am and who I'm with, so there's no need to get into that any further. I have a problem that I hope you can help me with. In return I'm going to help you with your problem."

"What problem do I have?" asked Fred.

Vincenzo ignored his question and continued, "There is somebody or some group that has been harassing some business interests *we* have. If you need to hear a word that describes *we*, Fred, it is Mafia."

Alarms were going off in every part of Fred's brain. To have Vincenzo openly state a fact that had always been intensely denied by the mob meant something drastic was about to happen. He desperately wished Vincenzo had not admitted that to him, unless of course, Vincenzo was giving himself up.

Vincenzo continued, "The family has taken all they intend to take, and it's my job to find out who is responsible."

"Whoa there, Vincenzo! Why are you telling me, the FBI, these things?"

"Because I need your help, Fred."

"Surely, you know we are not in the business of helping people like you. We are in the business to destroy your corrupt and illegal activities."

"Don't call me Shirley, Fred. And please, don't give me your bullshit about our corruption—worry about your own. Your fucking Bureau has enough shit going on to earn its place in the hall of horrors, and has had that honor for fucking forever. Don't forget, you're not talking to the general public or a media guy or a politician. You are talking to someone who knows your business as well as my own."

Fred didn't offer any arguments. He knew there were problems in the agency like everywhere else and the Mafia certainly contributed. He asked, "What kind of help are you looking for?"

"I need you to run these facts through your computers to see if there are any similarities going on in other parts of the world." He slid the sheet towards him.

After a moment or two and seeing Vito's name, Fred said, "Yeah, I read about that in the newspaper. I hear there is a big reward for the people or the diamonds. How much are the diamonds worth?"

"Ten million."

Immediately, Fred knew he had made a mistake in asking; under the circumstances he didn't want to know that either. He looked over the list and kept asking questions he didn't want to ask. Vincenzo answered openly, without fear that it would be going any further, which was obvious to Fred, and that bothered him more with each answer. This continued until the waiter arrived with the room service.

The waiter stayed near tableside to assist pouring wine, fixing drinks and doing waiter stuff. There was only light conversation about what was going on in the world of sports and politics during dinner. Afterward, the waiter gathered up the dishes and an empty bottle of wine and left.

Fred said, "I really enjoyed dinner tonight and I must admit that being here in your company is sort of exciting. Good-guy, bad-guy having dinner together, you know what I mean?"

"Of course, I do. I try to never eat and converse with cops, but, like they used to say, 'shit happens.'"

"Well, Vincenzo, you must realize that I'm not going to help you. I intend to tell the bureau about this meeting and I suggest, in the name of chivalry, that if you have any concerns about being in our country, that you be gone by noon tomorrow. That's the time I'm due at the office. I hope you're not offended, but at least I'm being honest with you."

"Fred, I appreciate honesty, so thank you." He got up and walked to his briefcase on the desk and pulled out a sealed manila envelope. He handed it to Fred and said, "I'm glad to know that you are an honest man,

Fred; that's why I picked you to work for me. I haven't seen those pictures, Fred, but I know what they are; that sort of stuff turns me off. They were given to me sealed and have been given to you with the same seal intact. Take a look inside to be sure the negatives are there, too."

Fred opened the envelope, and he pulled out an eight by ten photograph. His faced turned ashen gray, his life-spirit seemed to melt from within. Then he cried like the screaming faggot he really was. There were pictures of him in various motel rooms with various men doing various things—all of them disgusting to most people.

Fred didn't know it, but Chief McDonald had found some very competent people to arrange and photograph the scenes.

"Rest assured, Fred, no other copies were made; you have everything there is. They belong to you." He handed Fred the briefcase they had been in, and said, "Put them in here. The case and its contents belong to you." It was packed with hundred-dollar bills.

Fred was in shock; the money only made it worse. "Take it, Fred. It's yours. That's three hundred thousand dollars and it offers a lot of added security for you and your family."

No answer came from Fred, only a dumb look.

"If you don't want the money, take the pictures anyway. I can always get new ones without much difficulty. If you are truly honest, as you keep telling me, you'll admit to being a queer and make the best out of it. I know your wife isn't aware of your sexual appetite and neither are your four children. Of course, the Bureau isn't going to tolerate this behavior so you might lose more than your family when everyone finds out about your little escapades. And needless to say, Butch, one of the guys in the pictures is surely going to be hurt, too. Let's see, he is the chief of staff for your American president, isn't he?"

Fred managed to speak, but he still wasn't thinking, "I have all of the proof, so I can deny anything you say."

"Fred, stop being stupid; you know I can get anything I want on you. I can even frame you and there's nothing in the world you can do to stop it, other than killing yourself. But, why do that when things are just starting to go your way. We're not asking much from you, and you can keep your secrets and have enough money to enjoy many more perverted pastimes. In two months there will be another briefcase delivered to you with cash, but, hopefully, no more pictures. When you associate yourself with me, you buy all the privacy you want and I'll back it up if one of your play-mates ever tries something."

Fred was quiet, feeling shame and thinking about new possibilities in lustful fantasies. New possibilities were winning.

"Do everybody a big favor and take the money and pictures and leave. You're going to enjoy freedom from exposure, wealth, plus we can do a few things to make sure you keep going up that ladder you have been climbing. Do you think you'd like living in Washington? If you don't want to go up, how about a lateral move, say Los Angeles, San Francisco would be even better; you would have lots of playmates out there. Or... " Vincenzo didn't finish the sentence.

"Or what?"

"You will not leave this room alive and your wife will get the photos as will your boss."

"Let me take another look at that list, Vincenzo," Fred said as he sat back down.

ST. CROIX

EARLY IN THE MORNING, THE SOUND OF DISTANT ROOSTERS AND LOUD shrill calls of the Caribbeans's early-morning three-thirty-birds were in-terrupted by a timid knock on the screen door of Sidney's apartment. The boy obeyed the command to come in. He didn't feel good that early morn-ing, but a lot better than last night's brush with death. Sidney thought he looked a little rough, but he wasn't concerned. Sidney had been up long ago and ready to start his morning run, but decided to wait for the boy. Today was the start of the boy's physical training.

The boy was wearing his only pair of shorts and had swam to shore carrying his shirt in a free hand to keep it dry, and he had no shoes.

Sidney said, "Leave the shirt here. We're running this morning, but differently than we have been doing. No matter how bad you hurt or how hard things are, don't quit. If you don't quit, things will get better and one day soon you will be happy you endured and will probably be able to stay up with me."

Outside, Sidney started at his normal pace of a slow jog. The boy kept up with no trouble or heavy breathing for almost a mile before he started huffing and slowing down. Sidney increased his pace as if he were running alone; the boy started whining about wanting his father to stop, his side hurt, he was out of breath, and his legs hurt. Sidney didn't bother acknowledging the whining boy; he kept running and never looked back. If he did, he knew he would see the little boy half running and walking, with tears on his cheeks and he would be holding his side where the sharp pain resided.

That pain was to be expected when people were out of shape. After a couple of miles, Sid stopped and lay down under the shade of a big mahogany tree. He exercised, alternating between one hundred sit-ups and one hundred push-ups until the boy came staggering along. The kid was slow, but he had not quit, regardless of the pain. He had done what he had been told to do, and Sidney had that feeling of pride once again.

Sid continued his push-ups as the boy fell into the grass under the big tree. His face was white, his body was covered with sweat and his chest heaved to pump more air into starved lungs. Nothing was said for a few minutes until the boy's breathing returned to normal, then Sidney said, without breaking his push-up rhythm, "Think you'll live or do you think a little exercise is going to kill you? I was beginning to believe you were sitting back there on the road crying like a little sissy."

"I'm not a sissy."

The boy had expected a *kind* remark, even praise because he had completed the ordeal, not another sarcastic remark poking fun at him. He responded in Spanish "*¡Ustedes muy malo!*" It was in Spanish because he was thinking in Spanish and had only been angry in Spanish and didn't know mean words in English.

Sidney said, "That means *you're a fucking asshole* in English."

The kid repeated it in English while looking directly at Sidney. His dad had to fight the urge to laugh, thinking it was fun to have an adversary. He loved competition and could already tell it wouldn't be too many years before the boy might have the upper hand. He muttered to himself, "He'll make a hell of a pirate."

After Sidney finished his pushups he told the boy it was time to move on. Little Sid got up painfully; his leg muscles were twitching and his calf muscle cramped hard as he stood. Sidney showed him how to move the leg to relax the muscle while massaging it to increase blood flow that brought in the needed oxygen. His dad also suggested pinching his upper lip at the same time. In a minute, little Sid was okay and able to stand.

They walked at the kid's pace for another mile. During the walk, he explained, "In physical training, pain is only a signal that you're not in good shape. It simply means you have to exercise more. Don't worry about pain, it'll go away. One day you'll be able to run all day without feeling tired at all, but you have to make the effort to get there.

"Starting today you are going to be developing your body. You'll be feeling pain the next few days, but tough it out. The first month you are going to be working on your legs and endurance. That translates into a lot of running and exercises like push-up and sit-ups; then a little weight training, but not too much. You can't really start heavy lifting until you're older and your bones are strong enough to take the strain."

The boy showed his biceps muscle and said, "For a little kid, I'm strong already."

"You're going to be the strongest kid pretty soon. Do you like to fight?"

"Mother said it's not nice to fight."

"She was talking about girls. Are you a girl?"

"No way!"

"Good. By the time you become a teenager, you are going to be the best fighter around. By the time you're a grown man, you'll be the best fighter wherever you go."

"Doesn't fighting hurt?"

"Only if you lose. Sometimes you will get hit hard and it will hurt, but remember, it's only pain and that goes away. Never be afraid of pain; always be positive that you're going to win and know that you're the toughest guy around."

Cachorro had a wicked smile on his face and asked, "Even you?"

That caused a flashback to the time he decided to take on his father. He had loved fighting and was very good at it. As a little boy, he had been beaten up lots of times in fight training. By the time he was thirteen, he won all training fights where men were paid to fight him.

On his seventeenth birthday, he decided he had enough of his old man's bullshit about keeping in shape. He walked up to his father and boldly said, "I'm in perfect shape and I am going to kick your ass if one more word is said about it."

His father, surprised, said, "What are you going to do, pansy—hit me with your puny little fist? Be careful, boy, or I'll make you cry, so get outside and get into shape, you little sissy."

Sidney had swung out with his lightning-fast left fist. He didn't remember when he realized what a mistake he had made, but it was somewhere close to the end of the ten-minute fight they had.

He had fought well, but his father kicked his ass from one end of the house to the other. The interior of the house was in shambles.

His father's only noticeable injury was a broken nose and several bleeding knuckles. Sidney XXIII ended up with a broken nose, two eyes swollen shut, the loss of two front teeth, a damaged and very painful jaw, and several bruised, if not broken, ribs. He remembered lying on the floor too hurt to get up while looking at his father standing over him. Sidney XXII had a smirk on his face and said, "When you get in shape, pansy, try me again."

He never thought of trying the old man again. He knew that had he not been his son, and the heir to the family tradition, his dad would have killed him early in the fight. That same scene would surely happen one day between the XXIII and XXIV. *Hope I can do as well as my old man did,* he thought.

The boy found himself walking up a dirt path leading off the road through the thick growth of island scrub and mahogany trees. They walked to a small clearing, a yard untouched by trimming tools of any kind.

The area was an overgrown yard and behind it was a big house. It was all roof with screens as walls to keep bugs out. Instead of steps going from the ground up to the house there was a steep wooden ramp.

They walked into the house as Sidney yelled, "Anyone here?"

A man's voice came from behind one of the few interior walls, said, "Fuck, no."

Without responding, Sidney kept walking to the kitchen. He opened the refrigerator door and took a beer. He looked at the boy and said, "If you want anything, get it," and he went to the massive living room and sat in a big cushioned chair. Cachorro also took a can of beer and went into the sitting area.

The kid took a couple of sips and decided he didn't like the taste as much as Coke. He almost dropped the can on the teak floor when he was scared by the sudden appearance of an enormously fat woman who came out from behind a wall. She was wearing a dress that looked like a sheet with flowers all over it. It was very colorful and very big. He had never seen such a fat person and thought she had to be very rich to buy that much food. His eyes were locked on her every move as she waddled into the room with a big fleshy smile that showed the fun-loving spirit that lived behind the glob of soft rolling meat.

She looked at XXIII and said, "You must be Sidney. He said you'd be big and ugly," and she laughed heartily.

Sidney said, "Yep." His son giggled.

"Nice to meet'cha, Sid, I'm Rosie and I'm your new mamma." She roared another hardy laugh and said, "Any time you want to come sit on mamma's knee and cry your troubles out, come ahead, honey. Just don't let your old man catch you."   His father came rolling out in his wheelchair, laughing, and smacked her on her massive ass, saying, "Have you ever seen such a woman, son? God, all those years I been fooling around with those skinny little girls when I could have had Rosie. Shit, I've known her forever it seems. We were friends, but one night I got drunk and wheeled myself down to Jake's Bar. The next morning I woke up here in bed with my Rosie and in love. Damn, I don't believe I finally found the woman I been looking for all my life."

Sidney thought, *sure, you old fucker, we will see who comes out from behind the wall next week.* His dad was a little hard on the ladies.

As the older man wheeled himself into the room, his attention switched from the big ass of Rosie to the little kid sitting on the couch. He abruptly stopped his wheelchair and stared at the little bare-footed and bare-chested boy with his deep tan and sun bleached uncombed hair. His eyes locked onto the boy's eyes and he was silent. His face turned deadly hard—but not his heart.

He said, "This is the boy? This is the new Sidney, who the family responsibility will go to? This little boy who has only known kid's things is about to start a journey that very few people will experience. Complete freedom to come and go, to do as he pleases. To be a man outside of the world's societies and their pansy-ass ways, a solitary, powerful life, true to only himself and never ruled by man." He looked at Rosie and added, "or woman."

The elder Sid thought, *look at the little shit, half-sitting, half-leaning on the couch with a beer in his hands. He's frightened but I can see the spirit behind those eyes. He's ready, he won't run, he's Sidney tough, a natural Sidney. My son did good to spawn this little spitfire.*

Young Sid thought the old man was staring at him in meanness. He felt frightened and moved closer to his father for protection.

The old man finally moved and rolled his chair over to the boy. His face still showing no emotion, but there was plenty inside him. He wanted to get a closer look.

Nobody said a word; even Rosie was quiet. She could feel something very special was going on between the men and hoped it didn't mean that her lover was some kind of a young-boy-loving pervert. The old man reached over to feel the muscle in the boy's arm and said, "Show me your muscle."

The kid reluctantly raised his arms and strained with everything he had to make the slightly raised bump turn into a slightly raised lump. The old man was amused with the strain and determined expression on the boy's face. He rolled the wheelchair back a few feet, and for the first time showed a facial expression. He looked happy and satisfied that the new heir would do just fine—if he survived the training.

Sidney XXIII said, "Sid, this is your grandfather. Father, this is my son, Sidney."

Rosie broke in with, "My gawd, another Sidney! Don't you boys know any other names?"

They all ignored her remark, even the boy, for he felt something special was happening, too. He didn't understand it but could feel the approval from both men, they were proud of him—but he didn't know why.

It was a good feeling. It was like he belonged there, and given the choice at that moment, he would have chosen to stay there rather than return to his home and mother.

Sidney XXIII told his father, "I need your help training the boy for a while. He has his own boat in the harbor and will spend his nights there."

Old Sid acted grouchy about being asked to help out, but was actually delighted. He had been looking forward to teaching the boy many of the skills he had taught the boy's father.

He remembered his own grandfather during his training days as a child. His father was brutal in his ways at times and when things got too hard he knew he could go to his grandfather for compassion, not much, but certainly more than his father would give. That young boy sitting before him would be coming to him now when looking for someone to help with the bruised feelings and flesh.

It would be his job to turn the boy's tears into an understanding and knowledge that everything he was experiencing was for his own wellbeing. Learning the penalty of failure was pain; it was instrumental in keeping the boy alive. Not knowing failure's penalty would open every door that could lead to his early death and at the least serious pain or disablement. Or even worse than all of that would be capture. Capture wasn't a word to the Sidneys, it meant the loss of their most prized possession, freedom—and never had a Sidney allowed that to happen.

Sidney looked at his son and said, "Your grandfather was a great sailor, fighter, and protector of our family honor. He taught me everything I know and he'll do the same for you."

The boy had been puzzled by the wheelchair. He had never seen one before. He also noticed the old man's legs and wondered how he could sail and fight without feet, so being innocent and young, he asked, "What happened to his feet?"

Sidney answered, "He's in that wheelchair for only one reason. He forgot that he was the superior animal one night and the shark took advantage of his stupidity."

The older Sid flashed with anger at the remark but quickly realized it had been necessary.

Sidney continued. "The loss of his feet doesn't mean that he's not a capable man. Whatever you do, don't piss him off, and if you do, keep well away from him. He may be tied to that chair, but if he ever gets his hands on you—you're in a world of shit. But listen to everything he tells you; like me, he'll never lie to you."

Rosie broke in again; it was not her nature to be left out of a conversation, and she always had something to say. She asked, "How old are you, boy?" When she heard his age she asked, "I'll bet you're looking forward to going to school." He nodded his head yes.

The older Sid said, "Rosie, go take a hike. I want to spend time with my son and grandson without the babble of a beautiful woman."

She flustered up and said, "You old bastard," and left. As she left the porch, old Sid yelled out, "Don't come back until dark, and bring some chicken with you for dinner."

There was no response from Rosie and no one cared, including Rosie. She, like everyone else, didn't know much about her lover but recognized his self-confidence and power and that usually meant wealth or some other force that allowed him to do as he pleased. All she did was mutter, "I'll make him say he's sorry for chasing me out when I whoop my big old pussy on him tonight," and her body shook as she giggled.

Sidney told the boy, "During your physical training your grandfather will teach you different languages, world history and geography."

"What's geography, Dad?"

He'll tell you. He'll also tell you how to find out where you are and where you're going at sea or in a jungle. Everything he teaches you must be learned, because you are going to use the information or be lost or even killed. You are not going to be taught anything you don't need to survive, so pay attention and never be afraid to ask questions." That last statement was unnecessary: the kid never stopped asking questions.

"Starting tomorrow morning you will leave your boat after eating breakfast and run up to this house. You will do this every morning until you can get here in the same amount of time it takes me. I'll time the run tomorrow morning for you. When you do this then you will be given two days off to do anything you want. Until that happens, however, every day you will work out with me and take lessons from your grandfather."

The kid didn't mind, he thought it would be fun, but he didn't know if he would ever be able to run up the mountain as fast as his father. If anyone would've told the boy he would be able to do that in three months he would have laughed at them for being so wacky. In four months, he'd do it with ease.

Sidney stood up and said, "Let's go outside and see if you can fight." Outside, the little kid was growling and shaking his fist like the other kids did who had seen a karate movie. That was all he knew about fighting. He had wrestled with other boys before, and in the struggle, one of them would get mad and try to hurt the other by either pinching or holding him down real hard. But other than that, he didn't understand the concept of fighting. He had never even seen a fight by the older boys where he had lived.

Sidney watched him growl and hoot and circle around with his legs spaced wide apart so he could hop around. He lashed out a left hand with an open palm and popped the boy on the cheek. The suddenness of the slap's sting brought tears to the boy's eyes. Before he could cry about it, however, he felt two more slaps on his cheeks and he did cry then, but in anger.

The boy rushed his father with both arms flailing. With all the turmoil going on in his mind, the boy couldn't hear his grandfather laughing with approval nor did he see the smile of satisfaction on his father's face. Sidney didn't stop the boy from swinging other than to block the blows directed at his face.

Soon the kid was tired and still crying and he pulled away. He got angrier when he realized the men were laughing. He shouted like the little kid he was, "Why are you laughing? You hurt me and don't even care. You're mean!"

Sidney tried to conceal his amusement, thinking back to the first time he went through the same ritual. It was the start of the transition from childhood to pirate-hood. It had to be hard. It was the only way to get the man that was needed out of a little boy.

When the kid calmed down, Sidney told him to come over and sit next to him. He explained, "If you don't want to get hit then you have to do one of two things and they are your only options. One is attack first like I just did with you. Hit hard and fast so that your enemy only has time to worry about defending himself. That way he is not able to concentrate on hurting you. The second is to take the position as the defender, which is what you just did… Which way sounds better?"

The boy quickly responded, "The attacker."

Sidney continued, "You have to learn how to be the best fighter because when you grow up you cannot ever lose a fight, not ever. To lose a fight is to lose your life. Fighting is a very serious thing and you must do anything to win. You will be taught how to use various tools to be sure you win quickly. The faster you win, the less chance that you'll get hurt."

Grandpa added, "You'll have some sore bones while learning, but it's necessary in order to teach you the difference between winning and losing. Only after you're used to winning will you have the confidence to carry you through the really tough battles that lie ahead for you. Some fights are hard, some are ridiculously easy, but they all must be treated the same way. You must finish the fight as fast as possible. You'll be taught how to use everything around you as an aggressive weapon. A weapon means something that will disable or kill your enemy with the least possible exposure to injury to you."

"Kill someone?" The boy asked.

Grandpa said, "Yes. If he is trying to kill you, the only way to win is to kill him."

Sidney said, "We are going to do the same thing now. This time I want *you* to attack *me*. Think about how you might land the first blow. If you do, I'll not hit you back."

The boy thought for a few seconds, then resumed his karate position for fighting. He lunged in swinging a blow probably aimed at Sidney's shoulder. The blow was blocked with one hand and the boy's face was slapped hard—twice. The stinging blows produced the same results as before.

After the crying stopped, the same procedure was repeated. And again there were the slaps and advice during the rest of the day. The last effort from the boy was his best. His attack had failed, but instead of standing back with tears in his eyes, he immediately attacked again, taking his father by surprise.

The boy landed a small fist on the Sidney's cheekbone. Little Sidney was elated that he had been able to sneak in the blow and was proud of himself as he had planned the action. *Wish I could have hit him harder. I want to see him cry, too.*

Grandpa, who just returned from a nap, hooted with delight that the boy showed some initiative, and the father was happy the day was over. He wasn't really hurting the boy but didn't like making the boy cry. He didn't know why that bothered him. He certainly left a lot of tears on the ground in his early days of training.

Sidney said to the boy, "Okay, you got in by using your head instead of reacting to your emotions; good job. Practice is over for today. Tomorrow we'll work on your stance and that stupid noise you make. I guess you learned that from a movie or other kids, but we don't do things that way. That noise stuff is all show; it's meant to tell other fighters they had practiced the moves, it is no more than a sissy dance.

"If you watch the males of most animals during mating seasons, you'll see the same kind of dance; they are hoping to frighten the other away. You, on the other hand, are in combat and cannot let a frightened person run to warn others about you. When you get older, you'll never let someone who has seen you fight get away. Never let your enemy know how good you are or how you intend to fight. This may sound mean to you, but you have no choice, you are a special person. You are Sidney, the heir of the King of the Seas, and must learn to live above the fears and standards other people have."

"What's a heir?"

Grandpa rolled out in the field with a six pack of beer in his lap. He handed them each one and told the boy to sit on the grass.

He said, "You are the heir. That means that when your father retires you will own everything in the family. Now let me ask you two things, boy. One, why was it so hard to hit him? And, two, what are you going to do tomorrow to be able to hit him first?"

The boy responded, "It's too hard to hit him because he's so big and his arms are too long. Every time I get close enough, I get hit before I get a chance. I don't know what to do."

The old man said, "Sounds like you need to find a way to shorten your opponent's arms or make yours longer. Would that be good enough for you?"

The little boy smiled at the idea and asked, "But how?"

The grandfather said, "Look around for an equalizer. Something that will give you the reach you need: a board, a limb off a tree, or rocks to throw. All those things will keep him away from you. There are other things you can do, too. Throw dirt in his eyes so he can't see you. Fake a swing and kick him in the face with your foot. Find a piece of rope, net, bed sheet, curtains, anything you can find that will restrict the movements of his arms or hide your movements from his sight."

The boy looked surprised that his grandfather was suggesting that he hit his father with boards or rocks.

Grandfather then asked, "What are you going to do tomorrow?"

The boy took a little sip of the cold beer and said, "I'm not going to say it in front of *him*," and nodded to his father who was sitting Indian style a few feet away.

Both men laughed. Grandpa told several stories about fights he had been in where he used other objects as equalizers until all of the beer had been consumed. The boy's beer was self-limited to a few sips and he drank those only because he was thirsty. He didn't like the taste of beer; it was too bitter. He wished his grandfather had a Pepsi.

Sidney got up and told the boy it was time to go home and they broke out in a trot for the trip down the mountain. When Sidney reached his apartment, the boy wasn't in sight. Inside his apartment, he poured himself a glassful of rum and waited for the boy to arrive. It was important to

SIDNEY X THE PIRATE

keep him busy so he wouldn't find other kids to play with. The boy came into the marina parking area, huffing and puffing. Sidney was proud; the boy was really trying. He met him at the door and said, "Training is over for the day. Go on out to your boat, eat something and get some sleep. You have to be back here at dawn."

As the boy turned and started toward the water's edge, Sidney added, "It will get easier kid, give it time."

A thought came to mind: *Talking like that is babying the boy. Watch it Sid, you're getting softhearted... Fuck it... nothing's wrong with trying to encourage him. Shit, it's his first day.*

He watched the kid walk into the water and without hesitation swim very slowly out to the boat. It was very apparent a lot of effort was needed for the boy to climb up the boarding ladder. Once on deck, he laid there too tired to go inside.

Sidney downed the rest of the rum in his glass while thinking about the boy. *He'll damn sure sleep well tonight. Tomorrow will be tougher and he'll have to contend with his sore muscles after today's activities... Wonder what it'd be like to be... normal.*

He spent the rest of the evening at the deck bar listening to the almost drunk and the dead drunk talking about everything important in their lives. Their lives, attitudes, experiences and expectations were based on knowledge gained through their television eyes and stereophonic radio ears. Their basic need in life was to be beautiful, rich, and in love; they wanted be above the masses and drive outrageous cars, dress in Hollywood fashions, and talk the talk.

"Barkeep, gimme a fucking rum," he slurred.

BARBADOS

VINCENZO HAD JUST FINISHED AN INTERESTING INTERVIEW WITH AN-other robbery victim. The man had unknowingly given Vincenzo a seed to plant the first trap. Jason DeGotto had been the purser on a casino ship two years ago. The only reason the inept man had the job in the first place was because he was Carlo DeGotto's nephew, and Carlo worked hand in hand with Tony the Pop.

Jason was a notorious homosexual and totally unreliable. His banks were continuously found to be short, but, other than repeated warnings, it was overlooked due to his connection to the boss of bosses. He had been unfortunate enough to be attacked by apparently the same man. He was taped and tortured by air starvation until he broke down and told the man everything. In an effort to save his bank, he negotiated with information that he shouldn't have known. With a promise to not hurt him or take his bank, Jason divulged an operation called the Tribute.

The Tribute was a practice centuries old. It was an old Mafia way of passing on profits to the top echelon of the families. Modern day Tribute in the Caribbean was collected by a team of men trained to protect the Tribute at all cost, including their lives.

They flew from Sicily in the company's jet to Barbados where they visited each of the family's businesses and collected a set amount of cash or precious gemstones. The airplane went from island to island, making a loop of the Caribbean Basin. The last stop was Antigua, and then the aircraft, full of Tribute, was flown to Sicily for distribution.

The Tribute was collected three times every year. The same aircraft flew three other non-Caribbean routes as well—that Jason didn't know about. Jason, a dumbshit and a scaredy cat, would have surely told the robber of those, as well.

Of course, none of that information was volunteered from Jason during Vincenzo's questions. It had taken time, patience, and some well-placed punches to make him remember. He had never told anyone else about his feeble attempt to save his bank as afterward he realized how stupid he had been.

Vincenzo knew Jason's uncle very well and knew the uncle would have killed the boy had he known. In fact, he would have to kill him just to protect his own ass for telling *anybody* about the Mafia's most guarded underground operation.

That was perfect as far as Vincenzo was concerned. However, he was curious why the Tribute plane hadn't been bothered. *Maybe our security is too tough for the bandits. No… anyone who can show up in the middle of an ocean, rob a multi-million prize then disappear without a trace isn't go-*

ing to let security guards keep them away from that kind of money. Maybe they're lying low thinking the Winnie-whacker told us and would have extra security on board. Or maybe the thief didn't believe the story.

Then he reasoned that it'd be easy enough to keep a watchful eye out to see if it were true. *Shit! That's why it hasn't been hit. It's being studied to learn about procedures and timing before attacking. That's fucking perfect. And I'll damn sure be there when it happens, and I'll be the one with the bag of tricks.*

He was so excited by the new possibility that he forgot to bring in the nightly worthless-New-York-slut-of-a-hooker, and sat at his desk, beer in hand, and polished his plan.

ST. CROIX

It was rare, but the sun was high off the horizon and Sidney was still in bed and dressed in yesterday's clothes. The dull headache reminded him of last night's bout with the rum and no food. He usually drank to extreme, but usually ate lots of food before sleeping.

It dawned on him that the boy hadn't come at dawn.

He muttered, "The little shit must be sore enough to expect special treatment; he wants to be babied. Well, I'll give the little shit some special consideration—Sidney style."

Sidney's hangover put him in a bad mood, and without realizing it, he was going to take it out on the kid. If he had woke up after a night of drinking, good food, and getting thoroughly laid, things would have been different—especially if the lady were still in bed.

He walked out to the edge of the lagoon and yelled for the boy. Sally came out and started to say something but he gestured for her to be quiet. She had tried to give him a ration of shit last night about leaving a little boy alone on the boat and making him swim to and from shore. Sidney wasn't going to have any of that talk going on and vaguely remembered telling her that if she complained again about the way he brought up his son she could pack her shit and get the hell out of there.

Sally returned to her office. "Screw the bastard. I'm not going to jeopardize my job and home. He warned me to keep my fucking eyes and mouth to myself and I'll be happy to oblige the asshole," she muttered.

She had a little smile on her face as she thought about the asshole out there yelling for the boy. The smile turned into a grin when Sidney plunged into the lagoon to swim out to the boat. Her grin turned into giggles as he pulled himself up on the boat.

All she wanted to tell him was the boy tried to wake him up that morning, and he went to his grandfather's house. She had always been afraid of the horny grandpa. Unless he was smiling, he was the meanest looking man she had ever seen, except for a few times when her boss got pissed.

It was rumored that the old man Sid and his son owned the entire mountain and lagoon area. No one knew much about him other than he had supported the whore community, and they appeared to be the only people who knew him. Poor man lost his feet in some kind of an accident, but being in a wheelchair didn't slow him down when chasing cheap women.

Sidney quickly pulled himself out of the water, madder than ever. *Probably in bed crying for his fucking mommy. Well, he's going to have an extra hard day today for making me come get him.*

He didn't notice the open box of cookies and the open jar of peanut butter on the galley's counter. Nor did he notice the crumbs of cookies and half empty can of Spam or several empty cans of Coke. The mustard jar was open on the counter and the contents of the bread wrapper was half spilled out. All were pretty good signs that someone had gulped down a lot of food in a hurry.

He looked around but the boy wasn't there. He wondered if he might have fallen overboard last night and had been too stiff to get back on board. *Naw, he could have made it back to shore.*

He quickly went back on deck and scanned the water and shoreline for signs of the boy. Finally he swam back to shore. Sally met him and said, "He went to his grandfather's house early this morning. He tried to wake you up."

Sidney shot her an angry look and said, "Why didn't you tell me that before?"

Sally didn't answer but gave him *that* look women have perfected over eons; the one that said, "Fuck you."

He grunted and wandered over to the deck bar; he needed food and a couple of cold beers. *Hate looking like a fool— but sometimes it just can't be helped.*

☠

GRANDPA WAS SURPRISED WHEN ROSIE RETURNED TO BED FROM HER morning trip to the bathroom. "That nearly naked little heathen grandchild of yours is sitting on the front porch and singing something in Spanish. His father's not around."

He wheeled himself out to the porch and asked the boy, "Where's your father?"

"He's still asleep. I think he got drunk last night."

Grandfather asked, "Have you had breakfast?"

"Just a little one, Grandpa."

Sidney XXII smiled; *looks like I've just been given a new name. That's the first time I've been called a grandpa.* "Rosie, build two man-sized breakfasts for the men in your life. He and I have some hard work to do today."

Secretly, he was glad that his son wanted his help training the squirt. It gave him something to do and think about—other than pussy.

After breakfast, Grandpa said, "We'll work on three areas today. You have to exercise for an hour, fight-train for an hour and then learn language for an hour. Then we'll repeat the procedure. After you do everything three times, you can go home."

The exercise consisted of running, jumping, sit-ups and push-ups. A limb was selected on a tree that was a little higher than the boy could reach for a pull-up bar.

He told the boy, "To do this exercise, you'll have to run at it and then jump up to catch the limb. Then you pull yourself up."

The boy looked at him in a comical way, and then said, "You must be crazy, Grandpa, if you think I can do that."

"You want to be the strongest kid on the island, don't you?"

That reasoning appealed to the boy. He had a goal to work for. Grandpa's plan was to build his strength doing natural things for the next two years, and then he would start using weights to really make him strong. But, before that could happen, he needed to be naturally fit.

The first period of fight-training was spent sitting on the grass in front of his grandpa and listening to his instructions on how to hit with certain parts of the hand, elbows, knees, and feet.

It was during that period that Sidney showed up. He watched from the house and decided not to interrupt. Looks like pop's doing a good job. Sounds like he using some Norwegian words. That must be the first language he's teaching the boy.

THREE MONTHS LATER

CACHORRO COULD RUN ALL DAY WITHOUT TIRING. HIS FIGHTING SKILLS were developing nicely. His youth and reflexes made it hard for grandpa to duck some of the boy's punches. His grandpa loved every blow knowing his methods of teaching were effective. Not too many tears fell into the turf anymore, but a lot of sweat did. Fighting had turned into a challenging physical workout and lots of horseplay and little Sidney enjoyed both.

Learning languages wasn't fun, as most boys will attest, especially when it interferes with horseplay, but Grandpa made it easier by using the words mixed with English during instructions and conversations. At each hour session on language he would talk about sentence structure with the same words and spent very little time developing vocabulary. With frequent "attaboys," the old man was doing a good job with the boy.

Grandpa's daily routine worked well for everyone. Young Sidney retained everything taught and wasn't bored in the least; it was fun. Rosie was left alone to do something besides screw the old bastard. And Sidney was free three or four days a week to spend time away. It was a time in the year when he needed to research an upcoming raid he had wanted to do for a couple of years.

Four months after the boy arrived in St. Croix, Grandpa asked his son, "What do you think about me going sailing with the boy? I haven't been at sea since I lost my tootsies. Sometimes I miss the sea more than my feet, and I can continue his training and show him things about sailing and the sea. I know you wanted to start his seamanship after his survival training—but I'd really like get on the water again. We're ahead of schedule and the boy is smart and learns everything thrown at him."

Sidney answered, "He's your kid, too. You never asked me for anything before, don't start now. You're doing a good job, but the kid has to do it the hard way for food. You want to depend on him to find food for you?"

"Of course," was Grandpa's quick response.

Sidney asked, "Is Rosie going to go along? Can she sustain the huge body that you love so much, on forage food?"

The old man, thinking of going to sea again, answered serenely, "She stays here."

"Well, that works for me. I've been working on a raid that needs at least a month and could stretch out to three."

"Going to hit the Italians again?"

"Yeah, but it's going to be a tough prize to catch. Something I've never done before."

"What is it?"

"Tell you when I get back."

A few days later, Sidney picked up his father in the Jeep, leaving the wheelchair behind with Rosie. He rowed him out to the *Barracouta*, and Grandpa had no problem getting his body on board; his upper body strength was tremendous.

Sitting up on deck, Grandpa said, "Sidney, being back on a sailboat again after the years since my accident really feels great. I can't tell you how many times I've dreamed of getting offshore again with only wind to restrict my movements. It has been eating me up... you know how it is. We've been bred to live on the sea. I couldn't ask you to take me out, you've got to run the business, but this way I'll be doing what I love most, and teaching him how to become a Sidney."

Sidney sat in the dinghy and watched the boy pull in the two forty-five pound anchors. His father shifted around in the big cockpit on his ass rather than feet. He handled the sheets and the steering wheel. As the last anchor cleared the water, the jib was pulled taut, and with a snap of the sail being filled by wind, the *Barracouta* headed out to open water.

Cachorro went to the mast and hoisted the mainsail. With both sails up, the *Barracouta* fell off the wind and headed straight out to sea. Sidney remained on the dock watching his family sail away. As they cleared the reef, the trade winds filled both sails and she listed over to port.

He felt happy for his father; this was something he truly had been missing in his world of restricted mobility. *Wonder why I never thought about asking him if he wanted to go sailing?*

After pouring a glass of rum, Sidney took the Jeep into Christiansted to visit the library. He needed a little more research before his next raid. He found a book that would satisfy his needs; however, he had hoped to find something a little more comprehensive in the practical use of parachuting. The only book on the subject there was the *History and Design of Old and Modern Parachutes*. He didn't bother checking it out; he didn't have a library card. He stole the seldom-used book.

He had started his surveillance and planning two years ago. It had taken that long to identify the plane and map its route. His primary need after learning the where and when was to see who was the crew and how tough they could be. He was also interested in the airport crews who refueled and serviced the aircraft. He needed to know where the airport crews went after work to have a cold one. Later he returned to see what kind of security was used at night.

Sidney was fascinated by the project. It was to be the first air piracy the Sidneys had ever done in their five hundred-year history. It required knowledge that he didn't have: split-second timing and guts. But, the thrill of the challenge had consumed his thoughts as it slowly became a can-do reality.

That prize, and a Mafia treasure stashed in Cuba, would probably be the last raids he'd do in the Caribbean for a few years. He could finish Cachorro's training in the Mediterranean.

He found two bars the service crews frequented after work and one hotel the flight crews stayed in for the overnight flights. Three times a year, he had been on Antigua, their last stop. The crew overnighted there and he had been in both bars to listen to their conversations. He was in no hurry and the more he heard about their procedures, dislikes, and solutions, the better.

After six trips to Antigua, he knew everything he needed. He knew what actions would be taken to eliminate the possibility of a hijacking and the procedures to be used in case of an attempt. He knew what had to happen to open doors and escape hatches in flight and what happens when you do.

He developed three good plans, all using different techniques. His target was a converted Boeing 737. On the last trip to Antigua, he stole airport coveralls from a locker room and went to the airfield. He waited until all activity had stopped, then quickly made his way across the field and gained entry into the 737 through a cargo hold. Flight controllers were going home as the airport closed for the night. There were stacks of briefcases secured in the cargo web. He dared not to open a few for fear of an alarm.

Using the procedures described by a drunken electronics service man, he gained entry into the passenger area by removing a panel in the men's toilet.

Inside, he found the two security guards sleeping across from a big iron combination safe. He was sorry he hadn't brought Billy or the tape. To take the prize then would have cost him the Antigua Tribute, which was always brought to the plane just before take-off. He quietly walked around checking the doors. After reviewing what was needed to open and close cabin doors, he went back into the cargo hold, refastened the panel and left. The hardest thing he had ever done was leaving the prize untouched.

Emerging from the aircraft, he had felt very secure with his knowledge. He walked across the tarmac without being noticed. Thirty minutes later, he was back in his usual attire of shorts and tee-shirt and still had time for a couple of rums at the hotel bar, where he got lucky with a decent-looking hooker.

During breakfast the next morning, Sidney carefully read over the classified ads in the newspaper. Once again, he was in the market for a boat, but it would be stolen, not purchased. There were several that looked pretty good and each was circled with a pen swiped from the waitress at breakfast. Suddenly he had a better idea.

"I'll use the *Barracouta*." he muttered. "It will expose the boy to the type of work expected of him in the future, and it will be damn good for the old man." The only down side was, if they got caught, it would wipe out the whole family and the treasure would be lost forever.

"But what the hell, who really gives a shit. I'll find the *Barracouta* and see if father feels the same way about risking the family… Shit, he'd love the raid; this will be one future Sidneys will read over and over." He called an air charter company and hired a pilot and seaplane for the day.

Sidney knew his father would sail to his favorite area, the Windward Islands, and knew he would be within a distance of one hundred fifty miles based on the length of time they had been gone and the hull speed of the boat.

The pilot and Sidney had spotted several boats in the area *Barracouta* should be in; none were the *Barracouta*. Finally, he saw the *Barracouta*. His father was at the helm, the boy sitting beside him. A pass of one hundred feet over the boat confirmed it; the old man's angry face and extended arm with the pointed middle finger was a sure sign that he didn't appreciate his privacy being disturbed.

The seaplane landed directly ahead of the boat. Sidney hoped his father would slow down to see what was up—but he didn't. He sailed past the idling seaplane and was only fifty feet away before he recognized Sidney who was out standing on one of the pontoons.

The old man yelled, "What the fuck are you doing?"

The boy had a big smile on his face and was waving hello with both hands. He had never seen a seaplane before and was excited that his father would be in one way out in the ocean. Grandpa slacked the sails and turned the boat up wind, stopping its movement. Sid told the pilot to wait, then dove off the seaplane and swam the distance to the boat.

Grandpa was very curious and hoped Sidney wasn't there to join them. The kid was okay, but three people would ruin his sailing trip. Once aboard, Sidney said in front of the boy, "I raided a cruise ship a couple of years ago. My target turned out to be a very frightened Mafioso." He went on to describe the Tribute plane process to get money to Sicily.

Young Sidney asked, "What's a Mafia, Dad?"

Sidney said, "It's another word for assholes." Then he looked back at his father and resumed, "I have spent over a year finding this plane and confirming the purser had been telling me the truth. Since then, I have observed every flight that arrives in St. Maarten and departs Antigua. I have their actions and schedule down pat. I had intended to take the Italian's Tribute away from them before I sail to Europe this year to train Junior."

"Sounds interesting, but you are asking for trouble by hitting the same group so hard. They have to be really pissed already. They might be pansies on a one to one basis, but there's a hell of a lot of them."

"Fuck 'em." said Sidney, showing little interest in his father's opinion.

Grandpa asked, "So what brings you out here? I'm sure you didn't come by just to tell of this plan or even ask for my opinion."

"To make my plan work requires a boat to be in a certain position and waiting for me to arrive by parachute. I have worked out the details to do it by myself but thought it might be good for the boy. You might even enjoy some action, other than balling Rosie for a change."

"Really?" asked Grandpa in a genuinely surprised voice.

"The worst thing that can happen is all of us could be caught."

His father surprised him by saying without hesitation, "Fuck it! Nothing lasts forever, not even this family. Let's do it."

Without waiting for a response from Sidney, Grandpa went on, "Is it a big prize?" His facial expression said there was much joy in his life at that moment. His enthusiasm looked as if it was ready to jump out of the sparkle in his eyes.

Sidney answered, "It could be the biggest prize I've taken."

The older Sid showed his pleasure with a smile. His son had taken several prizes in the millions of dollars so this had to be something big. He wanted the details.

"I don't know for sure how much is involved, but do know that I'm going to have a very big bag with me the next time you see me."

The old man was so excited that Sidney felt a little guilty that he had never thought about asking him to get involved before. The only thing wrong with the man was his inability to walk, but his mind was good and he had more guts than any other man. And if any man or beast pissed him off and got within grabbing range, he'd damn sure kick their ass. He always had been the roughest, toughest, meanest son of a bitch in the world. Except for a particular twenty-foot hammerhead shark, nobody else had ever gotten the best of Sidney XXII.

Sidney said, "You need to sail into port and buy a good single side band radio. In one week from today, I'll call you on the SSB on the frequency of 12222.2. Your vessel's name is *Sunny Daze*; I'm *Sea Play*, both common boat names. I have listed the codes we will use to switch frequencies and talk about departure times, latitudes and longitudes, etc."

"Sounds simple enough," said his father. "But it sounds as if you are planning on jumping out of an airplane. Have you ever jumped out of an airplane?"

"Nope, but I read a book on it."

Young Sidney was excited, "You are going to jump out of an airplane? Wow! Is that the one?" and pointed to the idling seaplane.

"No, it will be a big one," then he pointed out some latitude and longitude coordinates on the wet crumpled paper that had been in his pocket during the swim from the seaplane.

"That mark is about fifty miles off Antigua; you'll need to be in that general area in two weeks. I won't have a definite time until just before the plane leaves. I'll check in with you every day at 0800, 1200 and 2000 hours. If you don't hear from me, then figure I couldn't make the call because I'm busy and on my way to these coordinates. If you don't hear from me by the next time, then figure that I got caught or I'm floating somewhere around those coordinates waiting for you. Any questions?"

"Nope, but that's a lot of water to find a floating man. Will you have a flare or a flag?"

"I'll wave to you with something, just go to that mark, I'll get there." Feeling satisfied with the arrangements, he then said, "Got to go. See you later," and dove overboard for the swim back to the idling seaplane.

Sidney had the seaplane land off the eastern shore of Fajardo in Puerto Rico. He paid the man a lot more than was originally agreed on and told him to be back in three days to pick him up for a return trip. The pilot knew he should advise Customs that he dropped off a passenger, but decided against it. A lot of people didn't bother with Customs anymore; it was just a lot of bullshit and paperwork.

A short swim to a rocky shoreline and a half a mile walk through the sparse growth of brush, and he was on the main highway. He thumbed until a farmer picked him up on his way to San Juan. He enjoyed the ride through the countryside but wasn't particularly happy with the one-sided conversation from a pissed-off farmer who complained about the prices of melons and the weather for the hour-long ride.

He got out at a rather large shopping mall; he was ready for a change of clothing. In addition to his clothes, he also bought a pair of thick socks, long, thermal underwear, a heavy jacket, and ski cap that pulled down to be a mask. A pair of heavy gloves was the finishing touch to his new wardrobe.

In a sporting goods store he purchased the rest of the gear he wanted: two inflatable life vests; a small scuba tank and regulator; a large inflatable balloon marker—the type used as a turning mark in some sailboat races—an inflatable one man life raft, and a fifty-foot long piece of one-quarter-inch nylon rope. The last item was a wristwatch that was also a stopwatch and altimeter. It was the first watch he had ever owned.

All of those items were certainly new to Sidney. He had only needed his knife, Billy, and a roll of tape on his previous raids. He was stepping out of his environment and would be working thirty-eight thousand feet above that familiar sea surface. He resented having to take so much stuff with him, but he had to survive in an extremely hostile environment. And for all he knew about jumping out of airplanes and freefalling 30,000 feet before opening the chute, he might not make it anyway.

He caught a taxi at the shopping mall and directed the driver to take him to the Marine Dream, a large marine electronics store. There he purchased the first navigational tools he ever needed; a handheld GPS ~global positioning system~, and a handheld SSB radio.

Sitting in the back seat of the taxi, he told the driver, "Take me to the Hilton on the beach area. There's a small motel near there." He couldn't check into the big hotel as they required identification.

He took a room in the motel and then ordered a big steak and a bottle of rum from room service. After a lengthy hot shower, he sat down to his meal and rum. Then he was hungry for some action and walked over to the Hilton.

In the casino he played craps, his favorite way to lose money. He played for big stakes, attracting the attention of the casino dealers and hookers who were hired to take care of big spenders. They liked to see someone play for the big bucks rather than the usual tourist who puts a hundred-dollar limit on the amount he'll allow himself to lose. After a couple of hours he was close to breaking even and quit playing. He tipped his table's crew a hundred bucks and said, "I need a woman."

The pit boss smiled and said, "Do you have a preference?"

"No. I'll wait in the bar."

Less than five minutes had passed before the girl arrived. Every pair of eyes in the bar followed her across to Sidney. Some were stunned at her beauty and a couple of guys let their mouths drop open. She was tall, five-foot eight, slender and shapely, with long natural red hair that hung down to her waist.

Sidney only saw pussy and didn't even offer to buy her a drink. Instead, he stood up and left money on the bar for his drink and motioned her to follow him. She looked nervously at the bartender for some sign that the guy was okay and not some kind of nut. But she got nothing back from the barman, as the customer hadn't spoken a word to him other than, "Double rum."

Much to her dismay, she followed him across the street to the motel. Foreplay consisted of dropping his clothes on the floor and sliding in bed, and then watching her undress. Standing tall and naked, she said, "It's three-hundred dollars—before."

Sid shrugged that was okay. She said, "I need it before we get carried away, Sweetie." He pointed to his shorts on the floor and said, "Get it from there."

The thick wad of bills found in the shorts impressed her. As she slid into bed, Sidney pulled her legs apart and quickly entered her. To her surprise, it was a long rough ride, and she almost reached a point of enjoyment before he finished. There were no comforting caresses or kisses or soft words most men do afterwards as the feeling for sex subsided. He got up and took a long loud piss with the bathroom door left open. He came back as she was sitting on the edge of the bed putting on her brassiere when he said, "Get back in bed. We are not through yet."

She objected, saying, "I have done what I was paid for and now it is time to leave. I have other customers to take care of."

Sidney said, "Bullshit, get your ass back in bed."

Looking at his hard, scarred body she knew that he was not a man to play games. The pit boss had said he was the serious type and had a lot of money, which could indicate that he was a criminal, and if there were any problems, use the phone to get security to the room. But she wasn't in the hotel. She thought for a moment and rationalized that if he planned to hurt her he would have done it already. She smiled and said, "That'll be another three hundred."

The girl was ravished many times during the night. The rough style had excited her after she resigned herself to pleasing her rugged customer and found herself climaxing several times during the night. The next morning, after his morning dump, Sidney came out of the bathroom and tossed the girl another three hundred dollars and said, "You were very good. You can leave now."

She was curious about the man, but knew better than to ask questions; she dressed, flipped her comb through her hair and waved goodbye. He acknowledged her wave as he ordered room service. He spent the morning checking his new equipment and became thoroughly familiar with the operation of each piece. There wouldn't be time to read manuals when the action started.

With his newly bought stuff packed in a large nylon sail bag, he left the motel and took a taxi to Fajardo. On the way he bought a six pack of cold Medala beer and a couple cheap cigars. He drank rum out of the bottle and smoked a cigar, much to the annoyance of the driver.

The wait for the seaplane was uneventful, just another cheap motel, lots of rum, a groggy head the next morning with the rotten taste of smoke and booze in his mouth.

"Shit," he said to no one, "surely someone in this entire world is smart enough to develop a product that can be put into your mouth to take that rotten morning aftertaste away." But it seemed that the only thing that would do the trick was a couple of cold beers. So he had a few.

The seaplane was on time and as soon as Sidney strapped in he said, "Name your price to take me to St. Maarten."

The pilot looked worried and said, "I would, but I'm not permitted to land there."

Sidney counted ten one hundred-dollar bills and stuffed them into the pilot's shirt pocket, and said, "I'm your brother; you wanted to show me the island and it's your day off, right?"

The pilot taxied out, saying, "Sounds good to me, Bro."

When St. Maarten was in sight, Sidney told the pilot to drop him off on the north coast and pointed the way. It was a long beach on the French side where clothing was optional and there was always a lot of activity around. Many boats anchored in the natural harbor and a seaplane landing was not uncommon.

Sidney jumped out of the plane in waist deep water and waded to shore while the pilot lost no time in getting airborne again. Sidney didn't stick around either, and hailed a passing taxi on the beach road.

He used a St. Maarten street address to show he was a local; thereby he wasn't required to put his passport number on the registration form as he checked into the Airport Inn. His equipment was laid out in his room and checked again. The scuba tank needed filling and the regulator had to be adjusted to operate at 38,000 feet above sea level. For a crisp one hundred-dollar bill, he arranged for a porter to take the tank to be filled. Then he placed a call to the regulator manufacturer and told customer service that he was going mountain climbing and needed to adjust his regulator. They were happy to assist, but later wondered where he could find a 38,000 foot mountain.

The only thing he still needed was the overalls that were used by the airport's ground crew. He would get the overalls that night then he could settle in and wait for the Italians to arrive.

Sidney took a drink from a rum bottle and sat in a lounge chair to mentally go over his plan one more time to be sure he hadn't forgotten something important. *When I get the air tank back, I better use some of the nylon line to make a special harness to keep it attached to me when I exit the aircraft. Damn, I'll be going over four hundred miles per hour. What's going to happen when I hit the wall of subsonic wind—a wall of super cold air? Shit, I have no idea if this is going to work. All I know with any degree of certainty is that I'm going to find out.*

That night he climbed over the airport perimeter fence to have a look around. He checked for obstacles and laid out the best route to the parking ramp. He was also shopping for a uniform. The field proved to be no problem to negotiate without being seen from the tower or any other concerned eyes. The locker room was unlocked from the parking ramp side and he quickly popped open one of the lockers. He took a fresh uniform that looked to be his size and everything else in the locker to make it look like a robbery, not just an effort to get the uniform.

Fifteen minutes later, he was in his room and pouring a glass full of rum. After the glass was empty, he was ready for sleep. It came easily and he slept hard until sunrise the next day.

After the bellboy brought in the air tank, Sidney rigged up a web harness that held the tank firmly in place on his chest, not his back. *I'll wrap myself around the tank to keep my arms and legs in tight like in a ball. I think if I back away from the doorway as much as possible to be able to run and exit as fast as I can, then leap out in a spinning tucked position, and that should reduce windage damage.*

During the day he constantly checked the parking ramp with his binoculars. He had scouted the plane every few months for the year and a half and knew it on sight. But the thought did pop up a few times. *What if they bought a new plane?*

Thanks to the ship's purser and Sidney's efforts to watch their operations in Antigua, St. Maarten and Puerto Rico, and he knew all of the stops the plane made; knew who took care of the details at each stop and who received the goods in Sicily. He knew as much about the operation as most any person connected to the tri-yearly flight process.

In St. Maarten, the plane would land, and a call would be made to a Mr. Ciro Renagi, the general manager of the Casa Cambino Resort. The plane would be on the ground for only two hours so Ciro wouldn't waste time. He was responsible for collecting and transporting the island's Tribute to the aircraft. He also supervised the loading of the briefcases and bags containing merchandise into the plane's cargo hold just before the plane departed.

A hop to Antigua would be next and the flight crew would leave the aircraft to rest up overnight for the flight to Sicily. It was very risky to approach the plane, as teams of men were stationed inside and outside the aircraft from the time it landed to the next morning when it left the ground. While security in Antigua was very good, the other stops only had two armed guards onboard with a flight crew of four men, also armed, but they were not professional shooters.

From Antigua it was straight back to Sicily. Security in Sicily was unbeatable, the plane and its treasure were untouchable. It would be met by several big black limousines full of armed men and a rental truck to haul the assorted briefcases and boxes of gifts to the mysterious Circle of Fifteen.

To maximize his prize, Sidney planned to board the aircraft as close to the end of the route as possible and Antigua was too risky. He'd board in St. Maarten very shortly after its landing and spend the night in the baggage compartment. His dirty deed to the Mafia would get started shortly after takeoff from Antigua the next morning when it reached its cruising altitude.

The plane was due to arrive in St. Maarten the next day, so Sidney was in his ready mode. No booze, no foolishness, mind and body locked on to the task at hand to do whatever was necessary to get the job accomplished. He would be happy when this prize was safely tucked away in the Cave of Snakes.

He loaded the bag with his gear, dressed in the slacks, shirt, sport coat and expensive leather loafers, and then took a taxi to the Casa Cambino Resort on the island and checked into a luxury suite. He called the bell captain to come to his room. Using an Italian accent, Sidney told him,

"Give this bag to Ciro Renagi. Do you know him?"

"Oh, yes sir. He is the manager here."

"You must give this to him personally. You are not to leave that bag lying around and you will not repeat the message I am going to give you. Do you understand me?"

The bell man, like all of the other employees, knew Ciro was more than a hotel manager. The hotel was owned by a few Italians that even the local government gave a wide berth. The man didn't have to be a genius to fully understand the seriousness of the hard looking man standing before him.

The bell man politely said, "Yes, sir. I fully understand your instructions and assure you I will personally be responsible to see that Mr. Renagi receives the package and the message exactly as you tell it."

"Good, I think you know better than to get Ciro pissed. You tell him this is to be delivered to Don Gugguci, in Sicily. It is to be put on the company's aircraft that will be arriving tomorrow. It *must* be on that flight. The bag contains things the Don wants for personal reasons. He stipulated it had better be on that plane when it arrives. It's okay for Ciro to personally check the contents of the bag, but under no circumstances is he to let anyone else. He is also not to handle any of the items in the bag."

Sidney gave the man a key to the padlock on the bag and tipped him with a one hundred-dollar bill. Before turning loose of the bill Sidney said, sternly, "You had best not fuck up the delivery or that message and don't even think about looking into the bag. If you do and Ciro doesn't fuck you up, I'll come back and take care of you myself. You understand me?"

The fear in the man's eyes told Sidney there would be no problems. Also he was sure the name of Don Gugguci would insure no hang-ups or missed flights. He had given permission to look into the bag to further reduce the possibility that Ciro would call to get clearance, as everyone was careful with all cargo on that aircraft.

THE TRIBUTE

VINCENZO WAS FEELING ANTSY AND AFTER SEVERAL DAYS OF BEING cooped up in the airplane with the same people, day and night, he was irritated at everything. Needless to say, the crew stayed clear of him; Vincenzo the Sicilian needed to kill someone—anyone. There were only two more stops to prove his theory and nail the bastards he wanted so desperately to catch. If it was a "no-go" then he'd have to ride every Tribute flight, and that was not how he wished to spend his time.

He had been careful setting up the operation; not one person outside of the flight crew knew he and his team were aboard. When they boarded the plane in Sicily, they were totally self-contained with several big coolers stuffed with food and kept cool with dry ice along with boxes of groceries. There was nothing they needed. When the flight crew re-provisioned at their normal stops they would be taking on exactly the same quantities in case the culprits had connections in flight service meals—if they did, it would have been apparent that extra men were on board. Also there was a possibility the food could be drugged to disable the crew, but it would not affect his own men.

Two men were always alert day and night, and for off-duty men there was no booze or women. They couldn't even look out of windows in fear of being spotted by the raiders. It was strictly business for Vincenzo's team. Besides his men, there were the usual two security guards traveling and doing their daily routines so there would be no deviation in patterns.

He was in Puerto Rico waiting for the flight crew to finish their pre-flight. Vincenzo walked through the baggage compartment looking at all the bags and attaché cases while thinking about any possibilities he might have missed. *Today is the next to the last stop. We'll be in St. Maarten for a couple of hours then head to Antigua for the night— like always.*

He was sure if the hit happened it would be in Antigua to get the most loot. He and his men had brainstormed every possibility on how it could be done; they were ready for anything. *Hitting us on the last stop ensures them maximum plunder, but they'll know we've always had more security there. If it's a big group of men that might be the place it'll happen— regardless of security.*

He knew the best attack would be a two-front assault. A helicopter could swoop in coordinated with an attack by an approaching airport vehicle and kill everyone in a quick firefight and then disappear in the helicopter. He had a fifty-caliber automatic rifle on board that would kill the helicopter.

If it were a one-or two-man hit, it would happen sooner and St. Maarten would be the best choice, as it offered near-maximum loot but no additional security. And since it was for a short stay and so close to the end, the flight crew would assume the pressure was off enough to let their guards down a little.

The bags were all new and in various sizes as fresh tropical fruits, drugs, and clothing made of illegal skins and furs from South American countries, were packed in tightly. Attaché cases were stuffed, too, but with cash, gold and gemstones.

He chuckled and said, "I'd like to snatch this load myself, if I thought I'd get away with it." Actually, after watching the routine, He thought: I *think I'd do it in Santo Domingo. Most of the large tributes have been collected and security is at its worst. Airport security was almost nonexistent and with all of the corruptible armed guards that work there it would be simple.*

Actually, Vincenzo had found a good reason at every place they had stopped to make the hit. Also, there wasn't a stop that he didn't fully expect the hit to happen. Each stop was to be the day he nailed the cocksuckers to the wall.

The aircraft left Puerto Rico on its way to St. Maarten; the team, weary of traveling, was happy that only two stops kept them away from their beloved Sicily. Vincenzo refused to share his private suite, forcing the four men to share one. That really wasn't a problem as two men worked for four hours and two were off around the clock, even while in the air. Vincenzo didn't fully trust the air crew either.

His men were beginning to miss the comfort of their own beds and their families and mistresses. They wanted this business to be over with and looked forward to tomorrow morning when they would once again be airborne, but be on their way home. Vincenzo wasn't in such a hurry, however; knowing that if the raid didn't happen then he and the team would be back aboard the next time it left Sicily. He felt certain the men who had learned of the flight were part of the same crew and would strike when it suited them.

Looking down at the beautiful green and blue water as the plane left the eastern most end of the island gave Vincenzo time to pause in his deadly mantrap. *Why can't I spend my time down there fishing or fucking on those beautiful beaches instead of traveling around, cooped up with a bunch of assholes? Usually I have a good life. I have everything I want, screw the world's finest women, eat the best food, am respected by all who know me, am free to do as I fucking want and I've managed not to develop any real enemies, or dangerous ones, anyway... Shit, that's exactly why I'm not spending time on beautiful sunny beaches, fucking or fishing. I've got it fucking made in the shade.*

That thought energized him and he went into the main cabin to invigorate his men; he wanted them not to be just ready for the raid, but enthusiastically looking forward to it.

ST. MAARTEN

Sidney made his first call to *Sunny Daze*. Grandpa responded appropriately and gave him his position. The coordinates given were well away from his actual position by using the code Sidney had engineered. A 1 needed to be added to the second number, a ~3 to the next, a ~4 to the next, and a ~5 to the next. A coordinate of 067:34:22 really would be 070:19:22.

Sidney told *Sunny Daze*, "I should be leaving site ~2 today unless you hear otherwise."

The same message was repeated at noon that day; the conversation was casual, sounding just like two cruisers trying to get together. There was no call at eight that night. Sidney was elsewhere.

He had spotted the aircraft just after it touched down on the runway. Before it came to a stop on the parking ramp, he was inside the airfield's perimeter fence and halfway there. He walked like he belonged there, even scooped up dried grease on the tarmac and pushed it under his finger nails and wiped the rest on his pants' legs as many mechanics had a tendency to do. He looked the part and would soon have to act it as well. When he got to the terminal's maintenance building area, he slipped into one of the pickup trucks and drove it to the newly arrived jet.

A man wearing slacks and a sport coat, to hide his shoulder holster and weapon, was already outside. He met Sidney before he reached the plane.

Sidney said "I've been told to stand by in case the aircraft commander wants me to handle any problems before you leave."

The guard shook his head and thought that was smart to have a mechanic standing by in case of a problem. They were on a tight schedule.

Sid stayed in the pickup and the guard continued walking around stretching his legs and warming himself in the afternoon sun. The other guard always stayed inside and out of view.

The crew left the aircraft in ones and twos to walk around in the sun while waiting for their precious cargo. After a few minutes, no one seemed to pay Sidney's presence any attention, except the one guard who stayed close by. He casually got out of the truck and mingled briefly with the flight crew while working his way closer to the plane. When he reached it he knelt by the wheels and inspected tires, landing gears, and worked his inspection to the cowling around the engine.

When the pilot came over to look over the same items for his preflight, Sidney said, "Everything looks A-Okay. Your tires might want a thorough look-at in another thirty landings, but they're fine for now. Since there doesn't seem to be any need for me, I'm going to lie down in the truck. A little nap will be good for me; I had a long night last night. Wake me if you need anything. If I'm not there, I'll be back. I may walk over to the terminal to get an Alka Seltzer to cool my pipes."

When the outside guard changed places with the other so he could get some time in the sun, Vincenzo asked him, "Anything out of the usual going on?"

"Nothing but the mechanic on standby; there's no problem there, he's just a worker told to fix any problems we might have. He doesn't give a shit about anything but taking a nap to sleep off a hangover."

Soon, a white limousine approached the aircraft from the opposite side Sidney had parked. With all attention directed toward the limousine, Sidney slid out of the cab and silently covered the fifty feet to the plane.

He quickly opened the small cargo door and threw his body in and rolled out of view. His movements had been quick; his timing perfect; no one saw his movements. And no one missed his presence on the field.

Three men got out and started unloading the limousine. Ten brief-cases, three duffel bags and Sid's big bag were loaded into the cargo hold. The crew's anxiety about the arriving cargo had dissipated; everyone except Vincenzo felt more relaxed. Sidney's lack of presence wasn't noticed as the maintenance van was parked in the proper area for work vehicles.

He heard footsteps of the last man leave the compartment and then the doors closed. Seconds later, the engines came to life. Five minutes later, he heard the engines roar and felt vibrations from their mighty power. Next came the bumping as the aircraft taxied over the typically rough tarmac. It came to a stop very briefly, and then the engines sounded like tornadoes as RPMs increased to takeoff power. The plane lurched with the brake's release, and then there was the hard jarring as the 737 bounced down the tropical runway.

The flight crew was relaxed; after all, they had made the same trip for years without a problem. Another reason they were relaxed was nobody knew this trip even existed, regardless of Vincenzo's suspicions—and if someone knew, they certainly wouldn't steal from them. It would mean certain and nasty death of the persons responsible, as well as their families. The flight crew hadn't been told the real reason for Vincenzo's team, only that it was a new security procedure being considered.

Vincenzo noticed the empty truck was still parked on the tarmac as they bounced down the runway and had a sudden feeling that something wasn't right. He motioned the regular guards to come to him.

"Why is the mechanic van still there? When's the last time you saw him?"

The first guard said, "I told you; he's really hung over and went to sleep. I guess he's really out of it and the engine noise didn't wake him. He's going to be in for a nasty surprise when his boss comes out and catches him."

Both guards laughed.

The second guard was tired of Vincenzo's intrusion into their territory and said, "Like he said, the man's asleep, relax. I watched him lie down and I checked on him. He's asleep. Quit worrying Vincenzo; shit we've kept the plane and the Tribute safe for years. We know what we're doing and damn sure don't need some big shot watching over us and telling us how to do our job."

The rebuff angered Vincenzo and he made a mental note to remove the asshole from future flights. Then, being paranoid, he wondered if he was defensive because he was working with the raiders.

Vincenzo said, "Don't you fucking be concerned about what I'm doing. All I want from you is for you to shut the fuck up and do as you're told. Everybody stays alert. Now get your asses down in the cargo hold. Go through the trap door in the pilot's cabin. I want you to look everywhere it would be possible for a man to hide. Have your guns ready; if he's in there, you're going to need them in a hurry."

The aircraft reached its altitude of twelve thousand feet on the hop to Antigua. Air temperature dropped to almost sixty degrees in the baggage compartment. Sidney was lounging inside his big black bag that he entered seconds after gaining entrance to the compartment. He didn't bother to put on his warm clothes, as soon they would be back at sea level and the tropical heat and humidity.

The engine's noise hid the sound of the trap door being opened. It also hid the guard's conversation about Vincenzo the Worrier. The man they used to know and fear—Vincenzo the Sicilian. They had a few laughs about Vincenzo and a smoke while they walked around casually looking for a man standing behind a partition. There was nobody except those who belonged there. And that was basically the message relayed to Vincenzo.

Sidney never knew the men were in the compartment; it was fortunate that he had not chosen to move around in the bag to reposition, or to fart when they walked past only inches away. He had planned not to move around while inside the aircraft either in the air or on the ground. He wanted no chance of discovery and had zipped the bag shut and locked the padlock to keep prying eyes from examining its contents. When he was ready to leave he would cut a slit in the bag.

The plane roughly landed and bounced down the taxiway and ended with a loud squeal from one of the brakes. Shortly, the sound of the engine's whining roar ceased. That sound was replaced with muffled voices of the flight crew preparing to disembark. Thirty minutes later, there were no sounds, but Sidney knew the two guards were wide awake and only inches above him. Each man would be armed with two weapons, an Uzi and an assault twelve-gauge shotgun. Also there would be three Antiguan men on the outside, each with an AK-47 and the same shotgun.

Sidney cut a small hole in the bag separating him from discovery. While peeking out, he thought, *I'd have to be nuts to try to take this aircraft here. Besides, they have the blessing of the local government and the Antiguans wouldn't hesitate a minute to blow anybody away who might threaten the Italians... Hope I don't fall asleep and snore.*

He had it all together—unfortunately, he was unaware of the additional team of four killers and Vincenzo who were also on board—and they were hoping someone like him would try to come aboard.

The night took forever to pass. There was noise outside a couple of times when the security crews were replaced, but other than that it was hot, dark and silent inside the bag. He caught himself dozing off several times during the night, but forced himself to stay awake. His legs cramped in the bag and it was sweltering, there wasn't any free flowing air, but still he didn't move. He wouldn't risk the chance of being discovered by the slight sound of a zipper being opened or the chance of making a noise while moving around in the bag. He wasn't even sure the door was closed and one of the guards could be in the compartment. Thanks to his training, he knew how to disassociate himself from discomfort and remained unmoving hour after hour.

Finally, he heard voices outside and in the cabin above him. The loud growl of a truck pulled up which had to be the fuel truck. He heard the cargo compartment door open and *imagined* that he felt a slight rush of fresh, cool morning air. A man's footsteps were heard walking towards him, and then around him. Then several clumps, thumps and sounds of briefcases being stacked up in one of the cargo racks next to him.

Now if only someone doesn't try to move my bag I should almost be

home free... That is if I survive the next hour... That's the cargo door clos-
ing. That's a relief... There go the engines—now I can move around.

As the plane taxied, he slit the bag open with his big knife and stiffly
crawled out on his hands and knees. The compartment was pitch black
except for the small beam of light from his miniature flashlight.

As the aircraft raced down the runway, he began laying out his gear.
Everything had to be ready. As he rigged his gear he went over his game
plan. He had to stay on schedule. He figured that every minute in flight
would take him approximately six miles closer to his intended drop zone.
And six miles was a hell of long swim in the seas of the Atlantic Ocean.

The plane would reach its cruising altitude of thirty-eight thousand
feet in ten minutes, then level off and go on autopilot. He should be about
sixty miles offshore then and that'd give him eight minutes. That'd be all
the time he'd have to take the crew, load the goodies he wanted in the bag,
check his position on the GPS then call his position to his father.

That was when he'd jump out of this perfectly good airplane at an incredible altitude and speed for his maiden parachute jump. He muttered,
"Hope I know what I'm doing. I'm a seaman, not a fucking bird."

The busy few minutes ahead didn't allow him to dwell on the horror
of the jump. He needed every minute between take off and the climb to
altitude to get ready.

ANTIGUA

VINCENZO STOOD ALONE IN THE SHADE UNDER THE AIRPORT'S OUTSIDE
observation area. He watched the Tribute aircraft taxi to the runway;
increase the engine's speed and release the brakes. In a moment it was
airborne and on its way back home. The martini in his hand was nearly empty as he mused over the last few days. He was disappointed. The
bastards didn't try to take it. Now he'd have to do it all again on the next
trip—unless he found the pricks before then.

Then he had a pleasant thought, *maybe I'll take a fucking broad next*
time. Spending time with a bunch of ginzos with hard-ons ain't much fun.

As the plane disappeared from sight he said aloud, "And I'm going to
take a hop back to St. Maarten to spend a couple of nights at Casa Cam-

bino, have dinner with my old pal, Ciro, and pounce on a couple of his hookers. Then, damn it, I'll have to return to New York and visit with the FBI faggot and the chickenshit attorney."

ST. MAARTEN

In St. Maarten he checked into the resort and left a message for Ciro that he expected to be entertained. The telephone in his room was ringing as he entered the room. It was a happy Ciro and they made plans for a late dinner and entertainment. Vincenzo welcomed the break; he was tired of the constant hustle and bustle of the traveling during the past week. It was nice to take a leisurely shower then stretch out on the bed in the cold air-conditioned room, watch television and nod off into a long nap.

That night, the two Mafiosos met in the bar where they enjoyed drinks during conversations about business.

Ciro asked, "So what brings you to my part of the world?"

"I've been riding shotgun on the Tribute flight."

"That's somewhat overkill isn't it?"

"No. It was my idea. I'm looking for someone who has been hitting our properties lately. You remember what happened at the bank here? Well, I think that might have been the people I've been looking for."

"I thought it was done by a wacko Rastafarian."

"Don't think so. You haven't had or heard of any more trouble have you?"

"No, things have been peaceful around here, which I guess must be true for the big guys in Sicily too."

"What do you mean?"

"When Don Gugguci starts parachuting and scuba diving it must mean he has more time on his hands than I do."

"Don Gugguci! Parachuting? You got to be shitting me."

"Well, the message I got was Gugguci personally was eager to get the stuff and it had to be taken on the Tribute plane."

Something about that bothered Vincenzo; if he had more time, or fewer martinis, and if the ladies had not shown up at that moment, he might have tried to get a call through to see if the aircraft was okay. But the girls were beautiful, sexy and eager for some fun. It was the early morning light that peeped over the horizon that brought the party to a halt as the sleepies took over. Vincenzo woke up at noon that morning and crawled over the warm body of a sleeping hooker to place a telephone call to Tony in Sicily.

"Tony, this is Vincenzo, did… "

"Where the fuck are you?" Tony interrupted with an excited yell. "I've been trying to find you for the last six fucking hours. Where the fuck are you?"

"I am in St. Maarten, why? Is something wrong?"

AT 38,000 FEET

WHAT VINCENZO DIDN'T KNOW WAS THAT BEFORE HE ARRIVED IN ST. Maarten, Sidney had put the warm clothes on; the temperature was rapidly dropping, but he was still soaked in sweat from his environment in the bag and his rushed activities. The air tank was tied to his chest, as was the regulator. The ski cap was rolled up making no attempt to cover his face until he was ready to jump. He strapped the parachute on according to the instructions. Billy was in hand and his knife was strapped into position on his belt.

Every briefcase was locked so he broke the hasps with a twist of his knife. The contents were poured into the big bag. He worked quickly because when his wristwatch timer sounded a chime it was time to leave. When it sounded, he still had six more briefcases to go, and since he never left a prize behind, he spent another two minutes to empty them into the bag.

He was ready for the next part of the raid and moved to the forward hatch. Carefully, he raised the hatch enough to see and listen to what was going on. Two men at the controls were talking about the weather coming up before they would see the Azores; their attention was focused. The third man, the navigator, was sitting with his feet only inches away from the hatch. Sid positioned his heavy bag under the ladder so he could pull it up with the cord that had been tied to it. With Billy in hand it was time to move.

He pushed the hatch open very quickly but was careful not to let it bang on a nearby bulkhead that might alert the others in the main cabin. His coiled legs on the ladder rung sprung out of the hatch and Billy tapped the navigator perfectly. The copilot turned to see what the flash of movement was but it was too late; Billy had him, too. The pilot saw that action but was too surprised to react and Billy sent the pilot on his last tailspin.

Sidney checked to be sure the autopilot was on; checked the heading they were traveling and the ground speed. Everything was close to the plan—or close enough.

The cockpit door was closed; the security guards were not aware of what was going on. The big, bulky bag was pulled up into the cockpit, then, without wasting time, Sidney took the nine-millimeter pistol from the pilot's shoulder holster. He quickly checked it to be sure it was loaded and that the safety was off. It felt odd—almost dirty in his hands; it was not a weapon of honor. He put the regulator in his mouth and tightened the strap as much as he could; the air flow valve had been turned on. The rope that connected him to his bag was securely tied to his waist, the extra line coiled over his shoulder.

Satisfied, he opened the cabin's door and stepped out into the cabin and took a firm grip on a handrail. Two men were sitting at the bar enjoying their first drink in two weeks and laughing at stories each had heard before. Two other men were stretched out in lounge chairs trying to sleep.

Surely, he was a frightful sight to the men at the bar. Nothing was said, but Sidney raised the gun and shot the window out next to one of the men. The cabin seemed to explode with the sound of the gun and the man sitting next to the window was no longer there; his body had been sucked out instantly. The other man followed him by three milliseconds.

After the hard suction ended, Sidney released the flight attendant's belt he had put around his bag. A few fast steps and he was down the aisle where the other two men were scrambling around in confusion, each trying to get oxygen masks that were dangling from the ceiling over their faces. Billy put them both to sleep without Sidney breaking his stride.

Two more men came out in front from one of the staterooms. Both were shot. Then another door opened and then quickly closed when someone behind the door heard the two shots. Sidney didn't have time to mess around with getting them to come out. Every sixty seconds added miles to his landing zone.

The rear door's safety lock was released and Sidney, standing well clear, released it. The blast of frigid air that struck him was overwhelmed by the fearsome sight of a lot of distance between him and the little white flashes of white caps way down on the sea's surface almost eight miles below.

Shit, this is high... No sense in putting it off; it's not going to get any closer. He backed away from the door to get a good run at the opening, then made the move forward—the one that meant it was too late to do anything but react to whatever was going to happen.

Just as he was ready to run, the stateroom door opened and two more men jumped out. Fortunately, they faced the plane's front, their backs were to Sidney. He turned and quickly, Billy said night-night to the hapless men.

He ran down the aisle while he pulled his bag in tight before jumping. Both arms wrapped around it and held on as tight as possible. Then he ran the distance to the hell that was waiting for him outside. The blast of wind instantly pulled the bag out of his grasp.

He was falling completely out of control. The piece of line attached to the bag had wrapped around his left arm and felt like it would pull his arm off. His tumbling caused the tether to wrap around him like a piece of cord around a stick. The blast of frigid air had rendered Sidney unconscious —and that was probably the only reason he didn't die of heart failure.

After falling to ten thousand feet Sidney slowly began to realize what was happening and knew he had very little time to get the bag's tether unwrapped. Not only was he wrapped up in the tether, so was his parachute. His knife had stayed in its scabbard, somehow. He managed to reach it with his hand; both arms were tied to his body. He managed to cut the strands away. As soon as he felt the chute was clear the ripcord was pulled.

It seem like forever—it was even longer than that—before the chute responded—and even longer than that for it to be fully opened. The sight of the open chute made Sidney want to sing with happiness, a feeling never experienced before.

His altimeter said he was close to a thousand feet off the sea's surface when he dug the radio out of his knapsack and called his father on the selected frequency while turning on the GPS.

There was no response, but he could see something white on the horizon, which he hoped was the sailboat. Water in his eyes from the wind and cold prevented him from seeing which direction the boat was traveling.

Wish I had read the section about steering the chute so I could cut the distance between me and whatever it is down there. Even if it isn't my boat, there's a good chance that those aboard will see the parachute and come to my assistance. That'll be their bad luck—can't leave witnesses.

Just before he hit the water, he called for *Sunny Daze* again. That time there was a response. "I see you," was all that was said. A minute later he splashed into the ocean. An hour later, he could see the sailboat every time he was on top of the big ocean swells. It was heeled over on a close reach and coming directly at him. The boy was on the bow, standing on the anchors looking for him.

Finally, Sidney saw the boy pointing at him while yelling his report to his grandfather. The boat pulled alongside of Sidney with its big sails flapping in the fifteen-knot breeze. The boat stopped and pointed dead into the wind; the elder Sid had not lost his sailing skills.

The boy was full of excitement and wonderment at seeing his father fall out of the sky in the middle of the ocean. That was a very strange thing for him and he was extremely proud of his father.

The heavy bag was the first thing out of the water, and then Sidney pulled himself up and over the gunwale. He lay on the deck for a few minutes basking in the warm sun. Only the kid was talking and he was talking enough for all three of them in his excitement. He had watched his father fall out of an empty sky in a big white sheet and now was lying here on the deck of his boat and they were days away from land. His father had to be magic.

Finally, Sidney's father asked, "How'd things go up there?"

Nonchalantly, he replied, "Okay."

After lying on the warm deck for a few more minutes, Sidney got to his feet and pulled his bulky and soaking clothes off. He didn't show it but he was damn sure happy to be back in his own element. Jumping out of airplanes wasn't for him; it was one of the few times in his life that he had actually been scared. Standing at the edge of the open door with the incredibly loud roar of engines and cold wind was terrifying; looking down thirty-eight thousand feet above the sea was unnerving. The highest he had ever been off the sea was a hundred or so feet when at the masthead of one *Barracouta* or another. He had decided when he stood at that doorway that he would never do that sort of thing again—ever, no matter what the prize might be. But he was happy he had done it; it would be good for the family log and he fully intended to make it known for future Sidneys to never try doing stupid shit again.

The old man told the boy to bring his dad a beer from the galley's ice box. Sidney drank the first one without stopping; the second took a little longer and he relaxed with the third; his thirst, as had the adrenaline rush, passed. He sat naked in the cockpit with arms outstretched, a beer in hand, feeling the heat of the sun bake his body.

Then he looked at the large bag in the cockpit. He wanted to see how large his prize was, but the sun's warmth was too good to disturb.

His father asked, "Where do you plan to hide the prize until you get to the snake?"

Cachorro excitedly asked, "What kind of prize? We're going to see a snake?"

Sidney told the boy, "Drag the bag over here." The boy grunted a few times getting the bulky bag to his father.

Sid positioned the boy in front of him and said, "The prize is in this bag. A prize is something the Sidneys, that's me, your grandfather and someday you, will take away from someone who doesn't deserve it. This is the way we support ourselves. It was the way all of my grandfathers supported themselves and it will be the way you will learn to support yourself and your son."

The boy was still wide-eyed and very excited. "You mean I can jump out of airplanes, too?"

"I hope not, but that'll be up to you."

Grandpa laughed. He had never seen his son show any sign of fear, but it was obvious that parachuting was a once-in-a-lifetime event for him.

Sidney continued, "There are rules about taking prizes. The most important rule is that you can never tell another person. If you do, the weak man's law that I told you about will come and take it away and put you into a cage to live for the rest of your life. You will never be free to sail anywhere you want to or do anything you want to do. If other people learn about this prize they will try to steal it from you.

"It's time for you to know that, while I took this prize, it isn't mine. It belongs to the Sidney X, that's Grandpa, me and you and your son and his and his. You must promise me that you know how important it is to keep this secret and that you will never talk about any part of it or our lives, to anyone."

The boy, without hesitation, promised; only a small part of him sensed the seriousness of the situation. Which was expected by the older Sidneys but it was a start that would take solid root before he was a teenager.

Sidney opened the bag and turned it upside down in the cockpit. The boy exclaimed a loud enthusiastic, "Wow! Look at all that money."

The older man was quiet, as was Sidney. The money was in bundles. Sidney counted the bundles, throwing the counted bundles to the boy to be put back into the bag. Sid counted twelve hundred bundles. Each bundle contained fifty one-hundred dollar bills, for a total prize of six million United States dollars. There were also gemstones scattered on the cockpit floor. They filled a quart milk carton.

The little boy asked, "How much is that?"

Sidney replied, "Enough for now."

The old man was pleased with the prize and impressed at what his son had done to take it. It was the first time a Sidney had ever taken a prize from the air; the sea and its shore had always been their way of life. The airplane had been so high that he hadn't even seen or heard it.

The older Sid asked, "Tell me what happened up there and the rest of the details. Should we be expecting company from the law searching for you?"

"No. Everyone was out cold when I left the aircraft. It was on automatic pilot and with the rear door open there wouldn't be enough air for the crew to revive. The plane will continue on course until it runs out of fuel somewhere far to the east of us."

Neither Sidney nor his father gave any thought about the people who might be under the falling aircraft when the plane's fuel was exhausted; neither did the little boy who didn't understand it anyway, but accepted it as a good thing.

The oldest Sid said, "When and if a search starts, nobody will have any idea where to start or even if there's a reason to search. The Italians will be pissed and suspect something, but they won't know if their money had been taken."

Sidney told his father, "Head the boat into the wind so I can get the dinghy off the davits. I'm going to stash the prize in her."

The boy's landlubberly assistance, which meant that he was in the way, but Sidney didn't mind his clumsy efforts; it was good that he wanted to help. The dinghy was turned turtle on the aft deck. He sliced a hole at the seam under two air section chambers and money was stacked inside the air tubes. The carry bag and cushions from the salon were positioned to remove excess space between the cash and the tube's top. That removed any possibility that someone could hear the sound of the bundles if nosey law enforcement types boarded them for a shakedown inspection. The repair kit for the dinghy was used to seal up the air tubes, making it look as though nothing had been done. After the glue was dry, the tube was inflated again and hung back on the davits.

His overalls, winter clothes, parachute and air tank were tied to a thirty foot section of chain he cut off the end of the aft anchor's rode, and dumped overboard in the blue-black water of the deep Atlantic Ocean.

With all evidence of the crime taken care of, Sidney was ready for his three "Rs", rum, food, and fun. He hadn't eaten or had rum in over a day. Then he'd take a nice long nap while Grandpa steered a course to St. Croix.

SICILY

Tony was always excited, but that day he was exceedingly so. "Vincenzo, what the fuck are you doing in St. Maarten?"

"I have been looking for the assholes, Tony. I've been watching the Tribute plane and had some extra guys on it in case they tried to take it while in the Caribbean." He wasn't ready to tell Tony that he had set a trap because he wasn't sure who might be involved with the raiders.

"Well asshole, if you had been in Sicily a few hours ago you could have just looked up directly overhead and you would have seen my plane go by. It flew in a straight fucking line until it ran out of fuel and crashed. Get your ass over here right the fuck now and tell me what the fuck is going on. You have your ass at the Tribute's crash site to-fucking-day!"

That night, Vincenzo would have given anything to know who was responsible for the wreckage around him. He was standing in a large pile of twisted metal, plastic and fabrics all blended together in what was once a beautiful jet airliner. There had been no fire when the dead mass of metal and men hit the ground. It had started its fall from over thirty-eight thousand feet after it was completely out of fuel. Torque from its downward spinning caused big sections of both wings to shear off, exposing the empty fuel tanks to open air. Parts of the fuselage ripped apart as well, exposing the internal tanks. Wreckage and defunct men had fallen the last mile or so straight down so most of the wreckage was within a quarter mile radius from impact. Bits and pieces of humans were found scattered everywhere. The captain and copilot were smashed beyond even a resemblance of being human.

If there had been a Tribute it consisted of empty black attachés, no money, jewels or anything of value was found —with the exception of a foot-high teddy bear adorned with a diamond and ruby necklace intended for Tony the Pop's mistress. Vincenzo looked carefully for the big bag with a parachute and diving gear that Ciro had described. There was no trace.

Vincenzo had thought seriously about going to Sicily with the crew, just to meet with Tony. He was curious who might be telling the raiders about some of the family's functions and thought it might not hurt to get a little dialogue going with Tony to see what happened. Looking over the remains of the plane, he was thankful he didn't. The scene in front of him did, however, strengthen his determination to finish the bastards himself, as soon as he could learn who was responsible.

Then it hit him: the scuba tank and parachute were not there; therefore it had been only one man. He looked at Vinnie, Tony's man who had brought him to the wreck site, and said, "No one but the flight crew was aboard. I had the plane searched just before they took off. The man who brought the bag to Ciro knew when the plane was arriving. He is unknown to Tony or anyone else, and neither Tony nor Gugguci wanted or knew about the shit in that bag. That's the motherfucker I gotta find."

Vinnie said, "I think that the first people to get to the wreck site took the money. How could the guy in the Caribbean rob them in midair?"

"Don't know, but it's apparent that bag carried the only means to escape the high flying aircraft. There's no doubt in my mind that one of the flight crew was responsible, but who? The DNA tests will tell us whose remains are not part of this mess, but I can't believe any of them would do this; I knew those guys."

Vincenzo kicked a piece of rumpled metal, and said, "I knew everyone's actions and whereabouts who came in contact with the aircraft. I knew for certain who was on the aircraft when the doors were shut and who was aboard when it left the ground."

Then he grimaced as a troubled thought occurred to him: *The only person I can't be absolutely certain of his whereabouts is the mechanic in St. Maarten. He was supposedly sleeping off a hangover in a work truck. But I had the guys check out the cargo hold, and he couldn't have been hiding in there. Fucking assholes, I'll kill whoever did this if it's the last thing I do on earth or in hell.*

The officials investigating the crash were in the process of looking for fingers or recognizable features of as many of the flight crew as possible. If the whole crew was found then it had to be an outsider. But how?

The officials knew someone had been on board and also knew in advance that the aircraft was going to run out of fuel and crash. An Italian military jet had investigated the aircraft after it flew over a restricted area and refused to acknowledge their request for radio contact. The pilot reported the rear door was open, and there were no signs of life on board. The military jet followed the big jet until the fuel was exhausted and then watched it change directions from eastward to downward.

THE TRIP BACK TO ST. CROIX TOOK A WEEK—OF RELAXATION AND FUN and instruction. They anchored off several uninhabited islands where Sidney and his dad taught the boy more about being a successful pirate. Sidney taught him more about survival in the wilds. Grandpa taught the boy many things about survival at sea, navigation and seamanship.

As they sailed into St. Croix, Grandpa sat at the steering wheel while the boy made ready the anchor. He thought about young Sidney; *everything sticks that I throw at him in the way of new information. It seems the boy is gifted intellectually. I hope he's as gifted in our ways of pirating.*

Sidney took his father home while leaving his son on board to keep an eye on the dinghy. On the trip, he asked, "Do you think it's too soon for the boy to see the cave?"

Traditionally, no Sidney had been allowed to see it until after they survived the jungle test. Some not until they had passed their rites to manhood by planning and executing their first raid at the age of thirteen.

His father responded, "I think the boy has the right stuff and understands most things, so it'd probably be safe enough. However, it's important to follow tradition for several good reasons. One… what if he *does* tell someone; after all, he is still just a little kid. Or what happens if he becomes under the influence of another person before he is adequately trained; someone who sparks the belief that our way is wrong. Two, what happens if he can't hack it when he kills his first man and it is obvious that he'll never make it. It has happened before, you know, and that puts a hell of a burden on the father who must kill his own flesh and blood to keep our secret of the Snake secure. Only a proven Barracuda can know of the treasure. If you get killed, he'll have full access to the treasure, and as a kid, could squander or worse yet, turn our family's treasure over to the government or a snappy talker." Snappy talker was Grandpa's expression of a belly-crawling con-man.

Sidney said, "I agree." The subject was never brought up again.

That same night, after tossing down a few rums at the deck bar he put the dinghy onto a dock cart and took it to his apartment. Under cover of darkness, he opened the air tubes; the money was stuffed into the bag once again. Feeling energetic, but not enough to go through the hassle of stuffing the money into the apartment's floor safe, he decided to take it to the cave. Finding the cave at night was no problem and it was always night inside the cave, anyway.

In the treasure cave, the bag full of jewels and millions of dollars was casually tossed over and it landed on more bags full of cash. The room was getting full of bags and chests of plunder. By the time his son started adding to the treasure it would be full. He needed to start spending money, especially the older cash; it gets old and sometimes obsolete. It was time to buy more land, and he thought about buying the land he liked at Ortega's area. It was remote, overlooked a beautiful valley, and probably bordered the sea. If necessary, he could dig a cave for new treasure.

That way of thinking was the full extent of his property management planning. Had they invested the money into the stocks or businesses, like society's acceptable lawmakers, the well-known families of wealth and fame, the Sidneys would surely rank among the richest families. But, it was more important to the Sidneys to remain unknown to the world. Their privacy was worth the difference between unknown riches and the unlimited riches they already enjoyed.

Thinking about the new land bothered him a little. *Time's approaching when I'll be going there after I dump the boy in the jungle. I like the kid. I remember how a kid alone in the jungle feels. Day or night makes no difference, for the first month I was always afraid and hungry.*

He laughed at himself. *Can't believe I had all that fear in me. Quit being an old fart, the boy will make it. It isn't easy and has never been intended to be easy. Every Sidney has made it—except two. Nobody knows what happened to them other than they just were not Sidney stock. Probably ended up in the bellies of jungle cats.*

His thoughts of the boy ended as he entered the accounts of his raid on the aircraft. Then he read through the log that night, looking for notations concerning the taking of sons to the jungle. He hoped to find a way to make the transition as painless as possible. He also was interested in reading about other daring raids, thinking that his last venture might have been the boldest ever in the family's history.

He read about how the sixteenth Sidney in the 1820s had been deposited on an isolated beach on the coast of Africa. There had been no warning, his father told him to swim to shore to get some fresh food. Only when he reached the beach did his father break the news to him that he would be on his own for six months. The fact that he had been deceived, as well as the sudden fear of being left alone in the jungle, angered the boy to the point of causing damage in his mental ability to cope. It made an incredibly mean man out of the once trusting boy. The young Sid not only survived the six months—he thrived.

When his father arrived at the appointed time to pick up the boy, he found a very vindictive kid waiting for him. The boy invited him to come ashore to see the habitat in which he had survived. Sidney the fifteenth was more than surprised when he fell through a trap door covering a hole nine-feet deep. The bottom two feet of the pit was covered with water— and the water was full of poisonous vipers that had been thrown in as his father's boat approached.

The boy stood on the edge of the pit, watching, while his father struggled to pull the many snakes' fangs out of his face, arms and legs. The struggle didn't last long and the boy didn't bother to bury his dead father; he left him uncovered, floating face up in the slithering pit.

That boy went on to record some of the most brutal acts of piracy the family had ever known. All of the Sidneys had been brutal, showed no mercy, and expected the same, but this man delighted in torture and pain. If it were possible for a family like the Sidneys to have a black sheep, surely he was the clear choice.

After killing his father, the boy stayed in the jungle for another month, not knowing what to do. Finally he decided to take his father's boat to sea. He had been sailing all of his life since he was born and was raised on that boat. This boy was also one of the few that had been told of the family tradition and shown the treasure prior to his test. Pirating was the only thing his father had prepared him for. The boy sailed north until he reached England, where he learned about killing in style.

In every port he entered, men of the established communities and men without law always decided to take the boat away from him—after all, he was just a boy. He accepted the lopsided takeovers and offered to stay aboard as the ship's boy. He acted the part well, but, at first opportunity, the new owner of the vessel and any crew that might be aboard would disappear. Usually the boy would wait until the crew was sleeping or drunk, then sneak in and cut their throats. Captains or owners were left for last; they would wake up to find they were hog-tied. The boy would drag him up on deck to see the mutilated bodies of the man's family, friends and crew.

Then he would put on his best little boy act, thanking the man for stealing his boat. He showed his appreciation for this act by slowly skinning the man alive, just as he had learned to do to the wild hogs in the jungle. He had learned in the jungle that he could skin a section and cut out the meaty flesh to be cooked for his meal without killing the whole animal. It was a waste to let big animals rot before he had time to eat them. The skin, wrapped over the exposed meat, helped slow the rotting process. Of course, the captains didn't like it any more than the wild boars did and had as many options as what to do about it—none. The boy slowly dispatched three men that way before arriving in his homeport of Le Havre, France.

He showed up on his grandfather's doorstep one day and announced that he had killed his father and told him why. He also told him of the trip back home. His grandfather was proud of the boy and took him in to be raised in the traditional Sidney fashion. Sidney XVI lived to the ripe old age of sixty-three. He died swinging from the top main mast by his neck when he attempted to take a British warship sailing out of London with the prize of Spanish doubloons that was being taken to Spain as an offering of peace. The English had liberated the doubloons from a Spanish ship over one hundred years prior. Reports were widely circulated about the event. Sidney XVI had killed the captain and two other men before he was discovered. He killed eight other men in the fight that followed. He might have made good in his escape, but he stumbled over a fallen man's sword blade and broke a leg. The chances of that happening to the fiercest fighter the seas had seen in a while were so remote that it made that Sid laugh. His captors, relieved that the battle had ended without any more of them being killed, thought it funny as well. There were no hard feelings on the part of the crew as the man had put up a hell of a fight—there were no hard feelings on Sidney's side either—he had grown up knowing the risk. The account was written in the log by his son, Sidney XVII.

The British crew never knew the man hanging from the rigging was responsible for the death of hundreds of sailors, the loss of seventy-eight ships and benefactor of much of the Crown's treasury. Nor would they ever guess that the dead man was the modern-day Barracuda, the legendary, phantom pirate feared by all men of the sea for hundreds of years.

Sidney VIII was another jungle problem; the boy was prepared as well as any and was deposited on a southwest African shore. When his father returned, there were no signs of his existence. No hut or tools or even a fire that had been extinguished long ago could be found. He couldn't even find the boy's bones.

His father returned to his home where he had two other boys, both younger. The second oldest was a complete waste. At age six, he already acted like a pansy. The boy was careful not to get dirty and loved to stay indoors. He had very little to do with other boys, as they liked to tease and punch him. The youngest was four years old and seemed to have a more masculine personality. He made the third boy the new Sidney X and trained him well. The boy grew up and followed family tradition until the ripe old age of forty-two, when he, like many other Sidneys, didn't return from a raiding trip.

The only other entry about boys in the jungle was Sidney V. The fifth

Sidney was actually two boys, twins. They were identical in every way; both rough and tough and competitive. Their father had very little to do with their training, however, since he was killed on a raid at the ripe old age of eighteen. The twins' grandfather continued the required training and decided that since both had the right stuff and both boys relied on each other, to train them both as equals. Unfortunately, three months in the jungle claimed the life of one of the boys. It wasn't a beast that claimed the boy; it was a sickness. The boy wasted away after ten days of high fever and the inability to eat anything. The surviving twin came through okay and lived to add much gold to the family treasure until he died at thirty-eight at home in bed from acute indigestion.

Sidney closed the log book and uttered to himself, "Think I'm going to tell the boy what's in store for him in two months. It'll help him become better prepared… Fuck tradition; he's my son."

In the years past, it was viewed as babying the boy if they were warned and prepared. The idea was to be tough enough to overcome anything that presented itself. That's what builds confidence more than the feat of survival itself.

He left the cave and was back at the deck bar an hour before last call. For last call he ordered a bottle of Cruzan rum and a couple of sandwiches to take out.

Sidney sat silently alone in the apartment chewing his food absently, occasionally washing it down with a gulp of rum from the bottle. There were food crumbs all over his stomach and rum that spilled from his mouth was glistening on his chin in the stark light of his bedside table lamp.

His eyes were glassed over, he was bored—wasn't happy; he just existed. Even though his mind was blank, somewhere inside was a longing for companionship. Not just an overnight fuck, but someone who would be fun company. Someone he could talk to about the boy. Someone who cared what he had to say or thought. Someone he could express feelings to. Someone who liked him for who he was. Those simple things—he had never known.

The next thing Sidney became aware of was a banging on his door.

He was still sitting upright in bed, the table light was on and there was a hint of sunlight outdoors. He opened the door to see his son who was on schedule for the day's activities.

As he walked to the bathroom he had a thought: *The boy seems to enjoy training... especially with his grandfather. Can't say anything, but kind of wish the boy liked me as much as he does my dad. Aw fuck it, what do I know about kids.*

Sidney took a fast cold shower, dressed in the usual attire and led the way out to the tropical outdoors. The boy stayed with him for the first mile with little effort. He was getting stronger and fit. The second mile was harder and Sidney finished the four-mile run about a half-mile ahead of the boy.

Rosie was in the front yard, waiting for little Sid. She had a jug of orange juice and some fresh out-of-the-pan hot johnnycakes waiting for him. Embarrassed that she hadn't been prepared for, or even expected Sidney, she waddled away but quickly returned with another glass of juice and a johnnycake.

On the run from the apartment to his father's mountaintop house, Sidney's mind had been lost in thought. He was thinking about what he had read last night on a raid Sid XVII had done in 1856, on the Cuban government. That story had always intrigued him.

As he sat on the grass eating his johnnycake he returned to 1856. Sidney XVII pulled a daring raid, probably the most daring, other than his recent adventure at 38,000 feet. XVII had captured a Spanish ship off the coast of Portugal one night. The captain, realizing that he was about to be drawn and quartered for putting up a tough fight, tried to make peace with Sidney by telling him about the Spanish gold in Cuba. With the right crew, it could be taken, but the right crew would be an absolute requirement. The captain had even given thought to the crew, ship and a scheme that would put him in position to take the gold. Sid listened and was genuinely interested in the plan. Satisfied the captain had told him everything he knew, Sid shoved his blade deep into the man's throat, severing his windpipe, therefore ensuring no one else would learn of the treasure.

The Cuban government had secretly been hiding one quarter of their gold reserve somewhere outside of Havana. The reason was twofold; one, to keep a large reserve out of Spain in case of a successful attack on Madrid by their enemies. If that should happen, then the Royals would have a substantial reserve to finance the taking back of Spain, or if things were too bad, they could live their lives of exile in the comfort they were entitled to. Two, since pirates and storms were taking a large percentage of the gold before it reached Spain, they decided to leave some in a safe outpost. When times were more stable they could bring the treasure to Madrid.

The treasure had been hidden in Saint Peter's Monastery de Cuba. The monks and one hundred soldiers dressed like brothers guarded it. No military uniforms were ever worn so nobody suspected that anything out of the ordinary was going on. In fact, the treasure was such a closely guarded secret that the sea captain, who was sprawled on the floor dying while gurgling on his own blood, had been one of only two Spanish captains who were aware of it.

While the information Sidney XVII had learned about the treasure was a remarkably lucky break, it did present problems. The amount of treasure was too much for him to handle alone. That was always a problem, as they never worked with crews. He had to come up with a scheme to either remove all of the treasure at one time or in smaller, unnoticed raids. Sid had decided to take it all in one move.

His first move was to take hostages. He kidnapped the wife of the island's Governor and their three daughters and only son and hid them in a cave he had learned about from a previous Sidney who had entered the information in the log.

He boldly approached the governor before anyone was aware of the kidnapping. He explained exactly what his men were going to do to the governor's family if he didn't cooperate. The thought of extreme cruelty to his lovely wife and helpless children prompted the governor to cooperate with Sidney.

The governor wrote out instructions to the soldiers' captain in charge of the monastery and another to the head monk. The documents explained that a decision had been made by the king of Spain to take the treasure to Madrid. That it was to be placed aboard the merchant ship

Allure for transport. To assure the vessel's identity would be kept secret, the entire company of soldiers would board another merchant ship, the *Princesa Alta a Mar,* immediately after loading the *Allure.* The *Princesa* was to be sailed to Dry Tortuga without contact with any other vessels and then return to Havana. That would provide the *Allure* with the time necessary for a head start to Spain before any possibility of leaks about the treasure could get out. Also, for security, the *Allure* was to be void of all crew other than the captain until everything was loaded and concealed aboard the ship. The governor had also been instructed to transfer command of the *Allure* to Sidney.

The vessel was loaded the next day during the early morning hours well before dawn. By noon, Sidney, and his skeleton crew of six men to help him sail the *Allure,* had cleared El Morro's deadly cannons at the harbor's entrance. He turned west to give the impression he was headed to Mexico until he was well clear of land. He then turned south and tacked towards South America. One more tack was made several days later and that brought him to St. Croix. By the time he arrived in his private lagoon on St. Croix, all of his crew had been dispatched. He cut the sails down to stop the ship and anchored in the secluded lagoon. It took two weeks to unload the Spanish treasure by himself. The *Allure* was then taken off-shore and scuttled.

The governor placed the capture of Sidney above everything else. Ships sailed to every known port in search of the ruthless pirate, the ship, or any of the crew. The governor never found his treasure, Sidney, the *Allure,* any of the crew—or his family. Sidney had described the cave's location in the Sidneys' Log, but apparently not to the governor. The poor family must have starved to death while imprisoned in the cave. As soon as the king of Spain found out about the governor giving away the treasure, the governor also had his neck stretched then chopped in two by the executioner's axe.

That story had always fascinated Sidney XXIII. It took tremendous courage to walk into the enemy's fort single-handed and steal the king's treasure. Some day he would do the same.

It was ironic that he had read that story again just before stumbling onto Vito's papers. The handwritten document in Italian about diamonds being taken to the Circle of Fifteen's Cuban depository was very interesting. It meant they had a major stash there. Unfortunately, there was no mention of where it might be, but he had sniffed a rich prize and it was only a matter of time and a little gray duct tape before he would discover their secret.

He had been targeting the Italians a lot lately as they owned so much of the gambling business in the Caribbean, Central and South America that they offered unlimited prizes. Also, they weren't hard to defeat. He had Hollywood hype to thank for building such a fearsome reputation surrounding the Mafia. The Mafia, unfortunately for themselves, believed all of that shit and didn't concern themselves with proper precautions. They relied on that reputation to make people leave them alone. Of course there was no fear in Sidney's thoughts—only plans of easy pickings.

Sidney knew the Cuban government certainty wasn't aware of the treasure; they'd seize it for sure. Someone made a decision to build a depository on an island that all countries had access to. It would be a cache of United States dollars and other widely accepted valuables like the diamonds. Like the old Spanish royalty, the mob probably stashed it to always have an unlimited source of cash in the western hemisphere for the selected few—the Circle of Fifteen.

Sidney muttered, "Guess I've lost all interest in going to the Mediterranean to let the Caribbean wops lick their wounds. I want that treasure."

Those thoughts had kept him entertained while munching on the johnnycake Rosie had brought for him. But the cake was gone and it was time to get back to business and kick his son's ass again with lessons on hand-to-hand combat. He needed to reinforce the need for being first to attack. And do it brutally so his enemy was not an opponent but an unsuspecting victim whose only interest was getting away from his attacker.

SICILY

The Italians in Sicily called a special meeting to take place immediately after the crash of the Tribute aircraft. It was a mandatory meeting with no excuses accepted. Ten men from around the world were summoned to join the five men in Sicily. All had known each other for most of their lives. Each man was at least tenth-generation Mafioso and equal to each other in every respect. No man had privilege but out of respect, the oldest took charge of the meetings. His name was Anthony Castero and he was only sixty-one years old. His *made* name was Tony the Pop; the *pop* had nothing to do with his age. He had been called Tony the Pop since his first killing when he was only sixteen years old. He had *popped* the main rival to his father's position in the organization at a birthday party being given for the man's daughter.

Tony the Pop had made the decision to kill the guy, Carlo Guanine, on his own. The man needed to be *popped*, Guanine was obvious in his moves to take over Tony's father's operation a little at a time. His father was nervous as hell about it, but there was nothing he could do; the man had always been careful to play by the rules of the governing heads. So claiming self-defense and survival of his family's position in the order, Tony took matters into his own hands. During the party, attended by every family in Sicily, Tony boldly stood before everyone present and calmly walked over to and shot the young debutante's father one time in the middle of his forehead.

In the midst of wailing women and shouting men, he then handed the pistol to the Don of Dons, Don Fatnani, and said, "It's done. That man has done my family a great wrong and every one of you knew it and you refused to intervene. It seems strange that a young boy is the only one with enough sense of right and wrong to correct a bad situation. If you disagree, Don Fatnani, take my life, but allow my father, mother and sisters to live a life of peace they deserve and not the constant threat of death or ruination from a greedy man. If you believe I acted with only right in my heart, I assume complete financial support for greedy Guanine's family."

He spoke very calmly and was ready to take the punishment because the man had to be stopped. The old Mafioso was delighted that new blood had the balls to act. They praised the boy, and the party continued. The only people outraged by his actions were, understandably, the victim's family. The dead aggressor's business underlings were wise enough to know that things had suddenly and irreversibly changed—as did their allegiances. And the boy, Tony, was a made man. Throughout his early career Tony had *popped* quite a few other people as well.

At sixty-one Tony was still very capable of *popping* a few more folks if it benefited him or the organization. And that afternoon he was eager to pump some lead into somebody.

Tony stood in front of the gathering that sat at a huge round table in his office. He announced, "This emergency meeting has been called because there is a rat in our organization. This rat is high enough to cause serious financial losses to us and possibly create major and long-lasting financial problems. We have suffered several thefts that cannot be explained in the last few years. Last week was the last straw: the Tribute plane from the Caribbean didn't arrive as expected. It took off on time from Antigua with the usual crew, plus four extra men Vincenzo had selected for additional security. Everything was fine, but the plane didn't land; instead it continued on in a straight course over Italy at thirty-eight thousand feet. It was picked up on radar and tracked by various airports but no one aboard would respond to radio contact. Finally, the aircraft ran out of fuel at altitude and fell to earth where it impacted.

"Nothing was left of our money, airplane or crew. We do not have a clue as to what happened. A military jet was sent up to investigate before it plunged to the ground. The pilot reported that the rear door was open as if someone used it to bail out. The pilots were slumped over in their seats without oxygen masks so they were apparently dead."

This was news to the ten men who had arrived during the last few hours. They stood and showed their outrage at the news with curses and balled-up fists backed up with vicious threats.

Tony quieted them down and continued, "We, Vincenzo the Sicilian and I, have started putting things together by listing all of the robberies involving our scheduled or regular runs where money was involved. We also looked into the casino robberies. There are quite a few instances that lead us to believe that information is being passed to the people responsible for these actions. Not only have we lost money, but people, too. You are all aware of Vito's death and we feel the same group did it. But, equally important, we are losing respect by allowing people to do these things to us. It must stop and strong examples must be made."

The room became noisy with discussion until Tony asked, "Which of you ordered a parachute to be brought on the plane?" Only silence answered. "Which of you sent a scuba tank to be delivered to the plane?" Still silence as each man looked to the other. He looked at Gugguci. "Did you check with your people to see if they ordered them?"

Gugguci said, "My people did not order anything. My people don't even know of the Tribute plane."

Tony picked up a piece of paper and showed it to the group, and then he said, "Of course we are going to do anything needed to stop this shit. The five of us in Sicily made a list showing a course of action to take to remove these people. I want each of you to take the time to study our ideas and add your own to the list. By tomorrow at this time we'll start the moves to bring this era to an abrupt halt."

The fifteen men worked on the list until late that night, taking very few breaks before retiring for dinner. The next day, the meeting resumed after breakfast and, by noon, everyone agreed the plan that had been developed was perfect.

Everything relating to the plan was to be controlled by Tony. He would be the only contact for all players. This would eliminate any possibility of friends and relatives of the other men from accidentally learning of the plans. Other than that everything was to proceed as usual.

After the meeting was over, Tony retired to his study to finalize and fine-tune the plan before setting it into motion. By midnight that same evening, he was satisfied. Whoever had been hitting the organization was living on borrowed time.

The next morning, Tony made telephone calls while enjoying breakfast on his patio that overlooked the rugged beauty of the Tyrrhenian Sea. This was a much more enjoyable place to work than the confines of his elegant office/study.

Between bites of the Boluga Molska and sipping on ice cold Crystal, he had a friendly conversation with his friend on the other end of the phone line.

Inspector Jameson was more than happy to assist him and didn't ask why Tony needed information from Interpol. A computer search of all burglaries with and without homicides connected to gambling operations, certainly made him curious, but he understood that questions were never asked of Tony. His well-paid, under the table job was to comply and forget, period.

Before Tony had finished his breakfast, he had made the same arrangements with the Scotland Yard of Britain, Interpol, and the Italian and French governments. If there were patterns to these criminals, this amount of information would certainly highlight it.

After breakfast and a long cold shower, Tony returned to the patio to finish his workload for the day. He placed two more calls. One to an American named Paul Chance and the other to a Chinese man. His name was too complicated to remember much less pronounce so he was known only as Chong. Both men had done work for Tony many times in the past. They were used to investigating people, places and things when the organization wanted to keep a lot of distance between the police and whatever they wanted information about. Those two men were at the very top of twenty or so private detectives in the world.

Tony's conversation with each of the men was very brief. "I'm not asking what your schedule looks like. I'm telling you I need you in Sicily at my office in five days. Be here for lunch."

His workday over, Tony changed into his tennis togs and went to his backyard tennis court. That morning's players—the newest US Supreme Court judge, an Australian governor and Britain's Finance Minister—was volleying, killing time while waiting for him.

VINCENZO WASN'T INVITED TO THE CIRCLE OF FIFTEEN'S MEETING, AND never would be. It wasn't even possible for him to attend; it was a matter of birthrights and that was something Vincenzo Jones didn't have thanks to his slut of a mother who had loved the American dollar during the war.

While the meeting was in progress, Vincenzo made several telephone calls. High on his priority list was a call to Ciro. Before making that call, however, he had to speak to Don Gugguci, so he waited outside of Tony's meeting for Gugguci to arrive. When he did, Vincenzo asked for just one moment to ask him one question. "Did you recently take up skydiving, Senori?"

"Why do you waste my time by asking me such a stupid question, Vincenzo?"

"Pardon, patron, but it is something I must know. It might help to find the people who did this terrible thing to the Tribute plane. I was told that you wanted a man in St. Maarten to send you skydiving as well as scuba diving equipment."

"That is absurd. I've already told Tony that I didn't. I have no interest in those things. Shit, look at me. Do I look the type that would do those things? Who told you I wanted these things?"

"At this moment I don't know, but I will advise you as soon as I find out. These things were put on board the Tribute aircraft for you, but they are not in the wreckage. I have reason to believe the equipment was used by the people who killed our men and stole your Tribute."

"You find this son-of-a-bitch, Vincenzo! I want to know how he knew about the flight and I want to know who he is!"

The call to Ciro was next. "Ciro, who exactly gave you that big bag with the parachute in it?"

"According to my bellman, it was a man who checked into the hotel. I didn't see him personally. He sent the bellman to me with a message about the Tribute flight so I thought he was connected to the Circle. He knew Don Gugguci and that he would be receiving the package. He left the bag open so it could be inspected which I did personally. Being highly connected, I thought that if he had wanted to see or talk to me, he would have. I was hesitant to show bad manners by asking him to expose himself to me. However, I called him three times during the night, but he was either out or asleep."

"Did it ever occur to you that there might have been a fucking bomb inside the scuba tank? Did you even think about looking inside it or the other stuff?"

Ciro had the sudden feeling he had just entered the well-known world of slimy brown and smelly stuff; "What's wrong Vincenzo? Was there a problem?"

"What name did he register under?"

"Hold on, Vincenzo, I'll get the register," said a nervous Ciro.

Vincenzo heard Ciro get on the intercom and direct the other person to bring him the register. One minute later, Ciro was reading aloud the names of new guests that had arrived that day, until he got down to what he was looking for: room number 455. "His name was Vincenzo Gambi; the passport number was O43122288 from Sicily."

"Any bets on the validity of that number?"

"The desk clerks are supposed to see the passports, but I'll admit it is not pushed if the guest doesn't produce it. All we are required to have by the government is the number."

"Ciro, find everybody who saw him and get me a description. You get that bellman and isolate him. He stays with you until I get there and I don't give a fuck if his mother is dying in the street in front of your place. He stays locked up. You understand me?"

"Sure, Vincenzo, whatever you say."

"I need the information from your witness today so I'll call you back in eight hours."

"I'll have everything I can get from them, Vincenzo, but if I might ask, what is going on?"

"Don't ask; just get me what I want."

Ciro wanted to do everything he could do to help. Accepting something for the Tribute plane had been stupid, and if the man who put it there was not legitimate, he was in serious trouble. Being honest about the situation was about the only thing he could do at that time. The mention of a bomb being in the air tank was a pretty good indication that the plane hadn't arrived in Sicily. If that was indeed the case he was no longer in a world of shit, he was about to jump out of his pile of shit to land in the sea of the dead.

He talked to everyone on duty that day to see if any had contact with the man in room 455. Meanwhile, his security men were dispatched to look around the island for him as well as the airport and cruise ship docks.

His only hope for survival was to produce the guy or find a trail to follow.

Vincenzo called Italy's passport center and gave them the name and hotel name and asked for verification of the passport. After a few minutes, the agent told him that wasn't a valid Italian passport. He had checked it out by name as well as number. There wasn't a Vincenzo Gambi, but it sounded familiar to the man. He ran it through the databases; the only listing of that name belonged to a well-known Italian pirate—who died in 1819.

Since he wouldn't be going to New York, Vincenzo called his man in the state attorney's office. He had indeed run Vincenzo's list through the computer people. There had been over five hundred incidents where tape was used to bind persons during a robbery. Only a few cases were listed during the last five years where a soft blackjack was used. There were no cases where tape was used to cover the airways to induce people to divulge information. There were no patterns similar to what he was looking for.

The FBI had a different story. They had run three separate searches—the Caribbean, United States and Western Europe—over the last five years. Too bad they didn't go back further; they would have seen another pattern in and around the Mediterranean.

"There have been eight cargo freighters robbed at sea. Each was out in the middle of nowhere and nobody saw who did it. Tape was used to bind and torture people. There were almost always lumps on the back of the victim's head."

"That sounds like our boys," said Vincenzo.

"There's more. Several hotels from the Bahamas down to Aruba have made statements about very important, *special* guests being attacked in their rooms, robbed and taped, many with sore heads when they awoke. There's nothing concerning casinos however; maybe they don't want outsiders to know?"

Vincenzo didn't reply to the insinuation that casinos had their own ways to deal with criminals dumb enough to steal from them. Instead he asked, "Any details on languages or the use of other weapons?"

"Nothing. Not a single description."

Vincenzo started calling casino operators he knew to see if they had experienced any of the same problems. A few had. Tony interrupted his telephone survey by calling him to his office.

"Okay, Vincenzo, update me on everything you know. We're pretty sure there is someone on the inside giving information; this thing with Vito and now the Tribute plane are not coincidences."

Vincenzo had to play it completely straight. Tony was more than shrewd—he was a conniving genius and extremely dangerous; very few men were better in spotting a con. If Vincenzo were caught holding anything back, there would be hell to pay, so Tony was told everything, including how he had tried to set a trap based on information the wimp had given the thief two years ago. Vincenzo also divulged that he was beginning to believe it wasn't a gang, but just one man and gave him the reasons. An hour later, Tony was impressed with the information he had learned.

"I apologize to you, Vincenzo; I thought you were just sight-seeing and whore-chasing. It appears you have been doing at least a little work."

"Well, boss, to be honest, I did get laid a couple of times."

Tony said, "We are stepping up our efforts, Vincenzo. I'm bringing Paul Chance and Chong in on this. Those are hard guys to beat when it comes to snooping around to dislodge somebody out of the woodwork. You will remain separate from their activities. They won't know about you and you will not contact them. I want no sharing of information with anybody except me. You keep me up to date, and answer to nobody else. If anybody fucks with you, have them call me before you whack 'em."

Vincenzo understood very well; Tony didn't trust anybody and that was one of the reasons he was still alive and on top of a very slippery pile.

"So, Vincenzo, what's your next move?"

"As you know, nothing was found in the way of the Tribute, only some badly broken attaché cases and an expensive Teddy bear. It'll be a while before they can tell us how many bodies and who they were in the crash, so there's nothing I can do here. I'm going back to St. Maarten to interview the guy who talked to the man who gave the bag of sports gear to Gugguci. I'll find that man because I think he's the asshole that's responsible or at least a part of it. If nothing else, I want to know how he knew to use Gugguci's name. If Gugguci is involved, then this will be the simplest way to find out."

"Don't go getting stupid on me, Vincenzo. You know fucking well Gugguci didn't have shit to do with this," said an irritated Tony. He had grown up with Gugguci and Tony trusted him completely.

"I didn't mean to infer that he did, Tony, but there could be someone in his organization that could be. I'm tracking every lead to an absolute conclusion."

"Well, be careful with Gugguci; if he thought you suspected him of conspiracy in this he wouldn't blink an eye, he'd just pull your balls off and cram them all the way down your fucking throat. And I wouldn't lift a finger to stop him."

"Believe me, Tony, I'm not even glancing at Gugguci and won't unless somebody in the know tells me face to face that his outfit is somehow involved. And under the circumstances, since I am so fond of my balls, I'll tell you first and won't move without your permission."

"Good. Get your ass out of here and find the bastards. I'll give you a healthy bonus if you do before they fuck with us again. If you don't find them, you better have a good reason."

As Vincenzo walked out of Tony's huge house, he wasn't happy. Fucking asshole! I bust my chops trying to find the sons of bitches. I set up a fucking trap that was right on and what do I get? Fucking threats!

He smirked and muttered, "What did I expect from the old Mafioso? No compassion or credit for what I've done; give him satisfaction or he'll break my fucking balls." He smiled, "But fuck it, I'm no different, maybe I'm worse. I'm about to lay some of the same shit on my pal, Ciro, and his unfortunate concierge and bellman who better have a damn good description."

He thought about spending the night in his apartment in the city but knew he had to get out of town that day because he knew how Tony worked. Tony was probably on the phone to put the word on Gugguci that Vincenzo the Sicilian was curious about a connection between him and the thieves. Gugguci would insist on a face-to-face with Vincenzo, and that was not going to happen.

Gugguci had a well-deserved and nasty reputation and a good way to get on his shit-list was to doubt his integrity. It was well known that in his early years his twin brother had ridiculed him for taking too much shit from the man they both worked for. It bothered Gugguci so much that he killed his brother in hand-to-hand fighting. Gugguci earned a lot of respect for it from the big guys and that single act served notice on everyone that Gugguci was a man to be trusted and he adhered strictly to family rules and to suggest otherwise was almost certainly an invitation to murder.

Vincenzo wasn't surprised to see two of Gugguci's men at the Catania's Fontanarossa Airport that afternoon. Fortunately, he couldn't get on the only flight to the Caribbean that day; all seats were taken, so he had opted for a Miami flight instead. He boarded the Miami flight unseen.

St. Croix

Little Sid lie on the ground with blood pouring out of his nose and tears of anger ran from his eyes. His anger had taken control of his actions and he kept trying to charge his father. Every time he got halfway up on his feet, another kick or punch would knock him down again.

It had been going on too long, but there was nothing he could do about it. If he didn't try to fight, then he'd get stomped where he lie. If he fought back, he got more of the same, but at least he was a moving target and not just a lump on the ground.

Grandpa watched the event as he sucked on a cold beer under the shade of the veranda over his back porch. He was cursing the boy under his breath. *You stubborn little shit! Quit taking the beating and learn! Quit letting your emotions take control of your actions. Man wasn't given emotions as a fighting tool, dummy! Man was given the gift of reasoning to control actions. All you have to do is realize that what is an unavoidable truth is you're going to get the shit beat out of you until your enemy wears himself out or you make your brains come up with a solution. Lying there crying and jumping right back into the jaws of the tiger is not going to save your skinny little ass.*

Finally, the boy rolled up onto his feet to get away from his father and ran like hell. Grandpa applauded, spilling his beer and yelled, "It's about time, you little turkey. I was beginning to think you like getting beat up."

The boy ran over to the edge of the clearing and stopped then turned around and yelled at his father. "You're mean! You're a bastard and I hate you! Just wait until I get big; you'll be sorry then!" He hurt mentally and physically; he had taken a good beating and was only a little boy but slowly—he was getting older and wiser.

Sidney said, "Don't run away, sissy boy. Come back and fight as a man."

The kid responded, "No way! I'm just a little kid!"

Sidney said, "Do as you are told, and do it without question. Now come back and learn how to fight. Don't make me chase you."

Once again the boy shook his head "No."

Sidney didn't say another word. He also didn't delay, and sprinted with the speed of a jungle cat towards the boy. He had closed half the distance to the kid before it registered to the boy that he was about to be caught. Little Sid started to run but was too afraid. He was afraid that he would be caught and punished even more if he tried to run. And he was correct.

He just stood there, but at the last second, he faked a move to the left and dropped to the ground just as Sidney reached him. Sidney tripped on the boy as he went by. The boy's movement had been timed perfectly. Sidney didn't see the boy drop until it was too late. He hit the ground and rolled, then sprang to his feet with the speed of the same cat and turned to face the boy in the same instant. But the boy was not there; he was on a hard run to his grandpa.

Sidney wasn't angry nor was he having fun beating on the boy, but it was the only way to train him how to stay alive as Sidney X. He felt like laughing at the way the boy out-foxed him but couldn't; humor would only sour lessons learned. He was proud of the boy's cleverness and speed but neither Sidney nor the boy could ease up. When the kid was on his own, he'd have to accept the fact that only his physical condition and brains can save him.

Little Sid finally figured out that he couldn't avoid the beating; therefore, it was impossible to win the fight, so he had to get away. That was his only choice. If he can't win easily then get out of the fight until he can control the situation. To get stubborn and let his emotions tell him to stand and fight was stupid. That guaranteed a beating.

The boy ran over to his grandpa crying, "Grandpa, help! He's going to hurt me."

Grandpa said, "That's your problem, kid; you have to help yourself," then he reached over into the cooler next to him and helped himself to a new cold beer. In Grandpa's mind the kid had been around long enough to know better than to ask for help. It wasn't the first time the kid had been in that situation; he knew that the fight would continue until it was over. All he had to do was keep his distance and lessen the beating or try very hard to win the fight.

Little Sid was given a chance to win; all he had to do was hit his father on the back three times. So far, he hadn't been able to get that close without slaps to his face or kicks to his mid-section or legs. But the memory of his charging father tripping over him and landing off his feet gave him something to think about.

He decided to start moving around his father. He started in to attack, then changed course, stopped and backed up, avoiding some of the blows from dear old dad. He continued with those moves until his father began to lose patience and darted in at the same time the boy did. Little Sid was ready and with perfect reflexes dodged the charge by dropping to his left knee and ducking. As soon as the ducking maneuver was completed, he jumped straight up and swung his body around, wrapping his arms around his father's neck. Without delay or thought, the boy hit him three times just under his right shoulder blade.

It was truly a time of manly rights. For the first time, the boy had attacked and won. Grandpa was excited and jumped up with joy, only to land on his stumps, and fell over laughing. Sidney couldn't believe it; the kid had been so fast he hadn't seen the move coming, and he was delighted to have lost. But it was a sweet-sour feeling since it was the first time anyone had beat him since his father—all those years ago.

Sidney briefly wondered if this was a sign that his time was over; that he was no longer unbeatable. Of course there was a huge difference in the way he fought enemies rather than the boy, but he had not been easy on the boy. It was a true victory for the little kid because he had won under the stated rules.

Sidney didn't say anything to the boy about the fight. He didn't con-gratulate him on his victory; after all, to do so would be making a game out of his training. In life you win or lose; the winner gets his own satis-faction from victory. Besides, he didn't have to tell the boy what a good job he had done, Grandpa was doing a good job of that while rolling around the ground in laughter and recounting the sudden moves and the three instantaneous blows on the back of the deadly charging bull. But because the boy had beaten him, the boy would be rewarded with the rest of the day off.

Sidney went over to the cooler and pulled three beers out. He mo-tioned for the boy to come over to where his grandpa was sitting on the ground. The three of them popped their beers and Sidney and son and son were grateful for the cold sting in their mouths as it poured down their throats. They had exercised for two hours then another one and a half hours fighting in the hot son. One of the true treasures in life was that first long swallow of ice-cold beer after a rigorous workout. The next best thing was the moment of relaxation in the cool shade and knowing that it was over for now.

The three Sidneys critiqued the fight, not telling the boy how to fight, but discussing the positive moves he made. This way the boy got another view of how things were and hopefully would build on his strengths and develop a style of fighting tailored to his way of thinking.

The kid had heard about keeping emotions in check after every fight he had been in, but now he had a good idea why. This was the first time he forced himself to quit taking the beating and think about the situation. It really seemed to work, and all of a sudden the dreaded fight was almost fun. He was extremely pleased with himself and Grandpa's laughter only reinforced his opinion that he was a bad little dude. He also started think-ing that maybe his father wasn't such an asshole after all. While he was very happy about that fight, he wasn't ready for more; his happiness faded briefly at the thought that there would be more the next day. If he was lucky maybe it would be Grandpa tomorrow—at least he could get away from him. And if not lucky, he'd be tricky and come up with a way to win early in the day to avoid the beating as usual.

After the fight discussion, Sidney opened another beer for himself and said, "Come here, Boy. It's time we discuss something important."

The boy, wide-eyed with curiosity, as usual, complied and sat in the grass before his father. "You are getting in pretty good shape physically. Being in good shape, being tough and being able to take care of yourself are the only things that are, or ever will be, important to you in life. You must start thinking that way and look for all kinds of challenges to make you more confident in your abilities.

"I'm going to give you a very tough challenge very soon that you must win. I cannot tell you what it is because to do so will only make it harder for you. I will tell you, however, that you'll be on your own. Neither I nor your grandpa will be there to help you. It may seem devastating to you at first, but always remember that I did the same thing at your age. Your grandfather and every single one of your grandfathers also did the same. Most survived, some failed because they were weak. We must do this to prove we are strong and brave enough to be Sidneys. Just remember these words when your time comes to prove yourself; you're tough physically, but you'll have to work hard to be tougher mentally, and only then can you succeed when your time comes."

The older Sid sat without saying a word, but was getting pissed off. *He's babying the boy. What's the matter, daddy? Afraid your little boy's going to be scared? It's part of the tradition that no warning be given before the jungle test. It's critically important to condition the young man to sudden hardships and adverse conditions in unknown, unexpected situations. That few months in the jungle has always proved to be the main factor that makes the Sidneys so self-reliant. That's the one thing that gives us an edge over every human adversary we'll ever have to face. The only way to learn about true courage is to have the all choices taken away.*

Sidney didn't go any further. He didn't think he went too far, but the look he was getting from his father strongly suggested otherwise. *Pop's pissed. Fuck him. I gave the boy fair warning and maybe those words will be helpful when he finds himself alone in the jungle.*

He finished off his long windiness with, "Just remember, every time you succeed in overcoming seemly incredible hardships or accomplishing tasks, raids or fights, those things are your badges of honor. Only you see the badges, but you know they are there and are well deserved. A rich man can buy anything he wants, but honor can only be obtained through actions."

Grandpa and young Sid had a much longer discussion about honor, bravery and self-worth. Sidney drank several more beers listening to the conversation. He wished he were more talkative and didn't know why he wasn't. His father could talk continually and it was practically impossible to shut the kid up. He felt left out when those two would sit around all day gabbing. For some reason the ability to verbally converse skipped a generation.

He had never given any thought about talking until Jandy made a big deal about it. His mind was always working; he was fully aware of what was happening and what was going to happen in his immediate surroundings. He muttered, "Just wish I'd find something to say more often."

During the ongoing conversation, his mind drifted away and into something more interesting. It didn't dawn on him that was why he wasn't talkative; he was a thinker. *Mafia's treasure in Cuba has to be known by more than the fifteen men in Italy. There will be guards in Cuba, guards to escort new deposits. Damn, wish I had known about this before I sent Vito to hell; he would've been happy to tell me: his wife still had lots of stuff to lose. I'd like to find out without messing with the Circle guys; it'll be a much greater effect on them if it just disappears one day. I'm going to take that prize.*

A name popped into his mind. "Ortega," he muttered, "in St. Thomas bragged that he was close to the Italians."

Ortega, king of smugglers in the Caribbean, should know who the Italians in Cuba were. Sidney was feeling refreshed and eager for the challenge. *See, Sidney, if you spent all your time jabbering you couldn't come up with these glorious raids. Poor kid will probably end up raiding Salvation Army boxes just so he'll have plenty of time to sit and chat. I'll probably need more logs for him if he writes of his exploits as windy as he talks about absolutely nothing important.*

SICILY

Tony the Pop sat on his patio enjoying a beautiful day; the to-tally clear sky had an almost slight chill in the air. A gentle wind made it cool enough to put on a light sweater—had not the warm rays of the sun made a difference. Lunch consisted of his cook's well-known Caesar salad and African lobster tails that had been boiled in olive oil and garlic. Several loaves of fresh bread were on the table. A glass of chilled California's Chateau Montelena Chardonnay provided a perfectly clear, crisp tasting balance for the food.

His guests were Paul Chance and the Chinaman, Chong. Both thoroughly enjoyed the casual lunch; no business was discussed, only pleasant small talk. Tony seemed interested in knowing what had been going on in their lives since he last saw them. Paul enjoyed the wine a bit more than he should and Chong much less than he should. Chong wasn't a man that enjoyed drinking or those who do. Actually, Chong wasn't a man who enjoyed anything—other than one almost uncontrollable craving.

After lunch, the men went into Tony's study, which was his special room. It was designed to offer isolation and security; a place to go for serious thought where there were no distractions. No windows were in the room nor paintings hanging on walls; no vases with colorful flowers, and no little gimmicks cluttered his desk. The desk was a large thick slab of glass resting on six vertical bronze legs. Its tabletop was oval, ten feet long and five feet at the widest point. Six straight-back chairs made of cast bronze were evenly spaced on one side. Each had a deeply cushioned back and seat to provide comfort after hours of sitting which was frequently the case when meetings were held in the study. Side tables were provided for the two visitors to put their briefcases on, leaving the table's surface clear for the work at hand.

The only thing decorative were the walls which were Honduras teak; its natural wood grain and golden color was preserved with an occasional wiping with a light oil. It appeared to be a very simple room; however, it wasn't. Filing cabinets, facsimile machines, an Alfa-geek's dream of a computer system, a bank of televisions for monitoring several stations, and a stereo system were concealed behind the teak. Also short and long wave radios gave him worldwide communications, as did the satellite telephone. Behind one wall was a well-stocked arsenal of weapons, another wall hid a full-sized map of the world. And, of course, there was a self-contained bar in the last wall.

The only way to gain access to these things was to use an electrical pushbutton combination switch located in the credenza behind Tony's chair. The switch released powerful magnetic locks concealed behind the panels.

Tony started the meeting by saying, "You guys have been called here to do a job for me. You'll have to drop everything else you are doing and concentrate on finding an asshole, maybe a group of them. The assholes have been asking for our special attention and now they're going to get it. You have a ninety-day window to tell me the names and where I can find these assholes."

He pulled out two sets of file folders and two CD disks. "I want you to work off hardcopies today, but all of your other work will be done on these disks after today. He then produced two laptop computers. He said, "These are special computers and you better pay attention to my instructions on how to use them."

He opened one and pointed to the power, on-off switch. "Do not push that switch unless you must destroy the computer. When pushed, you have five seconds before the computer blows the fuck up. You best be out of the room. The explosive device hasn't been activated yet, but it will automatically become active after you install the CD. Never remove that disk. If you do, it'll blow the computer the fuck up, too. That disk is for backup only—do it every day. If the hard drive goes down let me know; I'll have a man come to you to fix it. Each computer operates on a system unique to itself; they are not alike so nobody can figure out the processing. A real expert might eventually figure something out, but they would have to turn it on first without it blowing up. Any questions?"

Chong said, "Yeah, how do you turn it on without getting blown the fuck up?"

"Good question, Chong. There are two ways to turn it on. When going through security checkpoints like airports, push the power button while depressing the escape key. It'll display a standard Windows menu. The way you turn it on is to type in your personal password on the keyboard. Any more questions?"

Paul, thanks to the last two glasses of wine at lunch, was having a little trouble and was fuzzy about the words, "blow the fuck up."

Tony went through it again and Chong didn't mind going over the procedure again either. Blow the fuck up was pretty serious business to a couple of guys who blow the fuck up of a lot of things and persons.

Tony slipped them each a slip of paper and said, "These are your individual passwords, remember them and give the paper back to me."

He looked at Chong and said, "Insert the backup disk and then power up as if you're going through airport security."

Chong, without hesitation, went through the procedure. As soon as the Windows menu was on screen he wanted to shut it down. Then, nervously, he looked at Tony and asked, "How do I turn it off in this mode?"

Tony grunted, "And you smart fucks didn't have any questions when I asked you, eh? To turn it off you type the same password while depressing the escape key." Chong quickly made the moves and was relived it didn't blow the fuck up.

Tony then instructed Paul to start his to be operational. He typed in his password, *round-eye,* with the escape key firmly depressed. A menu appeared on screen offering five options. Option one: Known actions and updated remarks. Two: Current database of players. Three: Spreadsheet. Four: Expense account. The last option: Send.

Tony said, "The computers have unique 4-G Internet systems. Click on the 'Send' option every day before you retire. It'll automatically call a number and download the contents of your computer into my computer. I want this done every day even if nothing has changed. That way I'll know if you're fucking off on me and that, as you can imagine, is not going to be in your best interest."

Chong was told to start his up as well. Chong wasn't particularly happy about his password, thinking it was raciest. He started the program without difficulty.

Tony had them look at the expense report first and then said, "You are on expenses on this project. You have no reason to skimp, no reason to not turn over every stone, no reason not to investigate every lead. Travel first class. I want the job done right and I want it done fast, if not sooner. Expenses will be wired to a bank in the Cayman Islands. That same bank will be used to pay for your time in solving this matter. Each of you will receive fifty-thousand dollars a month for three months. If you haven't found the assholes by then you better have a reason. The man that gives the assholes to me collects an additional one-hundred thousand dollars."

Paul whistled and said, "I guess you do want these guys in a hurry."

Tony said, "These are not guys, they're assholes and now I'll show you why. Open your Known Actions and Updates option. Before going into these files I'll tell you what's on them. The assholes have targeted several of our people in the last few years. They specialize in casino operations and it doesn't matter if it's on land or aboard cruise ships. They also target private boats and even aircraft. All of the details surrounding every incident are covered in the report. By the way, this report isn't confidential—it's top *fucking* secret. You might have noticed there isn't a printer port on your computers, so you can't print a copy of anything. Also, the modem will only dial one number—mine. These assholes are going to be caught and extremely severe examples are going to be made of them. You might keep that in mind, concerning your own performances."

He ended up with a statement: "No one is aware of most of the actions in the files. If we hear about them on the street I'll have to think one of you is talking too much, and we all know that would be a mistake."

They both agreed knowing the penalty for having a lack of respect for the Mafia's private way of life. They went over the history recorded during the last twenty years from around the world. He had asked the various agencies for just the last few years but as they cranked up the big data bases, each pulled up actions that began as far back as data had been entered into computers. It turned out it wasn't a *new* show of disrespect after all. However, most of the activity in the last four years had taken place in the Caribbean. And the Caribbean bunch was his only priority.

Tony said, "Stay focused on the Caribbean problem. Some police agencies know about a few attacks, some don't. Most of this information is known by the big agencies, but hasn't been noticed. The big agencies normally don't operate in the Caribbean, except to look at specific drug-related crimes. Small town and island police won't know anything that isn't in these reports but you should check things out with them, anyway."

It was after ten o'clock that evening before Tony decided to give it a rest. He led the detectives out of the study into the brisk night air overlooking the usual awe-inspiring view. The black water of the Mediterranean was dotted with red, green and white pinpoints of lights from passing vessels and buoys.

A much heavier concentration of lights crowding the shoreline and the hills rose abruptly from the harbor. The ambience created by the view caused all the problems that the assholes were creating for a small group of people to seem insufficient to Paul. His glass of iced vodka helped minimize the feeling of importance that he had been feeling all day while listening to Tony rave on—and on.

Several more vodkas were consumed before dinner was served. The meal was superb and was very Italian. The California wine that complemented it was even better.

After a lengthy meal, and more wine than Paul should have consumed, the visitors were shown to their rooms. Tony had rules about foreigners working for him; they were not to be seen in Sicily when in Sicily on business. If they want to play then they can come and enjoy at their own expense. This suited Chong perfectly since he normally didn't drink and too much Russian vodka and Californian wine had already passed his lips. One glass of each had been enough to make him feel uncomfortable. The only reason he drank was because Tony didn't trust a man who didn't. He was able to conceal it, mostly, but the next morning he would discover the strands of pasta still clinging to his shirtfront, tie and the toe of his left shoe.

Paul was also ready for the sack; it had been a very long day, as he had traveled most of the night getting to Sicily from Chile, where he had been on surveillance.

At seven the next morning, it was back to the study for another full day going over past records and considering various known criminals who might want to do the family harm. The final stratagem couldn't be settled until they knew who they were dealing with, but one thing was a certainty: a trap would be set and sprung on Tony's assholes.

Tony planned to lure the assholes to the big shithouse in the sky with diamonds, as a measure of retribution. Vito had been a good friend, and the assholes had gone after his diamonds—and diamonds would be their demise. He also thought of the pain and punishment forced on Vito's beautiful wife and knew that before the assholes departed earth, he'd be sure they experienced three times the anguish. The assholes' utter disregard for life really bothered Tony. Ironically, when his side did similar atrocities, it had no effect whatsoever on him. As usual, everything was relative.

The missing Tribute and the dead crew and wrecked jet pissed him off, too. So did some of the casino robberies where he knew people who had been involved. Based on the facts as he saw them, the assholes were a mean bunch; probably one of the young Jamaican gangs trying to come up with enough cash to buy a vaulted position in the drug market. But he had doubts about that possibility; they could walk in and rob land-based casinos and banks easily enough and it was conceivable they pulled off the jobs aboard cruise ships. But Vito's yacht; only insider information could have pointed to the diamonds. And the same was true with the missing Tribute.

Tony was certain that eventually a name or two of someone who had prior knowledge of the events would surface. As he often said, "All things will be revealed—when covered with enough money."

When Paul and Chong arrived from Tony's study that evening, they were surprised to see six beautiful women waiting for them at the bar. While Chong wasn't much of a drinker, he was a serious womanizer—he was addicted to women and didn't give a damn who knew. During the course of the evening, he had two sips of wine and took every woman there to bed at least once. Paul was happy, too; he had gotten laid twice and stayed drunk all night. Tony didn't join the party—he had his private pair of girls waiting in his quarters.

After the detectives left Sicily the next day, Tony sat alone on his patio reflecting on how the meeting had gone. He was pleased and felt confident that one of them would find those responsible. Both had the gift for sensing things and had an incredible track record to prove it.

Tony had a list of names to call about possible leads. Some were low-level Mafia with connections in the Caribbean. Others were not part of the organization, but were friendly and helpful when asked for information or a favor. The first name on his hand-written list was Jose Ortega.

It was still early in the day in the Virgin Islands so he called Jose's office number. As expected, he wasn't there. In his opinion, Latinos didn't appreciate hard work and long hours the way Italians did. He tried Jose's hacienda in Venezuela; it took three calls before he got a good enough connection to Jose. The jungle compound was one of Tony's favorite places.

During the opening conversation, Jose was thinking, *why is Tony masking the real reason for his call? He wants something and doesn't want to come out and ask.* Finally Jose said, "Hey, Tony, what ever happened to the guys that held up that yacht, I believe it was the *Golden Boy?*"

Tony, relieved that he didn't have to come out with a direct approach replied, "Oh, yeah, we're still looking for the assholes that pulled that one. You got any ideas?"

Jose thought for a minute and said, "I asked around like you asked me to, but haven't heard anything."

Tony asked, "Are there any new kids on your block who might be playing with somebody else's marbles?"

Jose said, "Well, that's kind of a tough question. You know how people come and go in the business."

Both men were careful not to say anything incriminating, but weren't concerned with conversations involving public knowledge. Also, it would have taken an army to arrest either of them.

Tony said, "I can appreciate that. Would you mind if I came by to see the most beautiful place on your side of the earth for a day or two? Maybe we can do some hunting and go over some possibilities?"

"Sure thing, Tony, anytime, and stay as long as you want. You know we have plenty of room."

Tony said, "That's great, I'll see you in three days. Can I bring you anything from the civilized world?" Like most Europeans, Tony felt that only the old world was truly civilized.

Ortega laughed at the offer and replied, "No, we have plenty of bananas and rum; what else is there to want? But I do have a problem, Tony; I'll be away until the fifth of next month."

Tony replied, "That'll be fine with my schedule, if there is no conflict with another houseguest?"

"There's no conflict." Ortega, like any criminal with a long successful run, always took good care of his peers.

As soon as Tony hung up, he called his secretary, "Make arrangements to get me to the Ortega compound in Venezuela. I'm not sure how long I'll be there so buy one-way tickets for me and my travel crew. We'll be going somewhere else from there."

Before his next telephone call Tony had a brilliant idea. *The Cuban depository! If the assholes ever got hold of that information it'd be an easy ambush. The amount of money kept there would damn sure make them take chances—it's truly honey for the bee. But how could it be set up? Only fifteen men and their kin who guard the treasure know of the treasure and where it is. Besides it's unthinkable to expose the cache to potential thieves, and everybody fits that description when it came to that much wealth.*

He muttered, "And what the fuck would I do if I used the depository as the trap and they managed to beat the trap—and steal it, too? It would be the final insult and there's no doubt that I'd pay the price."

ST. CROIX

Sidney decided to take a day off and went to Christiansted. It would be the last time he was in civilization for a while and he felt like getting drunk. Besides, he needed to buy food anyway and the store was just down the street from Fred's Place. It was his favorite place in town to get shit-faced; it was a rough place, on the waterfront, and always full of drunken, derelict boat bums. Beer was cheap as was the rum and everything else there... including the women.

Fred's wife was tending bar and she was always good for a few laughs even though she was a wicked old bitch with a foul and loud mouth with a New Jersey accent. Her name was Lila Mae and she had the biggest boobs on the island. She always wore one of Fred's old tank tops to turn on or gross out the customers, depending on how drunk they were. Her true love in life was to drink and start fights between the patrons. Fred was the only living thing in the world who could control the woman when she was on a roll.

As Sidney walked into the grungy little bar he looked for Fred, but he had passed out and Lila Mae was in full bloom. She was standing on top of the bar chugging a bottle of rum that was spilling out of her mouth and running down her thin tank top. Her massive mammary glands were fully exposed behind the rum-soaked fabric.

The men in the bar—all six of them—were chanting and cheering for her to drink or spill the whole bottle of rum on her shirt. She did both, but most of it was on the front of her shirt and at her feet. When she was through, she threw the bottle across the room to shatter on a bare dirty wall. Then slowly she assumed the *Arnold Schwarzenegger* muscleman stance to best show her neck muscles while hissing "Yeah!" She slowly turned to face everyone to be sure they were looking. She was nuts, but she was having a damn good time.

When she saw Sidney enter the room and focused her eyes enough to recognize him, she yelled with a slur, "Siddy! Now there's old Siddy! There's a man that's not a fucking chicken shit to kill a bottle."

She dropped to her knees on the bar, then reached down behind it and came up with a new bottle of rum. She threw the bottle as a football and as hard as any NFL quarterback could. Fortunately, Sidney saw it coming and caught it before it could do any damage. The drunks, including Lila May, cheered the catch and started yelling, "Kill the bottle! Kill the bottle!"

Lila Mae never gave a man an even chance. She jumped up before Sidney knew how to react and started yelling, "Oh, shit! He's another chicken-shit, limp-dicker. You fucking limp-dickers ain't got no fucking balls." She walked over and put her dirty bare foot on the forehead of a guy sitting at the bar and with very little effort pushed him backwards until he fell off of the barstool. She yelled, "Look at that little *limper* bounce," and roared with laughter.

Sidney sat at the bar and opened the bottle of rum; he preferred to drink it straight from the bottle anyway while he watched the show. The wild woman went from patron to patron, doing her best to try to get the *fucking limper* to stand up and be hard like a man was supposed to be. All she got were laughs, which pissed her off more. Finally, it was *Siddy's* turn.

She said, "Siddy, you're a mean looking son-of-a-bitch and I never did fucking like you. But I never thought you were a fucking limper like the rest of these wannabe pricks. Actually, Siddy, you're an ugly fucker, too. Did you know that?" she asked in a sweet little innocent voice.

Before Sidney could respond, Lila Mae said, "Give me back my bottle of rum, you fucking limper. I gave it to you thinking you might have grown some balls since the last time I was unfortunate enough to see your worthless ass." Then in a dramatically poised, exaggerated pout on her face and sorrowful voice she quipped, "But I was wrong."

Then she made a sudden switch to hostility, "You're still the ball-less shit-sucker you were the last time you were here. Damn a fucking bear; I don't know why I put up with you bunch of pitiful limpers. Poor excuses for manhood are all I'll ever see around here. And you dumb shits wanna know the worst thing about yourselves?"

There was silence—any man who spoke knew he would take Siddy's place at center stage in Fred's world of shit bar.

Lila Mae continued, "The worst part about you all is you're too fucking stupid to know how worthless you assholes really are." And she laughed, but it was a mean laugh, not friendly. Everyone enjoyed the bitch-fit but no one was going to attract her attention.

She would have been more fun to watch if there were a bulletproof glass partition between her and the customers. No one knew what she might do next, including Lila Mae. She was known to do some really weird things, depending on how drunk she was. Several guys have had to be carried out because she knocked the consciousness out of them with barstools, bottles, and even her fist. On one occasion, she ran out of the bar screaming like the mad banshee she was and ran two blocks down the street to a construction site. She found what she wanted there, a two-by-four board, and ran back. Then she took a full swing at a guy's head. He was taken by ambulance to the hospital: he recovered but could never get the ringing out of his ears. He had made the one mistake nobody does twice: he called her a bitch. For some reason being called a bitch always set her off, drunk or sober.

Lila Mae eventually lost interest in Sidney. The bottle of rum he didn't return to her tasted pretty good and he enjoyed watching her attack the next hapless soul. He was having fun while everything at Fred's continued to deteriorate. She chased several tourists out who happened to wander in, offering Lila Mae a new set of victims she could terrorize. The regulars loved it and applauded. She was successful in starting a couple of sloppy fights; they weren't real fights, they were more like a couple of drunks rolling around and wrestling on the dirty floor.

Another tourist, a good-looking young guy with a shiny face, came in and made a terrible mistake. After Lila Mae finished chewing him out for being a no-brainer-piece-of-limp-dick, the guy thought he could match wits and insults—that was even worse than calling her a bitch. He said, "Get down on your knees, woman, and I'll show you a real man," and he hefted his crotch towards her.

She dropped to her knees so fast she almost bounced, saying, "Okay, big stud, give it to me!"

That caught him by surprise and he tried to recover by saying, "I would, you rabid bitch, but I'm afraid you would break your teeth trying to chew on my rock hard cock." He was having a good time trying to play the game with the rest of the guys. But what he didn't know was the rest of the guys were waiting and baiting him or any other man to try to get the best of Lila Mae—or call her a bitch. And he managed to do both in one sentence.

Lila Mae never gave fair warning. From her kneeling position in front of the guy, she reached up with both hands and grabbed two handfuls of whatever the guy had in his crotch. Then she squeezed as hard as she could and stood up screaming, "Okay, Mr. Rock Hard, let's see how many teeth break off now," and put her weight into swinging him around in a circle. The guy followed everywhere she went while screaming in pain; she had a death grip on his balls.

As she swung him around in circles she asked, "Where's that hard rock thing you like to talk about so much? All I feel is mush. Feels like you've been shitting in your pants. You ain't no different than the rest of these limpers, so go join your wannabe faggots."

She suddenly released her hold, and his momentum carried him to the bar where he knocked the guy sitting next to Sidney off his barstool. That man fell over and knocked Sidney off of his, and Sidney took the next man in line to the floor with him. Everybody was having fun—except the tourist with crushed balls—and the guy that Sidney had knocked off of his perch.

Unfortunately, the man Sidney knocked down was the male version of Lila Mae when he was drunk. Usually he'd get silent as he approached the dangerous level of drunkenness and someone would remind him it was time to go home. His name was Sam and he grew up with that problem; after twenty years of bar fights and jail time he had learned to go home when someone told him to. But that night, all eyes had been on Lila Mae and Sam had been ignored too long.

Sam looked up from the floor at Sidney who was righting his own barstool. He muttered, "I don't like you. And I damn sure don't like you knocking me on the floor when my back's turned. And I don't like all of the noise around here. I don't like the shit that's going on. And no son-of-a-bitch is going to fuck with me when I'm drink'n."

He quickly stood up and, without warning, gave Sidney the best punch he had ever thrown. It landed unhindered on Sidney's forehead.

The big fist would have been in his mouth, but Sidney saw it and was able to move enough just before it landed. Had it landed where it was aimed, Sidney would have looked like he was the one who tried to chew through the rock-hard crotch that caused all of the trouble.

Sam was a good fighter and sober he would be a tough match for any man. But he wasn't a match for Sidney, drunk or sober. Sidney was on his feet instantly and inborn instinct ruled that he was the aggressor and punched Sam twice in the face before he could react. Sam did the only thing he could; he fell back to the filthy floor of Fred's Place, unconscious.

Lila Mae was impressed. "Now that's the kind of fighting I likes!" She strutted over to Sidney and said, "Well, it looks like little Siddy here thinks he is a big man. He thinks he can just come in here and beat up on drunks, does he?"

Of course, everyone, other than Sidney, was egging her on to jump him. And she had every intention of doing just that. "Well, you wanna-be tough little limper, think you're man enough to try that with Lila Mae?"

When she finished the challenge she was standing only inches away from Sidney. Had it been a man he would have been snoozing with Sam. If he had an empty bottle of rum on the bar, he would have turned away and left. But neither of those was what he faced. Sidney, not given to pleasantries anyway, ignored the woman, sat down and continued to drink his rum.

She grabbed him by the shoulder and tried to turn him around on the barstool before punching him. When her hand clamped down on his shoulder, all she felt was solid muscle; she used all of her strength trying to turn him around. He didn't budge. His strength surprised her and only angered her more. She tried to push him off the barstool with no success, so she lowered her head and charged using her shoulder. To the drunks, she looked like a linebacker in blocking practice. She couldn't move Siddy and she was getting really pissed.

The guys in the bar loved it and were yelling encouragement to Lila Mae. She threw a punch at Sidney but he casually blocked it, as he did the next three punches while drinking from the bottle. Lila Mae reached the point of her endurance and was ready to run down the street for another two-by-four when Sidney decided to stop her attack. He caught her flailing arms in his hands and forced them down to her side; her strength was that of a newborn baby compared to his. She could not stop him from doing anything he wanted. She was helpless to move, run away, or even fall down. Then he pulled her so close she couldn't breathe. She couldn't struggle and realized her predicament and stopped yelling—fear had finally showed its ugly face to Lila Mae.

Sidney whispered to her, "It's time for you to go to bed now. I'm going to leave a hundred-dollar bill here to cover any business you might miss because you had to leave early tonight. If you don't leave quietly right now, and go join Fred in bed, I'm going to knock you out. Then you won't feel the pain as I break both of your legs. It'll be a long time before you chase anybody else out of here. The men in here won't be the only limpers. Do you understand me, Lila Mae?"

Her head nodded yes; her eyes were full of tears caused by an equal mixture of hate, pain and fear. At six feet tall and weighing one hundred eighty pounds, she had never felt so powerless. She had always been a powerful, aggressive woman and had never been manhandled like that before. Being out of control in a bad situation, she was smart enough to see through her drunkenness and realized she wanted no part of that guy. She was truly frightened for her safety for the first time in her adult life.

Sidney said, "Say goodnight, Boys—have fun. Leave what you owe and last one out, lock the door; and then you go join Fred." He released Lila Mae and she gave him a frightened smile.

She turned around and said, "I think it is time I go to bed. Goodnight, Boys—have fun. Leave what you owe and last one out, lock the door."

She walked straight into the apartment at the rear of the bar. Sidney sat there for a few minutes expecting her to return with a gun. If so, his knife, only a flash away, would be sent flying to bury itself in her throat. Fortunately, she didn't. The guys were hooting it up—jeering, cheering— and couldn't understand Lila Mae quitting like that. Sidney finished his rum bottle, put the money on the cash register and left.

It was a fresh new morning and two weeks after young Sid's first victory on the fighting field. Since then he had been able to score two more wins, and you could plainly see the confidence building within the boy. His increased level of confidence also signaled Sidney that it was time for the boy to go to the jungle. And it was a beautiful day to go.

Sidney was up at dawn. He made a trip to the cave to gather enough money to buy the land that he was so fond of near Ortega's place. He wasn't sure how much he spilled into the plastic garbage bag, but estimated that it was around three million dollars. Taking a look around before he extinguished the lights in the cave, he thought, *the next time I see this room I'll have the boy with me—if he survives. It'll be good to show this place to the next Sidney X. It has been my favorite place since I first saw it when I was his age. I hope he'll feel the same and remember that no one has ever seen our treasure except a Sidney.*

He made a fast trip down the mountain, and when he reached the apartment, the boy was sitting on the ground outside waiting to go to Grandpa's for the daily training session.

Sidney said, "Wake up, Boy, don't you remember? I told you to stay on the boat because we're going sailing today."

The boy moaned with embarrassment; he had been dead tired last night by the time he had returned home and was still half-asleep that morning and had forgotten. While he had moaned, he was happy about not going through the usual workout and fighting lessons.

Sidney, with his bag of three million dollars in hand, pointed to the pantry and said, "Load a bunch of canned food into some garbage bags, then take them to the dinghy."

Little Sid was puzzled: *Why is he bringing food? We catch our own food. Wonder where we're going?* The boy rowed the little boat out to the *Barracouta* and they made everything ready on the bigger boat to depart. An hour later, the pair of Sidneys cleared the lagoon's entrance.

Young Sid took the boat out of the harbor without instructions from his father; he was comfortable handling the big boat. The only instruction Sidney gave him was, "Clear the island then turn south-south-east. We'll be at sea for a few days before landfall so relax and enjoy the sail."

Sidney hauled the inflatable dinghy on deck and once again performed surgery on it to hide money. After the boat was repaired, he laid down on the aft deck for a mid-morning nap; it was a much-needed nap after last night's brawl at the little bar in town.

As he lay on the sunny deck of the *Barracouta*, he thought about last night's events. He didn't want to cause any problems in his own back yard, and was sure he didn't damage Sam. He suspected the next time he went to Fred's Place, Lila Mae may get Fred to put the scare in Siddy about fucking with his wife.

He watched the kid to see if everything was under control. He was right on course, so Sidney thought it was time for a nap. It seemed that as soon as he closed his eyes he was awakened. Something felt wrong with the boat. Waves and wind had shifted directions and the sun was in the wrong position.

He sat up and looked forward to see what was going on, and immediately he saw what the problem was. Little Sid was sitting behind the steering wheel fast asleep. The boy had been taught the importance of staying awake while on watch. That kind of action could result in a major disaster. If they had been closer to a lee shore the boat, the two of them, and three million dollars could have been lost. Falling asleep while steering was something that happened to all sailors, but it was Sidney's responsibility to instill good seamanship in the boy. He had to teach him a lesson.

Sidney XXIII was guilty of sleeping while steering, but he knew when to sleep and was always aware of the boat's sailing attitude. He would, as he just had, wake up when something changed. It was conditioning. He decided to give the kid time to see how long it would take for him to wake up.

The boat continued its dangerous pattern of sailing. She would head up into the wind, then stall with the banging of halyards, sheets and the popping and banging of the sails as they changed to the other tack. Then the boat would run down wind until she made speed before fighting to get into the wind again. It was a terrible racket and the boat's motion was enough to shake anybody awake. But not little Sid. Suddenly it dawned on Sidney that his son had died.

He moved to the cockpit, dreading what he would find slouched behind the big stainless steel wheel. The boy was sitting there with shoulders relaxed, and his little brown arms limply resting on the inside of his thighs. The face was a picture of peaceful innocence. Then Sidney heard it. It was slight but it was definitely a snore. He listened carefully to be sure and was reassured with his next breath. He didn't know whether to be happy that the kid was okay or pissed. All of a sudden he knew what to do to prevent it from happening again. He positioned himself so he was standing over the boy then scooped him up by his shorts and threw his sleepy little ass overboard.

Little Sid didn't wake up until he hit the water. The look in his eyes as he surfaced screamed, "What is going on?" He was very confused. The *Barracouta* was sailing away from him faster than he could ever hope to swim, and his dad was nowhere in sight.

A minute later felt like an hour to Little Sid. Sidney came on deck and shouted, "It is a hard way to wake up, ain't it kid? If you want to get a good sleep while you are steering, you better get used to waking up this way."

The boat kept sailing away and Sidney did nothing to stop it. The boy really knew he screwed up that time and knew his father had no intention of picking him up. He watched the boat as it rounded up into the wind, fell off and pulled further away from him only to head up and move back again. That told him he better swim to a point where he could intercept the boat at some point where it would stop briefly.

It took a while before he finally was able to grab hold of the man-overboard lifeline that trailed behind the boat. That was a sixty-foot-long piece of three-quarters inch double braid that was tied to a big snap swivel on the transom. Its purpose was to give a man overboard something to catch and haul himself back to the boat, should he fall overboard. It was a practice mandatory when sailing alone—unless someone was suicide minded—or Sidney XXIII.

But with all the exertion of the hard swim he was too pooped to pull himself on board. Finally, Sidney got up and grabbed his hand and lifted him on board. No lectures were necessary. The boy had learned another hard lesson and was sincere when he muttered his apology while he resumed his position at the wheel, very much wide awake.

Sidney went below to fix some beans and a glass of rum for lunch, and then went back to the aft deck to continue with his nap. Two hours later he looked forward to see the boy standing at the wheel, singing.

After fixing another rum, he went out and relieved the boy. He asked, "Why are you so tired today?"

The kid answered, "I was over at my grandpa's most of the night."

"What were you doing there?" Sidney asked, as that was very unusual. Grandpa Sid had other things to do such as his drinking and woman chasing.

The boy said, "He wanted me to come over and talk about edible plants and show me some pictures of some dangerous jungle animals."

Sidney could not believe that his father was such a softy. He was, in his own way, trying to prepare the kid for the next six months stay in the jungle.

"Well," Sidney said, "I'm glad."

Days later, Sid saw the first sight of land mass clouds and knew that soon mountaintops would be in sight. Soon after that he would have to kick the boy overboard to start his ordeal into manhood, according to Sidney X tradition.

Finding a truly isolated area was not as easy as it used to be. Even the jungles of Central and South America were changing almost daily. Between logging companies, hotels and the worst invaders—the ants of humanity, the ecotourism mob—who were going into raw lands to reap the benefits of monetary profit from tourists trampling over nature.

Therefore, Sidney had brought a chart and the best map available of the area to be sure there were no settlements a few miles inland or roads that could lead a boy to civilization. He was also interested in looking over the area he intended to purchase. If he could find a good cave he might consider moving there some day. It would only be a matter of time before moving would be necessary. St. Croix was growing rapidly with the edges of civilization creeping over the land like a cancer.

The area where he would drop the boy was still isolated. It was almost one hundred miles in any direction before any form of civilization was seen. And the terrain was tough, so tough that it would strongly discourage any attempts to cross it. There were plenty of rivers and streams in the area to provide water, and the area got rain most every day so fresh water would not be a problem. If the kid remembered all he had been taught about survival, he should have no serious problems—other than the things that wanted to eat him. And if he remembered the many lessons about dealing with animals, that wouldn't be a major problem either.

They arrived at the appointed place about three o'clock in the afternoon. Sidney was a hard man, but this was difficult for him. He had never been attached to anybody in his life. Not his father or the mother he never knew or any of the women he had bedded. There had been something empty in him all of his life. He had no idea what that feeling was, but it seemed to be filled with thoughts about the boy those days. Making the boy go to shore was the hardest thing he had ever had to do.

When the *Barracouta* was about fifty yards off the rocky beach, Sidney called the boy to come to him. "Son, you are going to swim to shore. Go below and put on long pants and a long-sleeve shirt, and shoes, and wear your knife too."

Then he realized he didn't even know if the boy owned a long pair of pants. Little Sid appeared on deck in a few minutes wearing a brand new pair of Levis and a thick cotton long-sleeve shirt. A pair of white socks was between his feet and the shiny new leather boat shoes.

Sidney was surprised to see the clothes and asked, "When did you get those things?"

The kid, feeling uncomfortable with clothes all over him said, "Grandpa had Rosie buy them for me the day before we left."

That brought a little smile to Sidney. His old man liked the boy as much as he did. Then a fleeting dark thought went over him. His dad had not shown him any concern when his ass was tossed overboard, barefooted, wearing a pair of old shorts, and no shirt. The only thing his dad had seemed concerned about was to be sure he had his knife.

Little Sid came up to his father and said, "This is the challenge you warned me about, right, Dad? This is the thing that you and Grandpa had to do when you were little like me?"

The boy was scared, but he fully accepted it and there was not a doubt in his mind that the time had arrived for him to become a man. He had been worrying about it ever since it was mentioned to him the day of his first victory, fighting his dad.

"Yeah, kid, this is it. You have to prove yourself to *you* now. You have to take care of yourself for a long time in the jungle. You have been taught how to survive in the wild, so do what you have to do to stay alive. In time you will even enjoy living in the wild; it is a good feeling. Do not sleep on the ground. Find a place in the trees, and a night fire may help you feel better if you get scared. You can go anywhere you want to while you are here, but you must be at this same spot in six months, for me to pick you up. You need to find a big tree and put a mark on it with your knife. Do that with every sunrise and when you have one hundred eighty marks, I will be here."

Sidney finished off his instructions with, "That's all you need to know, kid, so get your ass off the boat and go learn and make it fun. I'll have a couple of surprises that you'll like when I pick you up."

Little Sid sensed the concern and sorrow in his father and said, "Don't worry, Dad, I'll kick ass in there." He stood on the edge of the deck for a few seconds looking at the water and the waiting jungle. Standing there, he didn't want to go, but his grandpa had told him that to be the next Sidney X he had to do it—so he jumped.

The boy wanted his father to be proud of him so he wanted to show his dad he was not afraid. He wanted to have a big smile on his face when he said good-bye after he reached the shore. By the time the boy swam to shore and stood up to look back at his father and wave good-bye, it was too late. The *Barracouta* had her sails full of fresh breeze and was headed straight out to sea. His father was not on deck. The boy thought, *he must be below fixing another rum drink.*

PART OF SIDNEY FELT LOUSY ABOUT DUMPING THE KID ON THE BEACH. Another part felt shame about babying the boy. "That boy hit the beach with a whole lot more support than any other Sidney ever had, so why should I feel bad?" He muttered.

By the time he had finished the rum that he fixed as he sailed away, he had his mind on other matters. Important matters like "I wonder if Maria is going to be there. I need to get laid."

It took him a couple of days to get to the little village where he planned to leave the *Barracouta* for the next six months. When he arrived at the village, he knew he would have a problem getting the deep draft boat into the river and the sleepy little lagoon behind the village. There were big surf rollers from the northerly winds that had been blowing all day. The breaker bar outside of the river's entrance caused the seas to heap up and form ten-foot breakers.

He was at home with all seas, however, and what the average experienced sailor might think was suicidal, Sidney had probably done at least twice. After all, he was an original descendant from "the King of the Seas," as the pirates used to call themselves.

He sailed by the crashing breakers that were trying to force their massive volumes of water and momentum carried for thousands of miles over the shallow sand bar. He was looking for the best water, which would be indicated by several things like water colors and the size of the breakers. After he had picked his path, he headed back out to sea. He was going to have some excitement that day.

Several villagers saw the *Barracouta* sail by and ran out to wave their arms and yell warnings not to try to come into the river. It was way too rough and much too shallow with the big seas; the boat would be destroyed. They all felt relieved when they saw the boat turn out to sea. They all felt sick when they saw the boat turn in on an approach to the river.

Sidney had taken the boat out about a quarter of a mile from shore, and then made his turn back to thundering breakers. At that distance, he could see the wisps of spray blowing off of the backs of the huge forming breakers. More importantly, he could read the breakers to see where the deepest water was, and the distance was enough to get up to maximum hull speed. There was not a doubt in his mind that he could get over the bar. He didn't even untie the dinghy from the davits so at least his three million dollars would float to shore if the *Barracouta* didn't make it.

He had a good breeze coming in on his portside rear-quarter. So he started his run by pointing the *Barracouta* to a point on land that was downwind of the pass. The boat was sailing as fast as it was possible for the hull to go. As he got closer to the shallow water, the big swells started standing up, getting steeper. He was running at about ten degrees off of the direction of the waves. As he got nearer, the steeper waves would pick up *Barracouta* and try to carry her with them. But the big sails kept her moving where he wanted to go. She would lose some momentum as the big sea would pass under her, tilting the sails, allowing the air to spill, but Sidney compensated for every action that Mother Nature had built into her seas.

At the right moment, just before he reached the breaker-bar, he turned the *Barracouta* closer to the wind and was running a few degrees off of the waves so they were coming in on his port bow. The boat was leaning over, crashing through waves and hauling ass. He felt the *Barracouta* bottom out several times when the big waves passed and dropped him to the lowest part between waves, but between his momentum and the oncoming next wave lifted him off and propelled him away.

As quickly as he had entered the raging breakers he was out of them. All that was left of the massive waves was boiling white water and foam on the surface to sail through. He smiled; that was the first real fun he had had in a long time. Had he been trying to leave instead of coming in he would not have tried crossing those breakers that way. When he had to go out, he probably would have to start his engine, if it worked.

The entire village was on the beach and everyone was jumping up and down like a bunch of happy savages with cheers that Sidney had made the crossing. It was a feat that none of their experienced fishermen would have attempted. Sidney thought those people looked happy enough to have another pig roast and hoped he was right.

He sailed slowly into the lagoon and when in the same position he was in on his last visit, dropped the bow anchor. He threw a stern line to the children that were the first to arrive to welcome him. They ganged up on the rope and had a tug-of-war with the *Barracouta*. The adults arrived and stood back watching the children grunt and groan, while pulling the boat until it was as far as the bow's anchor line would allow.

Everybody was happy. Everyone except old Gaspar and he was only moderately happy because the return of Sidney meant his loss of position in the village as the man with the Jeep.

Sidney's Jeep was sitting right where it was when he left. Old Gaspar never did use the Jeep except to take people for a ride around the village. He didn't know how to drive very well and was afraid he would wreck the car. But he still had the most important thing about owning a car—prestige.

Sidney felt somewhat pleased to see the people of the village were glad to see him again. That was a rarity. Even his marina manager in St. Croix was never happy to see him when he returned. He visited many lands, but when he left, he left with high hopes that he would not be recognized if he ever returned.

It didn't take him long to find his way to Gaspar's bar. In fact, the villagers made a path for him to follow as they each greeted him on the way. Nothing had changed inside the bar, including the patrons. They were bitching about the militia that came by for their regular handouts, and, of course, there was the never ending bragging about who was the best fisherman. The roof still had the same holes in it that provided some interesting challenges when it rained. The floor had the same dirt on it and probably the same flies were buzzing around sampling the droplets on top of the rum bottle. Sidney felt at home.

He sat right there listening and drinking until he fell off of his makeshift bar stool. Then he happily staggered back to the *Barracouta* and fell asleep in the cockpit. His dreams that night were about a scared and lonely little boy alone in a dark and dangerous place.

The next morning he was up at dawn and went running down the beach. He ran for miles. It was the hardest workout he had done in a long while. At the end of his run, he lay down on the warm white sand listening to the crashing waves and the blood pumping loudly through his veins. It felt good to exert maximum effort and then relax and enjoy the feeling of his body pulling in the reserves to revive his strength. The feeling was so relaxing he took a nap. The nap stretched out to a deep sleep that lasted three hours. When he awoke he was rested, and after a leisurely swim in the ocean, he began a slow walk back to the village while enjoying the view and sounds of his surroundings.

It was almost dark when he walked into the village. On the trip back, he stopped and ate whenever edible food was found that appealed to him. The entire area was covered with the black spiny urchins which he had developed a taste for as a child. Also there was an abundance of little fish trapped in the tidal pools that he easily caught by using his shorts with the legs tied together to form a seine net. He washed everything down with coconut water.

When he returned to the village, all of his needs were well-satisfied except getting laid and getting drunk and getting a good cigar. He couldn't believe that he left civilization for an extended period of time without buying some cigars.

He walked into the village with the little kids playing all around him, and the few adults who noticed him gave him a friendly wave or greeted him as one of their own. He walked straight to the little bar, sat on the same make-shift barstool and listened to the same conversations and got just as drunk as he did the day before. And he was just as happy as he was yesterday. The next few days he did the same.

After a few days getting thoroughly relaxed, his nightly dreams about the little boy seemed to mellow. He also knew that if the boy was still alive by then he would more than likely be able to survive the ordeal. If he was not alive, there was no sense in worrying about it. There were the alternate sons he had, or he could knock up a few more whores. He wondered if his father had been concerned when he was the one in the jungle. He answered his own thoughts with, *"probably not."*

As he devoured a can of beans mixed with a can of sardines in olive oil along with a few swigs from the rum bottle, he found himself thinking, while chewing the concoction, that it was time to get laid. It was also time to see if Ortega knew anything or anyone that might help point the way to the Mafia's cache in Cuba.

He hoped there was enough gas left in the Jeep to get to Ortega's place. He yelled at one of the kids to go look at the gauge for him. The whole pack of kids that had been playing near the lagoon ran happily to the Jeep. Then the jubilant mob of nippers yelled, but not at the same time, that the needle was sticking straight up in the middle. To finish off his personal needs he went for a fast freshwater swim/bath in the clear water of the lagoon without seeing a crocodile.

Back on the safety of his boat he let the sunshine dry him and warm him all the way down to his bones. Then after dressing in his best shorts and tee shirt he went calling, not only on his best girl, but the only girl he knew.

The road to Ortega's place was almost the same as it was when he left, but it might have been a little rougher. He was stopped at the gate by the guards with their heavy burden of automatic weapons. Both guards assured him the Señor Ortega was not in the country and Jandy and Maria were traveling with him. The guards had no idea when he was to return. Sidney pulled out a hundred-dollar bill and gave it to the head guard. He said, "Go use the telephone inside and call this number. Find out when they are going to return."

The number he had given the guard was for the St. Thomas office. The happy guard returned with news that they were due to return to the hacienda in five days.

A disappointed and horny Sidney wondered if any of the village girls would be interested, but he quickly nixed that thought. The village people deserved more respect than to have a rum-soaked gringo messing with their daughters. He knew from experience that if he got laid in the village it would cause problems. It would establish competition between the girls that could lead to hard feelings from the girls' families towards him and it would damn sure piss off Maria. He planned on hanging around there for a while and certainly didn't have to worry about pissing anybody off. His world was full of enemies; he didn't need any more, especially where he lived.

He decided to use the five days to explore the land that he was so fond of. He asked the guard, who had pocketed the one hundred dollars, for making a telephone call if he could get some gas from Ortega's tank. The guard told him there was no problem and even pumped it for him. The guard refused payment for the gas and told him to have a nice day. A hundred bucks buys a lot in a third world wilderness.

The trip to the overlook was just as rough as the last time, but it was dryer. The mud puddles he had had so much fun wallowing in that night were almost dry, indicating it was the dry season. The dry season didn't mean much at that latitude with all of the jungle around. It still rained almost every day. The difference between the wet and dry season was that it stopped raining once in awhile during the dry.

Finally, he arrived on top of the cliff. The view was as spectacular as he had remembered. If anything had changed, it was better. He slid out of the Jeep and walked around, looking over everything while wondering how much trouble he was going to have buying the land. He was not concerned that the land might not be for sale either by individuals or the government. That didn't matter; everything was for sale. It was just a matter of different measures or money in how you convinced the owner. Money was a tool to be used to obtain the things you want, but there were other things that mattered, too, life and death things.

He made a quick return trip to the Jeep to fetch his bottle of rum and take a last look at the map. From there, he stood on the edge of the cliff and toasted what he hoped would be the newest addition to the family treasure. He enjoyed the view so much he decided to stay there overnight and start exploring at dawn.

After he finished the bottle, he went scavenging in the woods for the evening's fare. He returned with a good-sized rat and a handful of green plants. A fire with lots of coals had been built and the rat was thrown directly onto the coals. The heat not only cooked the animal but removed the hair and small extremities, like its little feet and eyes. He didn't like to eat things that looked at him or scratched his cheeks with its lifeless little paws.

Sitting under the open sky that night, he thought about many things. The wonder of all of the stars shining at night in an otherwise dark sky always provoked a feeling of contentment for him. At sea he had spent many nights looking at the universe. He never tired of it and usually only stopped looking because he would eventually pass out.

The next morning he took off to explore the property, and he hoped to find a natural cave. If not, he might have to dig one, and that would be a pretty tall order. It would have to be done by pick and shovel, the old-fashioned way. But, if he had to, he would. God only knows how many mines had been dug by a man or two doing all of the work. He pictured little Sid helping, but that only darkened the picture with the thought that little Sid might be resting in the stomach of some other creature at that very moment.

It was rough going as the vegetation was virgin. He had to fight to get through some areas. The vines, thorns, branches and undergrowth were just too much at times. By nightfall he had made his way down to the bottom of the valley, about a half a mile from where he had stood that morning. The stream in the ravine was crystal clear and moving fast over boulders and fallen logs. If there had not been so much water there would have been rapids. By the speed the water was flowing, he knew it was headed for sea level or a waterfall somewhere downstream. Or there could be a waterfall upstream feeding a lot of water to this area. A strong waterfall could be a good place to find a cave.

He opted to explore the most difficult direction first, so he headed upstream. He found a grassy little spot on the edge of the stream only one hundred yards from where he had started. There were no signs of big cats or other animals in the grassy area so he decided to stay there overnight. For dinner that night he feasted on snails taken from the rocks in the stream, and a good-sized trout he caught on the end of a pointed stick that he fashioned with his knife. That night, he drank fresh water from the stream because he had decided not to carry anything with him due to the rough terrain, including his rum.

Lying on his soft bed of harvested grass and looking at the beautiful nighttime universe through sober eyes, he thought of his son. He wondered if he was looking up from his tree into this same beautiful night sky. He wondered if the boy was tired or scared or both—and was Little Sid still alive. He thought about those things until his mind shut off and he slept.

At dawn he was hungry for another fish. Last night's trout had been tasty. He started a fire and while it was producing coals he went fishing. It only took a moment or two before the spear once again provided him with a meal. The stream seemed to be full of fish. In the morning's light he noticed a lot of green algae growing in the water, where the shade of the larger boulders kept direct sunlight away. He thought that might be a good salad for him that night.

It was a good thing he did eat that morning because he burned up a lot of energy during the day. His trip upstream was full of side trips to investigate anything that looked interesting. He had traveled about a mile upstream plus another mile or two on side trips. He found nothing but the beauty of nature. This was land that, more than likely, had never felt the soles of man's feet.

That evening he tried the algae and thought it tasted about like shit would. So he had frog legs with his fish that night. Dessert was several handfuls of a wild berry he had not seen before. They were slightly sour, but with a hint of sweetness to their taste. He enjoyed the berries and was glad to see they grew everywhere in the ravine.

That night he thought it might be better to take to the trees. He had spotted evidence of big animals feeding on the berries. It might be bears or big cats. Whatever they were had claws and that was a good enough reason for him to get off of the ground.

He had perfected sleeping in trees when he was a scared little boy in a terrifying jungle, probably just like his son was learning that night. He found a good looking tree to call home and there were vines growing on everything in the jungle, so getting up and down wouldn't be a problem. He selected a vine that appealed to him then climbed up a tree to cut it at the right length. His tree of choice was not a big tree, but it had all the right branches. He climbed up the small branches and gave each one a good stomp as he stepped off of it. The stomp was to break the limb. The broken branches then hung down by the outside of the bark acting much like obstacles or a barrier. It would not prevent a cat from climbing up, but it would slow it down, and it would stop a bear from following him up the tree.

About halfway up, there were two good-sized limbs growing at the same level. One of them faced the stream; the other ran about twenty degrees off of that. Using his vine, he laced a crude platform. It only had to be big enough to support his upper body as the limbs would support his legs. After it was complete, he laid down to try out the bed and knew it would be fine.

Then he got up and positioned himself just right and urinated on the tree's trunk so that it hit about six feet up and then ran down to the ground. That was a technique he also had developed as a boy. In his thinking, a big cat or bear might come along and pick up the scent. With it being so high up, they would think that a really big animal marked that tree and would look for a safer place to prowl. Actually, he had no idea if that worked, but he did it every night he was in the trees, and he was still alive so why take a chance.

The night passed by quickly and he had rested quite well in his tree-top penthouse. The vine he used to make his bed was unwrapped and then tied to another branch further down the tree. This was used to lower himself down since there were no reliable branches to use as hand-holds.

The morning marked his third day out and he still had a lot of territory to cover, so he decided to skip breakfast. Last night when the wind got very still, he thought he could hear a waterfall and he was eager to find it. The trip upstream was made by wading in the shallow water, using boulders to walk on. Very little way could be made walking on the bank. Both sides were too steep or the growth of brush and trees were too thick. A couple of times he had to swim across deep pools. But with every step, the roaring sound got a little louder.

Finally, about three o'clock that afternoon, he walked around a bend and the spray from a magnificent waterfall covered him. The fall was close to a quarter of a mile high and was twenty feet wide at the top. By the time it hit the rocks below, most of the water was spray. It was beautiful. He sat on a rock for a while admiring the fall and surrounding scenery. Then it struck him that there was a hell of a lot of water flowing for a waterfall that turned into mostly spray. Also, then he noticed that the fall was not the source of the river. He walked around the next bend. There was another fall from the same height but with a lot more water hitting the bottom. In fact, there was a tremendous amount of water being poured over the edge.

Sidney worked his way around to the back side of the waterfall only to be disappointed that there was only a recess in the rock wall, no cave. But, he did notice that the vertical wall extended straight down until it disappeared in the crystal clear water. The pool at the bottom of the fall was very deep. He wondered if maybe the pool had more water in it than had been there in centuries past. There was two feet between the rock wall and the wall of falling water.

He picked up a hefty rock to use as a weight to make him sink straight down. He took a deep breath and then stepped off of the edge of the recess. He sank fifteen feet straight down and, joyfully, saw what he had hoped for: The large dark mouth of an ancient cavern.

The stream of falling water had lost most of its momentum at that depth so Sid dropped his rock and kicked off of the rock wall to swim under the falling water. On the other side of the thundering wall of water, Sidney surfaced. A short swim later, he sat on a sunny rock near the edge of the pool drying off, while trying to come up with a way to explore the cavern.

Chances were good that it would rise above the water level, but how far back? He certainly could not take a chance to free dive to find out in case there was a current that ran down if the cave turned downward. The only safe way to do it would be to tie a long safety line to himself and use scuba gear. But he didn't have scuba gear and he didn't have any rope with him, and it was a hell of a long way to find some.

By the time he was dry, he decided to give it one try before resigning himself to go back to the Jeep and make a trip to civilization where he could get the gear needed. A good underwater lamp would be a good idea to have as well.

Sidney went into the jungle and harvested a few vines. These were tied together to give him a safety line almost a hundred feet long. Behind the falls, he tied the vine to a good-sized rock on the ledge and found another to act as weight for him.

He planned to make two dives. The first was to be straight down. He wanted to see how deep the pool was and how large the cavern's mouth was. The second dive would be used to go as deep into the cavern as the vine would permit. He had marked the vine every ten feet to give him an idea of where he was and when he reached the point of "must-return" because of air.

As he fell through the water, he passed the open mouth at fifteen feet and he could not see bottom. He kept falling. It was hard to tell about current as he had the rock pulling him down. He reached the limit he wanted to go at sixty feet and he still could not see bottom. He turned the rock loose and started pulling himself up as fast as his bubbles rose. He was ready for air when he surfaced, three minutes later. He pulled himself out and rested for a few minutes, and then he found another rock for his next dive.

Hanging onto the ledge, Sidney hyperventilated to pump as much air as he could into his system. He turned loose and swam into the cavern to see if there was an offshoot going up to a cave without water flooding it. His light was quickly turning into darkness. Swimming while hanging on to the vine was awkward, so he turned it loose, and soon it was easier going, and then effortless. He was caught in a current pushing him into the black void. He turned around and began swimming with all of his strength against the current, and headed back to the light. But, it was useless; he should have held onto his only connection to air, the vine. He was gaining more speed going into the blackness.

Sidney's last thoughts as he blacked out after he ran out of air were, *shit, how's the boy going to get out.*

THE HACIENDA

JOSE ORTEGA HAD RETURNED TO HIS JUNGLE HOME THE DAY BEFORE HIS important Italian guest arrived. Tony the Pop Castero was a good man to have on your side. In fact, as far as Mafia contacts were concerned, there was none better. Jose was not sure what rank he had with the Mafia, but it appeared he was very high if not the don of dons. There were a few men that seemed to enjoy a similar elevated status, but they always seemed to show just a little more respect to Tony than he did towards them. The top echelon were tough, dedicated, and were from the old families, and they took their business very seriously. Besides being a good contact, Tony was a fun guy to be around and usually very funny.

After Jose and the two girls had settled down and were relaxing around the pool with a refreshing drink, one of the security guards appeared. He was in charge of the compound so he had access to the house. He asked to be excused for the interruption, but needed to tell them about the visitor.

He said, "The man who was here some time ago came to see you five days ago. He gave me one hundred dollars to call your office to see when you were to return. You were not in St. Thomas when I called, but your secretary told me you were returning today. I gave that man the information."

Jose asked, "Who was he?"

The guard responded, "I do not know his name, but he has been here with you before." He didn't want to embarrass the Don Jose by telling him it was the man that he had rolled around with in the mud.

"What did he look like?" was Jose's next question.

"He is a hard man, Señor, dark from the sun, muscular body, black eyes. Oh, he was driving a Jeep that looked just like the one you used to own."

Jandy exclaimed, "Hey! That sounds like Sidney!"

They all agreed. Jose could not help but smile at the thought of Tony the Pop and Sidney the pirate being under the same roof. Especially since the Mafia had done everything they could to find the person responsible for the Vito murder.

Between the revelation in the back seat of his Mercedes and the hefty diamonds the girls received, right after the incident with Vito, he had proof enough that Sidney really did the dirty deed. It should prove to be very interesting to see what happened when they were face to face. He frowned with a thought: *My pirate friend better be careful or he will have the Italians up his ass before he sees it coming. He should not pick on the Mafia. They never forget or forgive.*

Sidney didn't show up that day or the next day, so Jose sent Maria and Jandy to the little village to see if he was there. About an hour after they left for the village, Jose heard the thumping sound of the rotors of an incoming helicopter. The helicopter landed on the manicured front lawn next to Jose's parked Jeep. When the chopper shut down, the side door opened and the bad-ass mobster, Tony the Pop, emerged. He was dressed like Jungle Jim, complete with pith helmet and trouser legs tucked into knee-length boots.

Tony let out a Tarzan yell while thumping his chest and yelled, "I love the fucking jungle! Let's go kill something, Jose!"

Following Tony were two stocky Sicilians not dressed in their customary black suits, but wearing black slacks and short sleeve shirts. Yep, they each had a pistol behind them tucked into the waistband and concealed by the shirts. Backup weapons were strapped to both ankles. These were Tony's personal guards, and they didn't like the steamy atmosphere of Ortega's jungle compound. They were much more at home in the air conditioned environment of Sicily. It suited their requirement to always wear a coat when in public. Suit coats were not required for image sake but rather security's sake. The coats concealed two shoulder harnesses on each man. One contained a specially made six-shot, twelve gauge shotgun that was only ten inches long. The other carried a nine-millimeter automatic; and you could be sure both men were very proficient with both weapons.

Jose met Tony in the yard and both men embraced in the usual manner. The bodyguards were introduced as Bruno and Mongo. Tony explained that those were not their real names, but nicknames that had been with them for years.

Jose was curious how they came by such Mongolian names, but thought he already knew why—just not the gory details.

Tony asked about Jandy and Maria, and Jose explained that they went to look for an acquaintance of theirs who was staying in a nearby village. He wanted Tony to meet the man as he was a very unusual individual. Jose, in reality, was just curious to see which personality would come out on top when the two got together. But more than anything, he wanted to watch that cocky motherfucker, Sidney, squirm when he learned Tony represented the mob and was very pissed off about the Vito murder. He also thought it would be funny when Sidney heard about the five hundred thousand dollar reward for the capture of the murderer.

Between Maria's antenna tuned in for reactions between the two men and his own ability to observe, surely they would know more about Sidney that evening.

The men went inside and put their things away and got more comfortable. At least Bruno and Mongo did, but Tony kept the jungle attire on. He still had to show it to the girls when they returned and he liked being dressed that way, anyway. It made him feel that he was ready to do some exploring. And that was exactly what he intended to do before he left the hospitality of Don Ziguia Ortega's oldest son.

If he was not able to learn anything about the assholes, then he would move on to Don Ziguia in St. Thomas. After that, he had four other men to see. Each ran a good-sized criminal activity that had connections in the Caribbean. Of course, none of them were anything like the Mafia, or so he thought. Tony, like the rest of the world, was just plain ignorant as to the size of the Ortega Cartel. And that was just fine with the Ortegas.

Jose's household staff took care to pamper the guests. Fresh drinks were served when the glasses were half empty. Cigarettes were lit for them and colorful hors d'oeuvres were served continually. The two men sat together talking about old times and what was new in their worlds. Tony was full of new jokes and his delivery with every joke was truly professional. Had he not been born with the spaghetti fork in his mouth and was fourth generation mafia, he could have certainly made the big time in show business.

Jose was having a wonderful afternoon. Laughing with Tony's sense of humor and drinking plenty of scotch; he was in a jovial mood and couldn't wait for the anticipated showdown between the pirate and the Mafioso.

Maria and Jandy returned that afternoon without Sidney. They explained that he had left the village days ago and had not been seen or heard of since. He didn't take anything with him when he left so everybody thought he would be back that day. Jose asked if his boat was in the lagoon. She confirmed that it was.

Jose was puzzled. There was nowhere to go in the Jeep. It was too far to drive to the nearest civilization. He doubted that the Jeep carried enough gas to get out of the jungle anyway. His guard said he had fueled up here but there were no extra tanks.

Tony was listening to the conversation with increasing curiosity. It was not like Jose to be so concerned about a man. He wondered if it had anything to do with Mafia business.

Finally Maria said, "I'll bet he went up to the cliff. Maybe he got lost in the woods." They all laughed at the remoteness of that possibility, remembering the bet Jose had made with him.

Maria continued, "Maybe he fell and is injured. Why don't we take a drive out there and see?"

Jose said, "Okay, Tony wants to do some hunting anyway."

He instructed Jandy to load up the cooler with drinks and a cook-out. He suggested that Tony's boys might be more comfortable staying there by the pool. Tony felt uncertain at that possibility. Those guys, or some other men, had always been at his side for the last twenty some odd years. He really did feel naked without them.

Jose sensed this and said, "Oh, what the hell. We can squeeze them in."

The thugs were not too happy; they rather fancied a leisurely evening around the pool with the cool breeze and efficient staff waiting on their every need. But this was business, and they took off to get their traveling companions, their guns.

The bumpy road to the cliff was filled with spilled drinks. Some of the booze made it to the insides of the occupants of the Jeep, but mostly it spilled over them. Everybody was crowded and practically soaked with rum, scotch or wine, but nobody cared much. Maria's ribs were hurting her, not because of the rough ride, but the incessant laughter at Tony's jokes.

They reached the cliff an hour before darkness settled in. They were dismayed to see the Jeep parked there. There was no sign of Sidney. Jose honked on his horn and called out Sidney's name several times. The response was always the same—nothing. They looked around the clearing and ventured into the woods looking for a sign that he had been there. There were no tracks or signs of broken limbs.

They stayed there for a few hours, eating and drinking and waiting for Sidney. But the party mood had vanished from the two girls. They were concerned. Sidney was sort of an odd duck, but it was a respectable bizarreness. Also, Jandy knew that Maria had more feelings than she let on about him and she felt sympathetic towards her. Maria had that inborn instinct to take care of any man that didn't have a woman to tell him what to do. And Sidney sure didn't have a woman. He was the loneliest man she had ever known.

The next morning, before dawn, Jose had four guards rounded up and on their way out to the cliff to search for Sidney. Jose reasoned that he might have gone exploring and either fell or had been attacked by one of the creatures of the jungle. God knows it was full of all kinds of things that would just love to eat a human, even a tough one like Sidney. Even the big-time mobster was up and ready. Still wearing his Jungle Jims, he was eager to get out into the jungle. His boys were not too thrilled however. It just meant they would have to protect their boss from things with fangs and sharp claws rather than just another human.

Jose and Tony and his thugs stayed together on the search. There were three teams consisting of two men. Each team was to walk downhill in three directions. They were to fan out. After traveling as far as they could, in four hours they were to return but spread out much more. Jose took the straight route down to the ravine. He thought that would more than likely be the direction someone would want to explore. If any team found a sign of Sidney, they were to fire the number of shots in the air that coincided with the team number they were, and then wait a few seconds and fire one shot if they found a sign. Two shots, if they found him dead, and three if Sidney was alive. Jose's team number was of course one. In the case of self-defense, against jungle creatures, the orders were to blow the fuck out of whatever it was being sure to use more shots than the codes called for.

Jose thought there were signs that someone had moved through the growth on the way down. Most of it was very dense and there were signs of broken branches and twigs on a few bushes. It could have been done by an animal; unfortunately, the ground was too hard to leave tracks. They worked their way down to the ravine before they found proof that someone did indeed travel through there. They found the remains of a campfire and the bones of a fish and empty snail shells. They fired one shot then seconds later one more. This would bring the other teams to them. It took a while for the teams to find them, so Jose's guards took off downstream to look for more signs.

Jose and Tony perched on a rock sipping scotch from a flask. Jose wondered for some reason if he had ever gone anywhere when he didn't drink. He started feeling guilty that he could not even go on a search mission without taking his hooch along with him. He took another sip and absently said, "Who gives a shit," out loud.

Tony asked, "Who gives a shit about what?"

Jose said, "Beats the shit out of me," and passed the flask to Tony.

About then, the other teams began arriving. Some of the men were sent upstream, the others downstream. Tony's and Jose's helicopters were flying a square search pattern, but none thought they would be able to see anything because of the dense jungle.

As the teams began dispersing, Tony's helicopter pilot came overhead and landed on the little grassy knoll. He managed to get the chopper down without clipping the trees with the rotors. He yelled out to Tony that it was impossible to see anything from the air. The growth was too thick. Then he added, "You got to come see the waterfalls upstream. Man, they are something."

Jose looked at Tony with interest about the waterfalls. He was not aware of them but wanted to see them. He thought that maybe that was were Sidney would be found. Jose asked the pilot if there was any place to land the chopper up there. The pilot didn't know.

Tony offered, "What the hell, we ain't doing shit around here. Let's go for a look."

They boarded the chopper. Fifteen minutes later, they were flying over the waterfalls. Mongo thought it looked as if the view was right out of a picture book. It was beautiful, with the wild river twisting through the dense jungle, then ending abruptly at a shear quarter-mile vertical fall. The river, just before it ended, split in two. The separate falls were only two hundred yards apart with one being much smaller.

They looked for signs of another human but nothing was spotted. Jose said, "It is too bad we can't set down here and walk back. We might cut off a lot of time on the upstream search. We know for sure he didn't come past this point anyway."

The pilot said, "No problem. I can perch on the big rock down there long enough for you to get out. I am low on fuel, however, and cannot hover while waiting for you. If Don Jose does not have aviation gas at the plantation, then I better return now so we have enough to get back to civilization, Tony."

"There is plenty of fuel for you at the hacienda," said Jose.

Tony and Jose agreed to get off; they would walk downstream to meet the team coming up. As they touched down on the rock that was almost big enough to land on, Tony shouted to the pilot, "Go back to the hacienda and refuel just in case we are not able to walk out. Come back before dark to check on our progress."

The pilot nodded his head that he understood.

It had been almost impossible to have a conversation in the chopper, between the noise of the thundering water and the whining of the chopper's engine and the beating of the rotors. With the chopper gone, it was still difficult to hear one another. You had to shout in order to be heard over the falls. But everyone was very impressed with the falls and the roaring sound was just part of the natural beauty.

Mongo and Bruno were the first to shift their attention from nature to the task at hand. They had had enough of the great outdoors and wanted to get it over with so they could get back to poolside. Also they wanted to be well clear of the area before nightfall. This really was a hard-core jungle and they didn't want to have anything to do with things that had more than or less than two legs.

Bruno was the first to discover that you do not step on the green short grassy-~ looking stuff that grew at the waterline on the rocks. It was slippery—and he went for an unexpected swim. The three other men got a good laugh while Bruno got a good bath.

They got an even better laugh when Jose said, "Hey, Bruno you better get your ass out of that water. This is South America you know, and we grow some really big crocodiles and thirty-foot carnivorous water snakes down here. And if *they* don't get you, there's a tiny fish that will swim up inside your penis."

Bruno's reaction, while it was instant, was one of confusion. He could not decide whether he should get out of the water first or pull his guns out to protect himself.

Mongo yelled, "Get the fuck out of the water, you dumb fuck. Those guns ain't going to shoot shit when you're in the belly of a beast."

It didn't take very long for the men to realize that walking out of the jungle was not going to happen. It might be possible, but they were not going to force themselves to go through that kind of aggravation. Especially for some dumb schmuck who got lost in the woods.

Tony was the first to express his sentiments by saying, "Fuck him; he wants to play Davy Crocket, let him, old Jungle Jim here is taking the rest of the day off."

He found a shady spot to sit and motioned Jose to join him. "How about popping that flask out again," he asked Jose.

Jose thought that was a hell of a good idea and joined him. They had walked enough to have gone around the bend so that the noise was not so bad. The scenery was outstanding and the scotch was even better.

After a pull on the flask, Tony thought it was a good thing he brought the big flask because it looked like they were going to be there until the chopper came back in a few hours. Tony didn't like waiting around with nothing to do. He was a mover, he needed action all of the time. The nature stuff was okay, but now he had seen it, so it was time to do something else. With nothing else possible, he decided it would be a good time to talk to Jose about his problem.

"Jose, you're probably wondering why I called and then showed up for a little visit, aren't you?"

Jose replied. "Well, Tony, I had hoped it was because you like my company or the raw beauty of my country."

"Of course I do, but there is more to it this time, my friend. I have a problem that I cannot seem to solve by myself. I need help in this matter and I hope you are the one who can help."

Jose responded, "Count on me to do anything I can, Tony. What exactly is your problem?"

"Somebody is fucking with my friends and we have not been able to get a lead on who it is. I need you to tell me about people your people are aware of that could be doing these things. I need to know if there are any newly formed syndicates buying large amounts of your product or your competitors' lines of goods. I just want names, and I will be discrete in my inquiries, but I have to know if they are using my peoples' blood and money to bankroll their start-up cost."

"What have they been taking away from your friends, Tony?"

"Well, you remember the deal about Vito being killed; his wife was also horribly mutilated and their friends were killed or beaten. They took millions of dollars in diamonds and cash. There has been a rash of robberies in our casinos aboard the cruise ships the last few years. The last straw was an undetermined amount of cash, but in the millions, stolen from a private jet airliner. They killed the entire fucking flight crew on that one, plus destroyed the plane, a fucking 737, worth millions. These people are ruthless and they have been getting information about our activities."

Jose, fishing for a job description without coming out and asking what his position with the Mafia was, asked, "Tony, what's your involvement in the investigation?"

Tony understood the nature of Jose's question and thought it was fair enough. Here was a man dressed in a Jungle Jim suit sitting on a rock in the middle of a wild jungle and drinking scotch from a flask, asking a man to divulge information on friends or business customers he might have. It was a fair question to ask.

"Jose, you have known me for years, but we don't see each other often. You live in the Caribbean and I stay mostly in Europe, but we have business interests that will sometimes pull us together and occasionally we even have had a little problem. But we have always respected each other's businesses and we both go out of our way to not cause any problems for each other. We both walk on the same side of the street. I enjoy the times I have spent with you and respect you as a man based on your personality not for your position in your organization. I think you have the same opinion of me."

"I do not know very much about your operation, Tony, and you probably know very little about mine, as well." Jose concealed the thoughts running through his mind. He knew a lot more about the Mafia and their mentality than Tony could ever guess. It was just too hard for an Italian to go against his inbred need to brag. So if you spent enough time with those guys, they were going to let you know a lot more than they were aware of.

Tony asked him, "What do you think my position is in this matter, Jose?"

"I had heard that you were right at the top of your organization, but it sounds like someone told you to handle it."

"Well, you're right on both counts. There are fifteen of us that make up the top. There is no one higher. But everyone agreed to a plan to stop these assholes and it is my job to do it, at any cost."

Jose was surprised at the openness of Tony admitting that he was the big fish in his pond. There were several thousand prosecutors of the various law enforcement agencies that would love to have heard that confession.

He knew for certain then that Tony was a man he needed to be able to count on in case he needed help from the Italians in the future. He also knew that he was going to give up Sidney to Tony, unless he could think of a good reason not to betray a man. It was becoming apparent that Sidney was lost and probably dead anyway. To give up a dead man was not breaking a trust made in the back seat of a car with the threat of death hanging over him. He was not sure that Sidney was the guilty party, but he could sell it to Tony easily enough. He would have to be very careful how he told the story. After all, they had told him they were looking for these people right after the Vito assault.

Jose said, "Tony, let me run a few things around in my head; I might have something for you," and he passed the flask to Tony.

Tony was pleased that everything was out and Jose had decided to give him something. He didn't want to push Jose for more than he was willing to give. He understood the nature of business in the worlds both men lived in.

Suddenly the jungle world and the calm mood between the two men perched on the rock were interrupted by an explosion. Jose and Tony jumped off of their rock and went around the bend to where the noise had come from. Mongo and Bruno were chasing fish around in a shallow part of the river. Bruno had his special shotgun out and was trying to shoot one of the fish. Another shot rang out then another. Then there was a victorious yell from Bruno as he scooped down and held up the partial remains of the fish for all to see. There was not much left of the slimy thing; only his head with the dorsal fin hanging by a thread of skin was left. The rest had been turned into fish food by the rain of twelve gauge pellets.

Mongo yelled over the rumble of water, "Let's get another one. We can eat it, but use the other gun, you dumb fuck." It was fun to watch the muscle-bound men jumping out of the water when one of the fish would turn and swim back directly at them. They were splashing around like a couple of children. Tony enjoyed the sight and went back to the rock to get the flask. They might as well have a drink while watching the children playing.

Both men managed to get a good-sized fish up on the bank. The bullets had taken a lot of the meat away, but there was enough of the fish left for a snack. Jose went up to the fringes of the dense growth of brush and gathered some twigs and small branches to make a fire. He told the boys to gut and clean the fish before he left to find the firewood. When he returned with an armload of wood, the boys were still standing around looking at the dead fish. With a little embarrassment they explained they had no idea how to clean a fish. Jose showed them how to gut it then scrape the scales off on one of the fish. When he was through, there was fish blood and guts all over his fingers and little scales were stuck all over his hands. He handed the messy knife back to Mongo, who reached out and took the knife with two fingers, being careful not to touch the gutsy parts. He tried to give the knife to Bruno, but he declined saying, "That's okay, you do it; I wasn't watching him because you were so interested."

Jose could not believe his eyes and ears. Two big highly trained killers could not stomach the thought of getting fish guts on them. It made his day, and his uncontrolled laughter made the thugs feel that they were no bigger, in Jose's eyes, than the dead fish with its guts smeared all over the place. They both looked around very gratefully to see that Tony had not witnessed their squeamish act. Neither of them had hesitated to blow the head off any man marked for death, and they would fight tooth and nail to the death; being covered from head to toe with blood and guts from a man in combat was fine, but not from some smelly fish.

Jose cleaned the other fish and made the fire. Then he collected some green sticks to hold the fish pieces over the fire. The boys just stood there and watched. Jose thought to himself that he had never seen two guys so useless in the woods. And it was their job to protect one of the most powerful men in the world, their boss Tony the Pop.

Thinking about the two useless guards made Jose aware that it had been twenty minutes or so since Tony went after the flask. He thought: *That son of a bitch is drinking all of the scotch.*

He walked off briskly to try to rescue a few swallows for himself. Tony was not at the rock and neither was the flask. In Jose's mind that meant Tony was in the woods taking a shit or was playing around by hiding until he drank up what was left of the booze. Jose looked at all of the obvious places but could not find the flask or Jungle Jim. Perplexed, he went back to the guards and told them he could not find Tony. That news caused panic in the two and they spread out with guns in hand to search.

Jose laughed and asked, "Who the fuck do you suppose is going to be down here putting the hit on your boss?"

The guards were not paid to think, they were paid to protect and their boss was missing.

Jose yelled, "Relax, he probably went up in the bushes to take a shit." His words were lost in the roar from the water.

As darkness approached, everyone was very concerned. The surrounding hills had been searched. Even the water pools had been investigated in case he had slipped and drowned. There was no Tony to be found, no flask or even any sign of Tony. Not even his Jungle Jim hat was lying around. That could only mean that Tony decided to walk downstream. Jose told the guards to start going downstream. He would wait there for the helicopter.

Mongo could not figure out why his boss would take off like that. He must have drunk too much from the flask and decided that silly jungle suit made an adventurer out of him. He would've liked nothing better than to kick him in the ass for taking off. If anything happened to Tony, the bosses were damn sure going to make Bruno and Mongo pay the ultimate price for being careless. It would not matter that it happened because Tony got drunk and wandered off.

The two of them seemed to overcome their timidness of nature and her obstacles. They swam the deep pools and traversed around the shear walls with little thought concerning their wellbeing. Their eyes were alert and saw everything; their ears were straining to hear anything above the sounds of falling water.

Jose sat on a rock thinking, *it's getting dark. What happened to that helicopter?* Then he had an even more unpleasant thought. *What happens if the Mafia thinks I set this up to do Tony in? That I'm involved in the Mafia assault thing Tony is concerned about. Shit, the first thing I need to do is isolate myself from his guards. I'm dead meat if they start thinking that way.*

Then he realized that by isolating himself from the guards it would be proof to the mob that he had planned it before sending the two of them downstream in order to give him time to escape in the helicopter. But where the hell was the helicopter?

THE JUNGLE

DURING THE DAY, THE JUNGLE WAS MADE UP OF A MYRIAD NUMBER OF birds, monkeys and other animals calling out to each other. The friendly chatter, however, died out around dusk as the majority of the animals stopped communicating in order to hide from the unimaginable number of hungry things that would be looking for them during the night as they slept. All were things with claws and big teeth or crawly things with deadly fangs moving silently through the dense jungle floor. And then there was the bandersnatch that his dad had warned him of—but didn't tell him what kind of terrible animal it was.

That first night had been the worst experience imaginable for a young boy—especially for a child used to having the company of other people around him, or the confines of his sailboat to keep him safe. Sleeping in an open jungle was terror in its extreme. He could not believe how noisy the jungle was at night or day. But at night it was a different kind of noise—spooky, bone-chilling noise.

The night went through its normal cycle designed to give all creatures an equal chance to live by providing the necessities, like food. The night's dominant noise was of the frogs. They were such a heavy population that their number must have rivaled the buzzing mosquitoes. There were frogs with deep croaks and there were frogs with high whistles and there were frogs everywhere in between. There were continual sounds he had never heard before. But worst of all, there was the occasional scream of something that had unexpectedly wakened to be in the jaws of another animal—or bandersnatch. That was always a loud, shrill and dreaded scream of pain, a final plea for help. Then it would be silent and the rest of the jungle world would come alive and scream for a moment at the painful passing of another creature of their world.

Little Sid didn't sleep a wink that first night but he did during the next day, and that was the pattern he had adopted as normal. His eyes were forced wide open by the muscles around them that reacted to fear and anticipation. He either stood or stooped with his back against a big tree all night and the heat from a good-sized fire in front of him. A spear he had fashioned from a limb was in one shaking hand and his knife was in the other.

The light of the fire sent out a message to every mosquito: *Here he is, fresh blood on the hoof, come and get it.* Out of desperation to keep the thousands of sucking insects off of him, he resorted to something unpleasant. As darkness rapidly approached he hurriedly looked around for some of the plants his father had shown him that would keep the bugs away, but he didn't see any. He knew that if he was close to water he could make mud packs and cover himself with the mud. That would keep the mosquitoes away. However, the nearest water was at least one hundred feet away and there was no way he was going out in the dark jungle. So he dug out a pit in the ground and urinated in it. That was how he made his mud packs. As the mud dried it became uncomfortable, but it was better than being bled dry by the bombilating swarms.

He remembered what was said about sleeping in the trees, but he didn't out of fear of falling out of it if he fell asleep. He'd be easy pickings if he had a broken leg.

That had been his first night alone and it had taught him several important lessons. He then knew that he should have found shelter before doing anything else. Instead, he puffed himself up as the great hunter and went looking for food and to cautiously play in his new surroundings. Actually, he did very little hunting and he ended up with a rat for dinner. He cooked the rat like his father had done many times with small furry things; he just tossed it on the coals. It tasted good but would have been better if he was more comfortable under his mud pack, had some water to drink, had some vegetables to eat, had somebody to talk to, and wasn't so afraid. Every time he took a bite off of the little animal, it reminded him of the part he played in the food chain. Just a little while ago, the thing in his jaws had screamed its shrill, panicky and final sound of fear and agony.

He made himself feel better that never-ending night by thinking of the daylight that surely must start any minute now. Finally, as things seemed to be at their worst, new sounds began. They were probably birds, but he could not tell for sure. He would soon learn that daylight would not come until the birds called the sun to rise. An hour or so after the birds began calling, the sky over the jet black tree line began to lighten. Very gradually, it became pale to the point that the trees took on color, slowly. Soon the night was gone.

The mosquitoes stayed around for a while even after the sun was up. They stayed until a breeze came up and then a few retired for the day. But with every step Cachorro made through the jungle, it flushed up biters that had been resting on the leaves and grass. He reached the ocean and dove in to bathe the dried caked mud off. It was refreshing and cool. The deserted shoreline stretched out before him in both directions. The thick jungle behind was noisy. He swam for a while, having fun until his eyes started burning from a lack of sleep. As he walked up on the rocky shore, he wondered why he just didn't stay out there last night instead of the scary bug-infested jungle.

Cachorro woke up later that day. By the sun's position, it must be about three or four hours before dark. He was glad he had caught up on his sleep, but angry because he had so much to do. He was starving and thirsty and he still didn't have a place to stay that night. Then he remembered his thoughts about staying on the shore. As he got up, he realized why he could not stay on the shoreline. He saw several big tracks of something with claws had been there overnight. He had to get off the ground before nightfall.

His father had told him not to drink jungle water without boiling it but he was thirsty so he did anyway. Then he went in search for a safe place to stay. He didn't care if he had anything to eat, but he was not going through another night like he did that night. The idea of staying on the shoreline really appealed to him. It was cooler since there was always a breeze, so there would be fewer blood-suckers. But he would be an open invitation to the big meat-eaters to come for dinner. He decided to move into the trees until he could think of a way to build something to give him protection on the shore.

Even the trees were not safe, but at least he could control the size of what was going to bite him. By being out on the smaller branches he could keep the big cats away. Snakes could be a problem, but at least they were not trying to eat him. He went to a nice big tree and climbed up but was soon stopped by a big male monkey with white testicles. The monkey raised hell trying to scare him out of his tree.

It didn't work; Cachorro was determined to make that tree his home, but the screaming monkey charged through the tree limbs and leaves in an attack. That worked very effectively and the boy got out of the tree before the angry monkey could throw him to the ground. After being chased down several trees by other protective males, he found one a hundred feet back in the jungle that had no monkeys. He had to be the first monkey in a tree if he wanted to live in one.

His second night was just as miserable as the first—plus he was starving. He just could not get comfortable. He couldn't stop thinking that something would crawl on him or bite him. The mosquitoes were not as bad up in the tree as they were on the ground. And he did feel safer from the meat-eaters. As he sat on his tree limb that night, he was thinking of ways to live on the shoreline. His first thought was to build a wall around him with sharply pointed spears. Then he thought that would just probably add a little fun for the cat before it jumped over it and ate him. Then he thought about building higher walls. Walls too high for the cat to jump over; then realized that would just cut off the cool breeze. The mosquitoes would eat him alive.

His father had taught him how to build walls by cutting poles the size wanted, and then stripping the bark off in long narrow strips. The strips were wrapped or laced around each of the poles to build a sturdy wall section. He had made a wind break using that method once before when there was nothing else to shield a fire that was used to cook dinner on one of his survival training nights. His mind faded to sleep then back to the thoughts of building a shelter.

Suddenly, he became aware that he had relaxed his grip on the branch he had been holding on to. He became instantly awake, but it was too late—he was on his way to the ground. He fell fifteen feet before hitting the first branch below him. The limb almost stopped him before it broke off and he continued the fall with his hands firmly clasping the broken limb.

He hit the ground with a thud and landed on his back. The force of the impact knocked him unconscious, which was a blessing, as he didn't have to endure the horrible feeling of having the breath forced from his lungs and the muscle spasms needed to refill them. He was unconscious on the jungle floor at night and the meat-eaters were prowling about.

THE DARKNESS

WAS HE BLIND OR WAS IT A JET BLACK NIGHT? HE WOKE UP TO A LOUD roaring sound and was thoroughly confused. His head hurt and he was lying on his back on a hard and wet surface, and it was raining on him. He was cold. His head was pounding with the noise and a deep pain behind his skull. He could not figure out where he was or what had happened. As his memory returned in little slices of time, the last thing he could re-member was a feeling of desperation. But where the hell was he?

He put his hands out to feel the surface he was lying on. It was cold and hard. His head cleared more, but it still was pounding and he didn't feel like moving. The cool rain gave him a chill. Feeling his head, there was a big lump on it where the pain was coming from. He then tried to sit up but his head told him that was not a good idea—and he faded back into unconsciousness.

Sometime later he awoke again, still lying in the same position in the rain. The pain in his head was as bad but his thoughts were clearer. He sat up straining to see something. There was nothing but blackness. Then he realized that whatever had put that lump on his head must have blinded him. That thought filled him with anxiety.

He sat there for a long time experiencing the thoughts of the newly blinded. It was a feeling of being lost and helpless. Both feelings were completely foreign to him. For the first time in his life, he could do nothing but sit there. He had neither plan nor idea about what to do. So he just sat there in the rain.

After a while, his curiosity took over and caused him to focus on what had happened. Then he remembered swimming underwater as hard as he could against a powerful current. Then the feeling of desperation returned as he recalled that he was being pulled down by the current and he had no control whatsoever over what was happening to him. Then he remembered his final thoughts and feeling of surrender as he accepted the fact that he was out of air and his time on earth was over.

He asked out loud. "Is this Hell?" If it was, there was an echo in Hell. He yelled, "Hey! Is there anybody here?"

Once again, his words bounced back to him over the roar in his ears. Perplexed, he began to realize that he was in the cavern he had been looking for. Maybe he was not blind after all. The water he had assumed was rain could be spray from an underground waterfall and that would explain the roaring sound. Those thoughts brought life back to his spirit—he had hope. He groped around feeling his surroundings. He had landed on a ledge sticking out of a shear vertical wall. The ledge was only two feet wide and he could not tell how long.

He muttered, "I must be a lucky son-of-a-bitch." If Sidney could have seen where he was, he could appreciate just how lucky he was. The underground waterfall fell two hundred feet to the bottom of the cavern floor. The only thing between life and death was a ledge that protruded out from a wall. The ledge was only ten feet down from the waterfall's start. He had been in exactly the right place, and as his unconscious body went over, he landed on the ledge. The slamming of his back on the rock caused him to expel any remaining air and water in his lungs and the reaction caused his diaphragm to suck in fresh air.

Sidney would have given anything for just a glimpse of light to see where he was and how he might get off of his rock without continuing down in the waterfall. He had no idea how far it went down and didn't care. He had already drowned once and that was enough for him. He would try to do the only option left open to him. That was to follow the ledge and hope it led to a way out. If it didn't, then he would probably follow the waterfall to see what happened. He really didn't have any other options other than resign himself to sit on the ledge until he died of starvation—but he wasn't that kind of man.

He started moving away from the waterfall on his hands and knees, keeping his left hand on the edge and his right hand out in front of his movement. The ledge was much longer than he had hoped. After traveling thirty feet on his hands and knees, the ledge became too wide for him to reach both sides of the ledge at one time. So he stayed with the edge of the ledge. Every ten feet he would put his left foot on the edge and move into the direction of the wall. That way he mapped out the ledge and could see that it was widening. As the width increased so did Sidney's hope that it would lead to somewhere. A couple of minutes later he could only feel a sudden drop off on all three sides—and a vertical rock wall on the other. He had reached the end.

THE JUNGLE

As the early morning birds began calling the sun, he became aware that he had fallen and was lying on the ground. This caused a spark of panic and he made a sudden move to get on his feet. This resulted in a thunderous sharp pain in his chest. And the pain got worse when he tried to breath. It was too dark to see, but he knew that a big cat had him in its mouth. So he jumped to his feet ignoring the pain. On his feet the pain almost made him pass out. He wanted to be sick. Then re realized that there was no cat, only pain. Then he realized that he must have broken something.

He had broken two ribs in the fall and bruised several more. He had no idea what was wrong with him, but just knew that he could not do more than take the slightest breath with the jabbing pain. The little boy in him made him cry. He was crying because he hurt and was afraid and alone. And there was no one to take care of him. It was also dark and he didn't know what to do.

The daylight came quickly that morning which helped the boy's spirits. But the pain kept him from doing anything. He had not eaten much yesterday and was very hungry. But he didn't know what to do about it. He could not hunt in his condition nor could he climb back up the tree. And why would he want to do that anyway, he thought. He would probably just fall out of it again.

He carefully walked out to the shoreline. The trade winds were blowing a strong wind that morning and it felt good. He found a place to sit down that was comfortable enough and spent the rest of that day there. He just sat there feeling sorry for himself and crying off and on, and used several of Grandpa's cuss words in conversations. He wished he could tell his father what he thought of him and the jungle challenge. Finally, he realized that it was getting dark again and he had nowhere to go.

He began to dwell on the hopes that his father would be real sad when he came back and found his bones lying there in a pile, strewn about by the animals. After spending the day acting like the little boy he was by feeling sorry for himself, he got mad. He was angry for crying and wishing that his father would be sorry when he found his bones. He was mad at his father for leaving him there and he was going to get even. He was determined to get stronger and meaner, so he could beat the shit out of his dad when he returned. He might be little but he could build a trap or just smash him with a club. The boy didn't know what he was going to do yet, but it was going to hurt, that was for sure. He had time to come up with a good plan, plenty of time. Five months and twenty eight days of time.

Anger brought life to the boy. He knew that he had to eat every day or get weak and die. There were plenty of snails around the rocks he could eat. That was not his choice of food, but that night it would have to do. He also was thirsty and that meant a trip back into the jungle to the stream he had found.

The trip to the stream was slow and stooping to drink was painful, but he drank as much as he could hold. He promised himself that was the last time he would drink the water without boiling it first. Also he knew that tomorrow he was going to find some container of some sort to hold a water supply so a trip to the stream was not required every time he got thirsty.

By the time he had made a fire on the rocky shoreline and caught a bunch of snails, it was dark. He didn't care because he was mad and had a purpose in his life. He knew he could stay alive. He had been shown how to stay alive by his father and grandpa. Nothing short of one of the meat-eaters could prevent him from surviving and getting his revenge. And the meat-eaters had better get him that night while he was defenseless because tomorrow he was going to have weapons and a good safe hiding place. He had gathered up enough firewood to keep a fire blazing all night if he stayed awake—but that wasn't going to happen.

The next morning he woke up in a daze. He was dizzy and sick to his stomach. The pain in his back and ribs was terrible, and he threw up. Throwing up caused the pain to reach levels he could not endure and he passed out. His face landed in the vomit and rocky sand. When he came to, the pain was just as bad. The position he had been lying in after passing out had caused the ribs to do more damage. And he was still dizzy and sick. He also had a very bad case of diarrhea that he could not control, and his pants were stiff with the foul mess.

He wanted to die. Out of desperation, he rolled over trying to find a position that would stop his back from hurting. It was not possible to find that position and he started getting the dry heaves. Of course that caused him to pass out again, but at least he was in a better position. He slept all that day and that night. He occasionally awoke only to heave and pass out again. The next three days and nights were spent exactly the same way.

The fourth day had brought a hard rainstorm that lasted until the following day. It might have been responsible for saving the boy's life. The rain provided a cooling agent for the boy's body that was burning from fever. The fever was caused by drinking bad water. Also he drank the rain, which replenished his depleted body fluids. By the fifth day, he felt better; he was getting used to the pain but he was awfully weak. By being so sick he had been immobile, allowing time for his ribs to convalesce. The boy felt like living again for the first time in days. And he was hungry enough to eat a feisty jaguar.

He started his new day by scavenging for food. He was going to eat a lot of something and was not fussy about what it was. The first to be devoured were more raw snails; He didn't feel like waiting to get a fire started when everything around was so wet. Next came several sea urchins, then thousands of tiny sea creatures that lived in the seaweed. He gathered the seaweed and combed it with a stick, knocking the tiny shrimp and crabs out to a little recess in a rock. He was able to collect a handful-size mound of squirming little creatures very quickly.

Eating the crunchy handful was another matter. With every bite he felt and heard the crunch of their body armor being broken but he kept reminding himself it was pure protein. It tasted like iodine smells and like salt. After his feast of tiny morsels he did feel better. Just to have something in his stomach was a big improvement.

It continued to rain periodically, and sometimes it was very hard rain. During the rain, he lay down to catch water in his mouth. To do this he picked a big wide leaf from one of the plants he found in the jungle and rolled it to make a funnel. The wide end was almost twelve inches across so he was able to drink as much water as he wanted.

With hunger and thirst out of the way temporarily, he decided to find a container that would hold fresh water. Now would be the best time to store up water, with the frequent rains. The first thing he found was a bamboo stand. He selected several of the largest stalks and cut them down with his knife. His ribs didn't fail to remind him of his injury with every swing or slice of the knife. Then he cut the stalks into sections, leaving one end sealed and the other open. These were placed out in the open and each had a leaf funnel in the open end. After a few good showers, he had all of the water he would need for a while. When that ran out then he could use his new-found containers to boil the water from the stream. He had watched his father boil water in a leaf one day. His dad explained that as long as one side was covered with water the leaf would not burn through.

Another day was nearing its end. The vast horizon signaled the close of the day with a fire-red sunset between the thundering anvil-shaped clouds. He still didn't have a safe place to sleep, but was getting used to it. After all, he had been on the ground every night so far and he was still walking around, sort of, anyway. His back was better but he certainly could not be climbing trees or engaging in strenuous activities. Just the chopping of the bamboo had been an arduous task.

He did manage to start a fire and threw more wood on top to dry. With this procedure he would have a nice bright fire that night to keep him company. Sitting there watching the flames leaping about, he became mesmerized. He was thinking it would be fun to have Grandpa there. He was still angry at his father, but not as much as he had been earlier. Given a choice of no one being there with him and his father being there, the boy would not have hesitated in choosing to have his father sitting there watching the blazing fire with him.

Little Sid had spent a lot of time with his father since his father took him away from his family. His dad was not a happy or friendly man, and he never said anything unless he was teaching him something. He never just chatted about fun things. Then the boy realized that in spite of his faulty personality and the fact that he dumped him in a wild jungle, he missed him. Then he started making plans about how to spend the coming months while he was sick. He was suddenly hit with a hard truth: While he was miserably sick with the fever he had lost track of time—and hadn't marked the days on the big tree.

That night he fell asleep sitting up and leaning on a good-sized bolder. The fire burned itself down to just a slight glow of red embers. It was a perfect fire for a big juicy steak, if he had one. Then he was jarred awake with fright by the loud growl of a jungle cat perched on top of the same boulder he was leaning against. The cat had picked up the scent of the seafood remains lying around, plus the smell of a human, of which the cat had no previous experience, so being a cat, he was curious about what that foul smell belonged to.

When the cat snarled, it scared the boy so much that he jumped up. That hurt him so much he roared with pain. And that in turn scared the big cat and it quickly disappeared into the safety of his dark jungle. It wanted nothing more to do with the foul smelling, and fearsome creature. The cat thought he was a huge monkey, but it certainly sounded and smelled much more dangerous than the tree monkeys.

That scare made it important to Little Sid to find a good shelter before the next nightfall. There was no more sleep coming to him that night. His mind was awake, his eyes wide open and the wooden spear and knife were at the ready. While waiting for the birds to wake the sun, he made up a plan of action. He was going to walk a few hours down the shoreline to explore. He didn't know exactly what he was looking for, but figured he would know it when he found it.

Preparing for the walk, he stripped off a long piece of bark from a green limb that he had broken off a tree. He used this to fashion a harness that would carry two bamboo sections full of water. The other sections were stacked together in a protected area. The mouths were covered with leaves, and a rock was placed on top. He didn't want some animal getting into his drinking water.

As the sun lit up the horizon, Little Sid set out. He was walking east, directly into the sun. Walking was not easy as the terrain was rough and his ribs were still very tender. He made his way around or over the rocky shoreline until the sun was almost directly overhead. He knew he would have to turn around if he wanted to return that day and be back before darkness set in. That is when he saw the sandy beach loaded with coconut trees just another mile or so ahead. That was a good reason to continue traveling eastward. Coconuts meant food and drink were just waiting to be picked off a tree.

He was a happy little kid when he finally arrived at the coconuts. Not only were the trees full of nuts, the ground was littered as well. The coarse rocky shore turned into a smooth sandy beach extending well out into the water up through the coconut trees to the edge of the jungle. There was an abundance of big land crabs that surely would be good to eat as well.

He celebrated the discovery of his new home with one fresh, just off of the tree, coconut. It was painful trying to hack his way thru the tough fibrous husk that protected the nut, but he prevailed. After drinking the milk and eating the meat and washing it down with several big gulps of fresh water, he leaned back against a tree and thought about how wonderful life was—until reality snuck back into the picture. He still didn't have a secure place to sleep that night.

There were only about three hours of daylight left by the time he decided what to do about his sleeping accommodations. The first thing was to gather a lot of firewood. While gathering wood, he found a perfect tree to build a platform on using driftwood and limbs he could break off. The old tree was just on the edge of the jungle and got the ocean breeze. The thick canopy offered shade from the sun and would stop a lot of the rain. He painfully managed to climb up to one of the big limbs then sat down to enjoy the view. Things were starting to go a little better for him. There were some vines hanging down around him that gave him the idea to use them to tie himself to the tree that night, and he would construct his platform the next morning.

The night came and passed without him falling out of his tree or anything trying to eat him. As the sun's rays began heating up the sandy beach, Little Sid was hard at work. He was gathering just the right pieces of wood he could find to build his house. He had his new home firmly planned in his mind.

The first problem he had to solve was how to anchor the floor to the tree limb so it wouldn't blow off. He ended up stripping long pieces of bark off of saplings. These were used to lash each board, plank or limb in place. When he finished, he had a solid floor roughly six feet square. Standing in the middle of his platform, he felt proud of his work. The hard and painful labor would be rewarded with a good, comfortable and safe sleep that night. He could hardly wait for nightfall. That was such a contrast, as every other night he had been alone he had dreaded the coming of darkness.

To further cat-proof his tree, he decided to sharpen more limbs into spears. These were tied all the way around the tree like a skirt. There was one opening just large enough for him to squeeze through. A cat would certainly be discouraged about jumping through the sharp spears. After that he gathered up a few coconuts and his water tubes and he retired to his new home. There he sat on the edge with his legs dangling down and swinging back and forth while munching on a coconut. Life was good.

He slept well that night. It was the first good sleep he had had since his arrival, other than passing out, and he wished he knew how many days he had been too sick to mark the tree. The next morning he sat down with his knife and put the same amount of marks on the tree as he had the first tree, plus two.

Sid's back and ribs were feeling better so he thought it would be good to have meat for his dinner that night. With two spears in hand, he went into the jungle to hunt. It was full of monkeys, birds and rodents of every kind, snakes of course, mosquitoes and even more bugs. He easily killed a boa constrictor about eight feet long. The snake was a powerful opponent and would have been the victor if he could have wrapped a coil or two around the boy's chest full of broken and bruised ribs, but the spear proved to be effective. He managed to drive it down through the snake's skull on his fourth jab. The spear pierced the brain, killing it instantly. The big snake's muscles, however, didn't know it was dead and kept wiggling about for several more minutes.

Little Sid decided he was going to skin the snake and make something with it. He was undecided whether to make a belt or a shirt or a bag to carry stuff in it or something else. It would have made a lot of belts, especially for a boy his size, and he didn't wear shirts so it would have to be a bag complete with a matching carrying strap. Skinning the snake was not an easy task but he managed.

The meat was beautiful and he had enough to feed lots of people. He hated the idea of throwing it away, but there was no way he could eat it all. He cut it in sections about two inches thick just like big pink steaks. He was now sorry that he had killed such a big animal. There really had been no need; the jungle was full of food. He ate all he could stuff down his stomach trying to justify the killing. Two thirds of the snake was to be thrown way until he got an idea on a way to use it.

The next morning he was down from his tree early and on the prowl for wood again. This time for the right sized sticks to build a trap for lobsters. His sore ribs still would not permit taking a deep breath to go diving. He lashed the sticks together with strips of sapling bark. When it was ready, he put a few sections of snake meat in it and waded out to a coral reef ledge drop-off and tossed the trap into the water. It floated.

With a long piece of bark he had tied to the trap to retrieve it, he pulled it back to him. His only thoughts were about how stupid he was and glad his dad didn't see him. He dismantled and rebuilt the trap around a heavy rock. This time it acted like the trap it was supposed to be and sank.

That night when the lobsters came out to forage for food, it acted like a trap very well and caught four of them. Three were returned to the sea unharmed and the fourth fed a very grateful boy. By the time Little Sid used up the snake as bait, he had eaten a dozen lobsters.

Time passed almost without notice; he was happy enough but lonely. If his grandpa were there it would have been great. He could show Grandpa how well he could hunt, fish and trap. He could show him the fine place he had made to live in. Little Sid could be proud that he was a survivor and a damn good man to carry the name of Sidney X.

His hatred for his father had subsided when he found this place and stopped being so afraid of everything. He understood that his jungle training was to make him understand fear and the worst of life's obstacles. Also, he knew his father and grandfather had to face the same experiences when they were his age. He could not picture his father sitting on a rock bawling like he had. He doubted that his father had ever cried about anything. He mumbled to himself, "He could probably cut a finger off and just laugh about it."

Little Sid was wrong; his father had cried his eyes out a few times during his first days in the jungle. So did Grandpa.

Since there was a thicket of bamboo nearby, he never returned to pick up the rest of his water. It rained most every day so he cut more bamboo and had a substantial water reserve. The food available was unlimited. He ate so well that he soon grew out of his clothes. The pants legs had been cut off to make shorts and the waistline was cut so as not to be so tight. He used a strip of snake skin as a belt. His shirt was used as a pillow when he went to sleep. Eventually, he started going naked. It felt better anyway. His hair had gotten long since no one was around to cut some of it off, and he liked it that way. He was feeling good and tough and his spirits were high.

Best of all, he was not afraid of anything. He had a fright once in a while, but fear didn't consume him as it had in the beginning. He had not seen a single other human or even a sign of civilization with the exception of a low flying helicopter one day. At first he thought about running out on the beach and waving in case it was his father. He decided not to; dear old dad wasn't supposed to come for him yet. He even had learned that the big cats were afraid of him. They never came around but he could hear them nearby in the jungle.

Being alone was hard on a person. A day or two wasn't bad, but a week or two does something. After a month or two, loneliness is a thing of the past. All that mattered was what life had to offer that day. His only links to the world of the past were the marks carved into the tree each day at sunrise. After ninety marks had been carved, any degree of loneliness vanished completely. He had found a friend.

It happened when he had heard a terrible racket behind him in the jungle. Something was being chased through the dense foliage by a big cat. The tree monkeys were absolutely going crazy. Little Sid picked up his spear to investigate. He was not trying to deprive the cat from a meal, as they both had the same rights to hunt and eat, but he was curious. By the time he found the cat, most of the big howler monkey he had been chasing through the brush was being processed as monkey shit in the cat's belly. Only the head and ribcage remained.

Directly above the partly devoured animal was a young monkey, sitting very still, on a tree limb. He was in easy reach of the cat, but its attention was on the meal in front of him. Little Sid moved towards the cat to scare it away. The cat growled a warning then stood up and carried his meal with him. Little Sid scooped up the baby and walked out of the jungle.

The little monkey had been scared so severely that it had become paralyzed on the tree limb while he watched his mother being chased then eaten. The monkey had done the thing that Mother Nature had designed him to do in that precarious situation, freeze. When Little Sid grabbed the little fur ball and pulled him close to his body for protection, the monkey grabbed him back. The monkey locked his hands around a finger and was not going to let go. He had just found another protector, another mother. Little Sid could not believe that the monkey liked him so much. The monkey didn't turn loose of his finger until he fell asleep later that day.

From that time on, the little boy and monkey were inseparable. The monkey followed him everywhere and had no desire to join its brethren living in the trees. That was just fine with Little Sid; he had something other than an object to react to and even talk to. He named his new friend Fred. He picked Fred because it was the name of a cartoon character he saw the only time he watched a television set. And that had not been until he had gone shopping for clothes with his grandpa's girlfriend, Rosie. She had let him watch the cartoon while she drank a beer in a bar while they were in town.

If Little Sid's father had not been so stern when he instructed him to mark the tree every morning when he first woke up, Little Sid would have forgotten. It was not so important to leave anymore. He was kind of eager to see his father just so he could show him he could take care of himself. And he was proud of that. His days were spent hunting or fishing with Fred. They would go swimming and climb coconut trees together. They went to sleep together with Fred usually curled up beside him. They were just a couple of unsupervised boys playing in the woods, having fun.

That came to an abrupt end one day when Little Sid decided to count the marks on his tree.

THE DARKNESS

DISPIRITED, SIDNEY XXIII SAT WITH HIS BACK AGAINST THE ROCK WALL for a long time in the black void. Finally, he stood up and felt his way up the wall. About four feet up, there was a recess in the wall. He crawled into the recess and by feeling around, discovered that he was in the mouth of a cave five feet high and ten feet wide. What he would give for a lamp, a candle, a match.

Sidney assumed a more vertical position to follow the cave on his feet. He moved one step at a time, carefully feeling everything around him as he moved at a snail's pace. His hope that he was on his way out of the cave soon faded, as he came to the end of the cave. Feeling around all sides of the cave, there was nowhere to go; it just stopped. It seemed odd for such a large opening to just end. Maybe it went vertical—he hoped.

He stretched up along the walls feeling for a hand hold to pull him up. A small ledge provided him with the lift to find another, then another. It felt like it was a vertical shaft, and if he didn't run out of ledges, he would know soon. He really needed the ledges to take him somewhere, as finding them coming back down would be extremely difficult—he was on a one-way climb.

Finally, he found a ledge that was wide enough to sit on and rest the strained muscles in his arms that had been pulling him straight up the shaft. He estimated that he had traveled nearly seventy feet since he left the cave's floor. He started to think about what he was going to do at that point if he could not continue, and then told himself to concentrate on getting out instead of flirting with fear.

He continued to find cracks that allowed him to get a few fingers into them or small ledges, but there were very few places where his feet could be used to let his arms rest. He reached up at one point, when he thought his arms were going to burn out from muscle stress, to feel a wide ledge. In fact, it proved to be not a ledge, but the floor of another horizontal cave.

He sat there feeling good but his arms were still burning and the muscles were twitching with stress. He was happy that he had reached a point where he didn't have to worry about how much longer he would be able to hold onto the vertical wall.

He took time to relax. In fact, he took a nap, since time meant nothing in his dark universe. He knew he could survive for about seven days without food and water. But if he hurried through the darkness looking for a way out, he could fall to his death in an instant. When he started moving again, it felt good to rely on his feet instead of his arms to move about the darkness. The walls were four feet apart and he had no idea how high the ceiling was; it was taller than he could reach. He walked and crawled over boulders and stalagmites in total darkness for hours.

As he walked, he felt up and down the walls for other openings as he mapped out the cavern. Several times he almost fell down vertical drops that his foot, feeling each step, would discover before putting his weight on it. It was so dark in the cave, he was not sure the blow on his head had not blinded him. Fortunately, he had plenty of experience in his family's three caves and a few others he had found. He knew there was no blackness to compare with that of the inside of a cavern.

He was about ready to sit down and take a break when his bare foot stepped into something slimy and gushy as it gushed out between his toes and then his foot slipped out from under him. He fell and landed in a pile of the slime. He felt the slime and recognized the stench—and he was very happy.

He was lying on his back in a pile of guano. That meant bats were in the cave and that meant that there was a way out—if he could find it.

After the joy of finding the bat shit the realization of the really stinky shit and the stickiness clinging to his flesh and clothes overwhelmed the joy. All he could do was to take his clothes off until he found water to rinse them out. He scrapped the fetid globs of shit off of the clothes and himself, and then wadded them up and tied them in a ball for easier carrying.

He yelled in an effort to scare the bats awake to see if he could tell which direction they would fly to get out. There were no bats, but the guano was fresh, judging by the smell. He muttered, "It must be night outside and they are out of the cave, feeding."

He continued traveling slowly while keeping alert, hoping to hear the bats. His every step landed in more guano, and while unpleasant, it was a good sign that he was going in the right direction. He began to realize that he had fallen into a huge cavern with more than likely an extensive network of smaller caves. It would be fun to explore the caves if he had a light and some food and water. With the discovery of the bats, he was not so concerned with the possibility of his survival. The worst case scenario was that the opening would be in the middle of the ceiling.

After a very long time of tracking the guano, it suddenly played out. He had not heard any evidence that there were bats in the cave and had not felt even the slightest breeze from an opening. That gave to speculation that maybe the bat colony had moved or been killed by some fast-acting disease, but his feet had not touched any bat carcasses which reduced that possibility. Running out of the guano field had a disheartening effect on him. Now he had no idea where to search. He then realized that, more than likely, the cave was tall and must have angled up into another cave system.

He worked his way back from the direction he had come for about an hour. He counted four hundred steps, about twelve hundred feet, to give him an idea of distance. Then he bent over and began running his hands through the filthy bat shit to feel the cave's floor. He was trying to find several small rocks about the size of a big marble.

After finding a dozen or so he dried them and his hands on his bundle of clothes. Then he threw one of them straight up into the air. He didn't hear the report of the rock hitting anything until it landed with a plop in the guano near him. He had thrown the pebble as hard as he could, expecting it to travel straight up at least one hundred feet. That indicated the cavern was quite high. Then he turned around and took twenty steps back to the end of the guano field. There he threw another pebble into the air. Once again, there was no sound other than a glancing blow on one of the vertical walls on the way down, and another plop. Another twenty steps and the procedure was repeated. Nothing changed all of the way back until he reached the edge of the guano field. At that point, when he tossed his pebble, it hit rock directly overhead; the ceiling was not more than ten feet off the floor he was standing on.

He took several steps back to throw his pebbles to locate exactly where the ceiling went vertical. He pitched several more pebbles while he moved away from the wall until his pebble hit the ceiling ten feet over head. He then made a right turn until he found the low ceiling and turned right again until there was a low ceiling. He had learned that there was a shaft about ten feet in diameter.

Sidney felt for handholds on the wall and began pulling himself up, one hand at a time. Finding the vertical shaft encouraged him, but it didn't mean he would be able to escape the shaft. It did, however, offer more hope than he had had just minutes ago.

About thirty feet up the shaft he found a ledge, where as he pulled himself up, and realized he had found what he hoped to find. It was the floor of another cave, and it, too, was full of guano. His spirits soared. The hunger that had been gnawing in his stomach was totally ignored. His senses were tuned in to find the faintest smell of fresh air or the slightest breeze or a shade of black less than total.

He worked his way forward with one hand on the wall to his right and felt his way with his feet and other hand. He kicked a lot of stalagmites and brushed by stalactites traveling that way, but that was the only way to walk without possibly falling down a sheer vertical shaft. He kept moving, searching for hours, until his body demanded rest. He had had almost no rest since he began his journey to find a way out. It was impossible to know how long he had been underground, but he thought it must have been close to two days, possibly longer since he didn't know how long he had been unconscious. Feeling frustration flood over him, he knelt down in the goo and laid down on the only surface available. Lying in the smelly, sticky substance didn't bother him much, he was asleep in seconds.

Squeaking from thousands of bats acted as an unwanted alarm clock—one that he ignored and went back into a deep sleep. Many hours later another squeaking alarm sounded, but that time he was aware of what was happening and jumped to his feet. At first he thought the bats were coming in for the day. Then he remembered the squeaking before and realized that he was totally covered with fresh bat shit. So they had come in, digested their evening's food and took a shit and then slept, and they were on the way out of the cave. He listened to follow the sounds. They seemed to go on for a very long distance before fading to nothing.

The trip, of course, was very slow-going. There were mountains of guano everywhere and he found himself getting irritable at the constant slopping around through it. When he started to feel that way, his conditioning as a survivor changed his thoughts to a more positive outlook. Thoughts like, *at least I am moving in the right direction to get out of here and there is absolutely nothing else to do but walk to freedom.*

As he struggled along, he passed a place where there was a sudden chill of fresh air, but he was so tired that he didn't notice it until it suddenly dawned on him that he had felt a breeze. He had resigned himself to trudge through the slime and had apparently shut down his thought process. He slowly backed up until he could feel the slight, but cool breeze.

It was coming from his left, which meant he would have to turn loose from the right side wall of the cave and walk an unknown distance to the left side. This he was not happy about doing because if he got turned around he could just as easily go back the way he came. He decided to travel like the bats do and send out pings. Not the sophisticated radar the bats use, but the rocks he would throw in the direction he was walking. He also would stay in the fresh air flow. It was effective, and soon he had his hand on the opposite wall. That wall seemed to make another turn, so Sidney followed it. The floor left no doubt that he was still in bat territory.

He went down that branch of the cave for a very long time. Finally, he heard a frightening but welcome sound. The flutter of wings, then the faint squeaking sound that soon turned into stereophonic screeches. The stampede of bats covered the entire cave. Sid had to lie in the guano to get out of the way from the flying mob. This was definitely the way out. It took an hour before the huge bat population finally settled down and Sidney could resume his search. Soon the guano rain started. It was a rain from Hell, with fresh globs and squirts covering him constantly.

No more than an hour later, Sidney felt a difference in temperature in the cave and shortly afterwards, saw a contrasting shade of black that, as he trudged along, became a very faint light. That light quickly grew in brilliance until it hurt his eyes. He had to stop for a while to let his eyes become accustomed. When he could see, he crawled up a fifty-degree incline to the most welcome sight he could ever imagine.

He was out of the cave at last. He stood there, naked, in the early morning light caked in bat shit and feeling like the king of the world.

His euphoria soon turned to hunger. He had no idea how much time had passed since he went stupidly for that swim underwater. It didn't really matter how long it had been, he was out, and he was hungry and thirsty and had a new challenge. He scraped and wiped as much of the bat shit off of him as he could with leaves, and went on the hunt. It didn't take long to locate some tasty roots to eat. Then he found a tree full of the berries that he had discovered before his trip through the cavern. He ate enough to feel satisfied for the moment. He needed to find water. The berries had provided some moisture, but he wanted water to gulp down and water to wash off all of the shit that was caked into his hair and every nook and cranny of his body.

He knew where the water was. He could hear it. The waterfalls were below him and off to the right. He could not see the river or the falls because of the dense jungle. To be sure he could find the cave's entrance again, he pulled vines out of the trees as he went downhill to the sound of the falls. These were laid out along the path he took. When he came to an impassable area, he would backtrack taking the vine with him. He used vines because he didn't want to mark the way to the cave. That cave was soon going to be his.

About the same time he saw the river, he heard men's voices. Because of the roar from the waterfalls he couldn't hear anything being said or who they might be. He moved in closer to see who else besides himself had made the effort to put themselves in such a remote area. As he got closer, he could identify one of the men as Jose, the other, he didn't know. All he could imagine was that Jose had returned from his trip and had come looking for him. When they found the Jeep he must have figured that he was lost and started a search. He was curious how long he had been missing. When he came to within fifteen feet of the men, he could barely make out the conversation.

The man he didn't know was telling Jose that he was in the inner circle of the Mafia. Sidney could hardly believe his good luck. The unfortunate circumstances of the last few days seemed to have paid off. He thought it was going to take years before he learned the identity of one of these men and have an easy access to him. And here it was served to him out in the middle of a jungle.

He crouched in a thicket of brush watching, listening, and thinking about what his plan of action should be. Finally, there was a blast, the sound of a gunshot and the two men got up and went around the bend. Sidney's thirst was screaming for the cool fresh bubbling water just a few feet away. He made a dash for the water as the men turned out of sight. He drank on his hands and knees like an animal, drinking greedily while washing his body.

With his thirst satisfied and the stench washed away, he looked around for the other men. They were still out of sight. He still didn't have a plan, but decided to keep out of sight himself until he did. He couldn't grab the Mafia guy in front of his friend, Jose, without creating problems.

He noticed the shadow of a man approaching. Sid quickly ducked behind a rock to conceal himself from view. The man he wanted walked over to within a few feet of Sidney and picked up a flask and took a long drink.

Sidney made his mind up about what he wanted to do. He quickly moved behind him and hit the man in the back of his head with a fist containing a palm sized rock. It worked as well as Billy. The man's legs went out from under him. Sidney caught him on the way down and slung him over his shoulders like a sack of potatoes. With the other hand, he scooped up the flask and the pith helmet that had been knocked off. He disappeared into the dense growth of jungle, taking the vine with him.

It was a long haul back to the cave, but that is where he had to go for a while. Before entering, he made sure all signs of his presence were gone. The thought of him trudging back into the shit covered cave might have been repulsive had not the thought of the mob's Cuban cache been so overpowering.

He took the man deep into the cave and put him down in a heap of the bat's droppings. Soon he heard a groan and knew the man was awake. He heard the man say, "Where the fuck am I? Hey! Anybody here? Damn, what the fuck is this shit?"

Then the man, obviously confused, switched to Italian and asked the same questions. Then anger and panic were taking over. Sidney remained quiet, but was only a few feet away. He didn't want to be too far away in case the man got away from him so he wouldn't be too hard to find.

He waited for a little longer before asking, "You looking for me?"

"Who the fuck are you? Where am I? And how the fuck did I get here?"

"You got here because I brought you here."

"And who the fuck are you?" Tony asked again.

"Who do you think I am?"

"You gotta be the guy Jose's looking for, right? Why did you bring me here? Shit, what is this crap I am sitting in, this stuff all over the floor?"

"It's bat shit."

"Are you fucking crazy? Get me out of here, you stupid fuck."

"Can't," was Sidney's response.

"What the fuck do you mean you can't? Get me out of here, now."

"Nope," was the next response.

"Okay, cocksucker, you don't know who you are messing around with here. You better do as you are told if you want to stay healthy."

There was only silence from Sidney. Tony started ranting, his anger building. He began swinging wildly, trying to connect with his captor. Sidney was not worried about the punches connecting; he was only worried that the man would move away from him and then remain quiet. That would make them even in the darkness. The man would probably figure he was in a cave and follow the bats out when they left a few hours after dark.

Sidney then said, "How bad do you want to get out of here?"

"What do you want?" Tony asked.

"Information is all."

"Information about what?"

"Tell me where to find your Cuban depository or you are going to be bat food."

Tony thought he had the man's location as he spoke and swung out with a big switchblade knife in his hand. But Sidney was not there and had heard the snap of the knife opening. Every time Sidney spoke, he silently moved.

Sidney said, "I will ask you one more time, then I'm going to break one of your legs if you do not cooperate. That will make it very hard for you to get out of here." Another swish of air as the knife was swung again.

"Fuck you! I don't know what you are talking about."

Sidney didn't hesitate. He lunged forward and grabbed the man and turned him over on his stomach as easily as a mother turns her baby over to change diapers. He took the knife away and held the man's upper body down with his legs, and using his upper body weight and arms, pulled on the lower part of his left leg, keeping the knee rigid until the kneecap broke with a loud snap. The man's screaming threats stopped and screaming in pain began.

Instantly, Sidney was off of the man. Tony wanted to pass out with the pain, but his anger would not permit it. Who was this piss ant thinking he could fuck with Tony the Pop.

Tony whined, "You, cocksucker, why did you do that? I told you I don't have any idea what you are talking about."

There was only silence from Sidney.

"Listen, you take me out of here, and I promise you I'll forget all about this. And I'll make it worth your while; you can name your price. You obviously have me confused with someone else. I don't know anything about what you want."

Sidney then said, "Your other leg is next. After that one is broken it will be one of your arms; then the other one. With no arms or legs you will never get out of here. This is not a good place to die, and in a few hours it will be dark outside and millions of bats are going to find you and feed on you."

Tony said, "Tell me one thing, asshole, who are you?"

Sidney answered quietly, "The guy who did your pal, Vito, and his yacht the *Golden Boy*. Thanks for the diamonds."

"You, cocksucker!" yelled Tony in a definite fit of anger. "Where is the rest of your crew? Who do you work for?"

Sidney said, "You wanted to ask me something and I told you. Now you are asking me more questions. It is your turn to answer a question. Tell me what I want to know."

Tony, trying to buy time, didn't respond to Sidney's demand, so there was another attack. And there was another broken kneecap. Tony had never wanted to kill someone as badly as he wanted kill that deranged bastard. He was so mad he tried to crawl over with broken knees to get his hands on him. But his tormenter was not there. Tony was screaming curse after curse and would have gladly died if he could just have gotten his hands on his tormentor.

"Are you ready to have one of your arms broken?" was a question out of the dark.

Tony was in serious pain and was genuinely frightened—his pulse rate was 180. It was the first time in his life that he was not in control. The other man was much too strong for him. He had done everything to try to break free of his grips the last two attacks, but he had been completely overpowered. Then he remembered the brutal things done to Vito and his wife and realized that he was going to experience pain until the man got what he wanted. He decided to minimize his losses. He had to stay alive, at any cost, just to kill the son of a bitch.

Tony replied to the last question, "No. I do not want one of my arms broken. I'll try to answer your question, but before I do, can I ask you something?"

"Go ahead."

"Are you responsible for robbing my casinos on board several cruise liners operating in the Atlantic Ocean?"

"Yes."

"How do I know you are responsible?"

"I am also the guy that took your Tribute money from your airplane."

That was all the proof Tony needed. "How do I know you are going to turn me loose if I tell you what you want to know?"

"In the first place, you got it all wrong. It is not *if* you tell me, it's *when* you tell me. You may not believe it, but you are going to tell me. You fucked up by not using your knife on yourself if you wanted to keep something from me. I hope you'll tell me before you are damaged too severely to survive—as Vito learned the hard way. In case you lie to me, I can get to you again. If you tell me too late, then you'll die horribly and I haven't lost anything other than a little time. I will find the depository eventually, anyway. I want to assure you this will not be an experience that you can even imagine the severity of anguish."

There was silence from Tony. The mobster was considering his position.

"One thing you can count on, Tony, that cache in Cuba will belong to me one day. I have every resource needed to find it, and nothing else to do but look for it."

Tony asked, "You seem to have targeted me. How did you find me? Is Jose working with you?"

Sidney answered, "It wasn't hard, and no on the Jose question."

"Where did you learn about the Cuban depository?"

"Vito. It was on a paper stashed with the diamonds."

"Why didn't you ask Vito where it was?"

"He was already dead."

Tony made his decision and told Sidney what he wanted to know. He took a chance by telling him where it really was thinking that it would be better to go against the stronghold rather than picking off another one of his friends until he found it. Also, he hoped the prick would get to the stronghold and they would not kill him. He wanted that pleasure for himself. And he was going to break some bones before cutting his throat and watch him bleed out.

Tony told Sid exactly where to find the mobsters' millions, but not any of the little things to make access any easier for him. After he was through, Tony was surprised when the man attacked out of the dark again. Sidney had Tony's arm in the deadly vice of his powerful arms.

"Last time for you to tell me the truth."

Tony, really afraid his arm would be destroyed, cried out, "That *is* the truth. The money and everything else is right there! I swear to God!"

Tony felt the grip loosen on his arm and he was thankful. He didn't see, feel, or even imagine the blow with the jagged rock that knocked a big piece of his skull into his brain. The second and final blow had been a waste of energy. Tony was dead.

Sidney stood up, out of the slime, and proclaimed, "Tony, you have fought me and lost. Your treasure will be mine and your bones will forever live here to protect my treasure for me and mine for as long as it is here."

Those were the words written in the family log as stated by his forefather when the Cave of Snakes was founded. Those words were also used when the first cave, the Cave of Spiders in the Mediterranean, was founded. In both previous cases, the name of the protecting skeleton had been known. Many pirates killed a man to be left to guard their buried treasures; only the dead could protect a hidden treasure.

Sidney liked the cave and the entire area around it. It was truly remote and would stay that way for a very long time. He would have preferred to have something closer to the ocean, but it wasn't that important. He had decided to leave the massive St. Croix treasure where it was for a while. This cave needed to be explored before bringing anything in there, anyway. He needed to find an access to the cavern without going through all of the guano, however, and he damn sure was not going to use the waterfall entrance. He was sure there had to be more entrances in a system that expansive, but its exploration had to wait. He had found the location of his next prize, and it was waiting patiently to be taken.

Sidney walked out of the damp blackness of the cavern into warm and intensely bright sunlight. He was covered again with guano. He resigned himself to wait until dark before going down to the river to clean up. The afternoon was spent lying under the shade of a large tree. His thoughts were alternating between his up coming raid, his son's ordeal, and napping. He didn't bother hunting. He knew people were in the area looking for him and, soon, the dead man in the cave. Therefore, if he killed something and cooked it, the smoke from a cooking fire could give him away.

Shortly after dark, Sidney was sitting in a shallow pool in the river. All evidence of the guano he had been covered with was gone. Also gone were the remains of the flask Tony had been sipping on when he had been knocked out. Sidney felt refreshed both mentally and physically.

After his long cool bath, he was ready for some meat. It was time to hunt. Normally he didn't hunt at night since there was so much competition, but he was good at it.

He would have loved to eat a fish but decided not to as there were still people nearby. He could tell that by the big fire on the riverbank only a few hundred feet away. He would have liked to walk around the bend to see who was there but decided not to because it would have been possible for him to be spotted. To go farther downstream would not do either as the river quickly turned into the narrow deep water which made his style of fishing very difficult.

He took his clean wet clothes and the empty flask with him to return to the cave. On his way, he heard the squirming of small animals under one particular bush. At first he thought it was a bird or two, and then realized it was too noisy and that it had to be a rodent—one of his favorite meals. Bird was tasty, but you had to kill so many of them to make it worthwhile. One stringy rat would last longer. And in the wilds, the time spent eating was as important as the quantity consumed. It made your mind feel that you had eaten more just because it was the same length of time a bigger meal would have taken. To have your hunger satisfied didn't require a full belly, mentally.

He caught two rats and managed to get bitten only three times in the process. They were cooked that night on a low fire, and devoured with berries. That night was spent in the big tree outside of the cave, and he slept as soundly as an innocent child.

The morning rays of sunshine had been preceded by the early birds calling out as usual. Sidney was perched in his tree and wide awake when the first light started peeking through the treetops. As much as he wanted to get started on his way back, he knew it was not the time. The area would be full of people looking for Tony.

They were not going to assume that Tony was lost in the woods. They were going to think someone had set him up for a hit—a hit that could not be traced like the Hoffa killing years ago. A smile flickered on his face when he thought of the hot seat that Jose had put himself on by taking a Mafioso to the point where he disappeared. It was humorous and Sidney wished he could witness firsthand how Jose would get out of the potentially dangerous predicament.

That left Sidney with a few choices. He could leave and try to make it back to the *Barracouta* and then sail away. Or he could walk out and act innocent about what had been going on. That would cause problems as the mobsters would surely have some serious interest in him. Or he could just hang out for a while then walk out and explain to Jose, after the mobsters left, that he had been exploring the area because he had planned to buy it. The last scenario sounded the easiest, but the other was more interesting.

He would have liked nothing more than to mess around with the gangsters. But that would have been stupid; after all, he had to take their stash in Cuba from them. Besides, he should not antagonize them anyway. They had supplied a lot of excitement and treasure for him during the last several years.

The Sidneys used to take from governments, but in the new age of wire transfers and trade credits, there wasn't much to choose from in the modern world. That made the cash market switch to those dealing in cash and goods like diamonds. This switched his most lucrative markets to the drug smugglers and the Mafia. Smugglers were not usually worth the effort as they usually had teams of men who went wherever the money went until it landed in the smuggler's nest. Also the big guys were wiring the money to offshore banks. And more importantly to Sidney, was the status or prestige of a particular prize. The Sidneys had stopped being concerned about the money a very long time ago.

As much as he wanted to return to his boat and visit Maria at Jose's place, he decided that it would be too risky for a while. Then he thought of another problem if he stayed out of sight: everybody would think he was dead and someone would take his boat and the dinghy with over three million dollars hidden in it. If they took his boat, how would he pick up the kid at the approaching time?

He thought about going back to the boat and sailing off to do the Cuba raid. Then he remembered the way he felt as he lost consciousness thinking he was about to drown in the cave. It was the sorrow of not being around to pick up the boy. He should have never done anything that would jeopardize the boy's return. The Sidneys needed the boy and it was his sole responsibility. He would have to be patient; the Cuban prize would have to wait a little longer.

That was the problem with being attached to another person—a loss of freedom. The same call that had beckoned pirates since time had begun was in him, but he had refused to follow wildness in his heart. The feeling of freedom and total abandon recklessness was usually a strong influence but not that time.

He put on the clothes that had been hanging on a tree limb overnight drying, and then started off downhill. He had no sooner reached the river when he heard the helicopter. He walked around the bend that separated the two waterfalls and saw Jose near the edge of the river looking to the sky. Sidney walked up to Jose and tapped him on the shoulder. Jose

SIDNEY X THE PIRATE

jumped and turned around to see who was there.

Sidney said, "Hello, Jose. What are you doing here?"

Jose's response was mixed. One second he was happy to see him, the next afraid of him, the next, confused. "Where in the hell have you been, Sid?"

"I've been camping."

"Did you see Tony?"

"Who is Tony?"

"Fuck who is Tony! Did you see anybody wandering around?"

"Who would be wandering around out here?"

Jose said, "We were looking for you and I was with a guy named Tony. He has disappeared. Have you seen him?"

"No. Why were you looking for me?"

"Because we found your Jeep days ago, but there was no sign of you. What the hell are you doing out here?"

"Camping."

"People don't go camping in areas like this," Jose said with a tone of distrust or disbelief. Sidney could not tell which for sure.

"Where were you camping?"

"All over up there," and pointed to the side opposite to where the cave was located.

That was the end of any possible conversation as the noise of the approaching helicopter and the falls roaring drowned out all other sounds. The helicopter landed on the same rock it had when the men had landed here almost twenty-four hours ago. After the chopper was up and away from the thundering waterfalls, there still was no conversation between Sidney and Jose. That was because the pilot was being called every name in the book and several threats on his life were promised. The pilot was trying to defend himself against the super-heated Jose as best he could, but it was almost impossible to get a word in.

As soon as Jose stopped to catch his breath, the pilot nervously asked, "Where the hell is Tony?"

Jose said, "Looking for you, cocksucker."

Jose's voice was strained from yelling at the helicopter pilot. He was also dead tired. He had not slept at all during the night as he had stared into the black edges of his campfire expecting to be attacked at any moment by whatever had eaten Tony. His attention and imagination focused on the night sounds of the jungle. It didn't matter that the waterfalls concealed those sounds as in his mind he heard very loud and clear.

He pointed sternly at the pilot to go back to the hacienda. He needed some food and a drink or two. He needed sleep too, but that could wait. He had to get everybody out in the jungle to find Tony. He also had to sort out a few things. Things like how Sidney just showed up after spending a week in the jungle without even shoes on. His instinct told him Sidney, the most wanted man on Tony's list, was responsible for Tony's disappearance, but why? Did he know that they were each other's enemy? Did Tony know? Also he had to be prepared to answer some tough questions from some serious people if they didn't find Tony.

Sidney sat in his seat, quiet as usual, and was scanning his new piece of land. That reminded him he still had to find out who to talk to about buying it. From his view in the helicopter, he estimated that the area he would take would be close to one hundred square miles of raw jungle and one hell of a cavern. The three million dollars would certainly not be enough money.

Maria and Jandy were outside waiting as they had heard the approaching helicopter. Both were surprised to see Sidney disembark rather than Tony. Maria was happy about finding him and just figured Tony had a good reason not to be aboard the helicopter. She walked over and kissed Sidney. It was an open sign of affection and something he had not expected or knew how to react to. But he was horny, so he kissed her back.

Jose stopped all of the chatter and romance by telling everyone to be poolside in ten minutes; that included all of the hacienda's guards. He wanted both helicopters re-fueled and to be ready to leave in thirty minutes. Then he put his hand on Sidney's shoulder and led the way to the pool, and he said, "Let's have a healthy drink before this all starts; besides, I have some things that we need to discuss."

The two men had time to fix their drinks, but there wasn't enough time for the discussion Jose wanted with Sidney; the other men starting arriving around the pool in less than three minutes. Everyone was eager to find out what was happening.

The helicopters were going to canvas the area all day looking for people. One team of men would be put down at the falls. They were to walk downstream. When they found the guards Jose had left, they were to build a big fire so the helicopter could see the smoke. Jose drew out some areas on a piece of paper giving each team the responsibility for searching each of them.

There he goes, putting foot prints all over my land, thought Sidney.

Ortega placed special emphasis on finding the bodyguards. There was a chance they had found their boss so that was the number one priority. Also he wanted them found to witness his efforts to locate their boss, the boss of bosses. Tony had been his guest when he disappeared, which made Jose responsible. And he would have to answer to that responsibility sooner or later. If Tony's guards were convinced that he had nothing to do with it then he would answer later; if they thought he had anything to do with it, they would make every effort to be sure he answered for it immediately.

After a plan had been established to search for the missing man, Jose instructed everyone to get going. He held back two men and told them to get into the kitchen to help the cooks prepare enough food for everybody for three days. When it was ready, they were to take it out to the truck on the cliff.

With everyone scurrying around, Jose made a telephone call. He talked to the St. Thomas office, telling them what had happened. Jose instructed ten men to be sent to his hacienda and wanted them to arrive that afternoon. He advised them his helicopter could not meet them at the airfield so they would have to hire one, but all arrangements would be made for them. He pushed the telephone switch to hang up and handed the telephone to Jandy to make the arrangements.

Sidney sat in his comfortable high-back wicker chair watching the events unfold. He was impressed with the way Jose got things done. The people always around him were not just trinkets or servants, they were his tools. The tools he used to get the necessary things accomplished, quickly and efficiently, in his business. Sidney was not used to such luxury. When he wanted things done, no matter what it was, it was his job to do it.

A thought flashed through him: *Maybe it is time to update our pirate business. The modern pirate, operating like Jose, would have a staff that would investigate possible prizes. Hire people to analyze the people involved, make all of the travel arrangements, and coordinate the timing of all of the players. Then others would be sent out to do the deed. These men would know nothing except to take the prize to a certain location, which would be some fancy Swiss bank for cash and some fence for the hard goods to be turned into cash, and hire investment people to investigate good business investments under different names... Shit... that'd be legit money.*

Nah, that'd take all of the fun out of it," was Sidney's reaction to the modern pirate. *Those thoughts did, however, plant some seeds that would soon sprout.*

Sidney saw Jose motion him over to the bar. Jose stepped around and was standing behind it. He said to Sidney, "While those guys are out there looking for Tony, let's have a few drinks and bring ourselves up to date on one another."

Talking was not one of Sidney's favorite pastimes, but the few drinks sounded good. He said, "Okay."

After a few minutes into the first drink and listening to Jose tell him everything he must have thought Sidney wanted to know about his recent activities, Jose's conversation turned into questions. "Sid, what do you know about this man, Tony?"

"Nothing."

"You ever hear about the name, Tony the Pop, Castero?

"Nope."

"Did you hear anything or anybody yelling for help last night?"

"No."

"You want to venture a guess who Tony works for?"

"Nope." Sidney finished his drink and pushed it forward indicating it was time for Jose to fix another. Jose had been doing all of the talking so his was not quite ready yet, but he gulped it down so he could make them at the same time.

With a fresh drink in hand, Jose asked, "Do you remember a man named Vito who was killed in a robbery?

"Vito who?"

"Vito Meridino, he was on the yacht, *Golden Boy;* remember him?"

"Don't think so."

"Damn it, Sid, I know you do. We talked about it in St. Thomas while in the car."

"Oh, that Vito."

"Yeah, him. Well, Tony is Vito's, and a lot of other guys like Vito's, boss."

Sidney asked, "So?"

Jandy and Maria were listening to the one-sided conversation trying not to bust out laughing. Sidney was the man of the fewest words they thought possible. What made it so funny was it was making Jose angry at the brief responses, and Sidney seemed to enjoy that. Once again, Jose was losing a game he decided to play with the mysterious stranger.

Jose realized that it was not going to get any better so he switched the conversation. He said, "Tony, in case you do not know, is a really big man working for the Italian controlled Mafia. He is the man that put a half a million dollars reward on the person or persons responsible for whacking Vito."

Sidney asked, "Oh. They catch them?"

Jose, looking irritated, said, "Not yet."

Sidney took the initiative to speak and said, "That jungle is a funny place to be looking for a bunch of criminals."

"He was helping me look for you, Sid. And now that he is missing, his group is going to think I had something to do with his disappearance. Shit, he was in my own backyard."

Sidney asked, "Did you?"

This irritated Jose even more. "Okay, Sid, I have to come up with some answers for those people and I have to know what you were doing out there."

"Camping."

"You don't have any camping gear. You are not even wearing any shoes. You are not even wearing your knife that I've never seen you without."

Jose hesitated allowing Sidney to respond.

"So?" was the only response he got.

"So, a man just does not go out in a savage jungle without gear, shoes or protection. Who is going to believe a story like that?"

"I do," said Sidney as he pushed his once-again empty glass towards Jose. He began to realize that he was not going to get another drink from his aggravated host, so he said, "Jose, I thought you knew that I enjoy living off of the land. I don't need those things that you *think* are necessary. I lost my knife when I got caught in the rapids."

Again he pushed the drink glass a little closer to Jose. Jose, thankful for any dialogue, put the glass away and fixed a fresh drinks for them both.

Jose looked over at the smiling girls and asked if they would step into another room for a few minutes. They both complied with the request without feeling belittled.

Then he said to Sid, "Tony thinks that whoever pulled off the Vito deal has been doing a lot of things to hurt the mob. Apparently, the mob is tired of being hit and has decided to do something about it."

"Sounds like a natural reaction to me."

"Maybe those responsible for these actions against the mob are not aware of who they are fucking with."

"Maybe they do."

"Maybe they think they do, but do not know just how ruthless these people are."

"Maybe they don't give a shit."

"Maybe they should."

"Maybe they think there's no reason for concern."

"Maybe, bullshit," Jose was getting tired of the game Sidney was playing with him. "These people are going to fuck you up, amigo, if Tony isn't found."

Sidney, also tiring of the "maybe game," said, "Well, it won't be Tony who'll be doing the fucking."

Those words were the words Jose feared he would hear from Sidney. He had hoped that Tony was just lost. *Sid knows something I don't about Tony—and I'm not going to learn shit unless Sid has a reason to tell me.*

Sidney said, "I'll tell you what. You give me a couple of good flashlights and a change of clothes, and I'll go back out there this evening and find him. If he is there and alive, I'll bring him back. I might be gone for two or three days. If I find him, I'll either light a signal fire or just bring him back in my Jeep. Is it still at the cliff?"

"Yes."

"Will that make you feel better, Jose?"

Jose was relieved at the possibility that Sidney had not wacked Tony after all. Sidney was happy that he had time now to explore his cavern using good flashlights. A couple of days would be enough time to see what the cave had to offer.

Jose was smiling as he yelled for the girls to come back. Maria came over to get a new drink and got cozy to Sidney as Jose was giving Jandy some more instruction on faxes to send out concerning their missing guest. He wanted the word out to Tony's associates.

Sidney felt the soft firmness of Maria's breast on his back, and that sent the appropriate signal straight down to whatever it is that pumps the blood into an erect penis. He stood up, turned to Maria, and said, "Let me show you something."

Without seeing, she could feel what he wanted to show. They both left the bar to visit Maria's room.

After the initial frenzied bout of mutual lust, the two occasional lovers lay in bed. He was near sleep with Maria caressing him. She said softly, "It's a good thing you are not around here more often. I would probably be in love with you."

That was the first time anyone had mentioned love to him. It brought to Sidney's mind a song he had heard in Fred's Place, by BB King. He was not a music lover or even paid much attention to it, but the lyrics of that song seemed to reach out and touch him in some way. The only part he could remember was, "Nobody loves me but my mother, and she could be jiving me, too."

That afternoon, neither left the bed except for a quick trip or two to the head for another kind of relief. It was a pleasant way to spend the day. Maria did all of the talking and Sidney did all of the listening about her life since they were together—things that Sidney had forgotten almost as soon as he had heard the words.

She also talked about Tony. Sidney was curious if she was on the payroll while she was in the sack with him. Jose had told him of her special talent about reading people on certain subjects. Was she using her voodoo magic to read his mind? He hoped so because he was thinking how good it would be to fuck her again before he went back to the jungle; which, of course, he did.

Sidney rolled out of the sack. It was time to look for Tony the Popped. Jose had been asleep in his chair out by the pool. He had not slept the night before and the drinks earlier in the day really zonked him. He stirred awake as Sidney and Maria came out to the pool deck. In his post-sleep awareness, he just sat there waiting for his brain to tell him what was going on.

Finally, he sat up and asked Sid, "Do you still want to go back to the jungle to look for Tony?"

Sidney answered with the customary, "Yep."

Jose asked, "How about some company on the trip?"

"No, thanks."

That made Jose happy as he didn't relish spending another night out there, especially the way Sid was going. He wanted the comfort of lying on his big soft bed covered with fresh sheets, fluffy blanket and the air conditioner set to freeze-me.

AT THE EDGE OF THE CLIFF AGAIN, SIDNEY WAS STILL IMPRESSED WITH the raw natural beauty of the land. There was nothing that suggested civilization was anywhere to be seen, except the small rough dirt road behind him. There was something about the place that seemed to be spiritually connected to him. Like all the Sidneys, he had wanted to be buried at sea when he died, but he'd rather be buried on this land, maybe put into the cavern.

Looking at the view that he was already calling home set his future for him. He couldn't wait to show the land and cavern to his son. *Maybe I'll take him on the Cuban raid... it's time for him to get involved anyway. It was time for the boy to start resuming the family responsibility of being the "King of the Sea—if he's still alive.*

Standing there with that thought, he wondered how the boy was doing. Was he alive? Did he turn mean as one of his ancestors had? He remembered being mad enough about being left there to kill his old man, too, but he did overcome it after he appreciated what the experience had done for him. He hoped that was the case with his son. He would hate to have to start over with a new kid, and he was getting too old to mess around with kids.

On the horizon, one of the helicopters came up and was hovering over a thin trail of smoke rising from the dense green of the jungle. They had found the guards. Then he moved off and down the hill. He used a different route that time, to eliminate a few miles. The shortcut would keep him in the jungle the full time rather than walking down the stream. This was a preferred route anyway. He didn't want one of the helicopters spotting him to see where he was going. The trip was a little rougher than anticipated, but he had done worse. He didn't mind the strenuous walk anyway; he needed the workout.

By the time he reached the cavern's well-hidden mouth, it was almost dark. He left his pack of clothes and food the cook had made for him and flashlights there and went down to the waterfalls. No one was there. Apparently, all of the searchers had been removed from that section before nightfall. He went behind the big waterfall to retrieve his knife that had been left when he went under the falls to explore. It was still there as was the vine he had tied to the rock, just in case he got lost. He untied the vine and it was swept away by the current.

"Boy," he muttered, "that was pretty stupid to turn loose of the vine, but maybe it was best. I may have never found that cavern."

When he reached the cave again, the bats were flowing out in a giant body, made up of individuals seeking exactly the same thing in life as the next one only an inch away. After the traffic passed, Sidney stepped into the cave and flicked on the flashlight. For the first time he was able to see the cave.

The guano was as high and as massive as he thought it must have been. There was very little of anything on or between the ceiling and the floor that wasn't covered with it. The mouth of the cavern was quite small, but just twenty feet inside, it blossomed out to a huge interior. Massive stalactites hung down everywhere and their cousins, the stalagmites, rose to greet them.

With a much bigger lamp he was sure the cave's interior would be spectacular. A little farther down he could see something khaki in color sticking out of the grey slime. It was the knee of Tony dressed in his Jungle Jims. He was still as dead as he was when he left him. He was not a very pretty dead man either. His head was covered in dried blood and bat shit. His mouth was open and it was full of bat shit as was his one remaining eye.

As Sidney walked by he said, "Fuck you some more, Tony the Mafioso. Have your bones been protecting my cave?"

He asked the question out loud, not expecting an answer and glad he didn't get one. There were several things he wanted to look for, but that trip was primarily just to get acquainted. He followed the main body downward; the beam of the flashlight was not big or bright enough to see any distance, but he was careful to keep it on the floor. He wanted to be sure where it dropped down. He thought he would have been able to follow his tracks in the guano, but the bats had done a good job of covering those tracks.

When he found the vertical shaft that he had climbed up to reach the main cavern, he was surprised and happy that mother luck had smiled on him; the shaft was right in the middle of the main cavern. He could have gone the other way just as easily, and he still could be stumbling around, going deeper into the cave. He passed the shaft and continued down the main body. It went on for a very long way before starting to get smaller and it began winding around more. The cave got smaller the more it twisted and turned around the harder sections of rock. The bat droppings thinned, then abruptly stopped.

At that point, he heard the first of many small streams of running water. It was an underground stream that surfaced and ran down through the cavern for about fifty yards before disappearing back into the rock. He tasted the water; it was cold and tasty. All the other streams he saw that day were the same. As he reached a point where he thought the cave might be ending, there was another opening leading in a new direction.

He put a mark on the starboard side wall then followed the new cave. Soon after entering the new section, his flashlight started to dim. It was time to stop his forward movement and rest. He had brought two flashlights with him, both with new batteries and spare bulbs. His plan was to go into the cave until one light went out, then rest and return to the outside with the other. With the flashlight's last brownish light, he found a place that looked suitable for a place to sleep. He turned the light off and settled in for a restful sleep. He was so deep in the cave that he could not even use the bats to tell the time of day.

Sidney had stirred around during his sleep trying to find a soft spot on the rock. There was none so he decided to get up. In spite of the hard bed, he felt rested, having slept for a while. He sat up in the total blackness listening and hearing only the ringing in his ears.

He wished the ringing sound could be eliminated as being in a totally black and soundless world would have been an experience that might put a better perspective on a loose idea that had been coming and going since he thought of making a change in his business. But, his ears had not stopped their incessant noise for as long as he could remember. He ignored it most of the time, but the absolute stillness made the ringing seem ten times as loud. It pissed him off. He thought that with all of his money he should go to a doctor and get it fixed.

Then he muttered, "Fuck it. They probably would tell me there is nothing they can do about it, and then it would really bug me."

A more pleasant thought occurred to him when he remembered that Maria had given him a couple of Cuban cigars before he left with a flask. The flask was amazingly similar to the one Tony the Popped had had with him. Without turning on his limited supply of light, he found the flask and took a long drink. It was a good rum, probably a Bermuda Black Seal.

Then he found one of the cigars and, after biting the end off, lit it with a match. He started to close his eyes when he lit the match so as not to cause night blindness when it was extinguished. Then laughed at himself—he was going to be blind anyway when the match went out. With the cigar well lit and rum flask in hand, he sat back with his back against the wall. He became fascinated with the red glow of the cigar. That red glow was the only light in his present universe. He moved it about like a kid would do with the end of a stick that had caught fire while roasting marshmallows. Watching the running flow of red streaks that followed his every move, it was almost hypnotic—especially after a few more swallows of delicious demon rum.

When most of the rum was gone and the cigar had burned down to the point that it went out because of saliva saturation, he decided it was time to start the long trip back. He had already decided to bring in ropes and food for the next trip. That was when he could seriously explore the lower cavern and some of the smaller side caves he had seen. He was more eager for his next trip than the return trip he must face now. He stood up, and turned on the fresh flashlight, keeping the almost expended one in reserve. As he started to walk, he noticed something peculiar. All of his cigar smoke had drifted farther down the cave. There was almost no smoke that had floated the other way.

Shit, is all he could think, *that could be an indication there is an opening that way. It could be miles away and travel through spaces much too small for me to get through. But, if there is an opening, it could be closer to the sea.*

He had to decide whether to follow the smoke or take the known route back to the outside. "Well," he told himself, "I came here to find a better entrance, so fuck it," and he continued going down the cave, but in a trot to save time.

At first he told himself he would only travel for an hour. By then, if there was no stronger sign of an opening then he would return. If not, he should have enough battery power left to at least get him close to the cave's opening. After all, he had made the trip in the dark before, so he sure as hell could do it again.

The hour turned into two. He just could not force himself to give up the hunt. At the end of the second hour he had lit up the other cigar so see what the smoke would do. It flowed more directly down-cave. The cigar was butted out to save it for more smoke tests later. On the next smoke test, an hour later, there was a definite smoke stream visible. Also the flame from the match leaned in that same direction. He knew now that he was not going to give up until he found the new opening. He could only hope that it was big enough to crawl through. He also hoped it was not inaccessible at the top of a narrow vertical shaft. In caves you can never guess how things will turn out—Mother Nature was full of surprises.

Another hour passed by; the cave had continued to get smaller and even more winding. Twice he had to push and pull himself through sections where the walls were too narrow to stand up and walk through. The last time, he had to use the butt of his knife to knock some old rock sections down in order to get through the tight opening. He was starting to have some serious doubts about his chances of being able to follow the cave to its conclusion. But he had made his choice hours ago and was determined not to quit.

Ten minutes later, he smelled fresh air. The air was good and saturated with the vegetation's fragrance of the jungle. He wasn't sure where it was coming from, but just the scent of the outside world was enough to renew his determination. Soon he saw light a little farther down the cave. He had to crawl on his stomach to get through, but finally he emerged.

It was either early morning or late afternoon; the sun was well below the horizon. He was in a jungle he had not seen before, and even the roar of the waterfalls could not be heard. He found a comfortable rock to sit on and drank the rest of the rum, smoked what was left of his cigar, and rested while waiting for the sky to tell him if it was a new day or a new night approaching.

Fifteen minutes later, darkness flooded in over the mountain peaks and through the valleys. The animal chatter patterns changed and nighttime had set in. Sidney sat outside on his rock just a few feet away from the cave's mouth, watching the growing illumination of the sky's stars.

There was a clear sky with a gentle breeze; it was going to be a pleasant night.

He sat up most of the night observing the heavens. There were several shooting stars that night, a sight that always had intrigued him. The night jungle was full of all kinds of sounds both from the dying and the living. During those times away from civilization, Sidney was a good man and loved the creator of all things without fear or expectations from his God, who had made such a wonderful world.

Just an hour before dawn, Sidney's eyes told him it was time to get some sleep. He crawled back into the cave feet first while keeping his knife out in front of him just in case one of the meat-eaters sniffed him out. Nothing found him, however, and he slept until the sun was above the horizon. He awoke feeling fit and completely refreshed and ready for another go at Maria's lovely body.

The cave's entrance was almost a quarter of a mile from the peak of the mountain top. He climbed through the jungle's abundant growth. At the top he could see where he was and how to return. He was upstream of the waterfalls by at least two miles and to the west by another mile. He sat on a large boulder near the mountain's summit observing his domain-to-be.

He thought about the best way to get into the area, while keeping it inaccessible to other people. It was too far to walk if carrying a good-sized prize. If he built a road, anybody could come up into his private world and that sure as hell was not going to happen. There would be no prying eyes; no militia with out-stretched palms. This was to remain a place impassable to all men.

The only solution he could come up with was to learn how to fly a helicopter and buy one. He could clear out an area to land it and build a house to live in with the timber cut to make the landing zone. Even by doing that he would be inviting the militia to come visit him by helicopter, so he had to give the matter more thought. He had plenty of time.

It took most of the day for him to get back to the cliff where his Jeep was parked. On the driver's seat was a basket with a note pinned to it. The note was in a woman's handwriting, probably Maria's. It read, "Bet you are ready for some refreshment by now, hope you enjoy." It was signed "Love."

Sidney dropped the note, his thoughts were on the basket of goodies before him. There was a thermos and a few sandwiches. "Coffee?" he muttered. "Who wants hot coffee?"

While taking the cap off the thermos, he looked around and under the seat thinking that maybe they hid the rum as a joke. There was no bottle of rum to be seen. However, as the lid came off the thermos, he did smell rum and not coffee, and it was in a thermos to keep it cold.

Sidney quickly forgave "Love" and was happy. He ate a couple of the sandwiches, not because he was hungry, but because they were there. He had eaten earlier that day on roasted snake and a plant called *Zepina*, which tasted like spinach. He also had snacked on the berries so abundant in the area.

The thermos full of the cold rum gave up the last of its contents as he arrived at Jose's hacienda. He walked back to the pool area where there were about twenty people milling about. Sidney recognized six of them as Jose and his crew. Some of the others appeared to be from the Caribbean, judging by skin color and clothing. The rest were definitely European and most likely, Italians.

Jose and the girls stood as he entered. Jose's whole expression screamed "Where is Tony?" But his calm voice asked, "Any luck finding Mr. Castero?"

"No," was the response as Sidney walked over and dove into the swimming pool. The water was refreshing and he had been thinking about a cool swim since he was stuck in the tight walls of the cave.

Jose seemed nervous and came over to the side of the pool and said, "Sid, there are some people here I would like you to meet. They have all come here to find out what happened to Tony."

Sidney, swimming on his back, spit water straight up into the air like a whale and said, "Good luck."

The short indifferent answer pissed Jose off. *I should just tell the mob that Sid whacked Tony because he learned that Sid was the guy that whacked Vito, and be done with the obnoxious prick.* But he knew he would not because of a promise made in the back seat of a Mercedes one afternoon. *But who gives a shit about promises to a dead man.*

Instead, Jose told him there were some clothes in Maria's room for him so why not change and join them for a discussion about Tony.

Sidney, still doing the back-stroke, said, "Okay."

He left the pool and tried to entice Maria to come with him to get dressed. She didn't go. In fact, she tried to ignore Sidney because she knew that if she did go with him, it would be an hour before she would be able to get him to return. She worked for Jose and knew the jam he was in. The boys from Sicily were not there for a friendly visit. And neither were the Ortega men from St. Thomas. All were armed and ready to shoot anything that needed to be shot.

Sidney returned wearing somebody's clean clothes and padded out in his bare feet to the bar. As the bartender fixed him a drink, Jose introduced him as a friend. Jose only introduced four of the other men and they all were from Italy. One man was older, about sixty, and the others ranged from thirty to fifty-something. There were two other Italians who were not introduced. Those two looked to be muscle-bound and somewhat square in relation to height and width. They were more bodyguards.

Jose asked him about his search. Sidney decided not to mess around anymore and decided to go ahead a give them the information so he could get on with his evening. He didn't feel like going through an evening of questions and answers.

He said, "I walked all over the area we talked about, Jose. I didn't see any sign of Tony or any evidence that someone else had ever set foot in there. I did see plenty of evidence of big cats, jaguars. In fact, one treed me for three hours, which is very unusual. The only time a jaguar will hunt a man is if there are too many in an area that their normal food source will not support or if it is a rogue cat. Based on what I saw, I think there are too many cats in those mountains, and if no one has seen the man, then he has probably been eaten.

"I honestly feel, based on my knowledge of the jungle, that his bones at this very minute are lying in an underground burrow and being gnawed upon by a family of jaguar kits. Those woods are too difficult to traverse, especially a man used to city life. Tony should not have gone into the jungle by himself."

"Bullshit," was the response from the older Italian. "Tony was not a fucking fool. He would never let a cat jump him without a hell of a fight. There would have been blood all over the place."

Sidney nearly smiled and responded with, "Have you ever seen the big cats hunt? When they hunt as a family they work as a team. Usually the big male will get into position, and then walk out to let the intended meal see him. The victim then will go into the bush to hide from the beast. The female and other cats are waiting in the bush and will just lie there until the victim works his way back to them. Then with a sudden spring from behind, the cat grabs the man's neck in its jaw and breaks it. That is how they kill the larger prey, they break its neck. They don't bite to break it; they just give it a good shake until it snaps. No blood is spilled until the body is carried off and dropped in their lair. It is not unusual for the dead animal to be gently carried or dragged without even a sign or a trail to lead other carnivores to the upcoming family feast. The family joins up and everybody digs in to reduce the body into a pile of scattered bones."

Sid was very convincing with his tale and it appeared that most of his audience believed him. A couple of the Italians didn't care; they just wanted to kill somebody because somebody let Tony be killed.

Jose couldn't believe how long-winded Sid could be at times.

One of the obnoxious Italians seemed to be very interested in who Sidney was—where he came from and what was he doing in the same jungle as their boss. Sidney continued playing the part of being civilized by responding to the man's questions. Two rums and lots of questions later, the Italians' interests seemed to fade. Sidney, not impressed with the crowd, managed to get to Maria and convince her it was time for a nap.

The nap lasted for an hour; afterwards, Sidney dressed and prepared to leave. He told her to tell Jose he was going back to his boat and he would return in a few days after his guests had departed. She argued that he should stay overnight in case he might be able to help find Tony. On his way out of her bedroom he said, "Forget Tony. There is nobody up there; he is history."

He didn't want to leave her that night to drive the rough dark road back to the village, but decided it was best. The Italians were pissed off about their boss and with an evening full of booze, it could lead to more problems. He had already put Jose into a jam with the mob, and if he stayed there he would end up killing the rest of the spaghetti-eaters if they kept pressing him, as the one had already done. Besides, he wanted to kill the others anyway.

He also wanted to tape up the old man to see if he could confirm what Tony had told him about the prize. The others would be killed just to piss off the mob. It would be a good idea to let them know somebody was not much concerned with the bully techniques and mentality they seemed to pass down through the generations. Sidney had no respect whatsoever for the man that puffed himself up as a bad man and hired several other men to do the actual dirty job of confronting the enemy. And that is what the Italian pansies were best at doing.

When Sidney arrived at the village, the people had long since retired to their beds. Even the dingy little bar was empty. So, that night, Sid caught up on his sleep. The early morning light told him it was time to rise and run. He had actually been looking forward to taking another run down the isolated and beautiful beach as he had done before.

As before, he stayed away the entire day. He ran, walked, swam and slept. The sun was close to the western horizon when he returned. The people in the village were happy to see him again; some had become worried that he had been gone for so many days. He explained that he had been camping and there was no need to ever be alarmed if he didn't return for months. If he didn't return after a year, the village could have his belongings including the boat.

They also said that Señor Ortega had come by to see him and that he had some men with him. They waited for two hours for him to return. Jose had left a message for him on his boat.

Sidney acknowledged the news as he disappeared into the village's dark and only little bar. Gaspar had heard him coming and had already poured him a glass of rum; it was sitting on the bar in front of the only vacant stool. He sat on that same stool until he had enough rum to numb all of his senses and forget the Italians.

He woke up the next morning and went for another run. That time it was not for a full day, just a few hours. He made a shorter run as he had a busy day scheduled. He was going fishing in the lagoon. He always was able to think better when he was fishing. And he had some thinking to do. It was time to start laying out his next raid. He dug out the old fishing pole that had come with the boat, a bottle of rum, and a can of Spam. A piece of canvas was rigged on the forestay and lifelines to give him a shady place to sit, and he fished. The Spam didn't prove to be the best bait in the world, but it didn't matter. He was cool and comfortable and that was all that really mattered.

About sundown, he had used only one piece of Spam on his untouched hook, but had munched on the rest himself as he drank rum from the bottle. He heard the sound of a Jeep coming through the jungle. It turned out to be Jose's Jeep with a lone occupant.

Maria stepped out of the Jeep and stood there with hands on her hips and legs at a firm stance. She looked like a mother that had come to get her errant child caught playing hooky from school. All she had to do to complete the picture was to repeatedly tap her foot, showing her impatience.

She yelled out at Sidney. "What are you doing?" Her voice was almost sarcastic.

He yelled back, "Fishing."

With the anticipated short reply, she pulled on the stern line to pull the boat closer to shore while thinking, *at least the asshole could come help me get on the boat.*

He didn't help, but she did manage to pull the twenty-two tons of sailboat close enough to shore to jump aboard. She went up to where Sidney was sitting amid the two bottles of rum and a dead can of Spam full of flies.

Sidney looked up at her and gave her a devilish smile. He was feeling no pain and was nuclear horny. He pulled her over for a little kiss, but received only an icy stare. There was no friendliness in her looks or actions. He wondered what he had done, but was not going to give her the satisfaction of asking.

Instead, he used rum diplomacy and said, "Shit, it's just like the old man used to say, 'A woman is pretty to look at, fun to fuck, and meaner than the devil if you piss 'em off.'"

She seemed to not notice the remark and finally she asked, "Where in the hell have you been? Didn't you get Jose's note?"

Sid said, "Oh... Forgot to read it."

"Damn it, Sid, Jose needed your help. Those guys are not going to leave until they find Tony or kill somebody to even out the score. Jose has brought in some of his men for protection, but doesn't want there to be trouble between the Ortega's and the Italians."

"So what does he want me to do, wave a magic wand?"

"He wants you to help defuse the situation somehow. I don't know exactly what he has in mind, but he seems to think you might have some ideas on how to find Tony or get the heat off his back."

The rum in him made Sidney say, "I'll defuse those greasers completely if they don't stop fucking with me."

He just wanted to be left alone; to catch the elusive Spam-eating fish and drink some more rum. And get some pussy, too. He put his pole back down and tried to pull Maria in closer again. That time she was not quite as cold, but almost. At least he was making a little headway.

She said everything she could to convince Sidney to return with her to the hacienda that day, but nothing worked. He was too stubborn and too drunk to listen or even care. All he wanted was to get her into bed, which she flatly refused. Finally, he promised to go with her first thing in the morning, if she stayed overnight with him aboard the *Barracouta*. She had no choice; Jose told her not to come back without him, and she was very likely incapable of beating him up and carrying him to the Jeep.

She made Sidney take her to the village bar as she intended to play catch-up with her drunken lover. She was not very fond of rum, unless it was ice cold Mount Gay, and all Sidney ever had on his boat was cheap and locally made and room temperature. She ordered the only bottle of vodka in the little bar. She drank it straight. After the first glass, it was not so bad. After the third glass, she didn't mind it at all. After the fifth glass, she had succeeded in catching up.

The next morning, Sidney shook her by the shoulder until she was awake. He said, "Get up; let's go."

That surprised her as she thought it was going to be a morning as tough as pulling hens' teeth to get him to go to Jose's. But he was up and dressed in his finest and probably his only shorts and tee shirt. Also, to her surprise, she was in no hurry to get going; it was her turn to be horny. Maria, with a smile that only beautiful horny women can deliver, had total control over poor old Sidney. She ravished him and he was beyond happy—he had visited paradise.

After the big event, they lay in bed with the feeling of peace and well-being between them. Sid even touched her skin in a non-sexual way. That made Maria happy; it was the first time he had shown any affection towards her.

She asked him, "Whatever happened to your son, Sid? Jandy said she saw you in St. Thomas and you told her you were going to pick him up to live with you."

"I did."

"Well… where is he? Did you put him in a boarding school? How old is he anyway?"

Maria was curious and Sidney had expected those questions to be asked sooner or later. It was what he got for shooting off his big mouth.

He answered, "Yeah, but I will go get him in a few months."

Maria wanted to meet the boy and asked, "Could I visit him sometimes?"

He said, "That will be hard to do. The boy is in a very remote location."

"My goodness, Sid; where did you send him? Alaska or China?"

"No. He's in a nature school. They don't allow visitors."

"Nonsense," she replied, "they have to let his family visit once in a while."

"Not this school."

"What is the name of this school?"

"Why? Do you want to call them to be sure they are nice to the boy?"

"Yes, as a matter of fact, I do."

"Sorry, they don't have telephones there." Sidney, usually not a talkative person, had a strong dislike for questions, especially about his actions, and was enjoying the grilling from Maria.

Maria had worked herself up thinking that she had to know who was taking care of the boy. It soon became apparent to Sidney that he had erred. She was not going to let the subject rest until she knew where the boy was. He decided to take her into his confidence, to a degree, by explaining the boy's whereabouts.

He said, "Maria, you remember how surprised you were about how well I managed in the jungle the first time we met. And how I have been camping the last week in the wilds without any of the things that most people need?"

"Yes," and nodded her head to show that she remembered.

"Well, that is because I went to the same school that my son is now going through. When he finishes, he will know how to take care of himself anywhere. It is a tough six months, but it is the only way to teach self-reliance, self-esteem, and to learn what the true natural laws of our world are. It is also the only way to learn of nature and the animals, the weather and everything surrounding us that most people cannot see."

"That sounds very interesting. Who are his instructors?"

"He is the instructor and the student. It is the only way you can learn these things."

She didn't understand what he said; it sounded like a new theory on education. In a few seconds she looked over at Sid and said, "You don't mean he is somewhere all by himself, do you?"

Sidney didn't respond because of the near hysteria in her voice.

"What is the name of this school, Sidney?"

"The School of Life. Only those who receive passing marks complete the course."

As Sidney spoke the words, he knew he had screwed up. He should have just lied to her. Now it was going to be the sweet little girl telling him what a contemptible prick he was for letting a boy be by himself in the woods. He knew what was coming but had not expected how severe her lip lashing would be. In minutes he was ready to tuck his tail between his legs and whimper—or knock the shit out of her to shut her up. He did neither, but was very tempted to do the latter.

What he did do was look her in her eyes and said in a sincere, no-nonsense voice, "Look, Maria, there is nothing you can do about this.

There is nothing I am going to do about this. His training is mandatory. I do not enjoy the thought of my seven-year-old boy being out in a wild jungle all by himself. I don't... "

She went berserk and interrupted him with "Seven years old! You put a seven year old in a savage jungle? Damn it, Sid! Are you crazy?"

"I went through the same six months at his age as did my father and his. Thinking about it makes it harder than it has to be, and it does have to be. Like I said, you cannot do anything about it."

He was wrong about her not being able to do anything about it. She started to cry. She was genuinely crying with sorrow at the thought of a scared little boy living all by himself with no one to protect him. It was the saddest feeling she had ever had. She would have cried a lot harder had she been able to see little Sid at that very minute as he lay on rocks with his broken ribs and painfully dry-puking and shitting in his pants.

Sidney realized her tears were affecting his feelings, so he decided to stop all of the emotional crap. Had he become any more concerned for her feelings, he would have agreed to get the kid right then. But instead, he got up and told her to get dressed; he was leaving to go see her master. That hurt her feelings on top of the sorrow she was feeling for the boy and she reacted the only way she could. She cried some more.

Later, she punched him in the stomach and said, "That's for your smart-ass remark about my master," and then punched him again and said, "And that's for being such a cruel and despicable father. If I were a man, I would beat the shit out of you until you told me where he was."

He knew she was serious and was a little concerned that she would tell Jose and the others and some of them might just try that tactic. He hoped not because he would have hated to hurt those people. Her good intentions would cost his son the edge he needed to survive, but he couldn't tell her that. Instead, he said, "Maria, I told you about my son because you asked. I told you about him in the strictest confidence. I hope you will not betray that confidence."

As mad as she was, she knew from the very beginning that he knew what he was doing. After all, he had that something in him that separated him from any other man she had ever met by a wide gap. Also the was this secretiveness thing about him: the surprise meeting he had had with Jose in the Mercedes that scared Jandy so bad that she had peed in her pants. There was something about the man that was almost alien to modern man. If he said something was as it was, then she should accept it as that was the way it was going to be and there had to be a good reason for it. Sidney was right: there was nothing she could do about it, but she didn't have to like it.

She told him, "You have nothing to worry about. I would not dare tell any of my friends that you left a little seven-year-old boy out in a jungle full of wild animals to live all by himself for a half a year. They would surely think I was crazy to have come up with such a story."

The last word on the subject was, "I will bring him over here so you can meet him after I pick him up. Then you'll see the difference between my son and any other eighteen year old." Actually, Sidney kept the age down for believability—there were very few modern men of any age that could match the kid's abilities in the wilderness.

The trip back to the compound was silent. Maria had nothing to say. Sidney would appreciate the silence as soon as they arrived. They had no more than stepped out of the Jeep when they were met by the men from Italy, followed by Jose's men who were trying to calm them down. The first Italian to reach him was one of the burly square bodies.

He was shorter than Sidney, but walked right up to him, blocking his way to the house. He stared up into Sidney's face and said in a heavy accent, "Okay shit-for-brains, where the fuck you been? We left word for you to get your ass here yesterday. Do you think we are here to play games with some fucking weirdo-of-the-fucking-woods?"

At that point, the strong-arm reached up to jam his finger in Sidney's chest to really drive the point home that they were important people not to be trifled with. Unfortunately for the Italian, his finger didn't make the trip. Sidney caught it in his right hand, and, with a fast jerking motion, broke it. At the same time, he sidestepped the man and continued on his way to see Jose. The guard was full of rage and with his other hand went for one of the guns he was carrying. Sidney saw the move and gave him a swift underhand backhand that caught him under the chin with the full

SIDNEY X THE PIRATE

force of Sidney's fist. The blow knocked the man unconscious, and he fell where he had been standing.

Sidney looked at the surprised faces of the other Italians and said, "He's kind of a grouch, isn't he?" He maintained his stride towards the pool area.

The men from Italy were confused; they had just seen one of their toughest dropped like a little kid. The men from the Caribbean were barely able to conceal the fact that they were elated. They had been bending over backwards to kiss Italian ass since the thing had begun. The more they kissed-ass, the more the Italians wanted. Jose was trying desperately to keep peace between the two criminal organizations. No one wanted more enemies.

Jose looked well-worn when he stood up to welcome Sidney. He was not aware of the incident that just occurred outside. He asked, "Didn't you see the note I left two days ago?"

Sidney replied, "Not until Maria showed it to me."

Jose was visibly irritated but decided not to press it further. Instead he gestured Sidney to follow him to an area away from the others. They sat on a couple of chaise lounges looking out into the jungle.

Jose said, "I have a problem, Sid. The Italians do not believe your story about a cat being able to take Tony out and not at least leave some signs of struggle or blood behind. We still have men out there looking and absolutely no signs have been found. These guys are not going to go away until they have an accounting of Tony, and they are getting extremely belligerent. It is increasingly difficult for my men to keep control. Hell, it is tough for me to want to keep them restrained. If we react like we want to, by kicking ass and sending them back to Italy where they belong, it would be an admission that we not only did Tony, but the other attacks on them as well. That will result in a lot of men being killed and the loss of millions of dollars. It will really upset business arrangements."

Sidney said, "What does your problem have to do with me?"

Jose, with the tired eyes of a man under siege said, "I don't know why or how, but I have the strongest suspicion that you know exactly what happened to Tony. What your motivation was, I do not know for certain.

I have not indicated this to anyone, not even the girls. Nor do I care. I know you have your own business to attend to and I would never dream of trying to interfere. I just need you to be honest with me so I can figure out what must be done to get these guys off my back."

Without giving Sidney a chance to respond, Jose continued, "I'm getting concerned about them kidnapping someone in my family. Or assassins taking my people out as fast they can in a swift act of irrational retaliation. These people are a bundle of emotions when it comes to protecting their own from outsiders. They kill each other like swatting flies, but outsiders had better not even think about it. I am an outsider, and they are about to do something. They will not let up, and I'm starting to think that somebody higher up in their organization is deliberately putting this pressure on me until I kill these men. That would tell the world that we are the slimes that started a war with them, and that would give them the okay to wipe us out."

Jose shook his head and resumed, "To let this happen, when the original confrontation had nothing to do with us, would be a real crime that didn't have to happen."

Sidney responded, "Isn't it customary or at least good manners to offer a guy drinks before making him listen to your woes?"

The remark sounded sarcastic, but it was said with a slight smile that said, "Relax, Jose."

Jose motioned to the bartender to come over. While waiting for the drinks they saw the Italians come into the pool area, supporting their fallen pal. The man with the broken finger was still woozy, but not enough to take the madness away. He yelled over at Sidney, "Your ass is dead meat, motherfucker." He meant it, too, and his pals were doing all they could to restrain him from pulling his gun out and blowing the finger breaker away. Sidney was not impressed.

The leader of the Italians used good judgment in not pressing the incident with Jose about his friend breaking the man's finger then knocking him out. First of all, his guard did get overbearing and therefore the Italian boss could not really blame the guy for reacting the way he did. But the way the man reacted was another matter. It was all so natural, so smooth, and it was not an accident. The man had snapped the finger then baited the Italian to pull his gun. He would learn more about that man before making a case on him.

The drinks came, the shouting from the wounded man quieted and the bartender left the two men to their privacy. Sidney looked at Jose and said, "I do appreciate your predicament. I must admit to you only that I'm the root of these problems. I have been zapping the mob pretty hard the last few years. I take things away from them because I do not like them and they are easy prey. They also have the tendency to have rather large caches which, of course, is also attractive.

"I value your friendship, Jose, and am aware that a man who refused to get rid of his problems by fingering me deserves my respect and help. Forget Tony, he's dead. I killed him and his body can never be recovered. Had I used better judgment, I would have waited until he was away from your protective responsibility. However, I reacted to circumstances that were more important to me at the time. For this I owe you."

Jose thanked him for his honesty and told him he had no intention of turning him over to the mob. Now that he knew with certainty about Tony he would negotiate something to show them the proper respect and honor.

Sidney said, "Bullshit, this is my fight. I want it and I will handle it. You stay clear."

Jose asked, "How many men do you have? You cannot hope to win a fight with a handful of men against a worldwide organization, Sid."

"I don't have any men, but I can assure you I am more than a handful. They do not know who is responsible for the things I do to their organization, so I come and go as I please among them and have all of the advantages."

Jose thought of the description of Vito's death and shuddered. He was glad Sidney was not going after *him*. Then he remembered the ease in which he had been taken in the St. Thomas parking lot. Plus the business about his five-hundred-year-old family history as pirates. Jose decided that Sidney knew what he was doing.

Sidney then said, "Jose, I can make all of this go away whenever you are ready, but according to my family's tradition, I must take something in return."

Jose said, "Just ask, it is yours."

"I want to own the area around the waterfalls for twenty miles in all directions. I will pay for the land and promise to keep it exactly the way it is forever. I want a guaranteed title to the land. All you have to do is find out who owns the land and set up a meeting for me."

Jose asked, "When do you want it and how much do you want to pay?"

"I want it as soon as I can get it and will pay any reasonable amount."

Smiling, Jose said, "That land is part of a land grant given to our family directly from the King of Spain a couple hundred years ago. Are you sure you can afford it?"

"Of course. How much do you want?"

"Well, we didn't know about the waterfalls and that is a beautiful spot," said Jose.

"Yeah, it is a beautiful spot—for a killing," was Sidney's response. Then he added, "The Ortega family is guaranteed access to the land as long as no damage is done to the property. I wish to own the land not only because of its beauty but the solitude it offers."

Jose, doing some mental calculating said, "Let's see that would be four hundred square miles of pristine, original forest. The lumber in there is worth a fortune, and when the lumber is gone, the land could be sold to some enterprising developer to build a golf course and resort hotels to view the spectacular falls for another fortune."

Sidney replied, "The land is not going to be changed or altered in any fashion, so the income possibility is moot. And no one will ever know about the falls."

Jose was not interested in selling part of his land, but his curiosity would not allow him to say so. He made a big tactical error then when he said, "Sid, the land is not for sale. I do not believe that my father would even consider its sale for anything less than enough money to represent a greedy profit. After all, he does not need money."

"What does he need, besides getting you out of this mess you are in?"

Jose knew then that there was going to be trouble unless Sid got the

SIDNEY X THE PIRATE

land. All Sid had to do was kill the Italians then disappear again. Nobody was going to believe Ortega if he tried to explain that a lone pirate was responsible for all of the Mafia's troubles. That would put him right on the front burner for sure.

Sidney said, "I will give you three million dollars now. You give that to your father as a show of respect from me. Tell him I wish to be a good neighbor and that he will never have any trouble from me. In fact, I would be surprised if he would ever see me. I will never sell the land, unless I tire of it, and in that case I will deed it back to the Ortega family fee gratis. Also, to satisfy his need for a healthy profit, I will pay ten million more dollars for the land in cash.

Jose said, "Well, you sure know how to offer a deal that would be hard to pass up. Pardon me, but I had no idea how lucrative the pirate business must be. When would you pay the ten million?"

"I will go for it later this week, just as soon as I clean up this mess with the Italians."

"You have three million on you now?"

"On the boat."

Jose could not help but think that a man who apparently had that kind of money sure ought to be able to dress better. He had never seen him wear anything other than shorts and a tee shirt. He wore no jewelry. He didn't even have a boat that you would expect a multi-millionaire would have.

"Under the circumstances, Sidney, I will accept your offer for my father. I will have Jandy draw up the papers and they will be ready pending your return." Jose was thinking that if he didn't return then he would have the land plus his three million dollars. Then he realized that he was plotting again. If it had been anybody else, Jose would have made sure there would not be a return trip.

PANAMA

THE OLDER OIL TANKER, BEING PULLED THROUGH THE PANAMA CANAL by the modern day mules, had a visitor on board. Vincenzo was there talking to the men who were aboard a year ago when it was robbed one night in the middle of the Caribbean Sea. The story he was told was becoming too familiar. It seemed the raider thing was nothing new to the shipping trade.

The captain, an older man in his sixties, explained, "For as long as there have been ships to sail the seas, there have been pirates to take the valuable cargo away from honest seamen. In the very old days, the ships would be boarded by a crew from another ship and the cargo taken, usually at a great loss of life. In these times, however, we have been bothered by a new type of pirate. In certain parts of the world, they are a small team of heavily armed men in small fast boats that storm the ship. In these waters and the Mediterranean there is another type of pirate, a solo pirate.

"I personally believe that most of our problems come from the same man. He works alone and is never seen or heard. How he gets on board and disembarks is a mystery. He is always successful in taking the ship's cash and all other valuables he can carry. He rarely kills, but many men have been found dead from blows on the head and slashed throats. It is widely believed among us, who live and work on the sea out here, that the Barracuda only kills if he has been seen and could be identified."

"Is Barracuda the name you have given this man?" asked Vincenzo.

"No. His name was given to him before I was born by other seamen. It is because, like the barracuda, he strikes without warning or even being seen and is away before the victim is even aware of the attack: which, also like the barracuda, can be vicious."

"How long has this been going on?" asked Vincenzo.

"That's a big part of the mystery. The exact same kind of raid has been happening for centuries all over the seas between Europe and the Americas."

"Then it is obviously not the work of the same man."

"Who knows for certain? The superstitious seamen feel it could be just that. Like the legend of the Flying Dutchman, the Bermuda Triangle, the Ancient Mariner, the Ghost Rowboat—there is no end to the unanswered mysteries surrounding seamen. All anyone knows for certain is nobody knows anything about him. It is always a single man and he speaks in the language of his victims. He is the most frightening experience a few had lived to tell about. It is a seaman's tale, but at least it is true. I know, because I have been bound and told in the same Norwegian language that my grandfather spoke to give up my ship's safe. I did only after my air was cut off and I lay there helpless on my cabin's floor. When I realized the Barracuda was responsible for my plight, I knew that I was only just another page in his history and I complied with his demands. Because I did, I did awake later, still bound and with a headache, but I was alive. It all happened so fast it was unbelievable."

"Captain, how do you know this pirate wasn't one of your crewmen?"

"Because, like in every incident, the entire crew must take lie detector tests. It was not a crew member and has never been on any of the ships visited by the Barracuda."

"How many people know about this Barracuda?"

"Go into any seaman's bar on the waterfront and ask around. He is and has been known for many years, no decades... what was I thinking? For centuries."

"Then it is possible for any number of men to copy this style of piracy?"

"Sure, that's possible, but it is not the case. There are two reasons why: One is that seamen are superstitious and would not dream of being the one responsible for copying the infamous Barracuda. Their fear of his retribution is too great in case the stories are true. The second is that there is a pattern to the Barracuda and it goes back many years. The Barracuda will only attack in the same region for five years or so, and then you will hear of his raids in another area for about five years. It is like he lets an area rest while he plunders another. It is a smart move. The efforts to catch him take about five years before the momentum is strong enough to mount any kind of action from the various lawmen. I'll bet if someone sat down in some fancy library that registered crimes at sea, you would see this pattern repeated for a very long time, certainly more than one generation of man."

This was the eighth cargo ship Vincenzo had visited with his inquiry. This was the eighth time he had heard the story of the Barracuda. At least he was starting to feel better that it was not a personal thing against the Mafia. But that in no way excused the asshole's actions. And now Vincenzo was sure he was going to be the one to hook, board, and break the neck of the infamous Barracuda.

VENEZUELA

"Jose, do you have any men in Cuba?"

"Of course, Sid, why?"

"I want you to call your man there and have him send you a fax. He should say that, in keeping with the policy to report outsiders seen with company contacts, he is reporting that a man from Sicily is visiting and was seen with our main contact in the government today. His name is Tony Castero and he is reputedly connected with the Sicily establishment. He is currently in Port Vincenzo and is traveling with two other men. One of them is an old Jamaican the other an Italian with a scar on his forehead. They're being followed and he will forward any new information as it happens. He is to ask you if there are any special instructions for him. When this comes in, show this to the old Italian friend. Also, show some obvious relief about the situation. Then make sure you put on the show about how insulted you are that they would not trust you, and all of the accusations they have made about you."

Jose said, "Yeah, I know the drill, best defense is a strong offense, but what makes you think they are going to believe that story? They'll just think that I'm doing this to throw them off of the track."

"Don't worry, they will believe you, and they will bust their asses getting out of here and getting to Cuba."

"Why?"

"Can't tell you, Jose. You go make your call now while I entertain your guests."

"No rough stuff, Sid,"

Sid walked over to the man with the broken finger. He said with apparent sincerity, "Sorry about the finger, but I reacted badly. I hope you will accept my apology."

"Fuck you," was the expected response.

Sidney then turned to speak to the older man, "You saw what happened. I had no choice. I really thought he was going to deck me."

The older Mafioso knew exactly what had happened, but decided to play it Sid's way to see what he was trying to do. He said, "Sure, let's all relax; we have more important matters to be concerned about."

Sidney then offered, "Why don't some of your men go with me today. We can go back out and take another look. I might have spotted a lair the other day that could be where the cat took his body. I didn't look in it as I was afraid I would have been attacked if the cat was in there."

One of the bodyguards asked with interest, "Where was it? Was it near the falls?"

Sidney said, "It was up the mountain from the falls."

That is when Jose made his entrance, his telephone call completed. Sidney told him they were going out to take a look at a possible lair to see if Tony's remains were there. Jose played the part well. He asked all of the questions you would expect about what was needed, how many men, etc.

Ten minutes later, Jandy let out a whoop from the office area and came running in waving a fax for all to see. She handed it to Jose and she was beaming with joy. The problem had been solved.

Jose read it and said, "I'll be damned." He handed the note to the older man and said, "Now whose balls are you going to bust?"

The man read the short fax. At first he responded with indifference with the attitude of who-are-you-trying-to-shit. Then his faced turned grey and his eyes widened. His jaws began to twitch as his anger began to whelm up inside. "That cocksucker," was all that was said.

The other men wanted to know what was going on and he showed them the fax. They all agreed it was just bullshit. It was a stupid attempt to get them away from the crime scene. Besides, how would he get out of the jungle without anyone knowing?

The old Italian sat down not listening to the others. He was the only one there who knew of the treasure in Cuba. He was stunned at the possibility that Tony the Pop had been the one they had put in charge to find the man who had been hitting them. And Tony that was doing it all along. Finally, he stopped the men from their treating remarks by saying, "It is true. We have been taken by Tony, but we still have time to stop him. I know where he's going, but we have to get there now. Load up and let's go."

Jose jumped in with his complaining about his treatment until the older man told him he was truly sorry, and could expect a delivery soon that would make up for his bad manners. Then he excused himself; he had to leave.

Ten minutes later, the helicopter lifted off and was on its away to Caracas International Airport. Twelve minutes later, Sid and Jose were toasting each other. Jose was dying too know how Sid knew they would react. Sid, in his usual long winded said, "Lucky hunch."

Sidney was very pleased with the older man's reaction for other reasons than getting them out of there. It meant the information from Tony was accurate. The older man was apparently one of the fifteen mob bosses, as Sid had guessed he would be. If the top dog had been there, another honcho would certainly be on hand to find out what had happened to Tony. The older man, Gugguci, had recognized the procedure to gain access to the organization's fortune in Cuba—the Jamaican and the Italian with the scar. The procedure required two days so that gave them just enough time to prevent Tony from stealing it.

This also changed Sidney's plans. In order for everything to work out right, he had to get to Cuba before the old Sicilian could discover that Tony had not been there. But, the only way was by private jet since he didn't have documents that would let him fly commercially. He asked Jose if he would have his plane take him to Cuba. Jose assured him it would be a pleasure knowing that Sidney had more work to do before the Ortegas were completely off the hook.

Sidney was not happy at the prospect of having to jump out of an airplane again. His last experience had been enough, but there was no other way to get into Cuba in the time allotted. He could not land for the same reason he could not travel commercial—no papers.

"Are there any private airports they can land at, preferably on the west end?" asked Sidney.

Jose told him, as he expected, "There is no way to land at any airport that will handle my Learjet. They all are run by the government and follow the rules to the letter. The Cubans are, understandably, very cautious about incoming aircraft, especially jet aircraft."

Sidney then asked, "Okay, then is there someplace where I can get a parachute?"

Jose gave him a big smile and said, "Sure there is. Jandy is a skydiver and has all of her own equipment."

Sidney looked at Jandy and said, "And I thought you were the smart one around here."

She laughed and went to her room to retrieve her gear. Sidney refused all of the fancy stuff like the altimeter, emergency chute and items that would not fit him anyway. The pink helmet did fit but was very tight. He decided to take it anyway, he couldn't afford the time it could take to revive if knocked unconscious on landing.

"There is no way to return this gear, but I will replace it if you insist on doing this sort of thing."

She said, "You better. I love the sport."

"Jandy, sport is pitching horseshoes or playing tennis, not throwing your body out of a high-flying airplane," offered Jose Ortega.

She laughed and showed Sidney how to fit the backpack on and how to open the chute. She argued that he needed to take the emergency chute, but he countered that if the main didn't open, he wouldn't have time for the secondary chute. She warned him not to jump less than a thousand feet. She tried to give him instruction on how to steer it, but he was not interested. He told her he only wanted to get on the ground alive. If he needed to alter his landing, he would learn how to steer it then. It was very clear to Jandy that Sidney had no love for parachuting.

Maria went with him to the helicopter and kissed him goodbye. She said, "Please take good care of yourself; you have a boy to pick up somewhere, remember."

Sidney had not thought about that. He wondered if he should draw a map and give it to her in case he didn't return. He decided not to because he couldn't trust her. She would probably get Jose to fly that damn helicopter over to find the boy. If something happened to him that was too bad for the kid. He would figure it out one day and find his way out of there. Also, the boy knew his grandpa was on St. Croix and should be able to get there somehow.

Three hours later, he was sitting in Jose's Learjet waiting for the crew to finish filling the fuel tanks. He had picked up a large scale map of Cuba at a marine supply store just outside the gates of the international airport. It wasn't much, but it did show some of the terrain and major features. He was hoping that he could bail out over a sugarcane field. That would help hide him on the ground if someone saw him landing. It would be almost dark when he would jump. The airplane would be flying at one thousand feet, then would land at the small airfield in Port Vincenzo, refuel, and go to St. Thomas.

After studying the chart, he opened a bottle of rum and took several big drinks. Then he stretched out on the lush seat and fell asleep. One of the crew woke him up about twenty minutes before he was to leave the airplane. None of the crew had ever done that sort of thing before so they were hoping that opening and closing the door would not be a problem. They also were hoping that the man jumping out would not bounce off the tail section, causing enough damage to make them lose control. But the boss man told them to do anything their passenger wanted so they were doing everything to make sure all went okay.

Sidney had also purchased another handheld GPS at the marina store. He had entered the latitude and longitude of a point of land he hoped to be able to land on. The GPS told him he was only ten minutes away at their present speed. Sidney asked the pilot to slow it down as much as possible, remembering the terrible beating he had taken the last time he jumped. By the time he had strapped all of his gear on, the GPS gave him two minutes. The door was opened without a problem and Sidney stepped out right as the beep of the arrival alarm went off. The ground below corresponded with what he had hoped to see. It was a sugarcane field that extended from the mountains inland to the edge of the sea. He was about six miles away from the town of Port Vincenzo.

The view from the aircraft was not as scary as the last time at thirty eight thousand feet over nothing but the broad expanse of ocean. The chute opened much softer than the jolt he had taken on his first jump. At five hundred feet, his decent had slowed substantially. He even played around with the steerage lines, but decided not to get carried away. He still hated being dangled in the air, and the sooner he was on the ground, the better. He landed, going faster sideways than he was going down, and he did a pretty good job of clearing out a good-sized path with his body being pulled through the cane. By the time he was standing vertical and had the chute off, he was a mess. The cane grass had cut his arms and legs with their razor-like edges. The cuts didn't bother him, but the thought of walking up on a big Cuban viper did.

He managed to clear the cane field without mishap. He brought the chute with him and buried it in the sand and rocky shoreline. He gave the most reverent burial any parachute had ever been given. He was very grateful it brought him safely back to Mother Earth at a speed that didn't crush his every bone.

He sat on a rock and pulled out the folded chart. Judging by the apparent shoreline he fixed his position. It would be a two-hour walk to the little town just outside of Port Vincenzo. He should be hours ahead of the Italians, but he had no time to waste.

He started his jog to town where he was on the verge of pulling off a tremendous raid that would shatter his enemy's illusion about itself—and cost them a major bundle. He was going to either have the best day of his life or it would be his last. Either way, it was a raid for treasure and it was happening. Sidney XXIII was at work, doing what all Sidney Xs loved most.

His first job was to find the Italian Carlo "Scars" Gambini. He was the third Gambini given the honor of protecting the Cuban treasure. His father and an uncle had the job before him. He hoped his oldest boy would be the next in line. The Gambini family was totally trustworthy to the Mafia. They would not hesitate killing anyone, even their own family to protect the cache. It was an honor they placed above everything else, even their deeply rooted Catholic religious beliefs.

Carlo was known as Scars since he was twenty-one and found himself on the wrong end of a machete fight in Cuba. Had his father not come along and shot the three would-be robbers, he would have been chopped to death. As it was, he ended up with a long scar on his forehead that went from his left eye and up past the hairline on the right side. His hands and arms were badly scarred as well, but the black priest robe he usually wore concealed those. He was not a priest, but, due to special considerations made by the church because of huge donations, he was allowed to come and go into the church in the robe. The priests called him Brother Carlo.

Sidney knew he would be at his home directly across the street from the old church and that was his target for that night. Supposedly, he was always at home or in the church twenty-four hours every day. He was always looking for strangers or anyone else who might be trying to find the cache.

The church was exactly where Sidney thought it would be, right in the middle of the little town's square. The old church was a classic small church; the walls were made of rocks and sections of coral that had been cut from nearby reefs. There was the traditional steeple with broken shutters that once concealed the bells. It had taken years to build the church, but that time and effort paid off since it was over two hundred years old. It would last for a few hundred more years or until the local politicians decided that a more modern building should occupy such a prominent place, as the little town would surely grow. All things evidently outlive their usefulness no matter if they were serviceable or not.

Across from the church was the town's square; a park with old shady trees and well-manicured vivid green grass to walk barefooted on. Park benches were scattered throughout. Young people in love strolled through holding hands and felt the hope of what the future would bring. Little kids were running around playing and making as much noise as their nearby mothers would allow. And the elderly people, still wondering what the future would bring, were mostly by themselves—having outlived the person that they had once roamed the same park with hand in hand.

Sidney, for some reason, was attracted to the expressions on the elderly faces that reflected feelings that had been developing inside them for years. It was of boredom; feeling lost with no one caring; being lonely for the love and companionship they once took for granted; and being unsure of tomorrow—would they have enough money, would that illness that had been flirting around get seriously bad? Worst of all was the feeling of resentment that they had wasted their lives and had not been to the places they had wanted to see; had not done the things they had wanted to do, and had not loved like they dreamed—and now it was too damn late. Those people were sad and ready to die just to get away from the sadness. To make matters worse, no one cared.

On the other side of the park there were a few shops, a bar, and one house painted white. That house had to be where he would find Scars. He walked out to the park and sat on a bench hoping to see Scars come outside. He gave it fifteen minutes before giving up on the possibility of catching him going into the church. That would have made his job easier, but now he would have to do it another way; there couldn't be much time left. The old Mafioso, Gugguci and company, would soon be arriving.

Sidney knocked on the front door and asked to see Carlo when it was opened by a small woman. She led him to the living room and offered him coffee while she went to get her husband. Five minutes later a man came in. His name obviously was Scars.

Sidney said, "Did Tony Castero talk to you yet?"

Carlos said, "No. Who are you?"

"My name is Alfonzo Ramerez. I have the same job that you do except my location is in Brazil. Tony brought me here and said he would try to call you to introduce me, but he is moving fast today. There is a major problem: Tony found out that a certain Sicilian is going to try for your cache. Gugguci is his name, and he is bringing in six men to take it and split from the family. You and I are to kill the bastards. They intend to kill you as well, but they are not aware of my or Tony's presence. You and I are to go to the vault armed and ready, and wait there until Tony and his men get here. Because of the possibility of you being killed, you are not to blindfold me as normal rules dictate to be sure that one of us knows how to approach the vault. As soon as Tony arrives, we will transfer your cache to a van and move it to another location until the problem has passed."

The thought of someone trying to take the treasure away from him angered Scars, but without question, he said, "Let's go," and went to get his weapon. Fortunately, Scars thought Tony was the finest man in the world, as he frequently sent expensive gifts and would call him with a couple of jokes.

Scars handed a pump action assault shotgun to Sidney and two automatic pistols. He picked up a canvas bag that sounded like it was full of ammunition and told Sidney that was all they would need. Scars led the way across the park and into the church at a fast pace. His mind was focused on one thing: blow the shit out of anybody approaching his vault.

Inside the church, Scars led him behind a drapery that hung from the ceiling. Behind the drapery was a single iron door that swung in so there were no visible hinges. The old door was ancient, but the device locking it was state of the art. Above the door was an odd-shaped hole in one of the cracks between the rocks that made up the wall. It was a hole that looked like many others with old construction. Scars inserted his index finger and Sidney heard a movement behind the old door. Then Scars produced a large key that matched the old lock on the iron door and opened it.

The hole in which he had inserted his finger contained the most modern electronic locking device. It was programmed to read his fingerprint. This activated another device that released and moved four iron deadbolts, three feet long and two inches in diameter, behind the door that retracted back into a wall. Closed, it would have been impossible to knock the door down. The iron door itself just opened into a corridor twenty feet long, three feet wide with a ceiling only five feet high.

Scars, proud of his fancy mechanism, asked Sidney if his was the same. He told Scars it was not, there was no electricity in the monastery where the money was kept. He told Sidney to watch him carefully as there were several conditions that had to be satisfied to go down the corridor.

All of a sudden, Sidney realized this must have been the same church his forefather raided when the long-past Spanish government hid their treasure. It was ironic how things never change he thought; *Once again the Sidneys are about to remove another treasure from the same vault.* He made a mental note to instruct future generations of Sidneys to raid this spot every fifty years.

Scars said, "All you have to do to return is pull a lever next to the vault door and that will give you thirty seconds before the traps reset. Every time you want to go to the vault you must disarm each trap."

Sidney wanted to ask what would happen if a trap was activated but thought he better not for fear of being discovered as a fake.

The first trap actuator was four steps down the tight corridor. It was a rock in the rock wall that protruded out slightly more than its neighbors. Scars pushed it in, turning off invisible laser beams crisscrossing the tunnel. Two more steps, there was another hidden switch and ten steps further there was a hole in one of the cracks in the wall that deactivated another. Five more steps was another, but it was a rock that had to be pulled up revealing a metal plate with one button. Scars pushed three long pushes, three short pushes, and then four long. That disarmed all traps inside and outside of the vault. Traps had to be activated inside the vault to eliminate the possibility of someone knocking down the walls to get at the treasure.

There was a key pad on the vault door that required the proper sequence of numbers to open. Scars didn't do it as he had no idea what the code was. Only the blind Jamaican knew those numbers. Sidney was almost positive there would be some device that would go off if the lock was tampered with or the wrong combination was used.

Sidney complimented Scars on the fine security system he had. Then he said, "I guess we have to wait for Tony and Blindman before going any further."

Scars, secure that everything was legitimate, said, "Yes, that is all we can do."

With that said, Sidney swung Billy out of his back pocket and caught Scars in the middle of his temple. Scars was dead before his body had completed its fall from the already-crouched position. He positioned Scars' body to lie as much out of the way as possible.

Finding the blind Jamaican would be more difficult. Tony had assured him that Scars didn't know where to find him. Only the men of the Circle of Fifteen knew of his location. The best he was able to get out of Tony was that he lived in a whorehouse in town. It was distinguished by the iron gate that closed off the short driveway into the house of ill-repute and good times. Unfortunately, iron gates were on every driveway in town according to the Spanish flair for ornate ironwork. One gate, however, had a distinctive design of hummingbirds circling a nude woman.

Sidney pulled the lever by the vault door and made his way out of the security tunnel. Outside, he began his systematic search for the hummingbird gates. He did this by jogging down the first street to the edge of the village then going to the next and running back to the other edge. It took an hour before he found the black iron hummingbirds. Everything behind the gates was quiet and the house appeared dark as if no one was there. He pushed on the gate and it opened easily. He was in a hurry as it was about time the Italians could be arriving by his estimation. As he got closer to the house a man stepped out of the darkness catching Sidney by surprise. "What do you want here?"

Sidney replied, "I am told this is the place to come for a woman."

"Go in," said the man as he opened the front door for Sidney.

Inside there was a living room with well-worn furniture. The air was heavy with cigarette smoke and cheap perfume. Sitting on the furniture were a half dozen women of all sizes and colors. All were young. An older woman, Sidney's age, approached him with a warm, friendly smile and asked if he wanted a drink. He refused. Then without rejection she asked if he saw anything he wanted. He pointed to a girl that looked to be fifteen years old. The woman complemented him for having such a good eye as she was the finest in the house.

The madam explained that was why she must have thirty dollars because the girl was in such demand. Sidney paid the woman and was led to a room upstairs by the girl without conversation. She went into her room and promptly took off her blouse. She held her small but beautiful breasts out for Sid to admire saying, "You like to suck on these?"

Then she removed her short skirt and pulled the red panties down to her ankles. She stepped out of the panties, leaving them on the floor and rubbed her bush saying, "Oh, I want you inside of me, hurry."

She then laid down on the rumpled old bed and spread her lovely, but often spread thighs. Sidney had planned to use the girl just to get upstairs, but he couldn't pass that up. He dropped his clothes on the floor and mounted the girl.

Inside her, his thoughts were only on how much he would like to stay there and screw that little morsel all night. His mind was not on the treasure, the Italians, or even venereal disease. He was focused on fucking. His attention soon shifted back to the present as soon as his lust had passed and had filled the tight sperm receptacle.

The girl, sensing that he had climaxed, made a move to get him off of her. He resisted.

She explained, "I want to get up to get you a wet cloth and then clean you up after such wonderful lovemaking."

Lying on the girl, he was thinking that there had to be a whorehouse somewhere in the world where the girl said something different. She only wanted to get back downstairs for the next thirty dollar quickie.

He said, "First, you have to tell me where I can talk to Jamaal Boggs, the Blindman."

During her continued effort to get out of bed she said, "I do not know him."

He said, "I know he lives here and he will want to talk to me because I have something very important for him. I also have something for you."

With that, he sat up and pulled a one hundred-dollar bill out of his pants. "This is your tip if you take me to his room."

She quickly snatched the money and said, "Come with me."

They dressed and went farther down the hall. She knocked on a door and said, "Blindman, there is someone here to talk to you."

A deep voice with a strong Jamaican accent replied, "Well, send him in here, girl."

Blindman had been supported by the mob since he was a little boy. He was born blind and had been left to fend for himself even before he could walk or talk. A priest found him in Kingston and he was raised by the church. When the boy was older, there had been a major fire in their church and all of the priests were transferred to Cuba.

The mob was already using the church for a secure area. One of the men took a liking to the blind boy and set up the security system for their treasure around his blindness. It was Blindman's only job and he was devoted to it. That had been forty years ago. The security system kept changing, but not the fundamentals. Part of the system required that there never be any contact between the two men, unless in the presence of a man from Sicily.

Sidney walked in and told Blindman in Italian, "Get dressed; we have to get to the vault. I am here at the order from Tony Castero. He is going to join us as soon as he arrives, but we have to act now. We are moving today and he will meet us at the new spot. The reason for this is there is an emergency going on at this very minute that requires drastic action, some of which has already occurred."

Blindman wanted to know more details before committing himself to any plans proposed by a total stranger. Sidney told him the same story as he had to Scars. He ended the story by saying Scars had been part of the plan and had been eliminated, and that he was the new guardian. With all of the name dropping and his language, there was no doubt that the stranger was from Sicily.

The story sounded okay to Blindman and he was not in a position to argue anyway. He had nothing more to lose by believing the man.

Sidney asked him, "Where can I get a car to transfer the goods?"

Blindman asked, "Why didn't you rent one at the airport?"

"Because nobody is to have a record of me being here. This is an extremely sensitive operation, and as far as anybody knows, I am not even in this country, and neither is Tony. I took a taxi to the church and planned to use Scar's car, but he left us before I could ask."

Blindman said, "My friend, Fredrico, owns a station wagon. It is an old model, but it still runs good. He lives a block from here."

Sidney pulled out some money and put it in Blindman's hand. "This is two hundred American dollars. Tell him I need the car for two days and have him bring the car to the parking lot here. We'll drive it to the church."

Twenty minutes later Sidney led Blindman from the old Chevy to the church just as Scars had done for him earlier. When he reached the iron door with the special locking device, he reached into his pocket. He pulled out the severed index finger that used to belong to Scars. The slight noise could be heard and the door was opened. Sidney negotiated the traps without difficulty.

Blindman was sure of the authenticity of the stranger when he stood before the vault. The key pad was shielded making it impossible for Sidney to see the combination. The vault door clicked indicating the electric locks behind it had released. Blindman pushed open the door and asked, "What now?"

"We load the Chevy."

The two men had to repeat the entering process seven times before the suitcases were loaded into the old station wagon. Sidney hoped the car's springs would carry the weight over the bumpy roads.

On the final trip, Sidney dragged Scars into the vault and positioned him in a sitting position with his back resting against the rear wall. His body was already getting stiff, so he formed a smile on Scar's face to get the last laugh on whoever discovered the empty vault. He wanted to leave enough evidence to suggest that Tony had indeed committed the crime.

Sidney thanked Blindman for the help and told him to go home and wait for Tony to arrive. "Tony will take you to the new vault where everything will have to be set up again. Tony said they would do some house cleaning before the church vault could be used again."

Blindman was happy they had been able to keep the treasure from being stolen and he certainly understood the secrecy behind the new location. He just hoped that he would be included in its security.

Sidney now had an unpleasant task. He went back to Scars's home and knocked until the elderly lady appeared. He told her Scars wanted him to wait there until he returned. She let him in and went to get him a cup of coffee. As soon as she turned her back, Sidney bounced Billy off the back of her skull and caught her on the way down. He positioned her on the floor and held her nose and mouth shut until her pulse stopped.

The Mafia was going to go berserk when they found out about the capture of the Cuban cache and he could not leave anyone behind that might give them his description. He thought about taking out the whore at the hummingbird whorehouse, but decided that he would be just another customer; she had not looked at him—with seeing eyes.

He had to find a sailboat moored somewhere between the village and Havana. His plan was to locate the boat, wait until dark, and then steal it. It would be loaded with the prize and sailed south, out into the Caribbean Sea and away from land for the five days it'd take to reach St. Croix.

As Sidney was driving in the old narrow streets, he came face-to-face with another car. Both had to stop and move over to within inches of the buildings to permit each to pass. The other car was full of Italians, the old Sicilian and his troop of mobsters. There was absolute disbelief in their faces when they recognized Sidney.

Sidney immediately resigned himself to the circumstances and flipped them a bird then accelerated the old Chevy. There was a crash and sounds of metal scraping metal as the station wagon pulled away. The Italians had to find someplace to turn around before they could pursue him.

The man with the broken finger kept yelling, "He's mine; that bastard belongs to me!"

The old man kept repeating to the excited hit men, "Nobody does anything to him without my say-so. He must be in with Tony."

ALL THINGS CHANGE, AND SHIT HAPPENS TO THE BEST OF PLANS. SID-ney's plan to leave Cuba had abruptly taken a change for the worst. Instead of a leisurely ride up the coast scouting for a boat to steal, he was now racing for his life. The race could have been enjoyable if he had a newer car. But the weight of the Mafia's lost treasure in the well-worn old car reduced his chances considerably. He could not outrun them, even if it did take them a while to turn around. And he would not be able to lose them as there was only one road leaving town. The chance of finding a driveway with an open gate was almost impossible so he would not try to ditch them. That would only work for a brief time anyway. They would get down the road and know that he was behind them. If he abandoned his prize he could easily elude them but that was not even considered.

He knew the only way to make good on his raid and keep the blame on Tony was to attack his pursuers. He would have to kill them and hide their bodies. The mob would think they were in the deal with Tony and that would keep them away from the Ortegas.

A plan formulated in his mind as he saw an isolated dirt road up ahead and to the left. He slowed down, made the turn and stopped the

Chevy. He left the driver's door open to give the appearance that he pulled off the road and made a panic-driven run for the trees up the hill. Instead he went back the thirty feet to the main road and hid in a low-lying bushy area near the main road. In less than a minute the new rental car zoomed past at full throttle. They saw the old car on the side road and slammed on the brakes.

Sidney heard the car accelerating in reverse, and then it spun around and went up the side road. They slammed on the brakes and slid into the rear end of the old station wagon, knocking the bumper off with the impact. Four doors on the new car opened at the same time and everyone, including the old man, bailed out. With pistols in hand, they were looking everywhere around them, while they cautiously approached the open car door. Unfortunately for them, they were not looking behind.

Sidney had moved forward with them at the same time. The last man in line was taken with a slit jugular's vein without a sound. The second man the same. Both had been dropped within ten seconds after they dove out of their car. The third man was the old Italian, and Billy put him away for later. Broken finger took the next thump from Billy, but he groaned loud enough to be heard by the others. The other two men turned at the same time and crouched down at the sound of danger. The one closest to Sidney died as the pirate lunged and jammed his knife blade into the man's stomach. That was a costly mistake. A knife buried deep into a man forms a suction that doesn't allow quick removal. That gave the surviving man the time he needed. He quickly fired off three shots—all of them hitting Sidney.

He was badly hurt but could not stop to think about it, it was time for action. He moved before the fourth shot could be fired and delivered a blow that crushed the gunman's windpipe. The gun fell from his hand and the man died as he writhed around on the dirt road while trying to get a breath of air.

Sidney looked at the damage done to him. He took two bullets in his abdomen and one shot had fractured his left arm. He was pissed off more than he was concerned. The shooting would attract a lot of attention from the police, and all strangers would be interrogated. He had to go somewhere to hide, to buy him time and to heal. There was no way he would be able to sail a boat by himself with the bullets in him anyway.

Once again, his plans had changed; he had planned to make these six men part of Tony's scheme by making them vanish, as he had with Tony, but now they would have to be found dead; killed by Tony the Pop Castero. He slit the throats of those still alive.

He remembered the cave used in times past where the governor's family had been hidden. He had never been there, but the description in the log included its location. He figured it was no more than ten miles from where he was so he decided to go there, in hopes it was still isolated.

Back on the main road, the old Chevy labored to maintain fifty miles per hour. When he reached the shoreline road he turned south, away from the big city of Havana. A few miles farther, he saw the marker he was looking for. It was a rock on top of a four-hundred-foot high hill. One side of the rock was flat. When he was able to line up his position to only see the edge of the flat surface he turned off of the road. The heavy Chevy made its way through the low-lying shrub and sparsely populated trees.

Twenty feet into the bushes, he got out of the car and painfully went back to the road to remove the Chevy's tire tracks. He was losing a lot of blood but there was not too much he could do about it. He had used his shirt and made a compress to put over his belly wounds. Fortunately, both were within inches of the other. Then he cut off the terry cloth seat cover on the Chevy's backseat and made a bandage to hold the compress tightly to him. Another strip was wrapped around his open wound on his broken arm to stop that from bleeding as well. He would have to set the arm later.

He continued driving the old car through the rough terrain until he came to a big rock outcropping. The cave should be directly to the left of that rock and be completely overgrown as it was when the other Sidney had discovered it. He painfully walked over to the area; the cave could not be seen until he was only a few feet away. There was a large opening but it narrowed quickly into the dark.

Sidney hoped the old Chevy had enough in her to bust through the tangled veins and old growth that concealed its mouth. Fortunately, there was not much soil covering the rocky surface so the plants had shallow root systems. The Chevy did a good job of working its way into the shelter of the cave. It took several attempts, but it did manage to push its way through.

Inside the cave he made an attempt to cover the opening again. He did the best he could under the circumstances and then went back to the car to pass out. Sidney woke up later; his stomach felt like it was on fire. He knew the bullets had to come out or he would probably die. Also his arm was telegraphing the fact that it was broken every time he moved, even slightly. The dizzy feeling he was experiencing indicated that a fever had started in to try to fight off the infections, but he knew that was not going to get rid of the new invaders in his body. Only the knife would be able to do that and it had better get done soon.

The thought of digging the bullets out of himself didn't particularly appeal to him but there were no options—and he had done it before. He tore up the terry slip covers for bandages and used a couple of small pieces to start a fire. Dead branches around the cave provided the fuel for a fire inside the cave. The fire was used to sterilize the knife blade and provide light for him to see by. He broke one of the rearview mirrors off of the Chevy so he could see his stomach as he dug for the lead bullets lodged in him. He had decided to delay setting the broken arm to see if he survived the surgery.

"No sense in putting myself through additional pain if I am going to die anyway," he muttered, "should've picked up the kid… damn it."

He would have given one of the suitcases in the Chevy for a bottle of rum at that moment. It would have made it a little easier to insert the knife blade in the already painful holes in his stomach. Thanks to his years of conditioning, the muscles in his abdomen had sufficiently slowed the projectiles to prevent them from reaching internal organs.

After the initial pain of sticking the knife blade into him, the pain seemed to mellow out. After the pain maxed out—it couldn't hurt anymore. So the thought of doing the job was the worst of it. The task was much easier than he thought it would be. Before he started cutting the bullets out, he looked around for something he could use to sew up the wounds. There was nothing to be found. He decided to let them bleed more to clean the interior of the holes out before covering them with thick terrycloth patches that unfortunately were not clean.

The patches were soaked in a minute and new ones were applied to the outside; leaving the old one in place. He hoped that as the blood congealed on the outer layers it would slow and eventually stop the flow of blood. He maintained his prone position and added patches until he fell asleep. The lack of blood and energy spent during the last twenty-four hours had sapped his strength.

During the next few days he would become aware that he was in bad shape. Most of that time he was either asleep or not conscious enough to know what was happening. He knew it was storming outside of the cave because water was running down the walls and dripping from the ceiling. The fact that it had been raining contributed greatly to his being alive. It provided badly needed water as it dripped on his face. The warmth of the fire had been extinguished days ago. But time didn't matter to Sidney; the present was the only time he was aware of.

One day, in the pale light of the cave, Sidney took another step towards survival. He tried to stand on his feet while figuring out where he was and what was going on. It took time, through the dullness of his mind, to remember the events that led him to be in the cave. He examined the dark red-caked terry cloth that seemed to be attached to his skin. His curiosity wanted him to remove the bandage to survey the damage but decided against doing it for fear of reopening his wounds. His arm was killing him as it had not been set and the terry bandage on it was caked as well. He realized that he felt terrible because his wounds were infected. He laid down and fell asleep and stayed asleep for another two days.

When he opened his eyes his head was clearer, but his body told him he still was running a fever. He had lost track of time so he had no idea how long he had been in the cave, but knew one thing for sure; he had been in there long enough to get very hungry.

His first task was to get another fire going. In his weakened state that was not easy, and without the cigar lighter in the old Chevy, it would have been impossible. With the bright light of warm fire, he felt, for the first time, like he might live. Looking at the floor of the cave, he was thankful that he was still in one piece; there were animal tracks all over the area where the imprint of his body had been lying in the loose dirt. The tracks belonged to rodents, probably rats. That would make his next meal easy to obtain.

An hour later, he was ripping a blackened steaming rat apart with his teeth, only chewing on it before hunger forced him to swallow. The first rat was devoured as a wild starving beast would have. The second went a little slower. Then he scooped up water that had gathered in a little pool from the rains and washed the meal down. With his immediate needs for survival satisfied, he once again began to feel tired. In fact, it was more difficult to lift his good arm than his energy level would allow. He wanted to sleep, but he wanted to put more sticks on the fire first as the heat felt as if it were healing him.

THE ITALIANS

The tragic news about the old Sicilian, Gugguci, and the deaths of the bodyguards was reported to Vincenzo over the telephone from people in Sicily, who had been notified by a longtime friend of the family, police chief Jose Grasso.

Vincenzo was in a hotel room that he had checked into two days ago in San Juan. After the upsetting news about Gugguci, he was told that everyone was looking for Tony the Pop and he was to stay there until he heard from them—*them* meaning the Circle, so he stayed put.

Gugguci was dangerous, but he was predictable and you always knew where you stood with him. Vincenzo had known him since he was a child, and was a distant relative. Gugguci was his mother's uncle. The man had put little Vincenzo under his wing early in life and was the only reason Vincenzo had managed to reach the rank he currently held in the organization.

The thought of Gugguci's throat being slashed by Tony was another major reason for Vincenzo to stay focused. He hoped the bosses would put him on Tony's tail, and he could work on it while pursuing the so-called Barracuda—who he suspected could be with Tony the Pop.

The men in Sicily were not so sure about the story of the Barracuda.

In fact, they were leaning towards the possibility that Tony and some others were involved in the other robberies. There was no doubt that Tony killed the team in Cuba. Blindman had furnished the solid truth when he had told him about Tony wanting the treasure moved and the locking device being reset to the new man's finger.

"Was the device reset to his fingerprint?" asked Vincenzo excitedly, thinking the print would identify the man with Tony.

"Blindman said it was. Changing fingerprints could only be done by one of the Circle of Fifteen."

"What language does Blindman speak?

"He lives in Cuba, he speaks Cuban for Christ's sake, and a little Italian," said the irritated voice from Sicily.

"I meant to say what language did the other man speak?"

"Italian and Spanish."

Vincenzo had a bad feeling about Tony. He had talked to Bruno while he was in South America with Tony at Ortega's place. Bruno was a longtime friend who had called to complain about some badass that had broken his finger. Bruno also thought that the badass was involved in Tony's disappearance. The next time Vincenzo heard from his pal, Bruno, it was when he called to tell him about the fax that took Gugguci and team to Cuba.

Tony's disappearance from a remote jungle and then the fax seemed fishy to Vincenzo. And who the hell was the tough guy that could break Bruno's finger, knock him out and get away with it? It had to be a mean mother—a Barracuda-mean motherfucker.

And how in the hell did Tony get out of that jungle unseen and be found in Cuba? Was that the work of one very clever and capable man, the Barracuda? He muttered, "I need to know who sent that fax."

Vincenzo had never met any of the Ortegas but certainly knew of the father and four sons. He was sure none were the Barracuda as they generated a fortune with their smuggling business, but Juan Ortega might know him. He decided to pay him a visit as soon as he finished his work in Cuba.

The next afternoon, Vincenzo was walking the streets of Havana. He knew the city was full of really beautiful young whores, but all his energy was focused in finding Tony and friends. He was a man with a mission. That afternoon, he sat in the hummingbird joint looking at not-so-first-rate whores, but the garden variety found in the poorer outskirts of town. He went upstairs to wait for Blindman to come back from his daily food shopping. When he returned, Vincenzo identified himself and told him they needed to talk.

"This man that came to you with the story about moving the cache; tell me everything you know. Describe him to me the best you can."

"As you can imagine I cannot see, not even shades of light, so I didn't get a look at the man. All I can say is he is very forceful and has a tremendous inner strength. I think I am alive only because I am blind. Unfortunately, poor old Scars and his wife could see. I think they were killed because they saw his face. He was a quiet man, speaks Spanish and Italian perfectly. I think he is Cuban because he speaks the Cuban dialect."

"Any idea how big he is? Is he a black man, white man, or Oriental? Any clues along those lines?"

"No. Everyone is the same for me. I did touch his arm one time when I helped him carry the treasure. His skin was cool to the touch and very hard with muscle, the surface was tough, as if he spent a lot of time in the sun, and he probably is not a very young man to have such sun toughened skin."

"Who can I talk to at Scar's place that might recognize him?"

"Nobody now."

"Anybody around here see him?"

"Sure, Roseta, she works here, but she ran away when she found out he was a very bad hombre. She is a foolish girl, always full of rum and smokes marijuana all day when not pleasing customers. I'm sure she could not remember him."

Another fucking blind alley. Doesn't this guy leave anybody alive that has seen him? He then asked Blindman, "How about the car he used. Was it a rental?"

"Yes, but from a friend of mine, Federico, but he didn't see the man."

The next morning Vincenzo drove out to where the police said the murders of the Italians had taken place. He wanted to look around to see if maybe something might have been dropped to give him a clue as to who or how many there were. The police reasoned that it had to be at least three men by the way the bodies were spread out and the nature of the deaths. One man could not have killed six men by cutting throats, stabbing and crushing windpipes.

That was bullshit, thought Vincenzo as he was beginning to believe that the Barracuda must be someone to be very careful with. The warning had not gone unheeded. At the scene, he saw the red stains soaked in the dirt road where his friends had caught up with Tony or the Barracuda. Or was it the other way around? Then he noticed something else. Drops, sizable drops of blood going off in a direction in front of where the rental car was found. So the man must have been wounded and crawled off to another car.

He went back to the police station and asked the man in charge if there had been a check with the local doctors to see if a wounded man had been there, possibly with a gunshot wound, since the police found a gun that had been fired four times. They had not checked. Vincenzo pulled five hundred dollars out and pushed them into the police chief's breast pocket and said, "Find out today. Call me at La Parador de Vista in Havana."

Later that night, he received the call from the police; there were no gun wounds or any other injuries inflicted by knives since the murders had happened; it was another blind alley.

That night Vincenzo got drunk, and just before he called to have a girl sent to his room, a thought came to him: he was trying to figure out how the Barracuda found out about the depository. That was one secret even more closely guarded than the Tribute flight. There were less than twenty men in the world who knew of the depository, and only a few of them knew where it was.

He instinctively knew Tony could not go against the family; he could not be responsible for the theft. "But Tony is missing... was he taped up like Vito and many others and tortured until he told the Barracuda everything he wanted?" he muttered.

SIDNEY X THE PIRATE

Then the fax from Cuba shows up a day or so after Tony's disappearance without his bodyguards? That doesn't make sense, he thought. *Everything seems to revolve around that friend of Ortega's... the man nobody knows... other than Jose Ortega...* Just coincidence? Maybe, but it was more of a possibility than any other leads he had, which was a grand total of none.

VENEZUELA

JANDY WALKED INTO JOSE'S OFFICE AT THE HACIENDA CARRYING A FAX for Jose. It was from Sicily and from a man Jose had met only once. While he had not known the man well, he knew a lot about him; he was one of the Mafia insiders. The fax was short but the message carried a very important subject matter.

It stated, "I understand we owe you an apology about our associates' actions on their recent visit. Please accept my apology for their actions and be assured that the Ortega family will never be subjected to that behavior from any of our people in the future. Unfortunately, neither Mr. Gugguci nor the men responsible for this offense will be able to respond to you personally. It appears that Tony Castero had conspired against the family and Mr. Gugguci and his men were killed. It will be generously appreciated if you advise me of any news you may have concerning Tony Castero."

Jose was delighted, curious, and astonished at Sidney's abilities. Jose had no idea what had happened to Sid, but it had happened two days after Sid went to Cuba. And that was two weeks ago. Since he had not heard from Sid, he thought one of the bodies must have been Sidney's.

Jandy showed the fax to Maria and both were horrified. Neither knew that Sidney's destination, when he left them, was Cuba, nor did they know that the fax from Cuba had been a ploy, and they had not been told what Sidney had said to Jose.

"Do you think this had anything to do with Sid?" Maria asked Jose.

"Why would it?"

"I don't know but he sure as hell didn't like those men."

"You think one man could successfully attack and kill those professional thugs?"

"Sid might; he's a tough one. Why was he in such a hurry to leave after those guys took off?"

"He didn't say. Maybe he was in a hurry to get the money to buy the land."

Jandy said, "Let's load up and go to the village to see if he's there."

Jose didn't want to spoil their fun, so he agreed. However, Jose was sure that Sidney was either dead or in jail. A single man just doesn't go up against six hard men like the team sent to Cuba. Those men had been killing folks since they were kids. Then he had second thoughts when he remembered some of the things Sidney had done and reconsidered; maybe it was an even match. The one thing he knew for sure was that six men were dead and he was off of the hook as far as explaining anything about Tony. Sidney had succeeded, making good on his word.

The trip to Sidney's boat was a jovial event with drinks being poured and lots of laughter. But inside each of them was the fear that they had seen the last of their strange friend. After all, he had plenty of time to get back with the money unless he couldn't borrow that much.

When they arrived at the boat anchored in the lagoon, everyone called out to him but there was no response. Jose went aboard to check if Sid might be there and be sleeping or dead. There was no sign of Sid having been there. Then he lightly began looking around for a good hiding place for the three million dollars that supposedly now belonged to him. After a few minutes, he took the challenge of finding the money and called the girls to come aboard.

He explained that Sidney had purchased the cliff property before he left and there was three million in earnest money on the boat somewhere, and they were going to find it. Maria went to work using her special skills. Jandy started working from the stern forward and Jose started at the v-berth. Every compartment, forty-four of them, was opened and searched.

Two hours later, there was not a nook or cranny that had not been looked at, prodded or felt. Maria had the feeling the money was enclosed in a tight area and had concentrated her efforts looking in the bilge from bow to stern. She had even found a screwdriver and removed the cover plates on the water and fuel tanks. Jose ran his arm down and around each of the tanks feeling for a bundle of cash. Nothing was found. The only place they had not actually looked or felt was inside the mast. But tapping the metal end of the screwdriver on the side told them it was consistently empty. In desperation, Jose held up his hands as a sign of surrender and told the girls they might as well leave.

Jose was surprised that there wasn't money on the boat because he never figured Sidney as a bullshitter. Then he thought of the possibility of the villagers stealing the money. He knew they would not consider taking anything from someone else, especially Sidney. They really seemed to like him, but he decided to ask the head man anyway.

The head man was visibly insulted at being asked such a question about the honesty of his people. After pissing off the man, Jose apologized and gave him a hundred dollars to fund the next pig cook-out. He then told him to be sure to tell Sidney to come see him when he returned.

When they returned to the hacienda there was an uninvited guest sitting at poolside. They were told of his arrival by the main gate guard.

As they walked in, the Italian stood up with a warm, friendly and apologetic look and said, "Mr. Ortega, please excuse me for dropping in on you like this, but it is important. I have been told that you are a good friend to my family in Sicily. My name is Vincenzo Jones; please feel free to call one of your friends to validate my standing with Sicily."

Vincenzo had no intention to give any warning to a guy who could easily dispatch six trained men plus elude capture for years as a pirate. When it came time to face that man it would be on his own terms.

"That will not be necessary," said, Maria, "I have met you before, in New York City, two years ago. You are Vincenzo the Sicilian, right?"

He agreed and that was good enough for Jose Ortega, so he asked, "Well, Vincenzo, what can I do for you?"

"As you know, we are still looking for our wayward friend, Tony Castero. I know Sicily sent you an apology for Don Gugguci's men being rude and I assure you that will never happen again. Did you know that the old Sicilian and his men were killed by Tony in Cuba?"

"Yes, that was included in the fax from Sicily."

"Well, that old man was like a father to me. I cannot believe he is dead at the hands of Tony; they, too, were friends. Since I know both men so well, Sicily wants me to find Tony. I don't want to bother you, but if you could take a few minutes to tell me everything that happened here, it might help me find Tony."

Fat chance, thought Ortega. He told Vincenzo the same story as he had before to the others. Both girls sat there listening and added a point or two, just to be included in the conversation.

They told of the hunt for their friend who had been camping and the story about how comfortable the man was in the jungle, and that he often camped out.

"He sounds like an interesting person. I wonder if I might be able to talk to him?"

"Not now. He's away."

"Oh, that's too bad. How long has he been away?"

"I don't know for sure. He owns land out in the jungle and spends a lot of time there, but he hasn't returned as far as I know." Ortega didn't know why he didn't tell the man about Sidney's boat, but he didn't feel like getting involved any further with this business between Sid and the mob.

Vincenzo asked several innocent questions about their friend. Enough answers came back to give him a pretty good description of the mystery man. Several things matched—he was a sailor, his skin showed the signs of extended exposure to the sun, he was a powerful man and didn't have much to say. He was gone a lot and had been away for about the same time frame as the Cuban raid. Vincenzo was very careful not to push the questioning and switched back to Tony when he had enough to assume he might be on the right trail at last.

The meeting was interrupted by the sound of an incoming helicopter. "That must be my ride," said Vincenzo as he got up to leave. Again he apologized for the intrusion and left.

The three of them looked at one another trying to see if anyone had any idea what was going on. They had only questions.

Time passed and still there was no sign of Sidney. Jose began to seriously believe that one of the dead men found in Cuba had been Sid. Otherwise he would have at least come back for his boat. Maria seemed to be distressed about his disappearance more than she should. They knew she was fond of Sidney, but she was acting in a way that said something more.

Finally, Jandy talked to her about it over several glasses of wine one night. Maria was happy to have Jandy to tell about what was bothering her. The loss of Sidney was one thing, but she had seen men she loved die before. She didn't know exactly what he did for his existence, but by his actions and demeanor she knew he was hardly a saint. The thing that bothered her so much was the thought of the little boy out in a jungle all by himself. She would think about the boy waiting for his father to show up to rescue him, but now that would not happen. And she didn't know what to do about it. She had promised not to say anything about the boy, but if Sidney were dead the promise wouldn't matter. Jandy agreed the promise was no longer valid when it is between the living and the dead. They decided to talk to Jose about it the next day.

Jose was called away the next morning to visit his family in Columbia. His wife had called and told him one of children had gotten a severe case of break-bone fever. Jose left before Jandy or Maria had a chance to tell him about Sidney's boy.

When Jose returned, almost two weeks later, he was told the complete story. By then the girls had worked themselves into a frenzy over the little boy. Maria figured that Sidney must have left the boy on the coast between the village and Panama, a stretch around six hundred miles long. She studied maps taken from the atlas and what she could get on the Internet through her computer. There were no detailed maps, but they were good enough to tell her there was a lot of wilderness there and very few, if any, roads.

She convinced Jose to search the coastline by helicopter. She knew he would not refuse so she was packed and was ready to depart. Packed with the essentials; two picnic baskets packed with goodies made by the chef, iced down rum and beer, and binoculars for the three of them to use. They would have to stop to refuel and could surely find a place to stay at night.

Jose went along with her plan for a couple of reasons. He never passed up a chance to go on an adventure, especially when there was plenty of iced rum and the girls were going, too. They were a lot of fun to be with and occasionally Jandy would get drunk enough to let him screw her. She liked Jose and he was attractive and not a bad lay, but normally she had nothing to do with him because of her job situation and his wife. She believed in the old adage, "Never shit where you eat—unless you're hungry"—that word could be replaced with horny.

The second reason he was willing to go on the search was his curiosity about the boy. He was fascinated that a seven-year-old boy had been left to survive in a wild jungle without adult supervision, companionship, tools or weapons. He now understood how Sidney had been at home in the bush and was able to survive so easily in the wild. If the boy was still alive, Jose had a lot of questions to ask about his father. Jose gave one chance out of one hundred that the boy could still be among the living.

They would end up spending a week covering the shoreline looking for a small boy by himself or even signs of life. They saw people in areas near civilization, but nothing in the remote areas. For the most part, they traveled at fifty knots over ground speed to give them time to look into the trees. All they saw was a lot of pretty scenery and dense jungle.

By the time they reached Punta Gallinas, Jose was ready to quit. He convinced Maria that it was pointless to continue searching to the west. They would return slowly and look more carefully in some of the areas on the way back.

The pilot, however, became concerned with a heating problem with the helicopter and had to land at the town of Maracaibo to send for a new recirculation pump. The week waiting was agonizing for Maria, but Jandy and Jose had already accepted the very real possibility that the boy was jaguar fecal matter by then. By the time they arrived back at the hacienda, Maria shared their belief.

Later, Maria's depression was interrupted abruptly one afternoon with the arrival of the same helicopter that the men from Italy had used on their visit to the hacienda. That time there were only two men besides the same pilot. One was a big American the other an Oriental. The Oriental appeared expressionless, but the American was very visibly angry. Their visit to the hacienda caught everyone by surprise. Even Jose didn't know them.

The combination of the unannounced arrival of the strangers and the nasty attitude of one of them was enough to cause Jose to react with equal hostility. His order to leave his compound was flatly refused by the strangers. They not only refused to leave, but the American pulled his pistol out and stuck it under Jose's chin before any of his guards could react to protect him. He then ordered Jose to go inside where they could have a little chat.

Inside Jose's house, the Chinaman told the American to remove his weapon and apologize to Jose. After a somewhat sincere apology from the American, the Chinaman took control of the meeting.

He said, "My name is Chong. My angry friend is Paul. We have been sent here to get some information about some of your friends. The reason we barged in on you unannounced was that it was necessary due to circumstances. We believe you have had a long-standing relationship with the people we are looking for. We also know you are aware of the nature of their business. The missing men's business partners have hired us to find them. The partners have given us the assignment with a promise of lots of pain if we don't succeed. They also gave us sixty days to come up with something, so we simply do not have time to show the proper respect. Once again, please accept my apology for the visit and Paul's lack of restraint."

The explanation made Jose feel better about the rude intrusion and could even understand the strangers' position. They had their backs against a rock wall and the guns of the Mafia were pointing directly at them. He asked how he could possibly help them.

The American and the Chinaman had prearranged to act out their parts. The bigger American was acting the part of a hostile personality, sort of a loose cannon. The Chinaman was more intellectual and had it together. He was the one to do the talking as long as the conversation went their way. When or if it faltered then the American would offer re-inforcement with threatening gestures. Actually, either man could play both parts equally well.

Their performance was quite good. Jose knew the men were in a po-sition where they had nothing to lose and they had to be good at what they were doing because the Mafia bosses had hired outsiders. That single point proved just how good they had to be. If the mob used outsiders instead of the abundant pool of talent they had, then these men had to be reckoned with. Jose knew he was in a dangerous position if he tried to be cute or withhold information.

They were trying to get a lead on Tony Castero, and his trail ended in the woods around Jose's compound. Jose agreed and went on to explain that they received information that Tony was seen in Cuba with a couple of other men. When that news came in, the six men from Italy took off to Cuba. That was the last he had heard from any of them.

Jose asked Chong, "What exactly happened to the other men?"

Chong replied, "I don't know, but apparently Tony found them first. They were all killed in a fight."

Jose asked, "Were there any other people killed?"

"We have not been able to find out yet. There was some blood leading away from the scene, but no bodies. The only other thing left at the crime scene was a rusted old bumper off of an old Chevrolet."

"How many men does Tony have with him?"

"We're not sure, but know he had at least one. A different Italian was there to set it up to take something away from the boys from Sicily."

"What was that?"

"I don't know but it must have been important; it sure pissed off the wrong people. In fact they were so angry both Paul and I woke up one morning with guns in our faces. They thought we had been involved."

"What would make them think you two were involved?"

"Because we were working for Tony. He had hired us to find some people that had been fucking with them. Tony was the man put in charge to find and punish these people. Now it looks like Tony was the ringleader all along, and we were part of the deal. Fortunately, both of us had very reliable alibis or someone else would be having this conversation with you."

Jose had a thought: *Sid had planned this thing because the mob had something he wanted. Apparently he had been successful.* He told the two visitors, "Well, ask any questions you want. I will be happy to assist you any way I can. I can appreciate the quandary you are in."

Paul finally said something in a civil voice, "Just tell us everything you saw and heard when Tony was here."

Jose told him the whole story and everything he could remember including the search for Sid. Sid was explained off as a friend that was a recluse and liked to live in the woods by himself. The investigators saw no value in pursuing more information about some wacko in the woods, when their time was getting perilously short. They thanked Jose for his good manners after the rude treatment and asked if he minded if they talk to some of the other people in the compound just to see if they might have overheard something that didn't seem to be of any importance, but might tie in with another small bit of information they had heard before.

Jose said, "Gentlemen, you have the run of the compound and please feel free to ask anyone anything you wish. After all, I want only the best of feelings between the Italians and my family."

Paul's attitude changed for the best. In questioning the staff, he was now a warm, smiling man with seemingly only concern as a motivation in finding an old friend. Chong was the same and they talked to most of the guards and house staff about conversations they might have had with Tony or his men or even might have overheard. They kept coming up with nothing useful. But they did keep coming up with a name of the only outsider present at the time. Sidney was the reason Tony was in the wilderness to start with. His name was there as the only one they felt could find him if Tony had been lost. His name was there when it was explained that Tony, more than likely, was the victim of a big jungle cat. And his name was there, with Tony's, as having not been seen since Tony's disappearance. Also Sidney's description fit the man in Cuba who was working for Tony to move something important. The man's description matched what the blind man could give them and the whorehouse madam's worthless description. That man had also rented a Chevy that had not been returned.

By design, the last two people they talked to were Jandy and Maria. Paul took Jandy, and Chong had Maria at the same time. That would eliminate any possibility of story collaboration between the two. Both men's natural instinct told them they were on a trail that would give them some answers. The Sidney connection was definitely suspect. They had learned years ago to pay attention to the little things that may not be terribly important by themselves, but like the aroma of something cooking, you cannot ignore it.

Jandy told the same, basically true, story as Jose had and that was about all she knew. She was not aware that Sidney had Jose's man send the fax that led the other men away. She was not aware that Sid had anything to do with Tony or the mob. All she knew was that Sidney was a very capable man and relayed that to Paul. She also expressed concern about his whereabouts since he had been gone for so long, leaving his boat in the little village, unattended. She also told them about looking for his little boy. He was supposed to be in some kind of survival training program and might even be alone.

Paul asked when the last time she had seen him was. She replied that he boarded Jose's helicopter to go into town for something and that had been weeks ago. About the only thing she didn't mention was Sidney borrowing the sky diving equipment. She didn't know what it was used for but it had something to do with her boss, so that information was out of bounds.

Chong went through the same routine with Maria. The only notable exceptions were that her story was more emotional. She had deeper fears about Sidney being dead. She was also very concerned about the boy. Those two subjects seemed to occupy most of her thoughts when on the subject of Sidney. The only other difference was that Chong found out that the last time Sidney was seen was when he boarded Jose's helicopter no more than thirty minutes after the Italians got word to go to Cuba.

Both Chong and Paul felt sure that Sidney had arranged to get Tony out of the jungle somehow, and he then flew to meet Tony in Cuba and make the set-up.

The intruders stayed there re-asking questions to Jose's pilot and the house staff for several hours. They were, without being obvious, getting a perfect description of the man named Sidney. When they were satisfied they had all they were going to get, they boarded their helicopter and disappeared as abruptly as they had appeared.

Jose went to talk to his pilot. "Did you tell them what I told you?"

"Yes, of course. I said I dropped him off at the airport and returned to the compound." He did not mention that they had met up with the jet pilot for a fast trip to Cuba.

As the helicopter left, Jose turned to the girls and said, "That fucking Sid pulled something off. It has the Mafia jumping up and down with anger; they are even hiring outsiders. Maybe that's why we haven't heard anything from him."

Jandy and Maria's faces went white at his words. They assumed they had known everything and that even Jose had written Sidney off as dead. Jandy took another look at the disappearing helicopter. It made a hard turn back to the left, heading for the village and Sidney's boat.

The villagers all came out to see the noisy machine settling down on the sandy beach. The wash from its rotors was blowing sand everywhere; it even ripped the tin roof off of one of the nearby huts. The two men emerged from the chopper as the sound of the helicopters engine was being turned off. They planned to be around for a while.

The head man of the village approached the men as they exited the chopper. He was visibly upset that they would come there and blow sand over everything and rip roofs off. If they needed to land they could have done so farther down on the beach where it was all open. Without exchanging the usual pleasantries the villagers would extend to any visitors, the head man said, "Look what you have done. What is the matter with you?"

Chong responded with a sincere apology by saying, "I am terribly sorry sir, but our helicopter lost all of its hydraulic pressure and we had to land here or crash. We certainly are more respectful of your village than to land here and do the damage we have done. Please accept this as a token of our sorrow at the mess we have caused."

He handed the man a thick wad of bills totaling over four hundred dollars. That was exactly what the village elder needed to show his authority to his community. The man apologized and more than paid for the mess stirred up by the whirling rotors. Also it appeared that the landing could not be helped anyway.

With everything in order, Chong told the man they were on their way to the village to see his old friend, Sidney. He pointed to the sailboat anchored in the lagoon as he spoke. Chong was smiling and very friendly, so the man had no reason to suspect anything other than the truth. The village leader told Chong that Sidney had not been on the boat in a long time. Some friends of his come by once in a while to see him, but he has not been there. When Chong inquired who these friends were the village man told them it was Maria, Jandy and Don Jose.

Chong said that he had been friends with Sidney for years and was told he might be back in the next day or two. So they would wait to see if he did return; which, as it turned out, was a good idea anyway, as it might take a few days to get the helicopter fixed. The villager agreed that things have a way of working out and if they needed anything to let him know. He pointed out the little bar and the house of Señora Bolanos. The señora made food to sell if they were hungry.

Paul had the pilot act like he was working on the helicopter while he and Chong went to search Sidney's boat. They were looking for anything that might tell them where he was, or going, or had been, or what his plans were, or anything else that might give them a clue as to who Sidney was.

They were much more thorough than Jose and the girls had been. They were methodical, and looked at everything they picked up, examined it for the smallest hint of something that might give them a clue. Some of the things they found that Jose missed were a phony battery that could be used to hide contraband and a small hand-held GPS inside of the navigation station.

Paul turned it on and let it warm up before manipulating the controls. Those controls did several things; it gave the present time and position, speed and distance traveled, and it stored in its memory one hundred way-points. Way-points were fixes in latitude and longitude set up by the navigator when he wanted to go to a certain point, anywhere in the world.

Paul clicked one way-point off after another. The coordinates of each were noted on a piece of paper. After pushing the select button four times there were no more way-points. Paul felt sure he had found pay dirt. Sidney may or may not be there, but he had been at each of those locations or they would not be in his GPS.

When he told Chong of his discovery, both were eager to leave in order to see what they would find at the way-points. They also knew their approach would have to be a careful landing as there was a good chance that their old boss, Tony the Pop, would be there as well. If so, they would be dead men unless they were in total control of the situation or be ready to die. It appeared to them that Tony was playing a no-quarter asked or given game

They restrained their departure for a while to give credence to their crash-landing story. Besides, they needed to get a chart out of the chopper to see exactly where the coordinates were. Also, they had been busting their asses for over a month, non-stop. It wouldn't hurt to take an afternoon off, maybe even do a little fishing. Paul had noted a couple of fishing rods on the boat's back deck and the rubber dinghy hanging on davits, and it was a pretty day, a day made for some relaxed fishing in the picturesque little lagoon. Chong was all for it, after they checked the charts.

The only chart covering the area in the helicopter was a large scale chart of the Caribbean Sea. The latitude and longitude would show them generally where to go but a much smaller-scale chart would be required to pinpoint the exact location. The first way-point was on the island of St. Croix. The second was a point out in the middle of the Atlantic a couple of hundred miles east of Antigua. That made them think that something was screwy; why would anyone want to put a way-point out in the middle of nowhere. The third appeared to be about where they were and the last was on the coast a couple hundred miles away. They decided to discuss it over fishing poles and went fishing.

The dinghy was lowered into the water while Chong talked to the children playing nearby about getting some bait to fish with. In no time, one of the kids produced several small dead fish the men used as bait.

They rowed the dinghy to the far side of the lagoon to cast up under some big overhanging tree limbs. Both men heard the warnings from the children about the fierce crocodiles in the lagoon and felt a little insecure about the aged rubber of the dinghy being between them and the slashing jaws of the crocs. But the danger was not enough to deter the men who had a longing for a restful afternoon of fishing.

During the afternoon, both men had a few small fish hooked, but nothing they considered keeping. Their reason for fishing was not for eating or killing fish, it was a diversion; a change of pace and a time to enjoy themselves. Paul had latched onto a bottle of Sidney's rum and the men occasionally took a pull from it. As the rum hit bottom and the sun warmed their frayed nerves and sore muscles, they relaxed and really began to enjoy themselves. Chong even laughed a couple of times, something that was totally out of character for him.

Chong's thrilling moment came when he hooked something really big. There was no way to control whatever had the other end of his fishing line. Paul tightened the drag so it would stop reeling line out. Paul had done a fair amount of fishing and feared it was a big snook that would swim into the nearby roots of the mangrove trees, and wrap the line in the roots and break the line, letting the fish escape. That was a common trait with snooks and was one of the reasons why they were so difficult to catch.

Paul assisted Chong by rowing to catch up with the fish so there would be less pressure on the fishing line. That way Chong could reel in, shortening the scope of line between him and the fish. It was a race; the fish was headed straight for shore, its eyes focused on a tree root he could use to break the restrictive force that was pulling hard against its mouth. The other participants of the race was one human who rowed as hard as he could, trying to keep up with the forceful thrust of the fish. The other, which weighed over five times as much as the fish, was doing all he could to hold the rod's tip up to keep as much spring between the fish and the dead stop of the reel. It was a battle that would last for almost ten minutes and its conclusion would be a fish tale that neither man would have ever expected.

The fish fought valiantly. Both men were soaked with sweat and swore at the fish constantly. Finally the big fish reached its point of endurance. It accepted its fate, gave up the battle, and rose to the surface on its side. The big gills of the fish were opening and closing slowly trying to get more oxygen into its system for maybe one more run at the thing that prevented it from freedom.

The two men stood up marveling at the monster fish they had beaten. It was a big snook almost three feet long and weighing an estimated thirty pounds. This was truly a trophy fish and Chong had every intention to do just that to the magnificent creature.

Chong reached over to pick up the fish as you would pick up a bass or a trout, or most other fish, but never a snook. He put his fingers under his gills to lift his head out of the water. The fish gave a sudden shake of his head and Chong quickly released him with a yelp. He pulled back several bloody fingers, as the gills were razor sharp.

While upset at the cuts on his hands, Chong was not deterred from bringing in the fish. His next attempt was to grab the other end of the fish and muscle him up that way. Once again, the fish began shaking its head and body violently as Chong pulled its tail up and over the round curve of the inflatable's side. The gills once again found something to cut that caused its release. The sharp gills cut the fabric of the inflatable in several places, letting the air that supported their only protection from the hungry crocs escape.

In a panic, the fish and the pole were dropped and both men got to the other side of the dinghy to try to keep it from going under water—a move that proved effective. They found themselves sitting on the other tube looking at each other, and they started laughing at the idiocy of the situation. After they settled down and were sure the dinghy was not going to dump them into the water, they began to survey the damage. Their survey quickly ended with a big surprise. The inside of the cut tube was full of United States one hundred-dollar bills and there were a lot of them.

Paul managed to row the dinghy back to the sailboat while Chong did what he could to hold the deflated side out of the water. Both were pleased to have made it back without interference from the local crocodiles. The dinghy was put back into the davits and lifted out of the water so they could retrieve the money.

Later, after counting out three million dollars, they had no idea what to think of the mysterious Sidney. Who would go off and leave that much money in an unattended boat for such a long time? Neither of the men had much nautical experience, but even they knew that dinghies had always been a favorite thing to steal, worldwide.

Paul told Chong it was time to check out the locations indicated on the GPS. They left the boat and told the helicopter pilot that he just fixed the chopper. The men waved a friendly goodbye to the village people as the rotors once again began blowing sand and tin roofs off as it rose up from the sandy beach.

There was not enough fuel on board to check out the one location to the west of them without first going to Caracas. By the time they could do that it would be dark, so they opted to take the evening jet to San Juan then take an island seaplane to St. Croix.

On the plane they studied several charts they had purchased. The coordinates for the north Venezuelan coast looked to be an uninhabited area. The other was definitely out in open water and it was several miles deep—much too deep to represent a good fishing hole. The last was the entrance buoy off the north coast of St. Croix.

The plan had been made for them to arrive by seaplane in the town of Christiansted. They would not be working together as added security for each other. Tony the Pop would certainly have his men on the lookout for the pair of them. They would independently investigate the area in the harbor where the entrance buoy led. Communications with each other would be by hand-held VHF radios set on an unused frequency.

The time spent in the airliner had been well used to develop the best plan possible for their next step. With the plan all set, for the time being, Paul said "I'm going to catch a few winks," and turned to face the window with a pillow behind his neck.

Chong was still interested in looking over the coordinates and was shuffling one chart, then another, looking at different aspects of each. Slowly he developed a smile that turned into a big grin. He shook Paul by the shoulder, disturbing his attempt to nap.

Chong said, "Paul, look at this," and pointed to the coordinate marked in the mid-Atlantic. He had drawn a line from Antigua to Sicily on a large chart and the latitude and longitude landed right on the line. Paul was not impressed, and tried to roll back to face the window.

Chong stopped him with, "Remember the jet the mob had that crashed after running out of fuel. Well, it was coming from Antigua and was supposed to land in Sicily, but it kept flying directly over Sicily until it crashed. That was one of the things Tony was so upset about. Apparently, it was carrying some big cash and someone might have dropped it over the ocean where a boat was waiting."

Paul said, "Then someone was a dumb-shit. The report was that everyone aboard the aircraft was dead as it flew over Sicily. A military plane sent up to investigate it said the rear door was open at thirty-something thousand feet. There's no breathable air at that altitude."

"Maybe a skydiver bailed out with the goodies. And, I would bet my share of the three million bucks, they were picked up right here where these latitude and longitude lines cross."

Paul believed that Chong might be right. Then he asked, "Could that three mill we found be the mob's cash?... Maybe Sidney is the man we've been looking for all along?"

Paul offered, "Or maybe it is his share. We need to find out how much was taken. With that information we can divide it by three mill and that'll give us a head count for the gang. Then we need to look into who on board parachutes."

Chong added, "A highly skilled parachutist. Doing a nose dive at that altitude would take a lot of experience."

Both men were thinking that if that was the case, they could be up against a pretty tough adversary. They had handled tough men before, however, and knew how to be prepared for that toughness.

"That guy, Sidney, may not work for Tony; Tony may work for him. I don't think Tony is the type of guy that would jump out of an airplane," Paul said.

"Another possibility is Tony is not part of the picture, Paul. He had acted very sincere in his desire to catch the people that were hitting on them. If Sidney was responsible for the mob's grief he probably wouldn't need Tony."

Chong was quiet for a moment while in thought, and then he said, "Then again, Tony was no push-over; he was a tough guy himself. Maybe he was working with Sidney until Tony had no further need for him. Maybe that was why Sidney didn't go back to pick up his three million bucks—Tony the Pop had popped him."

Both men were awake with anticipation. There was a fresh challenge that both men were eager to overcome. They had started by looking for an organized group that was targeting the mob. That had turned into the suspicion that it was all being done from inside the mob.

Chong said, "You can't jump out of an airplane and pick yourself up by boat, too. Tony was not what would be considered an outdoors kind of guy, and they had never heard of Tony showing any interest in boating. It would take a knowledgeable sailor to find that tiny X shown on the chart out in the Atlantic Ocean, so it's extremely doubtful that it had been Tony in the pick-up boat by himself. And there is absolutely no doubt that it wasn't Tony who bailed out of a high-speed airplane at thirty thousand feet."

"That means there had to be at least a minimum of three men, if Tony was part of the action." However many men were involved, the investigators felt they were closing in on them. They had the scent, and it was of a vicious and cunning adversary. It would be extremely important to be sure this adversary didn't turn the tables on them by picking up their scent. That could be deadly.

CUBA

IT HAD BEEN WEEKS SINCE SIDNEY WAS SHOT AND HE WAS BEGINNING TO feel better. He had not left the cave other than to do a little foraging at night for plants to eat and gather some dead sticks for firewood. The cave supplied an abundant supply of meat, but his wounds had been serious enough to keep him on his back most of the time. He was eager to get going again; however, each time he would move around for any time at all, like when he foraged, his body would remind him how weak he was and send him back to his backseat bed. He had managed to unload the treasure in the back of the old Chevy station wagon and use the backseat for a bed. It proved to be comfortable and the station wagon kept the ever-seeping drops of water off him.

He spent a lot of time trying to figure out how to get his prize out of Cuba, safely. In his present state, he could not do it. That left him with two options; wait until he was better, or leave it and come back later to pick it up. He decided to wait until he fully recovered; he had nowhere else to go anyway. He had two months before he was due to pick up the boy.

One of the two months was spent mostly on his back. Then he made himself get up and start working on building up his strength and stamina. Within two weeks he had explored a good part of the old cave. He found the remains of the governor's family that his forefather had left there. That must have been horrible for a mother to watch her children slowly die of starvation, but it had contributed greatly to the Sidneys' fortune—and the cave's rat population.

THE DAY ARRIVED WHEN IT WAS TIME TO LEAVE OR MISS THE DEADLINE to pick up the boy. He had not bothered to see if the old station wagon would start or not. If it didn't then he would leave the treasure where it was and return with the boy to retrieve it. That night he turned the ignition key on, and after several seconds of the engine spinning over, the old battery gave its last bit of power and the engine started. A hole in the tangled vines and thick growth was made again to get the Chevy out. He replaced as much of it as he could to keep that place private. It had served the Sidneys well, twice.

It was about midnight before Sidney pulled into a small fishing village. Everything was quiet except for the barking of several dogs scattered around. The small harbor had an abundance of fishing boats. Rowboats were pulled up on the shore and the slightly larger sailboats were scattered around and on anchor. Sidney pulled up next to one of the rowboats. After pushing it into the water he began unloading the Chevy's cargo into the boat. The rowboat could not handle all of the weight and bulk of Sidney's prize, so three trips had to be made to the sailboat he selected.

When all was loaded aboard the sailboat, he made one last trip to shore. On shore, he walked around the village until he found a small store. He broke in and filled a bag with anything he could find to eat. He also took a newspaper. He wasn't interested in the news, but wanted to see the date; his ordeal in the cave had caused him to lose track of time. Outside, he knew every house had chickens that ran loose, but was afraid the squawking of a freshly caught chicken would wake up the neighborhood. There was plenty of fishing gear on the sailboat, so he would have to give up the idea of eating a land animal for another week or so.

His trip across the Caribbean Sea was uneventful. The only moment of concern was a few miles off the south coast of Cuba. A Cuban gunboat pulled up behind him out of nowhere. When they were one hundred feet directly behind him the ship's big searchlight was turned on. The bright light blinded him as the gunboat pulled up alongside to look him over. Sidney passed himself off as a Cuban fisherman and with his beard, he certainly looked the part. The Cubans were satisfied and wished him good luck, then moved off into the darkness.

He knew how much time he had to make the rendezvous with the boy. He was mildly concerned about if the kid had survived the last six months. Sidney really hoped he had; the kid had potential. He was intelligent and tough. Best of all was his ability to understand circumstances for what they were, and was willing to fight if unfavorable circumstances needed to be changed. In short, he was a gutsy kid.

As Sidney approached the area where he had dropped the boy off, he had to go slowly, scanning the shore carefully. He didn't have the modern-day GPS he had planned to use to find the exact spot so he had to feel his way in by opening all of his senses to be aware of the way things were when he was here before. He remembered the big tree on the edge of the jungle so that is what his eyes were looking for. However, the spot he was looking for could be anywhere in a fifty mile stretch of shoreline.

At night he had to sail offshore to avoid the reefs then back in to resume his search at daybreak. The trade winds were blowing at a steady fifteen knots which made anchoring in the rough seas impossible, especially with the make-shift anchor the little wooden sailboat had.

On the third day, Sidney saw the tree he had been looking for. He began sailing in a big circle offshore waiting for the boy to see him and come to the beach. By the end of the day, Sidney was convinced that the boy had not survived. The seas were still too rough for his anchor or try to beach the boat. He decided to sail in to within fifty yards of the shoreline and swim in. To do this, he tied the steering tiller so it would keep the boat turning to port. It would be a sloppy maneuver, but the only other choice he had was to leave, not knowing about the boy, or wait for the wind to die down. That time of the year, the trades could blow for a month or so with very little change. He made a practice run to see if the little boat would head up into the wind and come-about in a manner that would keep her sailing. He was not concerned for his safety even if he had to walk out of the jungle, but hated the thought of sinking the boat with the mega-prize aboard her.

It took three times around to position the tiller just right so she would be about fifty yards off when he swam back out to her. When he approached the beach the next time around, he dove and swam to shore without looking back. His commitment had been made so there was no sense in worrying. After he reached shore, however, he turned to see the boat working to get through the wind and the rolling seas. It made the turn clumsily, but it succeeded. Sid was developing a real fondness for the little boat.

As he walked around the boulders on the rocky shore and made his way into the jungle, he saw a sight that jolted him with reality. Leaning against a large bolder were two bamboo tubes that had been made to hold water. Both had once been covered with a large banana leaf that had turned brown to black then shriveled to nothing more than a crusty patch of veins. Those water tubes had to be several months old. The tree the boy had used had only a few marks on it. That could only mean something had happened to the boy.

Sidney went on into the jungle looking for signs of the boy's existence;

there were none. He scouted the likely looking areas where a body would be dragged and eaten by the cats, but there were no bones to be found. He realized that it would have been possible for the boy to have drowned in the sea or even been attacked by a shark as his father had been. He went back out to the shore and walked up current a quarter of a mile. Not finding a body or bones, he went down current about a mile. All along he kept an eye on the little sailboat doing its dangerous circles in the heavy seas. There were no signs of human existence anywhere. Sidney resigned himself to the apparent facts.

His thoughts now were about the next Sidney. He had not been impressed with the other choice in the Dominican Republic so he would have to start all over again. That meant finding some whores to get pregnant and raise the boy for six years, and then start the training process again.

"What a piece of bad luck," he uttered. "That boy would've made a good Sidney X."

As he came back to the circling boat, he saw it had lost ground, but it was still a safe distance offshore. It would be doubtful if the boat could have made two more revolutions without going ashore. His time on the beach was over; he dove in and intercepted it just as it slowed and approached the wind.

He untied the tiller and headed the boat offshore once again. It would be dark in a couple of hours and he would just keep going out. There was no sense in waiting around the area. He tied the tiller down to keep it running northerly so the big swells were on his beam and he slept.

During the early morning hours he woke up to the unpleasant thoughts of losing his boy and the need for a replacement. Just the thought of going through all of that again prompted him to take another look. Was that tree the one he had marked? Of course it was; it had the marks. What about the water jugs? He decided to turn around and take another look.

He shortened the sail so he was just making headway as he traveled along the shoreline. He looked intently, hoping to see some sign of life, but there was none. By nightfall he realized that he had been hoping against odds that the kid would be there. He turned out to sea for the night and before dawn had once again convinced himself to take another look.

The next morning he was moving eastward with shorted sail; looking for signs of human life. As darkness approached again, he resigned himself to face reality and turned back to sea for the last time. If the kid couldn't make it then it was better to find out now, before entrusting the family treasure to him. "Too bad, boy," he said aloud, wishing there was a bottle of rum aboard.

Three hours after dark that night the wind stopped blowing. There was not even a breeze. Sidney was a couple of miles offshore and bobbing in the ocean swells like a cork. It made sleeping difficult as the round-chimed boat rolled with every wave. Usually the wind in the sail would keep the boat somewhat stable, but now every time it rolled up on her starboard gunwale Sidney would roll down. Finally, he gave up trying to sleep and decided to fish instead.

As he was lowering the hand line overboard with a flashy piece of his shirt tied on as bait, he saw something that made him want to shout with happiness. There was the flickering of a fire on the shoreline. It could not be seen always as the boat was in and out of the wallows of waves. But he watched long enough to be sure there was a fire and it was not his imagination. That was a definite sign there was life on the beach, and in this remote part of the world the odds were very good that it was the boy. But there was nothing he could do to reach the fire. He would just have to wait and wallow until the wind returned.

The wind did slowly start its westerly direction again the next morning shortly after the sun came up. Sidney steered in the direction of the fire he had seen during the night. When he reached the shore, he found a charred area on top of a rock but no one was around. He went into the jungle calling the boy's name, but there was no answer.

He continued on sailing eastward towards the area he had not looked before. He continued in that direction until he happened to turn around to see smoke rising several miles behind him. Sidney turned to sail with the wind to his back while watching the smoke getting closer.

When he arrived at the fire, it was obvious that it was a signal fire. It had been built behind a rock to protect it from the wind, and green branches were piled on to make more smoke than fire. Again, he walked into the jungle, shouting, "Hey! Anybody here?"

There was no response, and he could not see any sign or footprints of anyone on shore. He rationalized that the fire must be a marker for a fisherman well offshore.

He swam out to his boat and pulled himself in. He stood and took one last look at the shore. He was surprised to see a dark head covered with sun-bleached hair pop up from behind a big rock. The next thing he saw was the dark head had an enormous smile on it. It was his son.

Sidney felt so happy he had tears in his eyes. He yelled, "Sidney, get your ass out here!" Of course, he would never be able to show the emotion he was feeling at that moment, but he damn sure felt it and he was glad. He was also glad he was far enough away so the kid couldn't see the wetness around his eyes.

Without hesitation, the naked kid came out to the surf and began swimming out to the little boat. One hand he kept out of the water; holding a furry monkey. The kid was a bundle of excitement and chatter as he arrived at the boat. He was very happy to see his father again, but would have been just as happy if it had been any other human. He had not seen another person in six months. Sidney grabbed hold of the boy's arm that was holding the monkey and pulled his naked body into the boat. The kid had outgrown his shorts and had adjusted completely to being naked.

Not knowing exactly what to say to the kid, he said, "Well, I see you made it and you brought us a monkey to eat for lunch."

With all of the emotion whelmed up in the boy—and the excitement of being found and the pride of surviving his ordeal and the fear of his father eating his friend proved to be more than the boy's system wanted to handle: he started crying.

Sidney felt bad for the boy, but he didn't know what to do. He certainly understood the feeling of standing before his father after surviving the traditional test into manhood. He had stood naked just like his son was doing and cried just like his son was doing and his father just stood there not knowing what to do just like he was doing. He knew the six months were hard on a man, and the pride one gets in himself for being able to make it was a tremendously powerful emotion. A feeling very few modern men would ever feel. He decided the best thing to do was leave the boy alone and he changed the sail's angle and turned the boat out to sea again.

Sidney XXIII asked, "Why didn't you come out when I was calling you two days ago, and again today?"

As the boy got control over himself he said, "I lost track of time when I got hurt from falling out of tree, and I moved into a coconut tree forest east of here. I got back here last night and lit a fire. Today I was asleep." And with a stern look he said, "You can't eat Fred; he's my friend."

Confused at the statement, Sidney asked, "What did you say?"

The boy said, "The monkey is not lunch. He is my friend and his name is Fred."

Sidney was sorry about Fred; he really wanted to eat something that didn't spend all of its time swimming. But he could wait a few more days. Soon he would be back in St. Croix, the land of cheap rum, trashy women, and a huge piece of steak off of an old tough island cow. Yummy.

After the chatter and excitement of telling his story of survival, the boy became silent. He was different from the little boy who had been dropped off six months ago. The kid now seemed to be happy with his own company. He was totally self-assured. His pal, Fred, clung to him as if he depended on the boy to protect him from the new and bigger monkey—as was the case. The endless chatter that had continually come from the boy was now a thing of the past. He was now full grown in many ways. From that point on, he would learn how to become mentally hard as his mind and body developed into physical manhood. He also would be treated like a man from that point forward.

The next part of his training was something that Sidney XXIII had been looking forward to. He remembered his excitement and wonderment when he went through it and knew his son would feel the same. In fact, he was looking forward to getting back into the cave himself. The next lesson would be to learn the family's history, and be shown everything about the family history—the logs, and of course, the Sidney X treasure.

To start the lesson, he told the boy to go into the cabin to see part of his reward for passing the test into the family. The boy, with Fred on his shoulder, went below and Sid heard a loud, "Wow, look at all of this stuff, Fred. Where did you get it, Dad?"

Sidney replied, "I took it away from some people in a raid just like I did when you picked me up in the middle of the ocean. You don't need to ask any more questions about it right now as I am going to explain everything to you when we get to St. Croix."

That was the end of that conversation. In the next few days, little Sid spent a lot of time below playing with the treasure and counting money. Sidney had tossed the suitcases and put everything in heavy-duty black garbage bags. The Mafia, preparing for the worst, had socked away only things that could be exchanged quickly. Besides more United States dollars than the pirate cared to count, there were boxes of gold bars; one box of platinum bars, which was the first Sidney had seen; boxes of diamonds and boxes of mixed gemstones. It was impossible to place a value on the treasure, but there were millions of dollars taking up space in the old boat.

They arrived in the little harbor of their marina at night. The Cuban fishing boat needed only three feet of water so he was able to get it very close to shore. Sidney wanted to be careful unloading the boat of its precious cargo. In the islands, anyone seen unloading bundles at night quickly drew attention to themselves, as there was a fair amount of drug smuggling going on. Unloading at the early morning hours was the only safe time he could move the treasure.

When the sun was off the horizon, Sidney saw Sally doing her morning routine and she gave him the normal response, and things were just as they were last time he had arrived unexpectedly. She eyed the little boat several times waiting for Sidney to offer an explanation about why it was there and not the Morgan, but, of course, he didn't have anything to say.

Sidney got shit-faced before noon and stumbled off to bed with instructions for the kid to go see his grandpa and be back at dark. Little Sid and Fred were stopped by Sally, who offered to make lunch for him. Little Sid never turned down food, and with Fred's help, he ate two cheeseburgers and a full pitcher of ice tea. Sally made a mental note to talk to the boy's father about letting the animal eat off of the kid's food. But then she thought it was probably his father who showed him how.

Sidney woke up at dusk and went back to the bar. He needed a cold beer to help wake him up and a couple of hot dogs to satisfy the growler in his belly. When his son showed up, Sidney bought a couple hot dogs for the boy and a banana for Fred, but they were too full to eat. In a half-drunk mood he thought, *what kind of monkey is it that won't eat a fucking banana*, but he said nothing.

After dark, both Sidneys went to the apartment. The boy was given two bags to carry and when he saw his dad carrying four bags, he picked up another bag. They would have to make two more runs to move all of the treasure.

They went to the mountain, and halfway up, the boy realized that he carried more than he wanted. He had tried to impress his father that he was a strong boy since he learned to live by himself. Halfway up, Sidney wanted to tell the struggling boy to leave one of the bags and come back for it, but decided that would only insult the kid, so he said nothing. The boy toughed it out and made the trip, but only after a lot of stops and heavy breathing. The boy looked confused when his father told him to drop his load next to a rock outcropping and led him back down to get another load. That time the boy carried one bag less.

After four trips, all of the bags were at the rock outcropping. On the last load, Sidney had brought up a new bottle of rum for the occasion. He thought it was too bad his father could not be there, but that was impossible.

Sidney looked at his son and said, "Sidney XXIV, tonight you learn about your family and will be entrusted with our family's secret. It is a thing that no one has ever known about us in over five hundred and forty years. It must be kept a secret for the rest of your life, as well as the son you will have to replace you when you get older. It was your grandpa's responsibility to protect this secret until I took over. Now you shall learn it and start preparing to assume the role of protector of the Sidney X treasure."

The kid remained quiet. He knew there was going to be something important explained to him after he survived the jungle and was happy that the time had arrived.

Sidney pointed to the rock he was standing next to and told the boy to roll it over. The boy, with a little difficulty, turned the one hundred and twenty-three pound rock over, revealing an old iron eye-bolt attached on the bottom and a narrow hole in the ground where it once sat.

"This is the entrance to the Cave of Snakes. All treasure caves must have a name that signifies a meaning for it. This is called the Snake because an enemy of our family, known as the Snake, is in it to protect our treasure forever. Nobody except the selected male members of our family has ever been in here, except for one other man, Snake, a long time ago, and his bones are still here. I'll show them to you and explain later."

The boy, looking down the narrow dark entrance asked, "How do you get in there?"

Sidney explained, "This shaft is the only way in there. You go straight down for fifty feet without it getting any larger."

He tied a line to the eyebolt with a bowline knot. Then he tied the rope to one of the bags of treasure and lowered it to the bottom.

"I'm going down to untie the rope, and then you are to tie the next bag on and lower it. After all the bags are down you're going to shimmy down on the rope."

The boy was not too keen on the idea of crawling down the narrow black hole in the ground, but his father did, and so would he. Shortly after his father disappeared, he saw an illumination below; his father had lit a lantern.

When he lowered himself he was surprised to see a cavern that had a ceiling about five feet high. Sid showed him several oil-soaked torches on the wall and gave him quick instructions how to make and maintain them. Also, he pointed out the oil lanterns and explained how they had been replaced with battery-powered lanterns. The replacement batteries were easier to replace than having to lug fuel up the mountain. He found one of the lanterns and switched it on. The light, much brighter than the burning oil torch, bathed the rock walls with the yellow glow. The boy thought how spooky it was down there, especially on the outer edges of the lighted area, as it quickly turned to blackness. And then there was the matter of a dead man's bones protecting the family treasure. Was that a ghost?

Sidney picked up two bags and took off down the cavern. The boy didn't need to be told; he was not going to be left in the dark. He quickly grabbed two bags and followed. He noticed that he had a much easier time walking through the cavern as his father had to stoop over to keep from banging his head on the hard rock ceiling.

The cavern angled down for a while, and then his father pointed to another branch that turned back up again at a steep angle that required steps. Sid explained that one of his grandfathers had chiseled the steps that led the way up. As the vertical climb dead-ended at a larger cavern, Sidney waited for the boy. He took another electric lamp off the floor and handed it to the boy and instructed him to turn the lamp on and go inside the bigger room.

The boy complied, cautiously, and was amazed at the size of the room and how it was cluttered with all kinds of stuff. There were big plastic bags strewn around as well as many wood and steel chests. There were also weapons lying around everywhere. He, like everyone on earth, had never seen anything like that before.

Sidney said, "Look around through the chests and bags. All of this belongs to you as much as it does to your grandfather and all of the sons of Sidney X. This is the Sidney X treasure. It has been collected for five hundred and forty years, and you are expected to protect it and add generously to it before passing it on to your son."

The boy was excited at the massive amount of riches laid out before him. All of the gold; the coins of gold and silver, jewelry and even a king's crown like one he had seen in a book. Plastic bags were stuffed with all kinds of money, but the thing that impressed him most were the weapons that were everywhere. He picked up one sword only to drop it and grab another.

His father had said this belonged to him, and little Sid wondered if that made him rich. It would be a while before the boy would be old enough to understand just how rich he really was. This introduction to the Cave of Snakes produced the same excitement and emotions that a normal boy would experience with his first trip to Disney World.

"Take your time. I have to make an entry in the family log about how I took this prize, and then we will go over the log."

The boy, with a big knife in his belt and sword in one hand and an old boarding axe, came over after Sidney had made his entry. Little Sid said he was ready for some fighting now as he jabbed the air with the big sword and sliced away at an imaginary foe with the axe. Sidney was impressed with how formidable the boy looked. He might be young, but he already had the hard body of a young man. His time in the jungle had improved him tremendously.

Sidney said, "Okay, you look like a dangerous pirate with all that stuff; now come over here and listen to how crafty and ferocious you are going to be."

Pointing to his entry on the log he said, "This is what happened in order for me to capture the prize we just brought in. Every time we raid and capture a prize, we must enter the account in this log. Only the truth can be entered. All of your ancestors have always diligently entered their accounts here. You will start reading those accounts tonight to learn what was expected from them… and the same things are expected from you. It is important that the log be maintained for the future Sidneys. This log is more of a treasure to us than all of the stuff in this room. It records the daringness and cunning necessary to be the true "King of the Sea," a title our family has had since we became pirates over five hundred years ago." He handed the heavy book to the boy.

"What's diligently, Dad? And are we really kings and pirates?"

"We are the best of the pirates, therefore, the 'Kings of the Seas.'"

Young Sid started turning pages, impressed with all of the entries, then settled on the last entry. After reading for several minutes he whistled and said, "You were shot with bullets three times?"

"Yes."

"You dug the bullets out yourself?"

"Yes."

Again the boy whistled. Sidney got up and started arranging some of the things in the room thinking he would have time to sort things out and maybe count the money. If he decided to move the treasure to his new cave, then he should know what would be required to get it there. He needed to do something about the money, but didn't know what would be best. In a way he liked it there, taking up space in the garbage bags, but it was going bad. Some of the older bills were practically falling apart. As he moved about, he heard the boy exclaim time and time again, "Wow," or give one of his whistles of astonishment.

The boy would read aloud when a particular story fascinated him like when he bailed out of the high-flying jet. He was truly amazed at his father's feats, and soon it was obvious that the boy had found the deep sense of family pride that was tantamount to be a Sidney X. The speed in which he read indicated again the kid was a quick learner, but there were a lot of the words that he didn't know. Most of the words would take him awhile to learn their meanings, since they were in different languages, but he, like his father, would learn those languages.

At one point, when reading about Sidney XII, where he decapitated a Chinese man during a sword fight, the boy asked, "What is a Chinese man?"

Sidney explained that they are from the Far East and showed him on a map where China was. He explained, "They are small people with eyes that are narrow, not round as yours are. If you fight one, be careful; being small, they are very quick. It is best that you kill him quickly before he can hurt you."

The boy said, "I saw a Chinese man today, Dad. He came over to talk to me while you were taking your nap."

Sidney, not very interested, asked, "What did he want?"

"Nothing, he just said that the boat looked like it needed a lot of work and asked me my name. He also asked if you were a fisherman and was I named after you."

Sidney didn't like nosy people and especially people that asked personal questions. "What did you tell him?"

"I said I didn't know if you made your living fishing. All I know is you travel a lot, and that I was named after you and my grandpa."

"Don't talk to those people and don't answer questions about us. Our life is very private and we will keep it that way."

The boy went back to his reading and whistling and Sidney went back to sorting. The boy started nodding after an hour, but he was trying valiantly to stay awake to read. He was so interested in the log, but it had been too long of a day for him. Sidney told him they would come back tomorrow and many more days so he will have plenty of time to learn everything about their family. He turned off the lamps in the cave and led the boy out.

The fresh night air was welcomed as they emerged from the tight hole in the earth. With everything back in place they returned to his apartment. Sidney said, "You go to sleep. I'm going into town to get laid."

The boy asked, "What is laid?"

"If you don't know, it wouldn't do you any good to know what laid is anyway." Actually the boy knew very well what laid was; it was his grandpa's favorite pastime. He just hoped for details.

Before heading to Fred's Place he stopped at the Deck Bar to get a cold beer. As he sat down, the bartender asked if the drunken tourist had found him earlier.

"What did a drunken tourist want with me?" Sidney asked.

The bartender said, "This guy came here from the states and fell in love with his new-found tropical paradise. He decided he wanted to buy a marina and he loved this one. He left here a couple of hours ago to find you and I haven't seen him since." "What did he look like?" asked Sidney.

"He's an Oriental; looks like he is in pretty good shape and about forty or so. You didn't see him, I take it?"

"Nope." The reply was casual, but the Chinese man had also talked to his son, and that sent a warning shot over his bow.

As he drove out of the marina on his quest to get laid, Sally saw him but could not get out in time to tell him about his visitor that afternoon. It could wait until tomorrow, or so the visitor had said. She hoped Sid would sell the place to the man. He seemed nice, and it would be refreshing to work for someone you were not afraid of all the time. Besides, her boss's mysterious comings and goings, and the special packages that she deposited in the wall safe, made her suspicious of her boss. She was not too optimistic about him selling it, however, since his family had owned the land forever. Sally knew the rules about talking to strangers about Sidney, but that had been different. The man was genuinely interested in the marina, and her. He absolutely guaranteed her the same position if he could buy the place. Sally was so caught up with the nice man's dream to own the quaint marina that she was not even aware of all of the information she had given him about her boss.

When the man asked if Sid liked sailing, Sally told him that he certainly did and he owned a forty-six foot Morgan, but had no idea if he had sold it since he came in on a smaller fishing scow. It wasn't unusual; he had owned a lot of sailboats.

Later, when asked, she had no idea where the old wooden sloop came from. It was new there, but maybe he kept it in some other place. She could not fathom why he would sail in on an old junker like that, especially with all of his money. She had not seen a boat like that one since she lived in Cuba, twenty three years ago.

When asked what line of work the owner was in, she sarcastically said, "When I first started, he indicated that he was an independent news correspondent, but he may be an investor," but suggested with a wink that may not be the case at all. "Whatever he does, he has plenty of money, but doesn't spend much. He apparently doesn't believe in banks as he never wrote checks. He gives me cash to pay the bills, and my salary."

"By the way," she added, "Would it be a problem to continue paying me in cash?"

"Of course not, no problem at all, Sally." Then Chong asked, "Does the owner enjoy working around the marina?"

She responded with a laugh. "He has never done a damn thing to this marina. He tells me to get it done. Whenever he's here all he does is drink at the bar. He's always popping in and out and stays gone for weeks, even months, at a time. He pops in, gets drunk, checks his mail, and disappears again."

The prospective buyer asked, "Oh, they deliver mail here?"

"Regular mail, no. There is no mail delivery on the island other than Federal Express and that is what he receives here."

Then the man said, "I guess he's too busy fishing or bar hopping with his friends to be interested in working around the place."

Before she could answer, he added, "Where is his wife or girlfriend?"

She snorted a mock laugh and said, "That man ain't got no friends. I have never seen him with anybody other than his old man, and they ain't friends either. His dad is another hard-case recluse that used to live here, but he lives on a mountain that he owns. Poor man, maybe I would be a recluse too if I had lost both of my feet like he did. I have never seen or heard of a wife, but I guess he had one somewhere 'cause my boss is a spitting image of him, but with more wrinkles. If he does have a wife she must be a strong lady to put up with that mean bastard. He scares me to death sometimes. If you get a chance to see my boss with his shirt off, look at all of the scars on him. God, it looks like he has been in terrible knife fights all of his life. He never smiles or laughs at anything. He never shows any kind of emotion."

"Sounds like he is going to be a hard man to bargain with. Wish I could get my friend Vincenzo to talk to him for me, but unfortunately he only speaks Italian."

"Oh, that will not be a problem. Sidney speaks Italian and several other languages perfectly. Is your friend Vincenzo here on island with you?"

"No, but it won't take long to get him here."

"Good," was her response then she realized how much favoritism she was showing to the prospective buyer. She apologized saying, "My goodness; I don't know what got into me to talk so much."

The prospective buyer reassured her that their conversation was just between the two of them; no one, even Vincenzo, would ever know they had the chat.

Sidney's trip into town to visit Fred's netted him a terrible headache the next morning, and a passing thought about whether something had been sexually transmitted to him last night. He had ended up with a well-worn hooker.

"Well," he muttered, "if she was carrying something it is too damn late to worry about it now." That feeling was not new to him as he had bedded some of the worst looking things to be found, and he never used a condom. The score to date was clap five, all the rest none.

Lila Mae held no grudges from their last encounter, Fred was still in the back room drunk, and Sam only gave Sidney a passing frown. So everything was as usual at Fred's—some things change, most things don't in the Caribbean.

By the time Sidney got back to his apartment, the boy had already left. He wrote out a scribbled note that he was going to see his grandfather. Sidney decided to join them after a brisk run to force the booze, his headache, and hopefully, last night's memories out of him.

When he arrived, his father was sitting on the porch listening to the boy tell about his last six months. Monkey Fred was, of course, there, watching the boy's every move. Grandpa was on his third beer judging by the empties under his wheelchair. The cold beer looked inviting, so Sidney nodded hello to his dad and went inside to get himself one.

His dad yelled, "Bring two."

Sidney didn't see Rosie around and thought, "Well, as usual, the old man ran another one off."

Back on the porch and when the kid stopped yapping long enough to take a deep breath between stories, Sidney asked, "Did the boy tell you that I took him to the Cave of Snakes?"

"No. When was this?" His father was very much interested; that carried sufficient meaning. It meant that the boy had met the requirements in Sidney XXIII eyes to become the new Sidney X, the protector of the treasure.

"Last night," replied XXIII.

Then he asked the boy, "Why didn't you tell him?"

The kid innocently responded, "You told me to never tell anyone."

The two older Sidneys were pleased. Now there could be openness between the three of them. It would make training easier and a lot of the stuff could be cut out now that the boy knew things were going to get a lot more serious. After reading the family log he would understand that killing was just a part of doing business in their world and should not be considered as an issue of right or wrong. No quarter given or asked was the only way a pirate can expect to survive.

B.R. EMRICK

Grandpa asked, "Did you read anything in the log?"

The boy's eyes lit up and said, "I was just starting to read some of your entries when I had to leave last night."

Before anything else was asked by the old man, the boy said, "Boy, Grandpa, you should read about dad's last entry. He took such a big prize. It took us four trips to get it all to the cave."

Interested, Grandpa asked the boy to tell him about it. The boy told the story in the same detail in which it was written. The older Sid once again was tremendously impressed with his son's abilities to pull off incredibly difficult raids. But that job, in particular, reflected pure genius by dealing with situations that developed during the raid.

He looked at his son and said, "So you found the Mafia's Caribbean bank. That makes me very happy and it sure as hell is going to cause those bastards to start killing a bunch of folks trying to find out who did it."

Sidney said, "Let 'um. They don't have a clue. Besides, I've been working the Caribbean pretty hard for the last five years; it is time to move into the Mediterranean for a few years. That's where the boy will train."

The oldest Sid asked, "You will be using the Cave of Spiders for your base?"

"Yes."

The youngest Sid asked, "Why is it called the Cave of Spiders?"

Grandpa explained, "Because you drop down a shaft and there are several tunnels that lead off from it. Only one is ours and the rest lead miles and miles to nowhere. It is a very good hiding place and only a mile from our boat house."

Sidney, looking at his empty beer, asked, "You will be going with us?"

The old man was pleased to be asked even if it was because his son didn't want to do all of the training. He answered, "Sure, I'll go, if you get me another beer." The old man then added as an afterthought, "I'm due for some European pussy anyway."

"By the way, I have dedicated a new cave, Sidney said to his father. "It is a totally secure area in a very isolated place. This island is getting too crowded. In fact, yesterday some American tourist came by and wants to buy us out. The next thing you know, developers are going to start racking the books trying to find a way to take our land due to some loophole in the law. We don't need that attention. With so many people moving to the island, it's only a matter of time before someone discovers our cave. I plan to move the treasure to the new cave when we come back from the Med. I'm taking the seaplane to St. Thomas tomorrow to buy the land from the family that has owned it for a couple hundred years."

"Makes sense," said the oldest Sid. "How would you move the treasure to your new cave?"

"Beats the shit out of me, I'm still working on it."

"You said you have already dedicated the cave?" asked his father.

"Yes, it is the Cave of Pigs. The bones of Tony the Pop Castero lie there. Tony was a top man of the Circle of Fifteen. He was squealing like a pig when he found it necessary to tell me what I needed to know about the Cuba stash.

"Sidney, my boy, when you piss off the Mafia, you really do it in a big way."

MIAMI

IN THE MULTI-CULTURED CITY OF MIAMI, VINCENZO WAS DOING HIS homework. He had been there for a week, chasing whores at night and spending most of the days in the University of Miami's library. He was rapidly becoming an expert in pirates. He had read Defoe's "A General History of the Most Notorious Pyrates" plus a dozen other books on the subject. It seemed like the man he was after was, without a doubt, a pirate. His methods were the same as they were hundreds of years ago. Brutality and swiftness were the bywords of the pirate trade. One thing he kept reading was if the victim gave up the "prize," as pirates called it, they were usually unharmed. Those that offered resistance met a harsh death that matched the degree of effort they had spent resisting the inevitable.

Another book, the "Sands Register of Lost Ships," listed all of the ships that had been destroyed or were missing since the sixteenth century. There were an unbelievable number of ships that were missing and presumed sunk. A side notation by each noted the cargo carried and the possibility of piracy due to the cargo. Sometimes there was even speculation which pirate~s~ it might have been.

There had been plenty of rogues of the seas, and most had met a fitting end, either with a cutlass in their gut or at the end of a rope provided by one government or another. Those terms were accepted by the pirates; they asked for and gave no quarter. They would be delighted to blow up the captured ship with the powder magazine, if they could take their victims with them. The governments delighted in catching the scoundrels and would bring the bodies of the more notorious pirates, embalmed in tar and hanging in chains from the ships' rigging as they entered harbor.

Vincenzo had scanned a list of names, some recognizable most not, of pirates who had been caught in the act of piracy and their just rewards:

1212 EUSTACE THE MONK AND CREW, BEHEADED.

1572 KLEIN HENZLEIN AND CREW, BEHEADED.

1670 BLACKBEARD, KILLED IN FIGHT.

1695 ADMIRAL TEW, KILLED IN FIGHT.

170I CAPTAIN KIDD AND CREW, HANGED.

1718 MAJOR BONNET AND CREW, HANGED.

1722 BLACK BART AND CREW, HANGED.

1722 SIDNEY X, A SINGLE HANDED PIRATE, KILLED IN FIGHT.

1726 CAPTAIN BELLAMY AND CREW, HANGED.

1726 WILLIAM FLY AND CREW, HANGED.

1780 CAPTAIN JONES, A SINGLE HANDED PIRATE, KILLED IN A FIGHT.

1815 BLACK CAESAR AND CREW, KILLED IN FIGHT.

1854 CAPTAIN GODON AND CREW, HANGED.

Several books made reference to pirate philosophy, and they all tended to quote Captain Bellamy, who, as an outspoken pirate, defined piracy better than any lawman or pirate. He had just captured an English ship whose crew refused to join him under the flag of Jolly Roger when he first stated with his bloody sword held high over his head in front of the captured crew, "Damn ye, you are a shaking puppy, and so are all those who will submit to be governed by laws which rich men have made for their own security, for the cowardly whelps have not the courage otherwise to defend what they get by their knavery. But damn ye altogether. Damn them for a pack of crafty rascals, and you, who sire them, for a parcel of hen-hearted numbskulls. They vilify us, the scoundrels do; then there is only this difference: they rob the poor under the cover of law, forsooth, and we plunder the rich under the protection of our own courage; had ye not better make one of us, than sneak after the arses of those villains for employment?"

Vincenzo was surprised. Those thoughts ran along his own. Time didn't change much when it came down to human nature, at least not very quickly.

There was one very old and tattered book that contained less than one hundred pages that he came across, titled "Flags of Terror." He had always thought there was only one pirate flag, the black flag of the pirate with the skull and cross bones. The little book had drawings of actual flags or banners used by many of the pirates. The earliest Jolly Rogers to appear were not on black backgrounds, but blood-red to warn their victims they would show no mercy if they resisted. It wasn't until 1700 when the black flag became popular. The pirates during that time sailed with the black flag hoisted as they approached their intended victim, showing good quarter was offered if there was no resistance. If there was resistance, the blood-red flag was hoisted which meant, "No Mercy."

There was Captain Low's flag; a red skeleton on a black background.

Blackbeard's was of the devil's skeleton holding an hour glass and a spear pointing to a heart dripping with blood.

Captain Condent's contained three skull and crossbones.

Black Bart's flag was of a pirate standing next to the death figure, each holding the same hourglass.

Calico Jack's was of a skull leering over crossed sabers.

Sidney X was on a blood-red and tattered flag. There was a skull with a broad-blade boarding knife shoved into the eye socket of a skull. The other eye had a tibia shattered at one end. A barracuda half circled around both the knife and the skull. There were thirteen smaller tibia bones scattered at the bottom.

All this account stated was "Hung at sea on July 17, 1791 by Captain Clifford Jones, after single-handedly killing most of the ship's crew, but was caught when he fell and broke his back."

Something was amiss. He had remembered seeing that name before in the list of executed pirates. He looked it up again and was puzzled by the discrepancy. The first pirate's name was Sidney X, too, but he was killed in 1722; also a single-handed pirate. There was a sixty-nine year difference. The name was too unusual to be a coincidence. Things like that had always intrigued Vincenzo so he decided to spend a little more time to see which account was true. From then on, he started looking for any reference to Sidney X. Another thought popped into his head: *My number-one suspect as the possible Barracuda was named Sidney.*

Looking back at the flag, it was right there, another startling coincidence. There was a barracuda on the old pirate's flag. Another coincidence came to him: both of the old pirates worked by themselves and so did the modern-day pirate that had been terrorizing the Atlantic and Caribbean for as long as any of the seamen he talked to could remember. The books he had been reading listed many accounts going back into the fifteen hundreds that had been committed by a single man using similar tactics.

I need more information about this modern-day Sidney. That will have to come from Jose Ortega or one of the girls working for him... I need to get one of the girls alone, without Ortega near, to learn their secrets. Can't trust Ortega; he seemed to be holding something back about his reclusive friend when questioned. He could get his information, but it would have to be obtained using—the hard way.

ST. CROIX

Paul and Chong had separately driven to a spot in the rainforest to discuss their strategies. They both felt good about what they had learned so far and knew from experience that they had to proceed at exactly the right pace or spook their prey.

They were not sure if they should notify the Italians and share their information and speculations with them then or later. After a lengthy discussion, it was decided it would be best to wait until they were sure Sidney was the man behind their problems. There were still a few things they were not sure about, and they would wait until they had sprung their trap before making definite statements. They still didn't know about Tony, and the relationship between him and Sidney.

After everything was clear to each of them on the plan of action, they parted. They were to meet back at the same place the next morning to update the action plan.

Chong drove directly to the marina. It was time to meet this man named Sidney Xavier, face-to-face. When he arrived, he found Sally sitting in the office doing her morning paperwork with a mug of coffee on her desk that had turned cold an hour ago.

She was pleased to see that Chong had returned as promised. She dearly hoped that Sidney would be receptive to Chong's offer, but held out no real hope that he would. Chong was prepared to enter into negotiations that would give him the excuse he needed to hang around and get to know the mysterious man. Everything in his plan had a purpose, and also made it difficult for his target to wiggle off the hook that he was setting.

Sally told him that Sidney had left that morning on an early run which he usually did. She expected that he could be back as early as an hour, maybe two, or it could be late that night. She had tried to catch him that morning, but she didn't see him leave. Chong told her he would look around the marina while he waited; he needed to inspect it for negotiation points anyway. Sally offered to show him around, but he politely declined the offer.

Two hours later, Chong was in the office asking if the owner had shown up. Sally, with the same cold mug of coffee on her desk, said he had not, but hopefully, he would be back soon.

Another two hours passed and Chong was still waiting. A trip into town for lunch used up another two hours, but Sidney still had not returned. A trip around the island took four hours and produced the same results. Mr. Xavier had not returned.

The next morning, Mr. Xavier was still not back—yet. Chong asked how to find his father's place. Sally told him, but cautioned him against bothering the old man. There were some stories about him; he could get mean towards strangers.

Chong was surprised to see that the elder Mr. Xavier had the only house on an entire mountain. The mountain, he would find out later, was owned by the Xaviers. Sally had been correct in her assessment of the old man. He was indeed a cranky bastard.

The only thing the old man told him was, "I haven't seen the fucking asshole except for briefly yesterday. I'm not his fucking keeper and could care the fuck less where the fuck he is. Now, you turn around right now, you fucking chink, and get the fuck off my mountain before I blow your tourist ass the fuck off."

That evening, Chong returned to the marina, as he did the following morning—as he did each morning and afternoon until Sidney did finally show up.

With the flash of a stolen FBI badge with Chong's photo on it, he checked the airlines, ferries, and seaplanes to see if the man had left. There was no record of Mr. Xavier buying a ticket. Chong and Paul started thinking that perhaps they had spooked Sidney, because Tony was part of the team, and, theoretically, he would have given Sidney the detectives' descriptions. However, Sally kept telling him that it was Sidney's normal pattern; he would often disappear, to return unannounced. In the island lingo, "He be gone to come back."

They were running short on Mafia time and felt they better tell them something to buy them an extension. All they could do was wait it out; there were no other trails to follow. Also buying more time had some other benefits, as well. They had three million dollars to blow on fine wine and beautiful women.

THE ENTRANCE TO THE CAVE OF SNAKES WAS A QUARTER MILE OF HARD-going from the elder Sidney's house. The day the two younger Sidneys had disappeared, they had walked down to the cave and retrieved the money needed to finish the land transaction. Back at Grandpa's, Sidney had called a taxi to take them to a chartered seaplane.

In St. Thomas, Sidney went to Ortega's office and introduced himself to the family patriarch, Don Ziguia Ortega. Jose wasn't there but had talked to his father about the deal. His father was intently interested in Sidney. He didn't know the details about him other than he was part of a family business similar to his own.

Also, Sidney's grandfather had sent his own grandfather off to the other world. Ortega thanked him for the family bible he had given them, but he didn't ask any questions about it. He assumed that Jose's description that his family was in the pirate business was enough. Ortega was impressed with the Sidneys' newest member; a quiet and already muscular lad with a deep tan that screamed "I am of the sea. I am the King of the Sea," just like his father's attitude suggested.

Ortega, without insulting Sidney, asked about the money needed to complete the transaction. He indicated that twelve million dollars in cash was hard to move around with banking laws as they were.

Sidney told the boy, "Give Ortega your backpack." He then looked at Ortega and said, "It isn't difficult."

He had taken the full amount from the cave thinking he would use the three million on the boat to finance his new base in the jungle and to travel to the Mediterranean. Ortega accepted the bag with a cursory look into it, but not counting the cash.

"Well, Mr. Xavier, it seems that you must be in the right business to have so much cash lying around."

"It appears so," was Sidney's response. "Do you have the papers ready now or when can I expect to receive them?"

Ortega said, "Since such a long time had passed since you made your offer, I thought the deal was off. In fact, my son thinks you're dead."

"I have been busy, and as you can see, I am not dead."

Ortega told him he would have the papers drawn up and sent to Jose. He assured Sidney they would be in order.

Sidney was satisfied the papers would be in order, knowing if they were not, he would make sure they damn sure would be correct, and maybe signed in blood. If cash was not good enough to make the transaction flow smoothly, then a little gray tape terror would always get the job done.

He asked Ortega to rent him his airplane and crew to fly him to see

Jose that day. Ortega flatly refused payment, but immediately got on the intercom and told his secretary to arrange it.

By nightfall the two Sidneys were departing the Ortega Lear jet at the semi-private airfield outside of Caracas. All customs and immigration procedures had been arranged as usual by Ortega's secretary in St. Thomas. Basically, all that was required was Ortega to assume full responsibility for anyone he brought into the country and pay the yearly bribe to the Minister of Immigration.

Sidney had to admit there was something good about modernization. It was nice to have someone else to do all the work, leaving the Ortegas free to spend their money. Once again, he thought that maybe the time had arrived to update the business.

That evening was spent in a small hotel outside of the airport. Sidney had a shopping list in his head of some things he needed to buy before going into the jungle.

The next afternoon, they boarded Jose's helicopter that had been instructed to pick them up, once again by Ortega's secretary.

Little Sid was having a big time. He had completed six months of survival training, was officially accepted into the family business, shown the family treasures and trusted with the dark secret of their history, had ridden in a seaplane, a jet airplane, and now was flying in a helicopter—and he was suddenly rich—and he had not been in a training fight for the last seven months. He thought, *this is a much better life than playing in the Dominican jungle with a bunch of poor kids.* He rarely thought of his mother or siblings anymore.

After an hour or so, the helicopter circled Jose's hacienda. After adjusting for a sudden wind shift, the chopper was set down at its usual place on the manicured lawn. Sidney had asked the pilot to drop them off at the village where he kept his boat, but the pilot said he had orders to bring them to Jose's place. For maybe the first time, Sidney didn't bully the pilot to do as he was told. They departed the aircraft as the noisy helicopter's engine was shut down.

As they walked out, they were met by Maria and Jose. Jandy was trailing behind. Maria walked up to Sidney and asked, "This is your little boy?"

"Yes, Maria, his name is Sidney, and he is not a little boy."

Seeing Maria standing there, with her generous breast and flawless skin on her beautiful face, Sidney felt the old need for her flood over him.

Maria ruffled the boy's hair and said, "All seven-year-olds are little boys."

There was moisture in her eyes and tightened skin around her mouth as she fought off tears and the emotions she had been living with since Sidney had told her about the boy.

She moved away from the boy positioning herself directly in front of Sidney and unexpectedly kneed him in the groin, and then followed that with a punch brought up from her waist to land on his lower jaw. She had put all of her strength into both blows.

The blows were well-timed and her strategy was good. She had been planning it every day since her emotions became too strong with worry about Sidney and fear for the boy. Normally, she was not a violent person, but the thought of the boy alone in a wild jungle drove her to show Sidney what she thought of his macho needs in raising a child. She knew she would have to hit him when he least expected it.

Her blows were ineffective. Sidney's reflexes were too good. What Maria didn't know is Sidney lived every minute of his life expecting attacks. It had been the way he was trained to think ever since he was seven years old. He moved enough so that the knee missed its mark and the punch to his jaw was only a tap as he pulled his upper body away as the punch was on its way.

Fortunately for Maria, his instincts were good enough not to send a retaliatory blow back to the attacker, which would surely have caused a painful injury to the beautiful woman he wanted to bed.

What was unfortunate for Maria was the little boy's reflexes. He saw the attack and acted immediately. His first move was to kick the woman in her stomach, and as he turned to send a hard backhand to the back of her head, his blow was stopped by his father's foot.

Sidney said, "It's okay; she is my friend. Do not hurt her."

Maria was on the ground withering around trying desperately to get a breath of air. She had no idea what had happened. Everything had happened so fast that she was not even aware who or how she was struck. Jose was confused and Jandy was horrified at both violent attacks.

Jose was in awe. He had never seen a man react to a swift attack so naturally and he certainly never dreamed that a little boy would be capable of making an instantaneous decision to attack anyone that posed a threat towards his father. The backhand punch aimed at the back of Maria's head could have killed her if Sidney had not been able to block it. Where did he learn to fight so young in life? Maybe Sidney was right: his name was Sidney and he was not a little boy. And once again, Jose experienced the feeling he had had before when confronted with Sidney's abilities involving ruthlessness.

Jandy rushed to help Maria. Maria could not do or say anything; she only wanted to breathe again.

Sidney looked at Jose and asked, "What was all of that about?"

Jandy, clearly upset, yelled up at Sidney, "You bastard, you've been driving her nuts with worry about the boy and you for months. I wish it were you lying here in pain, not her. What is wrong with that kid of yours? Did you teach him in that jungle that it is okay to go around kicking women in their stomachs?"

Young Sid stood there at ease, thinking his father had some weird friends. If they didn't want to get punched, then they shouldn't punch other people, especially Sidney XXIII or Sidney XXIV.

His father answered Jandy while helping the breathless one get some air, "My son doesn't know any of you. When Maria attacked me he reacted the proper way. Neither he nor I will apologize for his actions. As far as what I do or what my son does is of no concern of any of you, so do not interfere. Maria will be okay in just a moment,"

Young Sid was impressed that his father had talked so much. *He must like these people*, he thought.

Maria gave him a dirty look as she was starting to get her breath back. Sidney thought, *Shit... there's no way I'm going to get any pussy tonight.*

He asked Jose, "Can I use one of your men to take me to my boat?"

Jose said, "I'll take you. Besides, we need to talk. After all, I understand we are neighbors now."

Sidney had made no effort to console Maria. It was not because he was mad or upset it was just because he didn't think about it. He figured she would be a little friendlier in a day or two, and then he could get her in the sack.

Jose had been around long enough to know that the best way to get along with violent types was to understand what actions should and should not be done. Sidney, and now his son, were specialized people, apparently trained to have limited values for a reason. After all, five hundred years of successive pirating required specialized needs.

Since his own family was in a related business, his training had been specialized as well, but not to the extent of the Xaviers. He was brought up to be just as ruthless, mentally, but expecting that there would always be others to do all of the dirty work. He was taught all of the finer things in life; attended the best schools and had grown up with the leaders and the elite of many societies. But, in reality, Jose had killed many more people than Sidney. The difference was Jose had employees that did all of the nasty work, while he sipped scotch on the veranda around his tropical swimming pool.

Another difference was, Sidney killed one-on-one, eye-to-eye, and it was done only to survive. Jose issued orders to get rid of people he didn't know or hadn't even seen. It was just someone in the way of someone else trying to do something to make money for their cartel. Or, it could be the killing of a political figure to give one of his friends a better position in an election. Or it could be a thirteen year old boy in a street fight for neighborhood control of the daily crack sales in Detroit, Miami, Austin, or any other town. Or it could be a woman struggling to support her family of four children and her own habit for Jose's street product, who finally loses track of how many hits she had that day and overdoses. Jose killed more people every day than Sidney had done in a lifetime of ruthlessness. Jose was aware of their differences and he accepted the deaths of innocent people in the name of business, as easily as he accepted Sidney's situation.

On the trip to Sidney's boat, Jose talked about everything he could, except what he really wanted to know. He didn't want to talk in front of the boy, so he decided to wait until they arrived and the kid could run off to play with the other children of the village.

When they arrived, the boy ran over to the boat instead. He called it his boat so Jose assumed that it was. Certainly any seven-year-old child who could walk in unannounced with twelve million dollars in his backpack could afford a sailboat.

Before Sidney and Jose made the short trip to the lagoon, the boy yelled, "Hey, Dad, somebody cut up the dinghy."

Sidney looked at Jose, but said nothing, waiting for a response.

Jose said, "It wasn't me, but I think I know who did it. That's what I wanted to talk to you about, but didn't think it would be a good idea in front of the kid."

Sidney said, "My business is his. There will never be anything you cannot say in front of him." As he finished that statement he boarded the boat.

It looked as if it had been thoroughly searched. Sidney looked relieved when he opened a cabinet drawer over the never used refrigerator. He pulled out two bottles of Cruzan Rum and tossed one to Jose. "Let's drink while we have this talk," and he led the way to cockpit.

"There were two men here looking for you. They told the village leader that they were friends of yours and were supposed to meet you here. They used your dinghy to go fishing and were barely able to get it back to the boat as one of the air tubes had been cut. People in the village watched as they dug something out of the dinghy but couldn't tell what it was. I figured it was the three million dollars as I had already looked everywhere else for it, but we didn't make this mess."

"Fuck that, who are those men?"

"These men are the same that came to see me. They have been hired by the mob to find Tony and the men who are working with him. They are outside talent, which means they know what they are doing. There were a couple of slip-ups during their private interviews with some of my people that gave them some reasons to want to talk to you."

"Exactly what were the slip-ups?"

"These guys are on the clock and they either perform and get paid, or they get whacked for fucking up. The mob has gone completely berserk trying to find the men responsible for their woes."

"I'm so sad. What were the slip-ups?"

"Nothing that pointed your way really, but a possible combination of things led them to have more interest in you. Things like why did Tony come to see me? Why was he in the woods looking for you when he disappeared? Why did you leave a half hour after Gugguci and his men? They got a description of you from everyone there; maybe it fit the one they were looking for. Then there was the three million dollars they found. The average boat bum doesn't leave that kind of money lying around. Like I said, they didn't learn any one thing that suggested you were involved."

"Describe these men to me, Jose."

"One is Chinese. He is about five and a half feet tall, weighs about one hundred fifty pounds. He speaks English with no accent. His name is Chong. I don't remember hearing his last name."

Jose continued, "The other one is a North American. His name is Paul Chance. Weighs about two hundred and is maybe six feet tall. Sandy hair, good build."

Before Jose finished the descriptions, Sidney knew that indeed the men were good at their work. It had to be the Chinaman that had talked to the boy and Sally. He didn't hear anything about the American. He had no idea how they located him, but now that they had, it mattered.

"Shit," Sid said aloud and went in the boat. He looked for the GPS. It wasn't there. He remembered that he had played with the damn thing to get used to using it. He had put the location of where the boy was, the pick-up point for the Tribute plane raid, and his marina's location. "Fucking modern doodad nailed me. That was stupid of me."

Hopefully they didn't divulge my identity to the mob. If they had any sense, they wouldn't until they had questioned me first. They don't want to look stupid to the people that had hired them. But they would surely do so to buy them more time if needed. I need to stop that info leak quickly. Then he made his first decision on the matter, and that was to drink the bottle of rum in his hand and take care of the rest tomorrow.

Halfway through the bottle, Jose brought up the Cuban thing saying that the private detectives mentioned that Tony had taken something important away from the family. Then Jose blatantly asked, "How important was it?"

"I don't know; didn't count it." was Sidney's answer and nothing else was said.

Jose talked to the boy for a while. He was very interested in learning how the boy thought. The scene on his lawn a few hours ago was a complete shock to everyone, except Sidney and the boy. Both of them thought it was perfectly natural to react swiftly and with aggressive action. In conversations, however, the boy seemed to be a normal seven-year-old. The big difference was his lack of interest to play with other children. He was contented to be at his father's side, even though there were never any enlightening conversations. The boy felt at ease doing anything he chose to do, including taking a swig of rum from his father's bottle. However, he did profess to like cold beer more than the rum. Jose suspected that given the choice the boy would have opted for a Coke or Pepsi, like all kids his age.

Sidney interrupted Jose's thoughts by saying to his son, "I want you to take the *Barracouta* home, by yourself. You will need to spend some time overboard cleaning the hull of marine growth since it has been sitting here for so long. But, do not do it in here. The lagoon is full of big crocodiles. You'll wait until the tide is at a full high during a calm sea then take it over the sandbar outside the river's mouth. After you're outside, you'll anchor and clean the bottom."

Then almost in a parentally manner, he looked at the boy through the bottom of his bottle of rum and asked, "Do you think you can do that by yourself?"

The boy, unsure, asked, "You mean I can sail the boat to St. Croix by myself?"

Sidney, slightly irritated that the boy had mentioned St. Croix, said, "Yes, by yourself. I have to leave here and I don't want you to arrive until I get some things settled."

Sidney went on to tell him the compass course to follow and how long it would take, and what time he should leave there to arrive at his destination in the morning hours. That conversation went on for fifteen minutes.

Jose was astonished. Apparently, Sid could talk a lot if he was instructing the boy. Even Jose thought he could navigate the trip after listening to Sidney explain it, and he wasn't a sailor. He thought, *so that was how the boy had learned the fighting reflex he had; dear old dad had indeed provided.*

Jose offered, "Sidney, I can have one of my men go along to help him."

"That's not necessary. He sails the boat by himself and knows how to navigate and he knows the area he is going into very well. He'll be okay."

It was hard to believe the kid sitting there would be on his own in the open sea for days by himself. But why not, he was in a hostile jungle for six months by himself. Jose was glad he didn't have to do either.

Sidney, without concern for Jose's presence, told the boy about the two men who were looking for him. He explained that he was leaving now to find these men before they told others where to find them. If something happened to him, the boy was to get his grandpa and learn about the snake and spider. Then he got more secretive and whispered to the boy, "Tomorrow I will take you to the Cave of Pigs."

Jose was dying to know more about the snake and spiders, but figured they were the code names for the centers of the Sidneys' activities. For a minute he imagined these were treasure caves, and then scoffed at the idea, thinking he had seen too many pirate movies.

Sidney realized that it really had not been necessary to go into all of the conversation he just had in front of Jose because he would be alone with the kid most of the day tomorrow anyway. He said, "Enough of this talk; let's get drunk."

He got up and led the other two to Gaspar's little bar in the village. As always, his reasonably clean glass filled to the top was waiting at the same barstool.

The boy begged off after a not very cold beer and two sweet soft drinks that were made in Venezuela. He went outside and took a long walk down the beach. He noticed that, for some reason, several of the village girls around his own age acted funny when he walked through them. They smiled and innocently giggled and seemed to want to follow him around. But he was too powerful for that. He started running down the beach, quickly distancing himself from his would-be admirers. He didn't understand why they acted so peculiar and soon forgot all about it.

Jose and Sidney did get drunk that night—so drunk that Sidney started philosophizing about the problems with the world. But it didn't matter since neither of them could remember anything after the second bottle anyway. Anyone else in the bar was not at their level of drunkenness, so they were left out of the conversation since they could not understand the slurred discussion.

The next morning as everyone woke up and started moving around, Sidney tuned on the single side band radio and hailed the high seas operator. Through the operator he placed a collect call to Sally. She was so surprised to hear from him, since he had never bothered to call her before, that she almost refused to accept the charges.

Sidney said, "I'm sailing, but will be back in six days. Is that tourist still interested in buying the marina?

She happily responded, "Yes, he is. He has been coming by the office every day to see if you have returned from wherever it is you went."

He said, "I'll be there in six days. Arrange a meeting for us the evening of the sixth day from now. I might want to sell the place."

Sally sounded very pleased and told him there would be no problem. What she didn't tell him was that the Chinaman was not only in the office every day, but in Sally as well. There was a one-sided romance blooming.

Sidney started his Jeep with ease since Gaspar kept it in perfect running condition. He asked Jose if he could have his pilot take him to Caracas when he was ready, and Jose assured him there would be no problem. He then told Jose he was going to show the boy their new property and they would be at his hacienda later. Jose offered to come along, but Sidney declined.

Jose said, "It would save you from having to bring the boy back to the village before coming to the hacienda."

Sidney assured him that was not a problem since the boy was a good driver. If Jose had been watching the boy then, he would have seen a big surprised looked on the kid's face. He had never driven a car.

As soon as Jose's Jeep had widened the gap between them, Sidney stopped the Jeep and told the boy to get behind the wheel. By the time they reached the cliff, the boy was feeling pretty good about being able to drive. He was also thinking for a seven-year-old there was not much he had not done. Of course, there was no difference in his attitude about that and most other boys about their life's experiences, however full or limited.

The boy really appreciated the view of the mountains and valley before him. He was particularly impressed when his father said, "You, your grandfather and I are the sole owners of everything you can see from here. If anyone ever tries to take it away from you, those people must be dealt with in the harshest terms. It is not only beautiful land, but is also full of plants and wildlife to live off of, and it has a huge secret cavern. This is the Cave of Pigs. This cavern will take a lot of time to explore, and we will do that, but we need to find another entrance. I feel sure there should be another entrance closer to the sea."

The boy looked up at his father and said, "How did you find it, Dad?"

He explained how he originally found the cave without going into all of the details. Then he told how he had found the entrance, hoping to instill some knowledge of moving around in lightless caverns. He also emphasized the importance to remember how to find the cave's entrance in case something happened to him. If it did, then he would be the only man in the world to know of its existence. Also, in that case, it would be his responsibility entirely as his grandfather could not help much because of his legs. It was not exactly wheelchair country, but it could be adapted after a house was built. It would be possible to build a house deep in the woods or over one of the entrances. However, he should not do anything without thoroughly exploring the cave. It would be important to know if there was only one way in.

Then he added, "I had planned on you and me spending a lot of time exploring this cave system on this trip. That's why I brought all of the stuff on our way here."

He was quiet for a second, and then said, "I have changed my mind, Sid. Instead of you sailing back to St. Croix you will stay here. I'll be back in a few days, and then we can get into the cave."

"Why do you have to go to St. Croix?" asked the boy.

"I have to kill the two men who are trying to find me," was the matter of fact answer.

The boy didn't show any emotion; he accepted it as fact the second he heard it from his father.

Sidney led the boy through the jungle on the way to the cave's entrance. Occasionally, he pointed out a particular landmark, and emphasized that he should be careful not to travel the same route so as not to establish a trail. If everything worked out the way he thought it would, then the Sidneys could be very happy with the Cave of Pigs for generations to come.

The pirate first took his son to the waterfalls and showed him how he found the cavern. Sidney strongly recommended against using that way to get inside. He also stressed the importance of finding where the water flow went. It could lead to separate caverns or other streams on the surface. It would take a lot of time to safely explore the entire underground area. Then they worked their way up the mountain to the entrance.

Sidney took two flashlights out of the backpack. He explained what the slimy stuff that covered the floor was and it produced the expected results from the boy who was holding his nose. After walking through the guano, Sidney found what he had been looking for. A lump on the cave's floor was a mixture of guano, cloth, and bones wrapped in shrunken skin.

Sidney explained to the boy, "These are the bones that will guard this cave and our fortune after we move in here. These bones used to own the prize that I brought back from Cuba, and that prize bought this land for our family. I took his fortune and his life because it is the Sidney X way. His bones and spirit, as pirate tradition, will serve us to keep all others away from our treasure. Let no man enter this cave unless he is a Sidney X. Any other man who enters and learns the location of our treasure caves must die. There has never been an exception to this rule nor will you or your descendants break the rules of the bones."

The next stop was the smaller entrance. Sidney said, "As of now, if we had to bring the treasure here, this would be the better entrance. The reason is a lack of bats in this section leaves everything a lot cleaner. The treasure chambers we choose must be free from all contaminates and well away from any source of moisture. Moisture comes from moving fresh air, streams, dripping ceilings or bat's drippings."

The boy thought that dripping bats was funny and he chuckled at his father's attempt at humor.

Then Sidney asked, "Do you understand everything I have told you, and can you find your way here?"

The boy answered that he could. Sidney didn't ask if being inside caves bothered him, as he had been watching his expressions when he occasionally would flash a beam from the flashlight on his face. His expressions had been relaxed as if he felt at home—there was no fear, only excitement, on Sid's face.

He told the boy to lead them back to the Jeep as they exited the cave. He wanted to be sure the boy could find it again and the best way to learn the route was to lead, not follow. The kid did know the way; he had a good natural sense of direction.

Little Sid drove all the way back to Jose's compound. His average speed to the cliffs had been very slow, however, as he gained confidence the rate of speed increased. At one point, Sidney had to tell the boy to slow down as the Jeep bounced wildly off deep ruts. Of course, a lecture on safety would have helped train the boy to drive safely, but none followed.

All Sidney said on the next big bump was, "Slow the fuck down. You can't kill yourself until you have trained an heir to follow our family tradition."

The boy chuckled.

They pulled into Jose's compound and parked the Jeep near the helicopter. Nobody came out to meet them as they were not heard driving up. Sidney found the girls and Jose sitting by the pool going over piles of papers spread around the floor between them.

Jandy was the first to speak, "Oh, look! The mean man and his little bodyguard have returned."

Jose got up to greet them, giving a hard look towards Jandy. She saw the look and then stood up and apologized for the remark, letting her natural good manners take charge. Maria just looked up to acknowledge them, but said nothing. Her feelings had been hurt more than her stomach by the boy she had wanted so badly to protect. She was not sure if she hated Sidney for turning the boy into a ruthless animal, or if she should have compassion for the boy. After all, it wasn't *his* fault that his father made him so mean. She was confused and her emotions didn't do anything to help sort out the best approach to take.

The eye contact Sidney had tried to make with her was ignored. She would not look at him. He didn't dwell on the rejection; he accepted it and moved over to the bar.

With a glass of rum in hand, he spoke briefly to Jose about the land transaction. A bill of sale on the land had arrived via fax. After reading it and he was satisfied that everything was in order, he had his son sign it, and the rest of them witnessed the seven-year-old boy sign it Sidney X. Jose faxed it back for his father's signature and notary seal.

Sidney said to Jose, "My son will come by to pick up his documents in a day or two."

Maria overheard the part about the boy picking the papers up and wondered if that meant that Sidney was leaving again. Was he leaving the boy by himself again? Was he leaving without saying anything to her? He had not said he was sorry or tried to console her hurt feelings in the least. Was he leaving without making love to her? Was he such an unfeeling brute that he was incapable of thinking of others?

She knew the answers, and it only made the feminine instinct stronger: that man needed to be in love and have someone to care for him. She was in love with Sidney and was going to provide for him what she thought he needed. One day he would get smart and realize that he needed her; she had time and no other romantic interest.

Approaching the boy would be another matter. If any kid ever needed a female influence in his life that kid was the one. She had wanted to hug the boy when she first saw him, and to tell him he was safe. And she wanted to take care of him, too. Her time spent worrying—and the concern she felt for the boy—had been rewarded with a hard kick to her stomach. Maria was not aware of the potentially deadly punch that had been sent by the boy, but blocked by his father. Had she known about that, it might have made her realize there are some things that were beyond her scope of understanding.

Maria's thoughts were interrupted when she realized that Sidney had said goodbye to her and was leaving. The sound of the helicopter warming up indicated that he was leaving soon. She could not let him go without talking to him. She got up and walked across the floor, taking notice that young Sid was in the pool, playing with his monkey. She was afraid of the boy to a point where she felt more comfortable knowing he was not too close to her.

The boy hardly noticed her approach to his father and was not concerned. In fact, he wondered if he had overreacted a little when she attacked his father. But either way didn't matter much. He and Fred were having fun splashing each other with the cool water of the swimming pool. He wondered if they had enough money to buy a swimming pool where they were going to live next. Little Sid knew many things most children would never know and there were things they knew that he would never know. Money was one thing that he had no concept of. He didn't equate the treasure and bags of money as spending money. It was just the family treasure, and that was something that was to be protected and never talked about. Even if he had known the family treasure placed them among some of the wealthiest people in the world, it would not have registered with him. His father had the same thoughts about wealth. Wealth only mattered to those who do not have it.

She took Sidney by the arm and gently led him away from the others. She said, "Sidney, I need to talk to you."

By the time they reached her room, she had tears forming in her eyes. She tearfully hugged him and said, "I am so sorry I hit you when you arrived, but I need to explain why I did it. I am not that kind of person."

Sidney responded, "It's okay, there is no reason to dwell on the incident." Then he offered a weak apology for the boy saying, "I wish the boy had not reacted so quickly. He didn't know that you and I are friends."

That made her cry—every time she thought of the boy attacking her made her cry. Her sorrow and tears couldn't soften Sidney's indifference. He embraced her letting her cry; he couldn't think of anything to do or say so he just held her. Her closeness was getting him aroused, but something inside told him it was not the time. Besides, he had to be in St. Croix in the next few hours.

Finally, Sidney said, "Maria, I must leave you now, but I will be back in a few days. The boy is staying on his boat, why don't you go by to see him. He knows you are my friend now and you have nothing to fear from him. In fact, you will find that he will be protective of you. Just do not treat him as a child. He may be young, but he is not a child. He doesn't need a mother, but you might become his friend."

In Maria's mind, that was all she had wanted—to be involved in a nurturing way with the boy. And to have Sidney ask her to check on him was the best part. He kissed her briefly on the lips while grabbing her ass, then said, "I wish there was more time."

She knew exactly what he meant, not quality time to talk and discover each other's thoughts, but time enough to fuck her brains out. But that was okay; she was making progress. She asked, "What's so important that you have to leave now?"

He responded, "Some men stole three million dollars from me. I work too hard for my money, so they need to give it back."

She was curious but didn't ask. Instead, she kissed him and rubbed her pelvis against his and said, "Well, hurry back." She knew a thing or two about life as well.

Sidney went by the pool to tell the boy he was leaving. Before he left he quietly said, "The woman, Maria, is going to come visit you. She wants to be your friend; do not hurt or scare her. She is my special friend, so you take care of her."

"Sure, Dad. When are you coming back?"

When Sidney went to board the helicopter he was surprised to see Jandy with a packed suitcase ready to leave as well. She explained that she had been called to go to the St. Thomas office. She was taking the original deed to the land with her.

By the time Sidney had left the compound, the boy and Fred were getting ready to drive back to the boat. Maria intercepted them, however, and easily talked him in to staying a little longer to have some cheeseburgers and French fries. The boy was always hungry, but had learned long ago in the jungle to ignore the feeling; however, a cheeseburger was

SIDNEY X THE PIRATE

his favorite food and he eagerly accepted. Fred was given his own cheeseburger, without the meat, that he tore apart and ate the parts he liked. The boy's manners were not much better than Fred's, but she would soon change that.

VIRGIN ISLANDS

Instead of sharing the seaplane, Jandy took a commercial flight to St. Thomas as that was where her car was parked. She arrived there shortly after six that same evening. She was not aware of the man who stayed well behind her as she walked through the St. Thomas airport. She took her car directly to her apartment up on Crown Mountain.

She loved the place with its view of the harbors of Long Bay, Elephant Bay and the small islands of Hassel and Water and the hundreds of sailboats anchored. She rarely got to stay there, however, as she usually came with Ortega and would stay at the family compound on Molab Cay.

That time it was different; she was there to meet with an attorney who had called a few days ago about settling some facts about her father's death in a hospital two years ago. There apparently was reason to believe that malpractice was involved, and he needed a deposition from her. That seemed strange to her, since he had died of prostate cancer, but she wanted to do the right thing, so she agreed to the meeting at eight o'clock the next morning. That was okay, too, it would give her a little time off from Ortega, the jungle, and mounds of paperwork that never got any smaller.

Instead of being in a hurry to look over the panoramic view, she should have been more careful about locking her apartment door. But it was too late. Vincenzo was inside and the door was locked. He lowered his briefcase to the floor and silently walked up behind Jandy and grabbed her with one arm and covered her mouth with his other hand.

She surprised him by being much stronger than he had expected and it turned into a wrestling match, during which she had seen who her attacker was. When that was apparent to Vincenzo he had no choice but to slug her, he did so, knocking her unconscious. He had hoped to be able to talk to her as an unknown assailant and scare her to get his information so it would not get back to Ortega—it was too late for that to happen. She would certainly be pissed when she woke up and would try for revenge through her boss, Jose Ortega.

"Shit, if she hadn't seen me I could have used the old tape trick used by the asshole to find out what I want," he muttered as he carried her to the bedroom and tied her hands and feet to the legs of the bed. He tied her with stockings that were found in the dresser drawers.

The briefcase was set on the bed and opened. He took out a syringe already prepared with sodium pentothal. He had brought it along as a last resort, but he was going to get what he needed one way or another. The Barracuda had run out of line and was about to be reeled in.

As the drug took effect, cold water was thrown in Jandy's face to revive her from the punch. A gag was already over her mouth. Vincenzo had not had much experience using drugs to make people be more cooperative. He had always found that fear and pain were the natural ways to get what he wanted.

She started acting docile and was cooperative. Vincenzo asked, "Jandy, how well do you know this friend of Ortega's named Sidney?"

"Nobody knows him. He won't talk to me," in an obviously drugged response.

"How does he make his money?"

"Don't know. Nobody knows anything about him."

"Do you know what his name is?"

"Sidney X is all I've heard."

That sent a jolt up Vincenzo's backbone. He asked, "Have you ever seen him with a funny-looking flag, with a skull on it?"

"Yes, on his arm."

"What do you mean?"

She tried to point to the opposite wall, but because of the bonding, was unable to. She didn't seem to mind, she just motioned with her head to look at the wall.

He turned and noticed a framed poster hanging on the wall and went closer for a better look.

"You bastard, I've got you now," Vincenzo muttered. He was looking at a poster with a picture drawn on it. "Just look at that fucking tattoo. It's the same fucking Jolly Roger or I'll fuck myself."

"Good idea," said a drowsy Jandy.

The only difference was that there were twenty-three bones and not the thirteen shown in the book.

Now he knew what the man known as the Barracuda to the world's seamen looked like; a feat that, apparently, no other living man was fortunate enough to claim.

He went back to Jandy and asked, "Where does Sidney live?"

"Don't know." She was starting to come out from under the drugs and was getting reluctant to cooperate. Therefore, Vincenzo resorted to some of his old tricks, using the tools of fear and pain.

He asked again, "Where does he live?" and twisted her middle finger back towards her wrist, causing her to cry out in pain.

"I don't know, but think he said St. Croix."

Vincenzo tried several times to get her to be more specific, but there was nothing more to tell and she had two badly disjointed finger joints to prove it.

"When will he go back to Ortega's hacienda?"

She cried when she answered "I don't know," expecting more severe pain.

"When is the last time you saw Sidney?"

"Today."

"Where?"

"At Ortega's hacienda."

"Why didn't you tell me he was there?"

"Because he left there when I did."

"So, where the fuck did he go to?" Vincenzo was close, but afraid he would not get his information.

She was silent for a few seconds so he grabbed a little finger on the same hand and begin pulling it backwards. She wailed, "St. Croooixx."

For once being a very beautiful, proud, self-assured woman, she was a pitiful sight lying there blubbering; the bed wet from her urine as fear and pain made her lose control over her body functions.

Vincenzo stood there looking down on her and knew there would be no forgiveness coming from her, and she would surely seek retaliation through the Ortegas. He moved closer, and put his strong hands on her slender throat and squeezed. He squeezed the life out of the once-jubilant and gorgeous woman.

The apartment was made to look like there had been a robbery. He thought about making it look like a rape and robbery, but decided not to go that far. He was a torturer, a murderer, and sure, he had raped before, but he didn't like the idea of fucking a dead woman. He took her jewelry and was fascinated by a big diamond that she had concealed around her neck.

ST. CROIX

SIDNEY'S TRIP TO ST. CROIX HAD BEEN A FAST ONE, AND EXPENSIVE. While waiting to board the chartered seaplane to St. Thomas, he came upon the idea of buying his own aircraft. When he flew, he often used seaplanes in order to circumvent customs. If he had his own seaplane he could come and go as he pleased. It would speed up moving the treasure if he could find an entrance closer to the sea. When he finished with his business he'd get more information.

The plane flew first to St. Maarten where it was refueled. Then it stayed low on the water to St. Thomas's north side. There it gained altitude quickly to resemble a take-off on the prying eyes of the radar screens. The plane then flew to Christiansted's seaplane landing area, dropped altitude and flew on the deck to the east end and landed between the outer reef and the beach. He had the pilot taxi to within fifty yards of the shore before he dove in for a quick swim to the beach. It was getting dark, and the pilot gunned the engine and was up again after spending one minute in the water.

He had not landed near town or his marina as it was important that no one see him until he accomplished his mission. He didn't know what the two men who were looking for him looked like, but the description he had on them should be enough. There was also the possibility there were other men as well. Also, he knew the two men would have been given a good description of him if they had not already been watching him.

A mile away from where he was there was a little beach restaurant. People would be arriving there to enjoy an evening meal. It was a perfect place to steal a rental car.

Sidney drove away in a new Cherokee that a trusting tourist had left the keys in the ignition. The first-time visitor to the island, thinking he was in paradise, had no idea that people steal things like cars there. Tourists were a Godsend to the local thieves.

About a mile away from the turn-off to go to his father's house, he pulled the car off the main road and left it on a seldom used dirt road somewhat overgrown by the jungle. He wanted to stay away from places that could be under surveillance, but he needed to get to the Cave of Snakes. Preparations had to be made that night. He moved through the edges of the jungle along his father's road unheard and unseen. Near the house, however, he heard a man sitting in a place that gave him a good view of the house. Sidney didn't disturb the man.

His task in St. Croix was to make everyone involved in finding him, disappear. There would only be speculation about what had happened. He could not have the Mafia know about him. That would restrict the freedom he had cherished all of his life. Also it was important that nobody knew that he was even on island to connect him with the disappearances. Especially with the Chinaman who was hanging out in his marina.

He spent the night in the Cave of Snakes. Most of the time was spent digging out the covered original entrance from within. The next morning, after two hours of sleep, he resumed the digging-out process. After he got a hole large enough to crawl through, he covered the opening with several transplanted bushes so there were no signs of the cave. The new opening was near the shoreline and only a quarter mile from his marina.

Sidney walked silently through the woods until he had a good vantage point over the marina. He noticed a new rental car parked by Sally's apartment.

At eight o'clock, a Chinaman emerged from Sally's apartment and drove off in a rental car. He continued his watch over the marina; looking for the big American and any other unusual people hanging around. It was easy to see the difference between locals and strangers; you could tell by the way they dressed. Most of the locals were in the lower income bracket, since they had abandoned their careers in the States to become boat bums. And that was how they dressed; old shorts, old shirts and flip-flops or old boat shoes. A man trying to fit in could dress the same, but the "old" would not be apparent. Also there was the longer hair and in many cases, a day or two growth of beard. Locals didn't much care about appearance. If they occasionally wore something new it would be obviously the cheapest thing they could find, so cheap it would scream "tacky."

He considered going to his father's house to pick up some binoculars that would make surveillance much easier. But he didn't want to risk setting off any warnings that he was on island. He knew that to fully cover the island would take as few as seven men. One man at the airport, one at the seaplane base, one at his father's place, and two more that would relieve the other men for rest periods and possibly roam the downtown streets. Then there were Paul and Chong. The extra men would be easy to remove; his main mission was to isolate Paul and Chong.

By noon, he felt comfortable that there were no other men hanging around the marina. He made his way down to Sally's place and waited for Chong to return. There was no hurry; he was ready and willing to wait for his prey. And he waited for several hours before the blue rental car reappeared and parked in front of Sally's apartment. Sidney could have used a little imagination to devise a plan to lure Chong away, but he was a man of few words and believed the direct approach was always best.

Sally would make her usual trip to the deck bar around ten p.m. to collect the day's receipts and then take a shower, and that is when Sidney would make his move. He positioned himself so he could hear and see everything going on in her small apartment. He was amazed at the way Sally had practically attacked Chong when he arrived. Sidney never had a clue she was so horny and was sorry he had not sampled her himself.

After a fast and furious session of sex and another fifteen minutes of caresses and soft conversation, Sally was out of bed and in the shower.

Sidney, quickly and with stealth, entered her apartment and walked into the bedroom. Chong was lying on his back with his eyes closed, smoking a cigarette. Without a sound, Sidney's Billy did a good job on his head. Sidney stuck the cigarette into his own mouth and rolled the man to a sitting position. Picking up one hundred fifty pounds of unconscious man would have been very difficult for most men; however, he picked up the naked man and threw him over his shoulders. With his free hand, he gathered Chong's clothes and shoes. He left the apartment and threw the unconscious man in the backseat of his car. Then he drove the rental car out of the marina and wedged it into the thick roadside bush so it was completely out of sight.

He carried Chong to the new opening of the cave and pulled him inside. He had given him a tap that should put a man down for about a half hour. The half hour was about up and Chong began to groan. In the total blackness of the cave, Sidney could hear his captive moving, trying to figure out where he was and what was happening. His mouth was taped shut as were his hands behind his back.

When Sidney was sure the man was awake and aware of his predicament, he said, "I understand you have been looking for me."

There was a muffled reply that tried to come from behind the tape. Sidney didn't understand what was said but he could guess. He then said, "You have three million dollars of my money. Where is it?"

Again, the muffled response. Sidney then said, "I also understand you are looking for Tony the Pop."

Then another muffled sound.

Sidney said, "Now that you understand what your position is, I'll take off the gag so you can enlighten me."

Chong's first words were, "Who the fuck are you? Where the hell am I?"

"Cut the bullshit, you know who I am by the questions I just asked you. Trust me; you do not want to play games with me. Neither of us has time for that. I am going to lead you to my office to show you something, and then I think all of your questions will be answered."

Sid helped Chong get to his unsteady feet. After a five minute walk through the black cave, Chong could see a dim light in the direction they were traveling. He had wondered if he had been blinded by the very obvious blow to his head, and now knew that was not the case. They were in a cave. The light got brighter as they turned around a bend. Then he could see the lamp on the wall responsible for the light. Chong was thinking, *no wonder they had not been able to find him, the man was a mole.*

They entered a room where there were other lamps, and Chong could not believe his eyes. Sidney pointed to one section and said, "There is the Cuban cache, and that garbage bag on top of the others over there came from the Tribute flight. I have brought you here in order to offer you something. You know some things that I need to know and you are going to give me answers, and any attempts to lie or deceive me will be futile. You do not have to worry about making the right choice for your answers. You only have one decision to make: that is, how painful your death is going to be. You see before you untold wealth. This has been accumulated for over five hundred and forty years and all of it by me and my forefathers. We are pirates who have been operating around the world continuously, since the first Sidney X. I am Sidney the twenty-third. My son is the twenty-fourth. I am telling you this so you will believe me when I tell you are going to die within the hour. I know the ways to make sure you tell me. Just like your buddy Tony told me about the Cuban treasure."

"Where is Tony?"

"Tony has a new job now, his spirit is guarding another cave I have just like this one. As you might imagine, he didn't want to tell me what I needed to know about the Mafia's most prized possession in Cuba, but he did. Unfortunately, Tony was stupid and died terribly. He died listening to and feeling his bones slowly being broken, one at a time. He cussed a lot, passed out several times, pissed all over himself and shit in his pants, and cried like a little baby before telling me what I wanted. I don't understand why a man would want to die that way."

He was quiet for a moment, and then said, "Before we get started, I want you to fully understand that you are going to be dead and nobody will ever find your body or even know what happened to you. They will never know that you saw me or answered some questions. There is nothing you can say or do to change those facts. So consider your last moments, go out easy. I promise you will feel absolutely no pain if you cooperate. By the way, I know a lot more than you know, and if you lie to me one time then the deal is off. I will take your information the painful way and you are definitely going to regret it. I am going to give you one minute to decide which way is in your best interest. Make your last decision a good one."

As he finished that last statement he slapped a piece of tape over Chong's mouth then another over his nose. There was a struggle and Chong tried to kick Sidney, but it was easily sidestepped.

Chong's struggle only lasted seconds. He was an intelligent man and realized that things were as they seemed. His time was up, and all he could do was try to make the best of it. He didn't owe the Mafia any favors anyway. He slumped and sat on the ground right next to a very old chest with its contents of sparkling gold coins.

With Chong's action, Sidney knew he had made the only logical choice he had. He removed the tape and asked, "How do I find Paul?"

There was hesitation, but he answered before risking the chance of a peaceful death. "He is staying at the golf resort on the west end of the island. At night he watches your father's house."

"Have you talked to the boys in Sicily about me?"

"Not yet; we wanted to be sure before showing our hand."

"How many men do you have looking for me?

"Five local men. They think we want you for a gambling debt. There is also Vincenzo from Sicily, a longtime hit man that is on your trail, too. I don't know where he is or what he knows."

"Describe all of the men on island to me."

He gave him good descriptions. Sidney was sure the man was telling the truth by the easy way he divulged the information. His last question was, "When are you to meet with Paul next?"

He answered, "We meet at the same place every morning at seven o'clock. It is in the old rainforest on a side road where there is a big mahogany tree that was twisted apart in a hurricane."

Then Sidney said, "I believe you have told me the truth. Is there anything else you would like to add?"

"Yes, I'm truly amazed about your family's activities and know my position is hopeless; can you tell me more about how your family has survived for so long?"

Sidney, walking around behind him, said, "Sure, I don't mind telling you something about our history." But, he lied. When he was out of sight he laid Billy directly on the back of his skull. Chong dropped straight down and he never had a clue he was hit. Sidney had lived up to his promise to make his death painless.

"Shit... I forgot to ask him about my money." Chong's body was carried away from the treasure room so as not to invite the creatures of the cave to come into the area and to keep the smell of his decomposing body removed as they would be working in the treasure room for a few months. He was deposited in the same small room the bones of Seaman Snake occupied. And it wasn't just Chong; he was going to have some company if things worked out right. To finish off Chong, Sidney slid the blade of his knife into his brain where the spinal cord meets the skull.

Outside, the cave's entrance was restored to look natural. Sidney had even dug up a big guardian plant and replanted it in the dirt covering the new entrance. With that completed, he walked quietly to his father's house. Paul was his next target. The other five men would be easy to take out—if needed.

He entered his father's house and caught the older man by surprise. Before his father could speak, however, Sidney gave him a sign of a finger over his lips to keep him quiet. Sidney went outside on the old man's front porch and walked around leisurely, taking in the cool night air. He figured that if Paul were there he would try to sneak up and take him unexpectedly, either outside or inside. If not, he would go on the hunt. That possibility was remote, based on the presumed intelligence of the man. He had been around too long to let his prey escape once spotted, especially when the stakes were so high. He would give the man ten minutes to make his play.

He stayed out on the porch for several minutes then went back inside. His position of control had vanished. As he entered, he saw a big American man standing behind his father with a sawed-off shot gun pointed at his head.

Paul said, "Well, we finally meet Mr. Xavier. I have heard something about you that makes me feel jittery, so don't make any moves that will certainly cost your father's head to be blown off."

Sidney was surprised; the man must have come in the back door and managed to catch his father off-guard. He said nothing in response; he just stood there, complying with instructions, waiting for an opportunity.

Paul didn't know it, but he was a dead man. If Paul shot his father, Sidney would have thrown his knife into Paul's throat before the boom sound went away. If he shot Sidney, his father would have done the same thing.

Paul pushed his father's wheelchair over to the telephone and dialed a number. Sidney wanted to get to him before he alerted anybody, but was powerless unless he sacrificed his father. While that was always a possibility, especially before letting the family honor be lost, it hadn't reached that point yet.

Paul said, "Let me speak to Chong, please... He is not there? Where did he go? Did he get a phone call?... Any chance he's over at the bar or just walking around?... When did you discover the car was gone?"

He hung up the telephone and asked Sidney, "Have you seen my partner, the Chinaman that was at your marina?"

"Don't know him, but I haven't been there yet. What's all of this about?"

Paul said, "No more questions unless I ask them. You sit down on the couch over there and do not move unless you ask me first. I mean even if you want to scratch your nose, you ask before doing it. I am very serious, and I have eight rounds of twelve-gauge buckshot, and will not hesitate to blow both of you apart."

Sidney's father was pushed closer to the couch, making sure it would be easy to kill them both, possibly with the same shot. Paul was smart and cautious; he knew his business.

As a distraction Sidney said, "You mean you would blow me to hell, not knowing where Tony is, or the Mafia's money? I don't think you're that stupid. The mob would have your head."

"That doesn't matter; that is later, this is now. I have no intention of letting you make any plays. If I kill you I can justify it to the mob; that's not of any concern to me. Not knowing where Tony is would just buy me more time anyway. They will not stop until they find him. And when I hand over your shredded remains as the man behind their attacks, I will be golden and I don't mean in skin color."

Sidney asked, "Well, what now?"

"We wait for a while for my partner to show." Paul made several more calls to the marina as well as the hotel he was staying in. Nobody had seen Chong all evening.

Paul started thinking that Chong was probably in a hotel room with another expensive hooker. After all, they had not expected Sidney to arrive for at least another three days.

Hoping to give Paul something else to think about, Sidney asked, "Well, if you're going to keep me and my poor old crippled daddy here, why don't you at least give us some food and drinks?"

"You get nothing but air."

"Come on, at least a cold beer."

"Fuck you, sleaze ball. You get nothing but what this gun is loaded with."

Sidney's father knew that Sidney was trying to make the man angry enough to lose his concentration. So did Paul.

Sidney only needed a split second delay in pulling that trigger to change the outcome of what was going to happen. One thing Paul was not aware of, was the old cripple was just as dangerous as his son, and he knew his son had certainly known that Paul was there.

Sidney's father got into the game. With an authoritative father's voice, he said, "Hey, don't make the man mad, son, his first shot is going to kill me, he can't miss."

"Fuck him. He doesn't have the guts to blow somebody's head off or kill me. He's just another American punk, a girly man; they're all talk and no action. They are worse that his Chinese partner; all they know how to do is act like the little squinty-eye roosters that jump up and down making childish noises. The chinks think that will scare people away so they won't hurt them. Why do you think they have yellow skin, Pops? It's cuz they're cowards, yellow from the spine out."

Paul realized the verbal attack was an effort to upset him enough for Sidney to rush him, but he was getting to a point where he'd love to blow him away and fuck the mob. He didn't blame Sidney for attacking him verbally; he would do the same if the situation were reversed. He was even playing a part by acting pissed at the remarks to keep Sidney focused on the verbal attack, rather than a physical attack. After all, he did need to keep Sidney alive for the reasons expressed by Sidney's earlier confession. All he had to do was keep him controlled until seven o'clock the next morning when he would meet Chong, who was an expert in extracting information.

The night was spent the same way, Sidney's verbal abuse, Paul's acting insulted, and the older man taking Paul's side at every turn. Paul held fast and remained cautious; he had not presented a single window of opportunity. At dawn Paul had just about had enough. He called in one of his other men and directed him to get one of the other guys and come to the old man's house.

Paul told them they were going to go for a little ride and they placed the old man in the middle of the backseat and Sidney on the right side of the car next to his father. Seatbelts were fastened on both. Another man held a pistol on the two men. Paul locked the rear doors and then sat on the passenger seat with the splatter gun pointing directly at the two Sidneys. The last man drove to the meeting place instructed by Paul. Chong was not there.

Paul tried the cellphone again, and as before, nobody had seen Chong. Sidney continued his verbal attack and said, "Maybe you could use your American pea-brain to see that your partner has split. He must have something of value and dumped you. He probably found Tony."

"What do you mean?"

"Chong's squinty eyes could see the light and his superior intellect made him understand the value of Tony's offer."

"What are you talking about?"

"Surely they approached you, too?"

"I don't know what you're talking about." Then it registered to him that Tony had made some kind of offer to Chong. And, apparently, he was not included in the deal. The realization made him turn quickly to the trees on the left looking for an ambush. He just flashed his eyes to that direction for a second, nowhere near long enough for Sidney to make a move. But, he had not even considered the old man.

The old man had moved with incredible speed and had pushed the gun barrel towards the front seat with his one hand as he swung his powerful other hand to deliver a knockout punch to Paul's lower jaw. The gun went off taking the driver's head, driver's side window, and part of the windshield with it. Sidney went for the pistol held loosely in the other man's hand. Sidney yanked it free and pointed it at the man. He raised his hands. Sidney shot him in the face.

Sidney said, "Leave the shotgun; it has Paul's fingerprints on it. It will make the others disappear."

His father asked, "What are you going to do with the asshole?"

Sidney answered, "He'll be joining Chong, the Chinaman who is waiting for some company in the Cave of Snakes. I'm going to stick you in the bushes while I take care of Paul."

He hoisted his father and slung him over his shoulder. Paul got a little tap from Billy just to be sure he didn't wake up sooner than he should. Sidney started jogging through the old forest. The big mahogany trees' canopies put so much shade on the ground that there was very little brush to slow Sidney down. He wanted to put some distance between the bloody car and his father.

Bouncing around on someone's shoulders was not the most comfortable ride the old man had, but he didn't complain. Sidney put his dad on a comfortable looking spot under a mahogany tree.

"Don't run off, I'll be back within the hour."

"Fucking smart ass," his father said.

Back at the car, Sidney scooped up Paul, slung the big man over a shoulder and ran into the bushes. Twenty minutes later, Paul was still alive but solidly secured to a wall in a totally black cave—in the same cavern as his not-yet-stinking partner. Paul would have to wait until Sidney returned to learn where he was about to die.

In Chong's rental car, Sidney pulled up to his father's home, and he carried his dad to his wheelchair. Then he went to the kitchen and came back with a cold six-pack of beer and a bottle of rum. He took two beers and the rum bottle and said goodbye.

Sidney tossed a cold beer to the old man. The senior Sid said, "Sit down for a minute; we need to talk."

He sat down and opened the beer, curious about what the man had on his mind.

"Tell me what you know about that man and his partner."

Sidney took about five minutes explaining everything he knew, leaving nothing out that could be important.

The older Sid then said, "The man named Chong probably didn't know it, but our visitor planned to fuck his buddy out of a half million dollar reward for you. He used my phone to call the boys in Sicily and gave them your identification and location; you have been exposed. Paul expected them to arrive here as early as tonight."

"That's good. It means I won't have to go after the other men already on island looking for me. Did Paul tell them anything about my presence in Venezuela?"

"No. It sounds like we are going to have a few problems from unfriendly heat put on us. What are your plans?"

"Pack up, Dad; I'll show you the newest land we now own."

"Is there any pussy around there?"

"There's not a lot of women around but we can work out something for you. It is damn sure a great place to disappear for a while."

"Sounds like I don't have a lot of choice since a plane load of pissed off wops is headed my way."

"I'm going back to the Snake to learn more from the American. I'll be back here in three hours, so be ready to leave."

PAUL WAS REVIVED IN THE CAVE OF SNAKES. UNDERSTANDABLY, HE WAS thoroughly confused. It was pitch black and his hands and feet were taped together, and the taps on his skull seemed to have had a cumulative effect on him. He was not the quick-witted man he had been earlier when he did everything perfectly to avoid Sidney's planned attack.

— 514 —

Sidney turned on a lamp and asked, "Can you hear me? Are you able to understand?"

Paul nodded his head, yes.

He said, "Tell me what you told the Italians about me."

He mumbled, but recounted the same story his father had overheard. "Do the Italians know of my connection with Jose Ortega?"

Paul's wimpy answer of "yes" was not what Sidney wanted to hear. Before he could ask him for specifics, the American shuddered, painfully, and then seemed to shrink as he slumped over with a long sigh. Paul had died, leaving a lot of things unanswered.

"You, prick. Where in the hell is my three million dollars?"

Back at his father's place, with a garbage bag full of cash, Sidney asked his father if he was ready to go. The older man had changed his mind about leaving. He said he could take care of himself and it would be best to have a pair of eyes and ears there to see if anyone was overly interested in him. That made sense, but Sidney knew the real reason, the old man would miss his girlfriends. He should've lied about not having many women around there.

VINCENZO HAD ARRIVED IN ST. CROIX THAT MORNING ON THE SEAPLANE from St. Thomas. He had checked into the Caravel Hotel and was walking the waterfront dock to get some fresh air and let his mind wind down. He needed to be clear-headed as he was near the lair of his enemy—a very dangerous enemy. He had studied the poster that he brought with him until he could recognize that face at a glance.

Tomorrow he would be fresh and would systematically start his tracking, but that day he wanted to enjoy the tropical view of the Christiansted Harbor while having a few drinks to relax. It was a day off.

Not many people were wandering about and that was even better. The steady trade wind blew its ten knots of cooling breeze in the tropical surrounding. His mind was locked onto the pleasant sensations he was experiencing and he was relaxed. He became aware of a waterfront restaurant up ahead on the boardwalk, and the thought of a perfectly made Bloody Mary would be a delightful way to welcome a new day.

Another man, carrying a bag, was approaching. When he got close enough to say, "Good morning," he stiffened in sudden recognition of the man. He continued to walk by and act normal as to not alarm the Barracuda.

IT WAS VERY QUIET, EXCEPT FOR A LOUD RINGING IN HIS EARS. HE DIDN'T know where he was at first, and then realized he was lying in a thick bunch of tropical foliage. He was covered with mosquitoes and his head hurt like hell. There was only confusion in his mind. Finally, he stood up in the middle of a tropical garden. Looking through the leaves of plants he could see more people walking the boardwalk.

After he crawled his way out of the growth of tropical plants, he stood on the dock checking his body for damage. Then he went for his wallet thinking he had been mugged; it was still there, his watch and ring were still on. The big diamond necklace, however, was gone. Suddenly he knew what must have happened. Vincenzo had seen his enemy and the bastard had seen the diamond sparkling in the light and had knocked him out and robbed him.

"You, cocksucker," he muttered. "Enjoy it while you can. You'll be dead meat before I'm through with you."

It was disturbing to realize how easily he had been taken. He didn't remember expecting anything, and the man could have killed him just as easily. Vincenzo was sure if Sidney had known the sparkler came from the lovely dead throat of Jandy, he would have never woken up.

SIDNEY COVERED THE WATERFRONT LOOKING FOR THE RIGHT BOAT TO steal. As he walked by a man on the dock he saw him stiffen in recognition, and thought it was one of Chong's men. As he walked by, he quickly pulled Billy from his back pocket and laid it on the back of Vincenzo's head. Sidney grabbed the man and pulled him deep into the bushes. That's when he saw a glimmer of something hanging around the Italian's neck. It was a big diamond pendant. In the dim light, it looked impressive, so he took it. Had he not been in a hurry, he might have associated the fallen man that matched the description of a hit man Chong had described, Vincenzo the Sicilian.

He had come to the waterfront prepared to leave; one boat or another was going to be his. All his shopping had already been done, and when he went aboard he had a second garbage bag, full of canned food, rum and a few cheap cigars. The boat he selected was a twenty-six foot fiberglass catamaran. Used, abused, but loved by someone, it had been sitting in Christiansted Harbor for well over a year. He was sure the owner must live in the States and would not miss it until he returned to the island.

By the time Vincenzo woke up, Sidney had managed to put miles between him and St. Croix.

VENEZUELA

Maria had just arrived at the lagoon where the boy was living aboard the Morgan. A day ago, she had driven him back to the boat from Ortega's house and the trip had been pleasant enough. The boy seemed to be unaware of any need to apologize to her for the kick. It was like it had never happened. Like most kids, he was not very interested in initiating a conversation with a stranger, but would respond to anything Maria brought up. She didn't want to spook the boy by asking questions she was naturally curious about, like where and who his mother was. Did he like his dad? Was he afraid in the jungle? Instead, to get a continuing conversation going, she asked him what his favorite foods were.

The boy responded, "Cheeseburgers, lobsters and coconuts."

She thought, *another long-winded conversationalist, just like his father.* Then she decided not to force her need for conversation. She decided to relax; if the kid was going to learn to like her, it would have to be the real person and not someone trying desperately to get a child to like her.

She soon found herself humming a tune she liked. The humming gradually turned to singing and she was having a good time. She loved to sing and hum and did it mostly when by herself. When she became aware that she was singing out loud she looked over at the boy, feeling slightly embarrassed, to see his reaction. He was sitting there, enjoying the song. He remembered his mother used to sing all of the time and that brought back pleasant memories.

The boy liked her singing and hoped she would keep it up, rather than go back to the stupid questions. He was curious about singing, humming, and the whistling the woman at his grandfather's house had always done. When they arrived at the lagoon, he asked Maria if she could teach him how to do those things. She told him it was easy and would come back the next day to teach him.

She was still afraid of the boy, but there were other feelings stronger than the fear in her. The boy was growing up to be as uncaring as his father and she considered that a waste of the human spirit. She was not going to let that happen.

The next morning, she had some things for the boy: four cheeseburgers in a cooler with all of the trimmings, and a harmonica with instructions and a book of songs titled, "Songs fun to Sing." They would have a picnic and practice the harmonica. She had never played one but thought it would be fun to learn, so there was another one for her. It had been Jandy's idea to buy a case of harmonicas to give to guests who were bored to tears in the remote compound.

He was elated at the food, but unsure of the harmonica. She led the way to a shady grassy spot under a bunch of coconut trees, and spread the same oversized tablecloth they used when they picnicked at the cliffs. While she was getting everything sorted out, she asked the boy, "Why don't you find us a couple of coconuts for coconut cocktails?"

That pleased the boy; he was good at popping coconuts open. He chose two big ones just the right color and using a machete, whacked the tops off in one easy blow, exposing the open part of the nut. They drank the milk then the boy sliced off two pieces of the outer husk to be used as spoons, and used those spoons to scoop out the soft meat.

A fire was made from the deadwood scattered about. Little Sid was an expert at that, too, and she cooked the patties she had brought along on a grill. The boy thought it was silly to carry the grill around and showed her how to make one using green sticks.

By the end of the afternoon, they were having fun, blowing all kinds of sounds through the harmonicas and laughing about each other's attempt. They had hummed songs, sang songs, but could not play songs, yet. She had found the vehicle to get through to the boy—music. He really was very bright and had much more self-confidence than she had seen in most grown men, even the men that were always around Ortega.

He would make a nice catch for some girl in a few years, she thought, *if only I can get that wildness out of him.*

Had Sidney known what was going on in her mind, he would have removed all possibilities of her ever seeing his son again. The wildness was a crucial part to be instilled into the boy to help him survive the life that lay ahead.

Maria went home that evening, but promised to return tomorrow with more hamburgers and hopefully, a mouth not so sore from blowing on the stupid harmonica.

The boy was happy; he had a friend. The other kids in the village stayed away from him because they were afraid of him. The first day he was there, some of the bigger boys asked him to go fishing with them. During the course of the day he proved to be far superior to any of the villagers. This brought hard feelings from the two boys who had always been best, and the expected male chest thumping—yes, even at that age—ensued, which as always, ended up in a fight. The fight was over before it began with Sidney breaking one boy's nose and rendering the other useless with a swift kick to the groin. From then on, they kept their distance.

The little children were always hanging around him, but they bugged him and he would run off so they couldn't find him. Therefore, he was happy to have adult company. And he wondered what those big tits felt like.

Maria made the trip three days in a row and the two of them became closer friends. They both were even getting to the point where they could play "Three Blind Mice" on the harmonicas.

During their time together, Maria got all of her questions in and he answered without much resentment. The boy liked her and still wondered about the tits. Finally he asked her, "Can I feel your titties?"

Shocked, Maria, in a very nice way, asked, "Has your father ever talked to you about relationships between men and women?"

"He said there wasn't much to talk about until I was ready for it. When I was ready, then I'd learn on my own. There isn't any big mystery about it; I watched Grandpa pork Rosie lots of times."

Maria wished she could belt Sidney for the way he was bringing up that child. Then she quickly remembered that if she was ever going to try that again, to be sure it was behind locked doors from the boy.

"Sid, you are at the age when boys and girls start thinking about sex. It is natural; there is nothing wrong with having those feelings. It is a feeling put into us by God to be sure our species is successful on earth. Without the sex drive, our population would dwindle, and like any kind of animal, we could not survive. Even your monkey, Fred, has those feelings, too."

"I know; he beats off all the time."

Maria was a little frustrated, she had never had anything to do with children, and now this conversation was going further than she wanted. The boy didn't seem to feel there was anything wrong with sex and seemed to have a basic or healthy attitude about it, but the details were going to come from someone else. She understood the best thing for her to do was to get out of it.

"No, Sidney, you may not feel my breasts because it is not the right thing two friends like us would do unless they were in love. I love your father, so it would not be right for me to let you do that. Besides, you are seven years old and should not be thinking that way towards a grown woman."

Little Sid thought, *all I wanted was to feel her tits, not fuck her, and I damn sure didn't want to get a lecture about it.* That was the end of the conversation about it forever, but he still wanted to feel those big tits.

☠

Sᴵᴅ sᴀɪʟᴇᴅ ᴛʜᴇ ᴄᴀᴛᴀᴍᴀʀᴀɴ ɪɴᴛᴏ ᴛʜᴇ ʜᴀʀʙᴏʀ ᴍᴜᴄʜ ʟɪᴋᴇ ʜᴇ ʜᴀᴅ done before when the water was rough. It was just as rough as it was then, but he had the advantage of not drawing more than three feet of water. He slid in without trouble. There were a lot of the villagers on hand to welcome him to the lagoon; all but a few were there because they were happy to see him. A few other people where there for other reasons.

A villager told him the boy had gone to the hacienda of Ortega with the woman, Maria.

He thought, "That's good, maybe they will get to be friends, but he better not try to feel her tits—those belong to me."

On his way to the lagoon, Sidney had time to reflect on his life and lifestyle compared to Ortega's. He had always lived wherever he stood at the minute. There were no plans for his life, other than for the next raid. No future, no expectations, no goals to work for; he never yearned for anything, and that had always been perfect for him.

He tried to visualize the boy carrying on for the family. The business of being a solitary pirate in the present day was much harder than it had been ten years ago. Throughout the five hundred years, each Sidney had to adjust to new methods and new markets, but the basic philosophy of pirating had always remained the same: Sneak, Surprise, Steal, and Survive was the pirates' motto from the beginning, and they still applied. They were known to pirates as the *quatre ~s de satisfaction,* the four S's of satisfaction, the basics of their business. But in modern times, the world was changing too rapidly.

Governments were cooperating to find the law breakers. The weird things they were developing in the laboratories, like communications and satellite tracking, were making his world too small. One of these days, he might sneeze while raiding, and a sharp crime laboratory technician will run his snot through one of their fancy instruments and be able to tell that the sneezer had been in Fred's place at three o'clock a week ago; was a Caucasian who smoked weed and drank booze, and the DNA compared to the world database of fingerprints could identify him.

He knew he could outsmart and outfight the authorities in most cases; but for a young boy starting out, it was going to be tougher. And how

SIDNEY X THE PIRATE

bad was it going to get in another ten or fifteen years? Science seemed to be tripling its discovery rate every five or ten years. How tough? Almost suicidal, and what would happen to the family if the boy was killed or thrown in some prison for life? It could mean the end of the Sidneys, and that thought caused him to shudder. He could not let that happen, and like his forefathers, it was his watch and only his responsibility to be sure the line continued; he had to start adapting.

He gave lots of thought as to what the Sidneys could do to maintain their heritage as "King of the Seas" without the disastrous exposure to getting caught or killed. He accepted the fact that he was going to make a change, but didn't know what or how. Some of the things considered were: switch over to land-based operations and rob museums of their treasures. That was no good as he was unfamiliar with modern ways of security, but the boy could learn. That, however, was too far removed from their old ways. They had always been men of the sea, they needed the sea, it was as important as the blood that coursed through their veins. And they needed action; to race in and take out what they wanted from anyone they wanted, and when they wanted.

Progress fucks everything up.

The one thing that got his interest, but he knew nothing about what it meant, was a term he had heard throughout the years—corporate raider. He didn't know what a corporate raider was, but after Jose had defined it, Sidney saw a new challenge, and with the wealth he had stored in a dark cave, it could be used to legitimately raid all kinds of businesses. He decided to look into it.

The idea of turning to drug running didn't appeal to him. They were just a bunch of dishonorable would-be bad guys. He thought that any man who risks so many years in a prison for the measly money made on a drug run was in an entirely different world than he was in. Ortega's position was different; he took no risk—just profits. *Maybe I should have several sons and each could be raiding while I, like Ortega, would stay safe and guard and maintain the family treasure. No... then I'd miss all of the adventure and action.*

Counterfeiting was a cowardly way, and there was no interest in living the life of a coward.

They could live the life of gentlemen and not do anything, like the royals in Europe; living off the empire their forefathers had taken from others until their own offspring became so fat, pampered, spoiled and useless that either the government in the form of taxes, or some enterprising crook, took it away from them.

Another thing he was not going to do was become a member of a government. His family belonged to the world and was never restricted to man-made boundaries that said, "You can't go here or there." Who in the fuck gave the governments the right? Surely, it was God. And he would not support any government in the form of taxation. They didn't do anything to help him get his treasure, other than, of course, to supply much of it. And he didn't subscribe to their laws, the laws of man, which were unnatural laws anyway. Man was designed and built to do the things he wanted to do, not be led around by a fat bunch of self-serving, greedy assholes who knew how to win public approval from the herd of the fat followers. No matter which new course he followed, he would never lose his freedom.

But, there was time for those thoughts later. His present priority was to see the boy, then do his best to get laid. Maria made it clear when he last saw her that she was certainly more than willing.

Also, he wanted to find out if they had heard anything from the Sicilian named Vincenzo. That was one loose end he wanted to nip as soon as possible. With him out there, a shot in the back could happen most anytime. For the first time in his life, he had to watch his back, and he did not like it. It was unpleasant to be restricted by a few punks from a crime family. If the Italians persisted in hunting him, he was ready to declare an all-out war against them. It might sound foolish, but he had methods and the knowledge to take the leaders out one at a time. Before a war, however, he was going to lie low while training his boy in the art of piracy when getting relocated to the Cave of Pigs.

TEN O'CLOCK CAME FIVE HOURS AFTER THE LOCAL ROOSTERS DID THEIR jobs of waking up everyone. Vincenzo's sleep was interrupted by the roosters, and as a city boy; he could not imagine why someone hadn't killed the island's rooster population. He had a headache that would not go away. He remembered his attack and didn't know whether to be mad or grateful, but knew that he would feel a lot better about it after he tracked the asshole down. All he wanted was to have the bastard be aware of who he was before he sent the Barracuda back into the turbulent sea of Hell, where he belonged.

He was in no shape—yet— to take on a man that had handled him so effortlessly. He opened the doors on his mini-balcony to look over the sleepy little harbor. It was just as picturesque in the day as it had been yesterday.

Streams of people, mostly tourist, were walking the boardwalk. He could pick out the cruise ship tourists: Most were fat and a pinkish white and wore matching shorts and shirts. The men seemed to have a dress code that said it was okay to wear sandals while on vacation, but someone should have told them it was not necessary to wear black socks, too. All the people were happy with their swiveling heads trying to take in everything at once while paying very little attention to where they were walking.

He decided to order room service, enjoy a leisurely brunch, and look for the Barracuda from his perch on the overhanging balcony. He probably lived close by since he was there yesterday.

Now that the asshole had seen and robbed him, a direct approach would be out of the question. *Sidney will think I'm coming after him for the diamond, and that could make my job much harder. The man, from all reports, is extremely dangerous. I'll have to catch him unaware and from behind; with my gun at the ready, safety off and my finger on the trigger.*

A look through the telephone book didn't reveal any listings for Xavier. He either had an unlisted number or none, or he lived there under another name. He sat there until two o'clock that afternoon before going out. He went to a photo store down the street and ordered a dozen copies of the poster he had taken from Jandy's wall. The clerk, whose mind was on things far away from the office, told him to come back in a week.

Of course, he thought she was kidding; after all, in the real world, they do that kind of stuff in a minute. It took a half hour of arguing and a one hundred-dollar tip paid up front to get her to promise to have it ready tomorrow morning.

The next morning, eager to get out and start looking, he went to the photo shop.

"It's not ready, yet," she said after waiting on three other customers.

"Damn, lady, why not? You promised it would be here by ten this morning and it's past ten already."

"Don't you be doing no cussing at me, mis'tar."

"I wasn't cussing at you, I just said damn."

"Don't you be doing no cussing in here! This is a Christian place and we don't allow that kind of talk. You go away. I'll call your hotel when they come in."

"Why aren't they here now?"

"I don't know mis'tar, I just work here."

"Well then who can tell me?"

"I don't know. As I said, I just work here. I sent them off to Puerto Rico."

"You sent my fucking picture all the way to Puerto Rico to make a fucking copy?" He knew he had made a grave mistake.

The woman now came from around the counter with a lethal looking club, raised high in the air. She had the meanest African female expression on her face one might expect if she caught you eating one of her babies—alive.

"You sinner. You better take that mouth of yours out of this place or you're going to be doing some explaining to your maker." She was serious, and he was gone before she cleared the counter.

Outside, he yelled, "I'll be back this afternoon."

"No you won't. You better not be, mis'tar. You a fool if you do. You best keep your distance. I said I will call you when they come in here."

"Fucking cunt," he said only to himself, as he turned away in defeat. *Shit, I'm here to take on a brutal murderer single-handedly, and I just got humiliated and chased away in fear of a beating by a small and skinny reli-*

gious woman… I paid an extra hundred bucks to get normal service.

He decided not to wait around the hotel for her call. Instead he wandered around town keeping a sharp eye out for the man known as Sidney the Barracuda. He stopped off at several bars and would casually ask if the bartender knew Sidney Xavier and described his features. Several said he sounded familiar but had no idea where to find him. Three times he went back to his hotel to inquire if he had received a phone call, each time the answer was the same, "No sir, Mister Jones."

The next day, he went to the desk at least a dozen times and every time he received the same response. Trips to the office became so frequent that the two women behind the desk would sing out to the tune of an old popular song about Mr. Jones. "No calls, no phones, Mr. Bones," as he walked into the lobby. It attracted a bemused smile on anyone else around, and then the two women would break out in giggles.

Each time it pissed him off more. If they knew they were messing around with one of the world's foremost hit men they wouldn't be so fucking cheerful. Then he thought, *Yeah I'd bet it would scare them so much they would run over and get that woman at the photo store to chase me off the island.*

Later, much later that night, he walked into a dirty little bar on one of the back streets. It was Fred's Place. Tending bar was a dirty, old, incredibly horny, hag. She had the big eyes for him and let everyone in the bar know it. Vincenzo took it in stride after he realized that besides being dirty, horny and a hag, she was also shit-faced. Her attention switched from him to the next guy who walked in, saving him. The newcomer was drunker than she was and gave it right back to her; they were having a good time. A couple of beers later, it calmed down enough to ask about Sidney. To his amassment, she announced, "Sure, I know Siddy, he a mean one, that son-of-a-bitch."

"Where does he live? I would like to go by and say hello."

"Out on Salt Creek somewhere; probably in the fucking marina on a boat since he is as fucked up as he is," she drunkenly replied.

The newcomer in the bar sitting next to him drunkenly said, "Yeah, he's fucked up alright. Take this to your good ole fucking buddy," and swung his huge fist up out of nowhere, knocking Vincenzo off of the barstool. The man then stood up, downed his drink, and left without saying another word.

"That's old Sam, he's a melancholy sort ain't he?" said the horny hag with a smile hidden behind her fat lips that hid the open spaces in her mouth where several teeth used to be.

The old man, Sam, had a good punch on him, and it was enough to make Vincenzo feel woozy. With the help from one of the other drunks, he got back on his barstool. The drunk got into Vincenzo's face and said, "Welcome to St. Croix; you gonna love this fucking place."

The next day after checking on his expected telephone call that had not come yet, he rented a car. Armed with the simple roadmap provided by the car rental agency, he easily found Salt Creek. He bought a colorful baseball cap and cheap sunglasses, smeared white sunblock over his face, especially his nose, and looked like one of the other thousand tourists on the island. When he reached the marina, he drove by slowly examining everyone.

The place was full of beat-up boats and weathered people to match them. Guys with beards, or at least several days of stubble, walked around with a Budweiser in hand. Most wore no shirt or wore one that wasn't all there because it had either been cut off to make it look like an escapee from the rag bin, or it was full of holes from age and rips. In the civilized world their clothes would be considered as rags. The few women he saw were at least dressed, but in the clothes a woman in the civilized world would have discarded years ago. There was no Sidney to be seen.

There was a little open air bar right on the dock that looked promising. At least he could get a cold beer and hopefully a little information without getting knocked on his ass or chased away again.

"Shit, I've been here two nights and have been beaten up two times and chased out of a public store. And I thought Sicily was a dangerous place."

He had a couple of beers and asked the lady working the bar, "Sidney around today?"

"I haven't seen him. Who are you?" Sally asked.

Vincenzo didn't know how to respond to that question. He didn't want to say he was a friend in fear she would send someone off to bring Sidney there. He damn sure didn't want a face-to-face with the man, even in a public place. And he didn't want to appear that he was looking for him for a reason; they might think he was a cop. Probably cops were not overly welcomed around there. Before he could answer, she helped him find the right answer.

"Are you Chong's friend, Paul?"

That struck a bell. Tony had told him Paul and Chong were trying to find the asshole, too. "Yeah," he answered.

"He has been waiting for Sidney to show up. He was supposed to be here yesterday."

"Where is Chong now?"

"I don't know. He left suddenly two nights ago, and I haven't seen him since. I was hoping you might know."

"What was Chong's interest in Sidney?"

"Oh... I thought you were his friend that was going to help him buy this marina from Sidney."

"Sidney owns the marina?"

"He owns the marina and all of the land around it, including that whole mountain over there."

"Chong didn't tell me what the investment was to be. That's a lot of land. Where does he live?"

"Over there," and she pointed the way to the duplex.

"You are sure he is not home?"

"Positive, I was just in there cleaning up."

"Where else might he go?"

"Sometimes he goes up to see a crippled old man that lives on his mountain. You might go up there and ask him. If you find them, tell Chong to call me, okay?"

"Sure thing lady, how do I get up there?"

She gave him directions and went to serve another customer that was banging an empty beer bottle on the bar, chanting "more whiskey, more whiskey, whiskey for me and my mates."

Vincenzo drove directly up to the only house on the mountain. He got out, making a lot of noise and slammed the door. As he approached the front porch he was met by an extremely tall woman. She had to be six feet six inches tall and was big boned, not a skinny woman. *Shit,* he thought as the ominous looking woman approached, *if she tries to kick the shit out of me too, I'll shoot this one.*

"You lost mister?" she asked in a pleasant voice.

"No ma'am, I'm looking for Sidney or Chong. I was told they might be here."

A gravelly voice from within the house yelled out, "Come on in."

At that moment he was on dangerous turf. Did that voice belong to the Barracuda? He had talked to Paul several times before on the telephone and knew it was not his voice. If it was Sidney, he had to go in ready to kill. His pistol was tucked in the waistband of his shorts, directly behind him in the small of his back.

He walked up and stepped on the porch very much aware of his surroundings. His nervous system was stretched tight and his muscles only needed a millisecond notice to grab the gun and start shooting. His attention was fully focused on the woman and anything else that might suddenly appear. He was not going to be sucker-punched from behind as had happened the other day. The woman stepped in front of him and opened the screen door, allowing him to enter first.

Inside was much darker than the outside that was being covered with the blaring hot rays of sunlight, but there was enough light to see nobody was in the room—other than an old man sitting in a wheelchair. He was wearing shorts, so it was plain to see the man had no feet.

"Hi, my name is Paul Chance, and I was told a fellow named Chong might be here. Do you know him?"

"Sure I do, he wants to buy the marina down the way. What are you to him?"

"I was offered a chance to buy into the deal. Did the transaction go through already?"

"Afraid I wouldn't know. That has got nothing to do with me. Did you look for him down at the marina?"

"Yeah, but they thought he might be up here with the fellow that owns the place, I'm not sure what his name is; Sidney I think. Is he around?"

"I haven't seen him either. Maybe the two of them went off fishing or over to Puerto Rico to do some serious whore chasing. Where are you staying? I'll ask them to call you if they come here."

"Why don't I just wait here for them, would you mind?"

"Shit no, it'll give me somebody to talk to. I don't get much company and I sure can't go traipsing about on my stumps. How about a cold beer?"

Vincenzo said, "Sure, that sounds good." He was glad to relax for a minute and relieved that the Barracuda was not there. Then he added, "I noticed your feet, mind if I ask what happened? Lose them in a war?"

"Nope, birth defect. My mother was a raving slut that smoked cigarettes, dope, and drank whiskey during her pregnancy," was Sid's response as he wheeled his chair over to give him a beer.

After a few sips of the cold brew, Vincenzo said, "What can you tell me about this fellow, Sidney?"

"Oh, he's a sweet boy. Comes to visit me a lot and he's about my only visitor except Emma Lou here. She comes over every day to fuck my brains out."

Vincenzo looked over at Emma Lou, to acknowledge her, but she was sitting there with indifference to the conversation. Then the older man told her she could go home for the day.

Shit, Vincenzo thought, *if that's a hooker then this guy is really hard up. St. Croix has to have better looking whores than that.*

She got up to leave. Vincenzo got up to be polite and said goodbye. As he did, old Sid saw there was a foreign object stuck in the man's waistband.

Vincenzo was glad for the woman to leave. Now he could drop all pretenses and get tough on the crippled old man to find out where the hell Sidney was, and where the best place was to whack him.

A few minutes after the screen door was shut, Vincenzo said, "Well, I need to leave, too, but I need to know where I should look to find Chong and Sidney, and don't give me anymore shit about power fucking in Puerto Rico. Where is the best place to find them?"

"You don't sound so friendly anymore, Paul. Did I piss you off about something?"

"I got some bad news for you, stumpy. You are going to tell me every-thing you know about your friend Sidney, and it's going to hurt you if you don't. Now where can I find him?"

"I told you; I don't know," he responded with a whine. "How come you need to know that anyway?"

Vincenzo walked over to the wheelchair, faking a smile until he was close enough, and then shot off a lightning-fast punch to the cripple's head. He would stun him with the blow and then tie him to the chair for some serious Q&A. He was going to have his information on the Barra-cuda even if he did have to beat the shit out of a crippled old man.

The cripple's head, however, was not there when the punch went by. It dropped, as did the cripple's body, and Vincenzo felt the pain of crush-ing strength around his waist from the man's arms, throwing him to the ground. A flash of pain hit him directly on the forehead.

Sometime later, Vincenzo became aware that he was hog-tied and ly-ing in the middle of the floor. He looked around the best he could and saw the cripple sitting in his chair, drinking a beer, smoking a cigar and snacking on peanuts while watching the Dallas Cowboys take a trounc-ing from the Tampa Bay team. Vincenzo remained still, looking for the asshole Sidney, who must have come up from behind him when he ap-proached the cripple. He couldn't figure out, however, how he had missed the old man; he had an open shot at him and was only two feet away when he had swung.

Shit, he thought, *what kind of island is this fucking place. I've been beat up by an old cripple man with no fucking legs and chased and beaten by two women and knocked on my ass by a drunk. Next, Sid will probably show up, and he's bound to put heavy pressure on me to find out what I know, and then I'll be zapped and thrown in a garbage pile or taken off shore and fed to the fucking fish.*

He wasn't happy, but knew that eventually it would be his turn. He had done those things to countless people—when it happens, there ain't shit you can do about it so don't dwell on it; just do whatever it takes to stay alive.

The football game reached the halftime and the old man in the wheelchair turned for the first time to acknowledge that Vincenzo was even there.

"Well, Vincenzo, how do you like the game?"

Vincenzo had not used his name so he was alarmed, and he had left his identification papers in the hotel's vault.

He responded, "It would be a better game if I could sit up to watch it and didn't have my hands tied up so I could eat peanuts and drink beer with you."

"Well, if you didn't go around picking on poor old cripples you would be sitting up drinking beer, eating peanuts, and I would have even let you smoke one of my Rafael Gonzalez cigars. They have been aging for a year now and are without a doubt the best cigar Havana can make. Do you like cigars?"

"Sure, I enjoy a good cigar occasionally."

"Ah, that's too bad, Vincenzo," he said, showing pity that he would not be getting one. The old Sid was not going to waste one of his treasures on a dead man. "So how did I get like this? Sidney did it, right?"

"That's right, Sidney got you."

"So they call him the Barracuda, uh?"

"Well, actually, it should be pronounced Barracouta to roll the Rs."

"Where is he? Can I talk to him?"

"Sure. Go ahead and talk."

"Where is he?"

"I am right here talking to you, stupid."

Vincenzo was not in the mood for games, but there was little he could do about it. The only option he had was to stop talking.

"I mean the guy that has been robbing ships and casinos for a few years. The asshole the seamen call Barracuda, Sidney X."

"Which Sidney X are you talking about?"

"Hell, don't tell me there is more than one?"

"Sure, there is. There are three Sidney Xs. My son and his boy are away, sailing off the coast of Venezuela."

Then realization of what was just told to him sunk in. The two entries concerning Sidney X spread over seventy years apart was not a coincidence or a mistake. "Are you trying to tell me your name is Sidney X, the Barracuda?"

"My name is Sidney X, but I stopped being the Barracuda when a shark took my feet. It's a little hard to capture prizes in a wheelchair. My son is the Barracuda now and has been doing a good job, especially with your people, don't you think?"

"You know who I am?" asked Vincenzo.

"Certainly; both Paul and Chong told us about you. That's why I am here instead of sailing with my boys. I have been waiting for you."

Shit, shit, shit, Vincenzo thought to himself, *now even old men in wheelchairs are playing me like a fucking puppy.*

"Where are Paul and Chong?"

"Those two are dancing with the devil these days. They didn't hold up too well while they were with my son."

Vincenzo thought, *two Sidney Xs in the eighteenth century and now there are three Sidney Xs, pirates all.* Paul and Chong were too smart to be taken by one man, then Vincenzo realized that he was smart also, and look where he was—and who did it to him.

"I'm assuming Chong and Paul were not good house guests so they were shown the door—to hell. Where do we go from here, Sidney?"

"I am going to go take a leak, then ask you a few questions, then you are going to say hello to your pals, Paul and Chong."

"Yeah, I guessed that is what you had in mind. Would you answer a couple of questions for me before you send me on that one way trip?"

"Of course. What do you want to know?"

"Tell me about you. I have been doing some research on pirates. I saw a couple of references made to Sidney X who were around a long time ago. There were two separate records about them being pirates. One was killed and other was of a pirate flag."

"No shit. I had no idea the public had any knowledge of the Sidneys."

"Who are the Sidneys?"

Old Sid pulled his shirt off. Vincenzo could not believe the muscular body sitting in the wheelchair nor could he believe he had the same tattoo as the pirate flag shown in the book. He counted the bones. There were twenty two.

"We have been around for a very long time. We are the least known pirates in the world, but have been the 'King of the Seas' for over five hundred consecutive years. We are born and raised for one purpose, to be pirates. So don't feel bad about you being taken so easily; you had no say in the matter. We are trained by our fathers starting at the age of six to be the most lethal mother-fuckers on earth."

"Shit, untie me and I'll show you some bad," said Vincenzo.

"What? You mean with that little pop gun you came in here with? If you had made a move to get that thing out of your belt you would have tasted steel from my little knife here." Out of nowhere he produced a custom made, stainless steel knife with a polished wooden handle and a ten inch blade.

"At least your pal, Paul, had enough sense to come in with a short barrel shotgun, but that didn't help him either."

"Who are you guys?"

"I just told you. There is no mystery. We are just born and bred pirates and love it."

"What happened to all of the money you have taken away from us? You could live in a mansion anywhere in the world you want with that much money."

"Hate to tell you, but it was just thrown into our cave with the rest of our treasure. That money means nothing to us other than it is the *prize*. We have millions upon millions of dollars in our treasury and can spend it anytime. When you know you have it, why spend it; what is it going to buy anyway? If I had a fifty-room mansion on the Riviera would I be any happier? Sure, comfort is important, but how comfortable can you be. I eat, drink, smoke, and fuck anything I want now. And the view and weather are perfect."

"Under the circumstances, Sidney, with all that money you probably are right, but you sure have bad taste in women."

"Yeah, that's what my son keeps telling me, but pussy is pussy, who gives a shit what it looks like. As long as it is good and friendly, that's all that counts. As you get older—which by the way, you don't have to worry about—you realize that the ugly ones are going to be much more appreciative about the fuck and will be better companions and usually have a better sense of humor."

Sidney then asked, "Now are you ready to answer a couple of questions for me?"

"I doubt that I have any choice. I have talked to a lot of people who have been in my position with your son doing his handiwork. I suppose he learned all of that from you, right?"

"I don't know. I think he is wimpy about getting people to talk. It has always been much easier for me. I really don't care how I leave someone. I know he leaves most of his people alive. I never did. That's why you are lying here all tied up right now, because he left people around to talk. Believe me, that was not how he was brought up."

"It seems I am in for a bad time of it," said Vincenzo.

"Not unless you want it that way. Sure, you're a dead man, but that doesn't mean you have to feel it or go through the experience. You cooperate, and I guarantee you will never be killed any better than by me. I absolutely can assure you that you will be here one instant—fat, dumb, and happy, and then in the next world the next instant wondering, how in the fuck did I get here?"

"I think I'll opt for the easy way. What do you want to know?"

"Who knows what you know?"

"The big guys in Sicily know most of it. They don't know about you, obviously. I called them yesterday and filled them in on what I had learned. I told them about Sidney's connection with the Ortega family and that he hangs out there. I am afraid unless I show up to tell them he is no longer in this world, they will swarm over this island and Ortega's place until they get him and maybe even you."

"That's too bad. I had hoped my son learned to be more careful. He knows he should have never started hanging out with other people. Now his getting known has gotten him into this mess."

"Did you say he has a kid who he is training to take over?"

"Yep. Ain't it wonderful?"

"It may be wonderful for you guys, but it's pretty rough on the rest of us," Vincenzo said with a smile.

"Too bad. That's what the world is all about though, meat eaters eat meat. How soon do you think it will be before the Italian swarm arrives?"

"There is a bunch due in here any day. I don't know how soon they will take men to Ortega's place."

"So give me the names of the big guys in Sicily."

It really bothered Vincenzo to even think of rolling over on the Circle of Fifteen. Those were the men he admired most of his adult life. Those were the men that kept the world's family together, the ultimate power. He could not tell him who these people were, knowing they would surely suffer as the other victims had. However, the memory of the terrible things that had been done to others, and would be done to him, bothered him more, so he talked freely. He not only gave Sid the names, but where they lived as well.

Sid asked, "They want to see a dead body that can be identified as the Barracuda?"

"And get their money back."

"They can forget that. It is our money now and nobody has ever taken anything from the Sidneys. They can have Sid if they can take him, but not the money, nor the boy. Anything else you want to offer? I got to go take that leak now."

"Mind if I smoke one of those cigars before I go?"

"Sorry, Vincenzo, but I just can't waste one of my beauties on a dead guy."

And Vincenzo really didn't see or feel a thing as he left the living world—and still, after 200,000 years, no one knew what he felt or saw in the next instant.

THE TELEPHONE RANG LOUDLY AS ALL CALLS AT THREE O'CLOCK IN THE morning will. Calls so early in the morning always meant bad news, and that was the case that morning. It was Ortega's brother. He was angry as he told Jose Ortega the news about Jandy. She had been found by the police after a call about a prowler from a neighbor. They investigated and when nobody answered her door, they broke in and found her body. She had been robbed and choked to death.

Ortega was grief stricken by the news; she had been like a wife, a sister and his best friend for years. Of course, he was mad as hell about it, but he remained calm. "Any idea who did it?" he asked.

"Not a clue, but a white guy was seen going down her walk earlier that night. That is what prompted the call to the cops."

That was somewhat unusual, a white guy doing robberies in St. Thomas? He told his brother, "Check with the cops to see if they had any other robberies that fit this pattern where a white guy robs and kills."

"I already did that, Jose. I thought it was funny, too. Most white guys there were usually too fucked up or drunk to rob people unless they were looking for dope or booze. That pattern is reserved for the young black men on St. Thomas who lost a job and needed to feed a family. The last white guy that committed a burglary and killed the victim took place four years ago."

Jose Ortega thought of Sidney at first, but knew he would not harm Jandy, and certainly would not bother making it appear that it was a robbery to hide the killing. If Sidney killed somebody, he would have cared less what anyone thought. His next thought went to the Mafia. Had they spotted the big diamond she was so proud of? Were they questioning her to find out where she had gotten it? That was more than plausible.

The day Sidney arrived, his son, happy and excited, ran out to see him. Maria, with wet, red swollen eyes followed. When she came closer she burst into tears. Sidney reached out and grabbed the boy by his arm and said, "I told you not to hurt her."

The boy said, "I didn't. She has been doing that a lot lately."

"Jandy has been killed," she blurted out.

The words, "Who did it," spoken from Sidney were enough to scare anyone with the tone of icy coldness in his voice. Ortega had just stepped out in time to hear Sidney's response. That was enough to assure him his pirate pal had nothing to do with her death.

Ortega said, "Don't know yet, Sid, but we are looking."

"Where was she and when did it happen?"

"She was found in her apartment in St. Thomas the day you two left here. The police say she was robbed. They also think it was a white man as one was seen leaving her place that night. You were not there?"

"They took her diamond, didn't they?"

Maria, suspicious about how he would know about that, unless he was there or took it, asked, "How did you know about the diamond?"

"I gave it to her," he answered.

"It was not in the apartment when the cops went through it, or they might have taken it if it was left there."

Sidney reached into his pocket and pulled out the diamond necklace and put it in Maria's hand. "I knew it belonged to either you or Jandy. I found it in St. Croix."

Maria had several urgent questions to ask, but Sidney said, "Ortega, let me use your telephone. I'll find out who did this."

He dialed the number of his father in St. Croix.

"Any visitors?" he asked without the preliminary greetings.

"Vincenzo Jones was here. He's not among us anymore. Are you down south?"

"Yeah."

"There are going to be some visitors coming by to see you. They know who and where you are; hide the boy before they get there. They don't know about me or the kid."

"Take care, Pop, and do what you can for the boy, he will be back there as soon as we look over the Pig."

"I have the names of those who want you. Do you want them?"

"I think the Pig is more important right now."

"Okay son, wish I could be there to help you."

"You have done your part very well. Goodbye, Pop."

Ortega overheard the conversation. It sounded like a final farewell from a son to his father. He was surprised to learn that Sidney even had a father. He toyed with the thought of an older version of Sidney and wanted to meet such a man to see if indeed the whole bunch of past Sidneys were the same. It also sounded like he was passing the responsibility of the boy over to his father which could only mean Sidney was in grave danger.

"The man who murdered Jandy was Vincenzo, the Sicilian." Sidney explained to Jose. "He confessed just before he died. Jandy was killed to gain information about me. I don't know how we became connected, but Vincenzo sniffed it out. You and Maria must leave here right this minute. The Mafia knows about me and that you and I are friends. They are coming here to look for me and possibly give you a bad time."

"That's ridiculous; those guys know better than to mess with me or my family."

"Well, they want me bad enough to take some losses."

"Let's all go, you and the boy, too. I can assure you will be safe at our compound in St. Thomas."

"The boy and I are safe. We are going camping and they won't find us until I am ready."

"Well, I am not leaving either; they won't fuck with me."

"Look what they did to pretty little Jandy. The Circle of Fifteen has ordered the team in here. You have to go. If you want to stay here and deal with their hassles, go ahead; it's your ass that'll take the beating, but get Maria out of here."

"I would like to know who those bastards in the Circle are. We could put a stop to this shit real quick."

"The Circle of Fifteen belongs to the Sidneys; don't interfere."

Ortega could tell Sidney was way ahead of him and shuddered at the thought of what was in the future for those men of the Circle. Then he decided to take Sidney's warning and told Maria to get the pilot; they were leaving in fifteen minutes.

"Jose, I would like to speak to you in private for a minute before you leave," said Sidney.

Ortega led him to his office and closed the door.

"Ortega, you don't know me very well, and I don't know you very well either. I have been on my own all of my life and have known very few people. I'm not even sure what the term friendship really means, but guess I would consider you as a friend. At least I trust you, and you've been told something about my family's history as pirates. I think those days are numbered, and it's time for the Sidneys to adapt to the changing world, without losing the principles of personal freedom that we strongly believe in. I am going to stop this business between the Mafia and your family the only way possible. That is to give them me. I could kill the men on the Circle, but that takes time. During that time, they are going to be giving you a lot of shit and more people are going to die if they think you're protecting me. It is part of my basic makeup not to let you, a friend, pay a price for my actions."

Ortega tried to interrupt him, but Sidney continued, "I want you to do something for me in return. I want you to be a friend to my son. Maybe offer suggestions, guidelines to help him grow up to be better suited than I was to live with modern society, but not to bow to it , just to live with it. Schooling would help, he is a smart kid, but you must never interfere between the boy and his grandfather. You do not want to get my father pissed at you. He is much more vicious than I am, believe me."

Ortega smiled at the possibility that anyone could be worse than Sidney, but he did believe him; after all, those men had five hundred years to perfect the meaning of being a bad dude.

"If you ever meet him, tell him about this conversation and tell him everything you know about us. He would be a good man to have on your side. He will finish training the boy, but if you get any ideas how he may do something different to adapt, then quietly work the ideas in. Your type of business is out of the question. He doesn't need money. The important things are to preserve our freedom and honor with him, and the challenge of taking the *prize* are what we have been bred for. Please respect this in the boy."

"Isn't there another way out of this?" asked Ortega.

"Yes, and it might happen, but I wanted to tell you these things in case it doesn't."

"I won't let you down, Sidney. As far as shifting gears into a different type of business, are you talking about learning the corporate raider?"

"Yeah, something like that."

Outside, the helicopter being started indicated it was time for them

and selected leaves from several bushes were added to the knapsack to give them some greens to eat.

They walked by the bones of Tony the Pop and slowly searched for the tunnel Sidney had crawled up in the total darkness to reach that level. The boy found the vertical drop and they climbed down and were happy to get out of the piles of guano. Sidney was amazed that he had found it in the complete blackness before. He wanted to see where he had landed when he was pulled into the water entrance of the cave.

It was an awesome sight, with the two small circles of lights from their flashlights playing back and forth over the jagged rocks and the shear vertical fall that went down farther than the light beams would carry. The roar of the waterfall was deafening. Falling on the ledge that saved his life and not going to the bottom had been a one in a hundred chance.

Satisfied there was no way to keep going in that direction, they took another side tunnel. At every change in direction, Sidney put two gashes on the rock wall with another rock so they would be able to find their way out again. It was going to be a slow process, but they had lots of time—as long as they remained in the cavern.

It had been Sidney's unbelievably good timing for Jose Ortega that Sidney left when he did. They had been gone about an hour when two helicopters sped into view of the guards and descended. The guards at Ortega's compound laid their weapons down and raised their hands into the air at the sight of a dozen men armed with Uzis and riot guns. The guards didn't mind pointing their guns at people to scare away the rare passerby, but a greatly unbalanced gun battle was beyond their pay grade.

Another helicopter landed in the little seaside village, blowing the tin roof off of Gaspar's bar. Heavily armed men bounded out of the landed aircraft as soon as they touched down. No one in the village admonished the intruders for the destruction their arrival had caused; they only ran to their homes and hid.

The invaders at Ortega's compound asked no questions, they just fanned out with guns at the ready. Some stayed outside; others swept into the houses, searching every room, ignoring the threats of the household staff to get out. Only after they were completely satisfied that Ortega and his friend were not there did they start asking questions.

The guards told them Ortega had gone to St. Thomas about an hour ago. The friend of Ortega was here, but he left at the same time to go camping for a few days in the jungle. He didn't know where, but they could look for his Jeep and he would surely be close by. Asked to describe the Jeep, he said, "Besides that Jeep over there," and he pointed to Ortega's, "it will be the only automobile you will see in one hundred miles in any direction."

One helicopter remained at Ortega's and the other departed to look for the Jeep. An hour later, the radio in the parked helicopter squawked, "We found the Jeep. There is no sign of the man. We will land here and await your arrival before searching. Run a heading of ninety-five degrees true for about twenty minutes."

The other chopper came to life and the small army ran to and loaded into the aircraft. As it disappeared, the guards looked at each other to see if anyone had any idea what that was all about. The housekeeper was on the telephone to St. Thomas to leave word what had happened.

The raiders set up camp where they found the Jeep. Someone reminded them this was the place where Tony had disappeared, either at the hands of the man they were looking for, or when the two of them instigated their plans to go against the family. Either way, the Mafia heavies were instructed to be on alert for anything out of the usual. They had come prepared to stay a while; their orders were to go there and stay until the bastard was caught or dead. They had provisions for two weeks on board the helicopters.

The same was true at the little village. The same was also true for the two choppers that landed in St. Croix.

THE SIDNEYS WANDERED THROUGH THE COUNTLESS BIG AND NARROW

passages. Some went vertical, some were impassable, and all were very dark without help from the flashlight. They stopped using both lights to conserve batteries in the five flashlights. When they were not moving, the light was turned off.

They had been in the cavern for an estimated four days and had found nothing to indicate there might be another entrance. Occasionally, Sidney would light up a cigar to see if the smoke would pull to one direction or another, but there had only been still air.

As the second light began to dim before failure, Sidney shut it off and made the decision to push harder on the third light and go further into the cave. They had been in a bigger cavern for about six hours and it didn't seem to be getting any smaller, so it made the going easier. Slowly the cave began to narrow again and they encountered more turns and vertical twists. It began to look like that branch might be petering out, but suddenly Sidney saw something on the floor of the cave—bones of a small animal. Then there were more bones and Sidney relit his last cigar. There was movement of the smoke. They followed the smoke trail to a running stream, where they drank their fill of ice cold spring water. While filling the two canteens, young Sidney saw a white fish swimming, then another, then a small school of blind catfish.

Sidney caught several of them and they feasted on raw fish. The rats they had roasted had been reduced to one rat. He was saving it for the halfway point on the trip back, if they didn't find another opening. There also had been the reserve food, Fred, if things got desperate.

It took about half a day to finally smell and feel the fresh air and three more hours to see a peep of daylight. As they climbed out to the setting sun, Sidney could not believe what he saw. Paradise in the purest sense of the word surrounded him. The cave's entrance was about two hundred feet above a lush jungle valley. A tiny lagoon was fed by the stream they had drunk from earlier. The stream continued on the other side of the lagoon to the Caribbean Sea. It was perfection. They worked their way down the hillside to the lagoon and over to the beach that was heavily populated with coconut trees, which made it perfect for Fred as well.

That evening, they sat under the stars of a beautiful Caribbean night, eating fresh food caught and cooked on an open fire. Both Sidneys were elated at being on top of the ground for the first time in days.

THE LEADER OF THE ITALIAN INVADERS' NAME WAS CHARLES DANIA, AND he was pissed off. They had combed every inch of ground they could traverse without a single sight of another human. He had convinced himself it had been a trick by Ortega to tell them the pirate was camping in the woods, but had probably gone with him to the Virgins.

"If this was a diversion to buy some time, it worked. It bought you a fucking week, but you are not going to like the price you are about to pay," he muttered.

It was the morning of the eighth day and he was calling it quits. Using the satellite telephone on board the helicopter, he called Sicily and explained the situation and what his intended plan of action was.

Sicily decided it would not be a good idea to burn Ortega's hacienda to the ground, nor the part about raiding their St. Thomas compound. After all, that was Don Ortega's turf and it would only be detrimental to business relations. They wanted one team to remain at the village where the boat was and one at Ortega's hacienda. The other team was to travel to St. Thomas and kidnap a couple of Ortega's key men. Care was to be taken not to damage the men in case the guy they wanted did come out of the jungle. Charles arranged for the three helicopters to meet at the hacienda at noon that afternoon. He wanted to pull the best men for the kidnapping.

SIDNEY HAD TALKED TO THE BOY AT LENGTH THE PREVIOUS NIGHT about what was going on and what would probably be happening. He gave him strict instructions on what to do when things started happening. The boy understood the importance of staying alive to keep the Sidneys in business, but he didn't like the plan. He didn't like the part about his father possibly being killed. But he accepted it as something that was meant to be. After all, his history was littered with dead, but courageous, fathers.

By the time the sun was just off of the horizon, they began walking down the shore. They would walk the twenty-seven miles back to the little village, rather than go back through the cave. They both had had enough of that. When they reached the village, the boy would sail back to St. Croix.

Sidney would make his way to Ortega's hacienda to see what had happened. He halfway expected it to be guarded by the Mafia until he was found. If it was, then good; it was time to finish the thing one way or another.

The twenty-seven mile walk turned into a seven mile walk and they trotted the rest of the way, taking them almost seven hours to cover the distance. When Sidney came to familiar grounds, where he had been before, he became cautious. They stayed off the beach and walked in the long shadows of the trees. As they got within sight of the village Sidney could see the rotors of a helicopter sitting among the trees. Then his mind went into gear planning the attack. If they were able to stay out of sight until he reached the village, the advantage belonged to him. If they had a man on guard with binoculars scanning the tree lines, he would have a much tougher time of it. To be sure he was not spotted, he stayed as deep in the trees as possible.

He instructed his son on the art of moving without being seen as the big cats do when they are hunting. But it was something the boy had already learned while living in the jungle. Sidney was thinking the kid had a knack for this sort of thing and wished he could let the boy go to the attack with him, but that was to risk the continuation of the Sidneys. The boy was being permitted to watch, however, as it would be good training for him.

The sky was turning dark as night approached, and a squall had moved in from the ocean. It was also a big help to have both. Darkness would provide him with cover and the rain would bring all of the men that came into the helicopter to group together in a shelter, either that or in Gaspar's bar. As Sidney worked in closer, in the downpour he could

SIDNEY X THE PIRATE

tell they were in the chopper as the little bar's roof was lying on the sand twenty feet away.

He watched the men in the helicopter. One man was seated at the controls, so Sidney would leave the pilot alive to furnish the transportation he would need. It was obvious that if they left a full team of men to watch his boat then they had to have at least the same number, if not more, at Ortega's place. To walk the distance would mean giving time for the other crew to try contacting the village team. When there would be no response it would surely alert them to a possible problem. Also he had walked long enough that day alreadyHe explained to the boy that what he was about to do was wrong. "You should never attack more than one man at a time. To do so changes the odds drastically that you will get hurt since you will be in the fight longer. Remember, the idea is to keep the attack as sudden and as short as possible. Watch my every move because someday you may have to face the same danger."

Sidney silently walked up to the open side door of the helicopter. Knife and Billy were pulled and ready. Little Sid was shaking with excitement watching his father do the same things he had been training him to do. The boy was proud and wished he had been allowed to help. His father worked his way to the edge of the open door, and then swiftly moved inside. In less than ten seconds, his father emerged and casually motioned his son to come to him.

They got into the chopper. Dead men and blood were everywhere. The pilot was unconscious in his seat. "Remember to walk in knowing your enemy is dead and he doesn't stand a chance against you, as you are the toughest man alive. You are indestructible, and if you get cut or shot, you know that it makes no difference. You are the Barracuda, no one is faster and none is as deadly."

"What do we do with the dead men, Dad?"

"We leave them as they are. The bloody massacre will send a powerful message to their boss."

He sliced the throat of a man with a crushed skull to show the boy exactly how it was to be done. He pointed to another crushed skull and said, "Now you do it."

The boy stood there. He had never killed or hurt a human before and it just didn't seem right. He hesitated and looked up at his father. Sidney had been there once before and knew the thoughts that were pulling at the boy. He decided not to push it; he was in a hurry and the boy was probably too young to get into the killing part of the business. There would be time for that later. After securing the pilot to his seat with duct tape, they left the bloody helicopter.

Gaspar came running out of the bar telling the village that Sidney had taken care of the foreign hombres, and the people emerged from their shacks, smiling and excited.

Gaspar ran up to Sidney, "You have done a very good thing. Those men were very bad; they had raped two young girls and were taking anything they wanted." He was so excited that he ran back into the roofless bar and came out with two bottles of rum that he gave to Sidney.

The boat checked out and it had not been bothered. Sidney said goodbye to his boy and told him to leave right now. While the boy checked his food and water supply, Sidney pulled out about one hundred feet of the anchor line and cut it free from the boat. The rope was coiled up and he took it with him.

He watched with pride as the kid hoisted his anchor, started the diesel engine and headed out of the lagoon. He watched as the boat maneuvered through the mild surf and then was in the clear. He was in deep water and the bow turned slightly northwest for the trip back to his grandfather.

Back inside the helicopter, Sidney freed the pilot and woke him up by splashing water in his face. The pilot became aware of where he was and looked around at the pile of dead men in the back cabin.

Sidney said, "there are only two reasons why you are not on that pile, and I bet you know what they are."

"You want me to take you somewhere in the chopper?"

"That's one reason. Yes, take me to Ortega's hacienda. The second reason is you have not seen my face. To see me is to be killed."

Then the guy became more aware and said, "Shit, you are the guy they have been looking for. Aren't you?"

"Could be. What do you mean *they?* Aren't you one of them?"

"Hell no, this is my helicopter. They chartered it and me by the day for an unspecified time."

"Just how many of *them* are there?"

"Two other chartered choppers with six men just like this bunch in each."

The pilot looked around as what had happened sunk in. "Did you do this by yourself?"

"Let's get going, pilot. Do what you are supposed to and you won't end up on the pile. Look at me one time and you're history." The pilot believed him and started his aircraft.

As they approached the hacienda, the pilot thought it would be a good idea to radio the other chopper to let him know they were coming in for a good reason. Sidney told him there would be no communications. Then he located the microphone and pulled it out of its connection. The pilot was frightened, but really had no options other than to do as he was told and be alert for any chance to escape from the bloodthirsty killer.

Sidney gave the pilot instructions. "You will hover at fifty feet off the ground. You will stay there for five minutes, and then land a safe distance from the other helicopter. You will not turn on any lights or make any contact with the ground until you land. If you do anything other than what I have said, you are going to die. Do as you are told and you will live. I need you to be a living messenger, so do not make me kill you. Understand?"

The pilot nodded his head that he did, but he didn't look at his captor. He didn't want him to see the fear in his eyes. He followed Sidney's instructions and took it down low and fast and approached from downwind, then stopped it in mid-air when he was given the word. He had done those things and had been stationary hovering for three minutes.

He could see the dark shadows of men running from the house to see what was going on. When he spotted one shadow come from behind another and the other fall to the ground, he decided not to look again until he landed. He spent the rest of his time watching his watch and borrowing a line from Sergeant Schultz, he said, "I see nothing!" At exactly five minutes after the killer had yelled "okay" he let his chopper settle to the ground.

Sidney had looped the anchor line he had taken from the *Barracouta* around the grab rail by the door. When he yelled, "okay", the pilot abruptly halted forward speed and Sidney leapt out of the door using the rope to slow his decent. As soon as he hit the ground he pulled one end of the rope through the rail, and it fell to the ground leaving no evidence that someone had left the aircraft. He then ran silently around the outskirts of the night lights, and he reached the house before the first man came out to see what was going on.

As they exited the house, Sidney waited until all twelve men were outside. One man was told to get on the radio of his helicopter to learn what was going on.

That has to be the other pilot, Sidney thought. Then he walked up behind each man and thumped them with Billy. Not one man bothered to look behind them, as their attention was focused on the hovering helicopter.

The second pilot came out of his chopper and yelled, "Carlo, there is no answer from Gary." Then he looked out over the lawn and there was no Carlo. A second later, there was nothing except blackness as Billy sent another into a deep sleep.

"You must be Gary." Sidney said as he jumped into the first helicopter. The pilot was extremely nervous as he had no idea what to expect. He was not a fighter, but realized that he might be in a fight for his life right at that moment. He had gotten ready to defend himself by placing his back against the bulkhead while holding an Uzi taken from one of the dead men on the floor of his chopper.

Sidney, seeing the man's condition said, "Put the gun down, Gary, you will not need it. You have done as you were told; you have nothing to fear from me. Now come help get those people in the other chopper."

Gary thought, *What the hell, I might as well believe him. If there is a problem between him and the Italians, they can sort it out. No reason for me to kill someone or be killed.* Before he put the Uzi down, he asked, "How do I know you are not going to kill me?"

Sidney, wearing a handkerchief, came into the cockpit. "I told you earlier; I need you to be my messenger. If I had wanted a dead messenger, there are plenty of others who already qualify for that position."

The two of them loaded the unconscious men into the other helicopter. As they were placed inside, Sidney quickly taped them up so they could not see, speak, or move. The last act was to revive the second pilot. A piece of tape was put over his eyes so he could not see the face of the man responsible for this. Gary felt much more secure seeing that the other men had not been killed.

After the crew was loaded up, Sidney said to the two pilots, "You two are going to top off your fuel tanks here and then fly directly to the Ortega compound on Molab Island near St. Thomas. I am going to give you a message to be given to the leader of the remaining team, but make sure that everyone in the team and the Ortegas read it. You two will not know the contents of the message to protect you from being killed by the Italians. It is highly confidential. The six men still alive must arrive in exactly the same way as they are now. I do not want them disturbed in any way, so I will be riding in the back of this aircraft. I do not want to be disturbed, even one time. Gary, you will leave first with your dead cargo. Chuck, you will follow him. Do you both understand and agree to do this?"

Both said, "Yes, sir." The pilot with taped eyes and hands said, "I'll need my hands and eyes, sir."

"Leave the tape on your eyes until you get in your chopper. I'll remove the tape after I write my message." Sidney and the two pilots went inside Jose Ortega's office and wrote the message to be given to the Italians, and then he made one copy for Don Ziguia Ortega. They were sealed in two envelopes and given to Gary. "I cannot impress too strongly, do not read this communiqué."

Sidney positioned himself for the ride to St. Thomas, sitting in the back. After the pilot was in place, Sid closed the door between the compartments and jammed it closed with a screwdriver. He heard Gary's helicopter rev up and lift off the ground and then Chuck followed. As it left the ground, Sidney slid out of the open side door and ran back behind the rising chopper while staying out of sight.

Four hours later, the pair of helicopters circled over the Caribbean compound looking for a good place to set down. They had followed

Sid's directions on how to find the place and had no problems. After all, how many small islands have only one very large structure on it with its own airstrip?

Their appearance attracted a lot of attention and everyone was outside to watch them land. Gary landed first, and the Ortegas and the Sicilian who took over Tony's position in the Circle, and Jake ~the Ripper~ Gugino, were there to welcome the teams. The returning teams could only mean one thing; they had caught the trouble-making pirate. Jake was anxious to see what was left of the man who had fucked around with the family and to congratulate those who caught him.

Gary opened the door and stepped out of the aircraft, leaving the door open. The expression on his face told Jake that something was wrong, and he ran to the door to look inside. Everyone outside could hear the cusses yelled from inside as Jake realized all of his men had been murdered.

Jake charged out of the aircraft and ran directly to Gary and screamed, "What the fuck happened? Did the villagers to do this?"

Gary responded, "No, Sir, it was the man you have been looking for. He did this by himself."

The conversation was interrupted by Chuck's helicopter touching down a few feet away. Jake ran directly to it to talk to that team to see what had happened. He was horrified to see everyone taped up and helpless. His men were told to get them free. Jake stayed inside asking each man, as the tape came off covering his eyes and mouth, what had happened.

Each one had the same story, "I don't know what happened. I went out to see Gary's helicopter, and the next thing I knew, I woke up here all tied and gagged. But I do have a lump on the back of my head."

Chuck corroborated Gary's story that it had been the work of one man, the man they were looking for. That is when Gary produced the sealed envelopes and gave one to Jake and asked to see Don Ziguia Ortega. He, like the others, had come outside and was standing near Jake. Gary thought he noticed a slight smile on Ortega's face.

The letters stated:

To whom this concerns:

Gary's cargo represents what happens if you try to find me, the Barracuda. Chuck's cargo is what you can expect to find if you stop your silly efforts to kill me. You have only been paying your dues to me for operating on my seas, for I am The King of Seas. I am free to take what I please from those who trespass and I have always been here; this is not a recent occurrence. Believe whatever you want, but the Barracuda has always been here and most seamen know it. Now you and your family do, too, so expect to live with your losses or get off of my oceans. As my laws dictate, you are given a choice to resist and die, or do not resist and survive.

The captured men I have returned to you will be the only demonstration of compassion. You better realize that you are not dealing with something you can understand, so just accept it. The Barracuda cannot be killed, cannot be seen unless he wants it, and travels in ways you could never understand. There were some members of your family who did not realize what I am until it was too late for them. Tony Castero, the old Sicilian Gugguci, and his men, Scars, Vito Meridino, Paul Chance and Chong, and Vincenzo the Sicilian Jones.

The next members of your family who will learn about me are the thirteen remaining men in the Circle of Fifteen. I know their names and I know where they live. If they persist in causing trouble for the Ortegas, or continue to look for me, then they will meet me, face-to-face. It's a face that will be the last thing they see. They can never be safe from me, even at thirty-eight thousand feet above my oceans in a private airliner. I come and go as I please.

The Circle of Fifteen should know that the Ortegas do not know anything about me. I occasionally mix with humans and that has been their only involvement. I will not bother them again. Ortega's grandfather became acquainted to me in 1860. I even demonstrated my generosity to those I like. I returned their old family Bible to the Ortegas. I have also shown my anger to many of your own by the sinking of the Virgin Princess in 1710 with all hands, including the Italians who were the priests and nuns and who were the Pope's personal staff. The Pope would have perished as well, had he made the voyage. Today, I still have the robes of David covering the bronze chest full of jewels and gold, and the Pope's goblet given to him by England's Queen Ann. It was neither my first hanging nor my last. And everyone I allow to hang me pays a terrible price that is very satisfying to me.

To confirm that, you might go back in your own family history to Don Grasso. The king was the son of another English dog that thought he was King and hanged me in 1791. He was one of your first family heads, and, like the Ortegas, I liked the man and would occasionally visit his family. I do not believe he has any direct descendants in your Mafia family now, as I killed the Don, his wife and his four children aboard the Fancy Lady in 1739. He died a terrible death because he tried to resist my demands. He watched his wife being mutilated with my knife, and then beheaded. Next he watched as I cut off the heads of each of his children. None-the-less, he told me what I wanted after he felt the pain of my knife. Why he had betrayed me and where the bounty the Spanish King had given him was kept. This bounty is still in my sanctuary today—sitting next to your tribute.

If these things are not enough to give you reasons not to pursue the Barracouta, then you, the Circle of Thirteen, Gino, Anthony, Georgo, Sergio, Carl, Gevonni, Joseph, Victor, Ronaldo, Carlo, Frank, Roberto, and Jake should think about the worst way you can die and your worst fears will come true. That is a promise.

King of Seas,

Barracuda

Jake finished reading the warning just as Gary asked Chuck, "Where is the pirate, Chuck? He was aboard your chopper, wasn't he?"

"Yes. He was back there when we left. He couldn't have jumped out unless he committed suicide or fell out."

That had everyone's attention. Was this not a human after all? Could he really come and go as he pleased? He had left the helicopter somehow and he did take out twelve highly trained men by himself, without them even knowing it. He also took out some very impressive people like Tony the Pop, Vincenzo, the best hit man who had been in the family, and Paul Chance, who was a tough man, too. All of the guards and crews of boats had the same story. Maybe the Barracuda was more than a man... a supernatural ghost?

Jose Ortega remained quiet while reading the letter. Of course, he knew it was Sidney's forefathers' actions in those early years, but he acted concerned and as a believer.

Jose Ortega said, "I knew there was something weird about him. I bet him twenty thousand dollars one time to go into a dense jungle and bring back a wild boar. He refused to take a gun, and he wore skimpy clothes and no shoes and disappeared into the foliage. When I returned, he was sitting there refreshed like he had not even left camp, and had caught a wild boar barehanded and brought it back to camp—alive! No human could have done that."

Maria, in the background, said, "That is true. I saw it myself."

Jose Ortega said, "So that's who is in the Circle of Fifteen. I bet they are going to wonder how the Barracuda knew that when nobody other than the Circle has that information."

Jake walked over to the senior Ortega and said, "Don Ortega, I must apologize for my rude behavior again. I was mistaken in my belief that your son had something to do with this business. We will leave now. I must get this information back to Sicily, and I am sure they will be in touch with you to pay retribution for our actions this week."

Don Ziguia Ortega sternly said, "Okay, Jake, take your men and go."

Jake politely said, "Do you have some place here where we can bury our friends? They are beginning to bloat and smell."

"You cannot leave them here. Drop them off in the Caribbean Sea."

Two days later in Sicily, Jake, the Ripper, Gugino was sitting in a meeting with the Circle. They were very interested in the story and the letter. They even made a few telephone calls to verify the things mentioned in the letter. After a very long day, it was decided that they didn't believe in ghosts, no matter how compelling the story was and the factual history, but they were good businessmen. If it meant losing a few dollars whenever this madman wanted to rob them, let it be. It was no different from their practices of collecting huge sums of money from labor unions and governments to be allowed certain franchises, just different styles. It was decided not to recognize the pirate as an entity, however; let the victims take care of themselves. Maybe one will be able to turn the tables on him someday.

THE NEXT DAY, DON ZIGUIA ORTEGA RECEIVED A CALL FROM DON CARLO in Sicily. He extended a profound apology to Ortega's family. The man responsible, Charles Dania, had paid the supreme penalty, and they could rest assured that that sort of behavior would never occur again. To show his sincerity, his expansive chateau in the mountains, complete with household staff, was given to the Ortega family forever. The deed was being sent by special courier.

Don Carlo ended the conversation with, "We have decided not to spend more time and resources tracking this madman; however, if your son's acquaintance is suddenly only an unpleasant memory and no longer a threat to our business, he could expect a major favor to show our joy. We could offer a five percent ownership in our Caribbean casinos."

The older Ortega scoffed. "Bullshit, they're baiting Jose to get rid of their troublemaker. They are scared right now, but it will fade as soon as they lose another prize or two. They are buying time to get their security up and let Sidney drop his guard. If that guy is your friend, you should tell him he had better lay off those people."

Jose agreed and told his father that he was returning to his hacienda to see if Sidney was still there. But there was something else in his mind. Greed had surfaced after receiving the Circle's statement. What those guys would give to be free of the Barracuda. That statement came through loud and clear with the gift of Don Carlo's multimillion dollar estate being given as a peace offering. Jose was very wealthy, but some people could never have enough money. More money equaled more power.

☠

Sidney didn't return to the hacienda when he had exited the aircraft. Instead, he faded into the jungle and found a comfortable place to rest for a day or two. His choice was in a big old banyan tree from where, if he climbed to the top, he could see Jose's hacienda. He would stay there to see if the Italians returned. If they did, he would simply make an all-out assault, killing as many as possible until they killed him. That was the only option left open. If they didn't return, then he would go down and use Jose's telephone to call his father.

Two days later, a helicopter passed overhead going to the hacienda. Sidney scurried to the top of the tree to see who had arrived. It was Jose's helicopter, but that didn't mean anything. It could be full of well-armed Italians. Jose disembarked, followed by Maria and the pilot. Sidney waited until dark to be sure there wasn't going to be another arrival.

Sidney walked into the pool area unannounced, startling Jose, who was sitting alone at the bar staring into a half-full drink. When he saw it was Sidney, there was a strange expression on his face. Sidney didn't know for certain if it was happiness to see him or dread. He probably had enough problems because of Sidney to justify the latter.

"Are you out of the soup?" asked Sidney.

"It appears so, but how did you manage to take all of those men? Did the boy help you?"

"No help was needed. What did the Italians have to say about my message?"

"They didn't know what to believe. I guess they checked on the stories you related and must have found out there was truth to them. They know you might have gotten the names of the Circle from one of the men you killed, but they are not certain how you got them. You have their names and that seemed to be the important factor. They don't know what else to do except live with your demands… for the present anyway."

"Are you concerned for your family's safety?"

"Not at all. The team leader, who chose to invade my father's compound and grab some of our people, was killed by the Circle. They also gave my father a hell of a piece of property in Italy, complete with a paid staff for retribution. We came out okay."

"Good. How about one of those drinks?"

They drank, but there wasn't much conversation. Maria was apparently asleep, and Sidney decided to leave her alone. There was something kind of strange about the atmosphere around there. He thought Jose would have been a little more upbeat about how things had turned out. Maybe there were other business problems he was concerned about. Jose was certainly in the kind of business that could cause concern and worry from time to time. He decided not to give it any more thought.

It was time for him to do something fun for a change; he wanted to go back to the new cave's entrance and start getting it ready. There was a lot of planning and physical work to be done before they could start moving the treasure. And now, more than ever, St. Croix and the marina were no longer their secret. Their property would still be there in ten, twenty, or even fifty years for whichever Sidney X had the watch, should that Sidney want to reactivate the Cave of Snakes.

Sidney asked to use the telephone and called his father. His father answered in only two rings. Apparently, he was concerned about the situation they were in. Usually he would take his time to answer the telephone, if he answered it at all, as the only people who ever called were his whores, and all they ever wanted was money.

"Pop, everything is okay for now. But you need to leave St. Croix for a while. The boy is headed your way and should arrive late tomorrow. I have instructed him what to do. You need to get a ride out to the refinery dock on the south side and wait for him. He will bring you back here to the Cave of Pigs."

"Yeah, okay, I understand. How did you get clear of the wops?"

"A little luck, a little bullshit, and lots of blood."

Jose could only hear a mumbled conversation. He was interested in who Sidney had called, but knew better than to ask.

When Sidney came back out to the pool bar, he finished his drink and went behind the bar and fixed another drink for them both. Jose did the honors next time.

Finally, Jose Ortega asked, "Was that your next of kin on the telephone? You must have taken him to civilization"

"Yep." Sidney didn't elaborate.

They alternated fixing drinks until the sun was near the horizon and Jose Ortega passed out in a chaise lounge.

Sidney went into Maria's bedroom and stood there watching her sleep. She was the most beautiful woman he had ever seen. He felt a need to hold her, to touch her, not in a sexual way; he just wanted to make contact with her. Standing there, the realization struck him that he wanted the responsibility to protect her forever. He wanted to spend all of his time with her. He thought, *is this what love feels like?*

When Ortega woke up in a few hours, the sun was bright and there was a note on the bar from Sidney. It said, "Went camping, see you in a few days."

Jose, like yesterday, was in foul mood that morning. There was something on his mind; something was distracting him from being his usual good-natured self. His mood didn't change for the next few days.

Maria noticed it just as Sidney had, but Jose was not talking about it. She was also hurt to learn that Sidney had come and gone without seeing her. Only the work that was stacking up made her not think of the situation. Since Jandy had been killed, she had to do the work that two had done before. When it became apparent that things were only going to worsen, she had a talk with Jose about hiring another woman. It was agreed, and Maria and Jose flew to Caracas. From there, it was off to St. Thomas to interview several candidates who were daughters of ranking cartel members. If no one was suitable, they would go to the Columbian compound to talk to more people.

After a day of interviews with dull—by comparison to Jandy—people, Jose Ortega got restless and left for his Venezuelan hacienda, telling Maria to find someone before returning.

Y OUNG S IDNEY HAD BEEN NERVOUS AS HELL FOR THE ENTIRE TRIP NORTH to find St. Croix. But he found it, and it was exactly where his father said it would be. He followed the coastline west until he came to markers leading into the ship's channel of the refinery. He could easily spot the wheelchair at the dock's edge with his grandpa sitting in it, drinking beer from a red Igloo cooler next to him.

Little Sid was a hell of a sailor for a kid, but he definitely was a lousy docker. He had never even tried to dock the big boat before, and he crashed into the greasy cero-soaked pilings and bounced off like a novice airplane pilot trying to make his first landing.

Grandpa, in his wheelchair tried to keep up with the forward momentum of the boat while telling the kid to throw him a dock line. When the boy finally found one and tossed it over, it landed only a foot away from Grandpa's chair. Unfortunately, it was the entire rope. In the boy's haste he had forgotten to tie the other end to the boat. Finally they got the boat stopped and tied to the dock.

Grandpa certainly had plans to show the kid how to maneuver a boat while docking. That was an embarrassment; how could the kid ever be the King of the Seas if he could not dock a boat?

The older Sidney tied a halyard around himself and his chair. The boy winched him up on the main halyard winch and lowered him and his chair into the cockpit. The cooler and a bag of clothing were also loaded, and they were off once again. The boat headed due south and the big white sails were set and the boat slowly disappeared over the horizon—unseen by the dozen men on St. Thomas who were looking for Sidney XXIII.

The return trip was fun; Grandpa did the navigating and it was his responsibility to find his father. Little Sid's duties were to keep a cold beer always in the drink holder on the steering console. Grandpa's return instructions were approximately twenty-seven miles east of the Lagoon del Crocodile. They were lucky with the weather; the trades blew ten to fifteen knots on the port beam, so they had a good ride.

When the old man and the boy arrived in the area of the Cave of Pigs, they saw where to go by following a small trail of smoke coming from the beach. Sidney was sitting under the shade of several coconut trees. He had seen the white sails on the horizon and knew it could be nobody else but his family, so he had lit the signal fire.

He had been sitting there for six hours, but didn't mind the wait. In fact, the time seemed to pass too quickly. At first he thought about Maria; he was confused over his emotions. He wondered if he should marry her, as she was the only thing in his life that had made him truly happy. He also thought that if he married, she would want children, and that would cause problems if she had a boy. He'd have to kill her to turn the boy into a Sidney X.

Then he thought about his son and the future sons of the Sidneys. It was time to attempt a change in their lifestyles without losing the benefits. It had been a challenge to make an intelligent decision when there were so many unknowns. His sphere of knowledge was very limited, but he was aware of that limitation. Much of the everyday experience the mainstream population took for granted was lost to him. His experiences revolved around bars, broads, booze, the sea, and raids for the prize. The only guidelines for going through life were the words penned by his ancestors in the family log. They were words that told of unexcelled bravery against incredible odds while capturing prizes from man and governments, and excitement and adventure were limited by each Sidney's own imagination.

Life's requirements were simple: live with courage and devotion to family, understand nature and respect the sea, be free and never bow to any man.

Moving the operation to the Cave of Pigs was a good start. It was isolated from the so-called civilized world where actions, like his own, were only allowed by governments or influential men. There, he had freedom from governmental influence and there certainly were no people around to cause problems. The sea was beautiful, and he had found a lake that would be a sheltered and concealed lagoon in which to keep the *Bar-*

racouta. A lot of digging would have to be done first in order to get the stream leading to the lagoon deep enough to get the boat in, however. That would be a body-building job for his son.

The idea of what to do seemed to explode in his thoughts. They could become salvage divers. He knew the approximate locations of hundreds of wrecks going back to the fifteen hundreds; wrecks where his forefathers could not get all of the bounty off the ship before it slid beneath the seas. And, in almost every case, it had to be close enough to shore for them to row the prize to land. Plus, it would be easy enough to add new wrecks to the list occasionally, so it would provide several lifetimes of adventure and riches. It would also reduce their exposure to the crime watchers as they became increasingly effective with all of their electronic doodads.

With the *Barracouta* anchored fifty feet off shore, the boy dove overboard and swam to shore. The older Sid pulled himself up on the gunwale and fell overboard. Both reached the beach at the same time.

Sidney waded out and carried his father to the shade he had been enjoying.

ON BOARD THE HELICOPTER, JOSE ORTEGA, RETURNING FROM ST. THOMas, was looking out of a window. Then he saw a sailboat on anchor. Though the boat was a couple of miles away, he could still tell that it was Sidney's boat.

"Probably trying to figure out how to get his boat in that lagoon," he muttered. "Think I'll pay him a visit."

N.

Sidney asked, "What do you think? This place beautiful enough for you, Pop?"

"Where's the fucking pussy?"

"We'll import whatever you want. How do you like this place?"

From where Sidney XXII sat he could see the ocean, the swaying coconut trees, and part of the little lagoon in front of the lush green mountain that rose up behind it.

"Yeah, it looks good. The boy tells me you found an entrance to the sea. How big is the cavern?"

"It is huge. The largest I have ever seen. If things ever really got bad, we could retreat into that thing and the authorities would never find us."

"Well, that's interesting, but what are you going to do now? You can't just leave the boat out there. As soon as the wind switches to the northeast, it's going to drag up on the beach. You might be able to walk out of here and the kid might, but I'm damn sure not going to crawl out on my fucking hands and knees."

"As soon as the tide is full, I am going to stick all the sails up, take her offshore and run her into the creek as fast as she will go. I can get her about half way up the creek before she bottoms out to a dead stop. She'll be stranded, but safe from the seas. Then we'll dig out the creek to the lagoon to float her in. No problem, mon."

"How am I supposed to get any pussy when the only way to find civilization is stranded on a fucking sandbar?"

"Relax, look around and enjoy nature for a week. It won't kill you. By then we'll know what we need and we'll have the creek dug out. Then we'll go to Caracas for your pussy and our supplies. We will need to make a trip every two weeks to buy more materials. I can get an apartment for you while Little Sid and I build a house for you."

"Why build a house? I thought you were going to the Mediterranean for a few years. I already have a good place to live there."

"I know, but I want to disappear completely for a couple of years. I also want to try another way to do business."

"There is no other way for the Sidneys. You know that."

"Well, I came up with a way that will be good for the family, the treasure, and the changing times. I want to talk it over with you later to see what you think. It is in keeping with our history and family honor."

"Better be. You're not so big I can't beat the shit out of you if you are trying to pussy out on our family."

Sidney picked up the older man, assuring him he was not going to do anything like that. He carried him up through the jungle to the cave's entrance. The older Sid tried to hide his approval of the view from the cave's mouth. It was a perfect place for a pirate to live. From their vantage point, they would be able to see any vessel approaching for miles in any direction. And the view was truly magnificent. Sidney told him of the waterfalls and the huge underground river that dropped off into blackness. The older man longed for his feet so he could explore the cave.

"I got to see these things, Sidney," said the older man.

"We will figure out a way to do just that, Pop. We have a lot of time."

Sidney started to pick up his father to return to the shore; it was time for him to drive the boat into the creek. Pop objected, saying, "There's such a good breeze up here, I'll stay here for a while and watch you."

Then he added, "Hey, boy, go get me a coconut and a bottle of rum from the boat. I might as well be comfortable while I'm waiting."

The kid turned then disappeared down the mountain slope. A few minutes later he could be seen swimming out to the *Barracouta* and pulling himself aboard. A few seconds later, he dove in with two bottles in hand, thinking that surely his father would want one, too.

The two men sat in the shade of the cave's mouth drinking rum from the bottles. The boy and Fred were splitting a coconut between them. Everything was at peace. Finally, Sidney said, "I think the tide is about as high as it is going to get today," and he ambled down the mountain. The boy volunteered to help, but Sidney declined the offer as no help was needed.

Sidney was walking across the sandy beach between the line of coconut palms and the gentle, clear surf of the Caribbean, when he suddenly found himself face down in the sand. He was confused at first, not knowing what had happened. Then he became aware that his body was on fire with a billion red hot needles sticking into every piece of his flesh. He was helpless, unable to move anything but his head. He was also experiencing great difficulty breathing; his mind was racing to learn what was happening to him. Finally, with a lot of effort, he was able to lift his face out of the sand. And that was all he could move.

His eyes were partly covered with particles of sand, but he forced them open. The eyes finally found and focused on something moving towards him. It was a man with a rifle in his hands. The man was the only friend he had ever had, Jose Ortega.

That is when he realized what had happened. He had been shot in the back and, more than likely, had been hit in the spinal cord. He was completely paralyzed from the neck down.

It had not been an easy decision to make, but Jose had made up his mind. He had decided that Sidney, no matter how impressed Jose was with Sidney's performance against the mob, was on borrowed time anyway. To give the Circle of Fifteen the man they had wanted so badly would improve the Ortega family's position and wealth immensely. That was important because he was about to become the Don; his father, Ziguia, was retiring in a year. It would obligate the Mafia to the Ortegas for many years and open several major doors his cartel had previously been denied. The increased revenue over the next decade, at the cost of this one man, could not be compared. It was just business.

When he was returning from St. Thomas, he realized there would never be a better opportunity. Sidney was by himself, doing his solitude thing. There would be no witnesses so Maria or Sidney's kid would never know what had happened to him. They would all just think that someone in the mob had found him.

He smiled at a thought; I *was right, I'm damn sure getting my way over the stubborn prick—one way or another.*

As he walked to the bleeding man sprawled out on the snow-white sand, he knew Sidney was dying, but was not yet dead as he held his wobbling head up watching him approach. A large part of his back was covered with blood, oozing freely out of the bullet hole. He felt cheap at shooting such a powerful man in the back like that, but that was probably the only way to kill him. He certainly had not wanted to go one-on-one in a personal fight.

As Jose came nearer, he cocked the rifle for its finishing shot—the bullet to Sidney's brain that would end his pirating days forever. As he stood over Sidney, he said, "Sidney, I am really sorry about this, but there was no other way around it. It means a lot to my family to take you down. I will do as you asked about helping with your son and will be sure he gets every advantage of my experience and influence I can muster. You are my friend, and I am truly sorry." He raised the rifle's sight to put the next bullet into the fallen warrior's temple.

Sidney couldn't speak—he was doing good just to get some air into his lungs—but he could hear and he could see. He heard the words of the back-shooter and he saw the movement of his son.

Little Sid was silently walking up behind Jose. He was calm, walked slowly, even casually, to within two feet of Jose. The boy's knife was carried out of its scabbard and was at the ready. Without delay, when he reached the point where he wanted to be, he swung his foot up between Jose's legs. The unexpected blow from behind that crushed his testicles caused him to drop to his knees with pain. The boy took another step forward and grabbed him by the hair with his left hand and sliced his jugular with his knife without any effort; just as his father had showed him on the helicopter. The sudden spurt of blood shot out six feet away from Jose's severed neck, and Jose fell dead in sight of the mortally wounded Sidney XXIII.

If Sidney could have smiled, he would have. He now knew his son was going to be one hell of a Sidney X. The moment of hesitation about killing the man in the helicopter was not important. The boy was a Sidney. The hardest thing Sidney had ever done in his life was to muster up the air and strength to speak. His voice was very hard to hear, but the boy dropped to his knees to lean close to hear what his father was saying.

"Remember when you asked me if you're smart, and I said don't know yet. Ask me after I get to know you? Well… son, yes, you are very smart. Don't forget this day; it's what happens when you let other people get close to you. Listen to your grandfather, he knows best. I will be dead soon, drag me far out to sea and turn my body loose to drift through the Caribbean. That way I'll still be… free."

Forty year old Sidney XXIII, the King of the Sea and anywhere else he happened to be, died with his face in the sand. His only friend was still pumping blood out and onto the same sand, and his son on bent knees was crying like a seven-year-old boy should.

Grandpa, on hands and knees, came to his crying grandson and punched him in the face. Little Sidney was knocked unconscious and his face planted in the sand.

Sidney XXII sat down and lit up a fresh cigar and waited for a half hour before the boy woke up. He was confused and when he saw the dead men and his grandpa sitting there with a smile on his face. The boy became frightened.

"You are, without a doubt, Sidney XXIV. And as a Sidney you do not cry—ever. You killed the man who killed the Sidney you are replacing. The cowardly man shot your father in the back and you made the right response. I'm damn glad, and proud to have you as my grandson. You and I will work as a team until you're ready to take off on your own. I have a feeling that you may be the best Sidney X ever."

Little Sid sat there not knowing what to do or say.

"Now, Sidney twenty-four, I want you to get up and come over here, and with your hardest punch, I want you to hit me in the face just as I did to you. That way you will be telling me not to treat you as a child ever again."

Sidney XXIV got up, walked over to his grandfather and punched him in the nose with his small right fist that knocked Grandpa down, but not out. Grandpa started laughing, and slowly, so did his grandson.

They sat down beside each other, and Little Sidney said, "I'm going to kill all of the Ortegas for this. Let's go get some payback, Grandpa."

Grandpa looked serious, "Not only the taco-eaters. We're going to nail the Italian Mafia, too. They paid a handsome price to Jose Ortega to kill your father."

"Yeah, Grandpa. Death to the spaghetti-eaters, too."

The End

THE SEQUEL TO SIDNEY X IS THE
MOVIE: SON OF SIDNEY X

OTHER WORKS FROM B.R. EMRICK

NOVELS

LAGOONIEVILLE
COLOMBIAN SECRETS
PIRATES, SMUGGLERS & VOODOO MEANIES
MAROONED ON SPOOK ISLAND
A SMUGGLER'S STORY
SNAKES IN EDEN
A CHEESEBURGER IN PARADISE
PARADISE BETWEEN EVILS
THE LAGOONIES OF LAGOONIEVILLE
KING ME, PEON YOU, HA, HA, HA!
THE ANCIENTS
SIDNEY X the Pirate

SCREENPLAYS

THE ROAD TO PANGAEA – action-adventure
NETHERWORLD – horror
SHENANIGANS – reality
A DEADLY ENCOUNTER – thriller
WITCHES OF THE LAGOON – horror
HAPPY COCO NUTS – comedy
DECEPTION AT 50,000 FEET – thriller
DON'T MAKE ME COME DOWN THERE – drama
ANGELS OF MASS DESTRUCTION – thriller
HAPPY ISLAND – drama
AN ADVENTURE WITH PIRATE GOLD – action-adventure
LIGHT MY NIPPLES – terrorists spoof

CPSIA information can be obtained
at www.ICGtesting.com
Printed in the USA
FFOW02n1046260716
26163FF